# THE SHE TIGER OF PARIS:

CONTAINING A HISTORY OF THE

## LIFE AND ADVENTURES

OF

A CELERATED FRENCH LADY OF FASHION,

UNDER THE NAME OF

## FELINA DE CAMBURE;

AND UNIVERSALLY ACKNOWLEDGED AS ONE OF THE MOST POWERFUL, AND THRILLING NOVELS OF THE PRESENT CENTURY,

**BY THE CELEBRATED FRÉDÉRIC SOULIÉ.**

TRANSLATED BY

JOHN TAYLOR SINNETT,

AND

MISS KATE HIBBURD.

PUBLISHED BY

SINNETT, 489, OXFORD STREET;

And Sold also by

VICKERS, HOLYWELL STREET; LEE, WARWICK LANE;

AND ALL BOOKSELLERS IN TOWN AND COUNTRY.

# PREFACE.

FREDERIC SOULIÉ, the Author of the She Tiger, is considered all over the Continent, one of the first Novel writers of the age. His plots are universally admired for their ramified form and skilful combination. In England we have no living author who is capable of a great plot: the novels of Dickens, Thackeray, Ainsworth, and all the celebrities of the same school, are mere stitches of chapter to chapter, and incident to incident. No plot is even attempted. The difference between Soulié and these gentlemen, in this respect, the criterion of high art in composition, is the same as that between Brunel or Stephenson, on the one side, and a few honest "navvies" on the other.

But plot is not the only gift of this accomplished Novelist: he excels in character, observation, and reflection; but above all in the delineation of woman's heart.

What can be finer than the pictures of human character in this Novel? Look at the Thoré family, honest Villon, the libertine Count, and Felina de Cambure! Look at Champmortain, Brias, poor Sylvia, and the Colonel. Observe with what powerful skill Montéclain is drawn! Montéclain the counterpart of Felina.

Again in humble life, can anything surpass the strong homely virtue of Farmer Bricord? The saucy vivacity, the quick affections of the soldier-servant Aly Muley? Can anything be more true to nature, than the artificial manners, the arrogance, the folly, the weakness of the honest farmer's wife, Léda?—a heart inflated by a theatrical career, and unprovided with the discipline of domestic education.

A book like the She Tiger, affords the student of human manners, a complete idea of French life and character. In peace, as well as in war, the basis of that character, is INTRIGUE; and all Englishmen who have dealings with that great people, must know this. There is a vivid sagacity, and moveable genius in the French, which urges them to act, and compels them to be occupied *in the mind*. They must always be making or unmaking; always be building up or demolishing. Their great enjoyment, however, does not lie in doing a thing, but in *devising the means* of doing it. They are proud of this talent, they glory in it; all their Novels are built upon this faculty, and every domestic fiction is but a separate confession or rather avowal of this instinctive propensity.

In the eleventh century, the unsuspecting Harold, lost his crown and his life through an INTRIGUE on the part of the bastard, William. The subtle intrigue of Cardinal Richelieu, prepared the way for the humiliation of Austria, and the absolute power of Louis XIV. The great French Revolution was a long congeries of intrigues. So was the advancement of Napoleon. By and bye, if peace endures, there will be a moral duel between France and England; *Intrigue* will be the weapon on the part of France, and *Principle* the weapon on the part of England.

JOHN TAYLOR SINNETT.

# TABLE OF CONTENTS.

THE

# SHE TIGER;

OR,

# THE FEMALE FIEND.

## CHAPTER I.

### THE THORE FAMILY.

SOME years ago, at a house in the Rue de Paradis-Poissonnière, a sign-board of a semi-circular form might have been seen, suspended from the arch above the gate. On this sign-board were painted the three following words: *Magasin de Porcelaines*, or China Warehouse. You enter the house by passing through a large yard, along the sides of which ran several pent-houses or sheds, leaving scarcely room enough for the passage of a coach between them. These pent-houses, rising no higher than the first story, were all of them surrounded with glass fronts, thus exposing to view the piles of chinaware with which the shelves of these vast and roomy warehouses were loaded.

The shed on the left hand side was entered by a glass-door. Within this enormous cage of glass, and standing face to face, were two smaller cages of wire; the first you came to contained an office desk in two compartments, made of oak and very high, at which the clerks, who kept the accounts, could either stand, or seat themselves on their high turning stools. At this double desk, the two scriviners sat opposite to each other. In the back part of this enclosure you descried large pigeon holes and an iron chest which no burglar could have forced, and which would have defied the genius of a Hure, or Hobbs, the great American picklock, to pick. At the time our narrative opens, two men were occupied at this desk; one of whom was about fifty years of age; this was M. Thoré, the master of the house; his countenance beamed with serenity and self-satisfaction, and bespoke the ease and respectability of his position as a tradesman. The other was M. Louis Villon, his clerk. Although M. Thoré was at once the best and weakest of men, he cherished certain principles of conduct which prompted him to do his utmost to belie both his nature and his disposition: for he used to say that no business could be carried on without rigid severity; and thus he had contracted a habit of speaking in a short and morose tone.

On this day, M. Thoré, with furrowed brows, and pouting lips, his elbows leaning on the desk, and his head resting on his arm, was employed in turning over, one after another, the account books which his young clerk on the opposite side kept handing to him; M. Thoré passed from leaf to leaf with grunts of ill-humour, whilst Louis Villon, the clerk, watched him with a cunning smile. The latter was a young man of five and twenty, tall and well-shaped, but his face, though handsome, was of a common character. Merely to have seen him, one would have guessed that he was one of those honest and hearty spirits by whom every duty of life is religiously observed.

The master had examined to the end one of the account books he was searching, and had thrown it on a table with asperity. Just as he was taking another from his clerk, he glanced his eye towards the other cage of wire, where two women were seated, and watching him with smiles. Now the meaning of these smiles in the case of the elder lady was this:

"Come, my husband is making believe as usual."

And in the case of the younger was this:

"Papa may do what he will, he won't find any opportunity to scold M. Villon."

M. Thoré having surprised his wife and daughter watching his motions with looks almost satirical, called out in a terrible voice:

"Well, what are you doing there? Do you think we shall balance these books by gaping at the crows?"

The mother and daughter instantly bent their heads over the ledgers they were reckoning up, whilst M. Thoré continued, with his eyes fixed on Louis Villon:

"As for you, Sir, you affect to be in order.

"You may depend upon it, Sir."

"Very good—very good," rejoined the master, resuming his inspection: "But stop—umph! (here he turned over the leaf) what's this? (he turned over another leaf). Zounds! this sum carried over is—no, the reckoning is correct." He turned over another leaf, and continued to grumble and frown, striving hard to find something to complain of, but without effect, and vexed that he could not make any room for a show of authority.

Meanwhile, the two women had resumed their task, and were making out the bills of the customers from the ledgers. The cage they occupied was adjacent to the glass front looking into the yard; it was richly furnished; the desks were made of fine violet wood; the floor was carpeted with a thick *moquette*, the seats were elegantly covered, and besides the immense stove which heated the warehouse there was a small German flue passing through their little retreat. In addition to the desks and pigeon holes in this favoured nook, there was a work-table and a frame for embroidery, which plainly told that these ladies' occupation was not confined to pen and ink labour alone.

Madame Thoré was a woman of about forty, whose calm, honest, and laborious life had left her beauty unimpaired. Age, however, had produced its expansion of the figure; her face had grown plumper and more ruddy, but not a wrinkle was to be seen in that coutenance so placid, happy, and well-featured. The shape was no longer elastic, but the plenitude of the contours still gave it a slender appearance; her feet and hands had continued perfect. Among women of fashion there are hundreds who pass for beautiful, and who seek to shine, none of whom could have been compared to Madame Thoré; but it was easy to see that she had given up all claims to beauty, and she owed her elegance to the extreme care she took of her person, and not at all to any idle desire to please or to attract attention.

It was fortunate for Madame Thoré that such was the case, for had she been one of those coquettes who wear their advantages to the last shred, she would have found in her daughter a rival whom she must have removed, to prevent her from intercepting every look, and seizing upon every homage. For in truth, Julia was the very dream of loveliness: tall, slender, flexible, hers was at once the majesty of a queen and the grace of a sylph. Her lineaments possessed that accuracy of design which too often exhibits itself as a fine mask to conceal vacuity of mind and apathy of soul. Not so in Julia, for thought dwelt in her brow, passion glowed in her eyes, and wit glittered in her smile; she was an angel, nay, more than an angel; she was a beautiful and charming woman.

Julia was sixteen years old, and carried her age with the decorous freedom of a good mind and a pure and simple heart; calm and reflective, she still had those freaks and sallies of childhood which urged her to run about like a merry little girl, over her father's spacious warerooms, without any regard to her finished beauty or to her grand lady attire. This was especially the case whenever her brother Charles returned from his workroom, with some flower or sketch, which she was sure to snatch out of his hand, without any pity for the intended receiver. Then would follow a race, peals of laughter, screams, an uproar which made the china ring. M. Thoré and his wife, with faces turned up, and Louis Villon, with mouth agape, looked with feelings of unspeakable joy, at the two fine tall children playing together; both of them charming, both of them gay, reckless, and never failing to close the contest with a hearty brotherly kiss; at such times Charles was sure to say:

"Since you have taken it from me this time, you may keep it; but if it happens again, I shall be angry." And it did happen again, and Charles was not angry at all.

At other times, Julia was thoughtful, and this she was with as much ingenuous openness as when she was gay. What was she thinking of at such times? Of nothing, she would have answered had she been questioned; and that would have been true. Only that said nothing has a name which she was not yet acquainted with; that nothing is the unknown stranger who calls all young spirits to him without their knowing whence the voice proceeds or whither it would guide them. Julia had never felt confused at the sight of any one, she had not yet listened to any hope, nor thought of any thing again. She was very partial to M. Louis Villon because he was an honest young man, who was very attentive and clever in her father's business; but she never laughed with him. When the business of the house obliged them to collate invoices or to examine accounts together, Julia called out or responded in a clear firm voice, like any other clerk with his companion, whilst the young man never said a word without trembling or making blunders, especially when they chanced to be alone. Had Julia perceived it? It is probable: but the young clerk's confusion did not at all embarrass her; she felt neither pity, nor annoyance: what she felt was indifference in the extreme.

Sometimes M. Thoré drew his wife's attention to the heavy sighs of M. Villon, and his radiant eye seemed to say that he rejoiced to witness a love which promised him an upright and able son-in-law, an excellent partner, and a successor who would keep up the prosperity of the house of Thoré, an heir whose personal property would one day be considerable. But Madame Thoré usually replied to these confidential glances with a soft shake of the head. Without being informed by any thing precise, she felt that her daughter's happiness did not lie in that quarter.

When M. Thoré wanted to know her reasons for this opinion, Madane Thoré was much perplexed to give them. As we said before, Julia liked and esteemed M. Louis Villon; she even frequently took his part against her father's fictititious ill-humour, but that was all; and Madame Thoré knew that woman's heart contains something else besides a rigid justice to him who is secretly preferred. That one is accused without cause, and defended without reason; to-day he is reproached for doing what yesterday he was asked to do; that one is laughed at, or pitied, cried up or disdained; in a word, that man is beloved.

Sometimes, M. Thoré would say that it was impossible for Julia not to love M. Villon, unless, added he, fixing upon his wife a look which he considered was deeply inquisitorial, unless she loves some other. But Julia did not love any one, her mother protested it, and was perfectly sure. however, Julia would sometimes fall into a revery, and when her mother appealed to her in her silent musing Julia blushed and always maintained she was not thinking of any thing. Her mother seemed to believe her; and was very careful not to question her too closely. She was too prudent to venture to give a name and a meaning to these vague aspirations of a young mind and heart, which begin to be conscious that the hour is come when a new life will open to their view.

The joy, the quietude, the security which had fixed their abode in this happy home, were increased for M. Thoré this year, by the brilliant result of his affairs. However, he had completed the examination of his accounts, and continued absorbed in the deepest meditation; his features still wore the expression of the keenest dissatisfaction. Truly, our worthy, M. Thoré, having nothing to blame, had found it impossible to scold his clerk, and give him a lesson drawn from his own manner of conducting business: so he was dissatisfied. Louis Villon was observing his patron attentively ever since he had thrown down the last ledger with vexation; Julia, as well as her mother, awaited the explosion without too much anxiety, but inquisitively. All at once M. Thoré's face grew cloudy, his forehead wrinkled, his eyebrows were drawn together, he threw up his head suddenly, and fixing a savage look at Louis, he said to him in a gruff voice:

"How much do you earn in my establishment, Sir?"

As Louis, two running clerks and two shopmen constituted the whole commercial house of M. Thoré, the worthy merchant knew perfectly well the amount of M. Villon's salary; still the latter, startled by the question, instantly answered:

"Why, Sir, I receive eighteen hundred francs." (£72.)

"Well," cried M. Thoré leaving the office with his hands behind his back, after the manner of Napoleon: "I will raise your salary to a thousand *ecus*."* (£120.)

"Ah! Sir, this is too much kindness," exclaimed the young man, "and my gratitude—"

"Enough," said the master with solemnity. "I am but just. We are going to have a few friends to dinner, if you like to join us you will have time to put on another coat."

"You do me too much honour," said the young man settling his pens and putting by the account books in a hurried manner, and immediately escaping from the warehouse.

Meanwhile, M. Thoré had entered the office of his wife who pressed his hand, whilst Julia threw her arms round his neck saying:

"This is so kind, so like you, papa."

"I have done what was right, nothing more," replied M. Thoré with sententious gravity. "You know me: I am pitiless, even cruel to the idle and wicked, great and generous to the good and diligent. I am just—always just."

"I say you are good," cried Julia kissing him again, "I want you to say that you are good."

"Come, come," said M. Thoré, "you don't know what you say, mademoiselle. But I will have no discussions in my house. It is five o'clock, and therefore time for you to go up and dress."

"I am going," said the young girl, preparing to close the account books as the clerk had done.

"Go, my child," said Madame Thoré to her, "I will put all these in order; I want to speak to your father."

Julia fled from the warehouse bounding like a roe, and sped rapidly up the staircase leading to the first floor apartment. On the landing place, and near the window from which one could see into the warehouse she had just left, she met Louis Villon, his head bent downwards and buried in deep thought.

"Well, M. Villon," said she merrily to him, "are you not pleased?"

"I—" said the latter starting. "Ah! your father has done for me more than I deserve—and I should be very ungrateful if—"

"Perhaps it thwarts your wishes to dine with us, and if you had other intentions?"

"I," said the young man, "I have no intentions, and assuredly I feel much honoured and very happy at your father's invitation."

"In that case, make haste, for you know that neither I nor mamma are ever long at our toilet."

Whereupon Julia went singing into her own chamber, whilst Louis laboured up with sorrow to the room he occupied on a higher story; and as he went up he asked himself why it would be a wise step for him to leave M. Thoré's house. Did he then already understand that the heart of that lovely girl, so good, and so candid, was never to return him a single atom of that all-powerful love which he experienced on her account?

However, M. Thoré had remained with his wife, and seemed to ask her how it was she had presumed to detain him thus, without previous warning.

"Well, my dear, what have you to say to me of such importance?" cried he sitting down like a king who is bestowing an audience upon a subject.

"Nothing more important than to inquire whom we are to have to dine with us."

"Why it seems to me you must know, since you sent out the invitations."

"Undoubtedly: I have invited M. and Madame Baucherat and their daughter; M. and Madame Lampin. But does not our Charles bring a friend with him?"

"Who, what friend?" asked M. Thoré.

"Well, his master; the painter in whose atelier he works."

"What painter?"

"God bless us," cried Madame Thoré, "why M. Victor Amab."

"Why do you ask me then, since you know it?" replied M. Thoré in the tone of Agamemnon.

"I ask you," said Madame Thoré with a slight imperceptible shrug, "because I know the gentleman's name and profession, but I do not know him personally. He is an artist, and since Charles has renounced painting on china to study historical painting, I hear him say such strange things, hum such singular songs, and relate to M. Villon such wild adventures, as lead me to suspect and beware of artists of every kind."

"Madame Thoré, I know whom I ought and whom I can invite to my house," returned M. Thoré with a self-approving nod of the head, "I am personally acquainted with M. Victor Amab; he will not be out of place in our society, since I have invited him to join it."

"You mean you have given Charles permission to bring him to us."

"That is all one, my love."

"You are right, but how does it happen that this young man, who has not been to see us once during the year that Charles has been his pupil, how does it happen, I say, that he has requested Charles to introduce him to us on this occasion?"

"It is an advantage he ought to have solicited sooner; but after all, every thing needs must have a beginning."

"Yes, yes," said Madame Thoré in an under tone, "every thing must have a beginning—well."

"What do you mean by that?" cried M. Thoré; "what signifies that word *well?*"

"I don't know—I was thinking of something else—I am going to dress, and I advise you to do the same."

Madame Thoré returned to her room, sadly dissatisfied, although nothing unusual had happened. Only, eight days previously, as she was sitting with her family in the second row of boxes at the opera, Madame Thoré had seen her son saluting a young man in the orchestre. She asked him who that young man was. "It is M. Victor Amab," he had replied. Then Madam Thoré looked more pointedly in the same direction, and thought she perceived that M. Amab was contemplating Julia with a kind of ecstacy.* As for Julia, she had remained a perfect stranger to this incident, being absolutely engrossed with the performance. The act being over, Madame Thoré wanted to know whether M. Amab was again looking at them. But he disappeared immediately. Madame Thoré thought he had left the house, but on looking about her, she

* It has been the fashion, for more than a century to translate this word *ecu*, as *crown*, whereas it is only equivalent to three francs, or half-a-crown.

* This is the first germ of the plot of this marvellous romance, and here the acutest reader but little suspects the wild, delirious and terrible scenes which are to follow.

remarked in the passage behind the opposite tier, a very elegant young man, with his opera glass rivetted upon her box. This young man was M. Amab. He saw that he was detected and turned away; but during the remainder of the evening, Victor continued in the same place, and, although he affected to be looking at the stage alone, Madame Thoré surprised him upwards of twenty times darting furtive glances at the box she was in.

"Did you observe your brother's master?" said she to her daughter, when they had returned home.

"Where do you mean?" answered Julia.

"At the opera."

"Charles pointed him out to you?" resumed the young lady.

"Yes; he sat opposite to us."

"I had something else to see," said the maiden exultingly; "*the Jewess* is so beautiful! Ah! that poor deluded Rachel! but she dies—as she ought—yes! she must have died afterwards."

Madame Thoré diverted her daughter's mind both from Rachel's misfortune and from their meeting M. Amab, and she herself had already forgotten it, when the very day on which our tale opens, Charles, as he was leaving home in the morning, informed his mother that he had obtained permission from his father to bring M. Amab home to dinner.

This expected introduction, after such a meeting, alarmed Madame Thoré, and that was her motive for endeavouring to glean from her husband who and what M. Victor Amab was; but from the way in which M. Thoré had answered her, she judged it would not be proper to acquaint him with her fears, M. Thoré would have treated it immediately as a serious business. He might perhaps have forbidden his daughter to look at M. Amab, and would have been sure, like most foolish fathers and husbands, to create the danger which he apprehended.

When Madame Thoré entered her room, she found her daughter finishing her toilet before the large mirror. Julia turned round on hearing her mother come in, and said laughingly:

"You see I have not been long, mother. How do I look?"

There was so much grace, so much openness in the lovely child, she was so attractive in beauty and youth, that Madame Thoré stood a moment to contemplate her. A thrill of pride and delight ran through her heart; but almost immediately there arose a mournful thought to subdue that impulse of maternal exultation.

"Come, mother," said the girl in her turn, "let me decorate you now, and make you handsome."

"You owe me as much," said her mother smiling, "for—"

"What is it?"

"Nothing," said Madame Thoré, "let us dispatch, the company are coming."

She was unwilling that her daughter should be able to finish the sentence inspired by the words: "Come, let me make you handsome," and to which she had answered: "You owe me as much." For, truly, did not Julia owe something to the mother who had rendered her so lovely, so handsome as to astonish her own mother. And as the old family doctor, M. Janson was his name, used to say: *beautiful enough to frighten you.* The expression though it may seem extravagant was a correct one; for very frequently Madame Thoré had herself trembled at so much perfection; often had she said to herself that so much beauty would draw too much homage and admiration around her Julia, for her life's happiness to pass through in its undimmed purity amidst such a throng of suitors and adorers.

The toilet proceeded to its close, rapidly enough, but scarcely was it concluded before there was a knock at the door of Madame Thoré's apartment.

"Who is there?"

"It is I, mother," returned a voice both merry and sonorous.

"You may come in."

## CHAPTER II.

### THE PICTURE.

THE next moment a fine young man with black hair, strongly built, with an eye boldly expansive, redolent of good spirits, strength and courage, entered the chamber. He embraced his mother and then advanced towards his sister. But before he embraced her, he walked leisurely round her and said with a nod of approbation:

"Nicely done!—very nicely done!"

"What means the gentleman?" asked Julia laughing.

"Come," said Madame Thoré, "Charles, have done with your workroom slang."

"It means that she she is as pretty to-day as—she always is."

Then he kissed his sister, smoothed with the tips of his fingers her long bands of flaxen hair, and said with a good humoured smile:

"Perfectly well done!"

"Tell me what the time is?" said Madame Thoré. "Is your professor come with you?"

"Not he," replied Charles moving across the room to his mother, and settling her curls with a smile of satisfaction; "no, he will be here at six o'clock, the fashionable hour—I say, my lady sister, do you know that mother is prettier than you?"

"Come," said his mother, "never mind my hair, but answer me."

"Very well done too—very well done!" cried the good humoured boy.

He embraced his mother again, and then tapping his forehead, suddenly exclaimed:

"Odds now! I was forgetting that Victor told me he would wait for me at the Opera Arcade."

"So you don't come directly from the workroom?"

"Yes I do, but he does not; the fact is this morning, I was much afraid he would not come at all."

"How so?"

"I will tell you the story. A duel this morning, in which he wounded his adversary. Therefore, instead of coming here at once, he has called on the sufferer to make inquiries."

"What! the gentleman who is to dine with us to-day, has fought this morning?" exclaimed Julia.

She uttered the words as though it were impossible that a man who, a few hours before had perilled his life, could come and seat himself quietly at her father's table."

"And much that he cares for it," said Charles as he was going away: "they fought at twelve o'clock, and down to eleven Victor was at work at his picture. I must go and fetch him; he is so shy, so timid, as not to dare to come alone."

"What does he mean, mamma?" said Julia, greatly surprised to hear a man called timid who had dared to fight a duel.

"Your brother is crazy and talks at random," answered Madame Thoré, who for her part well knew that there are men whom no danger alarms and who are yet confused by a look. She likewise knew that such men fascinate by means of the overpowering charm which is inseparable from strength when it yields to weakness ; is the old and pleasing story of the lion led by a child with a silk thread.

Madame Thoré hoped her daughter had not fixed her thoughts on her brother's last observations; but already that contrast of courage combined with timidity was a problem which the young girl endeavoured to solve. And already she felt curious to see M. Amab.

The mother was quite right when she said with affright:

"There is a beginning to every thing!"

This is an axiom: curiosity is the most dangerous beginning in love.

Three weeks had elapsed since the day when Victor had been introduced to the Thoré family. It was now the 31st of December. The merchant's warerooms were encumbered with boxes, packing baskets and such like; they were sending out goods for delivery, and making out invoices. All at once M. Thoré exclaimed:

"Tell me, is the invoice made out for that china service Louis Fifteenth pattern, Saxon style?"

"Another minute, Sir," said Louis Villon, who was entering a list of the articles in the ledger, whilst Julia was copying it on a fly leaf, both of them writing to the dictation of Madame Thoré, who was calling over each particular article in its place.

"To whom is this service to be sent?" inquired Julia of Louis Villon.

"It is to be directed to M. the Count of Monrion, Faubourg Saint Honoré, number—"

"Not at all," cried M. Thoré taking up the invoice and examining the total to see that it was correct," the invoices are to be sent by the collector to the Count; as for the service, here's the address."

Saying which, he drew from his pocket a memorandum book, and looked for a card on the back of which a few words had been written in pencil, and said:

"Let this service be sent to Madame Felina de Cambure, Rue Joubert, No. 20."

This little incident passed off without any observation from any one, and the delivery of the merchandise went on. The work of that important day was nearly over, when Charles suddenly appeared at the shop door, and made a sign to his father. M. Thoré responded to it by pointing with his finger to the apartment, and then turned round exclaiming:

"How now, M. Villon, what are you doing there looking at Madame Thoré? we shall never have done. Julia, your invoice book is not under the street door."

M. Thoré did his best, but with all his cunning, he could not prevent Julia from seeing a porter go by with a large frame covered over with green cloth, which Charles saw carried up to the apartment.

"Oh! mamma," she whispered to Madame Thoré, "it is Charles's first picture, I am sure it is: a new year's gift."

The mother glowed with exultation, tears were in her eyes; she pressed Julia's hand and only said:

"Let us be quick."

What remained to be done was soon finished, although M. Villon did not appear to participate in the eagerness felt by Madame Thoré and her daughter. It was even requisite to reproach him more than once with his dilatoriness. At length, the day's work was over. Madame Thoré and Julia hastened up to their apartment, whilst M. Thoré followed after, saying to M. Villon:

"Come and witness their surprise; they will be quite amazed."

"Is it so very fine?" said Louis with a deep sigh.

"It is a perfect resemblance," returned the majestic merchant.

So saying, the whole family arrived nearly at the same time, in the drawing-room where Charles had just deposited in the best light a fine portrait with a rich frame. Julia uttered a cry of wonder, Madame Thoré stood rooted to the spot; she was obliged to wipe her eyes before she could see; she held out her hand to her husband, then looking towards her son, said to him—

"Why don't you come and embrace me?"

Charles looked at his mother perplexedly. Meanwhile Julia cried out:

"Oh! how very like—it is papa himself—how very beautiful!"

She likewise turned to Charles, and said to him:

"How good this is of you, Charles, and how sincerely I thank you. Did I not tell you, mamma, he would give proofs of great talent."

The brother's countenance had assumed a look of disappointment. For him it was awkward to be mistaken for what he was not, and for his mother it was pitiful to have to contradict the kind and proud belief she had in her son. Still he was compelled to speak, and it was with a drooping head he replied:

"Alas! mother, I am not equal to this as yet."

"But it will come, it will come," cried M. Thoré stroking his chin and admiring himself in his image.

"Whom then is this picture by?" said Madame Thoré.

"Why it is by M. Victor Amab," said Louis Villon peevishly.

Madame Thoré became serious and Julia looked with eager interest at the portrait. This look was observed at the same time by her mother and by Louis; then Julia, muttered to herself:—

"Yes, yes, it is well done, oh! very nicely done."

"And after this one," said M. Thoré in high spirits, "we will have yours and Julia's too."

"No, no," said Madame Thoré softly, "a woman should have her picture taken only when she is young and handsome. Now I am too old."

But seeing M. Thoré knit his brows, she added with a smile:—

"You need not wonder. It is a very pardonable piece of coquetry."

"It is a naughty ugly piece of affectation mamma," said Julia, "you must have your picture taken—I entreat you—I will have it; papa, why dont you say you will have it?"

"Certainly," cried M. Thoré, "and I will have yours too."

"Oh! as to that," returned Madame Thoré, eagerly, "I will not allow it—a youg girl."

"Did you not say just now," resumed M. Thoré, "that a woman's picture should be taken when she was young and handsome?"

"Yes, but," resumed Madame Thoré, "with nascent vexation."

"Madame, doubtless meant to say," urged Louis eagerly, "that a young woman may have her likeness done after her marriage.

M. Thoré contemplated M. Villon, as if the latter had expressed some abhorrent proposition, or committed an act of unexampled impropriety. As for Julia, she was suffused with blushes.

"Are all the orders sent for delivery?" said M. Thoré, with great dignity.

"All," answered M. Villon drily, "but I have some calls to make."

Whereupon he immediately withdrew.

As he was crossing the anti-chamber, he met

Victor, who had found the door of the apartment open, and who said to him:—

"May one come in, Sir?"

"Ask the servants," replied Louis sharply, "that is their business."

He then went out slamming the door fiercely behind him, but instead of leaving the house to make the calls he had spoken of, he went and shut himself up in his room; there he strutted about striking the table, the bed, the walls, until wearied out with his own violence, he fell into a chair, saying:—

"Curse the caitiff, I will break his head one of these days."

Whilst the clerk was thus exhlaing his despair, M. Thoré drew close to his wife, who had reproved him with a look of regret for his harsh treatment of M. Villon, and said to him in a royal tone:—

"His attachment blinds him, I do not disapprove of it, but I wish to keep it within due bounds of respect."

"Assuredly," said Madame Thoré, "he was wrong to interfere with what did not concern him, and yet he may have been right, I do not think it proper for a young girl—"

Julia at the same time was whispering to Charles:—

"Is it not finely done?"

"Oh!" answered his brother—"Victor will be one of our greatest painters, he will acquire a great renown."

The conversation had proceeded thus far when M. Victor Amab, who had not seen any one to apply to; came into the drawing room and tapped softly at the door to announce himself.

"Come and be triumphant," said M. Thoré, holding out his hand, "these ladies are full of admiration at your master-piece."

"Are the ladies satisfied?" said Victor, bowing with modest diffidence; "may I then hope they will consent to let me attempt to paint their pictures also?"

"It is a settled business," said the china merchant.

"But it appears to me—" said Madame Thoré with embarrassment.

"We shall begin as soon as possible, shall we not?" said Victor delighted. "In the first place with you, madam," added Amab, "hoping to prevent a refusal by that attention."

"That of course," rejoined M. Thoré, "and Julia will come next."

"Certainly, I do not object," said Madame Thoré, "but we are in the midst of winter—the days are very dark, very short, the time that I and my daughter have to bestow, might not suit this gentleman."

"All my time is at your service, madam, if you will favour me with a portion of your own," said Amab with courteous persistency.

"Well, let it be so, when the fine season has returned."

"Oh! madam," said Victor in a voice of supplication, "the exhibition will be opened in two months, there will not be too much time in the interim to paint two portraits, how much so ever my models may stimulate me."

"What!" resumed Madame Thoré, "do you propose to produce our portraits, Julia's too, in the exhibition."

"Egad!" cried M. Thoré, "why would people be taken, if not for that?"

"No," replied Madame Thoré, "no: I may be very ridiculous perhaps; but I think the custom scarcely proper to expose the portrait of a young woman in public, amidst all sorts of pictures. 'Who is this?' inquires one—and such inquiry will be made—this gentleman's talent will make all his works observable. The people who do not know us may possibly make silly remarks, others will say openly:—'This is Mademoiselle Thoré,' and this will be repeated until my daughter's name becomes in some sort a public one."

"Well," said M. Thoré bridling up, "where's the harm?"

"It is never auspicious," resumed his wife in a determined voice, "for a young woman to be spoken of, whatever people may say of her."

"Well, madam," replied M. Amab, "that picture shall be left with you."

"In that case," said Madame Thoré, "it is useless to have it done for the exhibition?"

"You are right, we will only attend to yours; and, to save you the trouble of going out, Charles has promised me to dispose a place in your wareroom. By surrounding it with cloth and cutting off the light, we shall have all we can desire."

Any further opposition would have been discourteous, so Madame Thoré consented that the sittings should begin in the course of the following week. She had indeed felt some misgivings which had first died away and which were now reviving. But it was necessary to submit.

Since the day he had dined with M. Thoré, Victor had never set foot in the house; he had merely left his card at the door, and Madame Thoré had seen this indifference with pleasure; the attention with which the young painter had looked at Julia, during that dinner, had at first alarmed the prudent mother. But the frank manner in which Victor had explained himself during the evening, had quite reassured her.

As he was going to retire, he had gone up to Madame Thoré and had said to her:—

"Accept my acknowledgments, madam, for the kind welcome you have been so good as to give me; receive also my excuses for a very involuntary error, and which that ugly young lady at the piano, drew my attention to."

"Has she said any thing unpleasant to you? She is a very disagreeable little creature."

"No, madam; she spoke the truth—I felt she had, and I come to beg your pardon for my rudeness."

"If you deem the word a proper one, why do you deserve it?" said Madame Thoré.

"Why?" repeated Victor with rapture and glancing towards Julia; I am a painter, madam, that was what made me err, and that also is my excuse. Charles has told me how good you are Well, madam, understand me rightly; suppose I had to paint an image of the holy Virgin, suppose that in my embarrassment to express the divine chastity of that face, I had suddenly seen it revealed to my eyes, more beautiful than our greatest painters have conceived it. Thus imagine my joy, my enthusiasm. Excuse me, madam, these are an artist's thoughts and may appear very singular to you;—but I know a hundred of them who would pay, I dont know what price for such a model, were it one of those which money can procure. Well, I have had this study for nothing," he added laughing. "I have been indiscreet, and all to no purpose.—No" he continued looking at Julia again, "it does not belong to me to reproduce that purity of design, that transparent complexion, that limped eye, that perfect collective; and then her hands! ah! that makes one cruelly regret not to possess a great talent."

Madame Thoré examined Victor whilst he spoke in this manner, and though her feelings were shocked at the strange freedom with which the artist enumerated her daughter's beauties, she yet understood that she had induced M. Amab to seek to be invited to her house. There was not the least confusion, the slightest tremor in the painter's voice ; it was the language he would have held before a fine statue.

Madame Thoré's fears respecting this young man, were instantly lulled ; but that very night they revived with respect to her daughter.

When every body had left, Julia remained with her mother later than usual, more anticipating, more affectionate even than she was wont to be. Evidently she had something to say, and she was afraid to speak. Madame Thoré perceived it, and was too guarded to utter a word which might resemble a question. But the young maiden's curiosity was more enduring than the mother's prudence, and when the question was put to her :—

" Why dont you return to your chamber ?

" I am going ;" she said ; " but tell me, mamma, what it was Charles's master said about me ?"

" About you ?"

" Yes, a minute or so before he left, whilst he was whispering to you, near the fire-place."

" Why," said Madame Thoré in the most easy natural tone, " he said nothing at all about you."

" Ah !" sighed Julia vexed.—" Good night, mamma, good night."

Then she left the room blushing with shame and perhaps with grief.

The next day Julia did not play a single tune, not even a romance ; her gaiety was gone, and for three weeks she left off laughing, was absent and absorbed, sometimes sorrowful. Then the portrait had come, and Madame Thoré had remarked the ardent and impassioned look which Julia had fixed upon it, the moment she knew who was the author of the master-piece.

All that night, Madame Thoré did not sleep ; she brooded a long time over a plan to break off the engagement she had entered into to have her portrait taken, and consequently to authorize M. Amab to return to her house. Not that Madame Thoré was averse to the prospect of an alliance between Julia and the young artist.

He had no fortune, but fortune comes rapidly enough to men of talent. Besides, such an obstacle would not have arrested Madame Thoré for a moment, could her daughter's happiness have been secured by this union ; but by a strange presentiment, this loving mother had devined that this man brought with him a calamity for her. She had studied him well, and well considered him, and the result of that scrutiny was an opinion not in his favour.

However, he was a deserving young man, full of integrity and courage. He possessed that quality so charming in youth, of distrusting his present worth and relying on the future ; dissatisfied with what he did, he had sworn to do well, with that resolution which is itself a power.

When Madame Thoré had sent Charles to Amab's atelier, she had made inquiries as to his character, and had been informed that he was studious, well-conducted, orderly, and indefatigably diligent ; was not that sufficient to lull the fears of a mother, even supposing her daughter were to conceive a fancy for such a man ? Many others, less particular than Madame Thoré, would not have required better guarantees for a future son-in-law, and yet, she was afraid of this man, she did not like him. But little accustomed to explain those nice perceptions by which women judge so soundly without the intervention of reason, she would have been greatly perplexed to say why M. Victor Amab was so displeasing to her. Had any one asked her what she thought of him, and she had felt disposed to reply according to her impressions, she would have said that M. Victor Amab was an ambitous, selfish man. But had she been called upon to prove the truth of her opinion, she would have been quite at a loss to sustain it.

However, it was necessary to extricate herself from the irksome situation she was in, and, after long reflection, she asked herself whether she would not do better to let things take their usual course.

" My daughter," she said to herself, " has reached the age when the heart creates phantoms to live amongst ; it is not M. Amab that she loves, it is some fanciful being to whom she lends the qualities which attract and fascinate her. This imaginary being she will continue to love so long as she sees him in harmony with that creation. Would it not be prudent to show her the reality of her dream ? Either M. Amab is what I consider him, and Julia will find him out and be ashamed of her wild imagination, or I myself an mistaken on the young man's account, and it may be this love which is destined to secure my daughter's happiness."

Madame Thoré was released from her anxiety by this argument ; but what she could not understand was the suddenness with which Julia had fixed her thoughts on this young man. Doubtless, his manners were agreeable, and his person handsome, especially in that proud intelligence of look and expression which lends so much dignity to a man ; his conversation was sprightly and good natured ; but all that was not enough for Julia, with her candid heart, and delicate spirit, to accept him, at first sight, as the ideal of her dreams.

But Madame Thoré did not know all, she had not heard a confidential communication which Charles had made to his sister, on the evening of the day when M. Amab had dined with M. Thoré.

## CHAPTER III.

### SOME SECRETS ARE CONFIDED.

On that day, Julia had taken her brother into a little boudoir, and had asked him what he meant by that duel which M. Amab had fought in the forenoon ; for she could not believe he could work in his atelier only an hour before exposing his life ; and thence arose a thousand questions as to M. Amab.

" Ah ! her brother had replied to her, he is a wonderful man. I tell you.—He began by being an apprentice to a decorative house painter ; he used to stencil imitations of marble and granite for staircases ; then he took to thread painting. Before he was twelve years old, he had felt that he could do something better than that. When his day was over, he used to go to a free school of design, and in a few months he acquired there all that they profess to teach in three years ; afterwards he went to the Academy, under Sasse, always on evenings, because he had to gain his living by day to defray the expenses of his models."

" He has no relations then ?"

" His father and mother are dead, and they left him an orphan at eight years of age ; he was taken up by a painter and glazier, who taught him his trade for charity."

" Indeed " cried Julia in a tone of sorrow and pity." And you say he made great progress at the Academy ? It was there, was it not, he learned to paint ?"

" He did not advance so fast as that ; first, he attempted lithography, and when once he was able to do so, he began to work on his own account.—He made chimney fronts for fifteen francs. At that time, he never breakfasted, and there were days when he went without his dinner; by degrees, he caught the trade and got his hand in."

"You mean—?"

"I mean that he got his hand in, that is to say, he became clever; then he entered the employment of Leon Noel at a fixed salary, and earned his five francs a day; that was his good time, his harvest."

"What, do you mean that at present—?"

"It was then he saved up a little store to enable him to study painting by day light; he left off making lithographs, except at night, by candle light; here was fifteen hours' labour a day; it was near killing him.—More than that, when he rose again after his illness, he had not a brown copper to face the world with.—He was compelled to go out again by the day. At last he managed to do two or three pictures.—They were admitted into the Museum, but nobody noticed them, and he sold them for a hundred francs a piece to a jew. Any other man, I for instance, would have been discouraged; but this man possesses a character of iron; he lived upon bread and water, and still went on painting.—At one of the last exhibitions, one of his friends whose portrait he had painted gratuitously, put an article in a newspaper which brought him a few orders. Now, he is fairly launched; he also obtained the place of drawing master in a girl's boarding school.

"Ah!" cried Julia, "in a boarding school for young ladies!"

"Yes, yes," said Charles, without noticing the marked emphasis which Julia had laid on the words, "and that was precisely the cause of his duel."

"Indeed!" said Julia, "for one of his pupils—for one of the young ladies?"

"Not at all, not at all, for the mother of one of his pupils."

"For a lady;"

"Yes, and who was not worth the trouble, although she is very pretty."

"Ah! returned Julia, "who then is that lady?"

"The wife of a banker who wished to have her likeness taken, when her husband was from home, to give it to him on his return. She used to come every morning to the atelier. The portrait was finished in a month. It is a splendid picture; and I assisted to do the back-ground."

"Well, but what of the portrait?"

"Well, the portrait, when the time came to pay for it, the lady would not consent to the price agreed upon—she began to debate it."

"Perhaps she is not rich?"

"She has a hundred thousand francs a year.—Go, it is not the poor who bargain with you, but the rich; she wanted to give five hundred francs instead of a thousand." So Victor said to her:—

"Madam, you must pay a thousand francs for this portrait, or I will beg you to accept it as a present."

"Neither one nor the other," said the lady to him, "it is a service I wished to do you.

"Madam, I did not ask you to do me a service, and if I only charge you a thousand francs for this portrait, it is because I have no name to rely upon as yet."

"Will you take six hundred francs?" said the lady.

"A thousand or none at all."

"In that case, you may keep your picture. If you think I owe you any money, and desire to be paid, you can go to law with me, and let your canvass be appraised."

"Nobody shall appraise it," answered Victor.

And, thereupon, he coolly took his painting knife, and cut the portrait into four pieces, then turning to the lady, he said to her:—

"Now, madam, you are out of my debt."

"Did he really do that!" cried Julia eagerly, "that was right, that was truly noble!"

"You never saw a woman look so silly as that lady—she was absolutely stunned. Ah! Victor understands business in high style, I tell you," resumed Charles. "Men may set their own value on themselves," he often says to me; "I will live in poverty, but I will never bring down the terms of my art; this year my portraits are rated at a thousand francs, next year they will be worth two thousand; in three years we shall see what they will bring.—You see, Charles, that is the way people rise to fortune."

"And to glory!" said Julia enthusiastically, for she had not understood the bold calculations of a man who, fully self-reliant, fixes beforehand the cost and value of his talents, and resolves to abide by his own terms, convinced as he is they will be granted.

"It must have been, no doubt, with this lady's husband that M. Amab fought the duel?" added she.

"Why, no—and that is the strangest of all! I must tell you that the day before yesterday, in the green-room at the opera, they were talking about this adventure. In the midst of the conversation, a young man took upon him to say, that the account was not true that the pretended portrait never existed, and that the assiduous visits of the lady had another object that——"

"What object?" asked Julia innocently, observing that Charles had suddenly broken off.

"What object—I hardly know how to tell it you; a bad object,—yes,—it was wrong, you know something not agreeable to the lady."

"But what was it then?"

"A most silly insinuation," said Charles, "since I was present whenever she sat to him."

"But still what did he say?"

"How, dont you understand me? They said naughty things of the lady; they gossipped about appointments—of love."

Julia cast down her eyes and blushed; Charles, who felt he had ventured upon a story scarcely fit for a young lady to listen to, thought he would cut short his embarrassment by saying:—

"Then Victor went up and gave a formal denial to the young man."

Julia listened once more.

"He spoke to her these very words:—

"Whatever complaints I may have to make against that lady, I will allow no man to calumniate her; she may have been dissatisfied with her portrait, and have declined payment of it.—But if any one goes beyond this, he lies." Hence the quarrel and the duel with this young fellow, you understand?"

"Ah! that was well done! well done!" said Julia.

"Go—go—" resumed Charles, "you may believe me, this is a fellow of spirit who knows what he does; one may rely on him to give the right shape and posture to things."

Charles continued in the same strain, explaining in his own way the great art of assuming before the world, a bold relief to dazzle and astonish people. But Julia no longer listened to her brother; what Charles interpreted as skill, because he possessed the secret of his master's theories, Julia interpreted as disinterestedness, pride, and magnanimity, because she looked for the version in her own feelings.

Such was the confidental communication which Madame Thoré knew nothing of, and which had proved the origin or starting point of the interest felt by her daughter for the young painter.

However, scarcely had a few days more elapsed, before, without her having to think about it, the little nook where Madame Thoré was to sit was ready in her husband's warerooms. The truth is, that on more than one occasion and unknown to her mother, Julia had hurried the workmen. After that, the day having arrived on which young Amab was to come, the lovely maiden did not sleep, and rose earlier than usual; her mother said she looked fatigued; but Julia had put on the dress which became her the best.

Ah! woman, woman! bird of love and happiness, why must thy Paradise be crossed by the serpent! why turn and listen to his wiles!

## CHAPTER IV.

### THE DAWN OF LOVE.

During a month that Victor employed in painting Madame Thoré's portrait, nothing took place apparently by which a mother's foresight could be alarmed. Whenever Julia entered the temporary studio, whether to keep her mother company, or to watch the progress of the pencil, Victor was usually silent; except that now and then Madame Thoré detected the painter's looks riveted with covetous attention on Julia; but the admiration which lighted up the eyes of the artist was the mere curiosity of art. This man was so deeply absorbed by the passions of his calling as not even to guess the confusion he occasioned, and when Julia blushed, when her heart palpitated, when her voice faltered beneath that ardent look, Victor only deemed her more beautiful, nothing more.

During the long hours of ennui and attitude that Madame Thoré had to endure, she endeavoured to discover what was lurking in the soul of the young man; she questioned him about himself. He related his story to her, as Charles had related it to Julia; he told it without arrogance; neither blushing for his poverty, nor boasting of having subdued it. Julia listened to him like Desdemona, and loved him for the sorrows he had suffered, and yet Julia deceived herself. The indifference Victor showed for his trials did not proceed from that fine resignation which is rigid to itself, and pitiful to others; it was a strange apathy. The truth was, this man had never felt unhappy at being poor, what really afflicted him was not to become a great painter as fast as he desired.

His past life was untarnished, and yet it did not disarm Madame Thoré of her prejudices. She studied Amab more closely, for fear of being unjust, and saw that he was a man of honour, of strict integrity, endowed with every virtue to avoid evil, but with none to do good.

Madame Thoré thought that with such a character, this man must be meanly envious; to convince herself of the truth, she sought to discover what he thought of others. She imagined she had guessed the truth, on hearing him speak with contempt of some of our most popular masters, but she was forced to change her opinion, when she heard him speak with respect and admiration of some others. With Victor it was a matter of taste, an artist's enthusiasm; he admired and respected talent openly and freely whenever he met with it. Why then did Victor displease Madame Thoré? Why was she afraid of him? Because there was a something wanting to that powerful organization: *his quiet heart did not beat.* Was it only asleep? Would it wake up one day beneath the radiant light which the eye of a loving woman pours into the soul of him she has chosen?"

Madame Thoré still examined, still waited. Alas! poor mother! she saw her daughter gather every thought which fell from the artist, to carry away with her to her solitude, and there, with that laborious study, with that love for the beautiful, with that admiration for the genius of great masters, she saw Julia create one of those imaginary idols, to which woman devote themselves, and which crush the heart beneath their ruins, when a single breath of truth comes to demolish them.

Twenty times did that mother believe it had been better for Julia, had she felt an inclination for one of those bold seducers who advance directly to their triumph. Julia's virtue and purity would have been startled by a word of love; her pride of chastity would have revolted against an open attack; but here was nothing to raise fear; she was travelling alone along that road which removed her from her own peace without bringing her the nearer to Victor. Madame Thoré herself could not caution her daughter; she had nothing to complain of the artist. The man was perfect; he was as hard and brilliant as a diamond.

Madame Thoré was sad; she earnestly wished that her portrait was finished; she strove to pick a quarrel with him for his want of diligence; but how could she upbraid him with such a work for his defence?

There she was, more beautiful, more charming than she had ever been, young and beautiful as she had been before, so that her husband wondered how the painter had divined the past which he had never seen. Then the latter explained how he had in a manner beheld the mother in the image of her child; how by aging a little the young and fresh lineaments of Julia, and by rendering more juvenile the still handsome features of the mother, he had succeeded in producing that admirable face at the sight of which M. Thoré embraced his wife with pride, whilst Charles knelt before her to contemplate it, and which made Julia glance from the work to its author.

In presence of the artist's triumph, there was no murmuring; Madame Thoré seemed unjust to everybody, except to Louis Villon, who bitterly detested M. Amab. The clerk's jealousy had been more penetrating than the mother's tenderness. Sometimes these two would look sorrowfully at each other; they understood each other, but yet they would have been sorely perplexed to explain themselves; neither of them would have thought of accusing Julia, and Victor was above reproach.

However, Madame Thoré hoped in the susceptibility of love, she thought it impossible that Julia would not at last be offended by that apathetic courtesy, which was ever visible in Victor, as soon as the artist's curiosity was appeased. She sought not to remove the girl, but suffered her to listen to the young man, and hear him relate his future aspirings; the aim of all his desires was glory and power; never was the thought of a gentle affection, of an idolatry of the heart, mixed up with his dreams of ambition. In that life which he fancied, Victor scarcely assigned any place to pleasure. What we call the world was for him nothing more than a circus in which he hoped to be triumphant. This was a world which he looked for everywhere, at home, at people's entertainments, at the theatre; but all he asked of it was applause and power; as for his fortune, that came after this, and far behind.

Unfortunately, Madame Thoré was far from being

fully convinced herself that the opinions, as well as the actions of men, have quite a different aspect according to the point of view whence they are considered. She had placed herself to see and judge Victor, on the ground of reason and distrust. Julia was on the opposite side: that of love and credulity.

However, Madame Thoré might perhaps have gained her point at last, had not an incident, which we must now relate, deceived the beautiful girl as to the apathy she had ended by noticing. Not only did Julia's mother no longer fear to allow her to be present ae the painter's sittings; but she tried two or three times to leave them together on pretence of business. At first, she listened, and perceived that if a conversation had been opened, it went on; but if she left them in silence, that same silence continued. Victor only thought of his pencils and canvas. Madame Thoré thought she remarked signs of vexation in Julia, and resolved to leave time for that feeling to grow stronger.

One day, the eve of that when her portrait was to be finished, Madame Thoré had gone out. Julia had remained alone with Victor; she was looking at him stealthily, whilst with his eye fastened to the canvas, he continued engrossed with the contemplation of his work. At that moment Julia's heart was swolen with tears, she had at length recognised her love and Victor's indifference, but she loved him so much that what she felt was sadness not humiliation. By degrees she languished off into that desolate hopelessness which at once oppresses both heart and body; the work she held fell from her hands without her perceiving it; she raised her eyes towards heaven, and the feeling of which she had dreamed dissolving into the one that afflicted her, a tear rose into her eye. At this moment Victor chanced to look at her, became fixed with wonder, and as if struck by some sudden idea of inspiration, muttered the words:

"Oh! I ought to break my palette."

This exclamation roused Julia, and made her start.

"Oh! remain as you are," said Victor drawing near, "stay and let me look at you. Oh!" he resumed whilst his eye glanced with enthusiasm, "if you knew—but I dare not tell you."

"What is it?" asked Julia quivering all over.

"You will not be angry with me?"

"Why should I be angry with you? what have you done?"

"Well," said Victor considering her with a look which the passion of the artist kindled into a flame not unlike love, "I wanted to impart your beauty to a picture of the Virgin."

"What?" said Julia.

"Yes, assisted only by my memory, I have attempted to reproduce these charming features, and I flattered myself I had caught my idea after surrounding your head with a halo, and placing angels at your knees; but I have just had my eyes opened to my presumption. All I have done has been bad, pitifully bad. I have but this moment understood you; hitherto I had seen only your face, I have just discovered your soul. Oh! thank you, thank you! You have now given me a masterpiece," he added striking his forehead; "it is there—I shall owe you my glory."

This was certainly not love, but it was exultation, and that so young, so ardent, so earnest, that the poor weeping child listened to it with avidity, and thought she heard therein the voice she had so long waited for. Fond and obedient, she once more raised to heaven the eyes she had dropped when Victor spoke, and trembling, agitated, she allowed him to look at her whilst he hastily committed to a cartoon the first lineaments of that simple attitude, of that countenance so wonderfully animated. Then she snatched up her work on hearing Madame Thoré's approach, whilst Victor whispered to her:

"Say nothieg to your mother, she might forbiu me to carry away this memorial of you."

Saying which he eagerly concealed the sketch.

How she was embarrassed, how she felt ashamed the whole of that day! what a confession she had made! how easily she had accepted that contained in Victor's language (for she took it for a confession); what a proof of her love she had suffered him to take! how guilty, how wretched she felt herself. Oh! she would have been a thousand times more miserable, had she known that Victor had mistaken this submission of a suffering soul for the mere complaisance of a vain young girl.

The next day Victor arrived late; he was fatigued—He sat down coolly to his work, but as soon as he was alone with Julia, his eyes beemed again.

"Oh!" cried he, "I have laboured, and this time I hope I have succeeded."

Julia did not answer.

"Oh! it would be very kind of you," said he to her, "to permit me to behold you again as you were yesterday."

"Of what use would that be to you?" said Julia laying down her needlework.

'Of what use?" said Victor contemplating her —"why I shall owe you my glory—my life—yes, I feel I shall—and my gratitude will be eternal.

She assumed the same attitude, and when a noise came to disturb them, he whispered to her.

"Oh! you have indeed been kind, and never shall I forget it.

Then Julia looking at him, and without stopping to explain to herself the sadness which mingled with the hope she had conceived within the last two days, said to him softly:—

"You will not forget it, will you, Sir?"

Then suddenly, and for the first time, Victor asked himself, whether whilst seeking an occasion of honourable distinction, he had not obtained another triumph; he examined Julia more attentively, and felt that he was loved: a rapid flame glittered in his eyes, after which he seemed to seize and confine within him a second hope. Julia had watched him, had seen the ray of that light, and had said to herself: he has understood me, he feels happy, he loves me.

Alas! that look of Victor's did not mean that; the man had at that moment said to himself:—

"This young lady loves me—what can it do to serve me? where can it lead? I will think of it.

And on that day Madame Thoré's picture was finished.

---

## CAPTER V.

### THE DRAWING-ROOM.

HOWEVER Victor had not returned to Madame Thoré's house since he had finished her portrait; he had merely inquired of Charles the following day what were the habits of his family; and had listened to him attentively whilst his pupil had frankly related the honest pomposity of his father, the chaste and honest virtue of his mother, and the candid and trustful innocence of Julia. Then, after listening to this account, Victor had thought within himself, and had said:—

"I will not abuse this tenderness, I will not sow division in this family; it is sometimes enough to ruin a man in his profession when he commits a questionable act; what would it be if he committed a guilty one. Selfish man! he would be virtuous for his own sake."

The idea of marrying Julia had, indeed, presented itself to his mind; but that mind, engrossed by itself and by the spirit of advancement, had calculated on the spot, all the impediments which housekeeping may raise to clog the free existence of an artist. Amab wished to see Rome, and Florence, with their masterpieces, Africa, her deserts and prodigious vegetation; he desired to be free to go where he liked, to study every thing without constraint, both in art and nature. Domestic felicity, the delight of a harmonious union, the security of an acquired fortune, all these had appeared to him; but all had vanished before the breath of his ambition. This man sought not to be happy; he wanted to be great: that was his delight; so he repelled as promptly the idea of an honourable alliance, as the thought of a base seduction. The one might impede his progress, the other would not serve his ambition.

When Victor took this resolution, he did not think that the injury he had done was so serious, although he had guessed Julia's love. He absolved himself of the past, in which he had taken no part, and flattered himself he would be master of the future. "Really," said he to himself, "what could the most prudent mother, or the most punctilious father require of me? It would be not to see their daughter again, never to drop a word about her which might be reported to her and lead her to believe that she is in my thoughts. And that I will do."

But already Amab's silence depended no longer on himself; already a thousand tongues brought back the memory of him to Julia's heart, and he himself was to speak to her louder than all, in that sovereign language of art which so warmly impresses the fancy. In truth, the exhibition had scarcely opened, when some fine pictures of his began to be spoken of, but above all, and in a more lofty tone, a marvellous picture of the Virgin Mary.

Madame Thoré was thus reminded of what Amab had said to her the first time he had called at her house—and she had a presentiment of the truth. But Madame Thoré had resolved to know nothing. Julia, in the meanwhile was becoming every day more melancholy, more pensive, her mother could hear that she did not sleep amidst the silent stillness of the night; she saw her exert herself with effort to fulfil the once easy duties of their lonely life. Julia suffered, but did not complain. Doubtless at the first question from that mother's voice which so deeply penetrates the heart of suffering children, doubtless at the first word Julia would have said all, and confessed all. But what could it do? What consolation had she to give her daughter? Julia was not loved. The heart may be consoled for a happiness which is lost; but not for a disappointed hope. It persists in believing the realization would have come, had it not been driven away.

Every day, Charles urged his mother to go to the exhibition; she declined to go, postponed the visit, and every day Julia's despondency deepened its shade. At last, M. Thoré resolved to go and contemplate himself publicly in his image; it was necessary to submit.

Therefore Madame Thoré went to the gallery with a sense of keen apprehension; Charles's persistency serving to confirm her suspicions. After showing them every thing else, he at last led them up to his master's work. M. Thoré could not restrain a cry of astonishment which brought upon them the notice of a crowd of visitors. Madame Thoré stood transfixed, saying:—

"That is it."

She had not deceived herself.

As for Julia, her mother felt her leaning lightly upon her arm, and looked at her with anxiety: the lovely girl was as pale as a winding sheet.

"You are unwell," said her mother to her eagerly, and seeking to lead her away.

"No," Julia replied gently, resisting, "something like a choking sensation, that's all."

Her happiness had smitten her on the heart.

M. Thoré had forced his way through the crowd exclaiming:—

"Ah! how like it is.—Look then, wife, Julia, why don't you look, it is—"

"Is it not beautiful?" said a bystander.

"It is divine," cried another.

And one merry roysterer added:—

"If Amab has not a seat in paradise after this, he wont be used well."

Another gazer with more gravity replied:—

"He has opened the gates of heaven, and seen this supreme beauty there."

Whilst a third cried out:

"Where the deuce did he find such a noble head?"

That head was standing near, pale, with downcast eyes, confused, delirious with a strange delight, and with hopes unbounded; for all her doubts had disappeared. She heard the voice of Victor's love in that host of admiring tongues which were buzzing around her; was it not her image which she had secretly entrusted to him, which attracted this throng of gazers and prompted them to speak? She was so troubled and so confused that she hastily drew aside her mother, as if she had heard Amab's voice.

M. Thoré was obliged to leave the crowd and look for them.

"How, you did not observe M. Amab's picture?" he cried.

"It is very fine," said Madame Thoré.

"I don't mean that. Did you see nothing else?" said he swelling with joy.

"Nothing," said his wife pretending to look at another frame.

"What! you did not notice the likeness?"

"To whom?"

"Why to our daughter, my dear; to our daughter Madame Thoré—to my daughter," he added raising Julia's head.

"Yes, there is some resemblance to Julia, I must confess."

"Why it is absolutely her."

"No, no," said Madame Thoré trying to laugh, "that is not Julia. Don't weep Julia."

Poor child! her tears were choking her. Alas! perhaps she had deceived herself, perhaps it was not her that Victor had intended to paint! her mother did not recognize her.

Victor had been informed of all this, or at least all that Charles had understood; the clamorous amazement of his father, the surprise and confusion of Julia, his mother's diffidence, and Victor understood it all. But these assurances had not altered his resolution, and he would not meet Julia again: as he had reasoned within himself, her love would have stood in his way. And in spite of all his resolution, this love obstructed him; for it had planted a regret in his heart. Amab had not sacrificed his ambition to it, but his ambition seemed to him more difficult to satisfy than he had felt it hitherto.

---

## CHAPTER VI.

### THE ATELIER.

THE following day was a joyous one in Victor Amab's atelier; they were towards the end of a cheerful and sumptuous collation; the Museum had been open a week, and the crowd had continued to collect round a picture representing the Virgin Mary situated in one of the corners of the grand gallery. It was only a simple face, but that countenance was a masterpiece of colouring and thought. The artists admired the design, the model, the complexion, the drapery; the crowd extolled its expression, its beauty and grace. There was in that aspect a joy both sorrowful and holy; a divine hope seemed to radiate through tears; Mary felt beforehand all the greatness and the agony of her mission, she exulted in it and was resigned. How could it be explained? We shall not attempt the task: the pen has its secrets which none can interpret, the pencil has its mysteries which the pen cannot explain.

It was morning; Victor's pupils, among whom Charles was the most earnest, the most enthusiastic; a few of those friends whom success does not drive away, were relating the rapture, the admiration of the crowd. One cited the observation of a great nobleman; another, the discerning appreciation of a connoisseur; a third, the candid amazement of a child; a fourth, the honest delight of a mechanic, or the sententious approbation of a citizen: every one had his anecdote, his eulogy, and all assured Amab that he had at length shot ahead of all his competitors, and that the great masters would soon have to open their ranks to him.

And he?—oh! he was a strong, resolute man, for he received these praises well; he listened to them without affected modesty and without intoxication, It is true, a shadow had passed across his triumph; a painter of little talent had said:—

"Unquestionably, it is beautiful, but after all it is but a face."

This word, this galling remark:—"it is but a face," sounded continually in the ears of the triumphant artist, like a discord in the midst of that harmony of applause—and the insatiable pride of Victor was all the more wounded, that he could not help saying to himself:—

"Ah!" that man was right, it is but a face: he said so, others will therefore say the same: and this opinion is too well suited to their envy not to be believed; I have still to wait before the people will call me a great painter; well, I will take a canvas of twenty feet, introduce a hundred thousand men therein, like Decamps, or a few figures like Delaroche, and they shall call me a great painter, then. Yes, it must, and shall be."

And in the midst of his triumph, to him alone imperfect, Amab already meditated the picture which was to vindicate him for a chance remark.

Meanwhile, amidst the countless sayings which came and went in the workroom, they asked Victor whether that admirable creation was a conception of his genius, fraught with its own beauty and idea, or whether he had given life and immortality to a living angel.

To which Victor replied with a lordly smile:—

"That is my secret."

It was likewise that of Charles; but the master had requested his pupil to be discreet, and the pupil was one who looked up to his master as a superior being; he was the priest and apostle of his creed.

They were in the height and fervor of these congratulations and recitals of their young master's glory when a packet of letters was brought in for him. Most of them contained compliments; these he read hastily, handed a few to the company about him congratulating himself that he had so many friends.

By and by he opened another which greatly surprised him.

And truly the envelope was empty: he was about to throw it away thinking that it was one of those stupid mystifications which certain simpletons conceive, when as he crumpled it up he felt something move within the envelope. He tore it open and found at the bottom a heartsease and a myosotis which no doubt was intended to express to him: "Forget me not." Whom had he promised that remembrance to, now so modestly recalled? He remembered what he had said to Julia; his absence then had not banished her illusions. He grew sad, then gloomy, and at length discontented; he tore up the envelope, and hid the flowers in his pocket. Poor Julia! Yes, it was manifest, this love oppressed him, he became peevish, and it was perhaps his ill-humour which induced him to do that which, under any other circumstances, he would have looked upon as an improper joke, if not a bad action.

He opened the last letter of all, read it first, and then examined the handwriting: he read it a second time and suddenly exclaimed, at the same time interrupting the outrageous enthusiasm of one of those babblers of the atelier who win collections of sketches, drawings, and sometimes of small pictures by their incessant gabble:

"You are a man of talent. This is capital, prodigious! A. B. C. D. may go hang themselves! etc., etc."

Here Victor interrupted the parasite, as he exclaimed:

"I am more fortunate, gentlemen, than you think, and here is a rather particular rendez-vous."

They pressed round Victor with eager curiosity, who read aloud the following note:

"Sir,

A woman whose certificate of birth assures her that she is young, and whom a thousand tongues affiirm that she is handsome; whose heart tells her she is not a fool, wishes to see the author of *the Virgin in tears*. If you are not afraid of another admirer, come to-night, at ten o'clock, Rue Joubert—"

Here Victor broke off. The letter was signed FELINA DE CAMBURE.

"What number?" cried they on every side.

"That is enough," said Amab, "but it must be confessed there are some strange women in the Rue Joubert."

"Shall you go?" inquired the students.

"Certainly not, it is a *bonne fortune* which anyone is welcome to in my place,

Ten voices instantly laid claim to it. Among these Charles was the most eager, the most ardent; as soon as he put in his claim everyone else drew back. He was their king; of him they had said in the slang of the fraternity: "That he would have got Talleyrand to set for his picture," so tranquil and fearless he was in perpetrating his jokes.

Victor threw the letter to him disdainfully and recommended him to be prudent.

"Good," said Charles.. "I think the caution unnecessary, it must be some superannuated blue stocking' or some German baroness. Never mind, we will try and make it diverting."

A moment after Victor, having retired to the saloon adjoining his atelier, silently examined his two flowers. those candid messengers of the chastest and sincerest love, and said to himself with all the bitterness of a man, thwarted in his aims :—

"It is very disagreeable! it is very troublesome!"

This was the point of vitality the predominant idea, the master-feeling of his soul; then he began to reflect and became absorbed in deep thought and calculation. Was it love that had been rowsed within him? did he at length feel for the first time stirring in his heart that requirement of living in some one else, which is the complement of man's existence? or was it nothing more than the prosecution of a new thought; had he discovered that the persistent love of Julia might influence and assist his glory and fortune more than he had at first believed? Be what it might, Victor, when he returned among his friends, continued thoughtful and all but gloomy in spite of the joyous uproar in his atelier. At night, he called upon Madame Thoré and was told thht they were all gone to the play; he left his card and said to himself as he walked away :—

"Evidently, it is better so."

## CHAPTER VII.

### A TRICK.

THE next day, Charles related in the same workroom his visit to the rue Joubert. By his account, he had seen saloons hung with velvet, boudoirs lined with satin, Aubússon carpets, Martin's upholstery, golden lamps, a profusion of flowers, Venetian mirrors, intoxicating perfumes, and, amidst this scene of enchantment, a woman of regal beauty, with eyes black and radiant, a wild enthusiastic creature, fond, overflowing with passion, eloquence, and tenderness.

Charles had so much the reputation of an inventor, that his companions strove with each other to rally him. Victor, who was sitting with a cartoon before him, on which his abounding genius was sketching the outline of a great composition, suddenly interrupted his pupil's vainglorious account with the question :—

"And what did this superb creature say to you, when you told her you were not me?"

"I was very careful to tell her nothing of the kind, she would have had me thrust out of doors by one of the lackeys, for she keeps lackeys, she does."

"What you told her that you were——"

"I told her I was Victor Amab; and therefore I met with a welcome—oh! a most satisfactory one."

"That is very likely," cried the pupils.

Victor felt annoyed by this joke to which he had at first attached but little importance; but the idea that the power of his name had excited so much interest and admiration, soothed his displeasure, and stopped him as he was going to express it; he merely said :—

"I hope, Charles, you did nothing to commit me."

"What do you mean by that?" said Charles laughing.—"Make yourself easy, I take your glory to heart more than you do yourself, and I proved to the most beautiful of the beautiful that you know how to gather every kind of laurel."

An explosion of unbelief burst upon Charles, who suffered it to die away with the disdainful indifference of a man who is sure of a triumphant answer.

"Gentlemen," he resumed at length, "I have appointed a meeting with the lady here, in my atelier, that is in the atelier of the thrice illustrious Victor Amab; she is coming, and if I have invented a single iota, I declare myself unworthy to set my feet again in this august assembly. I had even planned a nice treat in this matter."

"Tell us," cried the giddy young men.

"Remember, I must not be mixed up in it," said Amab.

"You will not be included at all; only play your own part naturally. Some one will call and ask for M. Amab, and you will answer very simply: I am the person."

Victor at first declined; but the entreaties of his pupils on one side, and on the other the price which Charles appeared to set on his discretion with respect to the famous picture, a discretion too which Charles brought back to his mind by saying to him: "I was good-natured then, now it is your turn." Finally that absence of reflection, or rather that fatality which hurries men to say and do things which seem immaterial, and which affect and prejudice the rest of their lives; all this we say, determined Victor to lend himself to Charles's frolic. They wanted to know his project, but he refused to divulge it to the last. Soon after, a carriage having stopped at the street door, Charles ran to the window of an adjoining room, saying as he returned:

"Silencé, here she is.

Thereupon he vanished behind a large folding screen which had been placed there for the model figures to dress and undress.

Amab withdrew to the saloon which led into his atelier.

A slight peculiar tap was heard at the door, one of the pupils went and opened it, and stood as if dazzled as he saw come in a veiled woman, of commanding figure, who was attired with that luxury which requires a refined taste not to seem heavy and vulgar. "M. Victor Amab?" she said in a firm and articulated voice, whilst the whole atelier stood mute with surprise.

The pupil showed her the saloon; the lady went in.

Amab turned his head as the lady raised her veil so that they found themselves face to face, she, with her back to the students, he, boholding revealed to his eyes the proudest beauty he had ever admired.

"Monsieur Amab," she resumes,

"That his the name, madam," said Victor in a tremulous voice, so much had he been disturbed by the appearance of the woman.

At this answer, Felina, for she it was, fix'd her sparkling eyes upon Victor, and said to him in an altered voice:—

"You Sir?"

"Myself!"

Felina let down her veil, turned round, and swept the atellier, with a quick glance. Her strength seemed to fail; she staggered.

"A chair!" exclaimed Victor, who now began bitterly to regret the frolic he had allowed,

At that moment, Charles came from behind the curtain with a chair in his hand. The ill-starred youth had exchanged his working coat for a livery garment; he had a feather brush in his hand and looked exactly like a servant. He offered the chair he brought to Felina, and, as if the sight of her astonished him, he uttered a cry and let fall the feather brush.

Then Felina perceived him, and drew back with a muttered groan.

Victor surprised at the masquerading, said to Charles in a tone of authority :—

"Charles, what is the meaning of all this?"

"Alas, Sir," answered the young man, with

with that heartless brutality which induces your joker to slaughter a victim for a moment's laugh; it was madam who wrote you a letter, it was madam who had given you the rendezvous,—and at whose house I had the misfortune.—I mean the good fortune——"

"What man is this?" said Felina pointing to Charles with a quivering hand.

"Alas!" said Charles in a lachrymose voice, "I am the gentleman's valet-de-chambre.

"It is M. Thoré," said Victor angrily; "he is one of my pupils, madam."

Felina stood up, walked straight up to Amab, and whispered to him with a fiendish look:—

"One of your pupils, to whom you gave the letter which a fond woman wrote to you."

Amab wanted to reply—Felina lifted her veil, looked attentively at the pupil and the master; then after a short and dismal silence, she drew off saying:—

"We shall meet again, gentlemen."

The frolic had been played, but its success was a gloomy one. Victor was excessively dissatisfied and felt alarmed; as for Charles, he did not yet understand all the terrible gravity of such a meeting; but he had not raised a laugh, and he considered the sullen silence of the spectators as a failure.

"Psha!" he exclaimed after Felina had withdrawn, "she's an upstart pride.

Now we, the authors of this book, have related this scene in all its savage nudity; first, because this was how it happened; and then because this way alone can explain, as it appears to us, the feelings and actions it afterwards suggested to her who was the victim of this frolic. As for the rest, let this matter be borne in mind, we have invented nothing, neither the events nor the characters of the people introduced. We are writing a history, a true history, horrible as the events may seem; we have depicted portraits, and none but true portraits, however demoniac, flagitious, and abominable some of them must appear. Society is full of serpents with their venemous tongues, and the novelist who professes to describe the world, must expose that poison, or deceive his readers.

And this is the fittest place to introduce a chapter on reflection, and as many people are not fond of this revisal of the mind, it shall be a short one.

## CHAPTER VIII.

AN adventure like the one we have just related may possible appear incredible to some of our readers; many of them, though they may admit as possible Felina's unbridled lasciviousness, and Victor's impertinent disdain, will not believe in Charles's infamy; they will not believe that a young man can carry so far his impudence and baseness as to expose, to exhibit as a spectacle, before all his companions, the woman he has deluded. If his honour did not, they would maintain that the vanity of so charming a conquest would prevent them from taking such a course. Our readers would be mistaken: men like Charles are to be found in abundance.

These are fine spirited young men who begin life with a certain repute for jocularity, and of whom people say, when they appear: "Here comes Charles, he will make us merry."

These men accept the part of joker, and the better to support it they spare no pains, but exert all their mind and capacity. By degrees, success intoxicates them, and they must have it: if they find it escaping, they will pursue it at any cost, sacrificing honour, moral dignity, friendship itself, and in the end (if their popularity declines) their most tender affections, to win this admiration. Sometimes, they sacrifice to this longing for success, the world's respect, and the feelings nearest akin to honour.

Thus Charles had behaved, and, were it necessary we could name some illustrious models whom he had copied. This race of drawing-room comedians was especially prolific during the Directory; when they were called mystifiers. The present generation has given them the name of *blagueurs*, to the terror of our modest grammarians.

The woman who could do what Felina had done is likewise one of the phenomena which our period has produced. In truth, and it must be acknowledged by all who suffer their beards to grow, and by all who shave themselves, our present existence is wanting in excitement. Women especially are altogether deprived of those feverish conflicts in which they might employ that power and subtlety which in them ever abounds, and which our laws and our customs have removed from all serious affairs.

Let us not speak of the fine times of chivalry, not that we ever felt much esteem for those insipid tournaments in which they figured as queens of beauty; a poor meagre pastime which would not have been enough for their amusement, had there not been a chance of some brutal neighbour storming the castle where they lived with their husband, and giving it up to pillage and violation.

That time had far different attractions for women. Then they were betrothed in the cradle, then they were married and divorced; then they were killed and revenged; in fine they were the occasions of alliance and war. This was their good time: they were dreadfully unhappy.

Neither let us recall the League and the Fronde; then they instigated their brothers to fight against each other, their husbands against their lovers; then people killed their best friends to please them; then a man poisoned his wife and was afterwards poisoned by his mistress: this also was the good time, for woman reigned.

Afterwards they governed the state, concealed behind the curtains of the royal bed; this was still a good time for them, for they intrigued. Finally, after all this, they had the revolution, when they set men the example of an heroic death; this was a noble time, for then they were martyrs.

During all these different periods they lived; but now how can they be employed! What have they to think of, to interest them? Events are gone, and men are no more.

What passion is it that can be kindled by a deputy who enlightens the chamber* on the subject of the custom house tariff? What infatuation can be excited by the ablest orator who has been ranting and choking to curtail the salary of some consul at Malacca by fifty or sixty pounds? Where are they now those heroic deeds which save a nation? Where are they now those turbulent commotions which bring a country within an ace of ruin, and keep one's interest panting between right and wrong? Where are those incomparable steps which led from the Capitol to the scaffold? Nothing great survives, neither in selfdevotion, nor in hatred, nor in vengeance. The man who fights a duel is sent to prison, like a baker who sells his bread by false weight. All, every thing has fallen below zero.

* In France a member of parliament is called a deputy, and the house of debate is called a chamber, a it used to be called a hall in this country.

See, therefore, how the women are affected by those audacious scandals, those determined crimes, which are paraded before our courts of justice. In this steril world where they cannot find a single emotion to be gathered, this is like an oasis in Sahava. True, the trees are bald and ugly, the water beneath their shade is foul and full of rep tiles; but, good or bad, they hope to slake their thrist with it; in a word it is something else, instead of the same thing for ever.

People will say this is abominable! eh! honest gentlemen, why don't you compete with the thieves; woman desire no better than to warm up and glow with enthusiasm at the account of your noble deeds and adventurous enterprises, for it is the dulness in which you leave them which hands the palm over to these scoundrels. This same dulness it is which accounts for the success of a few men, who, in the fine arts, stand by the whole head above that boundless ocean of nonentities who speak, who paint, who carve, and who write: they at all events are worth something by themselves, they are always at war, first with poverty, and finally and for ever with envy.

And when I speak of envy, I mean not to allude to that which necessarily exists, from the little to the great, in the same career; I refer to that envy among the people, the envy felt by the cringing shopkeeper, the merchant, the banker, the clerk, the citizen towards any and every reputation whatever. A name that is too often repeated, and passed about, is importunate to their frivolous and vain insignificance; there is nothing too silly for them to fabricate and report to run down a name out of their own circle, and which is better known therein than theirs; this traducing usually proceeds in this mean and paltry way :—

" I am not a painter, or a sculptor, or an author, etc.; none can accuse me therefore of jealousy; well, I think that * * * is——" Then comes the abuse.

Well' these men perpetually run down by vulgar people, move and interest women, because their works excite them, make them feel and fancy. If it happens that the conduct of the woman whose fancy is thus agitated is chaste and reserved, this interest does not extend beyond their works, and a secret curiosity to see perhaps the man who has filled up some weary hour with emotion; but if, on the other hand, like Felina, the ties of modesty have long been severed, if the mind, instead of confining the senses within rigid bounds, is accustomed to carry them beyond those limits; if this woman has nothing to lose on the side of esteem and consideration; if, far otherwise, she longs to acquire a great renown by her irregularities, such a woman would certainly do what Felina did.—Such attempts are not unusual on the part of such women; but that which is really extraordinary is the event itself. It was indeed necessary to produce this result, that the same conjuncture should bring together, in presence of that woman a man as frigidly concentrated in his glory as was Victor Amab, and a youth as tainted with the vice of joking as was Charles Thoré. It was out of this fortuitous conjuncture that the other incidents and occurrences of this fearful story sprang. The beginning was terrible, so will the end be; but again we say it is true.

## CHAPTER IX.

### CORRESPONDENCE.

The day after the one on which this brutal scene had been played, Victor was in his apartment thinking of the scandalous adventure of Felina and the modest souvenir of Julia. His vanity was soothed by this double triumph. On one side, that lovely girl so pure, so modest, on the other that audacious courtezan so beautiful and proud; and both offering themselves to him. His pride exulted. And truly, he had but to wish and choose; and one might become the chaste companion of his life, or the other would be the dazzling mistress whom the richest, the noblest, and the handsomest men would envy him. But the latter, he had repulsed, and whether the thought of seeing that woman lost to him for ever, had provoked his wilful and absolute character, or whether this callous coldhearted man required the most piercing goads to drive him from the perpetual contemplation of himself and his aspirations, he regretted that Felina had escaped him. Besides, was she not likewise an admirable beauty of warm complexion, with lengthy hair and flaming eyes? Was she not an admirable model from which he might produce a marvellous Phryne?

Julia had delighted him. But had he not obtained all he required of her? With this singular man, Julia whose image he had reproduced, appeared to his fancy as a mistress whose favours had begun to tire him, whilst he had need of Felina for the picture he had just conceived.

We do not attempt to analyse Victor Amab, we knew him as we describe him; nature had created him, so to speak, out of one material; the mixture of alloy which particularizes all other persons was scarcely sensible in him. Such men are seldom seen in art; they are more frequently met with in the cabinet, but even there we could hardly cite above one.

Amab was thinking by what means he might succeed in recovering Felina, and was reflecting that nothing could ever unite them again, when M. Thoré's collecting clerk was shewn in and delivered to him a letter from his mistress. This letter was thus conceived:—

"Sir,

"I have no knowledge of the actual value of "things relating to art; if their cost were to be "rated by their glory, I should never be able to "absolve myself towards you for my picture and "that of my husband.; but I think I know you "set a very small price on the time you devote to "your works, and that sum I enclose. If I am "mistaken, I shall not be ashamed to be told so, "and shall always be ready to amend an error "which must be laid to the account of my ignorance.

"I am, Sir, etc."

"M. Villon," said the clerk, "told me as I was going out, to ask for a receipt."

Victor shrugged his shoulders and sat down to write. This was the answer:—

"Madam,

"I thought that Charles had explained to you "that I did not intend to receive the price of your "picture, nor of your husband's. Charles is more "than a pupil to me, he is my friend, and among "artists, there is a brotherhood which excludes "all bargains of sale and purchase. Permit me "to tell you, madam, you have spoiled the happiness I had felt in doing something for his "parents. Your note gave me pain. Still, madam, "if you think that all business deserves retribution, I have mine, which is richer, greater, and "more magnificent than any thing you could offer "me. Was it not in your house,—was it not "amongst you, that I found the ideal model of the "holy Virgin which has obtained for me so many "advantages? Do you think I have paid too "dearly for my glory in requesting you to keep "those two humble portraits which M. Thoré has "been kind enough to accept. Believe me, madam, "if you reckon what I have acquired in exchange, "it is I who shall never be able to estimate the "benefit you have done me. Be so good, therefore as to take back this money, I should be "ashamed to accept it, and you would be cruel to "offer it me again.

"I have the honour, etc., etc."

"Is this the receipt?" said the collector who thought it a very long one.

"There is no occasion for a receipt," said Victor returning the bank notes to the latter, "you will give all this to Madame Thoré."

Then, when the messenger was gone, Victor said:—

"Charles will hear all about it, and unless he greatly belies his habits of babbling; he will carry the news about that I refused payment for the pictures; the thing will spread; and that will look superb. True it will cost me two thousand francs."

Victor drove the thought away with disdain. This man however aspired to fortune, but he did not like money. He wanted to be rich, immensely rich, because, in our age, wealth is a representation of talent; but merely to satisfy his desires this fortune was not necessary. Amab had but few wants. Besides he was one of those who play the game of fortune on the large scale. And truly, what was two thousand francs (£80) to a man who expected shortly so set such a price on his works as none but kings and the princes of finance could sustain.

Victor was exulting in these reveries of the future, and pursuing in his fancy the consequence of this refusal from which he hoped shortly to derive a halo of popularity, when a new comer appeared. It was a lackey in livery with a note; the wrapper merely contained a slip of paper with these words written upon it:—

"Monsieur Amab is requested to deliver to the "bearer, the name and address of the person to "whom he gave up his place a few days ago."

"From whom do you come?" said Victor pettishly.

"From my mistress, Madame de Cambure."

"Who lives rue Joubert?"

"Yes, Sir."

"There's the address," said Amab with vexation.

The servant went away; Victor became pensive, and then dissatisfied.

"Charles," said he inwardly, "is handsome, merry, young, and all the ardour of this woman has reverted to him who had sufficient insolence to profit by her delusion. Come, it is useless to think of it any longer.

However, this proved to be a day for correspondence. Ten minutes after the footman had withdrawn, a street porter came in; he was likewise the bearer of a letter, the writing of which denoted that vulgar hand peculiar to common scriveners The artist fancied it was anonymous; and really there was no signature, but it was not exactly an anonymous letter, since it depended on Victor to find out who had written it. The following was the text of that letter:—

"Sir,'

"You are wanted to-morrow, at twelve o'clock, "on the boulevard Bourdon, with your seconds "and weapons. The party who will be there to "expect you with the same, will be in a coach-"house, opposite the provision store-house, along "the pavement lining the canal. You will have "no difficulty in finding the person, if you are not "afraid. In this latter case, you are requested "not to send a substitute. It is but fair to warn "you that if you avoid this meeting, you will ex-"pose yourself to annoyances which will make "you everlastingly regret that you have twice "proved yourself to be cowardly and base."

Victor was superior to a reproach of cowardice, he had shewn that; however this provocation disturbed him more seriously than had ever done the certainty of a dangerous meeting. There comes a time when the most careless man in matters of honour, conceives for his person sufficient regard not to expose his life to every body. Victor had reached that period; so it was by no means agreeable to him not to know the quarter whence this challenge proceeded.

He did not doubt that Felina had incited it; but he wondered within himself what kind of man she had appealed to as her champion. If he went to that meeting, he might possibly see before him one of those enormous bullies, whose swords pay for those good graces which age has to retribute with gold. Victor felt that if once he appeared, it would not be in his power to prevent the consequences of a quarrel which might be attended with the grossest outrages; besides, would it not be to acknowledge the adversary he might meet if he attended the rendezvous. He resolved therefore not to go, but he retained in his mind an irksome uneasiness.

And surely, it is an intolerable state of things to have to fear, whether in the open street, at a dining-house, in a public walk, or at the theatre, an affront from some unknown enemy, and at any chance moment. You watch every look, you feel uneasy at every notice, you stand on your defence against every man who approaches you or stops before you. Such a position is a loathsome torture.

Still even this suspense did Victor prefer to the risk of degrading himself by any ignoble altercation; but, for the first time in his life, he was dissatisfied with himself. He had been wanting in prudence, in dignity, in calculation; and he thought it was only just that the beautiful Felina de Cambure should seek to revenge herself in some way or other. Then, all at once, it occurred to his mind that Charles might perhaps be included in this measure of revenge, and that when asking him for the young man's address, Felina had doubtles had no other object than to get him more speedil- into her power. Victor experienced a moment of grave disquietude, Charles had not been to the atelier; it was already late. He wrote to him, therefore, by post, for he was unwilling either to go personally or to send to his house, after the letters which had been exchanged between him and Madame Thorè.

Consequently he waited anxiously for the morrow

## CHAPTER X.

### TRIALS OF THE HEART.

We must now turn back and tell the reader what had taken place in the Thoré family the last two days. We know that Victor had called there on the very day he had received the myosotis and the heartsease from Julia. He had found nobody at home and had retired after leaving his card.

When Madame Thoré returned home, it was delivered to her: and assuredly she would have suppressed it had not her husband been present. But M. Thoré was one of those men with whom it is unsafe to use the least artifice, for they instantly turn it into a blunder.

If Madame Thoré had not handed to him M. Amab's card, he would have called out to know what was going on, and if his wife had answered him that he should know by-and-by, he would have insisted to be informed directly.

"What do you mean by these mysteries?" he would have exclaimed at the street door; and he would have continued all the way up stairs: "I detest secrets. Everybody may know who calls to see me; I am like that ancient Roman who would have wished to live in a house of glass, and mine is not very unlike one—etc., etc."

Madame Thoré, unwilling to convert a mere visit into an event of consequence, handed the card to her husband, who cried out:—

"It is M. Amab's? Ah! so then he has called; it was what I expected.—He could not have done less.—That young man is greatly indebted to us, you know. I, and my daughter and you, will make him a great reputation.—I shall be very glad to see him. I want to point out something in Julia's portrait, for it is Julia in the disguise of the virgin.—Yes, I have made a remark: the frame is not so handsome as in our picture.—And besides that—but I will tell him all."

Whilst her father was delivering this tissue of nonsensical phrases, Julia had exclaimed:

"M. Amab has called?—oh! that was very kind of him."

"Wherefore?" enquired her mother.

"Oh! nothing particular," said Julia radiant with joy.

Victor had understood then the message of the heart'sease and the myosotis; for, he who had not called since a fortnight, had hastened there that very day.

She felt proud, she felt happy, the angelic girl thought herself loved. Absence, then, had not produced its effects on that passionate ardour which alarmed Madame Thoré: she thought it was time to take a course and bring on an explanation.

The following day, she came into the shop earlier than usual, and went up directly to Louis Villon's desk.

"M. Louis," said she to him, "give me two thousand francs."

Louis looked at her in surprise; M. Thoré was very systematic in his accounts. At the beginning of every month, the monthly allowance to defray all the household expenses was regularly delivered to Madame Thoré.

"What did you say, madam," asked Louis with a kind of terror.

"I asked you for two thousand francs."

And what for? excuse me!" continued the clerk opening the cash-box with a trembling hand, "to what account must I charge this sum?

"To mine"—

"Ah! very good—very good—to your account: Well," said he taking up a heavy note-case, "very well, and I must set it down in the day book as personal expenses—"

And so saying, he handed some bank notes to Madame Thoré with a quivering hand.

The lady examined the clerk and was at a loss to account for his terror.

"Why, what's the matter with you?" said she to him.

"With me, madam, nothing at all—you ask me for two thousand francs; it is my duty to give them to you."

"Of course," but you seem astonished at my application.

"Not at all" God help us! I suspose the time is at hand when these demands will return upon us one after the other—until the day when we shall credit our bankers, M. Gobert, with a hundred and fifty or two hundred thousand francs—Oh! that's a fine portion!"

At length Madame Thoré understood the terror of Louis; he had not been able to conceive any other reason for a sudden demand of two thousand francs, than the expenses incident on an approaching marriage—It was the beginning of a *trouseau*.

"No, answered Madame Thoré kindly, we are not about to marry Julia. If I ask you for these two thousand francs, it is on account of a debt which Monsieur Thoré ought not to have forgotten, and which must be liquidated immediately; I am going to send these two thousand francs to M. Amab.

"To M. Amab, said the clerk eagerly, holding out his hand as if he wanted to retake the bank-notes," and what for.

"It is the price of my husband's picture and my own,"

'And doubtless it is likewise that of the holy Virgin he painted, for I presume you will not leave the portrait of Mademoiselle Julia in his hands."

"I don't understand you, Sir, said Madame Thoré cooly." You will acquaint M. Thoré with the disposal of this money.

Yes, yes—I will enter it into the day-book, and yet, added he looking wistfully at the bank notes—two thousand francs for two or three weeks labour, it is a heavy sum Was it agreed upon? for if not, it would be exorbitant. Why, at that rate this gentleman would gain twenty or thirty thousand francs a year."

There are certain lawyers, grown rich with their talking trade, who think, like M. Villon, that an artist who has acquired reputation is sufficiently remunerated in his calling with a hundred louis d'ors per annum; and these lawyers are deputies, senators, who pass for men of understanding, and make our laws after having turned them to account; 'tis a sad thing this, for our country,

Madame Thoré was more reasonable than these gentlemen, for she answered M. Villon:—

"It is a moderate price, but I think it a proper one; it is what he asked of a lady who refused to pay him."

"Very good—very," said Villon; "but I can understand that such terms renders these gentlemen very impertinent."

"M. Amab appears to me most polite."—

"He, madam!" exclaimed Villon; ', he! why he thought—ah! you don't know.—He has the insolence to believe——"

"What do you mean?"

"Certainly, it is no business of mine."

"Explain yourself," said Madame Thoré to him; "have you any thing to say against M. Amab?"

"I have never so much as spoken to him."

"What has he done to you then?"

"What has he done to me? Excuse me, madam, excuse me; but I had believed—I had imagined—assuredly it was a silly pretension;—but until the day this young man came into this house, I was like one of the family—you were so very kind to me—and I said to myself that one day perhaps—well! I was wrong,

Madame Thoré listened patiently to these intermittent sentences broken with deep and heavy sighs, with looks raised towards the sky, with papers turned upside down, and account books driven out of place. The clerk resumed his seat, shut his cash-box with a heavy slam and betook himself again to his entries exclaiming in a tone of despair:

Item, one hundred and four sauce-boats; and thereupon he entered the article.

Madame Thoré could not help laughing, all at once she overheard her husband in the yard lecturing one of the shopmen, and said to the clerk in a hurried manner.

"M. Villon, I authorize you to apply to my husband and formally solicit Julia's hand."

Louis faced about as would a debtor in his distress if a bailiff's man had brought money to him.

"You said—madam—I must—"

"You must have spoken to my husband before night.

Madame Thoré had returned to her own particular office leaving Villon, astounded, intoxicated, mad. The next moment Julia appeared, and went and took her seat near her mother. Madame Thoré wrote a letter of a few lines, put it into an envelope, then openly inserted therein the two bank notes she had just received from Villon; finally she wrote the address, and carelessly threw down the letter on Julia's table:—

"Let this be delivered to the party it is directed to by the collecting clerk."

Julia took the letter, and had scarcely cast her eyes on the address, before she gave vent to a stifled cry.

Madame Thoré did not pretend to hear it, but requested M. Villon to go and conclude, in the adjoining wareroom, a scrutiny which would occupy several hours; she wished to afford Julia an opportunity to speak. The happy clerk went out.

Madame Thoré waited to hear her, but Julia said nothing.

The mother stole an unseen glance at her child. On her side, Julia looked fixedly at the letter. It was certainly the one in which had been put the two bank notes, the same they had told her to have delivered by the collector, as if it were an invoice or an order for goods—and that letter was directed to Amab.

That was a something which Julia could not understand, but which terrified and humbled her too. Then she looked at her mother as if to convince herself that she it was who had committed this enormity; for in truth, Julia might have understood such an act of brutality had it proceeded from her father, but from her mother it seemed inexplicable, a thing quite unexampled.

"Well, what are you thinking of?" said Madame Thoré to her.

Julia sat a moment undecided, during which she repelled the question which was rising to her lips, and answered with some bitterness.

"I am not thinking.—I was looking for my thimble—"

"It is on your finger."

"True.—I was wrong.—I have every thing I require."

She again took up the embroidery work she had laid down, clenching her teeth to stifle her sobs, holding down her head to screen her tears from her mother's look. Madame Thoré was on the point of opening her arms to comfort her. She had wounded Julia, and yet had failed to make her speak. However she wanted to measure this love by the courage that Julia would display in concealing her grief, so she said nothing. Soon after, she understood how powerful it was, when the collecting clerk having come in, Julia said to him in a clear and ringing voice :—

"Carry that letter to its address."

This obedience was the mask to a revolt. Still Madame Thoré remained immovable, for she had instigated M. Villon to take a measure which could not fail at last to evoke Julia's despair.

A frigid silence reigned between them ; but neither one nor the other felt sufficent strength to break it, when suddenly M. Thoré came in. His face was swollen with importance, his eye was sparkling, his gait was fierce and violent. He walked through the spacious warehouse from end to end, and every time he passed the front of the wire cage where his wife and daughter were at work, he delivered himself of a terrific sigh or a dumb groan. It was evident, he was waiting for some question, as to this furious excitement, to afford a vent to the anger which was raging in him. But his daughter was too busy with her own concerns to notice this awkward device, and Madame Thoré did not wish to come to her husband's assistance. The worthy trader, dreadfully disappointed not to have produced the least effect, had recourse to still stronger means ; he began to speak to himself :—

"It is incredible ! it is monstrous ! it is indecent !"

And as Madame Thoré did not even lift her head up, he took a piece of china, and smashing it furiously on the floor, he cried out like a sultan :

"I will not suffer such a thing to be done thus !—

"Why ! God help us ! what's the matter ?" inquired Madame Thoré, no longer able to affect to be blind and deaf.

"What is the matter, madam—what is the matter—I dare say you know it—a clerk to take upon him, suddenly—without any warning—without having sounded my intentions—who has the boldness——"

"What has he had the boldness to do ?"

"Don't you know ?—And was he telling me a oarefaced story, when on seeing my indignation, he dared to tell me that you had authorised him—what did I say, authorised ?—nay more, that you had enjoined him to.—Did he deceive me ?"

"No, my friend," said Madame Thoré gently ; it is true—and I thought I had done well—I thought I had acted in accordance with your own views."

"We do not always execute the designs we form —and moreover—if we did execute them—there is a suitable—yes, a suitable manner of doing so. But can you conceive any thing so extravagant as a man to whom you apply for a current account, who interrupts you ?" saying :—"Excuse me, Sir, I have something to say to you."—"Speak, my dear fellow, speak."—"Well, Sir, I wish to ask you for the hand of the young lady, your daughter."

At these words, Madame Thoré could not help smiling ; Julia started and looked at her father, whilst the latter went on to say :—

So it was."—Exactly as if he had said to me : "Excuse me, Sir, I forgot to tell you there was a ga in the waggon."

Julia turned very pale ; M. Thoré still proceeded :—

"And so it was you, madam, who thought fit to authorise M. Villon to conduct himself towards me with this impertinent coolness ?"

"If you only knew—" said Madame Thoré.

"I know," resumed her husband in a solemn tone, "that I loved you, that I married you, but that I did not behave in this manner ; I did not go up to your father, and cry out ; 'I say, tell me, Sir,—look yonder—I have a mind to marry your daughter !'—For, the longer I think of it, the more it vexes me—I was treated—"

"But, Sir,"—said Madame Thoré.

"Madam," continued M. Thoré with imposing majesty, "my father went officially to yours, and with due ceremony made a demand of your hand. Your father answered him favourably. Then, and only then, I dared to speak to him.—Not to mention the preliminary measures before taking this important step—the secret advices.—I had tested the ground, I knew whither I was going.—But in my case, they come up to me, and straight they ask me for my daughter, like a dozen of plates.—And it is my wife who authorizes such insults.—What an age this is ! What morals, my God ! what depravity !

This long effusion had quite exhausted the pulmonary strength of M. Thoré, who fell into a chair and began to puff and blow as an apology for sighing.

"I understand," said his wife gently, "I understand your vexation at a step which assuredly has not been taken with skill, but I beg of you to reflect that, you have long considered this union as a suitable match."

"That is possible."

"Remember that M. Villon is at a distance from his family."

"He might have written to them—"

"Do not forget that love is inconsiderate—

The look that Madame Thoré gave her husband undoubtedly contained a volume of reminiscences. Any one who had caught that glance might have affirmed, that the official step taken by the father, and so pompously quoted, had been the consequence of some private measure. M. Thoré assumed an air of radiant foppery: he rose up, moved towards the desk and said:

"God knows," I only wish for my children's happiness—but still it is desirable that things should be done in form.

Bless us, they are easily forgotten when passion hurries us along—" said Madame Thoré. You, yourself, have you not been forgetting all this while that the last person in whose presence you ought to enact such a scene, was our Julia, who does not know what countenance to keep, confused as she is with her good fortune."

Julia rose up, looked at Madame Thoré and left the shop, saying shortly:

'You are cruel, mother."

Madame Thoré was thunderstruck at the charge.

"What does she mean? exclaimed M. Thoré."

The mother began to weep.

"I will tell you the truth, my friend ; but I must speak to my daughter, I must go and speak to her."

She followed Julia into her apartment ; she found her in her room, pale with anger and grief.

"What signify," said she to her, the words you spoke when you left me ?

Julia subdued the violent transport by which she was moved, and answered :

"I was wrong to speak to you as I did, I ought not to have left the shop, I beg your pardon."

"But how, in what manner have I shown myself cruel with respect to you ?"

"I was wrong" I have said I was—it was foolish of me—I was wrong.

"Does this marriage displease you?"

Julia hesitated to reply: at that moment her father came in; he had heard the last question and repeated it.

"I have no right, said Julia, to answer my parents that a marriage which they consider a proper one is displeasing to me; but I declare to you with all the respect I feel for you, my father, and for you, *madame*—that never—no never will I marry M. Villon I will rather—yes? I will rather die!"

This answer so dry and so determined was nevertheless a proof of the controul which Julia had over herself. Her agitation was so dreadful, her pallor so alarming, that her speech was measured, in comparison with the emotion she felt.

M. Thoré saw nothing in it but a refusal which he thought excessively bold. Madame Thoré felt it as a bitter reproach. The proposal of such a marriage as coming from her father, did not at all surprise Julia; but this proposal coming from her mother, seemed to strike her as an act of treachery. Julia had relied upon her mother to rescue her from M. Thoré's designs, and it was she who was urging on their accomplishment. However, M. Thoré, who had scarcely recovered from his fiery denunciation of his clerks presumption, wanted immediately to renew hostilities against his daughter's disobedience.

"What does it all mean? This marriage shall never take place, did you say? Know mademoiselle, that *never* is a word which does not belong to the vocabulary of well bred young ladies."

"Father," said Julia to him with tender humility, "you are good and kind, you are—it is my happiness that you desire. Well, I swear to you, it is not there—it cannot be there. You will not compel me, *you*, to marry a man I do not love, whom I shall *never* love. Excuse the word—I feel I shall be very unhappy, to be obliged to disobey you; do not force me to disobey you; do not force me to resist you—have pity on me, father."

Madame Thoré listened to her daughter with extreme pain. The care that Julia took to exclude her from the entreaties she addressed to her father alone revealed to her in a new character that spirit of her child which she knew was firm, but which she did not take to be so resolute.

M. Thoré was much bent upon this union; it was a project he had long cherished. He knew the commercial value of Villon, and knew likewise he would hereafter inherit a pretty round fortune. But, as we have said, he was incapable of resisting a tear when shed either by his wife or his daughter. He did not feel courage to answer with firmness; but as he wanted to scold somebody, he turned round to his wife.

"Zounds! a *nice mediatrix* you are! There's your daughter in tears, M. Villon in a false position—altogether false—and I myself, what am I to do? I cannot now keep this young man—in my house—I must dismiss him, and yet he is the key—yes, madam, the master key of my business. What shall I do? Why don't you speak? After having done the mischief, give us a remedy."

"Well, Sir," said Madame Thoré, I will suppose that you did not tell M. Villon that you would acquaint me with his intentions—" ———

"His intentions were known to you, since you it was encouraged them."

"Undoubtedly; but Julia may be ignorant of them. Tell M. Villon that the time is not yet come—that hereafter—gain time.—At present, I wish to speak to Julia."

"No threats to your daughter above all, no system of intimidation; I wish my Julia to be free and happy.—At some future time, when she shall have reflected, I will argue with her—and—I hope she will listen to reason."

M. Thoré was preparing to leave the room at the very moment a servant entered with Victor's letter to Madame Thoré.

"A letter of business," said M. Thoré—give it to me, for in this house I must give my mind to every thing."

"Not so, my friend, it is a letter which I may want to shew to Julia."

"What mystery is this?"

"I will tell you shortly."

"I expect it," said the china merchant as he went out.

As if this letter had been a powerful auxiliary in the explanation the mother sought to have with her daughter, she hastened to break the envelope. The two bank notes did not escape Julia's glance, and a triumphant smile flitted across her lips. Madame Thoré read the letter and could not dissemble the vexation she felt. She had penetrated the personal character of Amab; but she was unable to understand the bold and calculating system by which he wished to rise.

She preserved silence a moment, and hesitated; a doubt stole into her mind; she asked herself whether she had not mistaken Victor's character, and desirous at length to extricate herself from the strange position she was in relative to her daughter, she handed the letter to her.

"Read this," said she, "and be candid with me."

Julia took the letter. The recent paleness of her face was succeeded by a gentle animation, then she blushed, next her eyes were moistened by tears; she looked at her mother who opened her arms as a suppliant, and the lovely girl flew there to conceal herself, saying:—

"Well, it is true, then—I do love him."

"Poor child!" said her mother embracing her, and happy once more to feel upon her own heart the heart of her daughter which had quitted her for a moment; but still sad, for she still retained the conviction that this love was a misfortune.

Then Julia said to her, between her fond kisses and tears:—

"Pardon me for not having told you of it."

"Alas! I knew it."

"You knew it!" said Julia much surprised, but however without any resentment for what she had just suffered, for all her anger had been melted by her mother's tears; "you knew it, and yet it was you who told M. Villon to ask for my hand."

Madame Thoré did not think it would be prudent to alarm her daughter's feelings, after what had passed; she wished to spare that soul whose quick sensibility terrified her, and she therefore answered with a smile:

"Did I not do well, since it was that which elicited the confession you should have made to me long since?"

"I did not dare, I saw clearly that you did not like M. Victor. Oh! if you had only liked him as well as you do M. Villon, whom you are always praising, I should have told you all. But, why then does he displease you? what has he done to you? Is it because he loves me without asking your consent?"

Madame Thoré took her daughter between her arms and pressed her head to her bosom; she wanted to hide the tears which rose to her eyes at the mistaken confidence of Julia.

"Pardon me, my child, for not asking you sooner for your secret; but promise me one thing, that you will never say a word, nor take a step, however trifling it may be, without my knowing it, especially in the case of M. Amab."

The young girl looked down.

"You answer me not.—Will you not make me this promise?"

"Oh!" said Julia embarrassed, "now I will tell you all."

"Then you have not yet told me every thing?"

"No—not all——"

And thereupon the lovely child, trembling, blushing, faltering, loading her mother with endearments, and twisting the ribands of her waistband, related to her, how she had allowed Victor to look at her, and how she had afterwards sent him that flower and that *forget me not.*

"But you did not write?—"

"Oh! mamma—"

"M. Amab is not sure that it was you who sent to him?"

"Oh! he must have guessed it; for he came here the same evening,"

"Never mind, he must not know it: you must not acknowledge it to him; I beg this of you, Julia. Believe me, child, I do not speak of M. Amab more particularly than of others; but no man thanks a woman for the imprudence she commits on his account, even when he solicits for it with earnestness; we always lose some portion of his esteem, and sometimes even of his love. You have entrusted me with your heart, let me protect it."

"Oh! thank you, mother, thank you!" said Julia joyfully."

Then suddenly recollecting herself:—

"But what countenance must I observe to M. Villon, at present?"

"You must know nothing of his application; continne towards him, simple and kind—he is an honest man, and a man of feeling.—Besides, he is unhappy. You don't yet know what it is to love and be disdained."

"But, why does he love me?"

There are none but coquettes and bad women who forgive the man they do not love for loving them: it seems to amuse and entertain them. As for the good and ingenuous, they have no pity on such importunate lovers."

Madame Thoré chid her daughter gently; and after that she consented to be scolded herself for her prejudices against Victor; for in vain she protested, Julia, guessed them all; she had understood that it was to humble her in her love for Victor, that her mother had written that letter to him in her presence, and had told her to send the missive and the money it contained.

Madame Thoré listended and allowed her to say whatever there was of fear and hope murmuring at the bottom of her heart; she harkened to that young fancy, expanding into dreams so charming, so fresh, so youthful, so tinted with the rose. The happiness which this little heart anticipated was so pure in its candour! It was that inexhaustible love which is constantly giving, and which asks for so little in return, that it seems impossible to deny it. It was an entire life settled beforehand with a husband, with a family, with the great cares, and little grievances which it brings along with it. And such was the purity of this ardent spirit, that nothing could be chaster than this youthful girl speaking of her husband, of her home, of her future family. She was like the angels, she looked upon it all from heaven; as yet her foot had not been soiled by the earth, her wings had not yet been torn with the thorns of selfish interests, she was taking her flight in a pure and shining atmosphere—and her mother listened to her still, admiring her thus, adoring her confidence, and yet saddened by the thought that she was perhaps advancing towards a region where the ground was barren, and the air chilling.

At last, the mother broke in upon this pretty prattle, and not to let the awkwardness of a meeting between Julia and M. Villon grow too embarrassing by affording them time to reflect upon it, she asked her daughter to go down with her into the warehouse.

And the maiden went down with a far lighter foot.

---

## CHAPTER XI.

### THE SHE-TIGER PROWLING ABROAD.

It chanced that this meeting took place in a manner much readier than Madame Thoré expected. Both of them, as they entered the shop, found M. Villon very busy in displaying to a fine woman the most costly articles in the house.

"All this is very beautiful," said the lady; "I see your house is one of the finest of its kind. Has M. Thoré been long established?"

"The house is one of the oldest in Paris; M. Thoré received it from his father."

"Ah!" said the young lady, affecting to look at a tea-service, "he is a young man, then?"

"No, madam, not so."

"Is he married?"

"Yes, madame. Look at this article; the English can show nothing like the delicacy of this tint.

"True, true—it is very pretty.—Has M. Thoré any children?"

"Yes, madam."

Just at that moment Madame Thoré returned down with Julia, as the lady was putting the last question.

"Those are his wife and daughter, madam."

The strange lady turned her head round and could not dissemble a sudden start of surprise at the appearance of the ladies. She examined them so attentively that it almost amounted to rudeness, but a strange kind of wonder and a look of sullen anger was mixed up with that insolence. Julia, however, and her mother returned to their desks after bowing to the lady;" who whispered to M. Villon:—

"Oh! those are Madame and Madamoiselle Thoré?"

"Yes, madam."

"I thought you told me M. Thoré had a son."

"That is the fact, but I don't think I mentioned it to you, madam."

Possibly not, I must have mistaken your meaning. Have the goodness to send me this tea-service.

"What name and what address must I direct it to?"

The strange lady was about to reply when she stopped.

"Don't send it to me, let it be packed up, and it shall be called for one of these days—let me know the price. I will pay for it now."

Whilst she was speaking, she looked at Julia with a threatening scoul and a sardonic smile.

"It is quite unnecessary, said Villon, and when the lady shall send for it."

"No, sir, I am going to the country—I had rather settle with you. The person who shall call for this china will send it to me.

Then, madam, to be sent to the country, it will require a box, and we must reckon for the package.

"Reckon what you like," said the lady impatiently.

All this time she had kept her eye upon Julia.

"Miss Julia, said Villon, will you make out an invoice for the English tea-service, number 5—"

Julia took a bill-head, and her mother opened a ledger.

"Madam, do you require an invoice in full ?"

"Yes, yes, said the lady, in a particular tone of voice, yes, I wish for a complete account.

Villon offered a chair to her within the ladies office, but she declined it and stood outside of the wire partition, whilst the mother and daughter were writing down the particulars as Villon dictated them

Madame Thoré looked up several times to see whether the strange lady persisted to examine them with the same curiosity. But she was immersed in deep reflection, and, whether she recollected the past, or was brooding over some future project, you might have read in her countenance full of sullen gloom as it was, that she was labouring under some cruel remembrance, or meditating some terrible revenge.

As soon as Julia had finished. she passed the invoice through a small wicket, saying :—

"Here it is, madam."

The latter took hold of it and examined it so closely that if M. Thoré had been present he would have said that the lady did not pay her bills without being satisfied as to their correctness. Madame Thoré was startled by it. The lady folded the bill carefully, and threw down the amount on the top of the desk. She then hastened away, without saying a word about her purchase, and without bending her head in reply to the repeated salutations of M. Villon.

Nobody suspected that a horrible misfortune had entered the house along with that dreadful woman.

"Umph !" cried the clerk, picking up the money from the desk, "what a singular customer."

"Singular, indeed," said Madame Thoré, and at the same time she handed the clerk the bank notes which Victor had returned, adding : "restore these two thousand francs to the cash account."

"These two—thousand," said Victor stupified.

"Yes."

"But how shall I enter this receipt ?"

"I took two thousand francs this morning, I return them this evening ; it is needless to put it into your accounts."

"Pardon me, madam," said Villon positively, the item is set down, I cannot take money from the cash-box without entering it ; nor can I return it without the same formality ; and you know, madam, that an entry in a merchant's account books ought not to be erased. I must therefore be informed—"

"Sir," said Madame Thoré hastily,

"Madam must have the kindness to tell me," resumed Villon looking down, "how I must—"

"Well," said Julia satirically, "write : *Refused by the party to whom they were sent.*'

"Can this be true ?" cried Villon in an altered voice, looking at the lady of his employer.

"Yes, said the latter, it is true—so settle it as you think proper."

Villon said nothing ; he took the money left by the strange lady as well as the bank notes, went to his desk where he first entered the item of the sale of the tea service, and then, in his running hand :—

"*Received* 2000 *francs, sent to M. Amab, and by him refused.*"

His hand shook as he wrote down this item, and, what perhaps had never before happened to a tradesman's book, a tear of love and despair fell upon and blotted that sum, of two thousand francs.

Meanwhile, Julia whispered in a low voice to her mother :—

"Poor M. Villon he cannot understand this disinterestedness."

"Silence, Julia ! silence !—he understands it better than you think."

The close of that day was sad and irksome to everybody. Charles, contrary to his habit, came home much later than usual.

## CHAPTER XII.

The next day was still more sorrowful. When Madame Thoré inquired for Charles, whom she desired to speak to in private, she was told that he had gone out very early, too early indeed to receive a letter which they delivered to Madame Thoré, and in the address of which she recognised the handwriting of Amab. As for the rest, this early excursion had nothing in it to alarm her : Charles was absolutely his own master. Setting aside the silly part of a joker which he had set up, he was an openhearted fellow who laboured with earnestness, who contracted no debts, and who led a life sufficiently orderly for his mother to shut her eyes to the little acts of freedom which on very rare occasions he indulged in, and which he was very careful to conceal.

And whilst upon this subject, let us observe that there are people who most clamorously denounce the hypocrisy of young people who deceive their parents with regard to certain little peccadilloes. They are at no loss for big words to qualify the impudence of those falsehoods and the dismal hereafter which awaits these wretches. Madame Thore wss not of this opinion : if she could not find an excuse for her son's faults in his solicitude to mask them, she at least could see therein a testimony of respect and deference.

Perhaps, in some other family than her own, she might have met some of those fast young men, who have the insolence to discuss with their own father, the right they have to sleep from home, to run into debt, to lead a merry life among whom the liberty of vice is one vice the more ; corrupt souls over whom family ties have no controul, for they do not respect them sufficiently to deny their misdeeds, and are bold enough to endeavour to make parade of their shameful behaviour.

Consequently, Madame Thoré was aware of her son's follies, and, under any other circumstances this early excursion would not have alarmed her. But there are days when every thing assumes a sad and sinister meaning, and it required all Madame Thoré's strength of character, not to send to M. Amab's house, to learn tidings of Charles.

She was plunged in this state of anxiety, when she saw the young painter arrive. And here the reader will remember that, on the previous day, Amab had written to Charles, and in that note* had requested him to come immediately. Yet already had two thirds of the day been spent without the appearance of his pupil in the workroom. Amab, alarmed at this absence, came to learn what had become of that young man, for he suspected not without reason that Felina's vengeance might have precipitated Charles into some snare.

Such, indeed, was his dread, and his fears must have been very serious to determine Victor to go to Madame Thoré, for he had felt and understood that Julia might interpret his visit as an impulse of his passion. "Well," had he replied to himself, if they give me to understand that my coming is regarded in that light, my answer shall be sufficiently clear as to my intentions.

How strange, how whimsical it was, that this love, which he was so indifferent to, should be always uppermost in his mind. It occasioned him

* Let the intelligent reader, especially if he is himself a writer of fiction, watch the thousand fine threads, with which this admirable Romancist, weaves and interweaves, his wonderful plot.

so much uneasiness and disquietude that he resolved to emancipate his existence therefrom.

We shall see what became of this resolution, and in what manner he executed it.

Madame Thoré had remained sufficiently guarded not to send to enquire at Amab's; but she could not repress a quick impulse of anxiety, which induced her to approach the young painter who doubtless was come to relieve her mind.

Julia mistook this behaviour for a more friendly greeting by which her mother intended to make amends for the wrong she had done to Victor, and thanked her for it from the bottom of her heart.

Victor received this eager demonstration with a mournful shyness.

"I am delighted to see you, Sir," said Madame Thoré, "for I was going to send to you to—"

"Madam," replied Victor hastening to interrupt her, "I suppose there is a subject upon which all discussion is at an end between us, I entreat you to let it be so."

M. Villon coughed aloud and crushed his pen on his desk.

"We will talk that over with my husband," said Madame Thoré somewhat coldly; "but I wished to know whether you had seen Charles to-day."

"No, madam, I have not seen Charles; I had written to him requesting him to call upon me."

"Is not this your letter?"

"Yes, madam, and as I have not received any answer, I fancied that Charles was unwell, and came hither to make inquiries respecting him."

The mother's heart was smitten through and through with an icy chill. She could not account for it, but she foresaw some frightful evil.

"How! have you not seen Charles to-day?" she inquired.

"No, madam."

"And have you no idea of the cause of his absence?"

"None at all," said Amab confused; for he now perceived that his apprehensions had been well grounded.

"You must have heard some illusion to a party of pleasure—previously intended with his companions? Do you suppose he has any reason or it may be some—occupation to keep him away?"

The manner in which the worthy matron pronounced the word *occupation*, allowed Victor to understand it in its fullest sense; it was as if she had asked him if Charles had not been allured to one of those assignations which have no name by which they can be mentioned in the presence of a young girl. Victor understood this; and desirous of gaining time to ascertain what had become of Charles, he answered with the embarrassment occasioned by the falsehood he had upon his tongue, and which the mother mistook for the trouble he felt in giving further strength to her suspicions :—

"It is possible he may have, as you say, some occupation which has kept him away the whole day. However, such is not his usual habit; he is very punctual, and if I find him in the workroom when I return, as I suppose I shall, I will scold him."

"So then, you have no misgivings?"

"None whatever, but I want his assistance, and expected to find him here; and, as I have told you, if I find him at my place, I will send him home to you."

Victor stood up and bowed.

Since he had come in, Julia, with her eyes bent over her work, had not raised her head. For her part, she looked upon Charles's absence as a pretext which Victor had seized upon with a lover's eagerness. His hurried departure, she now conceived to be an act of civility, one of those submissive indulgences by means of which a lover seeks to win the good graces of a mother. She looked up at Victor to thank him. The artist had stood up and was ready to go. This look changed his intention; he seemed to hesitate, and resumed his seat. At that moment, he determined to execute the plan and course of behaviour which he had laid out in his mind towards Julia. Then too, and not until then, Madame Thoré remembered that this visit was a perplexing one for herself and her daughter to receive. She attempted to throw the conversation far away from the thoughts which might be passing in the minds of both, and she said to Victor :

"It is for some new picture that you wanted Charles?"

"No, madam, I am not yet sufficiently burthened with labours to be obliged to set my pupils to work, and it is only to our great masters that it belongs to disdain certain details sufficiently in their productions, to entrust them to hands less skilful than their own.

"Still, you are undoubtedly preparing some new composition."

"I am always at work," answered Amab laying a stress on the words; "we have so much to do to become a great artist."

"Are you not already one?"

"Oh! no, madam, exclaimed Victor fervently, and as if he was glad to avail himself of the road now opened to him. It is by other toils, by other efforts than mine, that a man attains that lofty renown, that high and powerful position which is the crowning glory of the artist. To be worthy of the name of a great artist, one must have the courage to sacrifice thereto one's rest, one's health, —one's life,—if requisite;—far more than that, one's dearest hopes, even the dream of happiness which smiles upon you when you awake, When a man pursues glory, he must forget fortune; he must almost desert his family, if he be so fortunate as to have one; an artist's life, is a perpetual struggle a constant, an incessant renunciation of what we love. He is engrossed with continual study, with distant travels which consume those happy years of youth which others waste in pleasure."

"But likewise, when he returns, he is happy," said Madame Thoré, endeavouring to detect the real feelings of Amab.

"Yes, madam, when he meets again a family to whom he can say :—'Behold the glory I have brought back in exchange for the sorrows of my absence.'"

Madame Thoré could not help understanding the meaning so significant and obvious in these words of Victor. It was evident that Amab wished them to have a distinct sense for her who was listening to him. It was like an explanation of his sentiments and intentions. Madame Thoré determined that this explanation should be as complete as Victor could have wished to render it; and she said to him in a tremulous tone :—

"But the sympathy of his own family is not the only one to which he may refer his glory."

Julia was seized with a trembling on hearing these words; M. Villon made his stool turn about with a shrill groan, and Madame Thoré awaited a reply. Victor did not answer immediately, so much was he startled by the overture which was made to him. Proud man! he thought he was in favour with both, and had only to ask and receive. How little he could read into that mother's heart! How little he understood the subtleties and artifices with which women deal with love! At length, he summoned heart, and replied :—

"I am not so conceited as to believe that I can inspire so acute a tenderness—one that would be patient—and wait for—an uncertain return—perhaps."

Julia was half stifled; she could only breathe with difficulty—Victor continued :—

"For if it were possible for any one to like me for the little worth I possess, do you believe, madam, I should be so mad as to hope that this affection would survive absence?—for I shall probably soon set out. What chance would the memory of a poor wandering artist have over the homage, and the tender solicitation of all those who surround the heart he has left behind him? It would be too perilous a struggle to expose it to." And, added he with a sigh, "he would probably only return to disappointment, and deception."

Julia looked at him and did not take her eyes off until she met the severe look directed at herself by her parent. Victor continued :—

"Not that he would have a right to blame the forgetful girl when he returned home. What do we owe to one who makes us a promise which perhaps he may not keep? Can we reckon upon a heart which prefers the chances of a brilliant career, but venturesome withal, to the happiness which stood by his side? For my part, madame, if ever (here Victor's voice became agitated) if ever, I say, I could have hoped to possess a heart so tender and so constant, my own honour would have prompted me to say to it: 'Do not trust your dream of happiness to one of those capricious, fantastic beings who live with their thoughts as with their dearest mate; if you do, you may dread to see your hopes sacrificed by some vexation, some burst of anger in which you have no part. Do not look for your happiness in a man who cannot owe his own entirely and absolutely to you; do not let your weak and delicate spirit come in contact with one of those iron minds, which launched by their ambition like an arrow from a strong bow, tear and break whatever comes to impede them, and which often break themselves before they reach their aim.'"

Julia now trembled so much as to alarm her mother. Madame Thoré wished to break up the conversation, and said in a voice of entreaty :—

"You may be right perhaps; but Charles does not return—would you be so kind, Sir—"

"True, madam," said Victor with earnestness, "I am going to look for him, and I shall find him, I promise you."

Thereupon he withdrew. Poor Julia was almost stifled with her feelings. Her mother greatly alarmed whispered to her :—

"Well, you heard what he said?"

"Oh! mother," cried the young girl letting her heart gush forth, "how, noble, how good he is!"

"But you did not understand him then, exclaimed the terrified mother, he is going to leave, he said so."

"Well! mother rejoined the lovely girl with proud exultation, *I will wait for him*."

When a fire is widely kindled, every thing serves to extend it, even the water which would extinguish a small one: so it is with love.

Madame Thoré was silent; M. Villon listened, Had Victor spoken with sincerity? Madame Thoré at first thought he had, and she admired a man who sacrificed himself to cure a wound he had unintentionally given. But when she saw that all this had only served to develope still further her daughter's passion, she began to doubt, and she asked herself whether she had not to deal with a seducer of superior address. On the other hand, she was lost and could not make out the haughty and high sounding language of Victor Amab.

For her, glory and renoun were mere empty words, without meaning; but she understood .othing of those religious flights and extravagances which certain writers have rendered fashionable on the subject of art and artists. She could understand that a man had to labour hard, that to do so he forfeited his pleasure, and even neglected his wife, or his intended if need were; but in her plain style, that did not go by the names of sublime renunciation, and ardent struggles. In her eyes, a painter was a painter; but he was not a priest of art clad in his heavenly inspirations and his divine mission. She did not think it ridiculous. she was too little acquainted with artists to do that; but she was bewildered, uncertain, and, when she saw her daughter fascinated by such metaphorical language, she was quite disheartened, She then thought of her son who might be able to guide her with his information, and thus she was led to resume her former anxiety, when she saw that the dinner hour was past, and that Charles had not returned.

---

## CHAPTER XIII.

### THE HE TIGER.

The next day, Victor was in his workroom, congratulating himself on the courage he had shewn the day before, and saying to himself:—"This "yonng person must have understood me, or at "least her mother; it is impossible to tell a wo- "man more clearly; I cannot love you, and it is "silly of you to love me. Besides, what does it "all mean? it is but a romance conceived by the "silly girl herself—for, what did I ask of her? to "allow me to make a rough sketch of her face— "that does not amount to a declaration. She is "now well aware of the truth, and, really, if she "do not fully understand me, I must explain my- "self more clearly to her brother"

Then he recollected that he had promised Madame Thoré the day before to find Charles out and bring him back to her. He was going to inquire of one of his pupils, when there came into the atelier a young man of five and twenty at most, attired with the greatest elegance, of a noble countenance, already jaded, and overspread with sickly pallor blotted with purple veins which tell you that death is lodged in that living body. His complexion was fair but languid, his shape delicately tall, and his gate had a certain stiffness in it. A feverish light glittered in his large blue eyes. His lips pale and thin, his rigid nose, his wide and expansive forehead, testified to the intelligence, the spirit and the firmness of the young man. But no tender feeling appeared to find a place in that wild, passionate, and powerful nature.

He asked for M. Victor Amab in a soft gentle voice, which was jaded also, and after the latter had given his name, he said to him:—

"May I speak to you of business before these gentlemen?"

"It is for you, Sir, to judge whether the business muy be spoken of before others."

"Faith," said the young man, "I don't know, I am come to buy a picture of you."

"You may speak, then," said Victor smiling.

"I wish to have *your weeping Virgin*," said the young man; "is not that its name?"

This name had never before reached Amab except in Felina's letter; he asked himself whether this stranger had not some connexion with her.

"Such a wish is flattering to me, Sir; it shews that this picture has struck you."

"I have not seen it. It is a person who will absolutely have it, and to whom I am absolutely desirous to give it.—Such is the truth.—You see I use no stratagem. So, I beg of you," added he laughing, "not to bleed me too much."

"You make me quite curious," said Victor, "may one inquire who is the person, who is so absolutely resolved to have the picture?"

"She has imperatively forbidden me from mentioning her name. Why? I don't know. She is really the most capricious person——But after all, she will have it, and I obey.—Come, tell me your price."

"*She* will have it," the young man had said; "it was a woman then to whom he alluded, Amab no longer doubted that the purchaser had come to him on the part of Madame de Cambure;" and he replied by a question instead of a demand:—

"What would be your own valuation?"

"Felina told me that it was worth, at least, ten thousand francs."

"That was the name Victor expected, and which was to decide whether or not he should close the bargain. The pupils all exchanged looks: the picture had been liberally estimated."

"Well," resumed the young man, "does that suit you."

At the same moment Victor was informed that two ladies were waiting for him in his apartment; it was doubtless some order for a portrait. Victor told the servant to request them to wait in the saloon adjoining his workroom and which communicated with it by an entry closed with thick folds of old brocade.

If he had turned in that direction, Amab might have seen a hand lift up the portal, and a quick glance sweep over the atelier; he might also have heard these words escape a mother's anxiety:— "My God! where can he be?" words which were pronounced by Madame Thoré, for she it was. At that moment, his eyes followed the young man who having caught sight of a suit of armour in one part of the atelier, began striking it with his cane, exclaiming:—

"Faith! that is not amiss——

Then the purchaser turned round:—

"Well, tell me your exact price," said he, "what is it?—'"

In the mean time, Victor thought he understood that Madame de Cambure, the woman who had been so grossly insulted by Julia's brother and by himself, could only seek to possess the image of that lovely girl from some motive of vengeance. Perhaps, thought he, she wishes to obtain this work, which has fascinated her to so high a degree, only to destroy it. This thought alarmed Amab; and as the dandy repeated his question:—

"Sir," said Victor coldly, "my picture is not to be sold."

"There!" cried the young man, "I was sure of

it!—I shall always be taken in this way.—I ought to have sent you a dealer.—You refuse ten thousand——"

"Yes, Sir."

"Well, twelve——"

"No, Sir."

"Fifteen, eighteen, twenty thousand francs."

The pupils looked at Amab to whom such offers appeared an unhoped for good fortune; more than a fortune, the confirmation of his success. He was on the point of arresting the financial fervor of the young man by saying to him :—

"Give me,then 100,000 francs, and this picture is yours."

But he had said once that the picture was not for sale, and he would have blushed to make that assertion a speculator's feint; his pride would not let him.

"No, sir," he answered with an effort.

The young man waa amazed at the refusal, whilst the pupils admired the disinterestedness of their master, but they were still more astonished to see him set on his work an estimation beyond its value.

"Hold, said the purchaser at length, I have promised this picture as a gift. Be candid; tell me your price at once. I have indeed given away in an hour 80,000 francs' worth of diamonds for a ball—I can afford then to give thirty or forty thousand francs for a whim. I have promised it; take your advantage—I will pay what you like—fifty—sixty thousand—"

There was a kind of feverish stimulus in the language of this young man: it was the excitement of those unhappy spendthrifts, who are at once the slaves of a maddening passion and a consuming vanity—who still retain sense enough to see and feel the follies they commit, but who nevertheless persist in their errors with frantic irritation. They are like a man habituated to the intoxication of brandy, who knows it will kill him, and who drinks it with despair, but cannot refrain from it. Amab fully understood the character of his young visitor, and therefore interrupted him hastily saying:

"Neither for sixty thousand francs, nor for two hundred thousand, should you have this portrait. It is not to be sold."

The young man thus arrested in his offers, said with a bitter accent:

"Then, it must be the portrait of your mistress."

"Sir, said Amab haughtily, I allow no man to."

"Pardon me, replied the other, I know that you are a man of spirit: I heard them relate one of your duels, a somewhat singular one. I did not intend to offend you—But, acknowledge that if my supposition is unfounded—this is an inexplicable riddle."

"You may possibly have the key to it without suspecting it, said Amab to him."

"And probably I have said the word without being aware of it."

"Perhaps," said Amab, who thought that by naming *Felina*, the young man had led him to resolve not to sell him the picture.

The latter mistook this *perhaps* for a very different meaning; he returned to the idea that it was the portrait of an adored mistress and that Amab was offering up to it the sacrifice of his fortune; he replied therefore :—

"Egad! sir, you are quite as mad as I am—If however you should have a lucid interval, draw a bill at sight upon the Count of Monrion, and send me your *weeping Virgin*. I will trust to your honour.

"Do not expect this picture, Sir," said Amab, and be pleased to urge me no more—they are—"

"They are painful and irksome," said M. de Monrion in a tone of raillery "Are you a man to make an end of it like Queen Anne," and to exclaim: "You would tell me too much!" Well, sir, I will not behave like Mazarin, I will not suppose the case, and say: If you were offered a hundred, two hundred thousand, etc.—no, I here offer you a hundred, two hundred thousand—

"Sir, said Amab impatiently, we are playing a game only fit for children. I have refused you, because I have particular reasons to do so. Were I to accept the least of the extravagant offers you make me, I should not be an honest man."

"You are mistaken," said the count, "I will pay twice as much as I have offered you, to avoid the scene I expect to be exposed to endure, and double that again, to be able to say to a person. You desired to have it, you are obeyed. You will probably embroil me with her; I forgive you the injury you are doing me, but it is possible I may revenge it."

"What do you mean?"

"I scarcely know it myself," but Igive you warning that, perhaps two hours hence, I shall be your mortal enemy, farewell, Sir."

The young nobleman went out, and a confused murmur sped through the work-room: Victor Amab had refused to take two hundred thousand francs (8000 pounds) for a picture! Raphael and Rubens now were but two beggars compared with him. Amab stood for a moment silent and motionless; a deep sigh gushed up out of his breast; he had just sustained a terrible struggle: not that he could have believed in the possibility of so extravagant a bargain as that offered to him by M. de Monrion, but because there was between the real price of the picture and this exaggeration a medium which might have been a capital business for Amab. He now sought a consolation in the enthusiasm of his pupils, and desirous of imparting to this scene a signification which would show him in a heroic light, he said to them with a look of dignity:

"Gentlemen, the love of a man is like a woman's honour, far above all price."

## CHAPTER XIV.

### A MOTHER LOOKING FOR HER SON.

He had scarcely uttered these words, before he heard a gentle cry in the saloon where he had left the ladies who had been announced to him. He went thither, with a secret hope that they might have overheard the glorious comedy he had been performing. He was not mistaken, they had heard it; but a quick start of vexation took the place of the joy which Victor had felt at first, when he recognized Madame Thoré and her daughter. The care he took of his own glory, and perhaps likewise some regard for Julia's reputation, had just been too dearly paid for by Amab, for him not to feel some ill will towards her.

Madame Thoré's agitation was very great: it seemed to her that there could not possibly be a doubt of the insane passion of Amab. As for Julia, her whole being was filled and pervaded with an ecstacy which shone in her eyes, in her smile, in that divine but inexplicable delight with which happiness illumines beauty.

Any others than the ladies, would have seen in the vivid excitement which agitated Amab when he saw them, the actual truth, that he was vexed and displeased; but to eyes so prepossessed as Julia's, this passed for the confusion of a lofty spirit, surprised in one of its noblest sacrifices.

How happened it that Julia was there?" It

was the consequence of Charles' absence. Madame Thoré not having seen her son return, had at length conceived the most serious alarm. Already had Villon and M. Thoré run through all Paris in search of the fugitive.

After their departure, Julia had observed to her mother that they had not spoken of calling upon M. Amab.

"He would have let me know, if he had gathered any tidings," she had answered to her.

"Perhaps he has not had the courage?" the young maiden had imprudently replied.

"If he has not had the courage, there must have been some terrible misfortune!" the poor mother had exclaimed.

And, under the influence of this apprehension, Madame Thoré's heart had imagined misfortunes and disasters, not only impending but accomplished: perhaps even death! She had left her house in such a confusion of mind, that her daughter had insisted on accompanying her, and the mother had let her have her own way. To tell the truth, it must be allowed that neither of them had thought, at that moment, of any one but Charles, who then engrossed their minds. But what both of them had recently overheard had disturbed that sympathetic anxiety: the sister had forgotten her brother, whilst the mother still thought of her son. She hastened up to Amab, and taking his hands:—

"Charles!" said she to him, "have you any news of Charles?"

"None, madam," said Amab, delighted to see that subject started; "I have none at all—"

"But he must be dead then!" cried the wretched mother in despair. "My God! my God! my poor Charles, what is become of him?" What, Sir, don't you know any thing?"

—"Nothing, madam."

"Fear not to inform me of the worst, for your looks of agitation, make me understand, and forsee—"

"I pledge you my honour, madam, that I have no news of him."

"What did they tell you," inquired Julia, "where you went yesterday to look for him?"

Now the artist had not been any where; but on witnessing that mother's grief, he felt unwilling to appear to have neglected the duty he had himself undertaken to perform.

"He has not been seen."

"It must have been some quarrel," answered Madame Thoré anxiously, "It must have been a duel."

"He would have chosen his *witnesses** among his comrades, and these witnesses, whoever they might have been, would have apprised you of any misfortune, which had really taken place."

"Then it was some dreadful accident——"

"The police would have discovered that and would have informed you of it."

"But, what is it then?" exclaimed Madame Thoré writhing in despair, and falling on a chair where she began to weep

"A concealed enemy, perhaps," cried Julia.

Victor started and betrayed confusion: the young girl had touched the spring of his own thoughts and terrors, and had made them reveal themselves. Julia, whose eye appeared to see Victor without looking at him, noticed this agitation and drawing him hurriedly aside she said to him in a low tone:—

"Oh! if you have any trace, tell it me—look at my mother, it would kill her—and I—I should be very unhappy; it would be a dreadful blow to the family; you also must feel it yourself, for poor Charles loved you like a brother."

"Well, madam, return home," said Amab turning and speaking to Madame Thoré, who, when she saw her daughter whisper to the painter, believed they were anxious to conceal some fatal event and had just joined the group.

Amab at last had understood, if not felt, for feeling was almost a stranger to that iron soul, that he owed some good offices to a heart whose grief he was in a measure guilty of, and he therefore went on to say:—

"Return home, and have the goodness to wait for me there the whole day—I am going to inquire of somebody——"

"Who is it?" exclaimed Madame Thoré. "Oh! I will go myself."

"It is impossible," said Victor embarrassed, Madame Thoré penetrated his meaning, and, in her turn, drawing him apart, she whispered to him:—

"It is a woman, is it not?"

"Undoubtedly, but a woman at whose house you cannot present yourself."

"A mother's despair has a right to enter every where, Sir, were it even a house of infamy!"

'It is not that, madame, but I protest to you that you cannot, that you ought not to go there. Besides, you know nothing—you will obtain nothing—I will go thither instantly."

"Well, I will accompany you, I will wait for you, at the street door, unperceivod in a hackney coach."

"Madame!"

"I am resolved to follow you, Sir, absolutely resolved."

There is in a mother's determination a power which the most callous hearts submit to. So Amab consented.

A few minutes after, a hackney coach stopped at a few yards from No. —— in the rue Joubert. Amab alighted from it alone; having inquired of the porter, he went up to the first storey and asked for Madame Felina de Cambure: they told him that the lady was gone out.

He wanted to know at what hour it would be possible to see her. They answered him again, that the mistress did not give any account to her servants of what she meant to do, and that it was possible she might return in five minutes, as it might likewise happen that she would not return in a week, or remain in the country.

Amab could get no better answer. On coming down, he was greatly astounded to find Madame Thoré's coach drawn up opposite the gate. There, too, stood a small truck or hand-cart, drawn by a street porter; on this truck was a large box, on which was written: *brittle goods*, with the brand T. R.; it was the mark of the Thoré house; it was the box containing the tea service purchased the day before by that woman so handsome, so inquisitive, and so insolent; who had refused to give either her name or address.

"Yes, yes," said Mandame Thoré to her daughter, "it is this woman who has been the destruction of my son; but I will apply to the magistrates, I will expose her crime, I will snatch my poor child from her."

Already had Madame Thoré ceased to believe that Charles was dead; but she feared an evasion, an elopement with an artful courtezan; one of those bewildering passions which lead young men astray and destroy them; she thought of that woman's beauty, of the wild and fearful expression of her countenance, of the impudent investigation she had prosecuted at her house, and exclaimed:—

"O my God, into what wicked hands he has fallen!"

All her terrors appeared to her so many realities

* The French call the *second* in a duel a *witness*, and their practice is to have *two*, on either side.

as soon as Amab came and communicated to her the answer he had received.

"I guessed it was so, they are gone off together."

"God send it may be!" said Amab, whose fears were of a character far more serious.

"What do you mean?" said Madame Thoré.

"That such would be the foolish act of a young man, and would most probably soon have an end."

"But where is she? where are they gone?"

"That is what I hope to discover in a few days."

"In a few days, do you say?"

"Yes, madam."

"But I will know it in a few hours, I will.—The police shall have notice, and this frightful woman shall be denounced——"

"And suppose you were mistaken, madam?" said Amab; for he dreaded the idea of his name being ridiculously mixed up with a grotesque scandal, and was averse to all kind of *eclat* but that which served his purpose. Besides, added he, "Charles is of an age, in the eyes of the law, to be the master of his own actions. He was at liberty to go, if he thought proper."

"How could he do so, having about him no funds save the pocket money I used to allow him?"

And suppose he has obtained some by such means as to you would seem not quite excusable, would you suffer them to transpire?

Madame Thoré uttered an exclamation of despair; this new terror crushed the spirit of her grief, and she was easily persuaded and overruled by Amab, when the latter said to her:—

"You need not suspend your own measures in another direction, whilst I am busy on my side. But trust yourself to me; I pledge you my honour that I will take no rest and give no truce to the enemy until I have discovered Charles, and brought him back to you."

The afflicted mother accepted this protestation and consented to return home; but Amab who, to prevent the ill effects of her sorrows, had pledged himself to do more than he could really accomplish, Amab asked himself, when alone, how he was to keep the engagement he had just taken. Felina was gone; where was she hiding? How was he to discover that most subtle of women! that dark-minded *female fiend!*

There was but one clue which might lead to her track, and this clue was in the hands of M. de Monrion. But what excuse had he to apply to that man? what inquiries could he make of him? what right had he to go and ask him what had become of Felina? Amab, who was the most fastidious of men, and who carefully weighed whatever he did, faltered at these reflections. After hesitating some time, he suddenly started up, exclaiming:—

"Fool and coward that I am! I have dreamed an exceptional renoun, a life signalized by excentricity or agitation, and yet shrink from it when chance offers it to me, in a manner, ready prepared. Julia's love, Felina's anger—are they not two of those events which shed distinction on a man of genius? Did not Byron's glory owe something to the wild daring of his adventures? what need I fear? a duel? why, that would give me a figure and attitude in the public eye; and enable me to avoid the ignominious meeting which I am threatened with."

So Amab determined to call upon the Count de Monrion.

## CHAPTER XV.

### ONE OF THE VICTIMS OF THE SHE-TIGER.

The Count of Monrion lived in the rue du Faubourg Saint Honoré. When Amab reached the house, he was told that it was not very probable that M. de Monrion would receive him, in as much as he was then closeted with his uncle, the Marquis of Montaleu. However, Amab insisted upon their delivering his card to M. de Monrion, and almost immediately they came to tell him that the count was waiting for him. From the saloon, adjoining the one into which they were about to usher him, the painter could hear the sound of a most animated conversation. Amab paused through discretion.

"Go in, Sir, go in," said the valet de chambre, "the count, my master, wishes to see you instantly."

Amab went in. He bowed, but Monrion whilst returning his salutation, proceeded with his discourse.

"See," said he to his uncle, "here is this gentleman who can tell you that you had not been deceived, when you were told that I was flinging my money to the winds. I wanted to give him two hundred thousand francs for a picture which is not worth twenty pounds, I dare say, and I am still quite ready to let him have them, if it turns out that he is come hither to renew the bargain."

"I suppose that this gentleman, who has refused you already, still refuses," rejoined the old man to whom the count had addressed himself.

"Assuredly, gentlemen," said Amab, "and I came here with quite another purpose."

"In that case, my dear painter," resumed Gustave de Monrion, "the challenge I gave you this morning holds good between us, we are mortal enemies, and one of us will always be in the other's way, wherever we meet. I was going to write to that effect the very moment, the marquis of Montaleu, whom I have the honour to introduce to you, came in to rebuke me in fine set terms. How does it happen," said Gustave turning to his uncle. "that you never have the same command of eloquence in the Chamber? you would become a minister."

Amab was petrified with what he saw, and heard; he could not but admire the patience of the marquis of Montaleu, who had listened without rebuke to his nephew's apostrophe. He was a fine noble old man, who looked at Gustave with mournful astonishment, but without symptoms of anger.

"Count de Monrion," said he, "since you persist in dishonouring your name—"

"That which dishonours the name of a nobleman," said the latter with incredible haughtiness, "is not his bettings on the turf, or his ventures at whist, at the rate of a hundred guineas a fish, provided he pays for his stakes and horses. It is not his pouring his fortune into the lap of a courtezan, if he squanders that alone upon her. That which dishonours a nobleman, my uncle, is to belie the rules of honour, and the acts of probity; it is to use his name as a screen to escape the shame or punishment which base intrigues would invoke upon another; I have committed none of these crimes, Whenever the day shall have come on which a creditor can say that I have abused his trust, or a woman of respectability can raise her voice against me, and accuse me of destroying her character; the day on which a man can boast of offering me the shadow of an insult without my taking my revenge on the spot, on that day, you may indeed say that I have dishonoured my name as a nobleman. But until then, keep your empty and futile observations for those to whom they might apply better than they do to me."

"But, look at the life you are leading," continued his uncle.

"I know it," said Gustave flinging himself upon a sofa; "I am ruining and killing myself."

"Unhappy boy!" exclaimed the old marquis; "reflect that poverty—that penury may come before death."

"Be not afraid, uncle, I calculate better than you think: I have so well arranged things as to be sure to see my last shilling issue from my coffers on the very day that my last breath shall issue from my body; and, in case I should be mistaken, this last shilling would serve me to drive out that latest breath, should life prove more tenacious than I expected."

The marquis turned his head away.

"Oh! I understand you," resumed Gustave, "the subject is not agreeable to you; it deprives you of an opportunity to play the uncle with a fine burst of oratory, such as this," for instance:—"Nephew, I disinherit you."

"Reform your way of living, and my whole fortune is yours," said the good old marquis with tears in his eyes.

"It is too late," said Monrion; "we live no longer in an age when people believed in gold as a potation to restore the dying"

"Gustave," said the old man, and this name of tender familiarity touched upon a chord in spite of the young debauchee; "Gustave, there is a theme which I did not wish to recall to you, for I was afraid of polluting it by introducing it into this scandalous asylum; but, since nothing else can touch you I must remind you of it: Gustave, do you forget that you made your mother die of grief?"

"My mother! my mother!" he exclaimed.

The Count de Monrion took one step towards his uncle; his hands clenched, his lips convulsively trembling, he measured the old marquis with an ominous glance, whilst the latter looked on sad and without moving. The calm aspect of the aged nobleman struck the young man with awe. He averted his eyes; and, owing to some strange wandering of the mind, he fixed them long and earnestly upon a small cup of Saxon porcelain which stood on a side table; at that sight all his anger seemed to escape with the deep and painful sigh which rose up from his breast. Soon after his face resumed that expression of sadness combined with mirth which it wore when Victor had come in. He began to smile sarcastically, and turning to Victor, he said:—

"The man who touches with his finger's end either a woman or an old man is a coward, is he not? This at least is one of the axioms of our current morality. But what name ought we to bestow on the woman who takes advantage of her weakness, or the old man who appeals to his grey hair, whilst hurling at you one of those charges for which a man, who is a man, would have to answer with his whole blood?"

One might have thought that the marquis experienced a feeling of anger similar to that which had just disturbed his nephew, and, perhaps, to any other than his sister's son, he would have replied to this insolence by a challenge, and that in spite of his age and weakness. But this resentment broke out in a manner more cruel perhaps, for he answered:—

"Count de Monrion, there is no great difference, in current morality, between asking an old man for his whole blood and exhausting a mother's life in tears.

"What!" again, exclaimed Monrion.—"Take care—you come here to insult me.—Take care, Sir,—do not tempt my bad passions, since you are so well acquainted with them.—Do you wish me then to commit an act of shame to dishonour my last days?—Well, you shall not prevail.—There"—he added with a wild and savage laugh—"you see now I can be patient—say I killed my mother—that I poisoned her;—murdered her!—what more?—I will allow it all—speak—vociferate, say what you will—I listen to you—speak,—I say—why don't you speak?"

Monrion threw himself along a divan laughing like a spectre.—His face was ghastly—his breath was panting and arduous like the last rattle of the dying.

The marquis, who watched him with a steadfast eye, seemed to lose his strength—he staggered and hastened out of the room; but he could not leave the apartment, and let himself fall upon a seat, in the chamber adjoining the one in which this scene had occurred. Monrion advanced a step towards him; then stopped and said to Victor:—

"See what is the matter with him—commit him to the care of his servants—I am anxious to see the end of this——"

Victor passed on into the anteroom, where he found the old marquis rising from his seat with pain and preparing to go out: he offered him his arm.

"Heed me not, Sir," said M. de Montaleu to him in a mild voice, "it is a weakness unworthy of me in presence of such a wretch—but how could I help it? when I saw him there, so wan, so broken, so withered, so lost both in body and soul; when I saw death and vice laughing together on his white lips, I remembered that once handsome boy, so merry, so affectionate, who was the pride and love of his mother, and upon whom, I myself, had rested all the hopes of our family. I remembered that youth once brave, upright, and generous (for all that he was) who promised us so noble a future, and then, I was seized and overcome with a horrible despair.

"Oh! but you will surely try again."

"No, Sir, no—I have done with him—the hand of the fiend which has driven him to his destrucstill weighs upon him—and will never let him go until it has pushed him into his grave—God send he may not be driven to dishonour by the hand of that fatal woman!"

Here the old man was preparing to go out, when Monrion, who had overheard everything, immediately appeared, and said in a voice unusually serious and solemn for him:—

The hand which has driven me to my destruction, is yours, Sir; it was your cruel severity, your continual complaints to my mother, your bitter taunts at every thing I loved, your furious wrath against a woman who had escaped the effects of your hatred, that was what drove me to destruction. As for driving me to dishonour, neither her hand nor yours will ever be able to do that."

M. de Montaleu disdained to answer his nephew; he bowed to Victor and said to him:—

"If ever you have the misfortune to meet in your path with a woman whose name is Felina de Cambure, fly from her as if you had placed your foot on a venemous reptile. Farewell, Sir."

Saying which M. de Montaleu went out.

"Ah! that is it," exclaimed Monrion violently," always the same accusation. "Well then, the same shall the answer always be. For the first time in my life I hesitated, for she had exceeded the utmost limits of extravagance in her exactions, and I owed him a compensation—and yet I hesitated. But he came to speak to me about her again. Felina is always the last word in his rebukes, it shall likewise be the last in my life. Sir," added he turning quickly round to Victor, "Felina demanded of me that picture of the Virgin you have painted. Are you come to offer it to me at any price? If such be your intentiontion, only inform me what the amount is, and it shall be yours."

"I have already told you, Count, that this picture was not to be sold. And I now tell you," added Victor disregarding the sudden start of vexation which Monrion could not controul, "I tell you, I am too conscientious a man to profit by a caprice."

"Ah!" replied Monrion with a short derisive laugh, "you too, Sir," you treat me with pity, you are unwilling to take advantage of my rashness. Do you know that I did not require this treatment to demand satisfaction for the impertinence of your refusal?

"Count, you told me yourself that you were aware I was not the man to let such words pass by me unnoticed."

"Nor have I forgotten it. Let us come, therefore, to an understanding; to-morrow morning this picture must be delivered at my abode—or else I shall expect you in the wood of Boulogne with your witnesses. I leave you four and twenty hours to reflect."

"Reflection is needless; you shall not have the picture, nor will I fight on such a pretext."

"If you require another, I will give it you. But I candidly confess that the insult you will oblige me to put upon you has no other motive than my determination to have this picture, which I have promised to Felina. So you will gain nothing by it."

"Count, I shall be riding to-morrow in the wood of Boulogne, and if you choose to insult me there, perhaps you may find that an insult does not always resolve itself into a duel."

"Do you intend to kill me on the spot? Be it so," said Gustave, "it is as good a way of settling things as any other. Only I must observe, that you have just taken an engagement which authorizes me to treat you as the meanest of men, unless you keep it; but I am sure yon will not break your word. Let us talk of something else. You came here to see me—be so good as to tell me the motive of your visit. I am quite at your disposal, whatever you may ask of me—"

Victor was dissatisfied: it was not the fear of a meeting or of a dreadful action to be commited which excited this ill-humour; he had foreseen this danger: the ascendancy of M. de Monrion it was which made him falter. With all his skilful calculations and boundless ambition, he felt himself little and vulgar by the side of this young man, who sported so carelessly and recklessly with the wrecks of his life and fortune, merely to gratify a whim. Victor would not yield or be outdone by this extravagant vain glory, and coldly replied:—

"Since you are willing to offer me your services, I accept them."

"I thank you, Sir; tell me therefore in what manner I can be useful to you."

"I have need of your assistance to find out Madame Felina de Cambure."

"Really?" said Monrion, who could not help appearing astonished.

"I have presented myself at her house, and they told me she had left home."

"In that case," rejoined Monrion, you know as much as I do myself. I called upon her on leaving your atelier, and acquainted her with my ill success.—I was turned out after a few polite words on her part—which signifies that she will not easily forgive me for my want of address—and here I am."

"But you know where she is to be found?"

"Not at all."

"Shall you not see her again?"

"I shall see her again,"—said Monrion, in a sad and bitter tone.—"Yes, on the day when I shall have killed you for having rufused to sell me your picture, I shall again see her.—Or else on the day when you shall have killed me—she will return; but, in that case, I shall not see her again" he continued laughing.

"Excuse me, Count," said Victor with an air extremely foppish, "the business which induces me to seek an interview with Madame de Cambure is more important than either your death or mine. Have you no clue, no information to give me?"

"None; but I will do that for your sake, which I never did for my own."

M. de Monrion rang the bell. A valet de chambre came in.

"Attend carefully to what I am going to say to you, cunning rogue," said Gustave to him. "You receive my wages merely to play the spy upon me, and I know it.—Felina is always asking me for some favour or other on your account, in order that you may report to her whatever I do."

"Can the count, my master, believe any such thing."

"I am sure of it—I pay you too well for you not to betray me in a first-rate manner, Felina is not the woman to suffer you to rob me. But, in return for this treachery, you must possess some of her secrets."

"I swear to you, my lord."

"Even were it only to give her notice of what I am about, you must have means of communicating with her."

"If I knew it——"

"I don't seek to know it myself.—But this gentleman requires to ascertain it.—This gentleman, with whom probably I shall be cutting throats to-morrow or the next day.—He wants to see Felina, tell him where she is—I authorize you to do so.—Excuse me," he continued turning towards Victor, "I leave you alone with John; he knows what you require to learn.—Try to induce him to speak—I leave him in your hands.—That is all I can really do to serve you.—Farewell, Sir——"

Monrion, having said this, went out, and the valet de chambre said to the painter, who had been both amused and surprised by the above dialogree.

"You are M. Victor Amab, I believe Sir?"

"Yes, John."

"Well, it is very possible, Sir, that I may be able to inform you to morrow whether or not you can see Madame de Cambure."

"Where shall I be informed of this?"

"I will send you the information to your own house."

"I may depend on you," observed the painter.

"You may, indeed, Sir."

On which assurance Victor left M. de Monrion's house, without any better information than this indefinite promise.

---

## CHAPTER XVI.

### THE INSIDE OF A SELFISH HEART.

Meanwhile, he thought that this promise, vague as it was, might enable him to carry the shadow of a hope to poor Madame Thoré; he therefore went to her house to iuform her that he expected on the following day to see the person who would be able to give him some tidings of Charles.

Once more, whilst he was wending his way to the rue de Paradis-Poissonnierè, Amab began to reflect on his situation, and on the strange succession of events which in spite of himself were moving him along. Jealous of acquiring at whatever cost an extraordinary renown, he had

made real sacrifices to this ambition. But Victor only sanctioned the ill chances of an event so long as he himself proposed and directed the game; yet for some time past, he had been but the passive instrument of operations which were undoubtedly carried on for him, but not in the manner he could have wished.

This, on one side, the imaginative love of Julia had come to him; on the other, the impetuous passion of Felina, and because he had rejected both, he found himself exposed to a mother's grief, and to the fury of a poor demented libertine. Madame Thoré required him to account for the safety of Charles and Julia's peace of mind; M. de Monrion wanted to kill him for refusing to sell him a picture.

And all this, without reckoning Felina's vengeance, far more to be apprehended in her silence, than all the threats of M. de Monrion; without reckoning Julia's passion, Julia, who must think herself the object of his idolatry, since she had overheard the scene in the work-room.

Ten times did it occur to Victor's mind to take post and fly twelve hundred miles off, leaving all these people to disengage themselves as best they could from the embarrassments in which they found themselves. But that was a flight, and would make him appear to be afraid of M. de Monrion and of Felina; it would be to forsake Charles, and leave him to say hereafter, that his master was equally concerned with himself in the causes of the perils he had been exposed to. Amab did not hesitate a moment. He had at least the noble instincts of pride in what men weigh and discuss, if he had them not in what they do spontaneously. He determined to remain. Still, however, in the midst of all these events, and passions, there was one thing which he thought was in his power, this was to put a stop to Julia's love, although he had attempted it without success.

"Perhaps she did not understand me," he said to himself, "when I told her in her mother's presence that such a love as hers could not have any hope:" I am resolved, to-day, that she shall retain no doubt in this respect. It behoves my honour to destroy in Julia's mind, as well as in that of Madame Thoré, the erroneous ideas which may have been suggested to them by my refusing to M. de Monrion, to sell him my picture. On this side, at least, I will continue master to act as I think proper.

In consequence of this reflection, he hastened to call upon Madame Thoré, as well to acquaint her with what he had to say about Charles, as to execute his last resolution.

Were there not men, who, at twenty years of age, freely dedicate themselves to the priesthood, one would doubt whether such a being as Victor could possibly exist; and it might be argued too, that he who dedicates himself to the service of the church holds within himself the all-powerful zeal in which all other feelings are absorbed, whilst Victor, living in the world, must necessarily take his share in the passions which are its life.

Had he that chastity which shrinks from all irregular indulgence? In that case, Julia's love offered itself to him in the white robes of marriage, and all that environed that innocent betrothal was admirably calculated to sustain this felicity, if it came within the scope of Victor's wishes. There was youth, grace, beauty, spirit, enthusiasm, a good and virtuous family, fortune, intregrity: what more could he desire or dream of possessing?

Was it not towards these sweet asylums of life, towards these pure and lasting enjoyments that his ardent soul was directed?

Did he require the conflicts of the passions?

Did he mean to devote his life to the artful tactics of refined coquetry, or the insane fervour of an amorous Messalina! If so, why repudiate Felina?

Was it come to this that, for him, love was not the necessary complement of genius, that woman was not the first mystery to be studied and explored? Yes, such was the case with Amab. Starting in life from the depths of poverty, this man had weighed the value of every minute, and as he had prescribed to himself the order of his labours, so had he laid down the order of his life.

Let us explain. Whilst he was living in anxiety and pain on his daily wages, he never told his companions that any pleasure cost too much money: he used to say it cost too much time. This word *time* contained more precious things in his eyes than the word money: it included glory and the future. When he had acquired a firstling of fortune and renown, which would probably have induced another man to take breath and seek relaxation in the genial feelings and contemplation of the heart, or in the light occupations of an adventure; Amab only leaned on the ground he had ascended to, in order to climb still higher, and he said to himself with the same coolness as before, and without the least affectation of moralizing: "Either a wife or a mistress would cost too much:"

It was a sordid avarice for the treasure which was to make him illustrious. He estimated too highly the capital which had been his sole patrimony, to waste the smallest particle thereof, either in love or indulgence.

A day was perhaps fated to come, a far remote day it appeared, when Victor promised to himself the pleasures which serve to mitigate the burning cares of other men; but, until then, with regard to love, he had subsisted on little, or rather on nothing, or if we must be more candid and explicit still: *he had lived on black bread.*

In other matters, Victor was less austere. In truth, although he grudged himself what was necessary. he willingly allowed himself what was superfluous. He had a horse, he went to the Opera, and mixed in the world. Why so? why did he indulge in such diversions, whilst he shunned the most benign occupation? Because the time they cost him had a benificial effect on the time of his employment. The horse had been recommended for his health; not to appear in the boxes at the Opera, when every body went there, would have been to have yielded the palm to his rival, M. L *** Besides, it is there a man first forms those rich intimacies which he pursues in the world.

It was likewise with this object that Victor kept a rich apartment and a sumptuous workroom. Something of the shopkeeper existed in the artist. How could that consist with the indubitable genius of Victor? It was traceable to a feeling no less predominant than ambition which often despises the means it employs. The day may come when Victor, rich and celebrated, may paint masterpieces in a garret, naked and cold, provided this eccentricity communicates a new attitude to his fame; as on the other hand he may lavish the faults of his talent in extravagant freaks, provided they can be made to resound in the public ear.

Such was this selfish man at the time we refer to.

And now, was it reserved to a beautiful young girl, with a heart full to overflow of the purest, the warmest feelings, to make him deviate from this frigid and irksome resolution; or did such a victory pertain to the enticements of a bold and artful courtezan?

It was reserved for neither of them

That would have been his answer, had such a question been put to him. Consequently, as we said before, he had determined to demolish Julia's dream of love.

That was the point he had arrived at when he reached her abode.

Alas! how very far was the lovely and guileless Julia from suspecting so dire a calamity.

Sweet flower of sixteen! why should the perfume of thy love be squandered on a heart that does not open to them? Rosebud of innocence and beauty close thy cupola again, and let not thy sweets be wasted!

As soon as she had returned home with her mother, who had issued forth again immediately, Julia had striven hard to think only of her absent brother, who was perhaps lost, perhaps dead. But louder than the voice of a genuine sisterly affection, a voice was heard to speak, more powerful and more attentively listened to: it was the voice of Victor refusing the prodigal offers of M. de Monrion, and uttering the words :—"The love of a man is like a woman's honour; above all price."

Thus then, she thought, that image stealthily snatched was the young painter's dearest treasure. That image he had sanctified, the more chastely to worship it; for it was something more than his love, it was his religion. Ah! how proud, how happy did Julia feel thus to be adored! Ah! by what soft returns could she hope to requite this ecstatic worship? how she would have to love this man before her heart could acquit the debt, and she would be able to say that she was not ungrateful."

She had been only a few minutes at his apartments, and there, her heart oppressed with a family sorrow, and yet deluged at the same time with an unexpected joy, she had nevertheless seen and observed every thing; she had understood the picturesque luxury of the artist, she had admired the singular arrangement of his stock, those memorials of different ages, nations, and states; his weapons, his fans, his pieces of antique furniture; the Greek marbles, the Flemish wainscottings, the Roman bronzes; India, China, America, the dead and the living world, all was collected and displayed in that room darkened with its long and folded hangings, all this she had admired, and in all this, the charming child with her active and adventurous imagination had made herself a place, where she sat as upon a throne, happy, loving, and beloved, triumphant, wearing the name and glory of her husband as a diadem upon her polished brow.

There it was, in the nook of that high church window, in that ample chair of burnished oak, that her fancy seated her, fair and lovely, with her feet resting on a Persian ottoman covered and glittering with worn gold, and those little feet inserted in a pair of Turkish slippers.—From that spot, now hallowed in her dream of love, she watched her young and handsome husband standing in the atelier by his work, and followed his inspired pencil as it swept along the canvas; from that hallowed spot she heard a thousand times that voice which had raised her heart shortly before, when it said, "the love of a man is above all price." And yet that love had been paid, for Julia's dreams were no longer in the present time, they were on the wing and flying through the future. How happy, how blissful were those dreams! how charming they were, and yet how pure! for in this asylum where she had fancied herself, and where she saw herself the queen regnant of all that was Amab's, the noontide sun was pouring down its light, and the full bright day was present and looked on, as she took her place in her lover's home.

---

## CHAPTER XVII.

### THE COLD HEART AND THE LOVING ONE.

In the midst of these reveries, Amab was announced.—Julia was startled and wanted to fly.—As it had been anticipated that Victor might bring tidings of Charles; they had given orders that he was to be admitted. So Amab found himself alone with Julia. She was pale enough to have alarmed him. Cold and selfish as he was, his iron heart fell at the sight of that blanched cheek, nor did he feel that he had the energy to strike the heart of that young girl, whilst her mother was not there to hear her complaints and pity her distress. Julia saw his astonishment and sadness; inwardly she thanked him for his reserve. What an admirable reflector is love! The maiden's drooping heart was raised by this embarrassment of her supposed lover.

"Do you bring us any news of Charles?" said she to him.

"None as yet, mademoiselle; but it is most likely that to-morrow I shall have seen the person who is able to explain to us, at least I hope so, the facts of his disappearance. I am come to inform your mother of this much."

"She is absent from home," said Julia lowering her eyes.

Victor had continued standing. Had she offered him a seat, it would have been equal to saying to him:—"Stay,"—not to do so, was as much as hinting to him that she could not accept his visit in her mother's absence. She wished to leave him free to act himself.

"My mother is very grateful to you, Sir, for the trouble you are so kind as to take.—What you have just told me will doubtless restore to her a little hope; for we have learned absolutely nothing, neither through my father, nor through M. Villon, who have now directed their inquiries to another quarter."

Victor was no less embarrassed; he was seeking for something to say, and fancied he had found a subject- He had shrunk from the idea of striking Julia's heart in her love for him, but he would not have hesitated to open his mind to her mother. In like manner he would have dreaced to tell her mother the fears he experienced on Charles' account, yet he resolved to reveal them to his sister. By this means he transmitted the mischief he had to do by communicating it to the heart which he considered would be less sensible of it.

"I ought not to conceal from you, mademoiselle," said he to her, "that Charles' absence appears to me unaccountable. A man's intentions, in spite of his discretion, always escape him, in some unguarded word which he utters unconsciously, and which afterwards throws light upon his designs, when we recollect them; I have, therefore, taxed and sifted my memory well, and yet I cannot remember any thing which in him denoted the will to leave us either by himself or with another. I suspect some snare."

"Heaven preserve us! is it possible, Sir."

"Take courage, and do not let your mother hope that Charles has been induced to this flight by any fascination.—Charles had none that he loved——"

Julia cast down her eyes.

"He loved his family alone; his entire happiness was in its bosom. There must have been some violence——"

"Ah! speak plainly, Sir, you surely know something.—If you know it, tell it me; if there be a misfortune, I will try and lessen the horror for my mother. What do you know?"

"Nothing, on my honour—nothing, but I suspect, I fear——"

"What do you fear? oh! take pity on my mother, and do not hesitate to tell me all."

"Well, mademoisille, I fear that Charles has been the victim of an act of vengeance."

"On whose part? at whose instigation? Has he ever done any one an injury—he is so kindhearted, so cheerful?"

"A lively disposition is often a sad adviser it; impels us to actions which may appear pleasant but which are cruel, the wound we deal in our mirth is often the most acute."

"Is it a man he has offended? But no; a man revenges himself with weapons, and as you told us, we are informed of the consequences of a duel, when we have not been able to prevent one—can it be a—"

"A woman, perhaps," said Amab.

"Then said Julia, I cannot understand."

"Suppose—that Charles had insulted her in her pride—Suppose."

Julia was covered with blushes; Victor stopped in his speech. The young lady's confusion warned him that he was entering upon a subject doubtless scarcely fit for such ears. But this soft embarrassment had none of that scornful dignity which awes one into silence; it looked like a prayer that he would not abuse his power to tell her what he might—a moment after he resumed:

"But, really, I am alarming you without sufficient reason; I know nothing, I have no trace; but I am on the search, and my mind snatches at the least shadow of a probability. To-morrow, no doubt, I shall be prepared to tell you more. I was wrong to speak to you as I did. Do not repeat to your mother, therefore, what I have said, it would be causing her unnecessarily a very poignant grief."

"I will be silent," returned Julia.

"I shall feel grateful to you for it.

"You know that I can be discreet," she answered, looking on the floor.

This was as much as reminding him of the secret she had kept for him on the subject of that image he had carried off so stealthily with his crayon. The recollection made Amab start, he was disarmed for a moment by the appeal, and looking at his model, he thought he discovered new charms in that perfection of beauty. The painter's admiration was kindled again at this new aspect of that heavenly face. He forgot the selfish motive which had brought him there, and muttered in a low voice."

"Ah! had I but seen you thus, I would have made you still more beautiful."

The loving girl took heart and looked at him again, and as she looked all her love glided over to him in that glance, in a blue ray of light.

Then he understood her. Sad, and filled with despair for what he had just said, and touched by that pure and candid reliance of the soul of this innocent child on him—he continued :—

"Oh ! did you but know——"

"Silence,?' exclaimed Julia suddenly and drawing back, "there's M. Villon coming in.,'

Julia believed she had interrupted a declaration. She alone had said all by bidding Victor be silent."

It was indeed the clerk's voice asking for M. and Madame Thoré, as he hurried into the drawing-room. His eye measured them both with a rapid glance, and Julia's confusion, Victor's vexation were to him a proof that there had been an interchange of pledges between the two lovers.

Victor bowed to take leave. Julia offended at Villon's look, said aloud :—

"Do not forget that my mother will expect you all day to-morrow, to hear what you have learned about Charles."

She thereby explained the reason of Victor's presence and gave a pretext for his return, She alone had courage, because she alone had love.

Victor bowed to M. Villon and took his departure.

## CHAPTER XVIII.

### THE SHE TIGER AND HER WILES.

**On** the following day, Amab went out on horse back and took his ride through the bois de Boulogne. He had made up his mind to extricate himself, whatever might happen, from the awkward situation he had placed himself in. That very morning a note from Felina had been delivered to him by M. de Monrion's valet de chambre.

"You will see me sooner than you think," said the note.

Victor still had to dread the hidden designs, the blows in the dark meditated by this woman ; and, from what he had seen of the Count of Monrion, he did not doubt but that the latter would keep the word he had pledged of provoking him to a duel by some gross insult.

He had therefore determined to give defiance both to the snare, which Felina might lay to entrap him, and to the public insult with which Gustavus had threatened him.

Amab had thus been riding for nearly half an hour through the wood of Boulogne, without meeting with the Count de Monrion and without noticing that any of the mounted gentleman, who had crossed his way had looked particularly at him. He was beginning to feel more at ease regarding the threats which had marked him as their object, when suddenly he saw a horseman draw up his steed a few paces in front, and who was apparently struck at his sight. He was a very young man, almost a boy, to judge by the delicacy of his features, and the rosy-white tint of his complexion. But his thick black moustache lent to his countenance a more severe and resolute character.

No sooner had this cavalier perceived Amab, than instead of pursuing his road and crossing him, he turned his horse about and rode him for a few moments before Victor.

Amab, curious of seeing more distinctly the face of the party who had examined him so particularly, gradually gained ground upon him ; he had almost come up with him when the young man turned his horse's head again ; and suddenly found himself face to face with Amab and by his side.

Victor had not recovered from the surprise occasioned by this abrupt motion, before he had received a sharp cut with a horsewhip over his face. The painter, wild with anger, raised the cane he carried in his hand, but already had the young man set spurs to his horse, and darted off.

Victor rode forward immediately in pursuit of the coward who had first insulted him, and then betaken himself to flight. But the latter had considerably the start of him. He soon forsook the Acacia avenue where this scene had occured, and still flying, still pursued, he reached that part of Boulogne wood which almost extends to the Seine and which, at that time terminated close to a ferry-boat, opposite Suresne.

For some time, the man pursued by Victor, appeared to make it a sport to suffer him to gain ground and then to fly with greater rapidity, and to excite him in the race by the immediate hope to overtaking his enemy, a hope which was every moment deceived. But, by-and-bye, the strength both of horse and rider seemed to fail. Victor was on the point of coming up with them. The stranger attempted a last desperate effort, he drove the spurs into the bowls of his house ; the restive animal leapt up, then reared, and the rider rolled over the lonely grass road to which he had enticed Amab.

The latter in turn alighted from his horse that he might at length have satisfaction of his enemy ; but he appeared to have fainted, and his hat had fallen from his head a few yards from the spot.

Let our readers judge of Amab's wonder, on beholding long locks of black hair scattered over that pale and beauteous face. The black moustaches had disappeared, the waistcoat was partly open ; the insolent bravo was a woman : that woman was Felina.

Amab's anger was, in a manner, all diverted at once.

On recognising Felina, it passed from the burning lust of vengeance to that rage and vengeance which has no object to settle on ; then he began to consider that woman whose beauty he had scarcely had a glimpse of as yet, on the day when she had been insulted in so shameful a manner in his workroom. As on that occasion he had thought her beautiful ; but, for the first time in his life, Amab's heart experienced a different feeling from admiration for physical beauty. The bold behaviour of this woman who had entrusted to no hand but hers, the task of avenging her wrong, made him think that she was endowed with one of those spirits which a man might feel proud to cope with.

For the first time in his life, the painter could read in his heart the thought of subduing another heart. This is indeed the beginning of a great love, when the woman who has inspired it has skill enough not to suffer it to triumph too soon !

However, Felina lay without moving on the sward ; she fainted altogether, and, there were a thousand reasons passing like lightning through Amab's head, and prompting him to assist her ; if not from pity, it aught to be for vengeance ; if not to ask satisfaction for the affront he had received, it might be to ask her to explain the cause of the disappearance of Charles, if not of his death.

He went up to her, placed her in a sitting posture, undid the cravat which was stifling her, opened her white marble forehead to the air, and paused a hundred times in his eager attentions, to admire that haughty beauty ; finally, when a few minutes had elapsed he felt the deepest anxiety on finding that the swoon continued still, and that he could not afford any effectual relief to the sufferer.

Suddenly the sound of horses' steps was heard in

one of the side avenues. Felina started, and Victor was about to call for help, when he heard the thin piping voice of M. de Monrion through the foliage, crying out in a tone of raillery:

"Who the devil told you he had seen M. Amab in the wood? I was pretty well convinced that the little gentleman could think twice of it before he tried to play with me, a more serious game than that he ventured for the honour of his fair defaulter.

This was an allusion to Amab's duel for the unpaid picture.

Amab, who was kneeling by Felina's side, was on the point of standing up, but the hand he help in his own gently pressed him. He looked at Felina: her eyes partly opened and seemed to be striving to emerge from the darkness in which they were plunged. Her lips quivered as if her parched mouth had entreated for icy water. Quick and sudden startings pervaded her whole frame; and Amab was still watching Felina's face for signs of returning life, when Monrion and those who accompanied him were already at a distance.

Felina opened her eyes at last. She looked round at first for a few moments with a bewildered eye on every thing around her; then she fixed her looks upon Victor, and appeared not to recognize him. But all at once she uttered a cry and started to her feet so abruptly, that Amab was on his knees before her, whilst she was considering him, with eyes that flamed with anger and wrath.

How beautiful she was thus, her lips quivering, her nostrils dilated, her eye flashing, and her bosom heaving with palpitating breath. Amab forgot whilst he looked at her the wrong he had done to this woman, the insult he had suffered from her, and why he was kneeling there. As soon as he recovered his thoughts, he desired to leave Felina the difficulty of speaking first, so he remained still. Then, he was enabled to distinguish as they glided over that lively brow, a thousand conflicting thoughts, until a kind of astonishment was depicted at last in the still unmoving eye of Felina. Then only did she appear to perceive that she was standing before her enemy who was on his knees to her.

As if this attitude of the one in respect to the other had suddenly suggested the aim to which her vengeance was directed, there came a smile of triumph over Felina's lips. Her eye deluged Amab with a wild and burning light; but, the same moment, as if he had driven the thought very far away, a languishing sadness overspread her features. Her eyes seemed to be drowned in a veiled light, and her voice assumed the soft sounds of a flute heard from the remote silence of the wood, as she said to the artist:—

"Sir, I shall be at your orders, at the time and place you like to appoint: I shall have my weapons and bring my witnesses."

Such a provocation coming from a woman's mouth must call up a smile in the man to whom it is delivered, even when the amazon who offers battle speaks in a firm and imperious voice; but when her words are as soft as those of a child who supplicates and is afraid, when the eye, which is to guide the sword and pistol is modestly lowered beneath her enemy's glance; then, the man who is addressed no longer laughs with irony, but feels himself overcome with tender pity for the weak being whose spirit has exceeded her strength, for the feeble dare-all who would fight to be revenged, and whose arm is too weak to bear the sword she appeals to for redress.

"Madam," answered Victor, "you propose to me a combat which I cannot accept, and your weapons can never reach me, unless you are pleased to strike me unawares with your sword, as you did with your riding whip."

"Did I hurt you?" exclaimed Felina in an agitated voice, as if she felt uneasy at the harm he had possibly sustained.

And then the next moment, she seemed again to drive away this impulse of pity, and resumed in a broken voice:

"Since your disdain to demand satisfaction for the wrong I have done you, it is for me to ask you to account for that you have occasioned me."

"Oh! madam," replied Amab, "forget."

"Forget!" she here exclaimed hiding her face in her hands, "forget that you threw me into the arms of a villain! forget that you exposed me to the polluting derision of a crowd of coxcombs? Forget? Oh! such abominations cannot be forgotten. They would kill us—were they not avenged, and," added she shedding a few tears, "they still destroy us—even if we avenge them."

"Is there no means in the world to make you believe the deep regret I feel?" said Amab rising up; "is there no reparation that a man like me can offer to a woman like you, to be pardoned?"

Felina recoiled a step or two as if the better to search into his soul. She seemed to inquire within herself on what weak side this man could be assailed. Sometimes, she appeared about to speak, as if she had at last found the word she wanted; but immediately she stopped as if she feared to be conquered in the struggle by some false manœuvre.

Suddenly a more resolute thought seemed to present itself to her mind. She pointed her hand towards Amab, who stood motionless, and showing him the spot where, a moment before, he was on his knees before her, she said to him in a short and deeply altered tone:—

"There,—there, as you knelt before." And Amab did not blush to ask pardon of a woman in that humble attitude, and fell down on his knees again.

When he had done so, she advanced again close up to him and looked into his face as she had done before.

"Well," said the painter to her, in a voice of soothing repentance, "pardon! pardon——"

"No, no, that is not what I mean," she said in a voice almost inaudible, and seeming to pursue the track of a departed recollection; "no, it was not the word pardon you spoke to me just now," she added with a strange feeling. "You were on your knees at this very spot; you looked at me with other eyes—I thought I read in them——"

It seemed that Felina's reason was lost in the pursuit of some remembrance she could not entirely recall, and she said to Amab, with a smile almost bordering upon madness:—

"Oh! yes, you looked at me thus, and you spoke to me."

"What did I say then?" asked Amab.

"What did he say to me?" resumed Felina in a childlike voice and with a look into the real world. "Did he not tell me he would love me?"

Two tears escaped from her eyes upturned towards heaven.

"And if I tell you that I love you?" said Amab, who could not resist the enchantment which this woman exercised over him, and who wished to draw her back to the reality of their situation.

"Always thus," said she smiling in a strange manner, "always on your knees, always repentant."

"Always," answered Amab.

Felina leaned over him, as if her syren lips had sought Victor's forehead; but, as if it were a snake she had drawn near, she suddenly darted back exclaiming:—

"Oh mad! mad that I am! No, no, rather death than such an act of baseness! No, no, Sir, I hate you, I will never forgive you, never."

"Felina! Felina!" said Victor trying to retain

her, "there is no evil but what is willingly committed which is unpardonable, and this submissive love which was your dream and which here I offer you—cannot it make you forget?"

"Can you yourself forget?" resumed Felina looking coldly on him.

Amab did not answer and bent his eyes downwards. A new anger kindled in that woman's heart, and she then said to him in a tone of cruel raillery:—

"Yes, Sir, it is true," when I recovered from my swoon, I saw you on your knees before me, and a strange idea, a woman's idea came into my head, and I said to myself. "Yes, that would be a real vengeance! Yes, to behold languishing and kneeling before me the love of that man who so outrageously disdained me; to suffer him to consume his strength, his spirit and that genius which had fascinated me, in powerless desires, in useless prayers and in jealous, torments; that would be a real vengeance. But a moment came when I understood that I should not perhaps have strength enough to oppress you further. Then I returned to the project of killing you. For, however weak I may appear to be, however celebrated a man may be for his address, I should not fear to encounter him, sword in hand. No! she said furiously, "I should not have feared any one—"

A sigh of despair gushed from Felina's bosom, and she continued:—

"And I was afraid of you—I should not have dared to kill you, and you perhaps would have disdained to strike me; and therein there is enough of humiliation, Sir. Finally, just now," she added in a tearful voice, "I attempted to recover the first dream I had ever known; but it was no longer as a vengeance, it was as a consolation That dream, you have driven from me, Sir. I thought that I could have forgotten the injury; you have been careful to show me that you would not forget it. Farewell, Sir, the best course is for us never to meet again. To-morrow I shall have left France for ever."

Felina turned away when she had spoken. Amab hurried after her, saying to her:—

"But I am resolved to see you again, for I will love you, not in the hope of your loving me in return, but to obtain your forgiveness at least."

"Madman that you are," said Felina to him assuming all at once the natural and easy tone of mere conversation, "a woman's pardon is her love."

"Well, I will have yours."

"Never."

"Then you must prepare to repeat the word all your life long, for I shall never cease to sue for your love."

"But, to that end, you must see me again and that I will not allow."

"Permit me, in that case, not to leave you," said Amab to her, for there is somebody about whom I must speak to you."

"Oh! I know!" cried Felina with a start of impatience. "Well, you may reassure the tender anxiety of his mother, and his sister's too, if she still retains a thought for her brother. He is not dead."

"But where is he."

Felina laid her hand sharply on Amab's arm, as if to impose silence on him; she seemed to listen to some distant noise, and hastily replied:—

"Here, to-morrow, at the same hour, I will inform you of it."

Thereupon she sprang up lightly on her horse, and soon disappeared in the direction whence the voices were heard, and among which Amab thought he recognized that of M. de Monrion.

"Oh!" said she as she rode off, "he will come there, he will; but she! she! no matter!

The first scene in the comedy had proved successful; she went after Monrion, to play the second.

---

## CHAPTER XIX.

### EXCUSES, AND LOVE'S PROJECTS.

Amab, being left to himself, did not seek to understand the new feeling which disturbed him. Only, there seemed to be an entire age between the day he was in and the morrow. And that man, whose every hour had its appointed occupation and labouring ambition, asked himself for the first time in his life what he should do until the moment returned for him to meet Felina again.

However the recollection of M. de Monrion's name and the disdain with which the latter had spoken of him, soon recurred to him.

Up to that time, Amab had foreseen with spirit, but yet with displeasure, the probability of an awkward meeting with this reckless libertine; but scarcely had Felina taken her departure, before he felt, so to speak, the urgency of this meeting. He remounted his horse, and renewed his ride through the wood of Boulogne.

This search was for some time fruitless; but at last, just as he had made up his mind to return to Paris, Amab perceived Gustave who himself was advancing towards the Maillot gate.

Victor quickened his horse's speed in a manner to come up with the count at the same time as a party of gentlemen who were riding from the avenue of Neuilly. Amab wanted to have witnesses to the scene which he fully expected to take place.

When he had reached the count's side, he rode on a few steps in advance, and then turned his horse quickly round as Felina had done.

M. de Monrion likewise appeared much astonished at this abrupt motion; but on recognising Amab, he bowed and smiled, and said to him, with extended hand:

"Excuse me, M. Amab; you are a brave fellow, I say so aloud in order that all who are near me may hear my words. I offer you my apology for all my silly threats."

Amab conducted his horse by the side of the count and they rode a short time near each other.

"We no longer require your picture; there is another whim to be satisfied, and that, though it appears more difficult, will not perhaps meet with so great an obstacle as the duty from which they have absolved me."

"I congratulate you," said Amao to him, for he could not resist the frank and hearty manner in which M. de Monrion had spoken to him.

"You," said Gustavus to him laughing, "you—how very odd; and yet," he added with a sigh, "it is possible. Oh! the woman; the woman! But she insists upon it."

"She insists upon it," echoed Amab; "but of whom are you speaki[illegible], then?"

"You know her [illegible]," rejoined Monrion bitterly; "so much the better! never may you know her—you would waste your youth and genius, as I have consumed my youth and fortune."

Then he added saluting Amab carelessly with his hand:—

"But she insists upon it."

Victor could not doubt it, Felina it was who had prompted M. de Monrion to provoke him in public; it was she again who doubtless had just dissuaded him from this intention. He could not but suspect the price she had to pay for this disobedience.

At this thought, his heart was oppressed. On leaving Felina, Victor was in love; on leaving M. de Monrion, Victor was jealous.

Then, he felt that tumult of ideas, that confusion of feelings in which a man loses his resolution, in which his strength is exhausted, and in which he scarcely holds any longer to life save by a single point, and there he is linked to the being who has excited in him these strange and new anxieties.

The whimsical words of M. de Monrion had not alarmed Victor, he was as yet too ignorant of love to anticipate its dangers. He fancied it as a conquest and not as as a servitude. He did not even believe in the bondage of M. de Monrion, because the latter acknowledged it. He never suspected that inconceivable power which is denied, despised and yet submitted to.

The Count de Monrion appeared to him to be a fool who with his vanity made himself a chain which he disdained to break, and he would not have understood the words of a prudent man who might have said to him :—

"I will fly from the woman, for if I see her again, I shall love her, and from the day I should learn to love her, she would drive me to anything, not excepting crime, should she desire it."

Amab believed that there still remains a free feeling in the heart of man, when love has taken possession of it. Never had a more confiding victim advanced so boldly towards the snare in which it is doomed to perish.

Something however there was in the love he felt for Felina which terrified him. It was the life she had led. What then was the love he felt for her already, that such a thought should torture him? Did he feel that he could sacrifice his whole future existence to this woman, that he believed he had the right to demand of this woman to render an account of her former life?

"Oh!" said he to himself, "had I only met her in her girlhood, in her purity, before the world had fascinated and ruined her with its wretched levities and vertigoes! Oh! how I should have loved her, and how exactly she would have been the woman to have suited alike my soul, my ambition, and my purposes?"

It was during this dream which restored to Felina all the splendour of her former maidenly beauty; it was during this dream that, with his poetical imagination, he surrounded her dark glowing head with the white veil of a chaste vestal, that, by a kind of metamorphosis similar to that produced by certain jugglers by the deception of light and colour, this ideal portrait he thus conceived, lost by degrees its too obvious tints: the boldness of the forehead was smoothed, the flame of the eye was softened, the contraction of the brows was gently expanded, the scornful expression of the lips was converted into an angelic smile, and instead of Felina, the painter saw Julia's face radiant with purity, and glittering likewise with the love she felt for him.

What he fancied Felina to have been, Julia was at present: a heart without reproach and in which no vindictive feelings could exist; which contained nothing but what was good, and which had nothing to reject.

"Oh!" he exclaimed in a moment of natural impulse, and like a man who has just been struck with a dazzling ray of light, "that is the woman I ought to love."

As swift to execute his thought as he had rapidly conceived it, this strange man directed his steps towards Julia's abode.

What a singular whim of the mind was this desire to love the chaste and pure young girl, because he had felt a passion for the courtezan palpitate within him!

What is love? Is it a beverage of such intoxicating power as to parch and irritate the lips with thirst, even when they have imbibed it from a poisoned bowl? But why endeavour to discover a reason for that which so often has no argument for its basis? Victor's stubborn and selfish soul had just been roused from its torpor by a voice of enchantment: his hour was come. But for whose sake was it come. Proud fool! he still thought he could decide for himself, as if it belonged to man to decide any thing in love!

The truth is, that a lad of fifteen could not be more silly, than was Victor at twenty-five.

During the passage he had to traverse, between the Champs Elysées and Madame Thoré's dwelling, the painter had conceived and examined the finest reasons and motives to prove the necessity under which he was to love Julia. He had spoken to himself like a father, and had pointed out to himself all the advantages of an alliance with that honest family; he had calculated their fortune, and included his own vanity in the reckoning; he had argued that to whatever position time and his own talents might elevate him, Julia was a woman who would never remain below the place assigned to her. In all which, Amab proved himself marvellously wise and exact in his calculations.

In sober truth, one of the most fatal chances which mar the fortunes of ambitious men, is that of dragging along their paths of life a wife suited only to the arduous trials of their first poverty, and whom they are compelled to keep by their side, however awkward, inexpert, and vulgar, after they themselves have acquired the usage of the world, good breeding and power.* It is like the sign board of a glazier which some perfideous hand has put up over the entrance of a minister's hotel.

Yes, Amab was deeply sagacious in all the admonitions he applied to his own selfish nature; but the best reasonings, says La Bruyère and the great author of Tom Jones, "never have the least influence over the heart." A single word like the stab with a dagger will kill love, whilst the most eloquent sermon cannot affect it: and that is the reason why the noblest, the purest woman, the most chaste and perfect beauty, the finest and simplest wit, are powerless to produce a flame which is sometimes kindled by the fire of one obscene glance.

Such a look could never come from Julia's eyes; and it was doubtful whether Amab's wish to love her would flourish or continue barren in his heart. It was not easy to resolve this problem; but what was more easy to guess, was that Amab would endeavour to feel the love which he recommended to himself, and that whilst he hoped to be sincere, he would perhaps perform the character of a man in love when in Julia's company. Indeed, was he not going to her house for that purpose, and ought he not to do his utmost to convince himself?

As for the rest, what took place on that day at Madame Thoré's will serve to explain, better than all the reflections we could make, the part that Victor intended in his own mind to play, or to speak more plainly, the efforts which he made to call up a tender feeling which he considered proper and worthy of a man like him.

Meanwhile let us shift the scene and see what was taking place at Madame Thoré's house.

---

* The same idea has occurred to the accomplished author of Charles O' Malley, who has introduced a scene in one of his fine military novels, in which the ludicrous blunders and *naivetes* of a great general's wife, at an Imperial soiree at the Tuileries, are among the most conspicuous proofs of that writer's fine comic powers.

## CHAPTER XX.

### WHAT HAS BECOME OF CHARLES?

Gloom and anxious affliction still resided in the house; every step that had been taken by M. Thoré, by his wife, by M. Villon, by all the servants, had proved of no effect. The police having been applied to, had set inquiries on foot, and had declared their inability to discover a young man who had been missing and unheard of for two days, and on whose track none could give the least information. Charles had left his mother's house, the day before, at five in the morning, and Charles had not been seen ever since: that was all they could tell.

No message had reached him, unless it was Amab's letter, a letter which remained in Madame Thoré's hands; no friend had called to take him out, no previous habit could be quoted to indicate to what quarter he had gone. One man, and only one had said that he thought he knew a woman to whom he could apply for tidings of Charles. That man was Amab; that woman was Felina de Cambure.

Madame Thoré had wanted on the instant to denounce this name to the police, but she had hesitated, partly, because she could not well reveal a secret which belonged to Amab, and partly, because she doubted whether it would be prudent to summon the assistance of the police on so vague and uncertain a hint as that afforded by Victor. But that was not the chief objection by which Madame Thoré was restrained; the inquiries she had made relative to Felina had far more weight with her.

We must proceed at once to tell our readers, by what clue this loving mother had contrived to make out, in a few hours, a woman who was a mystery to persons who had been acquainted with her for many years, and whose subtle and extraordinary character we are painting without assuming to explain it.

If the beginning of this narrative has been noted by him, the reader may have remarked a very trifling circumstance, but which became of great importance to Madame Thoré when pursuing her inquiries. She already knew that the woman was most probably the same as the one who, on the pretence of purchasing some china had visited her warehouse, on the very day that Charles had been missed; and Madame Thoré had the more reason to believe that this woman had an interest in this disappearance, that M. Villon had told her with what eagerness she had inquired about the rich merchant's family. Finally as a last reason to suspect that she was concerned in this capture, Madame Thoré called to mind the refusal of this inquisitive stranger to give her address.

But all this was insufficient to put the mother on the track of this woman, and yet that track existed in her own house.

And truly, on the eve of New Year's day, a complete set of china had been transmitted on M. de Monrion's account, to a person whose address M. Thoré had privately delivered to M. Villon; and that person was Madame de Cambure. No sooner had Madame Thoré mentioned the name before the head-clerk, than the latter informed her of this circumstance. M. Thoré whose information went further, revealed to his wife the nature of the relations said to exist between M. de Monrion and Madame de Cambure. M. de Monrion was one of the customers to the house; there was consequently a means of ascertaining through him what had become of that lady.

But how was a subject of this kind to be broached to the young count, who might take offence on hearing his mistress accused of secreting a handsome young man. Besides, the Count de Monrion, notorious for his extravagant dissipation was not likely to be the man to listen patiently to the affections of a father or mother. Would it not be better to apply to one of his relations?

In that case, the difficulty and its solution appeared at the same time, for long since M. Thoré's house included among its patrons, the whole of the de Monrion family, and the Marquis de Montaleu, the young count's uncle and guardian, had always evinced the greatest kindness to this upright burgher family.

To him therefore they had determined to apply; and Madame Thoré insisted on going herself to call upon the old marquis.

We should deem it unnecessary to relate this interview, were it not calculated to disclose to our readers some particulars which will enable them to appreciate the previous conduct of Felina and foretell all that this bad woman might yet become.

A wife or a mother always obtains a larger share of a man's confidence than the most persistent friend, or the most tender father. The marquis had received Madame Thoré with that noble affability which does not fear to descend to respect towards an honest woman, although her condition be inferior to his own. He had listened to her patiently, but sorrowfully, and had concluded by saying to her:—

"I cannot believe that Madame de Cambure can be concerned in your son's abduction. Indeed what connection is there likely to be between such a woman and Charles, a mere child without any name (pardon me for saying so) to whom I presume you do not give money enough to indulge caprices surpassing belief."

"How does it happen then that M. Amab appears to have suspected she would be able to give us information?"

"This M. Amab is your son's master? Is he not the painter of a picture which is much spoken of?"

"Yes, Sir."

"Which he refused to relinguish to my nephew for an enormous sum."

"The very same."

"This picture was intended for Madame de Cambure, and M. Amab refused it; your son is one of M. Amab's pupils," said the old marquis taking notes as he preceeded; "I confess that, hitherto, I see nothing in these facts to warrant a charge; however, there is a circumstance, the mysterious visit made by Madame de Cambure to your warerooms, which might induce a suspicion that Charles may have been acquainted with this woman."

"Charles is handsome, young, and agreeable," said Madame Thoré who appeared to allow with regret those qualities which had formerly been a source of pride to her.

"If you understood Madame de Cambure, you would be of opinion that those are advantages which would fail to satisfy a mind so disordered; that she should be smitten in her wild fancy by a man like M. Amab, who is an object of public attention, is very possible, but by a handsome young man in obscurity, no."

"Still," resumed the poor heart-broken mother, "people say that these creatures do feel unaccountable preferences."

"You are mistaken with respect to Madame de Cambure: she is not one of those vulgar courtezans, who dispose with prudence of their fortune and their love. And yet this woman, is so extravagant—or rather so skilfull—If Charles can assist her in any of her designes—she will easily have won him over to her obediance. Hope, and desire, that this absence of Charles is caused by

something else besides Felina's will; it would be terrible to think of."

"You really alarm me, and fill me with terror, Sir, what kind of woman is she then?"

"She is the widow of a man who has left her a name which serves to protect her and class her above those whom she resembles. She is rich, but her position is of no consequence; let us talk of herself. Well, she is excessively passionate, she has delirious fits of anger, which appear to place her entirely at your mercy, and at the same time she possesses a cold and concealed cunning which covers up all her purposes. In a moment of pride and resentment, she will break and trample on the bonds she has imposed, and after that she will use indefatigable patience to reattach all those tattered threads; you shall see her, in the same hour, proud, haughty, unrelenting, then humble, penitent, devoted; she has glorious impulses to urge a man on to distinction, to labour, to honour, yet there is no tongue like hers to destroy in the most audacious language the noble feelings of honour and duty; tears, raillery, the most vivid eloquence, the coldest reasoning, she employs them all with unapproachable superiority: she has the most dissolute heart, the most impudent language I ever heard, with the loftiest soul, the most direct understanding, the noblest speech that was ever listened to; she crushes you with disdain or intoxicates you with flattery—oh! I understand her, madam, I have struggled with her, I wanted to rescue from her my poor Gustavus. I attempted to moralize, she did the same and broke with Gustavus. A week after, he threatened to blow out his brains, and I went and entreated her to soothe him. I reproached her with my nephew's ruin; she restored him the whole of his insane expenses, and a month after I thought it better to see him indulge Felina's whims than to know he was advancing to his ruin by paths still more flagrantly scandalous. Then, unfortunately, I threatened her—and then it was she swore to me she would be the destruction and total ruin of the Count de Monrion, and she has kept her word."

"But did you not anticipate her by warning your unfortunate nephew?"

"She warned him herself."

"And did he not sever this degrading attachment."

The marquis raised his eyes to Heaven and said with hopeless despondency:—

"Accuse him not too heavily. Ah! what a woman! She is the incarnation of evil. The following day he reduced his establishment; for six months he prepared himself, by the most rigid and assiduous study to appear one day with lustre in that chamber, in which since he was a child his father's seat has been opened to him. I thought he was saved, Felina had disappeared! vain and empty hope! she had not left him; disguised in the dress of a young man she acted as his secretary, assisted him, encouraged him, sustained him—all this time she had been employed to recover that dominion over him which a word had deprived her of. She took possession of that easy spirit—and then—then—"

The marquis averted his head and added: "Pray to God, dear madam, that your son may have nothing to do with that woman."

"Oh! if it were so, Sir, I would rescue my son from her, I would."

"Perhaps you are right," said the marquis: a mother who should go openly to Felina and say to her: 'I mean not to struggle with you, I come to implore your piety, I trust myself to your generosity. Restore me my son;' perhaps such a mother might move this singular woman, and perhaps Felina might ask her forgiveness for the sorrow she had caused.

This was what Madame Thoré had heard at the mansion of M. de Montaleu, who, moreover, had promised her to make inquiries.

After she had given an account to M. Thoré of the result of this interview, the china dealer, with the never failing assurance of fools, treated as a mere romance the pretended power of this modern Armida.

"All this," said he, "is good in poetry and novels, but in our age of enlightenment and constitutional freedom, we know how to manage such vixens; we treat them like hobgoblins which children are alarmed at; we disperse such phantoms with a good cudgel. I will call upon this woman, and treat her—in a way—"

Madame Thoré had no precise idea of what Felina was; but in her character as a wife, she knew too well by what harmless feints and stratagems she had always got the better of her husband's will, not to fear the abuse which a bad mind might make of the superiority of woman in this respect. She dreaded above all to provoke Felina's vanity, of which M. de Montaleu had shown her the fatal consequences. She therefore drew a promise from her husband that he would not offer to see Madame de Cambure, until Amab had kept the promise he had made the day before.

All this had been discussed when Julia was not present. But when once a young girl's curiosity is roused by a powerful feeling, it will pierce through a wall, and will leap over any space; it travels by incomprehensible roads. Let it not be imagined that Julia listened at the keyholes, she would never have thought of doing so; but the end of a conversation continued after she had entered, a chance exclamation during meals or office hours; some of those advices which people deem discreet because unmeaning names are invented to hide what they refer to, advices given by M. Thoré to M. Villon; a thousand strange reflections arising from the uneasiness of the whole house, a question apparently without motive, but to which the answer communicates a defin te meaning, all these isolated atoms dispersed through the air, and preciously collected by an attentive mind, finally assume a body, a shape and a signification. This is so true that Julia, to whom nothing had been told, knew perfectly well that Madame de Cambure was a dangerous woman, full of seductive wiles which few could withstand. She had seen her and knew how beautiful she was, and Amab, too, was acquainted with her.

This was the concluding word of that long and patient inquiry.

Consequently then, Julia had likewise learned to fear that fairy with her inebriating poisons, but it was not for Charles that she trembled, it was for Victor. The woman who loves possesses wonderful instincts; she suffers without knowing why, for evils which she is ignorant of. Silly women ascribe to their nerves the low spirits which at certain times oppress them; those who understand life say they are being deceived; and in nine cases out of ten they guess the truth. These instincts are felt a hundred miles off. How is that?

Whenever any philosopher shall be able to explain to us how it is that a carrier pigeon sent off to a distance of a thousand miles from its dovecote, in the darkness of a covered basket, contrives to return to its nest as soon as he is set free, we will endeavour to explain these inexplicable sympathies which bind one heart to another by an elective wire which bring to it confused but certain tidings of what it feels.

This must indeed be true, for during the whole of that day, Julia had patiently expected Amab's return, and it was not till about the hour when Victor met with Felina in the wood of Boulogne, that she had experienced a sense of anxiety, a restless and impatient suffering which brought tears along with it.

A man like M. Villon would have explained this in the easiest manner, and would have said: "At two o'clock a message was sent to M. Amab's, and the answer brought back was that he had just gone out on horseback; then, this uneasiness had begun; in effect, that gentleman who is secretly adored, whom they wish to cry up as a hero of devotion, in the opinion of the family, that gentleman who was to discover Charles, and upon whose word they relied so fully as to appear to think all other measures useless; that great heart, that genius, that cordial friend, is gone to take a quiet airing in the wood of Boulogne. See, therefore, how our pretty Julia frets, how she starts at every sound, hoping that it is he at last who is coming, and as time flies by, and four o'clock has already struck, then half past four, then five, she is too nervous and fidgetty to keep her place, she goes and comes without reason, she enters her apartment, opens the window to see if she cannot descry him at the further end of the street; all which is anger provoked by M. Amab's indifference; it is mere vexation and has nothing to do with ethereal sympathy, or magnetic affinity, or any such nonsensical stuff.

That would have been M. Villon's mode of explaining it, and it is not impossible that this man, accustomed for years to extort from figures all the facts they include, had fallen on the moral truth of Julia's manifold agitations. Perhaps M. Villon was right? But who would accept and be satisfied with such reason, but a jealous man like him?. And moreover is there any thing in the world more detestable than a man who calculates so coldly? Yes, certainly, there is a thing a thousand times more detestable: it is a man whom we do not love and who is right.

Now M. Villon was right in the opinion of her father and mother when he said that they ought not any longer to rely on M. Amab, that he would not come; that he was a man who cared but little for the affliction of the Thoré family; that at all events, they ought not to hope much of an interference which perhaps would rather protect the culprit than the victim, and a thousand other things which would have at length compelled Julia to relieve her heart, had there not suddenly been heard the sound of a horse's steps at the street door, and if almost immediately after Amab had not appeared.

## CHAPTER XXI.

### CUPID MAKES AN EFFORT.

JULIA sent a triumphant glance in M. Villon's direction, but the clerk did not give her the satisfaction to receive it; he had stooped his head over the ledger, and singular to tell, he suffered a slight tittering to escape him; positively the poor clerk's head was cracked, and his exultation was most unbecoming and rash.

"Well? well?" exclaimed the china dealer and his wife at once.

"Be comforted, madame, your son is alive."

Assuredly that was great news, and Victor had expected the enormous effect which it would produce. The effect did not fail, but when once this effect was exhausted, the questions followed, then the doubts, then the suppositions. "Where is he? What is he doing? Why did he go away? Have you seen him? Can he not write to us? Who gave you this assurance? Is it not a trap? A false hope? Can you rely on the person who spoke to you? Do you know him well? Who is it? What did he say when he told you about it?" etc., etc.

To all these questions Amab could return no answer, for the most excellent of reasons, that is, that he did not know himself.

Therefore he was obliged to intrench himself behind a crowd of ambiguous phrases, very solemn and fearfully compromising, such as this: "I have seen a party who knows what has become of Charles. Rely upon it, Charles is safe, I must not tell you more; I cannot name the person whom I have seen; I am to see him again to-morrow; I cannot take you to see him, it would be a breech of honour, it might increase the dangers Charles is exposed to. Do not insist, if you wish me to be of service to you."

And then followed a thousand other unmeaning trifles extorted from him by the objections and entreaties of Madame Thoré, and which to this adventure lent a very remarkable Venetian colour. The mother insisted, begged, supplicated, but it was necessary to desist at last, and to rest satisfied with the following declaration which the selfish man uttered with his hand laid upon his heart, or rather *upon his breast*:—

"On my honour I cannot explain myself more clearly; trust to my sincere desire to serve you, to my friendship for Charles; believe that I have nothing more deeply at heart than to restore peace and happiness to your house, and suffer me to follow freely my own course."

This was but slender intelligence, but still it was requsite to be grateful, and Madame Thoré replied:—

"I hope, Sir, the day may come when I shall be able to show you better than I can at present, the gratitude which will attend your kindness."

None but fools usually deal in these studied compliments; yet never was a happier retort than that aimed at Amab, who, as we said before, had arrived with the positive intention of engaging himself to Julia; for Victor having bowed in acknowledgment, and assumed a shy and timid look, as he replied:—

"It is not your gratitude, my friends, it is your esteem, your friendship I seek to merit."

"How could we withhold them after so great a service?" inquired M. Thoré; "we are all beholden to you, and should it ever happen—I don't know what—that I can do anything to serve you, be assured that I shall be ready on your first application."

"Stop, do not be too liberal," said Victor in a voice borrowed for the occasion, "perhaps I may ask you for more than you would bestow."

Madame Thoré quivered with anxiety; the lovely Julia trembled with joy; M. Villon shook with fury; M. Thoré alone remained tranquil, for he had not understood it. But it is sometimes fortunate that a husband, a father, or a patron is dull and impenetrable. When a man is called the master of the house, that is enough for him, and he need not always know what is going on under his roof!

As we said before, the cold-hearted painter had goaded his heart to embrace the chaste love of Julia, a love which his reason, his interest and his ambition recommended to him; the kind of declaration he had just made was the consequence of the facticious excitement he had called up, but it could not proceed further. All the fine illusions he had revelled in vanished before the object for whom he had evoked them. The presence of this angel of grace and beauty, whom he had wanted to place on the alter for his worship, congealed the ardour he fancied he was feeling. There was nothing in that beautiful young maiden to move his flinty nature; God had not given to this artist's cold and selfish heart, the understanding of mild and pure feeling. No? Felina must prevail.

This influence was so powerful over Amab, that he did not know what to say, and after a few perplexed sentences he took leave.

Oh! how deeply Julia loved him for the boldness he had shewn in revealing his intentions, and for his subsequent reserve. What sincerer, what completer, what humbler love could she desire. The evil, as we see, went on still increasing, and Madame Thoré gave it nutriment, for she could not interpret Amab's words otherwise than Julia did; only what this marriage was with the daughter, was a hope, with the mother it was a threat. Madame Thoré recalled in vain all she had seen or heard, she could not feel that her daughter was beloved. Whilst Julia full of the redundant fancies of her own feeling, never doubted that she was adored herself as keenly.

As for Amab, he left the house dissatisfied with himself, and was conscious that he had been cold, and awkward; he felt that he had not been able to profit by the good position in which he stood to show himself as he wished to appear, that is to say very loving. For positively Amab wished to be in love; he promised himself to return and really did return, for his hour he felt was come, and the skilful calculator had perfectly well understood where lay the suitable, the happy, the advantageous chance, and had chosen it. But his character even whilst it dictated this choice to him drew him back. It is a thing we fain would render intelligible to our readers, the struggle of the intellectual will, not with the transports of the heart, but with its apathy. We appeal to all men and to all women alike, whether it is not a hundred times more arduous to conquer indifference than the very intensity and madness of real love!!

There are in the world, and every one has met with some, spirits which, hardened by debauchery, by violent feelings, by wild and adventurous excesses, have lost the very faculty of loving what is simple, chaste, ingenuous: we can understand these. But is it posible for a young man whose heart has not yet been used up, to have the same apathy? This, people cannot help doubting; yet this is true, and, as it presents a phenomenon in human character, we strive to persuade the readers of this novel of its truth.

Yes, there are men to whom the Almighty has given a severe judgment, a powerful will, and to whom he has denied the love of good. Such men may succeed in winning over to matrimony a noble, a gentle, a virtuous woman; they appreciate her at her real value, and as far as depends upon their will, they render her the homage she deserves;

but their aspirings, their joys, their ardour, their adoration are reserved for idols they would dread to acknowledge: they honour virtue and make it an object of pursuit; but dissolution pleases and allures them. To these spirits, which ambition and selfishness have coldly and hardly steeled, it is requisite before a sigh can be drawn from them, to administer more pungent provocatives, more powerful solvents than the modest love of a young girl, her timid pleasures, and her pure and holy transports. "But in truth we know all this as well as the author," cries one; "when will he have finished his peroration? Does the writer of a fiction like this, flatter himself that he may nod and go to sleep at his pleasure, on his Pegasus, without being chidden. Is it not better to relate his story, and leave the disseration to his audience?" We cannot say. There are some people who believe that in the history of the heart, to dissert and to relate are all one.

---

## CHAPTER. XXII

### THE ARTS AND WILES OF THE SHE-TIGER.

About a week after his first meeting with Felina, a week after he had promised himself to fall in love with Julia and had done his best to succeed, Victor left M. Thoré's house at ten o'clock in the evening and rode to the wood of Boulogne at the full speed of his horse; he threw the reins to his servant in the neighbourhood of St. James's Park, passed along a wall lined and guarded by a thick copse, and stopped at last in front of a long pole which stood within the estate, on which pole was a large board with these words: *wolf-traps*.

This is so common a way of telling thieves: "You may come in by this direction," that it sometimes happens the rascals are led to suspect it. This time, however, the indication was perfectly true; there was not the slightest danger. Amab stole discreetly through the branches, and came up to a breech or opening which must have been very old, for already had the ivy and moss restored a verdant covering to the fracture. It scarcely required the foot to be raised even a step to enter on a level into the park.

At that moment Victor strove to remember the instructions which had been given to him: "When you come there," he had been told, "you will find a covered avenue, you may take it or any other—in a small park consisting of ten acres, it is not difficult to find out a house situated in the middle of it. There is a flight of steps leading up to the house; at the top of these steps is a door opening into a hall, the lamp burns the whole night; you will findthe staircase exactly opposite; go up to the first floor; pick your way through a wide passage hung with apple-green silk and decorated with fanciful birds, at the end of which you will find a velvet door dotted with large gilt studs, turn the handle, open a second door, cross a small anti-chamber, where you will find another light, then go through a saloon, after that a library, and you will find me.

Victor was unused to these Spanish assignations although he had imagined them, like all those who have sufficient elevation of mind, or who are unsophisticated enough to read romances as realities. Twenty times he had fancied adventures of a shady cast, and placed in such circumstances he willingly assumed a prudent carriage yet proud withall, marching forward, with his beard on his shoulder, as Sully says, and his hand on his dagger; but when he found himself confronting the reality, our hero was much perplexed. He instantly reached a fine covered walk which terminated on a fine lawn, opposite which he descried at once the house he was looking for. It was an awfully clear moonlight; so that he was fully exposed to every window of the dwelling; whether he chose to cross the lawn, or to take the circular path which opened its two long flowery arms to him; not the slightest shade, not the least mystery was there. By the light of that moon, our hero Victor thought he observed that this path, so treacherously exposed, was likewise newly raked, so as to betray the print of his foot, without alteration, to any jealous or scandal-loving eye which might examine it. This appeared to him far more dangerous than the wolf traps referred to on the pole.

Victor hesitated, but either his courage, his vanity, or his self conceit prevailed, without, however excluding his caution. He passed through the covered walk, struck the border with his foot, crushed the first slip of one of Tripet's rarest plants, then crossed the lawn, and, in three leaps had gained the *perron*, delighted to think he had so cleverly concealed his footsteps.

But there, a new terror came over him; the door was open, a night-lamp was burning in a large glass cylinder, in a copper frame suspended from the ceiling. This dull and flickering light seemed to droop and fidget by itself like a drowsy lacky sitting up for his master.

Victor thought that a man, perhaps two men, perhaps ten, might issue from the quivering gloom which this lonely lamp threw into the corners of that hall; he drew forth the Malay dagger which he had concealed in his pocket. A Malay dagger in the pocket of your paletot, after dark, will sometimes prove as convenient as a hand-gun to lie in wait for rabits.

Victor, armed with his dagger and with the shame he felt at having drawn it. darted up the staircase in three strides, and as the thick carpet laid over it suffered no sound to be heard, he faced abruptly about. At length the passage and velvet door became visible, he advanced, opened the door and entered the anti-chamber. There the same silence and the same security still prevailed; it was enough to dismay him. He went through the sitting-room, reached the library, measured it likewise, and lifted with a hand, which trembled though armed, a heavy *portiere* behind which he saw at length the chamber of Felina, and Felina herself half reclining in a large elbow chair.

"Ah! is it you," said she to him laying down beside her the book she held in her hand, "what is the time then?"

"Midnight," answered Victor in a low mysterious tone.

"Indeed, but it is true," she answered glancing at a small table clock close to her. "I had forgotten the time whilst reading these odes of Victor Hugo."

The painter was abashed.

"Why then don't you come in," continued Felina. "Ah! God help us! what are you doing with that?" she added pointing to the dagger he still carried in his hand.

"It was a precaution," he resumed with a look of embarrassment.

"But what apprehension?"

"The wood of Boulogne, is said to be the lurking place of certain people of a suspicious character."

"It is a report circulated by the lovers themselves to ramble their alone. Besides, you have been out of the wood this long time."

"True—but still—"

"Were you still afraid when in my abode?"—

"Excuse me," said Victor, who began to think it rather a strange reception; but people come into your dwelling as if—"

"As if on the public highway, you mean, Is it not very convenient?"

"Doubtless," said Amab; "but that opening in the hedge might have been closed and a private door contrived."

Felina laughed.

"Let me apprize you, my dear Victor, that nothing can be more indiscreeet and treacherous than what is meant as mysterious; if we have a door let in, it is because we purpose that *somebody* shall pass through it—If there is a rent in the hedge, and you let it alone, it is because you hope nobody will steal through."

"Then," said Victor, with ill-humour, "you must have a poor opinion of those whom you permit to visit you, to afford them so easy an entrance. In your place, I would have obliged them to climb over a high wall, bristling with spikes."

"No, when I intend to give a man a good reception, I must not expose him to the ridicule of appearing before me with his coat in tatters and his pantaloons torn; but what is the matter with you, my friend? sit down—are you unwell?"

Victor had come to an assignation of love, at least he thought so; he had settled the first moment according to his fancy:—

"Is that you, Victor? It is I, Felina. Hush! be silent—I am so afraid. Fear no more, I am with thee, etc."

But no, he had stolen in as freely as if he had knocked at the hall door; he was received at midnight as he might have been at noon: he thought it signified that he was being made a dupe of; he was vexed, and his presence of mind and spirit returning with his anger, he replied with great composure:—

"You have guessed right, I am unwell, and had it not been for the formal promise I made you, I should not have come out."

A swift but impenetrable smile of irony passed over Felina's mouth, but almost immediately she resumed with a serious and sorrowful look:—

"In that case you did wrong to come; in my opinion a man may sport with his life, but never with his health; to run the risk of being killed for a woman, is a fair chance of pleasing her; but to take cold—to catch a rheumatism, is vexatious to you—and to her likewise."

"That is as much as telling me that I have done wrong to run such a risk."

"Undoubtedly."

"And that I should do wrong to expose myself to it any longer?"

"Are you not comfortable here?"

Victor stopped just as he was going out; but he took a resolute course, and determined to confess himself defeated. This man was very brave at certain moments.

"Felina," said he, "why do you trifle with me and mock me?"

"I do not trifle with you, Victor! I am low-spirited."

"Your answers scarcely show it,"

"How so?"

"These jokes of yours about private doors, and rents in the hedge,"

"Why I told you what I thought," said Felina ingenuously; only you were determined not to understand me. I make a serious practice of what you call sprightly paradoxes. The way you came in, I perceive has disturbed you, you do not understand it at all. It was however the most convenient and the safest way: permit me to give you a short lesson, which may be of use to you in other adventures. And first of all, write this axiom in your note book: The best way to betray yourself is to hide yourself; between the man who assails another in open day in the midst of a crowd, and who plunges a dagger into his breast, and he who awaits his enemy by night in some lonely spot, the chance of success and evasion, is always for the first, if he have courage and a cool head. Caution is at once a sign of weakness, and a proof of guilt. I will give you a capital instance of it. I saw you, for I do not wish to play any longer the coquette with you; I was watching you behind the persian blinds, and I saw you leap into one of the garden beds to prevent your footprints from being detected in the path. Well, to-morrow, at break of day, my gardener would have raked the walk without inquiring whether those steps had come in at eight o'clock and gone out at ten, or whether they had come in at midnight and departed at daybreak. Instead of which, you have crushed, I daresay, some flower which will make him complain and vociferate all day to-morrow against the awkward booby who leaps into his borders: my friend, you really do not understand life? What, you are a bachelor, you have no one to account to for your actions, and yet suppose you had only one intimacy, you would be the greatest slave on earth.

"How so, then?"

"Your habits are most unaccountable. Everybody can see through you. Every one knows you by heart. You have one appointed hour for the workroom, another for your breakfast; then a third for exercise out of doors, and a fourth for visits; after this you are equally methodical with your dinner, the play, your evening parties, and the return home. I am convinced that your footman must have stared at you in amazement when you told him to bring your horse at eleven o'clock to Madame Thoré's door."

"How do you know that?"

"I don't know, I am sure of it. Well, it will be the same with whatever you may desire to do; every one will say: 'he is not doing to-day what he usually does, so there must be something new.' Something new, is so strange an event that we must forgive the world for the scrutiny they think they have a right to exercise on the intelligence of so great an occurrence. Be not astonished after that if your secret, supposing you have one, be suspected in two hours and discovered in twenty-four. As for me, I foresaw this danger as soon as I left my boarding school, and I took my measures as soon as I was at liberty to act for myself. Nothing in disorder can be better settled. Small shackles do not correspond with a great ambition. Petty requirements must not abide with lofty desires. I breakfast at any hour between eight and two, at home if I chance to be there, or elsewhere if not, it only takes me five minutes I dine between three in the afternoon and nine at night, when I do dine; and if I feel a fancy to sup it may be as early as ten at night, or as late as five in the morning. I go out on foot, in a hackney coach, on horseback or in a carriage, at the time when other people go out or when they are coming home. On some days I go to bed at nine, and get up at noon, on others I go to bed at noon, and get up at midnight. I come to the wood on leaving the Opera, and ten times have I stepped into a post-chaise on issuing from the ball-room. I go out to pay a visit, and, two days after I write to my people to come and join me at Boulogne. Gustavus took it into his head to be jealous, and unwilling to rely on the fidelity of a hired spy, he wanted to follow me. I kept him dancing attendance in his red quilted hackney coach at the doors of all my tradespeople, and at the most incredible places. Once when I had picked a quarrel with M. de Monrion as to the time, I started off mysteriously in a hired coach to go and set my watch by the clock of the Hotel de Ville, and then returned home. Gustavus had followed me; he inquired the cause of this promenade. I knew he had bribed my chambermaid, she told him the truth; he shrugged his shoulders and said: 'She is positively mad!' That was all I wanted. The struggle between us was a long one, but I was always too prompt to be overcome."

Victor was stunned. He was one of those men who dream and understand eccentricities in speculation, but who dread them in practise. Stupified by what he had just heard, he thought he had found something decisive and unanswerable, so he replied by this silly question:—

"But suppose M. de Monrion should take a fancy to come here at present?"

"Well, he would find the doors open."

"But if he found me here?"

Whether the objection did indeed embarrass Felina, or whether she disdained to answer it, she turned it off with a laugh, observing:—

"Are you aware that you are becoming a coxcomb?"

This retort brought back some of his peevish humour, and yet being unwilling to give way to a woman who so freely disclosed herself, he said.

"If I have committed this fault, it was you who enticed me to do it."

Ah! so I did," said Felina sadly, that is true.

"Do you forget that yesterday, in that carriage which bore us both towards Paris, when I told you my love and that you confessed your own, when I implored and you exhausted your denials; do you forget that it was you who promised me this meeting," and you said to me: "To-morrow, at my house—at midnight—my fears will be gone?"

"That is true," said Felina heaving a deep sigh, that is true, but I tell you frankly, even though the rudeness of the avowal may give you a still worse opinion of me than that you have; yes, I tell you frankly, you have been awkward and dull.

"Indeed!" cried Amab, in a tone which he vainly attempted to render careless and satirical.

"My friend, you must not laugh, I am speaking to you at present in all the sincerity of my soul," resumed Felina with her simplest look; learn then from me, "she added with a look both playful and confiding, that love is like certain diseases; for it, as for them, there is one fatal, culminating day, which either carries off the patient or begins his cure."

"And you are on the way to convalescence since yesterday," said Victor, with a raving smile.

"I hope so," said Felina raising her eyes to heaven.

"And you fear not a relapse, I presume;

Felina assumed a look both sorrowful and angry replying:—

"Oh! God help me! Victor, you are playing at wit when I am reasoning with you, when my heart is broken, when my tears are stifling me; oh! men never understand us."

"I confess," said Amab, that I no longer understand what you said to me yesterday, when I listen to you to-day.

Felina rose from her chair, moved pettishly a few steps, as if to withdraw, then suddenly returned saying:—

"Stop, this must be settled, listen to me, and hear me well, above all do not endeavour to make me out."

"What! you want me to—"

"I want you," said Felina peevishly, not to dwell upon my words and seek to discover in them secret sentiments, feints, stratagems, and all that! all that men who think themselves sagacious fancy they discern in what a woman says to them. I do not belong to the school of broken words and suspended phrases. I am free, my own mistress; I know where I wish to go, therefore I need not deceive either myself or others. I am handsome and witty enough to do without coquetry. Besides, you love me, Victor, and there is no artifice worth such an accomplice when we desire to deceive a man. Therefore, I can afford to be candid, and there is but one thing I require of you, and that is to listen to me.

"I listen to you," said Victor, who in his former interviews with Felina, fancied he had penetrated the turbid shadows of that existence and of that soul; "I listen to you," he continued.

"I loved you," Felina abruptly resumed, "I loved you from one of those insensate, and often vulgar caprices, which disturb and mislead the life unoccupied women. The sight of your picture of the Virgin made me fancy a something charming, innocent, ideal, in the soul of him who had so well pourtrayed it all in that divine countenance. With the same eagerness as that with which I should seek again the quiet and balmy air of the mountains among which I was born, if I could; I wanted to steep my soul in the fresh and youthful feelings I ascribed to you. I swear to you, Victor, if you had come yourself, you would have never known me except in my wild enthusiasm; perhaps I should never have seen you again. Had you been what I took you for, I would not have exposed myself to the remorse of destroying such a nature, I should have wished to pass over your career as an unknown fairy who had laid the first crown on your head.

"I was in the frenzy of my dream when I wrote you the letter; you were cold and insensible when you received it; you interpreted it as an old man might have done who was afraid of being ridiculous. Alas! at five-and-twenty you have faith in the experience of others; you have destroyed three parts of your life. You will reach an advanced age without having lived at all, and you will want to begin to live at an age when folly is no longer legitimate. On the day when you suffered me to be exposed to the most insulting outrage, I did not judge you, I despised you, and, for the first time in my life, I longed to be revenged on a person I despised; because I still loved you. You know the turn my vengeance took; the inconceivable folly of my heart protected you; not having been able to draw you into a duel the fate of which must have been unfortunate to you, I strove to render you sufficiently enamoured of me to suffer the tortures which would punish you cruelly for the injury you did me. I have succeeded;—believe me, Victor, do not put on that vexed and threatening look; you do love me, you love me acutely enough for me to abuse your love, for me to be revenged; but there is still a thing which I must not conceal from you, and that is that I love you still."

"Did you not tell me so yesterday?"

"Yesterday, I thought I was deceiving you, yesterday, I thought to mislead you. And yet yesterday—yes—yesterday perhaps there was a moment when I should have been happy had I been caught in the snare I had laid to entrap you. That moment, you suffered to pass away—that moment, I believed might return to my heart—and it was in good faith that I gave you this rendezvous.

"But, to-day," said Victor bitterly.

"To-day, is the morrow of yesterday," continued Felina; "to-day you meet with a woman who has been left alone, for twenty-four hours, to confront herself, a woman who does not shut her eyes to her own faults; a woman who has had leisure to sound the abyss into which you were not bold enough to precipitate her; then I reflected, weighed and calculated every thing, anticipated and supposed all. Well, from what I know of myself and of you likewise, Victor, I love you too much to dare to meet you again.

"Can this be! and after such a confession, can you condemn me thus?"

"It is not you that I judge, but myself that I comdemn."

"Felina, speak not so; you love me, you say?"

"Victor," resumed Felina, "let us not play and trifle like children. The woman who has said to you what I have just declared, ought not to suffer for the power her passion gives you over her. Hear me well—understand me fully—if I allowed myself to love you, I would not accept the luke-warm affection you might requite me with."

"But this love burns and consumes me; it fills and occupies my whole thoughts."

"Indeed, you are unkind—yes, you love me ardently, I know you do, enough so perhaps to ruin yourself on my account, if I were to accept the love you offer me; but I, Victor, will not suffer you to ruin yourself. What I admire in you, is your glory, your honour, your pure and irreproachable youth, your struggles with adversity, your triumph over poverty and misfortune; I admire in you, Victor, all these qualities which you cannot love in me. You know the life I have led, you know my fault—and you would have me bestow upon you as a mistress the most costly courtezan in Paris? But I will not. If God could kill or obliterate the past, and gave me in exchange millions of years of torment, believe me, Victor, I would purchase back at that price all my former life to devote to thee one hour of my existence. But give myself up to you, Sir, that I may see beneath the most ardent passion the cold judgment of the mind—no—no—I never will; I have found but one way of continuing worthy, not of your love, but of mine; and that is never to be yours. By not belonging to you, I shall perhaps believe myself worthy of having been yours! No, no, I never will be yours—never—never."

"Felina," said Victor kneeling before her, "no, you do not love me. Does love reason and argue like this, is it so strong to resist itself?"

Felina gently pushed back Victor's forehead which was bending towards her.

"Good God!" said she to him, "how very imprudent you are! You do not know what you solicit; for if I were so weak as to suffer myself to be persuaded, you would be too cruelly punished. I am jealous, fanciful, exacting; irritated at having broken my promise to myself, I should wish, as my excuse, to possess you so exclusively, that it would be a frightful torture to you. I should make you account for your every hour, your very minutes; I should spy into your thoughts, watch your ideas, and tear the canvas on which your pencil might trace some ideal beauty, by me mistaken for a real one. I should take the reflections of your genius for memories of love. I should shut you out from the world, sunder all your friendships, and lay a deadly hand on her whom you might hereafter prefer to me.—No—no, Victor, do not ask me to forget my oath. Fortunately I love you too well to let this misfortune light upon you. We must not meet again."

Never had any man's pride been more kindly soothed in its most hidden fibres. Victor was intoxicated, and replied in his most endearing tone:—

"Not see you again, can this be possible?"

"And why should we meet again? That you may fall at my feet once more as you have done; or take my hands and cover them with kisses as you are now doing; and look at me with bewildered eyes. All that may appear charming to you—but it is intolerable to me," she said rising suddenly.

She put her hand to her heart and muttered in a dumb tone:—

"Oh! this is dreadful!"

Then she paced the apartment with a quick and agitated step, carefully avoiding Victor's look, and averting her head; he rejoined her and looked into her face.

She was weeping.

"You weep!" he exclaimed.

"Yes, Sir, yes, I weep for being so weak, so mean-spirited, as to let your presence disturb me; for," added she with a gentle smile, "I should have been so happy to have been your friend, your sister; I should have liked that, and—"

She assumed an innocent child-like mien full of roguish archness.

"And if you would but be reasonable," she went on to say, "it would be so kind. You could talk to me of your studies, your projects, I would go to see you; you should relate to me your successes, your loves."

"My love! that is you."

"You see clearly it is not possible," said Felina sorrowfully. "Well, no, I will not meet you again, never, never."

"Well, I swear to be all you wish, and do every thing you desire."

"Oh!" said she ironically, "you are it seems quite the master of yourself, That is a most respectful passion of yours."

"Felina! Felina!" cried Amab, transported beyond himself, "You are pitiless."

"Well, so I am, it is true," resumed Felina impatiently. "But then how greatly I suffer, I am taking my revenge—and—come, hold your tongue. God help us! she suddenly exclaimed, here is the day beginning to break and we have forgotten poor Charles."

"True, I had promised his family, who question me every day about him, to bring them some tidings of him."

"You shall have something better still," said Felina. To-morrow, or the next day at the latest, you shall receive a letter from him. And now depart, go.

"Before you have told me when and where I may be allowed to see you again."

"I depart this morning for Fontainebleau; if you are at liberty the day after to-morrow at the same hour, we will sup here."

"Sup here—so then it will be again at night?" said Amab.

"Yes,' returned Felina looking downwards, "and if you dare to grant me the only proof of love—I ever intend to ask of you—then—"

"Well?" said Victor.

"I shall not be afraid," replied Felina—and now leave me, I am free; I sport with my character, but never with myself. If you return it will prove to me that you love me enough for me to confide in your honour.

Amab withdrew.—Felina watched his retreat through the window blinds, saying in a triumphant voice:—

"He will come ——. But she!'

A violent shudder of rage accompanied this last exclamation; she rang the bell furiously, a woman came in. Felina made some signs to her, to which the chambermaid replied in the same manner. But directly after, Felina resumed:—

"I forgot, we are alone—make haste, a great coat, boots, and a horse."

"I will fetch them, madam," said the pretended mute.

Twenty minutes later, Felina, dressed as a horseman and attended by a groom, took the road to Paris, in pursuit of Amab.

## PUBLISHER'S NOTE

There is some misnumbering.

## CHAPTER XXIII.

### THE JUNGLES.

GUSTAVUS DE MONRION was reclining on a sumptuous divan, when the dark and glittering Felina came suddenly and impetuously into the saloon; his eyes were raised to the ceiling, and his pipe, which was extinguished before he had finished it, had fallen from his hands, showing that he was absorbed by the deepest reflections,

"What can you be thinking of, my dear count?" said the She-Tiger to him in a dissatisfied voice; "it is more than a week since I last heard from or about you: you have neither written to me, nor paid me a visit."

"Ah! so there you are," cried Gustave, "I was expecting to see you."

"And wherefore, pray."

"To tell you, that what you required of me is entirely out of my power, altogether impossible."

"Poor boy!" sighed Felina raising her shoulders and throwing down her riding whip and gloves upon a chair which stood near, "call for some refreshment, I am dying of hunger."

The languid young noble pulled a bell: the valet de chambre, denounced to the painter as having been bought over to Felina's interest, came in directly.

"Take the lady's orders," said Monrion to him stretching himself again on the soft sofa.

Felina gave her orders and then resumed to Monrion:—

"By the bye, how does it happen that I find you so early out of bed?"

"I was going to retire to rest when you arrived."

"Did you pass the night at your club?"

"No, I spent the night here, in my own apartment, as Mr. Jean, your spy, can testify to you."

"And how did you employ the time?"

"I spent it on this sofa, with my own musings."

"You are mistaken," resumed Felina, sitting down at the table where breakfast had been laid for her, "you spent the night in learning and acquiring the word *impossible*, which formerly you asserted had been finally expunged from your vocabulary."

"And in your turn, you are mistaken," said Gustavus carelessly, at the same time picking up the long silk serpent with its amber head, which formed the tube of his pipe, "I have not acquired or learned the word, but I have discovered that it had a meaning."

"And who then has explained that meaning to you?"

"None but myself."

"That is to say," continued Felina knitting her brow, "that what I had demanded is impossible, because I refuse to do it.

"You are not lucky this morning," said Gustavus emitting a long puff of smoke towards the ceiling; "what you requested of me is impossible, because I refuse to do it."

A partial contraction gave a sudden change to Felina's features; when she continued in a tone of the most insolent indifference:—

"The less power a man has, the more he pretends to be bold and capable."

"That may be," said Gustavus; "and you, who lay claims to an iron resolution, ought to be an excellent judge of this matter."

"I declare it freely," rejoined Felina, "for whatever I have desired I have accomplished."

"Well," retorted Gustavus carelessly stirring the embers of his pipe; "I shall not accomplish what I do not desire; that puts us on a level, I think."

"You have aged wonderfully in a week" said Felina.

"Not at all, egad!" cried Gustavus; "never did I feel myself so young."

"In what fountain of youth have you been bathing?"

"In a blue eye, in a seraphic voice, in a halo of innocence and beauty."

"Ah!" said Felina laughing, "so you are caught! nothing can be better; I see I have no further call to be here, unless you would like to make me your confident; I half wish to make trial of the occupation, since I see you have chosen the part of Colin the shepherd, in the comic opera."

"The perfumed ambrosia of the gods," said Gustavus with a jovial foppery, "should be poured into vases of the purest and clearest crystal; the new love I feel requires a chaste and candid soul for its confident."

"You are wandering already in your sheepfolds, my dear count," replied Felina laughing; "your ambrosia is nothing more than cream cheese, and the vases into which it is poured are but pitiful earthen jugs; but, thanks to the papa's business, they may be probably manufactured in china."

Gustavus could not suppress a gesture of impatience, which he did his best to dissemble by stirring up his pipe again, well as it burned. Felina proceeded:—

"Do you know," said she, "that this M. Thoré will make you a very fine father-in-law?"

"A father-in-law!" said Gustavus, "what am I to understand by that?"

"Just what the term itself implies: I requested you to try what an elegant and lively young nobleman could effect over the heart of Mademoiselle Julia Thoré, and I now learn instead what a little shopkeeper's daughter can do with a poor lad who is very silly and very credulous. A week ago, when in default of the virgin portrait of this fair one, which you had been unable to obtain from M. Amab, I asked you to carry off the painter's model, since you had failed to seize his copy, you told me it was a matter of a week's business, and you set off with the looks of a conqueror. I trusted entirely to your tact; and here I am. I expected to meet a triumpher, I find a captive. But of all your former good qualities, I think you still retain one at least, and that is the art of doing things admirably when you really mean to perform them. You will not rest satisfied with a partial defeat, and I therefore suppose that in a few days' time. if you have not done it already, M. de Montaleu will present himself at M. Thoré's house, in order to ask the china dealer with all due respect to bestow his daughter's hand on the young Count Gustavus de Monrion.

"That has not been done," said Gustavus, "and it will not be done."

"It is doubtless a new impossibility?"

"Quite the reverse; I should be too much afraid of succeeding. I do not wish any harm to that lovely girl."

"Say rather," replied Felina, that you decline to accept M. Amab's legacy: but, if that be the case, what then do you propose to do with your passion?"

"Use it as a dream," said Gustavus sinking back on the sofa.

"You are perfectly right, the greatest of all human wisdom is to know how to limit our desires to what we can obtain, and as the realities of Julia's love belong to M. Amab, you have very judiciously allotted to yourself the only share to which you could pretend."

"Felina," said the young man with some disdain, "it is in vain you taunt and turn me into ridicule, all your jokes are thrown away. Julia is an angel of innocence and candour."

"That is what you should have said at first," cried Felina; "it would certainly have spared us both the foolish sallies we have exchanged, and would have spared me especially, certain words which I am sorry to have spoken."

"Ah! indeed," said Gustavus, "pray which words were those?"

"You know me," replied Felina in a more serious and affectionate tone; "you know that in spite of the errors of my life, you know that among all those principles, which I take to be moral, though others call them loose, which I have established for myself there is one thing for which I have always preserved a deep and sincere respect, I mean a profound and genuine passion, I mean love."

"Yes, that is true," said Gustavus, "and I have heard you in this respect excuse the strangest extravagances for the most worthless women, when a blind love was the cause of them."

"Yes, count," resumed Felina seriously, "you have heard me speak in that manner and you have seen me act accordingly: never under the false pretence of friendship, or of good offices, have I been to reveal to a man the faults of a woman whom he adored, nor to a woman the acts of infidelity of the man she trusted to. If I act thus, M. de Monrion, it is because love is not to be killed by such means, it is only tutored to give pain to the heart which cherishes it. I can understand that we seek to exterminate from this life the malignant being who injures us, but I cannot understand the torture by which we afflict him whilst his life is spared. I therefore beg your pardon for the suppositions I ventured to make, probably without any just grounds, as to the love between Mademoiselle Thoré and M. Amab. You love Julia, I respect her in your love, I see her now as you are pleased to behold her yourself, and I prefer your happiness to my revenge."

"You had a reason then to be revenged on her?"

"Ought I not to have one at present?"

"What had she done to you then, a week ago?"

"Does she not to-day deprive me of your heart?"

Gustavus had almost ceased to take an interest in Felina's feelings and affairs, for he did not pursue his inquiries further, and replied carelessly:—

"Confess that you are not free from fault in this matter."

"You are neither generous nor acute, Gustavus." continued Felina. "You speak of the happiness you owe to me as a crime and you compel me to tell you that I did not think you so foolish."

"Foolish? in what, if you please?"

"I told you that I would not touch upon your faith; for happiness consists in faith."

"So you persist then in asserting that M. Amab is the secret and discreet lover of the young girl?"

"I once more entreat you to forget that I suffered such a surmise to escape me."

"But what grounds have you to support such a supposition."

Felina shrugged her shoulders and rejoined:—

"You are mad, Gustavus, you resemble an inquisitive child, who must needs be informed of the secret of the doll she rejoices in; she turns it over and over until she has managed to break it; you will break your idol, too."

"Are you reluctant to assist me?"

"Yes, because you would never forgive me for doing it."

"What is your wish then?"

"Time is a good conqueror."

"Felina, suppose I ask your advice."

"A woman in my position never gives advice; she is believed to be jealous, and the very sun would be accused of obscurity if this jealous woman pointed at it, saying, 'there is the light.'"

"You have no longer any love for me then?"

"I no longer love you sufficiently to die for your infidelity, but I am yet too much your friend not to protect you against a folly or a misfortune."

"You deceive me, Felina, you hate this Julia, you seek her ruin, you told me so, and, as you knew I never would have gone with thoughtless levity to undertake the seduction of a pure and innocent young girl, you sought to remove my scruples by calumniating her."

"I confess I did calumniate her."

"For what purpose."

"To ruin her, as you said."

"And now? what is your object?"

"Now that my purpose has failed, I own that I calumniated her."

"Gustavus examined Felina's face, whose despairing and ironical expression seemed to conceal either a violent anger, or a profound sorrow.

"Felina," exclaimed Gustavus raising his voice, "you are an infernal creature! Well, hear the truth, I love that young lady, I love her to madness. No—I swear it to you, I have not exaggerated her merit: the aspect of that young and lovely face, in which as yet no passion has left its mournful stamp; that clear and serene voice, the echo of her clear and candid soul; that virgin look in which the mind's virginity shines as purely, all this sheds around this noble and beautiful child, a sweet, fresh and balmy atmosphere, which has revived my spirit. It is the delicious sensation of a man in a fever when he enters a fresh and perfumed bath. You laugh, Felina, but it is true, since I have loved Julia, I live more at ease. My chest is more open and free; I am not so certain that my death is at hand.

"Well," said Felina, "what more do you require?"

"It is something less that I should desire," said Gustavus attempting to laugh, "it would be that I had not heard what you said. Oh! I will not play characters with you, Felina; we have sworn to be frank towards each other, on the day we separate; well, I will be frank, for my part, for you told me, you no longer loved me. Well, I love Julia, Felina; but amidst the enchantment she has wrought about me, I still feel in spite of myself the drop of icy water which dissolves into rain the sweet vapour surrounding my soul. There is a hideous phantom continually darting at me a look of mockery through the lilies and roses of these cool and fragrant groves. I doubt;—will you come to my help? will you encourage me?"

"I can no longer do so, Gustavus," said Felina, I own it with regret; but such is the truth. Even were I to swear to you that Julia is innocent and that it was I who invented her pretended passion for M. Amab; even were I to affirm that is not true, that it was not during their private meetings that he painted that ravishing picture which was refused to you; even were I to tell you that what I said was dictated by vindictive feelings, you would not believe me. It is not the testimony of a woman you are deserting which can plead for and exonerate the rival for whom she is discarded. In spite of yourself, in spite of the confidence you may perhaps still place in me, you would suspect that some hidden and delusive thought induced me to say so, and you would perhaps be right."

"What! you are not ashamed to confess that when doing justice to Julia, you might harbour a treacherous design?"

"Between ourselves," said Felina laughing, "supposing I did not slander Julia, how could I wreak a better vengeance on your infidelity than to urge you to marry the forsaken mistress of M. Victor Amab?"

"I own said Gustavus moodily, that the idea of such a vengeance had never occurred to me."

"We cannot foresee every thing," resumed Felina; "but you certainly must perceive, that in an affair like this, I am too interested a party not to be a suspicious counsellor. It is your place to see, to ascertain, to guess. Has not this young girl a brother whom you might have the address to sound?"

"Truly," resumed Gustavus, "a brother who has been missing for one or two weeks, and whom I have been spoken to about; now I recollect it, it was in terms which make me believe that I am acquainted with the author of this young man's abduction."

"There have been tidings heard of him then?" replied Felina.

"It would seem so."

"From whom do they come?"

"From M. Victor Amab," answered the young count abruptly, as if the name grated on his ears.

"He knows then where the brother is?"

"Yes, undoubtedly," rejoined Gustavus with growing impatience, "it appears he has undertaken to restore him to his family."

"Suppose," said Felina, seeming to follow in her mind the combinations of a difficult mystery, "suppose that this young man were privy to the secret of Amab and his fair one; suppose he had threatened to expose the scandal, it would have been an artful measure to remove him for a time, and the probability is he will not appear again until they have obtained his promise to be silent."

"Why this is a tale fit for the Arabian Nights, that you are composing."

"I do not compose it; it is already made: this young man thus removed and whom nobody can trace out, M. Amab who knows where he is, and who however cannot or will not immediately restore him to his family, all this is not a story, I presume; or if it be one, I am not the inventor of it."

"In truth, you are right, Felina," said the young count; if one could see this Charles. Do you then think it impossible to trace out the young man?

"I confess that, for my part, I should not know how to set about it; but there is one thing which I can tell you, and that is that you have in your service a man, not so well instructed as yourself however, for he has not yet discovered the power of the word *impossible*. If he will undertake it, I think he will be more skilful by himself than you and I should be together."

"But this man, who is in my service, I know belongs to you, Felina," said Gustavus.

"Nothing of yours now belongs to me," said Felina with mournful dignity; "so long as you loved me well enough to deceive me, I required a spy about you; now that you consent to tell me, yourself, the true state of your feelings, this man has ceased to be of use to me; so apply to him or to any other you like. Farewell, Gustavus, I form no hopes for you, you have wounded me too deeply for me to say that I sincerely desire to see you happy, and I still love you too much to wish you any harm. I hope, however," she added with a bitter smile, "that this desire will soon come to me. So farewell."

"Shall I not see you again?" said Gustavus with the embarrassment of a man who does not wish to take upon him the responsibility of a complete rupture.

"Whenever you like," answered Felina; I shall probably remain in Paris for the rest of the week; at any hour you may choose to call at my house, my door you know is always open to men of sense and good breeding. Those are titles," she added with a smile somewhat satirical, which will always render a visitor welcome to me, and which, I hope, you will never forfeit."

At that moment, before going out, Felina stopped to survey a cup which lay on a velvet cushion, beneath a glass globe, which served as a cover. It was standing on a side table. It was the one on which the eyes of Gustavus had been fixed so long during his debate with his uncle, the marquis. The cup was rather a plain one, and did not seem to deserve so much care, nor so rich a place.

"Ah!" muttered Felina, "it was that poor fragile piece of white earth, which gave the first shock to my power."

Felina withdrew without waiting for Gustavus' reply; when she passed through the anti-chamber, Jean was there.

"This night meet me at the Bastille," said she to him in a low voice.

"I will be there," replied the valet de chambre; and the next moment his master's bell summoned him to his presence.

Felina heard it ring, and muttered, shrugging her shoulders:—

"Alas! poor boy!"

## CHAPTER XXIV.

### CERTAIN THINGS ARE EXPLAINED.

Before we relate what was the issue of Felina's advice to Gustavus de Monrion, and of her new rendezvous with the painter Amab, it behoves us to tell our readers what had been going on at the house of Madame Thoré for the last week. We must likewise explain some circumstances, which require to be fully understood and laid down, in order that the influence they must exercise on the various personages in this history may be rendered intelligible.

And first of all, let the optimists say what they will, and thereby we mean those people who maintain that the world is for ever the butt of calumny, and who consider it moral, happy, and full of virtue, we will venture to make one reflection, which, as it is directed against the natural man, and not against our social organization, cannot offend our modern Pangloses.

This observation is to the last degree vulgar and trite; but, according to our way of thinking, we present it much rather as an apology than as a charge.

Man, both physically and morally, is among all the animals of the creation the one which is most easily and completely hardened. The number of stripes which the slave man is able to support when gradually and progressively applied, passes belief; the mortal anguish and carking cares which are borne by the man of the world exceed all calculation.

Thus, Madame Thoré had said, and had believed that her son's death would kill her, and yet although ten or twelve days had elapsed since his abduction, it had not been necessary to call in a physician. M. Thoré had declared that he would shake both heaven and earth to discover his son, and yet these immeasurable words, heaven and earth, had bee limited to the police officers and the magistrates.

Certainly, we do not pretend but that Madame Thoré's grief was sincere, and that the resolution of honest M. Thoré was frankly and earnestly taken. The first day that the young and boiling steed feels the spur, he rears up, kicks and plunges forward, to disengage himself violently from the rowel which tears his flanks; but only let the rider hold on, and, for a whole month, prove to the noble horse that it is impotent in its struggle with a superior power, the horse will give way, submit, and its sore sides will grow habituated to pain, unless that pain yields to use. The heart of man is like that horse, at first strong and restive against pain; the first time it feels the spur, it rears up and strives to unsaddle misfortune, it shakes itself rudely and cries out again and again; but let misfortune hold on, and the heart submits, takes up its fate, and under this rigid horseman resumes its old pace and manner.

So it was in the Thoré family; Charles's disappearance had produced a revolution; they had hurried to and fro, they had taken measures, made complaints, the life of the whole establishment seemed hardly equal to the search for the lost son. But that first effort once over, it had been necessary to acknowledge that nothing had been gained, a second was made, but with no better result; no human strength could endure a state of existence which was spent in continual turmoil. They relapsed from this violent exasperation, into a worn-out despair, which in its turn made way for a more temperate anxiety, although Charles's disappearance had really left a shade of sadness over the family circle; but the attention to business, and a few stray words dropped at hazard beyond the sphere of this engrossing distress, had already relieved with less mournful ideas the gloomy background of this grief.

Madame Thoré had once ingenuously exclaimed: "My God! shall I then never see him again?" This cry was already far remote from the former one: "If I lose my son I shall die!" Between these two very different exclamations there was a world of space: the first was an open grave,—the second was a tomb already closed.

We desire not, in any way, to cast the least doubt on Madame Thoré's feelings by the reflections we have just been making; we merely wish to say that she suffered the common lot, when she endured her misfortune with more composure on the twelfth day than on the first.

Besides, this misfortune was not devoid of hope; had not Amab brought to them the assurance that Charles was alive. Since then, he had not indeed, produced any new circumstances, he could not produce any, he himself knew of none. Felina had said to him only: "The man is in my power, he lives, I will one day tell you on what conditions I shall be able to restore him to his family." Amab had repeatedly desired to know these conditions; but Felina had constantly put off these explanations, and he had learned no more. However he had continued to see her every day, since his first interview, when he had met her and pursued her in the wood. All that time Felina had employed in provoking Victor's curiosity and desires, intoxicating him with hopes, and racking him with deceptions, until the day had come, when certain of her dominion over him, she had fought her first great battle.

Every day likewise, Amab had called upon Madame Thorè, and every day he imparted to her fresh hopes of Charles: it was still necessary to answer questions, as on the first occasion, but when Amab had sworn once, twice, three times that he had nothing more to say; when he had protested on his honour that he was not at liberty to name the person by whom Charles, was concealed, they became accustomed to these vague and slender assurances. The certainty that Charles was alive was sufficient,—for their anxiety was dulled by habit.

As for the rest, Victor, had done his utmost to destroy the suspicions which he had himself communicated to Madame Thoré respecting Madame de Cambure. The unhappy man, really persisted in his incredible resolution to fall n love with Julia; and he persisted in it all the more that he felt Felina's power gaining upon him every day.

Men of powerful will and cold reasoning have singular fancies; the wildest of all, is to demand what they have determined to be good and advantageous to them, not only in spite of the obstacles which lie in their way, but in spite also of their own natural antipathy. I know a man who has suffered thirty indigestions, not for the sake of indulging a decided taste; but to inure himself to the eating of beef steaks, because, said he, "it is ridiculous not to be able to eat beef steaks like other people." Such persons are not common, but, still we meet with them.

Now Amab was one of these men; he had said to himself that other people liked beauty, youth, and virtue, and that he ought to be like other people; he had found in Julia whatever could promise a husband both happiness and respectability, and he desired to possess these excellent things. He came to taste them as often after as he could in order to habituate himself to them. He looked at Julia, he admired Julia, and by dint of admiration he began to think he was really in love; but when this struggle with himself was over, and he threw the bridle over the neck of his dreams, his vicious and depraved instincts turned him towards Felina, the capricious, the fantastic, the shameless, the passionate, the superb, the disdainful. I forgot to say that the gentlemen who wished to attach himself to beef steaks, like other people, liked better than any one cayenne pepper and the most pungent spices of the east.

This game of Amab's would have been nothing more than a curious trial of strength, had he alone been concerned therein; but, without gaining anything by it himself, he was destroying a poor child whose simple heart had been staked on these false pretences. Poor deluded soul, she had begun by adoring a dream and now loved a comedian. Nor was Julia the only dupe; both Thoré and his wife had become convinced that Amab was in love. They had spoken of it to each other, and neither of them had seen any cause to object to a man who possessed genuine talents and an unblemished name.

M. Villon alone, with the tact of a man in love, was still conscious that Amab did not love the fair maiden whom he pretended to adore. If Louis Villon could have been convinced of the sincerity of Victor's passion, his manly, honest and unselfish nature would have prompted him to submit, and so much did he love the beautiful child that he would have resigned Julia to the man she preferred. The clerk more than hated his rival, he despised him. Ten times at least it came into his head to provoke a quarrel with Victor Amab to demand satisfaction for this affected assiduity unaccompanied with love. Ten times at least had Villon resolved to leave the house, but every time something at the bottom of his heart had said to him: "Be quiet and stay where you are, Julia will want your help." And what were ten thousand real sorrows of his own, compared with one possible anxiety in her?

Another event of serious importance had happened at M. Thoré's house. This event was the introduction of the Count de Monrion to the house. But let it not be mistaken, the young count was only regarded in the light of a customer, not of a visitor.

The reader will recollect the day on which Gustavus had promised Victor to compel him to fight by insulting him in the wood; he will remember the meeting of Amab and Felina, and how the latter, on hearing de Monrion's voice, had hastened to join him, and had disarmed the hand which, only the day before, she had turned against Amab.

On the following day M. de Monrion presented himself at Madame Thoré's; but she was not within. M. Villon, on his side, was abroad; M. Thoré was dancing attendance at the office of the chief police magistrate; Julia alone was in the warerooms with the inferior clerks. Gustavus had put on a morning dress; he had decked himself out in the most proper manner of all; for he was attired with complete simplicity. Gustavus had certainly lost both his heart and his morals; but he had retained his elegance of manner. He entered that house, in which his person only was known, and, with the most perfect politeness, asked for M. Thoré.

"He is gone out."

"And Madame Thoré?"

"Likewise."

"Is there any one at home to represent her?"

"There is none but Mademoiselle Julia."

"I should be glad to speak to her."

They had conducted him to the office where Julia used to attend. The young lady was too much accustomed to such visits to be disturbed by the arrival of a handsome young man. She asked him what he wished for.

"Excuse me, young lady," said Gustavus, had I not been so anxious, I would not have troubled you for so trifling a matter.

"We are at the commands of those persons who are so kind as to honour us with their confidence."

Julia from her childhood had learned by rote this mercantile sentence and would have repeated it to a prince of the blood as well as to a waggoner.

Once more a thousand pardons, mademoiselle, but what I have to request of you will take some time to explain and may be very difficult.

"Have the kindness to explain yourself," said Julia sitting down and showing a chair to Monrion.

He declined it with a respectful bow and proceeded:—

"If what I have to request of you were but a passing whim, I should not come here to plague M. Thoré, or you, in his absence, about so small a matter. But in my eyes it possesses a grave and serious interest—it is a memorial."

Julia bent her head slightly,—intimating by the gesture.

"Let it be whatever it may, to me it is quite indifferent."

Gustavus looked at the girl, and that still and placid beauty, with its air of self-reliance, delighted him and almost led him to distrust what the perfideous Felina had told him. He continued:—

"My mother before she died—"

A sudden tremor altered the tone of his voice. Was it merely the memory of his mother or the remorse he felt in mixing that name with a feint of gallantry that disturbed him? Still it is certain that this agitation served his purpose admirably; for pretty Julia fixed her eyes upon him and paid more attention to what he said.

"My mother when she died," he resumed, left me, some pieces of china which are not perhaps intrinsically valuable, but which had belonged to her. "The one," he added with an effort, "in which she drank the last drop of the medicine which was inadequate to her restoration; it was the last object touched by her lips—"

"It has been broken perhaps?" said Julia eagerly.

"No, but somebody desires it of me, somebody I can hardly refuse."

"Well! sir?"

"Well! young lady, I wish to know whether there is any possibility of making me a second cup absolutely like my own—with its defects and minutest details."

"That I fear, would be very difficult."

"I must tell you beforehand that one unfortunate trial will not discourage me—I will pay—Excuse me—Money is so gross an argument that one is always puzzled how to advance it—I will pay for ten attempts if necessary—nay, twenty, thirty."

"Can you entrust us with the cup?"

"Could you send to my house for it?"

"What is your address, Sir?"

"You perceive how solicitous I am about this article—send me some person of trust, a steady—"

"The greatest care shall be taken—the name of monsieur?"

"I am the Count de Monrion, young lady.'

"Ah!" exclaimed Julia, "who could not help looking at a young man whose frailties she had heard of, as well as his scandalous life, his immorality, his impudence."

And yet that young libertine bowed to her as he withdrew with the deepest respect.

When he had returned home, Monrion said to his servants:—

"If any body comes from M. Thoré to inquire for me, I am not at home."

He wanted to reserve himself the right to return to the warehouse.

In this way it was that Gustavus had found his way into the Chinadealer's house, M. Thoré, having been apprized of the young count's desire, had sent to his hotel. But he was always out. The count had returned to the shop, and availing himself of M. Thoré's gossip, he had learned that Charles had disappeared, had taken advantage of that intelligence to offer his services, had returned once more to make inquiries, and every time had been, listened to, and admired pretty Julia.

This artifice had lasted a week; but dame seduction, as Scudery's novels have it, dame seduction with whom Gustavus had first set out for the conquest of this young girl, had basely deserted him. The unworthy ally had done worse, she had passed over to the enemy, and after the lapse of eight days, whilst mademoiselle Thoré was quite at her ease with regard to the Count de Monrion; the latter was already conquered and enamoured.

Meanwhile M. de Monrion had hitherto ventured to appear at M. Thoré's only in business hours. The after dinner time—those private and domestic hours, were sacred to Amab who then performed his part. As for Madame Thoré, she was alarmed. She wondered in herself what the Count de Monrion came to her house for. Was he not the man who had bid for her daughter's picture and had offered an enormous price for it? Was he not, or had he not been, Madame de Cambure's lover? Had not Madame de Cambure been mentioned by Amab as the person who knew what had become of Charles?

All these circumstances when collectively considered, concealed an indefinite but positive meaning; Madame Thoré worried herself to discover it, and after she had turned and twisted and put together these figures and particulars, she felt that lassitude of mind, which a man would feel after spending the night in vain, in attempting to arrange a chinese puzzle.

And now if any body wishes to know the starting point of all these events and occurrences—a very brittle and undistinguishable starting point,—let him be so good as to remember Felina's reflection on the subject of that little cup which stood on a side-table in Gustavus's apartment. And that reflection was really an allusion to the following circumstance.

One day—a day of pleasure and delirum it was, tired of seeing her young lover lavish upon her with boundless profusion his fortune, his health his life, his prospects; tired of seeing how easily she had persuaded him to sever the sincerest ties, his family affections, his earliest friendships—the terrible Felina looked into the past life of this man to discover something which his heart clung to more strongly than to the present, and Felina's whim had alighted upon this cup which she had desired, demanded, and which had been refused to her. It was on the day after this refusal that she had written to Amab, the letter which had since produced the events of this story. The love of women, like the ambition of men, is insatiable, not even the relics of the tomb are sacred to this all consuming jealousy.

The consequence was Felina had not forgiven Gustavus this last respect for a family memorial. It proved to her that there still remained a feeling in the soul of that young man beyond her influence. Her anger did not stop to calculate; she resolved to quit Gustavus, but for a man whose reputation should humble the cast off. we have already seen the turn of this attempt. Then came Felina's wish to get possession of the picture which had excited her love for Amab. She instinctively felt it was a rival's picture.

Gustavus, we have shewn, was so anxious to satisfy this desire of Felina's, that it took in him the form of self conceit, and his vanity was interested in proving that he was willing to sacrifice every thing, except his honour. He failed a second time, and was next employed to seduce Julia. Defeat still pursued him, and we have seen him enamoured and subdued when Felina came to ask him to render an account of that conquest which he had boasted he would effect in a week. Felina was defeated as well as he; but Felina was not the woman to forsake the vengeance she had resolved to achieve. She had laboured hard to prepare for this in her last interview with Gustavus. Haunted as she was by day and night by the recollection of the trick which had been put upon her, she was almost goaded to madness to see herself superseded, by a simple girl, and all her arts and lures baffled by one who had no art to use. Vengeance upon her, vengeance upon Charles, vengeance upon Gustavus, she must have!

Let us see by what new stratagems she pursued her fearful object.

---

## CHAPTER. XXV

### CHARLES UNDER RESTRAINT.

In the rue Charonne, on the right hand side, as you approach the *barriere*, there is a small door opening into a close of half an acre in extent.

This enclosure is planted with lilacs and fruit trees which, left entirely to their sap, have spread and expanded themselves so fully as nearly to conceal a low house, consisting only of the ground floor of rather a high standing, and a single story of attics above it. These attics are lighted by small oval shaped vent holes adorned with apple wreaths of sculpture, the whole being covered with an arched roof and lead coping. It is the hut of a gardner of an old mad house not far off, which has been converted into a private lunatic asylum. The ground floor of this abode consists of four small rooms; a winding staircase from one of these chambers leads up to the attics.

At the period of our story, one of these rooms was used as a kitchen; in each of the others, there was an iron bed and a few coarse articles of furniture. The windows, were secured by long iron bars, and still further to protect them there was a narrow grating of wire. This ground floor was a true prison. On the contrary, the attics were hung with silk stuff, and the floors were covered with thick carpets. Splendid furniture, Venetian mirrors, costly bronzes served to adorn the sitting-room, the bed-chamber and the boudoir of this upper story. However, there was nothing strange in this unless it were the contrast between the ground floor and this first story; only there had been opened in the ceiling of each lower chamber a private trap-door by which all that was either said or done could be heard or seen from the corresponding chamber above.

It was about ten o'clock at night, and two men were at that time lying in their beds in this ground floor. One of these men was only half undrest as he slept; he was about thirty, and it was easy to judge by his large hands and shoulders that his strength, in spite of his low stature, must be herculean. Owing to a caution the object of which we shall shortly explain, the sleeper wore a small chain round his wrist. This little chain was fastened at the other end to the collar of an ear pointed cur, with a grim snout, and stiff hair. This individual slept with that heavy slumber which belongs only to good men and to those who live on quiet mutton.

Another person occupied the second chamber. The latter, our readers are acquainted with him, was Charles Thoré. But the poor, the fine young man must have suffered dreadfully to be reduced to the state in which he is restored to us. Pale, lean, with a long beard, his hair in disorder; leaning up in bed, his eye fixed and haggard, his fists clenched, he was watching the peaceful slumber of his robust comrade. After a rather long interval of reflection and quiet, he turned slowly round on his bed, and flung himself upon his pillow like a man who has determined to try to sleep. At this motion, the dog gave a low growl and sat up on the mat on which he lay. The stretch of his chain slight as it was proved sufficient to rouse the sleeper who started up and whose first motion was to seize a heavy bull's hide which was lying by his side. The man looked towards Charles, and seeing him ensconced under his blanket, he began to growl too, and held his corrective weapon towards the captive, as much as to say that he would make him pay dearly for it the next time his sleep was broken.

However the silence lasted a few minutes; the sleeper had sunk back to his slumber; when suddenly, and although Charles had not stirred, the dog growled again and pulled his chain. The furious sleeper got up and went towards Charles to inflict upon him an absolute order to be still; but he refrained on feeling himself pulled in a new direction by the cur which was yelping with fury opposite the door.

The man, who was no doubt accustomed to this kind of warning, threw away his cudgel and went into the front room, where the winding staircase stood. As he entered by one side, the door was opened on the other. A woman came in, followed by a gentleman in a decent dress and with a respectable looking face. The lady was Felina, the gentlemen in decent attire, was Jean, valet de chambre to M. de Monrion.

Felina having made a sign to the keeper of the place who closed the door behind her, immediately went up to the attic.

"You are sure, Jean, we have not been followed?"

"Quite otherwise, madam: only I believe that

the man who followed us with a stick six feet long had no other motive of curiosity than to find out what we had got in our pockets."

"Then why did he not attack us?"

"It was yet too early, and besides that, one to one, is not the way in which generally, these gentlemen do battle."

"Zounds!" cried Felina taking off her bonnet and shawl, "you might have said one to two; unless you do not reckon yourself, which is not unreasonable, for you trembled—"

"For you, madam."

Felina disdained to hear this cunning repartee of M. Jean's, and hastily resumed:—

"For all that, this man's pursuit makes me uneasy. You know how to drive?"

"Yes, madam."

"When I shall have obtained through your artful contrivance what I require to persuade Gustavus that he is playing the part of a simpleton with regard to Mademoiselle Julia Thoré, you will go to the Faubourg Saint-Antoine. You must then dismiss the coachman, and bring back the carriage, so that the spy, if it is a spy, may bring the police here to-morrow morning, when the house will be empty."

"Must I go for the carriage all alone, in the middle of the night?"

"Lutz shall accompany you, he knows how to drive, he does."

"This rogue of a mute cannot hear any thing holy or unholy; if thieves should come across us, they will be upon our backs before he thinks of turning about."

"You shall look for him, and he shall fight for you. But we have something more pressing to do: we must think of our prisoner."

"But," said Jean, who seemed to relish very little the commission which Felina had given him, "is madam to be left all alone in the house with this young firebrand?"

"Why not? I have something to say to him which I desire you should not overhear."

"It is to be feared that this man, being exasperated with passion, may proceed to such violence, as those fair hands may not be able to repulse."

Felina looked at Jean with the most profound scorn, and said to him in a tone of supreme impertinence:—

"These hands are never touched but to be kissed. Go, master Jean, and send Lina to me—she might perhaps mingle her voice with the howlings which M. Thoré is about to give vent to, and with the arguments you are about to utter, and I do not wish to lose either a single cry or a word of your dialogue"

Jean immediately went down, undid the collar of the little dog, which flew rapidly up to the room above, where she found her mistress lying on the ground and gently removing the corner of the carpet over the trap-door through which Charles's chamber was watched by stealth.

"Well, Lina, well, my beauty," said Felina soothing the frantic carresses of the little bitch; "softly, my little pet, you shall sup with me, and soon we shall return to the hotel. Yes, you are pretty."

Then she took the hideous beast up in her arms like a child, kissed it with maternal flattery on its hairy forehead, saying:—

"Fie, then! you smell bad! Be quiet."

Then stretching herself at full length on the floor she applied her ear to the trap-door and her eye too, the better to watch the success of the stratagem she had come to attempt.

At that moment Jean entered the chamber occupied by Charles, who had heard the noise of the new comers, and who wondered in terrible suspense whether it was liberty or new tortures that they had brought him.

M. Jean was dressed in a black coat, in a white cravat, a satin waistcoat with a rolling collar, a single diamond ring sparkled on his finger, a costly cameo pin was stuck in the breast of his shirt, from his waistcoat pocket peeped the upper part of a valuable gold snuff-box, and a slip of red ribbon so narrow as apparently to shun observation gave him absolutely the look of at least a colonel who is not in parliament, or of a physician who has attended a minister's secretary. It was this latter profession that the valet de chambre aspired to, and it seems that he had already formally laid claim to it, for Charles Thoré said to him:—

—"Ah! it is you, doctor; are you come again to put the straight jacket on me and burn me with *Moxa?**

"Hush!" said Jean, "let us speak low, Sir."

Then he looked at Lutz, and added with a shrug of his shoulders:—

"I am mad myself, I think. No wonder after all I have seen and heard. I was forgetting that this mute cannot hear our conversation."

Then and as if he was at liberty to indulge the humane feelings of his heart, he offered his hand to Charles, exclaiming:—

"Poor young man!"

"What new misfortune do you come to tell me of, Sir? I perceive, you no longer believe that I am mad!"

"Alas! no—They have not been able to destroy your reason.—You are a strong man, M. Charles, ten others had they been in your place, and tried so cruelly, would by this time be at Bicetre. But what ten or twelve days have not succeeded to accomplish, a month's captivity might produce.—There is no resisting such trials."

"What! Sir they want to drive me mad then?"

"Yes," said Jean, in a tone of despair, "they want to see you mad—or at least to be able to say that you have been in that condition."

"That I have been!" said Charles stupified and alarmed; "I really fear I am mad at this moment, for I cannot at all understand you—"

"That is natural, very natural," cried the doctor "it requires a head of iron to invent such a complicated plot or even to understand the drift of it. Yes, Sir, yes, my friend, yes, my poor boy, they want you to have been deprived for a time of your reason; on this condition, and on this condition alone, you will be restored to freedom—unless you should at length really lose your wits—which will still better serve the purpose of the person who has sent you here."

"I am as much as ever at a loss to understand you, Sir. Why this condition does not appear so terrible to me. You say they want me to have been mad—Very good, let it be so, I have been mad,"

"That is well, extremely well, but it is not enough to say this—they will still require proofs, tangible evidence."

"What proof? what evidence? Must I go and proclaim a new prophet in the high ways, or get upon a post and recite a classic tragedy in fine arts and in rhyme? I have known but two madmen in my life, and this is what they did; one of them was a beadle who stood candidate for a porter's

* A kind of Caustic. The word *Moxa* is of dubious origin: it signifies any substance whose gradual combustion on the skin is employed for the relief of disease. This curative system was in use many centuries ago in Japan, China and India; thence it passed inty Spain and Portugal; bnt afterwards fell into disuse. During the campaign in Egypt it was employed in the French army, and thus it was introduced to French practise.

place and failed, the other had his play returned at the Odéon."

"That would not be amiss, not amiss—but you could not exhibit such symptoms of insanity without being free, and they wish to have proofs of your madness whilst you are still in their hands."

"Then Sir, be so good as to explain yourself clearly, I am quite ready to do whatever is required of me."

"The fact is I am myself greatly perplexed. In fact, they have given me permission to choose the means."

"But who is it? who is the person that gave you this permission?"

"Somebody."

"But that somebody has a name?"

"Silence; unhappy man? silence—perhaps at the moment I am speaking to you he may be hovering above us like a malevolent fiend—benevolent, I meant to say—Oh!—hush—hush!"

"Excuse me, Sir,—but you seem to be acquainted with the person who keeps me here under restraint if you wish to save me, you can go and expose him to my family—or denounce him to the police."

"I must retire, Sir," said the pretended doctor with well afflicted dismay, "I must leave you—if it is thus you receive the friendly terms I come to propose to you."

"Nay, doctor."

"Nay, Sir, who knows whether you have not exposed me to imminent danger by the very words you have spoken. They may imagine, they may believe," added Jean, raising his voice, "that I am capable of lending an ear to such insinuations, of yielding to suggestions which appear to be just, and they may compel me to share the captivity you suffer—If these be your intentions, young man, if these are the proposals you have to make to me—I must leave you."

"But," exclaimed Charles, "I told you I was ready to do whatever you liked—speak, command me—I am ready."

"I had an idea—yes, a medical idea—but you have altogether put it out of my head. However—stay—yes, here it is: *contraria contrariis*—it is a very good hypothesis, the result would be excellent—Tell me, have you a friend?"

"I have many friends."

"A devoted friend, I mean, one who has an interest in serving you in this matter, who believes himself bound so to do."

"In this respect, Sir, I have one who ought to come to my assistance, were he not a very selfish, unfeeling man."

8

"That is not the question—What is his name?"

"M. Victor Amab."

"Well—M. Victor Amab—very good—Suppose I were to say to you: "I can deliver a letter to M. Victor Amab—Write it directly, and I will be the bearer of it. What would you write to him?"

"Why, egad! I would inform him of the most likely reason why I am here—that his honour is concerned in procuring my release—that—"

"Not so fast—commit all this to paper."

"What for?"

"I have a plan."

"But what would you do with the letter?

"I swear to you by my father's death, and he was a member of the Institute in Egypt, you shall tear it up again before I leave this place—but write, I beg of you, and let it be a moving letter calculated to rouse this man from his insensibility."

"Faith," resumed Charles, "I see no great danger in it."

He began to write, and some twenty minutes afterwards, he delivered the letter to Jean, who kept saying to him every now and then:—

"Let it be touching, pathetic, with points and bursts."

The letter was thus indited:—

My dear Amab,

"I address you from a dungeon, a prison, a "madman's cell.

"That infamous woman, Madame de Cambure, had "me carried off as a punishment for your disdain "and for my happiness (in spite of all I endure, I "cling to that word). They want to drive me mad "or have it believed that I have been so. Inform "the police, let my family be warned. Let this "monstrous woman be arrested. My abduction "was managed in this way: The day after the "adventure of the workroom, I received a note "containing these words: "*On the Boulevard* "*Bourdon, at six o'clock—who dares to ask* "*forgiveness may be forgiven.*" They require "me to say that I have been mad—that is true—I "have been so. I went to this appointment with "my heart full of sweet recollections and delightful "hopes. There I met a fine tall girl who made me "a sign and walked on before me. This sign bade "me follow her, it was quite light—Besides, I "never thought of any risk—I am so thoughtless; "I followed her—She led me along the Faubourg "Saint Antoine, then turned into the rue Charonneé "and opened a small door on the right, close to "the lunatic asylum—I went boldly in—it was "seven o'clock—I came up to a sort of a cottage, "and went up to the first story. There she was "armed with all her attractions, and a sumptuous "breakfast had been prepared—I wanted her to "speak—and was told to refresh myself at table—I "obeyed—Five minutes after I sank upon a sofa, "where I remained in a heavy stupor—I don't "know how long—it was dark when I awoke—I "then found myself in a lower room, fastened to "an iron bed—By my side was the venerable form "of a worthy physician. They told me I was mad, "and was to be treated accordingly—suddenly "they deluged me with icy water, then they "scrubbed me over with brushes made of dog's "grass, and, ever since that time, at the slightest "noise I make, they sprinkle me with water—in "fact—But where is the use of these particulars? "am I still in the house they took me to? I suppose "so—However that be, my dear friend, make use "of these instructions to deliver me out of the "hands of that infernal creature. I rely on your "friendship; you know my attachment to you; "you know how faithfully I kept the secret of the "picture which has given you renown. My family "is grateful to you for your affection for me; it "will become like your own when they shall owe "you my deliverance, and among the hearts which "will love you, perhaps there is one whose "tenderness may appear to you worthy to repay "your devotion; for, I am not mistaken, you have "guessed that Julia is not insensible to the love "which inspired your masterpiece."

"Amab, it is not only on your friendship "for me that I rely, but on your love for another, "etc., etc."

Jean took the letter and read it aloud and in a tone of voice somewhat satirical; for he knew that other ears were listening to it. He interrupted his reading with marks of approbation.

"Well—very well," said he; "this is just the thing! this is what I required! the contrivance is excellent! it is perfect! perfect! quite perfect!"

"What do you mean to do with that letter?"

"Come now!" said Jean, restoring it to Charles, "let us reason together. This is a letter that you have just written as a rational man."

"I hope so," said Charles.

"It is not the letter of a madman."

"No."

"What then should you think a madman's letter ought to be?"

"Why something quite different, apparently."

"That is to say the contrary—precisely the contrary."

"Indeed!"

"Yes, certainly—You understand," said Jean in a tone of the frankest conceit, "I wanted to see what you could do being rational, to conclude by opposition what you ought to do being mad—So, now, understand me well: you begin your letter with these words:—"

"My dear Amab"—Write on the contrary: "Infamous Victor," You then add: "I write to you from a dungeon," say on the contrary: "In the delightful retreat to which you have lured me to bewilder my mind, by the most intoxicating pleasures."

"Stop—stop," said Jean scratching his forehead, like a man hunting for an idea. "Then" he exclaimed all at once: "Write—write. I have it all now: I have been informed of your shameful behaviour to a most worthy family—You understand—all this is so false!" cried Jean breaking off—that every body will say—why this young man must be mad!—"

"Be it so!" said Charles, but the plain truth is that nothing could be more irrational than that."

"Ah!" cried Jean seemingly delighted, "that is as it should be! I have found the means, go on—go on—you will be saved! Besides with such a proof I will answer for it you will leave this house before day.—"

"Indite then, indite."

"Yes, yes," resumed Jean, as if speaking to himself, and electrified with the aptness of his thought—"we must break the windows—the more the better—so write on. "You have basely abused "my confidence, cowardly seducer; you have dishonoured the pure and guiltless girl who put "faith in your honour."

Charles hesitated to write this last sentence, but Jean began to laugh outright.

"Ah! ah! ah! the effect will be certain—he was mad! they will say—Yes, indeed, poor fellow he had lost his wits—see he accuses his own sister "Unhappy fellow! Continue to write: She has "told me all—restore me my liberty—and if you "are not a coward, it is in your blood that I will "wash out the shameful wrong you have perpetrated."

Charles had written mechanically; but he placed his hand over the paper and said to Jean:—

"But, tell me, what do you purpose doing with this letter?"

"By the ghost of my virtuous father who died a member of the Institute of Egypt, I will send it to M. Amab."

"But he will take me for a madman!"

"Of course—and say so to his friends."

"And what next?"

"What next? you will return home and relate that you have been on a journey to the moon."

"And what then?"

"What then?" said Jean, "laying a stress on the words, so as to impress their weight on Charles, "if ever you happen to relate hereafter a certain adventure to which you allude in your first letter; they will not need to deny it with furious cries and exclamations, but will turn it off with a look of pity, thus: 'The poor boy has been mad! and the best proof that can be given of it, is found in the stupid, ridiculous things he said of his sister, who is virtue itself, and who he pretended had suffered herself to be seduced by M. Amab."

"Ah! I begin to understand," said Charles—yes yes—the stratagem is a good one—Truly, none but a madman could write such a thing, and if ever, as you say, I happen to relate the rather loose adventures of Madame de Cambure, she will say quite simply: "The poor boy has been mad! He fancied he came to an appointment made by me for some one else, and that at that rendezvous I placed on the brow of the scholar the crown intended for his master—" You are perfectly right—this would make every body believe that I had been mad—But it would make me appear a villain and a coward in my own eyes. You shall not have the letter.—

He snatched it up intending to tear it; but at that very moment, on a signal from Jean, the mute sprung upon Charles, and threw him back before he had time to destroy it. The struggle was a fearful one and in spite of Lutz's strength and the weakness which a long and severe abstinence had imparted to Charles, the latter was several times on the point of escaping from him; but Jean came to the mute's assistance, and they both were preparing to chain the unhappy youth to the bed, when Felina suddenly appeared saying:—

"Let the gentleman alone, the letter is not signed."

"It shall never be signed!"

"You shall sign it directly, this very instant. Leave us alone for a moment, and do you, Jean, go for the carriage—Lutz may go along with you"

"Madam," said Jean, "be on your guard."

"Go and return quickly. Did you not promise the gentleman that this very night he should quit this house?"

Jean left the room with a look of stuperfaction, saying as he went out:—

"What a woman!"

He was followed by the mute.

## CHAPTER XXVI.

Scarcely had they turned their backs, before Felina drew up hastily to the young man.

"Give me your hand, Charles," said she—Thank you—"What you have just now done was well, it was noble, it was brave."

The young man stood stupified at this friendly and abrupt manner of coming to the point.

"What I have just done," he resumed with confusion, "was very natural."

"No, Charles; courage, nobleness of mind, and sense of duty, are not natural to every body, and M. Amab, your master, is a proof of it.

"What has he done for you that you to accuse him in this manner."

"He has done exactly the very thing which you believe you falsely charge him with."

"What! my sister Julia?"

"You know she loved him?"

"Perhaps—but what matter!"

"Well, he has taken advantage of her weakness, and, during a rendezvous she granted him

"It is not true!"

"Do you believe him incapable of it?"

"I am thinking of my sister, madam."

"Whom you think innocent, and who is undone!"

"You lie! madam."—

"What motive can I have?"

"I know not; but this is a snare you are laying for me, and this letter was intended to ruin her."

"Was it not in my power to get possession of it?"

"It was not signed, as you said—"

"But I told you likewise that you would sign it."

"And by what means do you expect to induce me to sign it?"

"By a very simple means, that of telling you the truth."

"The truth? I don't really understand you."

"Listen to me, Sir. If ever there was a woman who had a right to avenge herself, I am one, as you must be aware. I wished to begin with yourself. All that doctor St. Jean has just communicated to you 'is true. In order to deprive you of the opportunity of ever revealing by what base treachery I was surprised, I wanted to drive you mad—I did not succeed—Every day I came here to watch the progress which I expected ill treatment and solitary confinement to produce, and every day I felt that my desire for your destruction became less eager. I was already thinking of some means of restoring you to life and of giving back your liberty, without danger to myself, when the doctor suggested to me the idea of making the world believe that you had been mad—I accepted the plan frankly, and felt happy to adopt it: for it relieved me of the terrible oath I had taken against you. I left it to the doctor to choose the nature and proofs of your madness; every thing was prepared beforehand; they were to deliver a letter to Amab at your father's house. There, the moment your writing would be recognised, they would ask to have it read. Doubtless, after what you were to write, the expected remark: "He is mad!" would have been in every one's mouth—That being done, you were to re-appear after solemnly pledging yourself to me to tell your friends that you knew neither where you had been, nor the strange delirium to which you had been a prey. You were to forget every thing, to remember nothing: neither what you had done, nor what you had written—It would thus appear a manifest fit of madness; it remained mith me to explain who I had chanced to be mixed up in it, if ever you had violated your oath.

"If I had once pledged my word, madam, it would be sacred to me."

"I believe you, Charles—what you have just done is a sure warrant to me that you would. But hear me still further. I had approved of the doctor's suggestion, as I said, and had committed to him the care of its accomplishment. On coming here, I will confess to you, I saw nothing in it but a joke; when the turn the doctor gave to the letter he required you to write, made me think of a new kind of vengeance against you, which I had never dreamt of as yet; for I knew that what that man was dictating to you as a falsehood, was a truth."

She paused a moment, as if collecting her thoughts.

"If you had signed that letter," she resumed, "I know not whether I should not have used it to ruin your sister, by showing it to every body. Be not surprised at what I tell you; my nature is such, and you ought, by this time, to know my character sufficiently to anticipate this, without my telling you—My will—my decisions, are as rapid and vehement as the thoughts which suggest them, an accident had thrown this opportunity in my way, I would have seized it as a means of vengeance; your noble spirit has taken it from me, I renounce it. Within this hour, ten different sentiments have all entered my heart and passed through it, and these feelings related every one of them to you. First I pitied you, then whilst Saint Jean was speaking to you, I could not refrain from laughing at your looks of astonishment; I thought you seemed so ridiculous. But, excuse me, it makes me laugh still to think of it—then all at once, when you refused to sign that letter. I saw you, as you are, brave, generous and open-hearted I admired you, almost loved you."

"Loved me!" echoed Charles.

"Yes!" she said with a soft sigh.

"Felina! Felina! do not deceive me."

"What you know of me, Charles, does not exhibit me, I hope,as an artful, cunning, treacherous woman. No, assuredly no, I am passionate, wrongheaded and, sometimes cruel, in a moment of anger I could kill;—but I cannot construct a plot, a perfidious combination. I love in my heart to be revenged,—what woman, what man, does not? I do not easily forego an opportunity to strike those who have injured me; that too is my nature. How then does it happen that I am here with you? Because at the same time that you have disarmed my anger against you, I have found a means of punishing the man—whose insolent disdain.—Oh! that man! that man!—added Felina with a terrific yell; you shall kill him."

She looked at him with eyes so full of ferocious vengeance, as to chill his very heart.

"Yes!" she continued, "you shall kill him, Charles. The world will think you did it for your sister, but I shall know you did it for me."

"Oh! yes, I will kill him," said Charles, if it be true.

"Well, Charles," exclaimed Felina, with sudden transport, sign this letter and you are free—you shall go yourself and bear it to the villian. I will accompany you to his house;—you shall see what kind of answer that man will return you. He will accept the offer, I hope, and you will kill him—will you not? Oh! do but revenge me on that man, Charles, and I will forget every thing—or rather, I will recollect it all—Charles, my weakness will not suffer me any longer to be revenged on you; revenge me therefore on him!"

It was a woman of supreme beauty who said this with tearful eyes, in a supplicating voice; and as she spoke and clung to him, her burning hands kept pressing those of the young man.

"And then I shall be free?"

"Instantly."

"And I may avenge my sister?"

"You forget me, Charles!"

"Can I not avenge you both?"

"Oh! yes."

"But—will you love me, Felina?"

"As I have loved you."

"Well, be it so—woe unto him!"

Charles produced the letter and signed it.

"Now write the address," said the She-Tiger hurriedly; "that is right, seal the letter. Stop, to explain everything, write on the back: 'I am free—I expect you in the wood of Boulogne,—in the Madrid avenue."

"At what hour?"

"At ten—I will accompany you. And now get ready to depart."

Felina whistled.

The little dog answered with a yelp, and the mute came to the door.

By an instinctive impulse, the prisoner laid his hand on the letter.

Felina then made a signal: the mute withdrew for a moment, and returned with clothes, linen and all that is required at the toilet.

Felina left the apartment, whispering to Charles: "Make haste, and do not forget the letter."

She went up to her decorated chamber whilst the prisoner was dressing. Jean was in waiting for her there.

"What is the time?" said Felina.

"About three," said Jean.

"Listen to me, in another hour, we shall be at Amab's door. Charles is to be himself the bearer of the letter to your new master."

"Himself. Ah! that is splendid?"

"It will be better."

"But how shall we prevent him from returning to his father's house?"

"I hold him in a prison," cried Felina, looking at her lovely hands, "whence he shall escape only when I choose to let him. Come, go now."

An hour afterwards, Charles and Felina, who had put on a male attire, driven by the mute as coachman, stopped at the gate of Victor's house. Charles had alighted with Felina and had inquired for M. Amab.

A servant in red breeches, a red waiscoat, and with a red face, answered him:—

"M. Amab is not at home."

"Is he already gone out?"

"Master does not sleep in Paris, and does not come to his atelier until seven."

"I will wait for him!"

"You are forgetting me," whispered Felina.

Charles looked at her. How beautiful she was, and how her eyes seemed to fill and overflow with love.

"Deliver your letter," continued she. "The appointment is for ten o'clock."

"But, a letter like this," said Charles.

Well, if I am right, it cannot be delivered too soon. If I have been deceived, an explanation will clear up every thing.

"And what am I to do in the meanwhile?"

"Are you already weary of your pardon?'

"But, my father, my mother?"

"Charles, you must not, you cannot return home without having the proofs of your sister's innocence, or else having had your revenge for her wrong."

"Friend," said she to the servant, "can you let us have paper, pen and ink?"

"Certainly, madam,"

"Well, here is a louis for you, and you must take the letter which will be delivered to you, and leave it at its address. Write Charles," she added in an undertone: "Mother, before the close of the day. I shall be with you."

"Who can tell?" said Charles mournfully.

"Are you afraid?"

What follies men are worked upon to commit with that word!

Charles wrote to his mother and left the other letter for Amab.

Felina made him re-enter her carriage.

"Where are we going now?" said he.

"To my house, at Boulogne, near the place of meeting. Ah! Charles, I would not tell you every thing; if this Amab should refuse to fight; if it be true, as I hope and believe for your sake, that your sister is not guilty, he will find me there; for already have I tried to compel him to fight, but he had the insolence to refuse the meeting."

The carriage rolled rapidly along.

Felina then related to him the account of the appointment she had made for Amab, and which he had not kept, and how she had looked every where for him, dressed as a man, and had struck him across the cheek with her riding whip.

And the heroic amazon recounted this to the young painter (for Charles too was a painter) with such charming smiles, such natural tears, such wild fits of anger, and such returns of tenderness, that Charles no longer thought of his father, nor of his sister, nor of Amab, nor of the meeting, when the carriage passed through the shady gate of the courtyard leading to Felina's villa. She alighted so hurriedly, and Charles followed her with so much rapidity, as not to perceive that the mute had thrown the reins to a groom and was following him step by step.

The She-Tiger went up to the first floor, crossed three or four chambers, then, on reaching a kind of boudoir, which was low, dark, and a very bower of love and delight, she suddenly turned round, and said to Charles:

"Wait for me here a moment—only a moment."

She went out alone.

But before shutting the door, she made a sign to the mute, who immediately pulled from his pocket the heavy bull's hide which it would seem, served him instead of a tongue, and, as he had given a few lessons of it to Charles, who perfectly understood it, the latter knew that it meant:—

"Come, go to bed, I did not sleep at all last night, you too must feel a want of rest."

After these words admirably expressed by pantomime, Lutz drew forth from another of the deep pockets contrived in that immeasurable top coat, the detestable cur whose ears were substitutes for his own, and having put on his chain fastened it to his wrist.

At the sight of this dumb play, poor Charles, overcome, confounded, maddened with despair, understood at last that he had been ruthlessly deceived.

Suffocated with contending emotions, he fell upon a bed of rest, whilst Lutz stretched himself softly upon his pallet.

## CHAPTER XXVII.

### FURTHER INQUIRIES AND FRESH PARTICULARS.

At the same hour, and whilst these things were taking place at Felina's, our friend Jean, who was no longer either the respectable and ribboned doctor of the rue Charonne, nor the red attired domestic at Amab's door, and who had received the letter intended for our hero—M. Jean, we say, returned to his lawful master, the Count de Monrion, and said to him:—

"Monsieur le Comte asked me for information relative to M. Amab and a certain young Thoré marvellously spirited away; I am now prepared to give him some."

"So soon? within four-and-twenty hours?"

"Within four-and-twenty hours."

This replaces you in my esteem. Come, tell me what you know."

"I request Monsieur le Comte to have the kindness to permit me to tell him how I obtained these particulars; he will believe them to be more authentic that I myself do not know them."

"Speak, I know you have studied law, and that you sustain your pretensions to the title of barrister, by being a loquacious babbler."

"I will begin," said Jean.

He took the attitude of a pleader, and opened his address in a nasal tone:—

"The best spy about the person of a general, is his aide-de-camp, or rather his quarter-master general; for the same reason, the best spy about the person of any man, is his valet de chambre."

"This belongs to Felina's school; only she practises what you merely profess."

"I have practised it."

"Yes, against me—I know you have, ungracious varlet."

"Never!"

"Do you pretend to make me believe that you were not in Felina's pay."

"I swear to you, on my oath, Monsieur le Comte."

I understand you—there are things which a woman must never acknowledge, and by analogous reasoning, you think there are certain shabby actions which a valet must always deny."

"Until death, Monsieur le Comte. At that moment, it becomes a matter of religion; we confess it, but never acknowledge it."

"Come to the purpose."

"Well, Monsieur le Comte, by virtue of the principle which I have expounded to you, and the orders you gave me two days past, I endeavoured to become as quickly as possible M. Amab's servant."

"And you managed to do so?"

"Yesterday morning."

"This begins to look tolerably clever."

"It was the simplest thing in the world."

"Well, for my part, I feel curious to know how you went about it."

Master Jean paused to reflect; he appeared to hesitate; but the vanity of the orator got the better of the lackey's prudence. He rejoined:—

"If you were a plain citizen—I mean a gentleman who has the arrogance to expect not to be deceived by his servants, who examines them, watches them, and loses half his time in coping with them, I would not tell you the truth; but you are a great nobleman, you live too far apart from your people to be reached by their faults, their vices, or their calculations. I may therefore entrust you with one of our little secrets. You are incapable of ever employing it to—"

"Perhaps I am not so generous as you imagine."

"That is not what I mean, Monsieur le Comte; you have something better to do than to recollect it and bear it in mind. Know then that every domestic who understands his situation and who has foresight enough to prepare for events, never belongs to Paris."

"Egad! you are right—whenever I have asked a servant where he came from, it has always been from the country. That remark induces me to think well of the Parisians.

A superficial observation, and altogether wrong. Monsieur le Comte, like all the moral statistics derived from the Academy of Sciences. The servant is born at Paris as well as elsewhere, his family live there, but only to his knowledge: for his master the servant always comes from the country and is never an orphan.

"Why so?"

"Because he is continually in want of a dying father or of a mother with a lawsuit hanging over her, to account for a sudden departure owing to a letter received that very morning."

"Ah! is that the case?"

"Thus it was, at least, that M. Amab's domestic explained the thing to his master, when requesting a leave of seven or eight days' absence, during which he proposed a substitute for whom he could answer as for his own body."

"And you were that substitute?"

"Yes, Monsieur le Comte."

"Has he answered for you?"

"I have deposited a guarantee for a thousand crowns as a pledge for my good behaviour and for the place on his return."

"Enough!" said the count disgusted, "But what have you ascertained respecting M. Amab?"

"I have heard nothing about him from himself, for that gentleman speaks to none but himself, that is to say he heaves dreadful sighs, and mutters romantic names in a low voice."

"But what names are they?"

"Julia,—Charles."

"Ah!" cried the count. But go on."

"I had learned from my predecessor who this Julia, and this Charles signified, judge therefore what my astonishment must have been, when, this morning, I saw M. Charles Thoré himself come to the house."

"What! do you know him then?"

"Monsieur le Comte forgets that I have sometimes been to take his orders to that tradesman."

"Rascal? M. Thoré is a respectable merchant; his house is one of the first in Paris."

M. Jean made a very humble grimace seasoning it with the following impertinence:—

"I likewise know that Madame Thoré is one of the most beautiful young ladies to be met with any where."

"Will you change the subject?"

"Well, Monsieur le Comte, this M. Charles came to the house, and not having met with M. Amab, he left this letter for him."

"Do you suppose I would be guilty of the baseness of breaking the seal of a letter addressed to some one else? Do you forget that when I was jealous of Felina, I never could consent to that meanness?"

"Monsieur le Comte can read the address at all events."

"The address," said the count taking the letter from him, and observing that the time and place of the meeting were written on it. "This looks very much like a duel," he added after having read it. "But why this duel?"

The count was here reminded of what Felina had told him about Julia and Victor.

"The reason for the duel is doubtless in the letter," said Jean inserting his finger under the cover.

"No matter, never!" cried Monrion, "never."

"Never, in your case! but if I—that would be quite another thing!"

"Miserable wretch! what have you done?"

"What I should have done before I came hither, if my master, M. Amab, had been at home, and if I had been able to dispose of only a few minutes to learn what you ordered me to find out."

"Base villain!" cried the count rising to turn Jean out of the room, but he stopped short on noticing the astonishment depicted on the lackey's features. "Well, what's the matter?"

"It is very deplorable, Sir, very deplorable. A young lady dishonoured, ruined—"

"It cannot be! it is impossible!" hastily snatching the letter out of the servant's hand.

Hurried away by this spontaneous impulse, Gustavus read the letter; he stood dumb, bewildered, distracted. The next moment, he threw back the letter to Jean, saying to him:—

"Go, go—I discharge you."

Jean withdrew contemplating his master with a look of pity, and Monrion was left alone.

"Oh! this is shameful!" he exclaimed aloud; "What, every where, still the same vice beneath the purest appearance of chastity. Youth, grace, openness, unblemished reputation—it is but one mask—the most deceitful of all. Oh! it is dreadful! Felina was right. That woman has an instinct of evil which enables her to detect it through the thickest walls. But no," he resumed, "that is not it—she knows the world! In every case of friendship, in every action, she bets on the base side and wins ninety-nine times in a hundred. But I must find out whether it is the intrigue of a hypocritical girl, or the misfortune of one deluded and misled. Ah! if it were so, woe unto this Amab! If her brother does not chastise him—it is I who will take charge of his punishment."

Then Monrion determined to go, the very next morning, to Madame Thoré's house, to know what he was to think of Julia.

On her side, Madame Thoré, lost in that threatening labyrinth, wherein she had been wandering at hasard, without a guide, had determined to come to a serious explanation with the painter. In order to understand what was the result of these steps, it will first be necessary to say how, after she had degraded Julia in the opinion of the too credulous Gustavus, the dark-minded and crafty Felina contrived to draw the selfish Victor into this satanic intrigue.

---

## CHAPTER XXVIII.

### THE SHE-TIGER'S DEN.

Once more it was night; the night too which had followed the momentary liberation of Charles and his transfer to another prison.

Amab had made his way into the park, like the first time; but on the second occasion he had passed through it without the least apprehension. He was now raised above all danger. Had he not conquered Felina's scruples the day before?—Unhappy man, he called them scruples,—had he not persuaded her, at least so he thought, that love forgets and pardons everything, and had she not said to him on that assurance:—

"Come, and if you grant me the only proof of love that I shall ever ask of you, I shall no longer tremble."

It seemed as if Victor ought to have known Felina well enough to tremble himself at such a restriction; but, Amab, in reality, did not concede to woman, a tithe of the pretensions which their language bespeaks, He was accustomed to solve many difficulties with his vulgar diction: "*It is all talk.*"

Moreover Victor flattered himself he was armed against them because he said to himself three fourths of them are actresses. He had taken all Felina's refusals for a mask of flirtation which she was impatient to throw off. All this in his eyes, was but a game of greater or less skill; because he suspected deception, he thought he was fortified against treachery, and never doubted how deep were his calculations.

"This reminds us of an anecdote which comes to us directly from Rome."

A young man who had ridiculed a courtezan said gaily: "Yesterday, la Bambinella wanted to prove to me that she had lost nothing in losing me: she offered me her hand to kiss; it was adorned with a splendid diamond ring. Alas! poor girl, she could not deceive me, the diamond was artificial."

Eight days later, the young man died; the diamond contained a poison, mortal, to those who touched it with their lips. This story may be true or not; it will serve at all events as an image to show, how Amab thought himself secured from every danger because he suspected a farce, which, unhappily for him, concealed a second, and far more terrible one than he imagined.

Victor fancied he was dealing with a mere flirt of the Gymnase theatre.

And yet Felina had given him a good warning, but vanity blinded him. He entered the villa light of heart, merry and spruce. He flew up stairs rapidly, passed through the sitting-room, the library, and entered the accustomed chamber, Felina was not there.

He saw an open door, went in and found himself in a boudoir, low, gloomy, mysterious, hung with black velvet with radiant ornaments. In spite of his mirthful disposition, this boudoir struck him as a dull one; the door through which he had entered closed behind him, and he stood face to face with Felina.

What ever people may say of the coquetry of our French ladies, it is far beneath that of the Eastern women. The fair dames of our belief and our society reign too much by the heart and mind to pay that worship to their beauty which is rendered to it by those woman slaves, who have no other power to exercise. The infinite art with which they languish their eyes, radiate their look and brighten their smile: the pencil with which they darken the eyebrow, and extend the eyelash; the waters with which they scent their hair, and dye their nails: the powders with which they smooth the skin and make the blue veins run over its dazzling white surface: all this amongst us is left to the ballet girls and silly old woman who cling to their youth when the season is gone.

If Felina had required all this aparatus to be handsome, she could have equally employed it; she understood life too well, not to know that most men value us rather for what we seem than for what we are. But with the exception of perfumes, and that fragrant atmosphere which instills delight, this fantastic creature had borrowed from the East nought but the costume she was arrayed in.

A thousand times more discreet than our European costume, it does not expose the charms, but lets them be suspected; it conceals every thing, but allows nothing to be disturbed.

We shall not attempt to describe the superb countenance of Felina, her flexible yet queen-like stature her snow white feet and ivory hands. Among all that silk, that gold, that gauze, which enfolded without dressing her, one thing above all was remarkable in that attire, its exactness. She had carried this exactness to the extreme, for she had even thought fit to stick in her girdle a small poniard the handle of which peered above a wave of silk, like the angry smile on the rosy lips of a sultana.

At the sight of this radiant beauty, the painter bent on one knee before her. He had the sense to think that he must be very ugly himself in the dress of an elegant Parisian, by comparison with this woman who appeared to him so magnificiently beautiful.

He told her his thoughts, and thanked her for her glittering adornment."

"Yes," answered she, "I love my beauty, and I enhance it as much as I can, to please those I like. Is not beauty a heavenly gift? You, on your part, love your genius, and should you not think yourself unworthy of holding it from the Almighty, if you did not place it on the highest pedestal you could?"

"It is an altar that your beauty demands, Felina, that your adorers might worship it on their knees."

"I accept your metaphor," said the She-Tiger smiling; "old and worn as it is, I accept it, and I will carry it on to see whether by joining our two heads; you and I can produce any thing new. Come, Sir, tell me, do you belong to my creed?"

"Love is the religion I profess."

"The deity of the christians does not receive every where the same homage," said Felina; "the children of Mahomet are divided amongst themselves; and love's believers do not all render it the same worship."

"Teach and instruct me then," replied Amab; "for I have as yet, for my part, but the candid religion of a child who prays to a power without even knowing it by name."

"Well," said Felina, fixing on Victor, her eyes half closed, "are you one of those who give to love the vacant hours of existence? one of those who assign it a share in the manifold occupations of life, like to the usurer in Gil Blas who heard mass every day at eleven to twelve, and who flayed his clients from twelve to four? Such are your honest and orderly people who never neglect their pleasure for business, and who do not neglect their business for pleasure."

"Do you call those people lovers?" said Amab smiling."

"Friend," said Felina, "these people have as much claim to be called lovers as most of our citizens have to be called religious."

"Well, I repudiate that worship; I will not belong to it at all."

"Are you then one of those butterflies for whom love is but an idle pastime, a seasoning which prepares them for the banquet or for delight;—one of those who celebrate their deity in glees and drinking songs,—rampant Bacchants for priestesses, and a wine barrel for triumphant car?"

"Oh! Felina," said Victor, "do you take me for a song-singer or a commercial traveller?"

"Well," resumed Felina, "let us have done with these mean and paltry subjects; and now, answer me candidly: is your love of those which in a woman looks for beauty, wit and radiance, in order to make a parade of its conquest, which love far more from outward inspiration than from inward feeling; which esteems a woman not for the happiness she bestows, but for the envy she excites.

Amab answered unhesitatingly, and yet his voice changed, for he was conscious he had in him a little of that alloy of which Felina had just spoken.

"No," said he; the vanity of such a triumph belongs only to men who cannot obtain other conquests, and I rate myself higher than that."

"There is likewise," continued Felina, "another conquest: some people love a woman as they do a fine piece of furniture, a handsome house, or to speak more correctly," said she laughing heartily, "who love her as people do a fine dress-stand. They cover her with showy gowns, with diamond ornaments, Indian shawls; they drive her about in silken carriages; they load her with lace, they encumber with jewels, they use her as a big doll to display the vanity of their wealth—and nothing tickles their foible so much as when they hear it said:—

"M. B—— or M. C—— is ruining himself through his extravagance for Madame C—— or Madame D——."

Amab was so eager with his answer, that Felina could not help smiling at his caution.

"You would scorn the offer of such love," he replied; nor could it exist under conditions suitable to me. But why all these futile dissertations of wit? Is it my love you desire to study, or my heart you seek to sound?" he added taking Felina's hand. Well,—it is that love which is a slave, that love which bows its head and implores."

Felina became sad, and gently withdrawing her hand from Victor, said to him in a faltering voice—

"What did you say?—what love did you refer to?"

"To that which adores, which obeys," said Amab in a supplicating voice."

"For ever?" asked Felina.

"For ever, I swear it!"

Felina appeared to make a violent effort over herself not to yield to the pain she experienced; and then added:—

"And will this love be without distrust, suspicion, defiance or jealousy."

"Entirely," said Amab who was entirely within her spells.

"It will be free from reproaches and retaliation?" she continued.

"Absolutely free from them."

"Happen what may?"

"Happen what may."

Felina had softly inclined herself towards Amab as if to read into his look;—her forehead was contiguous to Amab's brow. He wanted to draw still closer that perfumed mouth of which the breath he felt was burning him.

"Ah? you do not love me!" exclaimed Felina pushing him away abruptly, "and starting up with a gesture of despair."

Amab stood petrified, like a man who has scaled to the top most round of a ladder which is to deliver up to him the town he is besieging, and who is suddenly and rudely thrown down a hundred feet below the summit he was reaching. He felt a cruel vexation. However, Felina paced the chamber straining her hands, wiping her eyes, and heaving deep groans: it was necessary to say something to soothe this inexplicible anger.

"What love is it then, more powerful than that which gives every thing you would have?" resumed Amab with a bitter smile.

"The love that I require, Victor," answered Felina haughtily, "is not a slavish love,—nor a submissive, fearful one—such a love is either cowardly or hypocritical. The love I require—

She paused, and Victor resumed disdainfully:—

"What is it?"

"Why should I tell you? it would only terrify you, without persuading you. We cannot communicate our own feelings to others,—nor can we make a new heart for any one. You love me as you can, and I ought therefore to rest satisfied. The remainder is but a dream which I ought to forget."

"A dream!" cried Amab, as if indignant that she could have aspired to more than he offered her.

A sharp nervous laugh was Felina's first reply to Victor's exclamation.

Then she went and stood before him, and measuring him with a disdainful eye, striking her foot against the floor, and shuddering she said to him in a dry and insulting tone:—

"Ah! my dear Mister Amab, how childish I am still and how little I know of your sex!"

Felina's power and heartless nature were never so obvious as in these sudden changes of countenance, in these abrupt transitions from one sentiment to another. She appeared merry, easy; she seemed to delight in playing with words and thoughts, and all at once a darkening eye, a hopeless regret would shoot across that calm and pleasant sky. If the delirium of passion began to speak louder than this secret despair, and you fancied you held her at last in the bondage of love, quivering and breathless, at the same moment the expiring voice would revive to mock and taunt you, and the shudderings of the fever resolved themselves into convulsions of laughter.

Felina's last words, the tone in which they had been spoken, had confounded Amab; he felt himself to be the sport of a well acted comedy, and his wounded pride speaking at last louder than his desire, he remembered that he was alone with this woman, and that a moment comes when one may forget that weakness should be a protection.

He said to her, therefore in a tone which he had never dared to assume with her:—

"What! madam, you say you know but little of men: yet there is one who may have taught you to what extremities their bondage and madness may carry them. And your empire over M. de Morrion?"

"Ah!" cried Felina disgusted.

But she also subdued this new feeling and proceeded in a familiar manner:—

"That gentleman, whom I took for a fool, knows them better than I do. It is assuredly not from a superior mind; but society gives plenty of scope to the simpletons who despise men."

"Did that gentleman speak to you about me?"

"Not exactly about you;—no," rejoined Felina in a tone of levity. "Only, when he saw me exult in the reading of a book, or at the sight of a picture, and when he heard me exclaim in the ecstasy of my admiration. 'Oh! how I should like to know these highminded spirits! what a soul he must have to have discovered inspirations like these!' Gustavus laughed—and I was provoked by his ridicule. If, he would say, you wish to preserve this opinion, take care not to approach these heroes of your imagination; never go into their company—you would have too much to lose by staking your visions and illusions against the reality and matter of fact. This man, who exhausts his brain to lay bare the tenderest fibres of the human heart to reveal the secret of its most mysterious impulses, is a big cumbrous man, who eats a great deal, who laughs aloud and discordantly through his broken teeth, and whose vows are laid at the feet of some awkward city dame. That other who scatters diamonds and great fortunes over his dramatic conceptions is more closefisted than an Evangelical spouter. If you could see the rude tempers, the vulgar faces, and the groom-like manners belonging to that painter who has expressed in the purest ideal the imaginary figures of the German poets, you could scarcely believe that nature could bestow so bad a form on the genius it creates. No, Felina, he added, never seek to become acquainted with them. Those amongst them who are conceited perform a part, the skilful hide themselves; but not one amongst them possesses in himself the thousandth part of what he so liberally dispenses to others."

"And the language which M. de Morrion used in a general sense, you have at length found some one to apply to—is it not so, madam?" said Victor with sullen anger.

"Perhaps so," said Felina drily; "but it is not that which I could address to you."

"Indeed? and what else did he say—that excellent physiologist?"

"He told me, sir, that there are men among you, who make love a study, and woman a speaking book, which they translate and sell."

"I am not a romancist, madam."

"You, gentlemen painters, make her sit for a model."

"Can you believe it?"

"Did you not tell me so yourself? and when I strove to be jealous of that fair Julia who inspired you with your masterpiece, did you not tell me she had been to you nothing more than what I myself—perhaps—may be--a subject to be studied?"

"Love and admiration are easily distinguished"

"Yes, when love exists."

"Do you doubt mine?"

"What proofs of it have you given me?"

"Have I shrunk from anything you proposed to me?"

"And truly may you boast of it: you have consented to mount your horse a little late perhaps, to ride three miles in the finest weather, and come

into my garden through a broken hedge and open doors.

"What proofs did you require then?"

"What!" cried Felina whose anger rekindled, "have you never thought of any? not of one?

"But which is it?"

"What!—in your position as well as mine, has nothing occurred to you from your own reflections --if not on my account—on your own? What!—you have thought of nothing--of nothing?

Amab, driven to his wit's end, answered coarsely:

"I make no sacrifices for one who does not demand them of me."

"Ah!" suddenly yelled Felina in a transport of despair—"how foolsih—how mad I am! I have been striking his heart to evoke a single cry, a sob, a word to induce me to forgive him—but nothing --not even one—or worse still--self--nothing but self—"

Then she repeated disdainfully Victor's concluding words:

"I make no sacrifices for one who does not demand them of me. Ah!" she resumed—"selfishness—all selfishness!"

"Felina," said Victor angrily, "your disdain is turning to insult."

Felina faced about, and covering him with a look of superb scornfulness, she exclaimed:

"Am I to demand it, sir? ought you to let me ask it? But I, sir, I who am only a weak woman," —she resumed whilst a pallor overspread her brow, —"if I knew there was a man who possessed a secret which might be your ruin—why this man—I cannot tell how—but I would reduce him to silence—for your sake first of all,—to spare you one pang of anxiety, a single fear—and if I were like you--if I possessed that ardent selfishness which makes you the end and aim of all your passions,—I would still destroy him--yes, I would kill him to prevent his humbling me in the object of my love.

After this violent sally, Felina fell upon a sofa, and burst into tears.

Victor went up to her—and said to her in soothing accents:

"I understand you, Felina—and if you want—

He had once more sunk upon his knee before her;—he had again taken hold of her hand and was entreating her. She disengaged herself gently:

"Oh! no, sir," resumed Felina with more of sorrow than of anger—"You understand me not—you attach too exact a sense to the exaggeration of my words—people say such things they dont do them—but they should use a soothing word. Ah! must I then tell you all"— she added looking at him through her tears; "where is the woman, to whom the man she loves, proposes a crime and who accepts it? There is no such woman, believe me. Only, I expected—yes, I expected—a threat—a burst of rage, a transport of jealousy which would have made you exclaim at my feet:"

"No, no, Felina, the man who has insulted thee,—the man whom you and I cannot meet without blushing with shame—that man must not live.—Yes, it is true, I did expect that assurance—and then it would have been my place to fall on my knees, and ask pardon of that love which I should at last have seen break forth in frantic passion.—But no, nothing—it does not disturb you—it does not make you indignant—perhaps you have never once thought of it at all."

The sad and pensive language of Felina penetrated to the depths of Victor's soul and awakened feelings hitherto silent within him; he replied in a gloomy and bitter tone:

"Felina, you are mistaken, I have often thought of it."

"Is that true?" said she to him—and she looked at him as she spoke with a quivering eye.

"Yes," he resumed bending his eyes before that consuming glance;—"but such vengeances require a compensation which you are too artful in evading—not to be perfectly mistress of yourself."

A deep and heavy groan escaped from Felina's chest.

"O my God!"—she exclaimed, "I have not done enough to persuade him. Must I then tell him all? Well, Victor, when you are with me, when I am speaking to you, when I look at you! I no longer live in myself. The fascination which attracts me to you is so powerful, that nothing of my own being continues to belong to me, not even the thoughts I possess—not their most secret mysteries. I tell you all—and when your hands press mine, it seems to me as if my life goes out of me to mingle with yours."

"You love me like this, Felina," said Victor who at last took courage and surrendered himself to that wild and burning glance which seemed to warp him in its blaze. "You love me like this and yet you load me with ridicule and disdain."

"Because at the moment when I hear nothing, see nothing, feel nothing but what is you—because at the moment when love covers me altogether within its folds, separating me from the past, from the future, from the world, from its duties, from my faith plighted to another, from modesty, to leave me alone with you,—because at the moment when the world is nothing, or rather when thou art my world,—it is because at that moment, Victor—there is suddenly a phantom which starts up between you and me, which seizes upon me—bewildered in my maze of madness, and hurls me back cold and frigid into my life—yes, into my life such as you have made it for me."

Oh! Felina! Felina!—do not say these things to me.

"For," she continued with one of those sublime gushes of despair which agitate and rack the heart with goads of fire—"love may have led me to forget all—everything but that man—look—he is there—close at hand—by thy very side—he insults me, and you too—"

Nothing in the shape of woman ever shed such fiendish looks and longings for revenge, as those which fell from the She-Tiger at this awful moment.

She went on:

"Why do you look at me as if I were demented," she said with that desperate laugh which bursts out through tears! "Oh! what a superb conquest you are about to obtain, sir—what a fiend are you about to devote your existence to! What a noble love you are about entrusting your heart to—what a precious courtezan she is whose avarice you have overcome!—what a terrible coquette have you baffled in her wiles. Yes," resumed Felina, whose rage was so furious that she forgot the sentence she had begun, and completed it at random—"yes, whatever I may be, by whatever title you may love me whether you view me as the beloved and invisible fairy who watches over you,—as the devoted partner who travels with you step by step, or as the glittering concubine whom you would lead in triumph—still, do you hear—still—even at the moment when my passion may give me up to you like a common wench, I shall fancy I hear a voice whispering to thee:

"Poor dupe! that does not need much trouble—I can tell you."

"Felina, be silent"— said Amab with a sullen start.

"But I hear that voice, I do,"—she continued with dismay and pressing herself against Amab, who put his arm about her,—I hear it, I tell you, that voice—cannot you?

"Be silent—be silent"—

"Rather silence than voice—oh! it is enough to drive one mad—there he is—I see him—he pursues me—Ah!" she exclaimed, tearing herself from Amab's embrace, "shall I never find a man to deliver me from this phantom—

"But where is that phantom?—where shall I discover it again?"—cried Victor, whom this frenzy had gradually spread to.

Felina had stood up again, and pale, her eye fixed, her limbs quivering, she replied in broken words:

No—no—depart, hasten away—you terrify me—I will not—I cannot—be yours through a crime"

"Felina, I swear it, I will revenge you.

"No—no—I will revenge myself—it is time."

"Felina—where are you going?"

"What care you?"

Her eye was haggard; her reason seemed wandering. She tore herself out of the arms of Victor who strove to detain her.

"Ah! leave me, sir, leave me then," she exclaimed, rushing from the boudoir.

Victor followed her to the end of the chamber they had entered. He thought he saw, and did indeed see Charles buried in a deep sleep—It was like a fearful dream—Felina was already by his side. She held in her hand the dagger which she had just drawn from her girdle—Victor sprang upon her and snatched it away.

"Well, let it be so," said Felina to him, pointing to Charles—go, since you will have it so—yes—

Amab, urged by an infernal frenzy, stepped forward with the blade uplifted—Felina rushed before him.

"Ah! thank you," she said, snatching away the dagger and holding it off—"that was all I wished for—follow me"—

## CHAPTER XXIX.

### THE VERTIGO.

They stopped not till they had entered the apartment immediately leading into the boudoir. Both were pale and agitated, like those travellers, who, having lost their way, are by the force of a quick hand pushed back a few paces from the brow of a precipice, towards which they were unconsciously tending, and whose stupendous depth they were then able to estimate.

Amab had dropped down on a chair, exhausted and incapable of any exertion. Both remained silent—Felina kept her eye upon him. She asked herself whether she had sufficiently broken the energies of this man to ask him for that which she really desired at his hands. At last Amab, in his turn, looked at her. She turned away: he approached and sat close by her, she was weeping.

"Felina, what ails you," said he.

"Nothing," replied she in a tone of gentle resignation. I am weeping for myself."

"Do you doubt your power now?"

"Oh! no" she rejoined, falling on her knees before Victor, "I doubt it no longer, forgive me, forgive me."

"Oh!" said Amab, whose gloomy agitation had not yet entirely ceased, "this crime—I should have committed it."

"Have you then believed that I wished it?"

"What then meant that despair—those menaces?"

"It was but a trial, Victor."

"A trial" rejoined he with anger, "so, when, with this dagger in my hand, I was going to strike—you were calm, you looked tauntingly at the awkward automaton you were setting in motion."

"No, on my soul no," said Felina, in a tone of sincerity, "I have done in this case as I have in every action of my life; I have acted at random, and at first smiling at the idea as an easy game. But no sooner had I observed the thought of this crime flash like lighting into your look, no sooner had I seen you shudder and reel in the delirium into which I was plunging you, than I was siezed with a dizziness and looked upon the abominable thought in which you were concurring as being just and possible."

"Go, go," said she, "you alone shall know me thoroughly you alone will perhaps pity me. I have been so wronged by the world, and *you* also, *you* have done me wrong. Oh you did not know me and I pardon you. But will that put an end to my suffering? Will that render it unnecessary that I should dream of vengeance? Does it consequently follow that this man is not still there, close to us, still a prisoner, still completely in my power, whom I must, nevertheless, suffer to escape; for *I* will not slay him and wish not that *you* should."

"Are there not some more honourable means of compelling him to silence? Have I not already told you," said Victor, that I know how to handle a sword?

"A duel! for what cause. Were he aware of it, would he not hasten to say so, and would not his death render you odious, and (what is worse) ridiculous: odious for having smote the child of a family almost your own, ridiculous for having avenged, on behalf of a woman like me, an insult of which you were the prime author?"

"Yet this man," said Amab, "this man must be kept silent."

"Oh!" suddenly rejoined Felina, seating herself beside Victor, "I had indeed thought of something."

"What is it?"

"No, no," said she, "that also would be a crime; though" added she, there is no law to punish such crimes. No, do you perceive, Victor, I always combat that perverseness of spirit, which I must ascribe to my miserable life, and do not become sensible of the unworthiness of my projects until the moment when I am going to make you an accomplice in them. Yes, it is the privilege of those who have never done wrong to bring out in all its deformity the crime, which in its progress, it is intended should walk side by side with them. No, I say, do not ask me what I had thought of, do not force me to present myself to you in connexion with all the abominable and cruel thoughts that may enter the mind. Charles shall live, Charles shall be able to tell the whole world, that Felina de Cambure has surrendered herself to him as a prostitute; this is the penalty I shall have to pay for having loved you."

"But *I* will not have it so," said Amab, "but will force him to be silent."

"Can you?" said Felina sharply, "do you possess against him one of those secrets for which silence is given in exchange? Can you say to him "if ever *you* speak, I shall speak in turn? Is this obscure family, at the same time so respectable that it may not be threatened to be brought into notoriety through some shocking scandal? Is this father, who is so proud of his son, merely ridiculous? Is his mother, who must have been so beautiful, irreproachable also? Has not this young girl who loves you Victor, who resigns herself with such phrenzy to a passion which you do not share, has she not been led by this silly enthusiasm to do certain things, innocent perhaps, but sufficiently imprudent to enable one to threaten her brother with the revelation of them? This is no crime, this is an honorable use of an honourable weapon in self-defence. At all events the aggressor is the party to be blamed: for, by speaking, it is he, who authorises the party assailed, whose only wish is to be silent, to speak also. Well Victor, do you know of nothing that may save us?"

"Nothing" answered Victor.

Thus was the poison flowing gently into the ear of Amab, and accordingly he was anxiously searching his memory for some word or action which he might be able to employ against Charles: but all to no purpose, and he ended by angrily exclaiming:

"No, it is impossible, they are all invulnerable."

"Alas," said Felina with peculiar bitterness, "there are some persons who are truly fortunate!"

"Yes," rejoined Amab, "happiness is sometimes the companion of virtue."

"No doubt," said Felina, "and it is not their happiness that I envy; it is that virtue to which they have not even a claim."

"What do you mean?"

"What!" sharply answered Felina, at the same time rising from her seat, "had this young girl so pure, so invulnerable in her innocence, had she, instead of addressing her passion to one who has so long closed his eyes that he may not see it, to one who, forced at last to acknowledge it, has firmly kept aloof from it; had she, instead of addressing herself to you, who understood the duties of life in their strictest bearing, met, not a paltry creature like him to whom you have flung me, but a man constituted as almost all men are, I mean, in short, one of those in whose esteem a woman is of no account unless she bring him to-day a pleasure bearing a name different from that of yesterday's; yes," added Felina, with a sullen anger, "yes, had she addressed herself to any one but you, yes, this young girl, yet so pure, would have been a girl undone and, were her secret in your possession, you could impose silence on her brother. But you have respected him, and it is *I*, I alone that must suffer. Well, be it so; I will."

"Felina," said Amab sharply, "is it an act of cowardly villainy, and not a crime that you propose? Would you then have me seduce this child?"

"O no," said Felina, with a look of lofty pride: "you are mistaken, sir, I intend nothing, I ask nothing;" and then, shrugging her shoulders, she added, "you are mad. To what result would that lead."

"To that of avenging *you*, perhaps: and what do you expect as your reward? Have I not been on the point of perpetrating a crime in order to make you mine?"

"So, leaving the arms of this woman you would come to mine and claim my love; but would I give it? Oh, you do not know me, Victor. No, no, I have none of those incommensurable passions of Romance which absorb, in their violence, the puerile prejudices of love. I cannot, like certain persons, separate mind from matter. I would be loved like a queen, but am as jealous as a fishwoman. I will tell you my character: I am whimsical and full of contrarieties, if you will, but do not, therefore, annoy others; you shall not avenge me either by the death of the brother or the dishonour of the sister; I shall live with my shame, and shall, perhaps, inure myself to it, since you, the only person who could save me, can devize no means of rescue but such as *I* repudiate and you yourself reject.

"But how would you be served?" exclaimed Amab; I listen to you and, in your words, am watching to find a clue that may lead me into the right road; for, in my turn, I know you too, Felina; you would have your revenge."

"Yes, I would!"

"And, are you, peradventure, no longer undecided as to its nature, but dare not mention it to me?"

Felina, pointing with her finger to the boudoir which they had just left, replied: "After what passed there, do you say that I dare not?"

"Well, then! for once at least, be plain, replied Victor; do not overtask my sagacity; tell me what it is you have hit upon, and I will frankly tell you whether I have the power or the inclination to put it in execution."

"It would in truth," said Felina, "be so paltry an intrigue, after the lofty tragedies which we have just been acting; it would be so miserable an expedient, in so critical a position."

"But," said Amab, "out with it."

Felina had the art to contrive it so that the very thing which she was burning, with impatience, to impart, should be wrung from her word by word: she knew also, as it suited her purposes, how to invest the revelation she was going to make, with increased or diminished importance.

Accordingly she still replied: "No, no, Victor, should you refuse me, I should feel humiliated; and should you not refuse and success should nevertheless elude our grasp, you would not pardon me that I had induced you to take so foolish a step.

"Let me hear it at least, so that I may be able to judge."

"Did you not understand me just now," rejoined Felina, "when I asked you whether this young girl had done any act, I do not say *culpable* but barely imprudent, and when I added, that if it could be proved, it would be sufficient to compel her brother to be silent. Thus, to induce this young girl to leave home, unknown to her mother, with a view to an assignation which you would fail to keep is more than would be necessary."

Felina, who was watching to see the effect of these words paused. Amab appeared by no means convinced of the excellence of the expedient, and answered in a rather cold tone: "So many circumstances might frustrate such an intrigue that it would be awkward and imprudent to attempt it."

"I told you so," replied Felina, biting her lips: "it is impracticable; you ought not to consent to lend yourself to it; it could not succeed? Let us say no more about it then. However, my position becomes insupportable: the absence of Mr. Charles Thoré may at length awaken the attention of the police, and they would not, perhaps, like his family, rest contented with your daily reports. This young man must be liberated."

Felina paused again, and, reassuming that gloominess of expression which had struck Amab with dismay, she exclaimed:

"Yes, he must either be liberated or made away with."

"What is that you dare to say?" exclaimed Amab.

"Oh, sir," said Felina haughtily, "this is a matter that concerns none but myself, may I expect that, in case of disaster, I shall not find you among the witnesses who might contribute to secure my condemnation?

"But you shrunk with horror from such a crime," said Amab, in a fresh access of fright, "it is you yourself that wrested from my hands the poniard you had placed there: must this deadly thought present itself again to you!"

"I must," cried Felina, starting up in a fresh transport of rage, I must get out of my frightful position. Let us make an end of the matter, Victor."

"You can afford me no succour, is it not so? Well let me proceed on my own way."

"But what in the world do you mean?" said Amab, whose reason was staggering amidst those attacks which assailed him on all sides.

"What do I mean? Nothing—wha I wanted."

"Why, sir, I asked you only for a word, a letter, a note, which, perhaps, I should not have sent—What I wanted? Nothing. It was merely to appear desirous of avenging myself; but nothing, nothing," added she, furiously stamping with her foot, "nothing do I get. Well, be it so, sir, only do not complain if I take a violent course, you would have it so."

"But," said Victor, "this very note, did I consent to write it, would not produce the result you expect from it: Julia would not consent to an assignation proposed to her by me."

"You are diffident of yourself," said Felina, with bitterness; you doubt your influence with Mademoiselle Thoré: you shewed no such modesty in my case; but it is idle to discuss the question of her coming, since you are unwilling to write."

"But what am I to write? and how propose a clandestine meeting to a young girl to whom I have not even breathed a word of love?"

"I assure you sir, that that would not be at all puzzling."

"But how would you set about it?"

"Pooh, pooh," said Felina, in a tone of indifference; "this would do well enough"—

"Mademoiselle,

"In consequence of a singular occurrence, but which I am not permitted to explain to you, it depends on you alone to rescue your brother from his present position. If you have the courage to come to-morrow, and ask for him at the house to which you accompanied me, in order to learn what had become of him, your brother will be instantly restored to you."

"But this note itself, were I to write it, would protect her against calumny, by showing the cause of this meeting."

"Oh," said Felina, "objections for everlasting: the part I am playing, sir, is really too wretched; I am subjecting myself to the same treatment as the unfortunate man who goes to a money lender to borrow a hundred thousand crowns, and, in consequence of repeated refusals, gradually lowers his pretensions until, at last, he begs a hundred sous, which are also refused. I tell you, Victor, once for all, write that note immediately. You shall not send it, I will destroy it whenever you please; but write it, write it; God help me; write it, that I may be able to say I have got something however little."

Felina had taken such care to tell Victor that she was mad, that she abandoned herself to sudden impressions and whimsical fancies that he thought he was releasing himself from her importunities on easy terms, by satisfying her last whim; and did he not, moreover, keep reserved in his inmost soul a resolution to put Julia on her guard against the sending of this note. He wrote it therefore.

Then, having committed this petty act of cowardice, he turned towards Felina and said, as he presented the note:

"Are you satisfied?"

"Yes," answered she, with one of her most gracious smiles, putting the note which she sealed, into her bosom, and regarding Amab with the caressing and ferocious look of a sated panther which yet wishes to play with the remains of its victim.

"But at length let me know," said Amab, "what decision have you come to with respect to this unfortunate Charles?"

One of those extravagant ideas, which used, so frequently, to spring up in the mind of Felina, caused her to burst into a loud laugh, and she answered Amab:

"If I forced him to marry me, it would be the most certain way of forcing him to hold his peace."

"It would certainly not be the way to punish him," said Amab, in a tone of the greatest tenderness, for he wished to receive an equivalent for his complaisance.

"You are wrong to treat my idea with derision," gravely rejoined Felina; "there are but two men who can espouse me in a manner to justify me—either you or he."

"I," said Amab, who shuddered involuntarily at the word, and all whose desires shrank from the thought.

"Yes, really," resumed Felina, in a tone the most simple and natural, "for no one would ever give credence to an adventure like mine when you, who must be better acquainted with it than any one else living, will consent to give me your name."

Amab was dreadfully perplexed by this atrocious pleasantry.

Felina said to him with keen significance:

"It appears that in this last manner, I shall be able to inflict a cruel punishment on the one of the two men whom I have a right to complain of. Ah! you scarcely love me at all, monsieur Amab, she added smiling."

"Never touch upon such a subject," replied Victor in a sullen tone.

"Be it so," said Felina. I will never speak to you thereon, and I think we shall do well to remain as we are—Who knows? perhaps one day you yourself will ask to marry me? What say you?—Why do you not answer me?

"Because in truth," exclaimed Victor violently, "I know not what you require of me,—because I lose my way as I attempt to pursue you among the unsettled caprices of your mind and heart. Are you good?—are you wicked?—do you love me?—am I a simple tool which you are making use of for some unknown scheme? am I the person you said you expected in a lover of your choice?—I came hither with a heart inundated with blissful hopes;—I leave you full of shame and humiliation. Well, I tell you candidly, Felina, I am afraid of you;—I tremble for my love, you have too clearly shewn whither it might lead;—I believed I had understood you, and I wanted to overcome you;—but I confess myself conquered;—expel me if you like, but do not bring me back to scenes similar to those you have compelled me to endure;—I should not have spirit to support them: my body is exhausted, my mind dispirited—I can really bear no more."

The ruthless She-Tiger listened with triumphant looks to Amab; she seemed to inquire within herself if there was yet no point left where she might inflict another wound. Doubtless, she discovered one, for she laughed and answered the painter:

"Come! do you still believe one word of what you have seen and heard this night? Why you are crazy, my good friend, and I can assure you, that you have much amused me. I had promised Charles a farce, and he has had one;—unless he may have been afraid when he saw you enter so seriously into your part of Ægisthus."

"What!" said Amab, pale with anger,—"Charles"—

"Charles," said Felina tittering, "has been here this fortnight;—he abides with me, and time does not seem heavy on his hands."

"Has he heard what you have been saying to me?"

"He knew it beforehand."..

"And all that I have been saying to you?"

"You have said but little."

"Oh!" said Amab, "woe unto him!—woe unto you!—You have been revenged on me, I will be revenged on him."

"I defy you to do it," replied Felina.

"Farewell, madam," said Amab, "you shall see me again sooner than you think."

"I hope so, indeed," she answered with a gracious smile. "Return soon."

"Oh! madam, this is too insolent," said Amab driven beyond bounds, and feeling as if his senses were forsaking him. "Farewell—farewell, for ever," he continued, trying to open the door which with all his strength he could not manage. He then added:

"Do you intend likewise to detain me as your prisoner?"

"Oh! no—no, Victor," said Felina sorrowfully and more seriously,—"no, leave me under the impression that I have been mocking you;—leave me with the idea that I am the most audacious actress in the world, I shall not reproach you;—I have just explained to myself the last mystery in your character. So, I told you what was incredible, impossible:—I told you that I wanted to make you ridiculous in the eyes of Charles—I told you—but really it was too absurd a joke,—so absurd that I have forgotten it;—and yet you believed it immediately, without arguing it, without seeming surprised; neither your mind, nor your heart interfered to defend me;—what did you take me for?—a woman trifling with the shameful injury you had brought upon me. Go, sir, go, I seek not to detain you;—I know about you all I wished to know;—there is still time for you to steal unperceived out of my house. I would not expose you to blush, were it known that you came here."

Felina herself opened the door, by merely pressing it with her finger, although it had resisted Victor's utmost efforts.

"Farewell, sir," said she to him, "for the last time—farewell."

The miserable Amab was a prey to a bewildering vertigo; he looked at Felina, advanced a step towards her who was smiling, fell back again in dismay, and his head confused, his mind wandering, he darted out exclaiming:

"She will drive me mad!"

As she watched the departure of her victim, the She-Tiger repeated again what she had said every time he had left her before:

"I shall have him yet."

The day after this nocturnal interview was spent by Amab in a kind of mental maze, the consequence of the terrible shocks he had sustained. Left to himself and his meditations, he strove to find the meaning of what he had seen and heard, but in vain. Sometimes even, he doubted the reality of the facts, and asked himself whether the night had not been occupied with a fantastic dream, the recollection of which had disturbed his reason. But then he recalled to mind the words, the gestures, the looks, the very tones and accents of the subtle, dark-minded woman who had enslaved him, and he was too conscious that it was no fancied vision.

He attempted to write, and when his letter was finished, he dared not send it to Felina. He wanted to return to her, and when ready to go, he recoiled before the thought of facing once more that versatile and delusive phantom, that cruel and sarcastic fiend in the fair form of woman.

It was when he had again felt exhausted by this inward conflict with his recollections, that he took a decisive, sudden and irrevocable resolution.

This was never to visit Felina again.

Unwilling to expose himself anew to the infernal temptations inherent in that woman, he resolved to place between her and him a barrier which his honour would force him to respect.

He resolved to wait on the Thoré family and formally demand the hand of Julia.

---

## CHAPTER XXX.

### DARK AND SECRET SNARES.

**Before** we begin to relate the scene which took place at the china dealer's house, and the adventures which followed, we beg our readers to attend to, and mark with some precision, the hours therein indicated. The events contained within this single night are included in a space of time so narrow, that a few minutes' difference in their combination might have occasioned their total failure. But by means of an inflexible resolution, and an incredible audacity, they were so well arranged as to provide a place for each.

Imagine an experienced general who has foreseen the battle, who has divided his army into parts, who has fixed the hour of attack, who has traced its march, and who has foreseen a certain victory.

Such was Felina at the moment we parted with her.

And suppose in the next place, that the experienced general is suddenly informed that instead of accepting the battle, the enemy are preparing to leave their ground and take refuge behind impregnable forts. Then the skilful captain instantly relinquishes his combinations so exactly calculated, and replaces them by prompt attacks, forced marches, rapid movements, which are suggested from minute to minute by circumstances, and thus snatches back the victory which was about to escape him.

Such Felina was on that night when she appeared to have lost all.

The day which follows these unforseen engagements, there are sure to be critics who discern in the plans and combinations of the eve, a hundred points full of danger and ruin: there was a post undefended here, a passage by which the enemy might have escaped. The result of all these subsequent commentaries is, that the conqueror was rash and insane; and these critics are right. Still, the rash man continues to be a man of genius, for let people say what they will, there is no crown like success.

Seven o'clock had just struck. The Thoré family were collected together in the drawing room: contrary to his custom M. Villon was absent, for, since Charles had disappeared, the young clerk had been received on a more intimate footing by the family.

Whenever misfortune enters a house, with one hand it bars the door against those who are indifferent, and with the other opens it to the affectionate and devoted.

M. Thoré was a sort of mercantile aristocrat, who on very rare occasions condescended to admit M. Villon to his table; but this stinted hospitality had now been exchanged for a daily habit. Although Madame Thoré was more convinced than ever that the young clerk's passion would never be other than a source of annoyance to her daughter, she liked to see M. Villon about her—M. Villon who was ever ready to listen to her complaints, to have faith in her least hopes, to go out and pursue his inquiries at the faintest shadow of discovering her son.

It is true that, on this very day, M. Villon, had declared that he believed he had at length got upon Charles' track. The family were most anxiously expecting him and all their expectations were centred in him, for Victor had so often deceived the hopes of the family by promising more positive tidings, that they already began to look upon his pretended interposition as an excuse for his assiduous visits.

Meanwhile, Victor arrived as usual, but this evening the looks he wore were solemn, mysterious, and more pointed than usual, and after the first common-places had been repeated on both sides, he said to Mademoiselle Thoré:

"Madame, I am come here to say things, and disclose a secret which every body must not hear; will you be so kind, you and M. Thoré, as to grant me a moment's audience.

Mademoiselle Thoré whispered a word to Julia who withdrew all in a flutter of excitement, and guessed by the looks which Victor directed towards her, that she was in all probability the main subject of the interview about to take place.

She had hardly left the room before Victor began his address.

"Madame," said he, turning more particularly to the mother, "it is time for the painful position you are in and the false one in which I myself stand, to cease at once. I know where your son is, madam, and *perhaps* it is in my power to deliver him."

"*Perhaps* you say," exclaimed Madame Thoré;—"is he then entangled in some political matter, for I do not understand what other power than that of the government could detain him, the moment you know where he is."

"Madam," resumed Victor, "when I shall have explained to you the circumstances which have led to Charles' abduction, perhaps you may not find it so easy to disarm the vengeance whose blows all my efforts have up to this day only been able to suspend."

"But why did you not warn us sooner of this?"

"Because every day I had hopes that Charles would be released, and I wished to commission him to express formally a desire which my constant visits, I trust, have given you to understand."

"I hope you will believe, sir," said M. Thoré with all the fatherly dignity and importance he could assume,—"I hope you will believe that if I had not thus understood the frequent visits with which you honour us, I should have entreated you to render them less constant."

It would be impossible to describe the harmless pomposity of the worthy merchant as he spoke.

"You are right," said Madame Thoré hurriedly, "and M. Amab will permit me not to answer him at present on the subject of an application which does us honour; but we must think of my son,—we must think of Charles;—we all tremble for his safety, and I confess that what M. Victor has just informed us of alarms me so much that I entreat him to hasten to tell us, by what measures we may bring about the deliverance of Charles.

"That is all very well," observed M. Thoré gravely, with a toss of his head worthy of an emperor,—"but it was proper to signify to M. Amab that the chief of the family, which he desires to be received into, knows what is due to propriety and to himself;—now, M. Amab may proceed."

Madame Thoré quivered with impatience, and said in a tone of supplication:

"Speak, sir, speak."

Victor was just on the point of communicating to the family of Charles the sentiments he had resolved to reveal, when the door suddenly opened, and Count Gustavus de Monrion was announced.

This very unexpected visit would have astonished the Thoré family at any other juncture; it appeared both unseasonable and indecorous at that moment.

Monrion was greeted with one of those salutations which show the new comer that he would have done better to stay away.

Monrion, accustomed to the kindest deference on the part of the family, perfectly understood that he was interrupting an interview of the highest importance: he apologised saying to Madame Thoré:

"Excuse me, madam, for my awkwardness; I should not have come if I had thought I should have found M. Amab here; he will, I hope, have given you tidings more reliable than those I come to apprise you of."

A mother's heart opens to all who come to speak to it about its anxiety, and she replied to M. de Monrion with eagerness:

"What tidings do you allude to, sir?"

"I know most positively," said Gustavus, "that your son has been seen to-day in Paris; but M. Amab must be able to tell you this far better than I, for I have been assured that M. Charles had presented himself at his house, and had even written to him."

"The Count is mistaken," said Victor, "I have not seen Charles at my place, nor have I received any letter from him."

Victor had made this answer in the most confused voice, for Monrion's words had recalled to him under what circumstances he had seen Charles and he knew not how far Gustavus might be acquainted with this fact either by private intimation, or by Felina herself: All that related to that woman terrified him.

If, on the other hand, it is remembered that the Count de Monrion had called on M. Thoré being under the impression that Victor had seduced Julia, and that it was to escape from Charles' vengeance that he had caused his abduction, it will be easily felt and understood that the young painter's confusion must have tended to aggravate M. de Monrion's prejudice.

"Are you very sure," said he in the most serious tone, "are you quite sure, sir, that you have not seen M. Charles Thoré to-day, or at least that you have not had a letter from him?"

"Were it anywhere else, monsieur le comte," resumed Victor haughtily, "I should dispense with answering such a question, but in the presence of a father and a mother who may be alarmed by your language, in the presence of a family to which I desire to belong, I will not suffer a doubt to exist as to the rectitude of my conduct in this matter, and I swear on my honour that I have neither seen Charles at my house, nor received any letter from him since he disappeared."

Now it was M. de Monrion's turn to feel and appear embarrassed, not so much by what he had just heard as by the thoughts which crowded into his mind.

"Excuse me," said he to Madame Thoré, M. Amab desires to belong to your family, he said, did he not?

"Yes, sir, replied the china dealer's wife, greatly surprised at a discussion which she could not at all understand; "This gentleman has just now acquainted us with his intentions."

"Just now?" said Monrion, tittering; "then I understand it all."

Then he turned towards Amab and said to him with marked disdain:

"I can understand, sir, that there may be messages which a future brother-in-law should never have written, and which a future husband should never have received."

These words, inexplicable to every one present, had reference to that letter wherein Charles accused Amab of having seduced Julia and demanded satisfaction for his sister's honour—a letter which Felina had taken care to suppress as soon as Jean had shown it to Gustavus.

Monrion knew the letter; but Amab, who had not received it, was taken by surprise at the tone and language of Gustavus, and said to him drily:

"Count, I shall be obliged to you, to explain your enigmas to me."

"I think you will understand me, when I shall have told you that by soliciting the hand of Mademoiselle Julia Thoré, you have taken at once the most prudent and honourable part."

Having delivered these words Monrion bowed and was retiring, when Amab hastily stopped him saying:

"Count, you said that M. Charles Thoré had presented himself at my house, that I had received a letter from him; I swore to you on my honour that it was not true. Can you now inform me, you, how you became acquainted with these pretended circumstances."

Monrion was greatly embarrassed at this question; for it implied no less than to own he had commissioned his valet to watch Amab's steps, and that it was through the agency of that spy he had learned the appearance of Charles at Victor's door and the existence of a note the contents of which had been betrayed to him.

Gustavus hesitated only a moment: he was one of those men who have sufficient spirit to face the bad actions they have committed, so he replied:

"I confess that these particulars have reached me through a channel somewhat suspicious, perhaps."

"And which ought to have led you to doubt their correctness," said Victor, who was quivering with anger, "if you knew the hand which may have furnished them to you."

It was not till that moment that Gustavus remembered that Felina had advised him to apply to Jean to learn what he required about Amab; he instantly asked himself whether he was not the dupe of that woman whose hardihood and cunning he knew better than any one; he said to Victor:

"Have you any reason to believe that these assertions have been invented, that any one was interested in making me believe them?"

"Do you know," said Victor in a tone of mystery, "any one who has cause to be revenged on you? Is the party a woman? and is that woman called perchance—madame—"

"Felina de Cambure!" hastily exclaimed Madame Thoré, completing at once Amab's sentence and Monrion's thought, as it expressed the fear which she herself had always experienced since the ominous appearance of that woman in her house."

"Madame de Cambure!" repeated Monrion,

astounded to hear the name uttered by a person to whom he thought it was absolutely unknown; "Madame de Cambure!" he again resumed,—"but how and why can she be mixed up with the abduction of Charles?"

"Allow me not to answer you on this subject, Count," said Amab with embarrassment; "Madame de Cambure will be able to tell you the interest she takes in all this, if however she shall see fit."

"Be it so, sir," said the count, "and I will apply to her for information."

Whereupon Monrion withdrew immediately, with a pale brow, as he already suspected some infamous treachery in which he had been made to play a part both detestable and ridiculous.

Now let us allow Victor a sufficient space of time to relate to M. and Madame Thoré the greater part of the events in this narrative, and that with all the modifications which served to diminish in their eyes the cynical parts of the adventure, and show him, Victor Amab, as a devoted friend, who, since Charles had disappeared, had tolerated the immodest allurements of the lascivious Felina only to achieve the deliverance of his friend; let it be noted that Victor had come to M. Thoré's house at seven o'clock, that the Count de Monrion had arrived there at a quarter past seven, had left at half-past seven; let us measure the time that it took Victor to explain to Thoré and his wife Felina's system of vengeance, and the incredible schemes and intrigues she had set on foot to secure that vengeance, and let us see how the other personages of our story employed that time in their respective homes.

Awful, indeed, is woman in her vengeful hours!

---

## CHAPTER XXXI.

### AN UNEXPECTED ATTACK.

**Precisely** at seven o'clock, and just at the moment when Amab entered the china-dealer's house, M. Villon called upon Madame Felina de Cambure. The honest clerk had already attempted to make his way into the presence of the fine lady, by representing the name of the house he belonged to. He was dismissed with a degree of impertinence which showed him that he had chosen the worst recommendation he could have employed. Another time, and attired in a new costume, he had announced himself as an envoy from the Count de Monrion; this time, he had been allowed to await, in the antechamber, for the lady's answer, and an appointment had been made with him for the next day. But M. Villon's projects required a more proximate interview.

Villon attempted, therefore, a third ruse, in a third disguise, to obtain his admittance, and announced himself as a messenger from M. Amab.

This time the doors were opened wide to him, for Felina had said to her servants:

"If M. Amab should present himself, or if any one comes on his account, let the party be ushered in directly."

Felina had not doubted a moment but that Victor would return to her to ask her to explain all he had seen, all he had heard, and to ascertain at length the final resolution of that fairy of so many fantastic metamorphoses, who had continued so long to trifle with his feelings.

Felina had put off her ultimate victory over Amab until this meeting, and perhaps she had reserved her own defeat for the success of this last triumph.

The mere arrival of a messenger from Amab did not surprise Felina; considering in what a tumult of mind she had parted with him she had expected no more; all she wanted was that he should place in her hand the thread by means of which she was again to draw him back to her feet.

She received M. Villon with the most tranquil smile, the most modest look, like a woman who is prepared for a serious explanation; but she was greatly astonished, as soon as she was left alone with this messenger, to see him take off two thick mustachios from his nose, and a monstrous pair of whiskers from his cheeks.

"Madam," said the clerk to her in his gruffest voice, "do you recognise me?"

The She-Tiger, terrified by this mode of acting, ran to the bell, but suddenly checked herself for fear of committing an act of imprudence, having that moment recollected M. Thoré's clerk.

Felina possessed that faculty which affords to certain minds so great a talent for intrigue; this was to remember with precision the names, the places, and the countenances of those whom she had seen but once, as well as the very date of the most trifling occurrence.

The presence of M. Thoré's clerk in her house revealed to her that they were already on Charles's track, and she wanted to know the value of the information obtained by the family before she took any determination whatever.

"Yes, truly," said she at length, "I do recognize you, sir, you are employed by M. Thoré, and I beg you to explain to me how it is that you present yourself to me in so strange a manner."

"Because," said M. Villon abruptly, "I came here this morning in my employer's name, and the door was shut upon me."

"I never had any business with M. Thoré except the purchase of some china articles which I paid for, and I do not wish to be teased with offers of service, sir. In case I should require it, I have not forgotten your master's address; but once more I ask you, why you appear before me in so extraordinary a disguise?"

"Because," resumed Villon, with a look so melodramatic that it forced Felina to smile, in spite of the cruel anxiety she endured,—"when I presented myself here a second time, on the part of the Count de Monrion, I was politely requested to return tomorrow, and I wanted to see you this evening."

"I am not always at home to my best friends," said Felina, closely watching the intruder to study by what side she might contrive to deceive or terrify the man, in case of need; and you have at last, it appears, presented yourself in the name of M. Amab."

"That was most unwillingly," said Villon, "for he is a gentleman to whom I do not wish to be under any kind of obligation."

"Indeed!" cried Felina; "at all events, you are under the obligation to him of having obtained your desire, and since you are here, you can explain your object, you need no longer put on any disguise at all."

"If I have taken this disguise," said Vellon, "it is because the same man could not appear three times successively at your house from different persons, without exciting suspicions which might have caused the door to be shut against me.

"That was admirably weighed, sir; and on whose part do you come, among the three whose names you assumed as a recommendation?"

"On the part of none of them," said Villon, who was doing his best to sustain his anger in presence of that woman who spake to him with the most easy politeness, whilst any one else in her place,

would have called for help and have had him thrown out at the window. "I come on my own account."

"Indeed!" cried Felina who had been standing up to this time, and who now took a seat, and showed another to Villon, adding with a smile in which the most affable curiosity was apparent:

"And pray what have you to say to me?"

Villon had settled in his mind beforehand the sort of charge he intended to hurl at Madame de Cambure; he had indited a sentence in which he had stored all his facts, in a concise and crushing style to annihilate the culprit.

The moment he was summoned by her to explain his intentions, he did like certain lawyers, who, having learned their brief by heart, find themselves compelled, by the circumstances of the case, to disarrange their exordium, but who, the moment they find an opening to place the sounding sentences they have studied out of court, suddenly assume a Ciceronian attitude, and diffuse their pompous prose with so much emphasis as to amuse the younger judges and set the old ones asleep.

Villon, who had lost his latitude through the composure of Felina, had at length perceived his opening; he therefore poured out in a breath the following invective:

"How long, madam, do you intend to detain young Charles Thoré from beneath the family roof?"

Felina supported to admiration the eloquent effusion of the accountant, for she made a gesture of surprise, and the latter was thereby enabled to proceed, with swelling voice, saying:

"Do not interrupt me, madam, I know all: the night before last, I was at ten o'clock, at your door; I followed you to the place of the Bastille, in spite of the swiftness of your horses. I had an excellent cabriolet. On reaching the place of the Bastille, you took up a gentleman, who, judging by the gas-light, appeared to me old and had a ribbon decoration. You went with him to the Rue Charonne, whilst your carriage went and took up its stand at the corner of the Faubourg Saint Antoine. You went in by a little garden door to a house without any number. An hour afterwards, the gentleman came forth again with another man; a few minutes after that, they returned with your carriage; the coachman who had driven it to the Faubourg Saint Antoine was gone, and the man who had come out of your little house had taken his place. The carriage was left alone at the door, and these two men went back into the house: another minute elapsed; then the gentleman came out first, after him the strange man who got upon the coach-box; then you and Charles Thoré came out together and entered the carriage, which drove off."

Felina listened to M. Villon with an attention so placid, that the accountant began to lose his assurance. He fancied she did not understand him and never would he have dreamt that the She-Tiger felt the keenest admiration for the man who had found the means to obtain such precise intelligence.

"How is it," she said to him, "that you saw all that, and that you managed to distinguish every person so well, whilst none of my people perceived you?"

"Merely by hiding myself above the door, seated astride the coping stone, screened by a lilac bush overhanging the street."

"It was truly a capital post," said Felina, "but go on."

"Afterwards, madam, I acknowledge I did not follow you; when I got back to my cabriolet, your carriage was already out of sight, but now I know that you are acquainted with Charles's hiding-place; I know that you alone detain him captive, that your allurements have seduced him from his family, and in their name it is that I come to reclaim him of you."

"So you have warned M. and Madame Thoré of your discovery?" said Felina looking down.

"No, madam, for I wished to preserve you from a disgraceful exposure; for M. and Madame Thoré would have disdained to apply to such a woman as yourself, and would have charged the police to come and demand the release of their infatuated boy."

All M. Villon's grotesque ignorance, and all Felina's self command could not prevent her from feeling most acutely the grossness of this insult. Scarcely had Villon uttered the word police, before Felina started up before him, pale, terrible, and quivering with excitement.

"Down on thy knees! down I say! she exclaimed with such impetuosity as to make him recoil before that imperious gesture and fulminating glance. "Down on thy knees! Thou, and thy master, and his son, and all of you, shall perish for the insult thou hast just spoken."

Villon was a man of real courage, but it was the relative courage which does not extend to all the occasions of life. If Villon had been a soldier he would have been a very brave one. In any usual case, a meeting with one of his equals would have found him perfectly cool and collected; relying on his strength and youth, he would not have feared a quarrel with a carter. However, if he had been called upon to fight with a man of rank and fortune very superior to his own, he would have gone to the ground with less confidence.

So, in the measure of his thoughts, the accountant Villon considered himself Amab's equal, and would have gladly accepted a duel with him, whilst if the thing had been possible, he would have been at least embarrassed, if not alarmed, by a hostile meeting with the count of Mourion. But that of which he had no idea at all, was a woman like Felina, the haughty She-Tiger, with her flaming eye, who in so fiery and startling a voice could speak of death as the punishment of an insult.

Villon had retreated from the looks and action of Felina; he was confused and staggered by her words, and stuttered as he replied:

"Excuse me, madam, you did not understand me; I had no intention of offending you."

Felina, who perhaps repented that she had yielded to this transport of passion, covered Villon with a look of supreme disdain, and quietly resumed the seat she had just quitted.

"So then, sirrah," she replied, "whom do you think you are speaking to?"

Villon was driven from his latitude:

"Do you recognize me?" she cried.

"I have heard - I know that M. de Mourion -"

"Is a friend of mine, you mean; but has M. Charles ever spoken to you about me?"

"Never, never!" said Villon with earnestness; "I was not the confidant of young M. Thoré."

"Was it M. Amab then?" continued Felina not stopping to heed the word *confidant*, though it contained an impertinant allusion, and was also a discovery.

"No, madam," said Villon, who felt all his ill humour return at the mention of Victor's name; "I never hold discourse with that gentleman."

"Who then advised you to watch my actions; who led you to suspect that M. Charles Thoré was in my power?" said Felina, taking the most subtle advantage of the honest clerk's agitation to ascertain the full extent of the dangers with which her plans of vengeance were beset.

"Why madam, a thousand occurrences did this: first your visit to the warehouse, then something which fell from M. Amab, and which I did not hear, but Madame Thoré did, and which pointed you out as the only person who could possess any intelligence respecting Charles."

"But when was this hint let fall?"

"The very day the merchant's son disappeared; the very day on which the set of china was sent which you had purchased at our house."

"And the invoice of which Miss Julia made out for me," said the fiend with an infernal smile of inward satisfaction.

"Exactly madam, and it was this tea service packed up according to your directions, which you declined to let us send to you, and for which you would not leave your name, which you sent a livery servant to fetch away, that was seen at your door by Madame Thoré as she was waiting to hear tidings of her son. Such were the circumstances which induced Madame Thoré and myself to suspect, that this mystery contained a secret."

In spite of the serious aspect of her affairs, Felina could not help laughing at poor Villon's language, and especially at his singular confusion; she answered:

"In general, sir, every mystery contains a secret; but your discoveries will not obtain the release of Charles Thoré, unless I think proper to let him return to his family."

"What do you say, madam?" muttered the accountant, drawing himself up.

"Suppose, sir, that Charles Thoré happens to like me (don't you think I am worthy of it?) - suppose that he chooses to see me continually, to be always at my side; suppose that to effect this he chooses to fix his abode in the rue Charonne, or here, or elsewhere, what has the police to do with it? Charles Thoré is two and twenty, I believe; that renders him of age, the master of his actions, free to come and go, and I cannot see what right his family can claim to have him apprehended bodily at his own lodgings or at mine, like a secreted minor. Can any complaint be made of his conduct since he left his father's house? Have any unpaid bills been presented showing extravagant expenses? I think not. What then do you complain of?"

"Madam," said Villon much embarrassed at the derisive tone in which Felina spoke, M. Charles's family have feared lest he may have fallen a victim to some shameful snare."

"Are you not at hand to witness that he is perfectly well."

"To come to the point, madam, what do you intend to do?"

"Me, sir? I have no intentions in the matter. This question ought to be rather put to yourself. What do you intend doing?"

"Well," replied the accountant with all the dignity he could command. "I pretend to restore M. Charles to his honored family; and if he refuses to return home, I am resolved at any rate to see him."

"You wish to speak to him then?"

"I do."

"I shall not prevent you."

"Be so good then as to inform me where I shall be able to find him."

Despite all her assurance, and no woman had more, Felina felt herself driven back to her last intrenchments. The clerk with his plain-dealing and unvarnished frankness had contrived to break that plot so artfully woven. She took a desperate course; this was to suppress M. Villon for four and twenty hours as she had done with Charles for a fortnight. She rose therefore from her seat, saying to him;

"I cannot tell you where he is, but I can take you thither. Have the goodness to wait for me a moment, whilst I put on another dress."

## CHAPTER XXXII.

### THE SHE-TIGER PURSUES HER PLANS.

LIKE our experienced general. Felina maintained her order of battle after she had removed an unforeseen peril. She went, indeed, into her rich dressing room, and was occupied in attiring herself in her riding costume, when the bell rang to announce a new visitor. This time she hoped it was Victor, and she said hurriedly to the chambermaid:

"Show him in here—directly."

The room she was in was the farthest removed from the one in which Villon was waiting for her. Amab's arrival could not fail to alter her determination in some respect with regard to the clerk. She wished therefore to see him, and she was preparing to question him without delay, when Monrion stood before her.

"What you!" said she to the count, unable to conceal her surprise, in spite of the self command she habitually exercised over her feelings.

"Yes, it is I," returned Gustavus flinging himself into an arm chair, thereby showing that his visit would be a long one; "I am come to thank you for the information you transmitted to me through master Jean, my lackey."

"What information?" inquired Felina.

"Why! that unaccountable letter from M. Charles to M. Amab, accusing the poor fellow of carrying off the lovely Julia and of having seduced her."

"Who is pure and innocent, you mean,—do you not?" said Madame de Cambure, desirous of avoiding any direct answer, and of taking shelter in such epigrams.

"Who at least," returned Monrion looking fixedly at Felina, "will not have to blush for her fault, if she have committed one, since M. Victor Amab has offered her his hand."

Felina was thunderstruck.

"His hand!" she re-echoed with a sullen and wandering look.

"Does that disturb you at all?" asked Gustavus.

Felina continued still and silent for some moments.

"Gustavus," she exclaimed suddenly, "my life will be decided within this hour. Will you leave the hour to me, and I will afterwards explain to you all I have done.

"No, said Gustavus coldly;—I know nothing, I understand nothing of what is brewing; but I will not let you have this hour. I know you, Felina; in a shorter time you could ruin a family, set two friends to butcher each other—I will not release you this hour."

"Compulsion! restraint! do you intend, count?"

"No, but an assiduous attendance. If you go out, I shall follow you. Come, Felina, do not tear the skin off your pretty hands with your rosy nails; my resolution is taken—and we shall have a long conference, for I am come here to know the truth about M. Charles Thoré's abduction, and likewise the cause of your very marked taste for M. Amab's pictures; and then why you relinquished the desire you had for Miss Thoré's picture. Finally I am come to learn why you wanted me to seduce her, and what was your object in slandering her."

"Count," said Felina who had recovered all her composure during this last speech of Monrion's "I cannot prevent you following me, if I go out; but I have more regard for you than you have for yourself;—I will not expose you before my servants to perform a ridiculous part and one that would be pitiful: I shall stay, only I hope you will not oblige me to keep your company the whole time."

"Excuse me, excuse me," replied the count, this apartment is admirably adapted for entrances and exits, and I will not allow you to escape me whilst I have reason to suppose you would be occupied in plotting new mischief against me and others."

"I thank you, count," returned Felina satirically, "the lessons I have given you have not been lost, and you observe to admiration the precept you have heard me deliver a hundred times: 'When your enemy is undone and in your hands, crush him at once and without mercy.' I will stay."

She sat down opposite the count, and began to eye him so insolently that any man less accustomed than Monrion to Felina's strange manners, would have been exasperated by it.

"Well, sir, what do you wish to say to me?"

"I come here not to answer, but to interrogate."

"Well, I for my part, sir, refuse to speak."

"However you must consent at last to explain the whole of this scheme in which you attempted to implicate me."

Felina was silent.

"You are acquainted with M. Amab, and M. Charles Thoré?—Is one of these the happy man who has succeeded me in your good graces."

Felina did not move.

"So your mind is made up?"

"Yes, sir, it is."

"How solemn you look all at once."

"Of all the things I most detest in this world, there is none I loathe so much as ridicule, whether it alight upon myself or my friends. I know you, it were enough for me to continue still and silent in your company for an hour, to drive you to the most violent extremes of anger, and to urge you to break out into a storm of petulant fury, and fill the room with absurd clamour."

"It depends on yourself to avoid that scandal."

"And I will preserve you from it; but on one condition."

"A condition—I will have no conditions."

"Then I shall say nothing."

"But what condition?"

"To write to you what I will not tell you."

"Where will you write?"

"Here only."

"Be it so."

"You agree to the conditions?"

"I do."

No sooner had de Monrion uttered these last words, than Felina had rung. The pretended deaf and dumb chambermaid came in. The lady made a sign to her."

"What are you telling her?" inquired the count alarmed.

"You shall see," replied Felina with a disdainful smile.

The chambermaid returned the next moment with a desk containing writing materials.

No second sign—at least none which was observable—was exchanged between the chambermaid and the mistress. A single look was all that passed.

Felina sat down opposite a small table and affected to place herself face to face with Gustavus, so that he need not lose any of her motions. She then began to write very fast, interrupting herself however several times, as if she could not restrain the anger she felt under the harsh state of compulsion she had to endure, and this anger went so far, as to prompt her to strike the writing desk, two or three times, and disperse her pens and papers.

But Monrion only told her with vexatious coolness to go on.

"Continue, madame, continue," he said as often as she struck the desk.

She went on writing, and in about five minutes at most she took the paper on which she had been writing a few almost illegible lines, and tossed it across the table to Monrion, saying pertly:

"There, read that, sir."

Monrion stooped to pick up the paper which had fallen on the floor. The fleeting moment during which Gustavus lost sight of her was sufficient for Madame de Cambure to hide in one of her coat pockets, (she was dressed in male attire) two other notes which she had had the impudence to write beneath her lover's eyes.

Just as Monrion was going to open the note which Felina had so contemptuously flung at him, he perceived she had risen and was preparing to leave the boudoir they were in.

"You want to go?" he said to her angrily.

"Do you intend to compel me to stay with you, whilst you are reading the acknowledgment of my fault?" said Felina, half opening the door leading into the adjoining chamber.

Monrion faltered; he was ashamed to treat so rigidly a woman whom he had so fondly loved; so he said to her,

"Well, go, but this door shall be left open."

Felina moved rapidly away, and her eagerness reviving the suspicions in the count's mind, he pulled Felina back to him, saying:

"No, stay here!"

Felina let fall a look of scorn and exultation on Gustavus, shut the door herself and sat down in front of him. But that motion had sufficed the She-Tiger to throw into the next room the two notes she had stealthily penned, and when de Monrion attempted to read the note in which Felina said she had written the acknowledgment of her fault, he could make nothing out of the first ten lines of illegible scrawl, save the few following words written quite plain:

"Count de Monrion, you are a silly fellow."

The battle is now at its height. We left Amab relating to Madame Thoré the adventure which had rendered Madame de Cambure the sworn enemy of Charles; and now we are forced to leave Felina and de Monrion (to return to them again) in the midst of that violent scene produced by this impertinant note,—to follow the several movements of the other divisions of the army.

We have already said that Felina had found means to throw two notes out of the apartment where she was detained by the count. The deaf and dumb chambermaid, warned by the unnoticed glance from her mistress, was waiting for these notes in the adjoining room; she picked them up and read them. This woman was worthy to be the pupil of Madame de Cambure, or rather she was naturally the fittest auxiliary, the exact complement to Felina's extraordinary spirit.

It is worthy of remark that almost all superior minds either meet with or know how to discover these subsidiary spirits who understend them and serve them better than people of real personal merit. The Roman Cæsar had his Labinus; Napoleon had his Berthier;* and Felina her Dorothea.

When she had picked up the letters, Dorothea read them.

The first of them ran thus:

"To M. Villon, in the blue parlour.

"I am in the custody of the Count de Monrion, "who has sworn that Charles shall die, for having, "as he suspects, supplanted him. He has discovered the retreat of young Thoré. Go directly "to the Madrid avenue, in the wood of Boulonge, "where you will find Charles. Bring him away as "quickly as you can, and show him the accompanying letter. By the by, the horses are to my "carriage, take it for your use. The servant who "delivers this note to you will attend you, and "usher you into the presence of Charles."

On the second slip of paper was written:

"For Charles Thoré."

"My friend, you are free, your family yearn for "your restoration; I will keep you from them no "longer. If, after having seen what crime the man "who dreads your vengeance was on the point of "committing against you, you still doubt his perfidy, hasten home, and may you arrive there in "time to baffle the fatal scheme he meditates. "Forget not that I am obliged to send you away "My house is open all night."

Dorothea took the note, delivered it to her partner in the plot: or her pal as they call an accomplice in police slang. The domestic mentioned in the note received his instructions in less than a minute, went to look for Villon and immediately set out with him.

Villon hesitated a moment; but he was young,

* This is rather too cavalier a way to speak of one of the best soldiers in the French army. Alexander Berthier, prince of Wagram, was already a general officer in 1796, when Bonaparte arrived at head quarters at Nice to take the command of that army. He had fought in the American war under Lafayette, and besides great valour and skill, was the most orderly and systematic man at that time in the French ranks. His order and management were perhaps as serviceable as the genius and penetration of Napoleon. For eighteen years the Great Captain kept him by his side as his general quarter master and head of the staff; he made him a sovereign prince, first among his marshals, and loaded him with favours. He loved him acutely, never refused him any favour, and would have gladly given him one of his sisters in marriage. In 1814 when all his marshals deserted him to worship the new powers, he felt more grief at the ingratitude of this brilliant soldier, than at the falling off of so many others. For Berthier had been admitted more than any one to his intimate counsels, and had seen the deepest secrets of his great soul. The big dome which glitters in the air, could not stand without the structure beneath it, and who can tell how many superior spirits are fused into that name which twinkles for a thousand years in the eyes of men!

brave, and being moreover armed with pistols, and a large Catalonian knife, he resolved to go. One thought above all, put an end to his fears.

"If they want my life," said he to himself, "let them have it; did I not tell Julia that I would either restore her brother to her or die in the attempt?"

A minute or two after he had left the parlour where Felina had parted from him, Dorothea came in and searched a small dressing closet there. She then lifted up one of the small marble flags fixed in the hearth of a sculptured fire-place beneath which she found a small box, containing a letter. Then she stopped and read once more the private instructions from Felina to herself, and convinced herself that the note she had found was really the one referred to in those instructions. She read the note also, put it carefully into her pocket, took a large shawl which covered her completely, a long deep bonnet, left the house, and went for a hackney coach.

All this while the battle was raging fiercely in every part of the field: Amab was still relating his story, Villon was riding at full gallop to the wood of Boulonge, and Felina was arguing and disputing with the count.

Let us return to these.

---

## CHAPTER XXXIII.

### LITTLE MANŒUVRES.

When he had read the insulting note in which Felina had written: "Count de Monrion, you are a silly Fellow," Gustavus tore it up in a passion and trampled it under his feet.

"I have offended you," said Felina ironically to him.

"Yes," resumed Monrion, "for you have just told me a cruel truth. You are right, I was silly indeed to believe for a moment that a prayer could move you."

"Or a threat either."

"I was silly to believe that in any way whatever," said Monrion, "a word of truth was to be wrung from you."

"That is not what you said just now."

"Felina," said Monrion with emphasis, "I know not for what reason nor in what manner you wanted to mix me up in your intrigues with M. Amab. I knew I have been made ridiculous, nor do I care for that; but I will not be dishonourable.—I tell you, I will not, do you understand me? and I require to know what is the object of the farce you wanted me to play as well as that of the one you have just played yourself."

"I have told you three times already that I will not explain it," said she.

"Then why did you pretend that you meant to inform me in writing?"

"Because I required to do that to obtain in this very place, under your very eyes, some pens and paper, and send off two letters of the utmost importance to me."

"Which you have written?"—

"Yes."

"Just now?"

"Yes."

"Here?"

"Beneath your eyes."

"But where are those letters?"

Felina listened and said as she heard the rumble of a carriage driving off:

"Hark! there is the first setting out."

"What!" cried Monrion—"that door half opened for a moment."

"A moment, and an open door," said Felina, "have decided very great events."

"But the other letter," said Monrion, rushing forward to leave the boudoir.

"There it goes likewise," said she, making a sign to Gustavus as the sound of the street gate closing met their ears.

The count came back into the room with his doubled fists pressed to his brow. That man at that moment must have had the principles of good breeding very deeply rooted that he did not strangle the She-Tiger at once. Finally, he recovered himself a little, and said as he fell upon a chair:

"Always foiled—always duped! And you for ever the same shameless, the same worthless—"

"And you the same violent, insulting, unjust—"

"Forget not, madam, that it is my honour perhaps that I am come to protect, and ask you to account for. You told me, Felina, whenever the day shall come for me to speak in the name of my honour, you would tell me all. Have you done so?"

"When I told you that, Gustavus, I likewise said to you: 'Never make a bad use of the power which passion may have over me, and when I ask you to grant me an hour to plead my justification, grant it me.' Now I did apply to you for that hour, a moment ago, an hour to determine the fate of my life. This hour you refused me, and how did you refuse it?"

She glanced around her and next upon herself, as if to indicate her captivity.

"Oh! you are free at present," said Monrion to her.

"That is useless to me," she returned with disdain, "the mischief is done."

"What!" exclaimed the young prodigal, "another bad action?"

"You drove me to it."

"I?"

"Yes! had I but possessed an hour of liberty, I might have found my safety in the safety of the rest; you compelled me to seek it in their ruin."

"But what then have you done?"

"I cannot tell it you."

"Oh! you shall speak!" exclaimed Monrion with violence.

"I will speak, for I have a terrible dread of a blow," said Felina, "but I shall not tell the truth."

"You must and shall tell the truth."

"But how will you know that it is the truth, count? There is a gross and brutal address which induces people to say, when they want to force an avowal: 'Confess the truth—I know all.'—If those who have recourse to this stupid practice have energy enough to force a woman to speak through fear whilst they hold her in their power, they have then the chance that she will not dare to deceive them, for fear of being confounded, and they sometimes learn a part of what they desire to know. But you came here loudly proclaiming that you know nothing, that you understand nothing that is going on, and you want me to divulge everything. That is really too foolish."

Gustavus grumbled between his teeth; just so, Samson must have roared after Dahlila had cut his hair.

"Come," resumed Felina, "let us argue the matter coolly. Are you determined to believe all I am about to tell you."

"Your language and your looks betray you: you are going to prevaricate."

"Then, let us drop the subject."

Monrion unfastened his cravat and threw it off

"I am choking"—he muttered.

"Do you suffer pain, Gustavus?"

"Its very slow, is it not?" said he repressing with his hand the violent pulsations of his heart; "I am a hard one to kill."

"Have I passed so many nights at your bedside, Gustavus, for you to say this to me?"

"Ah!" cried Gustavus in a panting voice, "you have answered beforehand to those who will accuse you of having killed me."

"You are unjust and cruel, sir; you know better than any one how much I have been calumniated.

"Yes, certainly, and calumny will pursue you still—people will say."

He paused a moment as if collecting strength for an usual rebuke.

She bent her head down in dismay, for even the gloomy mind of that pernicious woman could not shut out every gleam of conscience.

"People will say" he continued, "poor Monrion! he died at the age of twenty-four worn out by riot, debauchery, nightly excesses, and the most dissolute pleasures—poor fool!" Why can I not issue from my tomb to reply to them: "You are mistaken—no, no—that Felina whom you accuse is neither the dishevelled wanton, nor the insatiable Messalina you imagine her to be, it was not through the senses, but through the heart she killed me! Love her, and you will have in her a character of ice, too proud of her beauty not to prefer it even to her happiness. What you will really find in her, is a spirit of fire which will wither all your most natural feelings, which will kill the faith of your soul, and reduce it to a barren soil, in which nothing that is young and fresh can thrive. You will love her, and that evil tongue will intoxicate you with words formed to lure you with the promise of happiness. And then when you shall feel your soul expand to those images, she will damp your ardour with some cutting mockery, some shameful doubt which will chill your heart, as the frost nips the flower in the bud when first it opens to the sun. You will believe in her, because she will one day have amazed you with the boldness of her sincerity; and on the morrow you will distrust everything she may say, from the empty and useless lies she will indulge in. You shall expect her gentle and confiding, she will come to you jealous and wild with anger. You shall fear to see her wrathful and irritated, she will appear before you tender and resigned. Yesterday she was by your side, and to-morrow, you hope at least, she will be near your. No! she has started off and fled a thousand miles away. You flatter yourself that you are released from such a torment, it bursts upon you again, more alluring, more radiant than Paradise! Every day some new surprise will break and shatter your joy, irritate your anxiety, and deceive both your hopes and your fears. Your thirst is excited every hour, but never satisfied. No, she did not kill me through the senses, but through my heart, which grated against all the angles of her whims—my heart shaken in every sense like a toy in a child's hand, and which, now bleeding—and full of pain, stifles me—stifles me—stifles me."

Monrion, exhausted by this excess of passion, fell back on the divan, his panting breath showing how much the unceasing torture in which he had lived had debilitated him. Felina approached him and wanted him to inhale from a bottle of salts. He pushed her away.

"Ah!" she said bitterly, "you do not love me any more."

Gustavus sat up and looked at her bewildered, scarcely believing she could have dared to utter the word *love*, after what he had just spoken.

The fiend smiled gently at him.

"Come, Gustavus! be calm—I seriously entreat you—I was wrong, I confess—but am I alone guilty?—And since you understand me so well, you must know that I would have perished before I would have yielded to a desire expressed in such a tone and manner as you employed!"

"Have I not seen my prayers as often rejected as my threats?—And in the same manner as you have defied me till I had raised my dagger at you, have you not suffered me to drag myself at your feet and writhe there in tears, without either my threats or my entreaties obtaining anything from you?"

"Hear me, Gustavus," said Felina sorrowfully, let us not dispute about the past, I might complain like you, but I will not. You have related to me the account of your new amours. I heard you patiently; I submitted, and did not reproach you; now you come to question me about my life. Have you the right to do so?"

"I have the right with respect to you, Felina, as I have the right with respect to any man who mixes my name in any intrigue—only with a man we have advantages."

"Which I would offer to any but yourself, Gustavus. You well know, that I consider women have a right to avenge their wrongs or to defend their honour with the same weapons as men, I have more than once proved the reasons. But you would not accept a challenge from me?"

"From you?—"

"And I myself—I could not." She stopped, a tear rose to her eye, and she said mournfully:

"To die by your hand—that would perhaps be better."

"Ah!" cried Monrion, "are you come to that—to wish to die?"

"Perhaps," said Felina in a firm voice. "How can it be helped? my life has missed its aim—you have ceased to love me."

"That word again!" said Monrion, "do you think I am one of those who are to be drawn back with such vulgar appeals, to a passion which you have entirely drained."

"No," said Felina softly. "I say this not intending it as a reproach to you, but as a truth. Besides, the fault rests with me. At all events, I tell you again, the object of my life has been missed."

"I confess I cannot understand you. I shall soon be dead, Felina, and you will remain behind me, rich—young, and beautiful."

"But defeated and baffled."

"Defeated?"

"Yes, and twice by yourself."

"By me?"

"Yes, said Felina; but already you are quite unconcerned in what is about to happen."

"What then is going to happen?"

Felina advanced with a friendly motion towards Monrion, and then added with gentleness:

"Leave me here by myself, and I promise you that nothing which will happen here this night shall reach you in any way."

"I should prefer to judge for myself of events; I should be surer to see my honour issue forth safe and sound from the ordeal."

"Trust to me, Gustavus, do not venture upon a dangerous proof."

"Dangerous—how so?"

"To tell you that, I should have to reveal my projects, and that I must not do. Only, I warn you. If you remain—beware."

Whilst she was thus speaking, Felina appeared to listen.

"Ah!" cried Gustavus, "is the hour then come for some great treachery?"

"Not yet," said Felina rising. "But hear me well, Gustavus—for the last time I ask you, will you let me be my own mistress and act as I think fit?"

"No—for the last time I intend to see with my own eyes how far you will dare to carry your designs, whatever they may be."

"You are resolved."

"Yes."

"Well," said Felina to him, "curse nobody but yourself in your dying hour, if execrations and remorse should sit heavy on your conscience; for the moment you refuse to let me act alone, you must perforce become my accomplice."

"Felina, I have been sufficiently warned, and all your artifices shall not avail you."

"You have been sufficiently warned, Count de Monrion, and you will leave your honour in this house."

"You are crazy."

"Gustavus," said Felina with a desperate effort, "I have still an hour before me—I have pity on you—I will tell you all; you will know me at last, and then indeed I hope you will consent to go."

"We shall see that," said Monrion aloud, whilst inwardly he thought: "I wonder what new fable she is contriving?"

For some minutes this singular woman continued silent, her elbow resting on the marble chimney-piece. She was calculating her means of operation. We should be glad to initiate our readers into the secret thoughts of this woman, and certainly, were it only a figure of our imagination, we should not hesitate to do so, even at the risk of ascribing improbable or flagitious motives to Felina's manner of speaking and acting. But the She-Tiger is a real portrait, drawn from life, and we are relating only, not inventing. And truly, it would be impossible for us to say whether the warning she had just given to Monrion was one of those impulses of genuine pity which are sometimes met with in the most perverted hearts, or whether it was only another of those insulting bravadoes which she was sure would not be trusted to, and which justified her afterwards when she said: "I had given you warning, it was you who had the rashness to encounter the peril."

However that may have been, Felina's meditation did not long endure; she rang the bell and said to Gustavus:

"I was to have supped out; allow me to put off this dress now become useless."

A chamberwoman came in.

"I rang for Dorothea."

"She is gone out, madam."

"Without asking my permision?" said Felina angrily—"Dorothea takes liberties which I cannot allow. Let her account be settled to-night. I am going to sup here."

The chamberwoman curtseyed and left the room. Monrion said to Felina:

"You forget that Dorothea is doubtless gone out to deliver one of your letters, and this mode of enquiring whether she is come back lacks your habitual address."

"Read my note again, M. de Monrion," answered Felina pulling another bell.

"What is the meaning of this?"

"That Dorothea is not gone out at all, that she has had no letter to carry, and that here she is."

And truly, Dorothea came in by another door.

Monrion turned round. A stealthy signal had been exchanged between the mistress and the servant. The latter had probably succeeded in what her mistress had desired her to do, for a smile of fiendish delight swept like lightning over Felina's mouth.

"Zounds!" exclaimed Monrion, who did not wish to seem either astonished or dissatisfied; "since Dorothea was there why did you ask about her?"

"To prove to you that you will not guess anything in my manner of acting; to prove to you that you will learn nothing except what I choose to acknowledge. Besides," she added taking a decanter and pouring some of the water into a glass, "you are so incredulous that, fully persuaded I am lying and continually deceiving, you would believe that this was poison if I said it was pure water, and that it was pure water if I told you it was poison."

"If I wanted to know the truth, I would request you to drink some."

"And I, like Cleopatra, would drink the poisoned cup."

"I, for my part, would look on and wait like Rodogune."

"Which shows you that your presumptive proof would be none at all. But I entreat you, Gustavus, to cease these trials of wit—we have far more serious things to treat of. Will you go for one moment into the room adjoining and allow me to dress myself."

"Formerly you permitted me to be present."

"I rather fear," said Felina smiling, "that this implies a suspicion and not a regret."

"I shall leave you to guess which."

"My vanity shall be chooser: I wish to believe it is a regret, and therefore I will not requite the last of your good feelings by a refusal. You may remain."

Felina took shelter behind a splendid screen of Berlin tapestry worked with the needle.

"I am in your way?" said the count.

"It is done," said Felina reappearing immediately, as if some fairy wand had conjured her male attire into a full sized *robe de chambre* of black satin, which she wrapped about her. "It is done," she continued tightening her waist with a flexible girdle with gold tassels. "But, in the situation in which we stand."—

"Modesty?" said Monrion jokingly.

"Why are you so rude to me," said Felina sadly, whilst in spite of himself the young nobleman contemplated that wonderful beauty.

He would not tell her it was precisely to escape from the power she exercised over him that he had, in a manner, sought refuge in that sarcastic taunt; so he replied:

"How then would you have me interpret these rigid precautions?"

"When a woman has ceased to be loved, she can never adorn her beauty too much."

"That is a stretch of modesty, which I presume you will scarcely pretend to claim."

"I am not vain enough to expect to make you believe anything."

"Except what is about to happen here."

"That you shall see."

"And is it so very extraordinary?"

"It is only an appointment between two persons of your acquaintance."

"A rare kind of appointment, no doubt?"

"Why no—a very natural appointment between those who love."

"Supposing it to be so natural, how does it happen that it is to produce results so important to you or me?"

"Because," said Felina, whilst a small table was pushed in with two covers, "because if the meeting is a usual one, the circumstances which have brought it about are very strange."

"It is a story."

"Which opens at your house, which was to have closed without you, and which, now perhaps, will only be unravelled by your agency."

"I am all attention."

Felina threw herself back in her seat, and looking at Monrion with her gayest smile, she began by saying:

"What a pity we have quarreled, Gustavus;

there might be at the bottom of all this the most delightful bit of roguery. But psha! you have left your goshawk plumes in the birdlime of the china dealer's yard; you are so nice in your honour so virtuous; a truce therefore with such folly—let us talk soberly."

She went up to the supper table, and said to the chambermaid:

"Take that cover away

"Is it my presence that renders it useless, who was it intended for?"

"For nobody but you, probably. Why did you lay the second cover, Lucy?"

"For the count."

"The count does not sup with me any more—it might expose him to evil tongues."

"And it might also be tedious to you, Felina."

"I hate you too much at present," said Felina laughing, "for you to be tedious to me."

"Suppose I asked leave to sup with you," replied Monrion in the same tone, "should I be in your way?"

"Not in the least."

"Which means quite the reverse. So, will you let me sup with you?"

"Leave the cover, Lucy," said Felina eagerly.

"I am dreadfully importunate, am I not?" said he drawing close to the table.

"Nobody can be more charming."

"Vexation quite becomes you."

"Your tyrannical looks suit you admirably, Gustavus."

"And they inspire you with inward longings to tear my eyes out."

"They almost provoke me to try and fascinate you," returned she with her fine eyes softly shaded, "if I did not know there are things in this world altogether impossible."

"Who taught you that word, Felina?"

"You, yourself," she returned helping him with a ravishing grace.

"Ah! that is true," said the count; "I recollect our discussion on the subject of Miss Thoré.—You are perfectly magical in the art of transitions, for I presume it is Julia you mean to speak about."

"Really, I was not thinking of it; a long time since I had recognized that there were things impossible for me, when you taught me that there were likewise some beyond your attainment."

"This relates to the disclosures you were going to make?"

"Entirely, and the time is come to speak."

They conversed in this manner both of them, with smiles on their lips and their souls embittered with gall; yet nothing in Felina betrayed the aim she contemplated. She had tolerated Monrion's presence so readily that one might have been led to believe that his presence was requisite, and yet she seemed to have no desire to detain him. If, on the other side, any one had imagined that she was capable of extracting from the slightest circumstance, a means of beguiling de Monrion; if any one had thought that in case of need, she would call the intoxication of the banquet to the assistance of her infernal schemes, one would have relinquished that suspicion as one watched the indifference with which she suffered Gustavus to act as he liked, without urging or exciting him to anything.

Felina's accomplices had left the supper room, each of them carrying off the order of march to be followed. The battle raged on every point, and the dark-minded woman had just received the important intelligence that her grand manœuvre had proved successful. She had singled out Monrion for herself, as the most dangerous of the enemy to be encountered. From sentence to sentence, from retreat to retreat, she contrived with the most refined art to entice him into the position she wanted, the ground on which she felt she should conquer him, and she reflected awhile before she engaged in this last decisive attack.

Monrion, however, waited for a few moments, and seeing that Felina did not hasten to speak, thus resumed the dialogue:

"Well, tell us at length what are these revelations that you promised to communicate to me."

"I am preparing to do so, count, but you must permit me to go back a little," said Felina.

"The night is my own, and I am all attention—speak."

---

## CHAPTER XXXIV.

### GRAND MANŒUVRES.

"Do you remember, Gustavus," said Felina, knitting her dark eyebrows, "do you remember the day when I had the fancy to ask you for a porcelain cup which still stands on the *etagère* in your drawing room?"

"I remember it well."

"Do you recollect the scene between us which ensued after that refusal, and the last word I spoke to you?"

"Perfectly well. It was a threat."

"You are mistaken. I promised you a lesson."

"Be it so, let us not stop to differ about words; it is then that promised lesson that now serves as the starting point of what is about to take place?"

"You have guessed it. I wanted to show you that there are men ready to grant me more than you denied me."

"If you computed the past as among the items in the account," said Gustavus bitterly, "you would have much to obtain from them before you could compare them to me."

"Learn this much, Gustavus," rejoined Felina with a disdainful smile, "the moment a man appeals to the past to defend the present, it is because either his heart or his coffers are empty, according to the mode of requiting the love he wishes to keep. 'After all I have done for you, can you suspect my love'—is a sentence which means nothing more than this: 'You have had from me all you could expect.' Now I conceived that such was my case with you, and that was a condition I did not choose to tolerate. I forget now how it was that the story of M. Amab and of the passion which had inspired his masterpiece was related to me at that period, but I longed to bring you acquainted with it, I longed to show you the value a man may set upon his love. I asked you for that picture, and I sent you to M. Amab's atelier that you might judge for yourself what large sacrifices a man is capable of to the woman he admires, a poor man, likewise, to whom you offered a fortune. You remember the ill success of your application. It was then that in my turn I attempted this illustrious conquest, and that I wrote to M. Amab a letter the consequences of which for the present it is not my purpose to explain, but which proved to me I should not be more successful than you."

"Ah!" cried Monrion in a tone of real pleasure, "you were refused, were you, what had been denied to me for a hundred thousand francs? How humiliating."

"More humiliating than you can believe. And, as I wanted to punish you for your refusal, I likewise wished to punish M. Amab for his."

"Plague upon it!" said the count, "the plot begins to thicken. Go on."

A RIDE THROUGH THE WOOD OF BOULOGNE.

Had any one observed Felina coolly, it would have been only at that moment that he could have suspected the desire she had to mislead Monrion's reason, and overrule it by some other power than his mind; she poured out a few drops of wine for him with a look of indifference and continued earnestly:

"Yes, my friend. I felt a moment of unspeakable vexation—almost of spite—and I applied to you to revenge me. I entreated you to deprive Amab of that adored model whose image nothing in the world could wrest from him. I was foiled again on that side—you deserted my cause like a coward. Then it was I resolved to punish that gentleman in a different manner. Illicit means having proved entirely powerless, I turned towards the moral influences; I committed a very good action. I denounced to Charles Thoré his sister's intrigue with M. Amab. None was ever so unfortunate as I am. The very day on which my disclosure was to have borne its fruits, Charles disappears almost miraculously, carried off I know not by whom."

"Indeed?" said Monrion, striving to collect and adjust the dates of all these abortive attempts, and who fancied he saw in them much confusion;—"but all this appears to me to have occurred very rapidly."

"Is it not so? and yet I was outdone in speed by that gentleman. Ah! Gustavus, he will be the best man among you all for skill in directing an intrigue. He has a mind always prepared for repartee. One last resource still remained open to me; I was going to have recourse to it this evening—and this evening, I was already defeated."

"I understood you very little before," said the young nobleman, "and now I don't understand you at all."

"This evening I meant to warn this virtuous family of the intrigue existing between Amab and Julia. Well, this evening, M. Amab demanded her in marriage. You brought me this news yourself, and you may remember my anger and astonishment on hearing the news."

"That is true. But tell me, Felina, when you engaged in this desperate struggle with M. Amab, had you no other motive, no other incitement than the provocation of being refused the picture he disdained to sell me?"

"I wanted to be revenged."

"Of a refusal?"

"Yes."

"But had you then any reason to believe that such refusal in your case could not occur."

Felina shewed her hand to Monrion:

"Have I not told you that the very day any other man should obtain in my heart the place which you occupy there, I would throw this ring away?"

"So, M. Amab—"

"M. Amab did not set a price on that picture which I had to reject. On that side he is unapproachable. He loves Julia."

"Plague upon it!" cried Monrion, his love is very awful!"

"Which did not, however, prevent M. Amab from thinking me handsome, and from telling me so far more frequently than I could have wished to hear it. But, as for paying a sacrifice of any mark for the love of Madame de Cambure, that only suits a lion like Monrion."

"Did he say that?" exclaimed Gustavus passionately.

"No, for I am not the woman who would suffer such insolence; but this is his thought, it speaks in his manners, in his disdain, in that inexplicable something, which we feel and perceive, but cannot define."

Supper went on, and during the restlessness of mind into which Felina had lured the Count, she had contrived to magnetise the vigilance he usually employed to watch over himself. She had filled his glass several times—and he had reached that point when a man can still give himself warning that he must not continue to indulge: a point which, when once it is passed, opens before it a gulf of folly, into which he plunges like a madman.

Felina availed herself of the burst of anger which she had excited in Monrion, and continued her story:

"Yes, my dear Gustavus, we are beaten; I by a gentleman, to whom I would have disdained to grant a minute to defend himself, and you by a little girl who has persuaded you of her seraphic virtue."

"Faith," said Monrion laughing, "you are probably not so ignominiously beaten after all since he is to marry her."

"Oh, no," replied Felina, "he is not going to marry her."

"How?"

"He is to elope with her—or rather she is to fly to him."

"When is that to be?"

"This very night."

"What meant the demand of her hand?"

"A mere pretext for a last visit to the house."

"Are you sure of this?"

"Come," returned Felina, leaning her elbow gracefully on the table, "let us con. the thing over as Figaro says. Have you seen Julia, this evening?"

"No."

"That's it! said Felina, "I was sure of it."

"How?"

"Let us proceed," she resumed: "M. Amab, one night when you called upon the Thoré family, was speaking sententiously I believe, to the parents?"

"I left him there thus occupied."

"Well, added Felina throwing herself back in her chair and laughing, "during that very time, the young maiden was making her escape."

"That is impossible," cried Monrion emphatically; "such an elopement—such a flight—why it would be a crime provided against by the law."

"And for that reason, M. Amab will be perfectly innocent of it; he knows as well where to conceal the young lady, as he knew where to hide her brother."

"Why he must be a demon or a returned transport then."

"I will confess to you, Gustavus, that this man has struck me with awe and admiration; and when Jean related to me his last plot, I bent my head in pity for you."

"Jean?"

"Did you not place him in Amab's service to satisfy yourself of the truth of what I had told you?"

"Yes."

"And afterwards did you not expel him, for having delivered to you a letter which confirmed the dreadful truth?"

"Well, he has continued in the service of his new master, and it was he who contrived every thing for this new and wonderful elopement."

"The count looked at her amazed, but without speaking.

"Gustavus," said Felina eagerly, "give me your honor, and promise me not to convert into a mortal quarrel, what, at other times, you would have treated as a capital joke."

"I cannot give you such a pledge."

"In that case I must say no more."

"But if my honor be engaged in asking satisfaction for this gentleman's behaviour," said Gustavus, whose head began to be heated, "I must punish him."

"You cannot punish him for his actions until you know them, and then I refuse to tell them to you."

"I begin to understand you. Did you not tell me that I should leave my honor in this house?—Felina—Felina—I must know all—I insist upon your telling me—it must be!"

"Oh?" said she, earnestly, drawing herself more closely to Gustavus, with that familiar abandonment which sometimes rendered her so persuasive, and speaking to him in a low voice, "if you would assist me to revenge myself, if you would revenge yourself at the same time—not by a duel, the man does not deserve to receive such a lesson from you—but as we revenge ourselves of a mean artist of an abject shopman;—but no—I feel you would not. You are no longer capable of a bold resolution."

"If I have been duped, Felina, I will have vengeance; of that you may be sure. Only, I shall retain the right to choose my vengeance."

Felina, who was a prey to the most violent agitation, exclaimed, without answering the count:

"Ah! there is a woman, to whom I likewise must humble myself. Ah! Gustavus, Miss Thoré acts like the Cid, she opens her career with a master-stroke."

"Shall you soon have done with these exclamations?" answered De Monrion sharply. "Come, tell me—what has been brewing?"

"Count," said Felina, placing herself again before him—"let us do better than seek for vengeance—let us laugh and look on. And yet," she continued, stamping furiously, "to be made such gross dupes!—it is dreadful! But what's to be done?" she added contemptuously, "with a man who admits of none but that stupid vengeance, the duel, and who will go, duped, mocked, ridiculous, nay, even dishonoured, to a meeting there to be wounded—perhaps to be disfigured."

"Oh! speak, speak, Felina," said Monrion, whose impatience and vivid anger increased every moment. "What signify these broken words, these lamentations, these threats, and what has Jean had to do in all this?"

"And what would you think," resumed the arch-fiend, leaning over him, and half mocking him with her smile, her look, and an impertinent shake of her head, "what would you think of a little girl who, fully persuaded of the love she has excited in the Count de Monrion, has made use of him to hide, not only her amours with another, but even her flight with him."

"You have lost your wits," he replied.

"That is possible," resumed Felina, with the same air of mockery. "But what would you think of a former valet de chambre belonging to M. de Monrion, who has actually come to my house, where the count is well known, to here, in the name of the Count de Monrion, a small apartment intended to screen the private amours of one M. Amab?"

"What!" roared the count, "has that rascal dared to commit such an atrocity?"

"What would you think," continued Felina, "of M. Amab, if, whilst he was soothing the father and mother of the young lady with his splendid protestations, the girl had stolen out of her house to come to the little apartment of which M. Amab has the key, and Count de Monrion the empty honours."

"I tell you it is impossible," cried Gustavus, whose head was bewildered by this tissue of intrigues and entanglements.

"And what would you think of M. de Monrion," resumed Felina, tittering, "if whilst all this is going on, he came and harshly demanded a woman whom he once fondly loved, to tell him all she knew about the honour of that dear young lady and the sufferings of good M. Amab?"

"I tell you it is all impossible."

"Should you like to see it?" said Felina.

"Yes. And to prevent your preparing some shameful deceit, I must see at this very moment."

"This very moment, be it so. And when you shall have seen it, what then?"

"I will wait for that man, and he shall pay for this insolence with his life!"

"And what of me," she said, "who will revenge me? No, no, M. de Monrion, that is not how I understand it."

"What then would you have after all?"

"Hear me, Gustavus," resumed Felina, "I have been insulted and despised by that man and his Julia. Women like me are made only for men like yourself. That is what they say. But, as for those precious conquests, those chaste beauties who spit on the face of a lost woman like me, men like you either respect or marry them; for I know you thought of doing it."

"A truce with your taunts and insults," said Monrion passionately; "only prove to me that what you have already told me is true, and I will as certainly evince that I know how to be revenged."

The emphatic tone in which Gustavus had uttered these last words sufficiently attested tha the galling satire of this unsparing woman had penetrated into his mind. His eye was as troubled and bewildered as his thoughts.

"What must you see to be convinced of the truth of my assertions."

"One thing only," replied the count, "Julia away from home."

"You shall have more than you ask," said Felina.

She pulled the bell sharply and said to the chambermaid:

"Tell the street-door porter to come up immediately."

The porter made his appearance a minute after.

"M. Guillaume," said Felina to him with vivacity, "has not the small apartment above mine been let for some days?"

"Yes, madam."

"Who was it came to hire it?"

"Why, madam," replied the porter confused, "I know not whether I ought—"

"Answer frankly; the count will not be angry."

"Certainly not," said de Monrion.

"Well, then, my lord, it was Jean, your valet de chambre, who came here and hired it in your name, and so it is entered in my books."

"Never," roared Gustavns, "never was such insolence heard of before. And what did the rascal say?"

"Blessed Virgin!" cried the porter still alarmed. I really—know not whether—"

"Speak, speak," said Felina, "it is now my turn to allow you."

"Well, he told me that my lord, the count, desired to have the apartment without anybody knowing it, because it communicates with that belonging to Mademoiselle de Cambure by means of a private staircase."

"You see, count," observed Felina pointedly, "we are put upon the stage in a most respectful manner: you engage private apartments communicating with mine; the measure is so artfully cautious, that poor M. Guillaume is quite perplexed to own it."

"But once for all," resumed Gustavus furiously, "what has been going on this week past with regard to that apartment?"

"Nothing, until this evening. But this evening—"

"Well, this evening?" said the count.

"Two ladies came here, one of them old the other young; the old one came into my lodge and asked me for the key of the apartment hired for M. de Monrion; she delivered me the letter which Jean had told me would be given to the persons who should present themselves as occupants of the apartment."

"And the two ladies went up?"

"Yes, my lord; only, after a short time, the elder lady came down again and delivered the key to me, saying:"

"If M. Amab (a gentleman who sometimes meets Mademoiselle de Cambure) should apply for it, you may give him this key."

"Ah?" cried De Monrion, whose altered features testified to the boiling rage he was in; "and is M. Amab arrived?"

"Not yet, my lord."

"Well, go and fetch me that key, go,—the apartment has been hired in my name,—I have a right to enter it, I presume."

But who can fathom the depth of woman's guile? Scarcely were Monrion and Felina left alone, before the latter suddenly changed her tone and manner; and instead of seeking to kindle the anger of Gustavus, she went up to him in alarm, whilst he was striding across the room with long ejaculations of fury, and said to him:—

"What would you do, for heaven's sake? Why do you want to go up to that chamber?"

"My dear Felina," said Monrion to her, looking at her with supreme disdain, "I am not the dupe of your vindictive vanity; a woman does not pursue a man like M. Amab with the headlong animosity you have shown, for merely refusing to satisfy one of her whims?"

"What do you insinuate?" resumed Felina, in a voice of embarrassment.

"I mean that all this anger bespeaks some cruel affront. I understand the lesson you wanted to give me; you have missed your aim, I am sorry for it; although, after all, such a successor as M. Amab is a proof how little you esteem me."

"Can you believe, Gustavus?" said Felina, in accents such as a woman speaks in when she bends her head beneath the burden of her fault; "can you believe——?"

Monrion, who felt persuaded from this well feigned confusion that he had guessed the truth, hastily interrupted her."

"I pardon you, Felina," he said; "but if I pardon you, I cannot forgive that gentleman! Ah! he assisted you to deceive me, on one side, and on the other, he no doubt was laughing at my respectful sighs with his fair Julia. By all the fiends!" cried Monrion, with a Satanic smile, "let him laugh who wins."

At that moment Dorothea came in and held out the key to her mistress; the latter strove to get possession of it, but Monrion snatched it from her.

"Stay—stay, I implore you," said Felina in vain; "I am not guilty, I take God to witness!"

"Enough, madam, enough," said the Count, pushing her from him; "you have even forgotten how to play a farce!"

And thereupon he went out, and hastily went up to the floor above. The next moment he entered the apartment, the key of which had just been delivered to him. It was at that time close upon eleven o'clock.

Heaven protect thee, unhappy Julia!

## CHAPTER XXXV

### VIRTUE IN DANGER.

Let us go back and see what had taken place at M. Thoré's house since Monrion had departed from it, leaving Amab behind?

The latter, as we have said, had considered that a full avowal of all that had passed between him, Charles and Madame de Cambure, was indispensable to explain with sufficient clearness to the china dealer and his wife the danger which threatened their son. He had therefore entered upon the narrative of that long and unlikely story, being interrupted every moment by the astonished exclamations of these worthy people. Amab could not lower his voice sufficiently, they thought, for it seemed to them that the walls of their house ought to fall in at the sound of those shameful exposures.

Several times Madame Thoré had partly opened the door of the drawing room to see whether her daughter, urged by a very excusable curiosity, were not upon the watch to overhear what they were saying. The first and second time that she did so, she saw her daughter setting in a small boudoir on the other side of the dining room, and to all appearance busily engaged with a piece of needlework. But the last time the mother looked out, the boudoir was empty and the light extinguished.

Madame de Thoré inquired for her daughter; the maidservant answered:

"My young mistress bid me tell you, madam, that she was tired, and was going to bed."

Madame Thoré, being now released from the fear of her daughter's listening to or overhearing a word of such impure adventures, returned to the saloon to learn the rest of them, and to advise with Amab the best means of rescuing Charles from the vindictive persecution of Madame de Cambure.

The discussion lasted some time, which is not to be wondered at; but that which is really surprising is that Julia,—knowing that she was the subject of so much interest in the saloon—should have retired to her chamber to seek repose and sleep. Love in general keeps young gents awake; and the truth is Julia was not asleep at all, and if she had employed this excuse, it was because she had to conceal something of unusual importance.

And truly whilst her mother and father were listening to M. Amab, an elderly woman had come and rung softly at her chamber door. To look at her so shy, so serious, so modestly wrapped up, to hear her speak in a voice so soft and free, none could have suspected she was the confidential servant of a very fine lady, the pretended deaf and dumb girl before whom Monrion used to speak without ceremony.

She had asked for Mademoiselle Julia Thoré, and the young lady unaccustomed to receive personal messages, wanted to call her mother; but the woman had suddenly prevented her saying in a whisper:

"If you wish to save your brother, send the girl away, and don't say a word."

The maidservant on a sign from Julia had withdrawn, and the disguised woman had then said in continuation:

"Here is a letter from M. Amab. He is at present in the house, is he not?"

"Certainly."

"Your father and mother are both engaged with him, I believe?"

"He is conversing with them at least resumed Julia."

"Very well. They would never consent to let you come alone, and it is only on the condition of your being alone that your brother can be restored to liberty. Read this."

Julia unfolded Amab's letter and read it, she knew the writing in a moment, for she had read and re-read a hundred times over, the note to her mother in which he had refused the price of his portraits, and although this letter repeated precisely what the old woman had just said to her, Julia hesitated.

"Make up your mind," continued the old woman; "another hour and it may be too late. Your brother's life is in danger; if he die, you will have none but yourself to accuse."

The merest prudence ought to have directed Julia to summon her father, her mother, to have had that woman arrested on the spot, and thereby to have compelled her to divulge the secret of Charles's hiding place. Dorothy took alarm at Julia's hesitation, and immediately added:

"There is one thing which I must tell you, and which M. Amab would not venture to avow, it is that unless Charles be restored to liberty this evening, and if your father and mother should be warned, M. Amab himself will be struck to-morrow. So, resolve."

Many men, older by several years than Julia, men of resolute minds, have not always in presence of such fearful threats and exposures sufficient self-command to escape so vulgar a trap; can we then wonder that Julia should be caught therein? can we then wonder that when her friendship for her brother was made the medium of this deceit, and her love even for Amab appealed to, that she yielded to her desire to save them both.

"What is to be done then?" said she.

"You must come with me to the rue Jaubert; but," added Dorothy quickly, seeing Julia prepared to accompany her, "nobody must know that you have been out; it is but half an hour's business at most. I will go before, and wait for you a few doors down the street."

Dorothy departed, and it was a few moments after this that Julia said to the maidservant to tell her mother that she had retired for the night. The same moment she gained the private staircase leading to the warerooms by which she was enabled to leave the house without being observed.

The clock was striking ten.

Meanwhile the conversation was continued in the drawing-room, and the conclusion of this private interview was as follows, on the part of the family:

"Engage your word of honour to this lady that Charles shall leave Paris to-morrow for a long time. Tell her that before he sets out he shall likewise pledge his word as an honest man never to divulge a word of the deplorable adventure between him and that lady; tell her that you yourself would disown him as a brother, if ever he broke that promise; give that lady every possible assurance that her secret shall be well kept; but warn her at the same time that unless Charles be restored to us this very night, the magistrates shall have notice to-morrow; we are but simple tradespeople, but we shall find powerful protectors: were it only M. de Montaleu, who, we are sure, will take this matter to heart. In him she will find an enemy who will be too happy to have an opportunity to be revenged for the injury she has done him in the person of the young Count de Monrion. Then, when Charles has been restored to us through you, we will think of your happiness and Julia's, for we must not conceal from you, M. Amab, that if your proposal is flattering to us, we think we can assure you likewise, Julia, on her side, is not indifferent to it."

After this last speech, Amab, bound by his confidential communications, bound by his formal proposal, bound, too, by the obligations he had just fastened on himself, and which no longer allowed him to submit to Felina's fascinations, Amab left for the Rue Jaubert, to convey to Madame de Cambure the ultimate decision of the Thoré family

## CHAPTER XXXVI.

### TRIUMPH AND DEFEAT.

It was nearly half-past ten when Victor left M. Thoré's house to wait upon Felina. Just as he reached her abode, that is to say a few minutes after Monrion had entered the apartment overhead, Amab found Felina ready to set out. Had she foreseen Amab's arrival? The thing is not likely, but she expected to see him that very night for she said to him, as he entered:—

"I was going to call upon you, sir, and I am delighted to see you."

"What would that visit have been occasioned by?"

"The necessity of extricating myself from a false position, and which I can no longer maintain, owing to the vigilance and activity of some one else. The time is come to restore Charles to his family."

"What is the powerful reason which thus obliges you?"

"The very simple reason, that some one has discovered that Charles was in my power"

"Has M. de Monrion at length suspected the mystery?"

"M. de Monrion has other things to attend to than to busy himself about Charles. The person I allude to is neither more nor less than M. Villon, from whom I this evening received a visit very unceremonious and full of threats, and who has allowed me but four hours to take my measures and set Charles at liberty. I asked him to let me have these four hours, sir, to enable me to deliver Charles into your hands. You alone, as his accomplice, have power to require that silence of him which I have a right to expect from both of you. Besides, what he might possibly have refused to M. Amab, he will, I am convinced, readily grant to his future brother-in-law, to his sister's betrothed—"

"What!" cried Amab, embarrassed, "do you know--"

"I know all, sir; "I have seen M. de Monrion. Be so good as to attend me, for it is some distance from this to the wood of Boulogne and then back again to this house; and I should not like, by a few minutes' delay, to have the police invade my house, and expose me to a scandalous uproar. It would not be just, I think, that I should always be made your victim, and in everything."

"My victim, madam!" said the painter with a look of surprise.

"I was the victim of your contempt and indiscretion, sir, as you perfectly well know; I am still that of your false oaths, for to them I have sacrificed a love on which I had learned to depend; and I shall still be the victim of your wavering habits, unless Charles Thoré is restored to his family in a few hours."

"Come then," said Amab, "I am ready to attend you."

They went down together, and set off for the wood of Boulogne, in a carriage which was standing at the door of the hotel.

Having reached this point in our history, we should like to let our readers be present at the mysterious and dismal dialogue between Thoré and his wife, who continued to converse in whispers, lest a single word of theirs might reach Julia's ears. They considered it most fortunate that she had withdrawn to her chamber, and that they were not called upon to reply to the questions she would have put to them, if by chance she had been informed of their hopes of soon seeing her brother again.

In like manner, we would fain let our readers be present at the scene which at this moment was passing between Monrion and Julia. We ought also to tell them the result of the letter which Villon had delivered to Charles; but as the narrative rather aims at showing the character of a woman too notorious, than to relate incidents at large, we will describe the scene which took place between Felina and Amab.

The night was dark; the carriage rolled swiftly along, and they had been driven as far as the entrance to the Champs Elysées before Amab and Felina had exchanged a single word.

Amab was deeply embarrassed by this silence, but perhaps he would have felt still more awkward had he been under the necessity of speaking to Felina.

As for the latter, she concealed neither her impatience nor her chagrin; her foot kept beating the floor of the carriage furiously; she several times lowered and raised the window;—she was warm, she was cold, she was stifling;—and then her teeth chattered convulsively.

From time to time, her handkerchief, raised to her eyes, seemed rather to force the tears out than to dry them.

As soon as they entered the Champs Elysées, she gave a violent pull to the string fastened to the coachman's hand, and had the carriage suddenly stopped.

"What is your intention?" said Amab, eagerly, to her.

"Suffer me to get out and walk a few minutes, I am stifling, I shiver with cold, I am burning, I should have a nervous fit were I to continue shut up in this way; it would be very ridiculous and unseasonable; I will not let myself be subdued by a feeling such as I now experience. I am accustomed," added Felina in a broken voice, "to be more mistress of myself than I am at present."

She alighted from the carriage, and turned towards Amab, saying:

"If you think it would fatigue you to walk, I will dispense with your attendance."

Amab felt how rude it would be for him to remain in the carriage by himself whilst Mademoiselle de Cambure was following it on foot; he got out in his turn and walked beside the lady.

"Wait for us at the Barrier de l'Etoile," said she to the coachman, "I shall walk as far as that."

The carriage drove swiftly away, leaving them alone.

The weather was cold, the sky dark, the avenues deserted. Felina began to walk with a degree of rapidity; Amab had some difficulty in keeping pace with her. All at once she stopped, her hands pressed against her chest, and she ejaculated in a smothered vo ce:

"No—no—it is impossible!"

Then she leaned against a tree and seemed ready to sink down.

Amab eagerly drew near her.

"What is the matter?"

"Nothing," she answered undoing the ribbon of her bonnet, and uncovering her head to expose it to the coolness of the night air.

"Do you feel unwell?"

"Not enough to prevent me from returning to my carriage."

"It is unnecessary."

She put on her bonnet in haste, and resumed her rapid walk, saying with painful vexation:

"My God! my God! to be so weak as this!"

Amab followed her with anxiety; he was afraid of that nervous fit which had been threatened; but his grief for Felina's suffering was not his only fear; he thought of the delay which this accident would create in liberating Charles, or rather in liberating him, for it was fearfully irksome to him to be thus alone with Felina. Do what he would, he could not help dreading her, but hate her he did not; he saw her in pain, and he could not doubt but that he was the cause of her sufferings. They occasioned him that sense of uneasiness which is derived from the wrongs a person does, when he is yet determined not to repair them. If Felina had appeared to him the day before in this state of desolation, he would have sued for pardon.

"She still walked before him, but her steps grew slower; her panting breath evinced that she was making fearful efforts to endure the weariness of this hurried walk. Several times she staggered, took heart, and then suddenly stopped short. Amab approached her, and Felina hastened to catch his arm.

"Excuse me, sir, it will soon be over; agitation, anger—even despair—"

As she uttered the last word, she once more wiped her eyes and walked on, leaning on Victor's arm. The latter, who attentively watched every action, thought he saw that her efforts over hersel were not quite useless. She appeared to compose herself and said, in a faltering voice:

"I thought I was stronger than I am; I was wrong to leave the carriage; it must be at the end of the avenue, and we must lose a great deal of time before we can reach it: a little patience, sir, I beg of you ——"

"Madam, I am quite at your orders; and if you wish to rest yourself, here are chairs."

"The truth is, there is one," replied Felina, bitterly, "who will not be so obliging as you are; we must make haste to arrive."

She drew forth a small watch, looked at the time, and exclaimed:

"So late already! My God!" added she, attempting to accelerate her steps, "what a fault, what a fault!"

"Shall I go to M. Villon, madam?" said Amab to her; "shall I tell him to wait?"

"Oh, sir, do I know where he is? Besides, M. Villon hates you. Did you not deprive him of Miss Thoré's heart? Let us make haste; that is the best thing we can do."

They walked on for some time in silence; but, in spite of her resolution, Felina's strength seemed gradually to become exhausted. She suddenly stopped, leaned against one of the barriers lining the edge of the avenues, crossing the promenade, and said, in a voice all but extinguished:

"I can go no farther, sir; no, never, never!"

Then she continued, bitterly:

"It seems to be your destiny to ruin me altogether."

"I, madam," said Amab, who already felt less concerned for the liberation of Charles in the presence of so genuine a grief endured with so much resignation; "I," said he, "I know, madam, the serious wrong I did you; but I cannot understand how, at this time, I can be the cause of the new sorrows that afflict you."

"You cannot understand it, sir—oh!" she exclaimed, with an accent of desperation, "those who have no love can never understand."

"Your grief is unjust, madam; I feel all that you must suffer, I understand all your fears; but I am innocent of them."

"Oh!" said Felina, proudly, "I fear nothing now, sir—I fear nothing now. You have just informed me that there are afflictions still more galling than those caused by contempt and the vengeance of a disconsolate family."

"I!" said Amab, still quite amazed: "has a single unbecoming word escaped me, and have I said aught to arouse in you these painful recollections?"

Felina uttered a smothered exclamation, pressed her forehead in agony, and, as Amab wondered at this new transport of grief, she suddenly resumed:

"It is not enough to show me his contempt by his silence—he must even tell me of it."

"What?" resumed Amab.

"Why," continued Felina, interrupting him with violence, "these recollections that you are unwilling to arouse—these recollections which you wave off with so delicate an attention, are very shameful then?"

"Why, madam—" began Amab.

"Enough, enough," said Felina, resuming her walk with fresh rapidity and under the impulse either of violent despair or fearful passion; "enough! your silence offends me, your words put me to the torture, your presence kills me."

Amab stopped, almost determined to follow Felina no further.

She stopped in her turn, and turning her head towards him, added with unmerciful irony;

"Come sir, come—do not be afraid, come—a woman may be killed, but she does not die immediately; besides, must not your pupil, your friend, your brother be restored to you this very night. Oh! come then—and above all leave me not alone with him so long as he is in my power."

Amab followed her, and she went on rapidly muttering to herself:

Oh! the wretches! the wretches!"

Amab, who saw Felina exciting herself with an angry thought, and who imagined he knew to what extremities such a feeling might carry her—Amab drew near to her, and in his most gentle voice, he said:

"Hear me, madam, if the word of two men of honor—"

What do you purpose doing for the next exhibition?" said Felina, interrupting him hastily, in a sharp ringing voice; "is it to be a scriptural subject or a historical picture? Do you intend to exhibit anything but portraits?"

"Excuse me, madam," said Amab, "but a discourse of this nature—"

"You will have the cross of honour, no doubt, this year, and perhaps they will entrust to you the painting of one of our churches?"

"Really," resumed Amab, I am at a loss to guess how you come to speak to me on such a subject—"

"What does it signify to you?" said Felina. "It is always a noble subject that of art—I used to love and cultivate the arts myself—sometimes I painted——"

"You! madam."

She returned no answer. Amab could see she was weeping; afterwards she added, as if speaking to herself, "Oh! I have done with painting now!"

"Why so?"

"Why, sir?" you ask me why? Oh! wretch that I am," said she, clasping her hands; "this thought will kill me!"

"What thought?"

"Why, cannot you understand," continued Felina, amidst tears and sobs, "that here, this very moment, I wanted to emerge from the dreadful thought which for ever haunts me? I gave you a word at random, I hoped to fly from myself—but I was instantly called back—yes, sir, I once loved the arts, and had for those men who win an illustrious name an enthusiastic admiration, which, one day, in its extravagance bereft me of reason. Well, sir, I will kill this love as I have destroyed another. I will see no more pictures, not even a brush; for if I did—I should be reminded—Oh!" she resumed, "is there any need of that to remember? Oh! no, no—God is implacable, and will not let us forget!"

"At least, madam," replied Amab, with humility, "you may rest assured that the deepest secrecy shall ever—"

At that moment, Felina appeared to compose herself. Was it weariness, was it resignation, was it deceit? She leaned on his arm, and continued in a gentle yet faltering voice:

"Oh! you are neither kind, nor generous; cannot you perceive that the very assurance you give me confronts me again with my misfortune? You offer me your word and that of another—I do not despise you enough to distrust you; and as for that other, I imagined you did not require to tell me that you would be able to silence him. Besides, believe me, M. Victor," she added bitterly, "I do not set so much value as you think on that secret, there are times when men without pity render women shameless. A woman's honour is like her beauty, sir; she takes all the more care of them, that she is about to lose them both; she plasters them over, she paints them, she enhances them with all the resources of art, above all" she added, wiping away a tear, "when she has a latent hope in her heart; but the very day this hope is lost, and when there remains no person in the world she wishes to deceive—her honor, her beauty, every thing is neglected. Oh! stay, dishonor me, sir, if you will—I have no more care, either for my honor, lost through you and on your account, or of my beauty which I hope will soon follow it."

"Why should you despair," said Amab, "why?"

"Oh! console me not, sir, you cannot do so. Suppose you stood by a mother whose beloved child you had killed,—would it be your place to comfort her?"

"At least, it is a crime I have committed unintentionally."

"And that is the most frightful point of all, sir: that is what would prohibit you from approaching that bereaved mother. But a crime may be pardoned: Gloucester persuades Lady Anne that it was through love for her that he killed her husband; he persuades Elizabeth that it was to restore her to the throne that he killed her children; and he receives his pardon. In the same manner we may say to an outraged woman: 'I betrayed you to another because I hated you, and yet I was mistaken for I loved you.' We may say to her; I thought you too happy, and I wished to make you suffer, and now I pity you.' But to tell her what you tell me is intolerable: 'I crushed you beneath the wheel of my chariot because I did not see you; be comforted then, for I ruined you because I did not deign to know that you existed.' No, no, Victor, that is not the way to console a woman. Be silent, believe me, and do not attempt impossible things. You are young, and the future is all before you, so vast, so glorious, so magnificent, that you must advance to meet it with a steady and resolute step. I understand ambition, I admire and honour it. To proceed to your aim, I can understand that you may place your foot without mercy on the heart that stands as an obstacle in your way. Proceed, and crush, if necessary, the vulgar feelings which may rise up as enemies to meet you. Burst the narrow bonds which might impede your cause, but do not act so from blind inattention. Get out of the way if a madman runs laughing in front of your horses. Do not drive away too savagely the beggar who hangs to the skirts of your coat. Do not call your slaves to scourge the enthusiast who proclaims glory and happiness to the prophet, because his voice is displeasing to you. The most loathsome evil is that which does nobody any good, not even to the malefactor who commits it. Vengeance is the right of a heart which values itself, cruelty is but the weakness of a bad man, and I had done you no injury—not I."

"Oh! the soft, the penetrating, the sad, the melodious tones in which these desolate complaints were conveyed to the ears of the young painter."

"Oh! if I had known you!" he replied, in a voice almost of repentance.

"What does it matter, Victor? The fond and doting woman who had written to you the letter you received, had she been old even and ugly—and those are great crimes;—had she been the most abandoned creature in the world—still she did not insult you."

"If you knew, Felina, how all my life I have dreaded ridicule; I was afraid—"

"I understand that, Victor; but in that case the letter should have been thrown into the fire;—you would not even have had the trouble to forget it,—not even to think of it. Oh! no, no, you deceive me, or rather you deceive yourself. Yes—believe me: acoustom yourself to look your feelings in the face, how bad soever they may be. It is not their evil thoughts which ruin men, but their deceitful appearances."

"Do you think, then, that I had been able to foresee."

"Had you said to yourself" said Felina, gently interrupting Amab: "I am going to ruin a woman for the sake of ruining her,' certainly you would have hesitated! Nobody commits a vile action, that is the true word, without having a motive."

"And what motive could I have had?"

"That of saying to your friends when you met together: 'My success goes beyond your enthusiasm; see, I am not merely applauded—I am loved—I am run after. Well, I care nothing for all that! I disdain this admiration, and hand it over to the first comer; I want something different.'"

"Oh, madam!"

"That is precisely what you said to yourself, Victor," resumed Felina, in the tone of a mother gently reproving her child; "and that is why you were unkind and cruel without cause; that was the occasion on which you drove your chariot-wheel over the woman who, on her knees, was clapping her hands, and exulting in your triumph; and you did this, Victor, when you had only to turn aside and leave her."

"Ah! had I been able to repair the injury, I swear to you I would have done it."

Felina did not appear to have heard him, but continued, in a tone of resignation:

"To-day, that you are killing me, I understand you better; you are less guilty."

"What do you mean?"

They had reached the carriage at this part of the conversation; and Amab, who was under the incantation of that soft, sweet tongue, who hung with admiration on the soothing reproaches which were gliding into his heart—Amab said to her, as he took his seat beside her:

"'To-day that I am killing you,' you said, 'I am less guilty.' Explain."

"Did I say so?" began Felina. "Well, I was wrong. I am tranquil now, and will remain so to the end. Forget those words."

"You are right, Felina; I cannot excuse the mischief I have done you; but I should be the most abject of all wretches were I to do you any more unintentionally."

Felina laughed with cruel bitterness, and continued, in a voice too much broken to bear the tones of anger:

"Ah! God help me!—they want to have you married, and you know I am aware of it; yet you say you intend me no further injury. Ah, Victor!"

"Excuse me; but it seems to me——"

"Since you reminded me of my words, take them all—yes," said she, almost exhausted, "to-day you are really killing me, and yet you are less guilty."

Amab started.

"Do not interrupt me!—I require all my strength to pursue the thread of my thoughts. My heart must not leap up to my head, to set it in disorder, as it did just now; my resolution is taken, inflexibly taken; but you must not think I feel nothing, that, I understand nothing. You are killing me—yes, sir; for, after all, either I am a woman who has yet some honour left—some pride of soul—a little genuine passion—a little self-esteem,—or else I am a brazen harlot, full of stupid vanity and furious passions. In the first case, what could I hope for to enable me to forgive myself the misfortune you brought upon me; I could only hope for your love to absolve me from my disgrace. Fond and empty hope, was it not, since you are going to be married to another? On the other hand, if I am the shameless and violent woman, whom, perhaps, you despise I must have dreamt, at least, of vengeance, must I not? Well, vengeance escapes me: and to insult my misery the more, you are about to marry the sister of the man who injured me; you honour him with your alliance, you side with him against me. Ah, Victor, do not stir up these thoughts in my soul—do not place me again in the presence of that horrible shame to which I am condemned; I should become once more what I do not wish to be—wild, raving mad—and capable perhaps of a crime."

Amab did not immediately reply; but his hand meeting Felina's, he gently pressed it, and said to her:

"Felina, I trust to your generosity."

"Ah! thank you," she answered eagerly: "thank you for that word; it is the first that you have used which is kind—and what is kind begets kindness—I want you to be happy without regret or remorse. Yes, I would have you so. You sacrifice me to another—can I complain! You loved her before you knew me—she is beautiful, far more beautiful than I, and I know it—oh! jealousy and vexation have not blinded me. She is beautiful, and your love for her assures me that she understands you. It will be her part to sustain your genius, and spur it on. Proud of you, rich in your possession, love will teach her to please you; she will accompany your triumph, and adorned with your glory, she will wish it greater still for your sake. Such is the future destiny of this woman, for she loves you—and I, I who had dreamt of nothing but your glory—I feel it here—had you only been mine, I would have made you so great that the world should have marvelled at our love."

Here the carriage began to roll over the sinking gravel of a dark narrow covered avenue.

Felina's voice, passionate, vibrating, passed into his sense like an intoxicating song of triumph, amidst the sweet perfume of her breath. Her hand trembled in his own.

"Oh!" he exclaimed, "why did you not speak to me thus yesterday?"

"I cannot say, Victor," replied Felina, "but I have been distracted this last month. I longed for your love and—oh! you do not know what the heart of a loving woman is. Men never suspect the immeasureable wildness of our dreams. And yet, Victor, you do not know me. I am not a perverse creature, my heart is not unfeeling, I am not a skilful actress. I am only a loving woman, who pines for your love in return."

"Ah! Felina, Felina," said Amab to her—could I out believe you—did you really love me."

"Do I love you! Why what more proof would you have, my God?"

"I would—"

"Stop"—she eagerly replied, "we are arrived."

CRIME AND PUNISHMENT.

At that moment the carriage entered the courtyard of Madame de Cambure's villa.

The clock struck twelve.

---

## CHAPTER XXXVII.

### A DEED OF HORROR.

MORE than an hour previously, and just as M. and Madame Thoré were beginning to feel impatient whilst waiting for the answer which Amab had faithfully promised to send them, when they were almost lost in conjectures and nearly paralysed with increasing fears at the unaccountable delay and whilst they were meditating the most unsparing vengeance against this woman, at the very moment they began to entertain fears for Amab himself as well as for their son, a violent knocking was heard at the door. They run out expecting to see Amab, but were agreeably surprised on beholding Charles who had been released by M. Villon.

This was indeed a moment of inexpressible and uncontroulable transport, nor could Charles himself resist its influence; but scarcely had he embraced his father and his mother affectionately before he exclaimed, looking earnestly at one and the other:

"Where is Julia?"

"She has retired to rest. Ah! then M. Amab has not deceived us."

"M. Amab," repeated Charles suddenly.

"It was he who went to Madame de Cambure, it was he in fine who by his prayers and threats obtained thy liberty," said Madame Thoré.

"M. Amab," said Villon dryly, "has had nothing to do with M. Charles's delivery; it was I who called on that lady, and it was I who had an interview with her, and it was I whom she deputed to restore to you your son."

"Ah! thank you my friend," said Madame Thoré."

"It is of no importance," added M. Thoré, haughtily, "to whom Charles is indebted for the liberty he now enjoys since he is restored to us again."

"It may be of some consequence, however," said Charles, "to know at what hour M. Amab started from this in order to obtain my liberty."

"I believe it was about half-past ten."

"As for me," said M. Villon, "I left Madame de Cambure's hotel at nine o'clock with the order in my pocket restoring Charles to liberty."

"And it appears to me," observed Charles, "that since leaving this house he has had plenty of time to learn the success which has crowned M. Villon's kind efforts, and time enough to come back and apprise you of the circumstances."

"Perhaps so," said Madame Thoré, "but what puts such things into your head. Why damp our present joy by these reflections?"

"My mother," answered Charles, with much sadness, "I wish to embrace Julia."

"Very well, come then, let us go and see her." And Madame Thoré led the way to her daughter's bed room, calling out:

"Julia, Julia!"

She opened the door, again repeating the name:

"Julia, Julia!"

But no one answered.

"Julia, Julia," screamed Madame Thoré, precipitating herself into the room.

"Ah!" exclaimed Charles in a terrible tone, and rushing also into the deserted room. "I am too late!"

Who can describe the shrieks? Who can paint the despair of this mother who for nearly a month had been kept in cruel suspense as to what had befallen her son, and who, now that he had been restored to her, felt her joy turned into mourning, having to bewail the loss of her daughter. They searched for her everywhere—they called upon her by name—they interrogated all the household, and at length they learned from the chambermaid that an old lady had called to see Julia, and that after the departure of that lady Julia had said she was going to her room. After much cross-examination the servant at length admitted that she had partly overheard the conversation between the elderly lady and Julia, and that she had caught the name of M. Amab.

"Madame de Cambure is right," said Charles furiously, "but the coward knows well enough that I shall punish him for this infamous seduction."

Let the reader bear in mind the tale which Felina had recounted to Charles, and remember at the same time how Amab had told M. and Madame Thoré of his criminal relations and that of Charles with Madame de Cambure, and then it will be fully understood in what confused explanations the mind of this worthy couple so constantly wandered. Villon accused Amab, and without hesitation came to the conclusion that he was a base and cowardly ravisher.

He vehemently exclaimed, "That he would follow him, and never desist from so doing, until he had severely punished him, perhaps killed him."

Madame Thoré, although more afflicted than the rest, had more judgment, and therefore was able to see in this mysterious event the hellish handiwork of Felina, for the honest woman readily comprehended the thirst for vengeance which that abandoned woman had been maddened to pursue by the outrageous treatment she had met with from her son. M. Thoré, in a voice of thunder, invoked the law, and thundered out for paternal authority, to aid them in obtaining satisfaction of the guilty wretch: and Charles, who began at length to see that he was the principal cause of this dreadful calamity, at once offered to confront every danger, and sacrifice everything in order to save his sister.

After repeated cries, terrible menaces, and continued lamentations, two resolutions were at last proposed in the midst of this prevailing grief. The first was to go without a moment's delay to two persons on whom rested their suspicions, Amab and Madame de Cambure.

These proposals having been agreed to, a new contest was started: Madame Thoré was for going everywhere at once; she dreaded the quick temper and violence of her son, if he should go to M. Amab's with Villon alone. In truth this violence might ruin all, if, as she thought, yet dare not say, Amab had been the blind instrument of Felina's vengeance.

Madame Thoré, in like manner, was afraid to let them go to Madame de Cambure lest she might prepare some snare which their inexperience might cause them unwittingly to fall into. She resolved to accompany her son.

As for M. Thoré, he wanted to go alone and everywhere, to make the whole affair public, in order to save and restore all or punish every one, as the case might be.

The result of all these various discussions terminated by it unanimously being agreed upon that they should all go together to the suspected parties. They therefore took a carriage and called first on M. Amab. He was not at home; it seemed he had not returned at all that night. Charles insisted on writing a few lines to him, and with this view he opened the door of his apartment, and hastily strode through it. But he saw that they had told him the truth.

"It is certain," said he, "that if he has carried off Julia, it is not here he has concealed her."

They next called on Madame de Cambure.

She in like manner was not at home; they then endeavoured to find out where she had gone, that they might follow her, but the lordly porter indignantly refused all further information. In vain they tried every possible means which prudence suggested to induce him to answer their inquiries: but all to no purpose, for they had miscalculated their man, who felt satisfied that he was studying his interest much more by obeying his mistress, who paid him well for keeping her secrets, than by accepting a few Louis to divulge them to the curiosity of strangers.

M. Villon endeavoured to gain over the porter by persuasion, M. Thoré by argument, Charles by curses and threats. But Madame Thoré used sweet words, and was more successful.

"I can readily understand," said she, "that if Madame de Cambure desires to be alone, she may have told you to say she is not at home, and of course you dare not disobey her. But sometimes there are circumstances which could not have been foreseen, and for which one would gladly waive every rule, in order to prevent a great misfortune from happening; for instance, the sudden illness of a friend who required your presence."

"I understand very well what you mean, madam," replied the porter; "however, I must tell you that if you wish to inform Madame de Cambure of a misfortune, no matter what, it will be quite impossible to do so now, for I swear to you she is gone out, first her calash drove off—"

"With me?" said Villon.

"Very likely, sir; but I never notice who rides in Madame de Cambure's carriages, nor where the postillion drives my mistress herself."

"And you dont know where we can find her?"

"Madame de Cambure never told me where she was going."

"Can any of the household inform us?"

"You may inquire if you like, madame; there are many servants here."

Madame Thoré quickly ran up stairs, and knocked at Madame de Cambure's door. Dorothy appeared.

"Madame de Cambure?" enquired Madame Thoré.

"I declare," said Villon, "this is the deaf and dumb creature who brought me the letter."

The woman uttered a hoarse cry, and immediately another servant made her appearance.

"Is Madame de Cambure within?"

The chambermaid consulted the deaf and dumb girl with a glance of her eye, and instantly she made a sign to her.

"No, madame, she is not at home."

"Are you sure?"

"Quite sure."

"At what hour did your mistress leave?" said M. Thoré.

"My mistress goes out when it pleases her to do so."

This answer was given in such an insolent manner, as to leave very little hope of their being able to glean any more information. Dorothy had already half shut the door, when all at once piercing cries were heard again and again from the floor above. These cries had scarcely reached those who were standing on the landing place, before Madame Thoré recognised in them the voice of her daughter.

"Julia it is Julia," she screamed, rushing up to the next storey.

As the daughter's voice had been recognised by the mother, so the mother's voice had been recognised by the daughter.

"Mother, mother," exclaimed the wretched girl.

Whilst the porter and his family were attracted to the spot by the united shrieks of mother and daughter, and whilst Madame de Cambure's servants were curious to know what would be the result of all this uproar, and whilst the neighbours who were aroused from their slumbers by the tumult which resounded from the grand staircase, were beginning to flock together from all parts, Charles Villon and M. Thoré himself pushed against the door, burst it in, and entered the room.

M. Thoré received in his arms his weeping child, her hair was all disheveled, her garments torn, she was pale, disfigured, bruised.

A man with haggard eyes, with foaming mouth, was standing in the room, his dress in the same wild disorder as Julia's. Charles, excited with rage and hatred, precipitated himself on this man, who, armed with a poignard, endeavoured to strike him; Charles, however, wrested it from him, and seizing him by the neck with an iron grasp, hurled him violently back to the ground, profusely bleeding from a wound he had inflicted.

Villon hastened to assist Charles, wishing also to reck his vengeance on the wounded man, who made a desperate effort to rise; but he started back almost stupified with astonishment, as in the wretched man he recollected the Count de Monrion.

Every heart was filled with hatred against this wretch, but still they stood in breathless silence, and contemplated the inanimate and bloody body of Gustavus, which gave no signs of life.

It would be vain to attempt to describe the outcries, the fury and confusion of the bystanders,—the questions they eagerly put for answer,—their threats of vengeance, and the feelings of pity and sorrow which were provoked by this terrible discovery. Some of the women tendered their apartment to the mother of this beautiful child, who was then unconscious, and who appeared to have been drawn into a foul and abominable snare. Others exclaimed that a man had been killed, and that the culprit must not be suffered to escape. It was like a Babel of tumult and confusion, whilst the prudent house-porter, as the magistrate over all his tenants, kept the street door closed, and whilst his daughter (every house-porter has a daughter) went in search of peace officers.

When they arrived the Count de Monrion was already placed in bed, a medical man residing in the house was attending him, who declared that he was not in a state to bear any inquiry; for, independent of the wound he had received, the count seemed to be attacked with congestion of the brain; whether it was occasioned by the wound or not, the Doctor was not prepared to say; but it rendered him incapable of understanding anything that might be said.

On the other hand, Madame Thoré had accepted the hospitality of a neighbour, to whose chambers the unfortunate Julia had been conveyed; and, on returning to consciousness, she had thrown herself into her mother's arms, giving utterance to these ominous words:

"Oh! hide me! hide me, mother! The looks that some who were present rapidly exchanged with each other had served as a cruel commentary to these words; and, doubtless, had Charles heard them, helpless, distracted, maddened, as he was, he would have repeated the cry he uttered when he first entered his sister's room, '*It is too late.*'"

Meanwhile the justice began to make inquiries respecting the affair, and the excitement assumed a new face.

Madame Thoré, who had contrived, in Julia's despair, to draw a few words from her, informed the officer that it was on the receipt of a letter from M. Amab, that her daughter had left home.

"M. Amab, then, is the name of the culprit,"

said the justice, "and consequently it is he who has been wounded?"

"No—the culprit is the Count de Monrion."

All looked astonished.

"Then, who hired this apartment?" enquired the officer of the porter.

"Why, the Count of Monrion did, through his valet de chambre, who is well known to all the household, for he often comes to Madame de Cambure with messages from his master."

"To whom was the key of this apartment then to be delivered?"

"To M. Amab," replied the porter.

"Has he been here to-night?"

"Yes, but, almost immediately after he came in, he went out again with Madame de Cambure."

"But what became of the key?"

"The key was restored to M. de Monrion."

"Then the key belonging to M. Amab was given to M. de Monrion?"

Here arose a second embarrassment.

"Well, but this may be explained. Who was it had the key, was it to be restored to M. Amab?"

"Why, the old woman who brought Julia the letter from M. Amab; but this woman contrived to slip a well filled purse into the porter's hand, on the part of M. de Monrion."

"Where is the purse?"

"Here it is."

The purse was adorned with pearls, bearing the coronet of the count, and the letters G. and M., which were M. Monrion's initials.

"But what brought this young lady here?"

"She came in reply to a letter from M. Amab, to demand of Madame de Cambure her brother's release."

"The young man, then, was detained as prisoner by Madame de Cambure. Let the young man come forward."

Here Charles drew up to the justice.

"You were carried away and kept a prisoner by Madame de Cambure, it seems?"

Charles hesitated, but replied, falteringly:

"It might have been by M. Amab, who well knew I should avenge myself on him for basely seducing my sister."

Here a cry from Madame Thoré interrupted her son, who could continue no further.

"Oh! then it was M. Amab who carried you off," continued the officer.

"I can't say."

"It must have been Madame de Cambure," said Villon.

"And why so?"

A general silence followed the question.

Although we must do the officer the justice to say that he did every thing in his power to arrive at the real state of things—nevertheless he signally failed to effect his purpose. As however, all things must have an end, so in like manner when the midnight hour struck, and every body began to feel weary and anxious to retire, the officer recollecting that a lady of great fortune, a celebrated artist, and above all a peer of France were implicated in this intricate affair, came to the conclusion after a few moments reflection not to push the matter any further.

However as both parties had sustained serious injuries, he arrested Charles and had him conveyed to prison, he also left a man on watch in M. de Monrion's room. The skilful officer took every necessary precaution and demanded the letter which M. Amab had written.

As it was necessary that one of Madame de Cambure's chambermaids should remain in the apartment it was decided that Dorothy should be sent for that she might take care of the sick-man. They next searched in every part of the room for the letter. Dorothy who seemed more anxious than any of the rest to find it, actually rummaged M. de Monrion's pockets, and it would seem that she was wise in so doing for there they found a great many letters. The first of these which was from M. de Montaleu burst upon them like a thunderbolt, for after having reproached his nephew for his scandalous intimacy with Madame de Cambure he demanded an explanation respecting his constant visits to M. Thoré's house. The enraged uncle could see nothing else in such behaviour but a preconcerted plan, which he felt certain would terminate in an infamous seduction; the accusation was dreadful, and the present event appeared to justify it.

But what astounded them most, and what seemed to render this intricate affair still more complicated was a second letter which the justice's clerk had taken from M. de Monrion's great coat pocket, and delivered to his superior, who after having perused it, said to Madame Thoré stiffly,

"What is your daughter's name, madam?"

"Julia, sir,"

"Is this her handwriting then?"

Madame Thoré examined it.

"Unquestionably it is."

"Well then, read it Madam."

Madame Thoré read as follows;

"Yes, I love you—find an excuse which will "enable me to leave home and which will serve me "as a pretext on my return, and I will go to the "place you have appointed.

Julia."

Madame Thoré who well knew the extreme love which her daughter bore to Amab, believed she had yielded to its resistless sway; she turned over the letter to examine the address, it was directed to the Count de Monrion.

The fatal letter dropped from her hands, a dizziness came over her, everything seemed to disappear from before her eyes, she felt as if she would go distracted. In the midst of the pale and glimmering light which the few tapers afforded, but one idea seemed to pervade the minds of every one present, it was that in the midst of the tumult and confusion which rose on all sides, the image of Felina seemed ever present. Like a bird of prey it continually hovered round this paralised family enveloping them with its busy circular flight until at length it descended on its victim with whetted beak and distended claws.

This vision had so strongly fixed itself upon the mind of Madame Thoré that she rushed towards her daughter and clasping her in her arms vehemently exclaimed:

Oh! come, let us fly I will have you—yes I will.

In the meantime Julia's letter had been picked up and added to the charge of accusation drawn up by the Justice.

Charles accompanied by Villon and a police officer was taken in a hackney coach to the neighbouring prison, while M. and Madame Thoré returned home with Julia whose tears had ceased to flow, a burning fever having succeeded to her agony of woe.

Thus after all the bitter anguish which M. and Madame Thoré had experienced in the loss of their son, and the desolation and dishonour which had crept into their family circle; this respected and esteemed father, this happy and loving mother who prided herself on her children, now beheld with heartrending grief their daughter betrayed and deserted, and their son guilty of the awful crime of murder.

Assuredly we might at once explain to our readers the still mysterious circumstances of this last scene—to them at least perplexing;—but if we did so, we should leave unfinished the character of the *She-Tiger*, whose portrait we have undertaken to paint; we should shrink from applying the last stroke of the brush which is to pourtray her as she was, as she is still.

For the She-Tiger is still living.

---

## CHAPTER XXXVIII.

### THE DECISIVE WORD.

Early on the following morning Dorothy who had committed to M. de Montaleu's old housekeeper the care of M. de Monrion, who had been restored to consciousness by the praiseworthy efforts of the police officer, hastily left the Rue Joubert for the purpose of rejoining her mistress in the *Bois de Boulogne*.

The day was far advanced when she arrived. She entered her mistress's apartment and found her in the little library adjoining which was her bedroom.

"I was apprised of your having come, and therefore I got up.

The deaf and dumb girl who spoke mysteriously said in an under tone:

"And he?"

"He is still asleep—What took place?"

Dorothy recounted everything that had happened.

Felina could not refrain from bursting out into immoderate fits of laughter at all the blunders which the Justice had committed.

"After all" said she, "whom do they really suspect?"

"M. de Monrion, thanks to the letter which I took care to slip into his great-coat pocket."

"In case the authorities should come to institute a search here tell me what have you done with the invoice which enabled you to imitate so well the handwriting of that little girl?"

"The invoice of tea! the tea service—Oh! I burned it."

It was evident nothing had been wanting to the completion of Felina's plans, not even that invoice which she had received with a menacing smile. From the first hour that she had visited Thoré she foresaw to what purpose she would be able to employ it. It might have been otherwise, it might merely have been an instrument accidentally put into her hands, and that circumstances afterwards suggested to her the idea of doing as she did.

"And Amab's letter?"

"Here it is."

"Give it me," hastily ejaculated Felina, taking it out of her hand and concealing it within a beautiful bookcase, which was covered with rich velvet, and bound round with gold, and which opened by means of a spring, when one of the precious stones, with which it was adorned, was slightly pressed.

There is little doubt but that this letter had not accomplished all that Felina had hoped it would.

"One more question was addressed to Dorothy, in a whisper, and, when asking it, she seemed to be cautious not to betray herself.

"Tell me! what became of the remainder of the wine which Gustavus drank?"

"I threw it amongst the ashes, and it kept the fire in all night."

"Good," said Felina, heaving a deep sigh, "you did quite right. I had forgotten that."

What could it have been? Doubtless a poison which Felina had administered to Monrion at supper. The horrible state in which he was found when the door had been burst open; the congestion of the brain, which had been alluded to by the medical man, might it not all have arisen from the fatal effects of poison? No human power could ever have extorted this dark mystery, either from the mistress or the servant, had not one of the accomplices determined to reveal the secret; but, before touching upon that subject, it is necessary for us to say a few words, in order to explain what happened between Amab and Felina. She had told him all, and he trembling full of alarm, could scarcely behold without shuddering, that woman whose very voice at one time seemed to intoxicate him with a maddening pleasure, and who had filled his soul with a burning love which none but herself could satisfy. He had heard all that she had to say, he had accepted every proposal she had made. She loved him, she was avenged. She had done what to her seemed right, she so haughty, so implacable, so cruelly wanton in the manner in which she recited the sufferings of her victims, that she seemed totally void of every womanly feeling. And it was with a contemptuous sneer that she thus addressed herself to Amab:

"Count de Monrion wanted to treat me like a prostitute, and the consequence is, he will meet with a disgraceful death. Another, (she alluded to Charles), made me blush before you—and I have sullied his name with his sister's dishonour—his hand with the blood of an intoxicated man. She had pronounced these words in a tone so unrelenting, and in a manner so heartless, that Amab began to entertain fears respecting his own personal safety, and said to her:

"It was well done."

Then she went on to explain to him how she had contrived to remove all suspicion from himself, and that it was the mad passion which she cherished for him that led her to commit these acts of desparation, lest she might lose him altogether. She had so well penetrated his soul, when telling him that he did not love Julia, that he never had loved her, and his reason for taking refuge in the society of that girl proceeded from the little esteem he had of himself, and not from any passion for her, for he never dared to believe in the well-deserved enthusiasm which he had inspired, she had so artfully possessed herself of the cherished wish of his heart, which ambition portrayed to him in its brightest hues, and having once arrived at this point, she well knew how to flatter his vanity; she told him that he was one of those men to whom the whole world should do homage, and that his genius had a right to dispense with the base bonds of morality. She so eloquently depicted the pedestal of glory on which she wished him to believe he stood, resting as it were on the broken hearts or ruined reputations, or sundered friendships, as the pedestal of conquerors rests on an army of lifeless bodies—she so persistingly maintained to him that if a man was determined to rise to the summit of power, it would be utterly impossible for him to do so, unless on the condition that nothing should arrest his progress—no, neither the tears of the woman he had ruined, the children he had cast away, nor the friend he had betrayed—she intermingled these wild sophisms with such secret smiles and tender carresses, she kissed, like a menial slave, his hand, with which she had once commanded him to strike an avenging blow—in fact, she had so bewitched and fascinated the unfortunate Amab, that at length, vanquished and borne down, he fearlessly determined to follow the course pointed out to him, and which had been represented to him in such brilliant colours.

Are you unacquainted with my hero? Know you not that this would-be-honest-and-ambitious man, confining himself entirely to his own meditations, was at length imperceptably dragged into the very vortex of crime? behold then how, all of a sudden, confronted by singular audacity and a powerful imagination, which proves to him that he wasted his time in considering those obstacles over which the bold leap without effort; he thinks himself clever, and is a coward—whilst he is only creeping, others fly. Finally, his soul pants to be one of those men who direct others: he follows whoever will employ his fictitious audacity, and becomes a powerful instrument in the hand that intends to rule him.

At the close of the explanation which Amab had had with Felina, it was clear that he was her accomplice, for he regretted not having assisted her in working out her infernal schemes. Thus, the weak-minded egotistical man was once more intoxicated with the fascinations of this artful woman. Just as Felina was leaving him, having previously, however, well-tutored him as to what he should say in case any persons should call, either from M. Thoré's family or the police authorities to make further enquiries, Amab said to her, as she was leaving the room:

"By the bye, what became of the letter which occasioned Julia to quit her home?"

"Well, since you particularly wish to know I must tell you that I have that letter in my possession."

"Oh! indeed; then give it to me."

"I will before long."

"But when?"

"On the day of our marriage."

The answer was a heartless and cruel one, and Amab turned pale. Felina in an instant perceived the hectic glow which mounted on his cheek, and when he was far away from her on his way home, she repeated triumphantly to herself the fatal words:

"*I shall have him yet!*"

---

## CHAPTER XXXIX.

### EXAMINATION.

Some time afterwards Amab was tranquilly seated in his atelier listening, apparently with great interest, to the recital of a scandalous affair, which they said had taken place in the Rue Joubert; they did not mention any names, but they spoke of a young girl as having been decoyed from her home by means of a deep laid snare; and they said that she had met at her lover's house, not him whom her soul adored, but the man who had dared to aspire to her affections, although she had repeatedly told him that she hated and abhorred him.

At these words one of the pupils jocularly remarked that the Rue Joubert was renowned for such ludicrous occurrences, and that it would have been highly amusing if all this had happened in the same house as that in which the charming lady of fortune resided, who had sent a letter to Amab which Charles had availed himself of.

These severe remarks made Amab tremble with rage, but he suffered their pleasantry at his expense to continue without appearing to take any more notice of it than if they had been recounting the adventures of Telemachus. However, the numerous and bitter stories which were circulated against him began to wound his pride, and he was at length about to impose silence on his pupils, when his servant (the one who had quitted his service for some days but who had lately returned) announced that the Marquis of Montaleu had called to see him.

The dangerous position in which Amab was placed fortified him with presence of mind: he laid down his paint-brush and palette, and hastened to conduct the Marquis de Montaleu into the sitting-room adjoining his atelier, and having expressed his high gratification at being honoured by such a visit, he offered him a chair; but the marquis refused, saying:

"Have you any objection to the gentlemen in your atelier hearing our conversation?"

"Certainly not."

"Then let us go there."

"If you prefer it," said Amab, completely thrown off his guard.

When he had ushered the marquis into a remote corner of his apartment, the marquis seated himself and for a moment was grave, sad, and absent, heaving many deep-drawn sighs. As to Amab, he stood before him like a man who knew nothing of the mystery which was spoken of by every one, nor of the misery which it naturally occasioned. A single night and a single lesson had marvellously improved Amab. Felina would have been satisfied with her pupil, and might have feared the consequences, for she knew he had a desperate adversary to deal with.

"You are acquainted, no doubt, with the occurrences which happened last night?" said the marquis.

"What occurrences?"

"You wrote to Madame Thoré, did you not?"

"To Madame Thoré? never that I remember."

"She pretends then that she received a letter from you."

"From me? It would seem from what M. de Mourion said that I received a letter from Charles but there is no more truth in my having written to Madame Thoré than there is in the statement that I received a letter from her brother."

"You had better then, sir, be on your guard, for I assure you there is murder, seduction, sequestration, and I don't know what not concealed under all this. It is a case which will end in a court of justice, if we ourselves don't bring it to some definite point this very day."

"It will end where it is proper that it should end—that is the business of those whom it may concern," rejoined Amab coldly.

"Let us keep our tempers, sir—did you not yesterday pay a visit to M. Thoré?"

"I did, sir."

"You explained to him the cause of Charles's disappearance?"

"I did, sir; —and did he tell it you?"

"No sir, you confided the secret to his honour, and therefore, notwithstanding he is almost distracted with grief for the safety of his daughter, yet nevertheless such a noble and generous-minded soul could not be guilty of so dishonourable an act as to break faith with you under any circumstance."

Amab slightly bowed his head, he felt himself relieved of a dreadful apprehension, for he had never ventured to tell Felina of the avowal that he had made to M. and Madame Thoré respecting the cause of their son's disappearance;—The old marquis continued:

"After having consulted with M. and Madame Thoré for some time, you left them in order to go and pay a visit to Madame de Cambure?"

"All this, sir, is quite correct."

"Well, then you went to see her for the purpose of:—"

"Excuse me, sir, but I don't see why any living soul has a right to interrogate me in the manner in which you are doing. Am I before a police magistrate?"

"No, sir, but it is to prevent your appearance before one, that I have sought this interview."

"I thank you for your kind consideration for me, on your part, but as I am not afraid to encounter the investigation which you seem to threaten me with I must request you to permit me to wait until then before I answer such questions, for the interrogator will have the advantage over you by being invested with unquestionable authority, which I shall then feel myself bound to submit to."

"Very well, sir," replied the marquis, shrugging his shoulders, "however, you remind me of my duty. I am a legislator, and it is my duty both to respect the laws which exist and to make new ones, and it is my business to endeavour as much as possible to keep the laws of the country respected as it is my duty to assist in creating new ones. Justice must take its course."

"I am perfectly willing that justice should take its course," said Amab, bowing with the air of a man who is well pleased to see that he is likely to get rid at last of a troublesome visitor.

The old marquis rose, took his hat in his hand, and looked about for his gloves and cane. He then turned round to make a bow, but it was evident that he did not wish to leave so soon. This feint to depart had been predicted to Amab by Felina in the following words:

"Perchance he may go down stairs, perhaps he may enter his carriage, and perhaps even he may go half way home; but be assured of this, that in a quarter of an hour he will return; for she knew well enough that as long as he should entertain the slightest hope of being able to hush up the affair, he would risk almost anything to do so, rather than let a public investigation take place which would drag his nephew's name before the censuring world.

Amab was silently admiring the wisdom of Felina who was able to understand character so well as actually to predict the very thing which occurred, when the old marquis said to him:

"Are you then going to imitate Madame de Cambure, and do you desire to bring disgrace upon Gustavus?"

"I may possibly demand an explanation of M. de Monrion for making false accusations against me."

"What accusations do you speak of?"

"It is a very serious charge."

"Explain yourself, sir, to what do you allude?"

"Pardon me, my lord, you came here to tell me of a dreadful event in which there was a murder, violence, and a letter, said to be written by me, whilst I have reason to fear I have been the dupe of some base treachery; - you seem to accuse me -- but what has happened? what has passed?"

"Why, don't you know that Mademoiselle Thoré was lured from her home yesterday by a letter from you."

"From me; but how can that be; when I tell you I never wrote to her."

"Well, that may be, sir; but are you not aware that she was conducted into Madame de Combure's apartments, and that she met there M. de Monrion, drunk, infuriated."

"M. de Monrion? why, I saw him at Madame Thoré's."

"That is true; and the letter I allude to was conveyed to Mademoiselle Thoré a short time after he left."

"Then I must still have been at M. Thoré's house?"

"Just so, sir."

"Then I must have written to her whilst I was with her?"

"This letter informed her that she alone could obtain the release of her brother."

"And could I have engaged her to undertake so perilous a task, when I myself, together with her parents, could not find means to accomplish it?"

"Excuse me, sir, I must tell you all. It has been surmised that the object was to draw this unhappy girl into the fatal snare which had been prepared for her."

"And I should have done this at the very moment I sought her hand?"

"I am telling you all the fears of minds in despair; but such a step might be considered as another link in the plot."

"In any case, then, sir, if you give me the credit of taking so much caution on such an occasion, would I not in like manner have taken care that M. de Monrion should not have profited at my expense by his baseness, for it was he who profited by it, he alone; and now, sir, in my turn let me ask you one question: this letter which was written by me, that is to say, the letter which is alleged to have been written by me, where is it?"

"It has been lost."

"Oh! indeed!"

"But Mademoiselle Thoré swears before God that it was written by you."

"It is a falsehood."

"Ah, sir! remember this child is dying - it is true she is delirious, but she would not be guilty of telling an untruth - you cannot deny it, sir, it was your writing."

"My handwriting," said Amab, who for a moment seemed to give way to this formidable difficulty. "But the apartment to which they conducted Mademoiselle Thoré, pray to whom did it belong?"

"To M. de Monrion. It was rented in his name, at least, by a certain valet-de-chambre, of the name of Jean."

At these words, Amab uttered a cry. "Oh, sir! sir, but this is dreadful, it is terrible, sir. The whole is a most infamous perpetration." As he spoke, he raised his eyes to heaven and gesticulated fearfully, and stamped his foot against the ground, so much so, that M. de Montaleu was obliged to calm him, and asked him what there was in the last words he had spoken to cause him so much uneasiness.

"What was conveyed in those words, sir? - but stop. Dont you recollect the first time that I had the honour of being introduced to you at M. de Monrion's house; don't you remember the picture which I refused to sell him at any price."

"Doubtless I do."

"Well, sir, as soon as you had left, your nephew swore that he was a man who could not suffer any living creature upon the face of the earth to refuse him anything that he set his heart upon, and therefore, as an exchange for this picture he would take my life - that he would insult me. I looked upon him as a madman?"

"He is mad, indeed," said the marquis.

"Well then, sir, on the following morning I met M. de Monrion, who shook hands with me, and joked. I do not well remember how, on the preference to be given to the original. At the time I did not take much notice of this; it would seem, however, that it was no light joke. Do you know, sir, what I learned this morning at home?"

"What was it?"

"I had a servant who asked me to give him a holiday for a week, and he recommended to me a comrade of his to fill his place whilst absent. I did not object to it. Well, then, I found this morning that my servant had returned without even apprising me of the circumstances. I was very much displeased at what had happened, and I asked him to explain why he had acted as he had done. At first he was silent, but after I threatened to dismiss him altogether from my service if he did not satisfactorily answer every question, he told me that the person whom he had recommended to me to fill his place, and whom I had accepted, was no other than M. de Monrion's valet-de-chambre, named Jean, whom, I feel confident, is the same person you just this moment mentioned. Well, this man sent back my servant this morning, saying:"

"You may go back to your old place, the farce is played out."

"Is this really possible" exclaimed the Marquis in utter amazement, but what object do you think they had in view."

"My lord," replied Amab drily a letter purported to have been written by me, but which I never wrote at all, was transmitted to Mademoiselle Thoré to entrap her in the snare evidently laid by M. de Monrion—as to the letter it has entirely disappeared—M. de Monrion actually had one of his agents in my very house who might readily have secured some of my papers in order to counterfeit my signature—the letter was forged.",

"Sir!" said the marquis rising.

"It was a count in the accusation which we had omitted to bring forward," said Amab in an overbearing manner, "but I shall not forget it."

"Did you ever write to Madame de Cambure, sir."

"Not once—besides what has Madame de Cambure to do with this affair: it was not she, I presume who sent M. de Monrion's valet-de-chambre to be my servant."

"But are you quite certain that you are correct in all your statements?"

"I can instantly satisfy you on that head by sending for my servant whom you may question as much as you think fit."

"Then you have not yet dismissed the rascal?"

"He leaves my house to-morrow."

"You will permit me to have him secured?"

"It is the very thing I meant to do."

M. de Montaleu was completely overreached by the audacious effrontery and the inexplicable mystery which enveloped in obscurity every circumstance connected with this intrigue. Like Madame Thoré he had only a faint suspicion of the culpability of Amab; as for himself, he felt satisfied that it was Madame de Cambure who, like a malicious and invisible fairy, was at the bottom of all this conspiracy; but he could not see on what charge to bring the accusation against her. Felina always contrived somehow or other to shelter herself from the crimes she committed by artfully causing the blame to fall on some innocent person totally ignorant even of her design.

The old marquis seemed at a loss to know what to say; at last, after meditating for a short time, he said to Amab:

"Will you allow me to ask you one more question: in your interview with Madame de Cambure what did she say to you?"

"She told me that yielding to M. Villon's appeal she had restored Charles to liberty?"

"And did not your own feelings urge you to carry this happy news to his family?"

"I believed that Charles was with them."

"Then you didn't go to convince yourself of the truth of Madame de Cambure's statement?"

"I was bound to believe all that she said."

"You place much confidence in that lady?"

"Well, you see that she didn't deceive me?"

"You are right, but you did not go and participate in the joy of your own family then, for you might, you ought, after your demand, have looked upon the family of Madame Thoré as your own, and longed to share with them their joy."

"After I had proposed for Mademoiselle Julia I received a very ambiguous answer, they postponed the decision of my happiness until the liberation of Charles."

"Well, but circumstances were in your favour."

"Charles might, perhaps, have to make confessions and disclosures, which in no wise concerned me. I thought some reserve becoming—and I still think it was opportune, since it is only through you that I have learned the certain return of Charles and the calamities of last night."

"And now, may I ask you, what are your real intentions respecting Mademoislle Thoré?"

"Ah, sir!" replied Amab, casting his eyes down.

The marquis looked fixedly at him, and then added:

"Pardon me, sir, but how came it that you were not aware that M. and Madame Thoré called at your house last night?"

"Because yesterday evening I left Jean, M. de Monrion's valet-de-chambre, in my atelier, and this morning I found that my own servant had returned, and his comrade did not think it necessary to mention this nocturnal visit."

"Then you did not pass the night at home?"

"I was but a few minutes since before a magistrate, now I am standing before a schoolmaster, I perceive."

"No, sir," said M. de Montaleu, sternly, "only my age and experience authorise me to say that it is not extraordinary for a man of your age to pass the night from home, were it not, just after he had proposed for the hand of a young girl."

"But, sir."

"This is serious."

"Do you threaten me?"

"It will be inquired into, sir."

Amab felt much perplexed; he knew that justice would not make any allowance for the chivalrous concealments of a discreet lover. M. de Montaleu began to gain ground; happily for Amab he suddenly bethought him of the advice which Felina had given him, and he immediately rejoined:

"Well, be it so, my lord, in a quarter of an hour my servant shall be arrested, and then, of course, he will be obliged to explain the reason why M. de Monrion sent his valet-de-chambre into my house as a sort of spy—and it will be inquired into, as you say."

"I know that you will never suffer such a thing. You dread an exposure just as much as I do; but now I feel certain that you passed the night at Madame de Cambure's house. Whether you are her dupe or her accomplice, it is out of my power to say. Farewell, sir.

## CHAPTER XL.

### THE SHE TIGER BAFFLED.

M. DE MONTALEU left M. Amab, in order to visit his nephew, who, thanks to the unremitting attentions lavished upon him, began rapidly to recover from the burning fever to which he had fallen a prey. The physicians had insisted on his being kept quiet for some hours before he should be informed of anything that might possibly excite him, and M. de Montaleu, availing himself of this moment of respite, had seized the opportunity of going to pay M. Amab a visit, Felina also took advantage of this favourable opportunity.

The old woman who had been left to take care of the wounded man, perceiving that he had fallen into a sound sleep, gently withdrew into an adjoining room.

Before we proceed further, we must inform our readers that the side of the invalid's bed which faced the windows was in a kind of recess, formed by hanging drapery, which, like the common bed-curtains, formed an enclosure or recess at the head and the foot of the couch; the recess at the head, if we may be allowed so to speak, formed a narrow passage which communicated with the antichamber into which the sick nurse had withdrawn; while the other enclosure at the foot of the bed seemed to have no aperture, so skilfully had they

managed to conceal behind the thick drapery which was hung round the apartment, a secret door opening into the back part of the closet.

This door communicated with a back staircase which, as Felina had said, went down into her apartment. It was by means of this door that she had gained her own room, whilst Victor on his side, had returned to his atelier, and it was now by this same door that Felina came up cautiously with the stealth and lightness of a panther drawing towards her prey. When she had penetrated into this recess, a profound silence, only disturbed by the short and heavy breathings of the sick man, pervaded the room. She stopped to listen. At the other end of the room a bell was gently rung. The old woman went to open the door, and Felina recognised the voices of some of her own servants, who came to enquire after the state of M. de Monrion's health. She availed herself of this circumstance which had been planned by herself, to engage the attention of the old sick nurse. She hastily drew aside the drapery which enclosed the foot of the bed, and leaning both arms on the side of the couch, like a person looking out of a window, she found herself at once face to face with M. de Monrion.

The latter, who had hardly fallen asleep, was awakened by the noise of the curtains. He beheld before him this unexpected apparition, but at first he gazed vacantly around, without being able to recognise Madame de Cambure. At length, he fixed his eyes attentively on her; his countenance beamed with the light of intelligence, and his memory gradually returned. Presently a bitter smile played round his lips, and a slight motion of the head, seemed to say:

"I expected you would come."

"Yes, it is I," said Madame de Cambure, in a low voice. "Alas! Gustavus, all that I predicted would come to pass, when you behaved so rudely and harshly to me, has now been accomplished. You have left your honour here, as I told you then."

Gustavus raised his hand to his chest, and placed it on the wound which Charles had given him, and Felina continued;

"In this place also you are going to leave your life, you mean to but no, Gustavus, at your age a man need not die, if he have a strong desire to live."

Monrion answered her again with a disdainful smile.

"You have no longer that resolution, say you; this wish has expired in your heart, has it not; because your fortune is dissipated and your name dishonoured?"

Gustavus raised his eyes towards heaven and heaved a deep sigh. There was more than a regret in the pain he now experienced, there was a sharp pang of remorse.

Monrion understood, at last, that a man of his distinction and rank, must render an account to others besides himself for the name and rank which society had endowed him with. About to be ushered into the presence of the Almighty, he believed he would shortly be called upon to account for the time which he had thoughtlessly wasted, the riches which he had squandered, of the abilities which he had abused. It was a soul-rending meditation, especially when he considered that all these choice blessings were undoubtedly intended for a noble and holy end, and when he meditated on these things he saw the extent of his culpability, and wept like a child.

"And yet," said Felina, again lowering her voice, "this fortune can be restored to you; your honour may rise up unsullied from the depth of the abyss in which you believe it to be buried."

Monrion fixed on her a look of distrust—and the She-Tiger continued:

"You know, I suppose, in whose hands you may recover your broken fortune?"

Monrion closed his eyes, and endeavoured to turn away his head not to behold the face of her who had despoiled him of his fortune, and who now exulted in her treachery, whilst he lay stretched upon the couch of death.

Felina did not desist from her purpose, notwithstanding that all the proposals she made were rejected with disdain. She continued:

"Although, to all outward appearances, you are dishonoured, and denounced as a guilty wretch, yet I hold in my possession documents which will take the crime from off your shoulders and place it upon those of another."

Monrion again fixed his eyes on Felina; the unfeigned astonishment which his whole countenance expressed seemed to say, that he wished from his soul that it could be so.

"Yes," added Madame de Cambure, whose voice glided like a low hissing through the silent room; "yes, if you desire it, Gustavus, to-morrow you shall be the victim, instead of the culprit. It shall be shown that your honour has been sacrificed to the wanton caprice of a hypocritical and abandoned woman. All this shall be satisfactorily proved, if you will only utter a few words."

"And what words do you want me to utter?" said Monrion, gasping for breath.

"Say to me, and swear it upon your honour; say but these words: "In another month you shall be the Countess of Monrion."

At this proposal the face of Gustavus continued unaltered, he merely raised his hand and seized the bell-rope, which was close beside him.

"Beware!" exclaimed Felina, in a tone of indescribable fury. Monrion rang the bell violently, sank back on his bed completely exhausted by the effort.

"Turn this woman out," said he to the sick nurse, who ran in on hearing the bell.

But Felina had already vanished, and the sick nurse raised her hands in wonder, muttering to herself, "God help us, God help us! he is delirious again."

---

## CHAPTER XLII.

### REPENTANCE AFTER SIN.

A SHORT time after, M. de Montaleu came to see his nephew, who, since the departure of Felina, had not made the least motion.

The sick nurse, who had begun to entertain new fears for the recovery of the invalid, informed M. de Montaleu of what had occurred; but he knew better than the old crone the real state of things, the porter having already told him of the secret communication between the first and second floors. He went into the little closet, and perceived by some of the folds of the drapery which had been shut in the door, as it had been hastily closed, that some one had recently passed through there.

"The fiend! the callous fiend!" he ejaculated, with passion.

This voice again aroused Monrion from the torpid state into which he had fallen; he saw his uncle, and raised himself up a little in his bed; he offered him his hand. The old marquis pressed it warmly in his, which Monrion gently raised to his lips. Tears started into the eyes of the old man, tears of joy and despair, for he had now regained the affections of the child he had so tenderly loved, and this was at the moment when he felt that a few short days would terminate his career, when dishonour threatened to accompany him to the grave.

He seated himself by his nephew, whose hand he still pressed. Monrion made a violent effort to articulate the following words:

"My uncle, after all the kind attention which you have so frequently shown me, I am going to ask you to render me an essential service; I want you to bring me here—to my death-bed, M. and Madame Thoré."

"Are you in earnest?" said the uncle.

"It must be done," continued Monrion, "and you must likewise bring the young man who so nobly and bravely avenged his sister."

"He is in custody," replied the marquis.

Monrion handed a paper to his uncle, who read the following declaration:

"I swear, that it was I who first attempted to strike M. Charles Thoré, and that it was in defending his own life that he wounded me."

He paused, and then continued:

"And moreover, you must bring Julia, too—the poor child whom I so cowardly outraged."

This time, M. de Montaleu made no answer, so extravagant did Monrion's request appear to him.

"Do this, my uncle," said Gustavus, without heading the astonishment of the old man; "do it, and I am sure you will have reason to be satisfied with me."

This last word sounded like an inspiration for the Marquis de Montaleu; he instantly stood up and said to Gustavus:

"Oh! thank you, my child, thank you; God, who has put this good thought into your heart, will restore you to us."

He hastened from the room to wait upon the miserable family of poor M. Thoré.

Scarcely had the marquis left the house before M. de Monrion called the sick nurse to him, and ordered her to push a heavy piece of furniture against the foot of his bed.

The nurse obeyed his orders, without knowing the reason why he gave them, as we humour the whims of an invalid.

This precaution having been taken, he called for pen, ink, and paper, and wrote with a trembling hand these words:

"M. de Monrion, who is about to breath his last sigh, wishes to have a few minutes' interview with M. Amab."

"Let this be delivered into M. Amab's hands," said the invalid, handing the paper to the sick nurse, "and then return as quick as you can."

He glanced towards the foot of the bed, and resumed, after a slight shiver:

"Remember, I do not wish to remain long by myself."

The sick nurse was just preparing to leave the room, when a ring at the bell announced a visitor: it was the doctor."

"Be quick and deliver my letter," said Gustavus "and whilst you are absent the doctor will keep me company."

The sick nurse went out, and the doctor and Gustavus, were left alone together. The former felt his pulse and examined him carefully.

"Doctor," said Gustavus, "how many hours, or how many days do you think I may still linger on?"

"I hope," replied the doctor, "that your recovery will enable us to reckon upon years."

"Hark!" replied Monrion, "I have a great crime to atone for, and it would be a crime to deceive me, I know I may consider myself a dead man, but I know not when my dissolution may take place, and therefore it is your place to tell me the truth, however dismal it may be."

The doctor appeared to hesitate.

"Take pity on me," said Monrion, "tell me when you think I shall die, do not think of my life which will soon pass away, think of my honor which I yearn to regain."

"Well then," said the doctor, "in four days hence, you will either die, or your recovery will have begun."

"Four days!" repeated Monrion, "that is very little."

"Yes, but I told you that you might recover."

"I don't wish it, doctor," rejoined Monrion, were it not that I have a last duty to perform, I would tear this bandage away and open this wound afresh. It is necessary that I should die, it is necessary for me as well as for the happiness of another. You might take all that I have said for a foolish vaunt were I to talk of committing suicide when in enjoyment of health; but when stretched on the couch of death it is otherwise. It is necessary for me to die, I repeat, it is absolutely necessary, and I desire death; only tell me, can you not exchange the uncertain recovery you speak of, for a few days of certain life?"

"What do you mean?" enquired the doctor in amazement.

"I mean to say, replied Monrion, "that instead of carefully husbanding what little strength I have left so as to bring on a long and weary convalescence—it may be possible for you to vivify this expiring vigour and increase it so as to render life more vital whilst it lasts though of shorter duration."

"Were I to do that it would be a crime," said the doctor, "and I will not do it."

"Then the thing is possible, doctor, and I am sure you will do it; for if you refuse me it will be the same as telling me that you wish me to die this very night."

"Well, I tell you what," replied the doctor after a moment's reflection; "pledge me your word of honour that if after the eight days which I shall employ in giving you artificial strength—if after those eight days have expired, your constitution is not completely exhausted—you will then entirely submit yourself to my care, and that having accomplished your last wish, you will abandon all thoughts of suicide."

Monrion did not answer immediately; he weighed the conditions which he was required to consent to, but at length he accepted them, saying:

"Upon my honour I will do nothing to accelerate my death."

Scarcely was the conversation finished, when the sick nurse returned; she had taken the letter herself to Amab and brought back the answer.

Monrion took the letter and trembled as he recognised the handwriting on the back, he hastily broke open the seal, and found but these words:

"He shall not go."

It was Felina who had written it for Amab; she was therefore with him, and had doubtless urged on him the same proposal as Monrion had rejected; and had drawn from him the pledge which Gustavus had refused.

Probably as the price of his honour and security this young and celebrated artist had been compelled to say:—

"In a fortnight you shall be the bride of M. Victor Amab."

"Unhappy man!" exclaimed Monrion, after he had read the letter.

Then raising his eyes to heaven, he added:

"Who can tell? perhaps it is a judgment on both of them."

The doctor, who had not yet left Monrion, ordered him to take a new kind of medicine, and waited until he saw the nurse administer it to him.

When Monrion had taken the draught which the doctor had prescribed, he relapsed into a sound sleep."

"This drowsiness," said the doctor, "will continue until night, but he mustn't be awakened out of it, for it would tend to bring his malady to a crisis, and he certainly would not have sufficient strength to support it. When once however he is thoroughly aroused, you may let any one come and see him who wishes to speak to him, for his strength will then have sufficiently returned to enable him to sustain a tolerably long interview with any one; but mind that you let none but M. de Montaleu enter this room until he has slept well and woke up."

"The doctor withdrew, and Monrion and the sick nurse remained alone."

Meanwhile M. de Montaleu had called upon M. and Madame Thoré. We need scarcely tell the reader, that as soon as he had learned the appalling adventure of the preceding night, the marquis had earnestly supplicated M. and Madame Thoré to suspend further proceedings. They however were too much absorbed in their deep affliction to give the matter their slightest consideration. They anxiously watched by the bedside of Julia, who had recovered just sufficient consciousness to immure herself in absolute silence and shrink from all communication.

At the same time M. de Montaleu had managed to prevent the magistrates from subjecting Charles to an investigation. He had promised to make strict enquiries into this terrible event, and each of them had too high an opinion of M. de Montaleu's honor to believe that he wished to profit by this delay to favor the escape of any delinquent, whoever he might be."

When M. de Montaleu left his nephew, he went first to Charles Thoré, for whom he obtained a temporary release on his own responsibility, independent of Monrion's declaration, his own rank as a peer of France, and his relationship to the victim, seemed sufficient guarantees of the prisoner's innocence, to entrust him to the marquis. When Charles and M. de Montaleu had reached M. and Madame Thoré's residence, their son had been completely gained over to the marquis's side, and he was quite ready to accompany him to M. de Monrion. M. and Madame Thoré were not, however so easily persuaded; they shrank from the idea of beholding face to face the wretch who had dishonoured their daughter. They demanded to know the object of this interview; and although M. de Montaleu did his best to explain to them what were his hopes; still he was afraid to speak with too much confidence on the subject, lest the wretched parents might have to retire from this solemn interview with a new and intolerable mortification. However, the supplications of their son, and the tears of M. de Montaleu, prevailed at last over all these objections; but when the marquis declared that it would be necessary for Julia to accompany them, they refused at once; they did more, they would not even allow so dreadful a proposal to be made to their unfortunate child. The discussion grew warm, and M. de Montaleu in vain had recourse to promises, arguments, and prayers. In spite of all he could urge, Madame Thoré remained inflexible on this point.

"No," said she, "I will not suffer my daughter to be killed in my arms, by making her such an odious proposal; innocent or dishonoured, my chief desire is, that her life may be spared to us."

The door of the little parlour where they were holding this discussion was suddenly flung open, and Julia, pale and feeble, entered the room, saying:

"And, in order that I may live, I wish to know what it is that the Count de Monrion can have to say to me?"

This time Julia had listened at the door; this time she had said to herself, that if on a former occasion she had heard the secrets which Amab had confided to her father, she would not so easily have been imposed upon by the fatal letter which had lured her into the snare where she had met her ruin. In fact, Julia had learned that it was M. de Montaleu who was in conference with her family. She knew that it was concerning her life and her honour that they were disputing, and this time she said that it was but right that she should know the sentence which they were going to pass upon her. Thus she had heard M. de Montaleu's proposal and Madame Thoré's objection, and she had entered to accept the interview which her mother dared not propose to her.

## CHAPTER XLIII.

### THE ATONEMENT.

The day was well nigh spent in bringing all these things to a favourable issue; because Madame Thoré wished to leave her house by night, to cross the street, too, at night, and to enter by night the house where she had discovered her deceived and dishonoured child, and where M. de Monrion was waiting for them.

When M. and Madame Thoré and their children arrived at M. de Monrion's, in company with the Marquis of Montaleu and M. Villon, Gustavus was still asleep. They found the doctor with him; he introduced them noiselessly into the room, where each sat down in silence.

M. Thoré seated himself near the recess, formed as we before said by the large folds of drapery which hung round the apartment. He had hold of his son with one hand, and of M. Villon with the other; grief had completely altered the foolish vanity of this man. He wept. Madame Thoré and her daughter sat down close to each other, but the parts of each seemed reversed from the ordinary state of things. On one side, it was the son who sustained the courage of the father; while, on the other, it was the mother who sustained the courage of her daughter. Madame Thoré held Julia's hand, but neither of them wept; for women have not only the spirit prompted by despair, but they have its dignity likewise. M. de Montaleu and the doctor, and soon after M. Villon, retired into a corner of the room, where, after waiting some seconds, the doctor said to the old marquis:

"M. Villon and I will shortly withdraw, for it will not be long before your nephew will awake."

A profound sigh which came from M. Monrion's bed seemed to answer these words, and an involuntary shudder came over everybody present, and fixed them to their seats: the fate of each was about to be determined.

The doctor and Villon were on the point of leaving the room, when Monrion, casting a searching glance around him, and observing the clerk's motion, and the doctor's, said, in a faint voice:

"Remain, gentlemen, remain; I have nothing to communicate but what men of honour and the friends of my family, and those of M. Thoré, may be permitted to hear, remain: for, if I had been able to assemble here all those whose word is an undisputable testimony, I would have done it. Remain, therefore, and listen with attention to what I am going to say. On the honour of a nobleman, it is true."

These few words seemed to have exhausted all M. de Monrion's strength, his head which he had partly raised up, sank heavily upon his pillow, and his breathing became thick and short.

The doctor made him take a few drops of a lotion which he had prepared.

Monrion recovered and made a sign with his hand to those present to draw nearer to his bed. They all advanced a few steps, all but Madame Thoré and Julia."

"You madam, and you particularly young lady, draw near," said Monrion.

Julia rose suddenly, advanced to the bedside of the dying man and stood up before him, while Madame Thoré sank into a chair which her son had given her.

Monrion gazed at Julia for some moments in silence; then, as if he had gathered strength in contemplating his victim, he said with a firmer voice:

"If the word of a nobleman is sacred before men, if the word of a dying man is sacred before God, believe what I am about to say."

Monrion drew breath, and then continued in a solemn tone addressing himself to Madame Thoré:

"Madam, your daughter entered this house immaculate, and she left it undefiled."

None replied to this declaration. Julia stood still and erect, but a bitter smile of disdain swept across her lips. Monrion who seemed to be exhausted after each sentence again drew breath.

"It is not enough," continued he, "that you should be satisfied as to Julia's innocence, it is necessary that the whole world should share your conviction. Listen to me then, Julia. It is not only with the outrage which I have done you that the world will seek to brand you; an infernal and pitiless hand is stretched over your fate. That hand knows well how to prepare the poison of calumny, as it knows how to compel its slaves to commit crime, not only will it be said that M. de Monrion has defiled the innocent daughter of M. Thoré, but it may likewise be said that he has taken M. Amab's mistress from her lover."

Madame Thoré uttered a deep moan and rushed towards her daughter; but Gustavus stopped her, saying:

"She understands me, your son too ought to understand me; he knows by whom this calumny has been spread."

Madame Thoré looked at her son who bowed his head saying:

"It is true."

"As for me madam," said Monrion, "I have heard your daughter's protestations, I have witnessed her noble despair, when in this very room she was as much tormented by the horror of my accusations as by the insult of my prayers. They had made me so drunk and reckless as to render me as ferocious as a wild beast; but they had not rendered me so stupid and dull as to deprive me of my memory. For two hours the delirium was prolonged and I did not believe;—but the delirium has left me, and I remember all, every thing; I have remembered and judged myself. I behold your daughter ruined by me, and still more by another."

Madame Thoré raised her eyes to M. de Monrion, as if to ask him whether it was to bear this she had come.

M. de Montaleu was silent, everybody else was afraid to speak when Madame Thoré said nothing.

Julia still stood up fixed and motionless.

After a few moments silence Monrion resumed, his voice becoming more and more feeble:

"In the midst of all the follies and faults of my youth there is one thing which I have at least respected, it is the honour of the name which I have inherited from my ancestors. There is a woman to whom I have sacrificed all my fortune, all my future prospects, and all my brilliant hopes; to this woman I sacrificed everything, my youth, my ambition, my love, my mother's life, my uncle's affection, the esteem and good opinion of the world—yes, I sacrificed everything to her—everything but my name. Yet to obtain this was the aim of her life; but I always answered her, and all who know me well know it—the whole world, indeed, knows it—that I will never ally the name of Monrion with that of a woman on whom the slightest suspicion rests."

Every one leaned anxiously over the couch of the sick man to hear his last words; they waited with anxiety the conclusion of this solemn declaration. Monrion, whose strength appeared to be increasing every moment, sat up in his bed, and added in a loud voice:

"My resolute resistance, my steadfast determination not to yield to the importunities of this woman has, I trust, rendered unassailable the last sanctuary of my honour."

"It is true," said M. de Montaleu, "and up to this day this sanctuary has been the only hope which remained to me."

"Well," said Monrion, stretching out his hand to Julia, "this sanctuary I here offer to you; this name which I have sworn never to bestow but on some irreproachable woman, will you accept it?"

Madame Thoré uttered a cry of joy, and Julia sank on her knees before the bed.

"This name will not only protect you against any infamy, it will also protect you against the calumny which they wish to brand you with. No one will ever dare to call in question the honour of the Countess de Monrion. I would not have offered you this name, had I not known that no other can offer the same amends."

The tears of Julia began to flow at this moment.

"This name," said Monrion, in a lower tone, as if he did not wish any one but Julia to hear it, "will not be a very cumbrous bond for you, the man who might render it hateful will scarcely have the time to give it you."

The tears of those who listened to Gustavus were his only answer. None dared to utter a word to express his thought; at length Monrion spoke again turning to Madame Thoré:

"Madame, do you reject my proposal?"

Just then the clock struck nine, Julia arose from her knees, and answered with dignity and firmness:

"I accept your offer, Count de Monrion; and if it shall please God to prolong your life, as I earnestly trust it may, I will be to you a faithful and a devoted wife."

Thank you, Julia," said Monrion, smiling and taking her hand, he pressed it to his lips, "I never do things by halves."

Madame Thoré had taken her daughter affectionately in her arms, imagining that she would have to console the despair of a heart compelled to forsake the man it adored; she was much surprised to behold Julia more composed even than herself She feared that this resolution concealed some fatal thoughts, and she said in an under breath to her daughter:

"This is a terrible sacrifice, but it is indispensable."

"No, mamma," replied Julia, "it is not a sacrifice—it is an honour which I will be worthy of."

Madame Thoré, whose ideas were now completely overturned, looked at her daughter with amazement. The girl understood her, and went on:

"Mother, you do not understand my real feelings; I have eluded your surveillance; this morning I sent a letter to him, for I requested why Count de Monrion desired this interview, and in my letter I asked him if he who loved me would do for me what another who loved me not was prepared to do, I gave him until nine o'clock, and told him to send his answer here—the hour is now passed, mother, that man is a coward."

Charles now approached M. de Monrion, followed by his father, the doctor, and the Marquis de Montaleu, each pressed his hand with tears of gratitude. M. Villon's turn having come Gustavus made a sign for him to approach close to his bed-side:

"You love Julia," said Monrion in a low tone of voice. "I confide her to your care—protect her when I am gone, and this will be very soon, depend upon it."

Villon, whose tears almost choked him, could not answer a single word, save by warmly squeezing his hand.

"It is not all," continued Gustavus, "I wish you to remain in this house with me until I leave it or go elsewhere."

"It is I shall watch over you," said M. de Montaleu, glancing his eye at the secret passage by which Felina had gained admittance.

"As you please," said Monrion. "I am going to put my life entirely into your hands, it will then be your place to take good care of it, only, my uncle, will you satisfy my last desire?"

"All that you wish shall be done," said the marquis.

"You know," replied Monrion, "that poor porcelain cup, which my mother used when she was dying; send it to me by somebody."

"If the marquis will entrust it to me," said Julia who had drawn nearer to Monrion, "I will bring it to him to-morrow."

"You!" said Gustavus, with a transport of joy, "have you the heart to set your foot again in this house?"

"I fear nothing now—I fear nobody—am I not your bethrothed?"

"Oh, doctor!" said Monrion, as the tears started to his eyes, "now I wish to live."

The doctor made no reply, and Monrion added, in a gentle tone:

"You are right—it will be better."

The next morning the bans which announced the marriage of M. Gustavus de Monrion and Mademoiselle Julia Thoré were published by the direcrection of M. de Montaleu in all due form; but as if to give these bans an insolent defiance, the announcement of a marriage between M. Victor Amab and Madame de Cambure was fixed for the same day.

The precarious state of Monrion's health could not admit of a long delay, and therefore M. de Montaleu obtained leave to hasten the ceremony, for fear of the death of his nephew in the interim: M. de Montaleu was desirous of avoiding the scandal which would arise in meeting Madame de Cambure in the same room, and before the same magistrate.

Notwithstanding all these precautions, the intrigues of Felina, were quite as active as the anticipations of M. de Montaleu, and she obtained the same favours as those which had been accorded to the Count de Monrion. M. de Montaleu dreaded so much meeting Madame de Cambure on the occasion of his nephew's marriage, that at length he adopted a strong measure, and he had so well succeeded in his plans, that eight days after he announced to Monrion, that, on the following morning the parish clerk and the magistrates had consented to come to his residence and perform the civil marriage in his own apartment.

Monrion heard all that his uncle had to say without making the slightest observation; then, when M. de Montaleu thought he had convinced his nephew of the necessity of acting thus, Gustavus said to him:

No, uncle, it is not thus that I wish to espouse Julia, if my strength should fail me, and I am unable to approach the altar, I must be carried there, I wish to have other witnesses present at this marriage besides those required by law."

"But," said M. de Montaleu, don't you know who else might be present.

"I know who you mean," replied Monrion, "and I hope they may be there. That Madame de Cambure and M. Amab will be married before the same magistrate and the same altar, as I shall espouse Mademoiselle Julia Thoré, is what I wish. This will be my revenge and my consolation."

The wishes of Monrion on this point were so inflexible that his uncle found himself obliged to submit.

M. de Montaleu, however, hoped that he would be able to make such arrangements that his nephew's marriage might precede that of M. Amab; but the hours had been already fixed, and therefore it became totally impossible to make any further alterations.

Thanks, however, to the delay occasioned by the slow departure of the affianced bride; thanks to the gentle pace at which the cortége proceeded to the mayoralty; they arrived at their place of destination a few moments after Amab and Madame de Cambure had departed.

It was a strange sight for the inhabitants of that part of the town, where Madame de Cambure resided, to see her leave her house in a magnificent equipage drawn by four high-mettled steeds, to see her numerous suite costly attired; and to behold her whose name had been familiar to every ear as irreparably linked with crime and deceit now radiant and triumphant. A few minutes after another cortége rolled slowly by, and, as it passed, the spectators caught a glimpse through the half-raised blinds of the carriage window, of the pallid features of a dying man.

Both went to celebrate the same kind of féte. She who was so sumptuously and magnificently adorned, was writhing under the maddening consciousness of wounded pride. While he who was exhausted and almost dying felt happy in his heart, because he was about to perform an honourable and generous action. But it was a much more pleasing spectacle to see Gustavus and Julia, after they had been married in the civil form by the magistrates, hasten to the church in order to sanctify by religion, their solemn union.

The imposing mass which had celebrated Felina and Amab's marriage was scarcely finished: the bride and bridegroom had left the sacristy, surrounded by handsome women and elegantly attired gentlemen—all were waiting under the porch of the church—a lackey in a loud commanding voice called for Madame Victor Amab's carriage, the splendid equipage and sumptuously caparisoned horses and riders were dashing noisily up to the church, when all at once they were stopped in their course, by the fatal chaise in which de Monrion reclined. As if the horses recognized the hand of him who had so often guided them, and as if they felt the damps of death issue from the ambulatory couch on which Monrion was stretched, they were seized with an unspeakable terror, and suddenly stood still, with their long necks outstretched and their ears pricked up. They sniffed with their smoking nostrils the almost lifeless corpse which passed before them. In truth, Monrion seemed completely worn out.

At this melancholy sight, mirth and gladness fled from ever heart; vows and promises were stifled. Every one silently withdrew as if to let a funeral pass, and although they were no longer within the church all took off their hats as if to a coffin.

Felina, who was the last to leave the sacristry with her bridesmaids, became surprised at the profound silence which had succeeded the joyous tumult of the assembled crowds. She arrived at the door of the sacred temple just as Julia accompanied by her father and de Monrion, still borne on his couch, and followed by M. de Montaleu, were about to enter; she stopped and looked at them as they passed.

Never was a more livid pallor depicted on the features of any woman: Felina's eye seemed steadfastly fixed on the haggard brow of M. de Monrion; it followed him to the altar. In vain whilst the priest was hastily performing the religious ceremony, did Felina's friends inform her that it was time for her to retire. In vain did Amab himself in a low tone entreat of her not to scandalize the number of friends he had invited by exhibiting before them her ungovernable rage. Felina was deaf to all he said, she did not make any reply, for she remained immovable in her place until the priest having received the mutual pledges of the two spouses, had given them the nuptial blessing.

On the evening of the same day, at the hotel of Madame de Cambure, a noisy orchestra seemed to animate an assemblage of fashionable dancers, bedecked with silks and diamonds. They laughed, they talked, they sang in all the excitement of thoughtless intoxicating revelry. Never was a marriage celebrated with more magnificence and pomp. Lights gushed out as it were from every corner of the room, which was decorated with gold and bronze statues. Valets, richly dressed, glided about with silver salvers, loaded with the choicest wines and most delectable fruits.

It was an enchanting scene, like the poetical dreams which imagination paints when we think of the glories of the Eastern clime.

At the same hour, a young girl, all alone, in a room dimly lighted by a single wax taper, was kneeling at the side of the bed, on which lay the lifeless body of her husband, who had given her his name and hereditary titles, at the very moment death had summoned him to another world. She raised her eyes to heaven and prayed God to enable her to preserve unsullied the name which had been so magnanimously bestowed upon her. But two partitions separated the festive hall from the chamber of death, but in that festive hall anger, disappointment, and despair mocked this false pleasure, whilst hope and calm resignation resided within the chamber of death.

However, the feast was ended, and Madame Thoré's maternal solicitude aroused Julia from her long prayer. At the dawn of day Julia went home with her mother, and in that virginal chamber into which she returned with the title of Countess de Monrion, she found no change save that there stood on a marble slab a small porcelain cup, which had once belonged to Gustavus's mother; it had a note in it, which had been written with M. de Monrion's own hand.

"The lips of my mother pressed the edges of this cup a few minutes before she expired, my lips have also done the same. Cherish it, as I have cherished it till now."

Julia in her turn took the cup, and putting it to her mouth, said aloud:

"I accept thy present, and take the kisses which thou hast imprinted upon it."

But elsewhere Felina, proud of her transcendant beauty, awaited in the nuptial chamber the husband whom circumstances had forced upon her. Amab entered, and notwithstanding that intoxicating passion she had inspired, he started back in dismay on beholding suspended over the foot of the nuptial bed the masterpiece which had gained him so much renown and so much misfortune.

Felina had hung over her couch the picture which represented Julia habited as the immaculate virgin. This was an insult and a blasphemy; moreover, it was a threat, portending evil to Amab's future happiness: he understood it so.

Whether this ominous prediction was well founded or not, will be seen in the sequel of this extraordinary narrative.

---

## CHAPTER XLIV.

### A BIRD'S EYE SKETCH.

In this work our object has been to show the phenomena of Virtue and Vice, as it is met with in the world. Most novels terminate with marriage, as if the rest of human life were a blank, or a happy valley, full of smiles and sunbeams, with shepherds and shepherdesses reclining in the shade of trees as happy and blooming as themselves, with white flocks in the foreground, and tinkling bells softly sighing in the wind. Many poets, and not a few romance writers, have left us this description of life beyond the hymenial altar. But if ever there was a time so tranquil and placid for the active beings and fluctuating spirits of this world, it must have greatly differed from our own. In France, and in most of the European countries, real life begins after marriage, and in the dark pages that we have still to write, in depicting the deep and unfathomable malice of Felina de Cambure, now Madame Amab, we shall find events of the most exciting character crowding upon us in each succeeding chapter. But let not malevolent critics, who seem to envy whatever is done to entertain other men—exclaim against our purpose, which is really to raise virtue, and to rebuke vice. The torturing scenes which are to follow, and the heart-rending misery which lacerates the feelings of the reader, as he follows poor Julia, now the Countess de Monrion, through the arduous path of rectitude, with calumny hovering about her like a malaria, are pictures of human life as it is, and no mind can be prejudiced by the contemplation. The triumphs of the wicked are very great whilst they last; but they are transient, and act as lures to punish those they seem to serve. But if those which virtue gains are fewer, they are more lasting, and they certainly are both greater and brighter. And having written this much in explanation, we beg to renew the conflict between vindictive malice and patient goodness, after an interval of a few years.

The curtain rises in the lovely month of May. Sweet and happy Month! Why does it end so soon?

On a warm and lovely morning, two horsemen were seen ascending a rough flinty byway, which turned its winding course along a hillock.

By the respective position of the riders, you saw directly that they were master and servant; by their garments they both were or evidently had been soldiers.

The first of them, who was mounted on a very fine Arabian steed, looked about thirty. He was fair, but the thick moustache and imperial he wore had a fallow colour, which lent a fierce expression to his aspect; whilst his greyish blue eye, his sharp aquiline nose, added to the tone of this expression, softened only by the particular grace of the mouth. The African sun had imparted to the rider's face that brown and torrid complexion which since a few years has grown familiar to the eyes of Frenchmen. This gentleman wore a riding coat buttoned to the chin, with that rigid nicety which bespeaks the habit of military life. A plain slip of red ribbon peeped out from his button hole.

His companion, or rather the soldier who attended as his servant, wore, like his master, both moustache and imperial. He was a small swarthy man, lean, slender, always restless on the saddle, and tortured with a continual itching to speak: he could not let any one pass by without enquiring how far it still was from the place they were at to the farm of Lavordon.

Meanwhile his master appeared prepossessed by some mental and sorrowful anxiety, and scarcely returned the peasants the salute which country people seldom fail to render a man mounted on a handsome steed and decorated with a red ribbon.

At length they reached the topmost part of the hillock they were climbing; at which spot the road narrowed between an almost perpendicular rock overhanging it on the left, and a turreted castle bordering it on the right.

This passage was the key of the valley they had recently ridden across, and of a second valley which here opened to the travellers in all its magnificence. Whether it was that the master wished to survey this prospect, or that he wanted to breathe his horse, he stopped and directed at the landscape before him an inquisitive and almost threatening look. After that, a bitter smile passed over his handsome mouth, and he was about to pursue his course when a jovial voice suddenly resounded above him.

It came from the old castle situated on his right. In fact, whilst the two horsemen were climbing the steep, a young man was pacing up and down a kind of terrace-walk between the two largest towers of this quadrangular castle. He was dressed in a brocade robe-de-chambre, wore a sort of Greek cap splendidly embroidered, and was smoking a cigar. This man likewise was between eight-and-twenty and thirty; his face was what the women call pretty, his shape perfectly formed, his manners elegant, with a touch of affectation, admirably suited to his soft, almost feminine look; moreover he was dark and bewitchingly pale. As he walked up and down the terrace, he had descried the two horsemen at some distance, but had not at first paid much attention to them, so absorbed did he appear to be with some inward anxiety.

However, the appearance of the travellers having probably struck him, he had entered one of the towers enclosing the terrace, had brought out a telescope and had examined them. By the astonishment depicted in his face, it was easy to understand that he knew them, but was not able to account for the motive of their coming. He resumed his cigar and his promenade, and waited for the two horsemen to reach the sort of strait we have already spoken of, then he leaned over the terrace wall and cried out as loud as he could:

"Ho! colonel."

The officer did not hear.

"Ho! most worthy Thomas Rien!"

The person thus denominated looked up to see whence the voice proceeded.

"This way, my lion of the desert," resumed the young man.

"M. de Brias, I believe?" said the colonel.

"Myself. What the devil brings you to this wilderness of a country—this desert Morvan?"

"You were saying?"

"Stop," continued M. de Brias, "come out of this break-neck lane, turn to your right, and about forty yards off you will find the iron gate which has replaced the portcullis of this Gothic manor; they will let you in without blast of trumpet. Aly Muley, for I see you are attended by your faithful spahi, will conduct Mogador and Penny to the stables, for I have not forgotten your illustrious chargers, and if you have no engagement either of pleasure or business, if you are not come to look for either a mistress or an inheritance, we will eat together a slice of boar's head, steeped with a bottle of old Madeira, which I won at Gibraltar from an old English gentleman, who asserted that the French were not good marksmen, and with whom I wagered two hundred bottles of this excellent wine that I would break his left arm at fifty paces, which I did." *

The colonel listened to the young man with a friendly smile.

"You said to the right—an iron gateway—very good."

He urged his horse into a gallop, and was in a moment at the gate; he leapt down as Aly Muley was saying to him in a very marked Gascon accent:

"Are we to breakfast here?"

"Yes," said the colonel, "but you must not get drunk."

"I shall keep sober," answered Aly.

A moment after, Colonel Thomas Rien was by the side of his host on another terrace overlooking the valley he was going to pass through, when the voice of Brias had arrested him.

"I would not believe my faithful telescope," said Brias to him. I knew you were at Paris, but I never could have suspected that having but one month to spend in France, you would come and squander the smallest portion of it in this abominable country."

"It is magnificent," said the colonel. "These rising grounds, bristling with woods, and dotted with neat habitations, that little rivulet intersected with causeways and gliding through the valley, these elegant mills buried in the pale foliage of the willow trees, those wide green meadows streaked with lines of poplars, present a most agreeable picture to the eye of a soldier who, for fifteen years, has seen nothing but a burning sky and the scorched campaigns of Algeria."

"At your pleasure, colonel. But I am a better diplomatist than you are a good soldier. I hate the landscapes of my native place, because they too often tell me—"

"That you have no office?"

"Exactly so."

"I heard so at Paris."

"And what do people say?"

"They say that you are embarrassed—that you have debts."

"Everything gets known. What more?"

'That the minister *entreats* you to set your affairs in order."

* Some Englishmen might be found who would bet upon the consequences of shooting even at their fellow creatures, when shooting was really going on; but no English gentleman would lend his own body as a target for all the grapes that Madeira has produced since its discovery.—*Translator's Note.*

"He tells everything, then, our minister: in that case, I have nothing more to inform you of as to the causes of my sojourn in these parts. And now, colonel, if you please, we will take our breakfast in that turret."

"Can you not have it served upon this terrace?"

"Very well. You shall enjoy at your ease our dull national verdure. And I, whilst looking at you, shall fancy myself at the bivouac of Isly. You are splendidly tanned, colonel: you must have met with a bewildering success at Paris."

"Marshal Soult received me kindly, and the king expressed his satisfaction to me in the most gracious manner."

"Good! very good!" said Brias helping the colonel, "you are still the same man as ever, reserved and impenetrable. The consequence is, I withdraw the question I put to you over this wall, when I asked you what brought you down to this cursed country."

"I am quite ready to tell you. But first, before I answer you categorically, I should like to have some information."

"A military habit; you don't like to advance until you have studied the map of the country. Well! my dear Thomas Rien, I will give you the historical, topographical, and psychological description of the country. We have here an admirable site for such a purpose. If your eyes are not good enough to follow me, here is my telescope to help you to distinguish the points and landmarks; shall I begin or would you like better to question me?"

"I am all attention, speak."

"Well! then," continued Brias, turning towards the valley expanding below them, "do you see on the right yonder, behind the hill opposite to us, the castle with its sharp gable ends, its weathercocks, its dove cote, and large sheet of water with marble border? You do not see it, but it is there."

"I see the gable-ends and dove cote."

"Well! that is the abode of Viscount Hector de Montaleu."

"Ah!" said the colonel whom the name appeared to strike.

"He is the son of the second brother to the Marquis de Montaleu, a peer of France, president of the council-general of the Nievre, whose house I will show you presently."

"What sort of man is this Hector de Montaleu."

"Five feet eight inches, French measure, (six feet English); fiery fair, a low forehead, as strong as the late Marshall Saxe; he drinks like a sand-hole, eats like a lawyer's clerk invited to dine with his master, and is a terrible sportsman. To you or me he would seem half a fool, but he is quite clever among the peasants, whom he always takes in when driving his bargains with them. He may be about five and thirty, and was quite an adept at the college of Juilly in grammar and philosophy. It is suspected that he would not mind killing with a blow of his fist any man who stood in his way."

"He is doubtless on the best of terms with his uncle the peer of France?"—

"Do you prefer the interrogative form of communication?"

"No; proceed, de Brias, I wish you to speak."

"That's right! Let us continue travelling along the height opposite. Look, now, I beg you, at that immense building the base of which is buried beneath a carpet of jessamin, clemates, and glycería; the large windows with their brick recesses seem to be watching us."

"Ah!" said the colonel taking up the telescope, "whose house is that?"

"Whose castle, you mean. It is there that for nearly the last two centuries the family of Rudes-

THE MEETING AT THE CASTLE.

gens has dwelt. M. Annibal Cesar de Rudesgens was formerly page to Louis XVI., then an emigrant, then a captain in Condé's army, after that colonel in the Austrian service, and at length, in 1813, he was married to Mademoiselle Van Marken, the daughter of the contractor of that name, who, if you are at all versed in the history of those times, died at the bottom of a dungeon, at Cologne, without the great Napoleon being able to force him to restore the least fraction of the millions he had purloined. The consequence was that the fair Artémise Van Marken brought her seducer, for there was one in the case, a portion of four millions of francs (£160,000), with which the brave Marquis de Rudesgens repurchased the castle of his ancestors, and became one of the richest proprietors in all the country round. Now, in a few days there will be a party at the castle, and as I intend to present you there, I must tell you whom you will meet."

De Brias took a glass of the old Madeira, and went on:

"The old marquis is a bit of a dwarf who tells you he was once a Narcissus, an Adonis, that artists took his likeness by stealth, that he danced like Vestris, fenced like Saint George, and fascinated like Lauzun. To hear him speak, he still retains many of these qualities, which produces on the part of Madame de Rudesgens scenes of jealousy which are richly grotesque. She herself is a tall, long, flat, raw-boned German lady, strait-laced, with ardent loving eyes, and five and forty years of youth engulfed in the anxieties occasioned by her husband's infidelity, though she is the woman to make amends if any swain were smitten with her mincing lures."

"So, it is to the party to be given by these two relics of a bygone age that you propose to take me?"

"Because besides these two Gothic moveables, the castle contains the daughter and son-in-law of M. de Rudesgens, that is M. de Champmortain and his lovely young wife."

"Oh! there is a young wife, is there?"

"Beautiful as an angel, and witty, even before birth, for she borrowed of her father all the grace, elegance, wit and fascination he pretends to have had, and of her mother all the tenderness, fortitude and spirit she will not acknowledge to have had, and she has left them all their faults and absurdities."

"She seems, then, to be an accomplished woman."

"Alas! not so. She has principles of inaccessible severity and a touch of devotion which allows Champmortain to plunge into all manner of wild adventures in which he spends his life, without any risk to his honour, and without his wife even knowing anything of it. She sees nothing but her missal."

"Is she not a fair woman?"

"Yes."

"With long hair, dressed in the Louis XIV. fashion?"

"The same."

"Well! my dear Brias, if she does not look at what is done at home, she willingly observes what is done elsewhere, and if the approaching-glass she was using just now is as good as yours, she must see us breakfasting."

"Do you think so?" said Brias confusedly.

"Look yourself. For even with the naked eye—methinks I still perceive a woman at the corner window."

"That is possible," said Brias, "she may be watching the return of her husband, who, on the pretext that he loses his way in the woods whilst hunting, does not return home every night."

The colonel bowed, and wishing to relieve his entertainer's embarrassment said to him:

"M. de Champmortain is not so sensible as he ought to be of the charms of Madame de Champmortain!"

"The count," resumed Brias, "having now reached the age when corpulency clogs and fetters the enticements of gallantry, got married in order to break off with his old habits, such as the jockey-club, the opera, the Café de Paris, etc. He held out three years. But one fine morning, about two years since, he fell in with a certain Madame Victor Amab."

"Victor Amab!" said the colonel with a little agitation in his voice: "you spoke to me, I think, about him in Africa; he is a painter who married one Madame de Cambure."

"Exactly so, the very same; continue to look at the hill before us, but down yonder on your left; look at that castle in the *renaissance* style, with its leaden roofs; it is there that M. and Madame Victor Amab reside. It is the old castle of the Monrion family which has passed into the hands of the said lady, by consequence of—"

"You mentioned all that to me in Africa," said the colonel, coldly; "you likewise told me of the singular marriage *in extremis* of the last Monrion with the daughter of a potter, a silly little ——"

"Silence, colonel, or I shall be angry. Respect, love, and admiration, should all be offered to the most perfect beauty, to the most refined wit, to the most finished elegance, to the most bewitching grace, to the purest virtue, to all that is charming and divine at once—to the countess Julia de Monrion."

The colonel knit his brows, and yet resumed, in a voice sufficiently still:

"This woman is a perfect prodigy it seems!"

"First, her position partakes of the marvellous. She is a widow, and if you fully recollect the story, I related to you, she might enter upon a second union with the maidenly garland she wore at the first. She is therefore a pure and candid young girl, with a title, a rank, a freedom of action, which generally implies an experience which she does not possess. Oh! colonel, if you only saw her in the drawing room of the old Marquis de Montaleu doing the honours of the house, with that superior ease, that benevolent authority, that perfect taste, which appear to belong only to a woman whom nothing can astonish; and could you see, at the same time, her surprise, her confusion, at certain questions; if you saw that maidenly mind, that maidenly person, that maidenly look, bearing so simply her name and title, supporting still better the glittering ornaments of the highest lady, guessing, rather than understanding, the little secrets of those around her.—Ah! colonel!—I cannot well explain it to you, but there is about her a charm so peculiar, so original—"

"She is here, then, with the Marquis de Montaleu?"

"Yes, for a month past."

"And doubtless, she has brought with her some member of her respectable family?"

"What completes the marvel, colonel is this—that whilst I was relating her story to you, nearly three years since, her father and mother were included among the victims of that terrific catastrophe on the Versailles railway. She is now an orphan. It was at that period M. de Montaleu took charge of her. He is passionately fond of her, and very naturally. But he will not hear a second marriage spoken of. This is the second time he has brought her down to this country, to remove her, I believe, from the fascinations which surrounded her at Paris; for he is as jealous of her as a miser is of his treasure."

"My dear Fréderic de Brias, has not this treasure something to do with your exile here?"

The young diplomatist heaved a deep sigh.

"You are a man of honour, colonel, and I may tell you that I had hoped to be able to follow the minister's good advice, and settle my affairs here. The countess has inherited a fortune of her own, amounting to twenty-five thousand livres a-year; the wreck of the former splendour of Monrion has given her about as much more, which already renders her a good match; but she will inherit the estate of the old Marquis de Montaleu, I am quite sure of it."

"You think so?" said the colonel, with a bitter smile.

"Which makes her a prize that a prince might envy. Montaleu has upwards of three hundred thousand livres a-year."

"But there's his nephew, Hector de Montaleu."

"Who, if he knew that his uncle had made a will in favour of the countess, would be capable of strangling the poor child to annul it; and, on the other hand, if he were certain that no will had been drawn up, would be capable of opening his claims to the succession of the marquis by some unlucky gun-shot."

"Impossible," said the colonel.

"I assure you he is a kind of brute-animal, with too little heart to fear God, and too little mind to fear the attorney-general. He is a mad dog hitherto muzzled by his uncertainty."

"And what does he do?"

"What does he do? He has fancied he shall win the inheritance by winning the heiress."

"Is he in love, then?"

"Do not profane the word, colonel. M. Hector de Montaleu had seldom ever raised his desires above the charms of some poultry-yard beauty, until he happened one day to turn the head of the poor young wife of a farmer, whose house you see yonder at the bottom of the valley, near the castle belonging to Hector de Montaleu."

"And what sort of woman is she?"

"It is a romance, colonel. A young girl, with wild extravagant ideas, who, after she had been educated at the *Conservatoire*, fancied she could easily settle down as a rich farmer's wife: she relinquished her ball-room conquests, her merry and joyous life of the stage, her dreams of fame and glory for a country existence. Now, colonel, you know what a country life is in the Nièvre: a poultry-yard full of dung, in which the filthiest marketable animals swarm together; a cottage floored with mother earth, wooden shoes to be worn as a necessity when you went out, the care of the poultry, the sight of the plough labourers, the bleating of muddy sheep, the conversation of coarse and discontented peasants, the winter evenings spent by yourself, the kitchen fire-side your only drawing-room, ham hung up to dry, bacon boiling in the pot: all this had very soon broken the enchantment of the fair Leda. Then it was she met with this fierce Hector—this percussion gun—Nimrod. All brute as he is, he still has a mode of expression, a sort of deportment and manner, which induced Leda (for that is her name) to make a hero of him—and our pretty Parisian came to have her Hector, just as she was on the point of resigning the virtues of Andromache."

"That at least ought to reassure you as to your rival's interference."

"Oh! egad! it is not he who perplexes me, and were it not for the arrival of Champmortain—"

"Champmortain! a married man!" said the colonel observing Brias.

"But he is a devil of a babbler," said Frederic confused.

"And Madame de Champmortain is inquisitive and makes use of her telescopes wonderfully."

"Colonel, I swear to you on my honour—"

"Excuse the jest—I do not wish to know the obstacles which obstruct your love affair—unless they lie in yonder castle, on the right, on the very hill where we are."

"There?" said Brias shrugging his shoulders. "No. That is the castle of Montéclain."

"Of the Marquis de Montéclain," said the colonel, "he who served as a volunteer some ten years ago, in the campaign of Constantine?"

"Himself. Do you know him?"

"He was wounded by my side after he had rendered me the service of ridding me of an Arab, who was aiming at me with his pistol—what has become of him since then?"

"Nothing—he has led precisely the same life: keeping actresses, giving parties, running horses on the race-course; he has revived the game of lansquenet, visited watering places, eloped with two ambassadresses, killed three or four men on the ground, and in spite of all these achievements, he offered himself last year as a member for the borough. M. de Montaleu was indignant, and having called a preparatory meeting, he related without mercy the whole history of the singular merits of M. Arthur de Montéclain, and had him dismissed once and for all. They are therefore mortal enemies."

"He has, I believe, immense estates in this country?"

"Yes."

"Does he live upon them?"

"No."

"What, then, is he doing here?"

"Nothing, for he was rejected in the same manner at the elections of the *conseil général*, thanks still to the old marquis. Just for the present, he hunts in the forest with Hector and his farmer Bricord, another Nimrod of the same strength as the young and terrible Montaleu."

"Ah!" said the colonel fixing an inquiring look on M. de Brias, "and who is this Bricord?"

"Oh! 'faith, the farmer, the husband of this Parisian Leda."

"Indeed," said the colonel in an altered tone, "is that unfortunate Bricord the victim of this blackguard Montaleu?"

"Do you know him too?" asked Brias, struck by the tone of passion and menace in which the colonel had uttered the last words.

"It is his house I am going to Brias, and I take God to witness that I will not suffer this worthy fellow to continue any longer the dupe of a worthless woman and a clown."

"Colonel, colonel, colonel," said Brias, raising his voice, "I offered you hospitality, you accepted it; you asked for information about the country here, I have given it to you, that you might turn it to advantage; but all that has been said here must live and die here—or else, colonel—"

"You and I must cut each other's throats, is it not so, Brias?"

"Certainly."

"It is extraordinary, that you who are a diplomatist should have so decided a taste for extreme measures,"

"It is my own fault if I am obliged to have recourse to them this time: it proceeds from my being too confiding. Had I remained shut, close, walled in and padlocked like you, I should not now be under the necessity of requiring your discretion at the point of my sword."

"Are you sure that would be the best means of enforcing it?"

"I doubt it; you are brave, and handle the sword skilfully. But if I kill you, I shall be certain that you will not betray me; if you kill me, nobody will blame me for an indiscretion which will have cost me my life."

"Well! Brias—I will be silent. But are you quite sure of what you say?"

"Faith, it was that stupid churl Hector who told me about it. But you, colonel, what powerful interest can you take in this Bricord that you wish to tell him so disagreeable a fact."

The colonel did not reply.

"How now, my worthy guest," said Brias, good-humouredly, "know you not that you are here in the castle of my ancestors? Know you not that from the height of these walls, whence I invited you to breakfast, one of my noble forefathers would not have failed to bar your passage, until you should have answered his questions, even supposing they had not obliged you to pay the right of way through this valley, whose mysteries I have just revealed,—even supposing, too, they had not stripped you of your effects, instead of harbouring you as I am doing? Ah! that was the good time: it was then worth while being noble and having a fortified castle; they pillaged, they plundered, they paid no debts, and they put people to the torture when they would not speak."

"You shall not be driven to such extremities to learn what you wish to know. I am come to see Bricord."

"You? What can there be in common between you and that brave peasant?"

"Are you acquainted with my history, Brias?"

"Yes, I know that you went to Africa at fifteen, about 1830; that you entered a regiment of light horse as trumpeter; that at eighteen you were quarter-master, at nineteen you had a medal, at twenty you were made a lieutenant, at twenty-four a captain and officer of the legion of honour, and that now you are a commander and colonel at thirty. I believe and I know that you are one of those of whom they make generals and marshals."

"I hope so," said the colonel, coldly; "but you do not know that all this fine fortune has been three times on the point of being destroyed; the first time at Mascara, where I had fallen beneath two shots, amidst a group of Arabs, who were preparing to cut off my head, when a brave soldier charged upon them all alone, rescued me from them, and bore me off to the camp hospital. The second time, it was during the retreat from Constantine. We had no horses left, and I had a wound in my leg which prevented me from walking. The same soldier took me on his shoulders and carried me thus for seven hours, which did not prevent him from fighting, since we were quite in the rear-guard; only I helped him by tearing up his cartridges, because his jaw had been crushed by a ball. This soldier, Brias, was Bricord. The third time, as I told you, it was Montéclain who saved my life."

"By all the infernal spirits!" said Brias, "this Bricord is a gallant fellow, and the next time I fall in with that clodpole Montaleu, I will pick a quarrel with him, and kill him like a young wolf."

"Think you that it would be a likely way to settle your affairs with the minister?"

"The deuce take the minister, and my debts above all! but tell me, Colonel Rien—how does it happen that with such a fine military spirit this Bricord should have left the service to come ——? Alas! alas!"

"It is my turn to tell you a secret, which I shall confide to your honour. This man who is so brave, so intelligent, and who has more common sense in him than you and I put together—this poor man was never able to learn either to read or write. I urged it on him, I commanded it, I pointed out to him the example of his comrades, my own, but all was vain—he never could surmount the difficulty. Between this intellect—in all other respects so fine—and the most ordinary teaching, there was an insuperable barrier. He tried—he persisted—he was near going mad. Then seeing that he could never hope to rise, he left the army, and it was at my recommendation that Montéclain gave him a farm of his to manage."

"You did not meet Montéclain at Paris, I suppose?"

"No, they told me when I called at his hotel, that he was in London."

"That may have been; for he only came down here a fortnight since. But what puzzles me altogether, is, that your friend Bricord, with his simplicity of heart and ignorance, should have taken a fancy to a wench who thought of nothing but novels and romances."

"Because he worships most fervently those unknown deities whom he must not approach; because he is so much ashamed of his ignorance that he very probably has never owned it to his wife; because Montéclain is not aware of it, and the honest fellow would not forgive me for disclosing the secret to you."

"Still he must have signed his marriage licence—"

"That he *was* able to do; I taught him to write his name; it cost me two months to bring about; he writes it, but it would be impossible for him to read it."

"This is very singular," said Brias, carelessly. "So you are come to visit your deliverer."

"When he left me, he made me promise him that, if ever I came into this part of the country, I would go and see him. I am come on purpose to make good my promise."

"And have you no other object?" said Brias, looking hard at the colonel.

"None at all," answered the latter, coldly.

"Are you expected at Bricord's?"

"No."

"Well! I am to dine this very day with Madame Amab; Montéclain will be there. Probably Champmortain will come too, and perhaps even the wild boar, Hector de Montaleu. Shall I present you?"

"Without notice?"

"A man like you, colonel, requires none. They will thank me; you are not only the lion of the desert, but the lion of fashion likewise. Come, and I shall owe you the obligation of being permitted to kiss Felina's pretty hand."

The colonel consented. A man of less levity of character than Brias would have wondered at this easy assent on the part of a man so reserved as Colonel Rien, especially had he remarked the derisive smile which escaped him.

## CHAPTER XLVI.

### HUSBAND AND WIFE.

Let us now direct our course towards the castle of the renaissance style, which Brias had pointed out to Colonel Thomas Rien as being the abode of Madame Felina Amab. Let us pass through a magnificent iron gateway, wend our way along a wide avenue of elm trees, the end of which brings us in front of a fine house, decorated with the most fantastic sculptures, either preserved or renovated with a care which lent to the old fabric the appearance of a work fresh from the sculptor's chisel, though it still retained the dun or dark brown colour, the all-surpassing touch, which none but time, the greatest of artists, can give to our temples and monuments.

Let us ascend the marble steps of the fine *perron*, cross the spacious hall, with its vaulty roof, and enter a sumptuous dining-room, decorated with rich side-boards overspread with costly plate. The table was already laid out for breakfast, two covers were placed opposite each other. Victor Amab was alone, and was pacing the room with a moody look, whilst a tall lackey, in morning costume, went to and fro preparing the repast.

Victor Amab had already ceased to be the young aspirant, full of haughty ambition, whose early career had opened with so much glory. A few years had proved sufficient to fix upon his brow, which was turning bald, the deep lines of some consuming anxiety. Premature wrinkles manifested that his youth had experienced the hardest trials, and there was something gloomy and restless in his eye, which plainly told that his soul's confidence in other men was dead.

After he had walked about for some minutes, he turned and said to the servant:

"François, has your mistress been told that breakfast is ready?"

"The breakfast bell has been rung, and madame will not let any one call her."

Amab heaved a deep sigh. It would have been too much for so trivial an inconvenience, but that sigh bespoke a long arrear of grievances and provocations which had accumulated for years.

However, he continued to walk about, till at last he stopped at the door opening into the park. He stood before the castle of M. de Montaleu.. At first, his eyes seemed to avoid it; but at length attracted by an imperceptible magnet to that abode, his look settled upon it. How many bitter regrets rose up in his breast! What hopeless, what desolate reflections were in that eye, as it rested on that distant house.

"There," the melancholy look seemed to say, "there dwell grace, innocence, peacefulness, benevolence, devotedness, and all those virtues which I disregarded. Here, far otherwise—"

Amab was terrified by the picture he had drawn of his own house, and turned suddenly away. Few men have spirit enough to face and examine the evil they have brought upon themselves. But this calamity was fated to return upon him in a thousand intolerable little instances. And truly, he detected the servant looking at him with a titter.

"The newspapers and letters must have come by this time," said Amab, sharply, "go and fetch them."

"They have been carried up stairs to madame."

"Very well," said Amab, peevishly, "you may go."

The domestic left the room, and Amab gave vent to a low but dreadful complaint.

He clenched his hands with violence.

Then he resumed his promenade, but this time it was with quick and agitated steps. A few minutes after, the servant came back, took one of the covers off the table, and placed it on the tray with the rest of the breakfast materials.

"What are you doing there," inquired Amab.

"Madame will breakfast in her own room," answered the lackey, carrying off the tray.

Amab's endurance was at an end.

He rang the bell furiously, but nobody came; he rang a second time, no notice was taken of it; at length, he drew the bell-pull several times. The servant entered with that insolent look which every lackey can put on when he has a good reason to give to one about to scold him.

"Don't you hear me, varlet?" said Amab angrily.

"I was carrying up madame's breakfast. I cannot be both up stairs and down stairs."

"Where is Louis?"

"Madame has sent him on an errand; he has been gone this hour."

"Where is Peter?"

"Madame has lent him all day to the gardener to assist in making baskets for the drawing-room."

"Wait upon me."

"Madame has just told me to go to Bricord's farm to treat for the little pony he is breeding."

"That is not your business, but the coachman's."

"Madame intends riding in the forest after breakfast, and the coachman has no time."

"This is becoming ridiculous!" said Amab, grinding his teeth. "Leave the room."

The wretched man sat down to table, waited on himself and made a scanty meal; when he had finished, he left the parlour and mounted the grand staircase with a resolute look. On reaching the first floor, opposite Felina's apartment, he seemed about to go in, when suddenly he stopped, hesitated, and whether from want of spirit, or apprehension of the anger which disturbed him, he passed on to the second floor, and went into a spacious atelier, where he threw himself down upon a sofa. Now that he was alone, Amab gave free vent to the wrath which he had found it so hard to restrain. Broken exclamations escaped from his bosom.

"Oh! wretch! miserable wretch that I am!" he cried, pressing his head despairingly between his hands. This must have an end. "It must!"

For the twentieth time, Amab had thus conceived a great resolution; the life they led him was insufferable, and he was resolved to change it."

Just as he uttered the words, *It must!* the door of his atelier was opened, and Felina came in, habited in the most elegant attire, still beautiful, still young, arrogant, commanding, resplendent. She carried in her hands the newspapers and letters by that day's post.

"Really, Victor," said she to him, as she entered, with the most gracious air, "you are not over-attentive; one might die in one's room, without your deigning to go up or down stairs to inquire about one's health."

"You will allow me, Felina," returned Victor, tartly, "not to admit this reproach; you have often enough cautioned me that I must not enter your apartment, until you thought proper to leave it."

"How, sir," said Felina, bitterly, "would you quarrel about a reproach which formerly would have appeared kind and flattering? You are out of temper; I will leave you."

"Not yet," said Amab, sharply; "we have some serious matters to speak of."

"True," resumed Felina, "you remind me of it; here are some letters which concern you, and which I request you to be so good as to answer, for I am not accustomed to such importunities."

—"What letters are they?" continued Amab, taking them from Felina, and reading them whilst the She-Tiger moved about the atelier examining some sketches recently begun by her husband.

The letters which Amab rapidly glanced over, were not calculated to soothe his vexation; they contained applications for money from his Paris tradesmen, almost all of them short and dry, some of them written in that insulting style which proves that the writer's patience has been pushed to the utmost verge. Amab threw them angrily on the table, exclaiming:

"Well! let them distrain, let them sell; I should prefer it to being for ever exposed to this endless persecution."

"Take care!" said Felina composedly, "it would be a grievous scandal for you; and I, for my part, would never endure the disgrace."

"Felina," replied Amab, "methinks you might screen me from it. Thanks to our marriage articles, your private fortune is safe from all legal proceedings."

"Do you not think I acted well?"

"I do not blame what I agreed to," resumed Amab drily; "but after all, you might in this instance have come to my help; for," added he with a nervous shudder, and taking the letters up again from the table, "here is a jeweller's bill, and I do not wear diamonds."

"Yes," said Felina, "they are those you presented me on my birthday: the setting of them is exquisitely tasteful."

"This other bill," continued the painter, "is the coachmaker's; and this comes from your horse-dealer's."

"You wished to have a carriage for your private use: I made these purchases for you alone."

"Finally," said Amab with rising anger, "here is a goldsmith's account; this at least must concern us both."

"That is possible," said Felina taking the bill; "let me see."

She read the letter, and then handed it back to Amab, saying:

"You did not read it to the end; this tradesman does not apply to you for the full amount of his goods, you see he acknowledges he has received half the sum due to him; the articles were supplied in the month of February last year, and as early as in April I had paid my own share in this account."

Amab groaned with furious wrath. The lady continued:

"You wanted to speak to me seriously, Victor; well, and so did I desire it; but really you have made me stand in such dread of explanations owing to your ill temper, that I even hesitate to give you good advice. Think you that I am not a cruel sufferer when I see you thus producing your own ruin and mine? for if you distrust me sufficiently to believe that I would leave you a prey to your difficulties, I esteem too much the honour of the name I have assumed as my own not to come to your relief. You lack order and foresight."

"It seems to me, however," said Amab, "that my personal expenses make but a poor part of the extravagant sums which are consumed and wasted in this house."

"I will not take offence at the tone in which you speak to me," resumed Felina with calm disdain; "you suffer, and I pity those who suffer; you complain of the extravagant sums wasted in this house; was it not understood between us that our expenses should be fixed at a stated amount? of this amount I take one share and you the other. Have I ever asked you for anything beyond what was agreed upon? Is it my fault if, beyond this stated sum, your caprices induce you to scatter money with incredible imprudence? Why did you order those diamonds for my birthday? did I require them? Why did you buy a new carriage when we had one already? Why order that service of plate which you were so anxious for? Because you saw your comrade, M. L——, give diamonds to his wife; and you would have the carriage because G—— has got two; and on returning from dinner at your friend T——'s house you tormented my life out until I consented to the extravagant expense of this service of plate."

"God help me!" said Amab, "did you not speak to me twenty times about Madame L——'s diamonds? Did you not come home sick and unwell in a hackney coach, because I one day chanced to use your carriage? Finally, you taunted me so bitterly on the meanness of our plate, that I wished to satisfy your desires, and not my own caprices, as you call them. And the gratitude you now evince is a fine set off against the struggle I make to please you."

"More reproaches!" cried Felina, "and yet I expected them. But tell me sir, is it not natural for a woman to desire what may elevate her position in the eyes of the world? I wished for those things which I saw possessed by others, who, in my estimation, have less talent than you have. What they did for their wives, methought you might well do for yours, and when I saw you solicit me so pressingly to accept it, did I not think, ought I not to have thought, you were not going beyond the bounds of your resources? have I been mistaken? Love, yes sir, the love which induced me to sacrifice my liberty for you, must have deluded me. Do you not possess all the talent I ascribed to you? must I admit that twenty artists whom you speak of with disdain, have more skill, more celebrity, more merit than you have? My whole heart refuses to acknowledge it; but after all, if the proofs are produced, I will submit to them—there will be no avoiding it."

Nothing can describe Amab's inward torture at these words, uttered in the softest and most serious tone. His pride was wounded in its most sensitive fibres, the deep conviction that he was the sport of a superior subtlety without his being able to bring it home to her, was like a torture to Amab.

"You are right," said he with clenched teeth, "I have but a moderate talent—a talent which cannot sustain the expenses of such a house as yours."

"We will reduce them whenever you like," said Felina, "but in the meantime, you must answer the persons who have not yet been paid."

"I have no money, and I know not where to find any."

"These four pictures already begun, and which may be completed in a fortnight if you work diligently at them, may be turned to account."

"They are sold—and if I must tell you everything, I have already been paid for them before hand."

"That is unfortunate, for I think that M. de Champmortain would have bought them of you at a price which would soon have relieved you of those bawling creditors who prevent you from continuing your labours."

"M. de Champmortain," said Amab gloomily, "it appears to me he is not the man you ought to advise me to have recourse to."

"I understand the motives of your very proper susceptibility, sir. When we came down to this place, I called to visit Madame de Champmortain, and she has not returned my visit. In a few days they intend giving a party, and every body within thirty miles round is invited to it, except you; it is an insult which I must endure."

"It does not prevent you from receiving M. de Champmortain."

"My pride has long been laid aside, Victor, I am your wife. I will not, I cannot embroil you with a man who is one of those who build up and demolish reputation. Besides M. de Champmortain is indignant at the behaviour of his family towards you—"

"Towards me!" muttered Amab bitterly, for he felt he was suffering an exclusion which he had a right to think was not meant for himself. "Always me!"

Felina did not or would not hear this complaint muttered to himself, and proceeded:

"It appears to me, at all events, that by shewing a little politeness to a man of good company, I have afforded you the means of avoiding scandalous proceedings. M. de Champmortain is in love with these pictures. Sell them to him."

"I have already told you that the amount has been paid to me beforehand."

"Has the time been fixed for your delivering them up to the purchaser?"

"Yes, as soon as they shall be finished."

"In that case they need not be completed for six months. You can paint them a second time."

"But I cannot throw them in the face of M. de Champmortain after I have refused them to him several times."

"M. de Champmortain is coming to dine here to-day: it will be easy to lead him on to speak of them again."

"What! M. de Champmortain is to dine here—again to-day. He comes here very frequently."

"He shall not come," retorted Felina coldly. "I will write to tell him that a sudden attack of illness will prevent your receiving him. I will do as much to MM. de Brias, Montaleu and Montéclain; for I suppose that it is not M. de Champmortain alone whom you seek to exclude."

"God help me! Felina I do not wish to exclude anyone; but more moderation in M. de Champmortain's assiduity would be more becoming."

"You are jealous?" asked she.

Amab returned no answer.

"Answer me frankly; are you jealous?"

"I do not suspect you, certainly;—but slander—may lend an unfavourable aspect to a friendly intimacy."

"Oh! misery!" muttered Felina, "is it come to this! suspicion to-day and ruin to-morrow. Enough, sir, I will receive no company; I will not stir abroad; these promenades, once my only consolation, shall be given up—people might believe—".

"But I don't say that—" cried Amab impatiently; "I merely make a remark, and have no wish for you to avail yourself of it as an excuse to tax me with harshness."

"Did I utter a word which even looked like a complaint?"

Amab had preserved all his anger; but by a singular chance or an admirable skill, Felina had placed a barrier between her and every opening through which it might have escaped. He continued silent a moment, and at length cried out;

"Look you, Felina, I am not satisfied."

"Do you think that my own heart is full of joy?".

"Felina, you love me no more."

"Say at once that I never loved you at all."

"That may be true."

"Well done, sir, go on—"

"But, after all, you see I am unhappy; I am in a most painful situation, and instead of advising and encouraging me, you put me on the rack."

"Sir," said Felina rising, "when your reason shall have returned, when you are more composed, I will come to you again."

"Come! now you pretend I am gone mad. Where are you going, Felina?"

"To my own apartment."

"Why do you take those letters?"

"To answer, to pacify your creditors; to gain time and find means to pay them by mortgaging some estate."

"But I will not suffer it," said Amab abashed; "I will pay them; I will write."

Felina shrugged her shoulders.

"Certainly—" resumed Amab haughtily, "and the price of these pictures will meet the claim."

"You have been paid before."

"I will follow the advice you gave me, I will sell them."

"Where?"

"At Paris."

"Where those who ordered them of you may chance to light upon them at your new purchasers. Here, in the country, the thing is possible—they will remain buried in the castle of the owner. But you refuse to see the only man who might save you."

At that moment Amab had on his tongue one of those fatal words which betray the shameful compromise which the heart makes with hard fortune. He turned round to Felina and said to her:

"Felina, do you love me?"

"Ah! Victor, Victor, is it right for you to doubt me?"

"When we love, we are afraid."

"Ah!" said Felina, "you do not love me well enough to be jealous of me."

"I!"—exclaimed Amab, "oh! Felina, Felina, you know that I live only for thee. Is it possible not to love thee? But thou, thou—

"I, yes, I love you—and I ought not, for you suspect me—"

"No, no, Felina, I will follow thy counsel. I will give those pictures to M. de Champmortain, for you love me, do you not? He is coming! so much the better; we will settle the matter this very day."

"Wisely resolved--now you are reasonable once more—and I will stay and keep you company."

"No—I cannot allow it. You are unwell, go and take your airing; I shall work with all the more courage that I know you are taking diversion."

"In that case, farewell for a while."

Felina left her husband. As she was getting into her carriage, her faithful chambermaid, the pretended mute, whom she had not parted with, offered her a parasol.

"Well, does the dinner hold good?"

"I have just managed to sell to M. de Champmortain his grand privileges."

"To atone for his small ones. Is master still in a passion?"

Felina smiled with disdainful pity.

"No," said she, "the poor man is quite exhausted."

Felina told the truth; a few years had proved sufficient to crush that ardent character, once so firm and vigorous. She had degraded his ambition and brought it down from the heights of glory to the depths of speculation; she had relaxed and enervated his spirit by leading him to pursue as his aim, those riches and that repose which he was never destined to attain, for, thanks to the luxury of the house, necessity returned after the most persevering efforts. She had done worse, she had worn out the artist's integrity in this continual struggle; she had hurried him into a labyrinth of perplexed affairs, which are sometimes excused in men of talent, but which carry with them cares, anxieties, and above all, dissatisfaction with one's self; she had wearied, she had withered everything as well in his mind as in his heart.

One thing alone, in Amab, had outlived this imperceptible degradation—it was that love of the sublime and beautiful which constituted his genius. But this worship he had been compelled to renounce; for Amab had not had the courage to drive the dealers out of the temple; he saw with grief that his noble talent was doled out in productions which he did not esteem, even when most largely retributed. Instead of being one of those men on whom a whole nation has fixed its eyes, expecting the advent of his new work, he was one of those fashionable artists, who are rated at a high price, but whose reputation is trucked. Consequently, the only feeling which was left to him of his powerful nature as an artist, had become a misfortune and almost a remorse.

He remained alone at his work; but his apparent reconcilement had not restored to his heart that spirit which is drawn from the renewal of confidence. Amab had left unsaid many things still murmuring within him, the offspring of anger, suspicion, and despair. Among the grievances which he felt most acutely was the bar which had been put upon him on his arrival in that country. He did not doubt but that M. de Montaleu was the origin of this interdict, but he had no longer spirit enough left to ask for an explanation, and he endured with impotent anger the discredit which had been thrown upon him by his marriage with a woman already too notorious for her misdeeds.

---

## CHAPTER XLVII.

### THE DOUBLE HOUSEHOLD.

The scene displays a wainscotted saloon of water-coloured green, with fanciful birds, with white-gilt tables rounded at the edge, and with green and rose-coloured drapery.

M. de Rudesgens, whose old but pleasant face we shall meet again, sat, or more correctly to speak, lolled in a deep *bergère*, or easy chair, enfolded within a striped robe-de-chambre, of calimanco stuff. Armed with a pocket comb, he busied himself in bringing back over the crown of his head the few and scanty grey hairs which his fiery and tempestuous passions had left him. He seemed not even to hear the very warm and earnest conversation which was sustained between his respectable spouse and his son-in-law, M. de Champmortain.

Madame de Rudesgens, with a *Quotidienne* (Daily News) in her hand, and her spectacles upon her nose, was sitting upright and rigid in her chair, all her features agitated and bristling with excitement.

Champmortain, a man about forty, whose look and demeanour were grand and dignified, was pacing the apartment with ill-concealed impatience, whilst the fair and lovely Sylvia, his wife, did not raise her eyes from the embroidery frame, on which her needle was drawing some fine leaves from a chrystal vase by her side.

"It must not, it shall not be, sir," said Madame de Rudesgens, in a dry and vibrating voice.

"That will be wrong, madame," answered Chammortain, striking his words, like his mother-in-law, as with a hammer.

"I shall not send an invitation to M. and Madame Amab; you are at liberty to see such people either at their house or your own, if my daughter deems it proper; but they shall not set foot in my house. I believe that is your opinion, Annibal?" she added, turning towards her husband.

"Ay! ay!" said the latter, who was suddenly arrested in his hairy exercise by this appeal; umph! they are neighbours, you know."

"The swineherd of the borough is our neighbour as well; and do you invite him? You make me strange answers, Annibal."

"But, madame," resumed Champmortain, "M. Amab is a man of the best company; I meet him in all the highest circles of Paris—he goes to the king's parties."

"What king?" inquired Madame de Rudesgens, in a tone like that of an angry parrot.

"What! madame," said Champmortain, "are you going to argue that question with me again? I know that you are as unwilling to recognise Louis Philippe as your father was to acknowledge Napoleon."

"What do you mean?" shrieked Madame de Rudesgens, snatching off her spectacles to discharge at her son-in-law all the fire in her looks, "what do you mean, sir? Annibal—this is an insult to my father's memory, my father, who died the victim of Bonaparte's tyranny. Well, Annibal, you don't reply."

"Oh! oh!" cried M. de Rudesgens, slightly scratching his nose, "I did not understand M. de Champmortain to say anything unfavourable to the political opinions of the late M. Van Marken."

"Let me entreat you," resumed Champmortain, "to leave kings in peace, and the dead likewise. For the last time, I ask you for an invitation for M. Amab and his lady."

"For the last time, I refuse it."

"In that case, madame," said Champmortain, I request you to grant me the favour of a private interview."

"If you please, sir," said Madame de Rudesgens, sharply.

"Will you permit us, Sylvia?"

Madame de Champmortain bowed her head and left the room without uttering a word, whilst M. de Rudesgens went up to his son-in-law, and said to him, with a light self-sufficient look:

"You will not prevail with her at all, my dear fellow; she never could endure a pretty woman in her company."

"What are you saying about pretty women?" cried Madame de Rudesgens, in an acrimonious voice.

"You are mistaken, dear Artémise," replied M. de Rudesgens, alarmed, and assuming a tone of gallantry, I was only talking of yourself."

"I am obliged to you," said the old lady in a bitter tone. "I see clearly that this Madame Amab has got possession of your heart. Men love none but creatures of that sort."

"Madame," said Champmortain, warmly, moderate your language."

"Champmortain is right," said M. de Rudesgens. Deuce take it! she is a very fine woman—"

"Are you acquainted with her, Annibal?" resumed the haughty Artémise, with a kindling eye.

"Whenever I meet her, I salute her, and she smiles at me. That is all—up to this time," he added, in a whisper to Champmortain.

Then he went out humming an air from the *Visitandines.*

Champmortain could not help shrugging his shoulders, whilst Madame de Rudesgens muttered:

"He deceives me, I am sure that he deceives me."

"Come, good mamma," said Champmortain, as soon as he was alone with his mother-in-law, "let us talk together in a friendly way."

"Annibal shall pay for it," said Madame de Rudesgens, without attending to her son-in-law."

"M. de Rudesgens has no concern in the business."

"He's a libertine, sir; yes, that is the proper word," rejoined the old spouse, in a lachrymose tone; and when you see how much I suffer by him, you want to introduce into my house a woman whose notorious beauty has already turned his head."

"If you stand in dread of Madame Amab because she is handsome, how is it that you invite Madame de Monrion, who is equally beautiful."

"Excuse me, my son, excuse me, Madame de Monrion is a woman whose virtue protects her from temptation, whilst your Madame Amab has a very questionable reputation."

"She has been much calumniated, and, between ourselves, if she wished to intrigue, she might I think, choose better for herself than to allure M. de Rudesgens."

"Why so, if you please?" said the lady, tartly.

"He is, I believe, seventy, or seventy-two?"

"Some men of forty there are who do not carry their age so well," said Artémise, addressing her answer to her son-in-law, with a very significant nod.

Champmortain bit his lips and resumed somewhat sourly:

"I warrant you that Madame Amab's virtue will continue unassailable despite the seventy-two years so well carried by your husband."

"He has two hundred thousand francs a-year, (£8000,) son-in-law, and this fortune, destined to be hereafter your own, is a powerful recommendation to certain creatures."

Champmortain changed colour, and felt all the more humiliated that he could not altogether disavow the justice of the observation. Yet he restrained himself, and continued:

"You will not, I am sure, *good mamma**," said he, "drive me to extremities, I entreat you, understand me well, I entreat you to invite M. and Madame Amab."

The old lady scanned her son-in-law with a searching glance.

"Excuse me, M. de Champmortain, but this persistency might lead me to suspect that you—yourself—"

"Is that it?" said Champmortain, drily. "In that case, I shall begin: 'One day that I had Cardinal de ——— to dine with me—'"

"Sir," cried Madame de Rudesgens, in affright, that abominable story again?—you dare to tell it to me to my face?"

"Upon my honour, I will relate it before the whole company, if you still refuse me."

Madame de Rudesgens bowed her head and heaved three prodigious sighs.

"You are ungenerous, son-in-law."

"You are not indulgent, good mamma."

---

* *Good mamma*, and *good papa*, are terms of endearment used in families by French children when speaking to a grandmother or grandfather. They are likewise used by married sons and daughters to the old people. This is one amongst the millions of the sweet socialities of life, in which that amiable people so much excel us. The French cannot understand that the whole sum of human life is to be spent in a fretful struggle to exist. When they are not pulling down thrones, and making revolutions, they see no harm in being happy; and this they understand so well, that every sentence they exchange, contains some kind word or other to cheer the hearts of those whom they address. With us it is the reverse: we taunt, we jeer, we mock one another, as if life ought to be nothing else but one long contest of selfishness and unkindness. Bulwer, Dickens, Thackenay, and Lever, have said so, as well as Scott and Byron.

"Well then, those people shall be invited."

"And let not a single word be said to Sylvia which might put ideas into her head which she neither has nor ought to have."

"Very well. But I implore you, let this be the last time that I hear this dreadful story called up."

"It shall be the last time if you like."

The next moment, Champmortain rejoined his wife and her father in the park.

"Well!" exclaimed M. de Rudesgens.

"She has listened to reason."

"So then, we triumph, we win the day," cried the old gentleman, delighted.

A cold and reproving look from his daughter cut him short.

"I mean that you triumph," resumed M. de Rudesgens.

But a short disdainful smile from Madame de Champmortain warned him a second time that he had committed a new blunder.

"I mean to say that my wife submits—I am going to send off a letter immediately," said Champmortain.

"I was so sure that you would succeed with my mother, that I have just dispatched one," said Sylvia, in a curt and pointed tone.

"You are always charming," answered her husband with a look of the most perfect satisfaction.

"It would have been as well to have included a word of apology to excuse so tardy an invitation," said M. de Rudesgens.

"M. de Champmortain will have the opportunity to do so for us," said Sylvia; "for I believe he is to dine to-day at M. Amab's."

"Psha!—" said the antiquated beau.

"Yes," said Champmortain, carelessly; "I forgot to tell you of it."

"You are mistaken," said Sylvia, coldly, "you did tell me of it."

"I—"

"Yes, you, sir, for you are incapable of forgetting what is due to my father and mother, by stopping out without giving us previous notice. It was I who forgot to tell them."

This little speech was delivered in a tone most precise, correct, and angular, after which the lady withdrew.

"Where the deuce has she learned all this?" said Champmortain; "I am sure I never mentioned it to her."

"Ah!" cried M. de Rudesgens, "the women know everything. My wife would snuff a rival three thousand miles off. Look, this very day I had scarcely uttered Madame Amab's name, and it almost brought on a regular scene. With such jealous women as these an intrigue is out of the question."

Whilst he was thus listening to the grievances of his father in-law, Champmortain had gradually reached a small door leading out of the park.

"Are you going out?" said M. de Rudesgens to him.

"Yes, I feel heavy; I want to take a little exercise."

"On horseback, it seems? for I can see your horses and groom behind yonder thicket."

"Indeed? well! I will take advantage of it, and instead of walking I shall ride; perhaps I may push on as far as Viscount Hector de Montaleu's, whom I am going to introduce to Felina."

On hearing this name, M. de Rudesgens fixed a look of astonishment on his son-in-law.

"The consequence is," continued Champmortain, "that I shall probably not return before dinner. It may be late in the night before I come home."

M. de Rudesgens had not withdrawn his eye from his son-in-law.

"Felina, did you say? Felina! How now! M. de Champmortain, are you deceiving my daughter?"

"I? deceive my wife?" said Champmortain, satirically, "That was all mighty well in your time; for, you have often told me yourself, there is no living in these days, we cannot play the truant now."

"Take care, Champmortain," said M. de Rudesgens, putting on his conquering look again; if it were true that you were deceiving our Sylvia, I would avenge her—"

"You shall not have that trouble."

"Never mind! only take care," said the old gentleman, with an indescribable look, "I will chouse you of your Felina. Ho!"

A cry like that of a wild cat issued from behind the door of the park. Champmortain sprang upon his horse, laughing heartily, and M. de Rudesgens found himself face to face with the infuriated Artemisa.

The next moment, Champmortain stopped the full speed of his horse opposite the farm of Lavordan, into which a strange servant was leading two horses of great value. Champmortain, who was a connaisseur, was about to alight and inquire whether they belonged to Bricord, who dealt in that traffic, when a carriage was seen entering the forest at the extremity of the road.

Thereupon he set spurs to his horse and rode off.

---

## CHAPTER XLVIII.

### THE FARM.

Léda had just entered the large room on the ground floor of the farm-house, the same that Bricord had had boarded, and ornamented with bright red calico curtains, in honour of his consort. Bricord was seated before a table, on which stood two glasses and two bottles, one of the latter already emptied; on the other side was Aly Muley, the servant, or rather the soldier of Colonel Thomas Rien. When Léda came in, she was pale, agitated, and trembling; she threw off the little cloth mantle which covered her, and would probably have crossed the room without stopping had not her husband called out to her in a joyous tone:

"Ah! Léda, great, good news! my colonel, Colonel Thomas, has arrived in the country; here is Aly Muley, an old comrade of the Turkish cavalry, whom he has sent to me in advance, with his luggage."

"Ah!" said Léda, in an abstractic manner, "your colonel arrived? so much the better for you."

"And, you see Léda, the best of the matter is, that he does not come, because he is passing this way, but expressly for me; only think, girl, seventy leagues, and nothing less for the pleasure of seeing me. Ah! thunder!—hold, Aly, only to hear what you are come to tell me; I would give my right hand, though to say the truth, it does not serve me for any great things, since the sword cut that spoilt my writing."

While he was speaking, Aly Muley rose, and addressing the farmer's wife, said to her, bowing, glass in hand.

"I drink, less for drinking's sake, than to wish you joy and happiness."

"Thank you, sir," said Léda drily.

"The lady got up, feet foremost, this morning

it seems," said Aly, resuming his place near Bricord.

"Perhaps she didn't sleep well," replied his friend, in a low voice, "and so is suffering from her nerves."

Aly looked at Bricord, made an expressive grimace, and drank off the contents of his glass at a draught.

Léda seated herself in a corner; there was a something wandering in her look; her whole frame quivered. Her husband, rendered proud and joyous, by his colonel's arrival, approached her, without remarking this agitation.

"Léda," said he, "I have a favour to ask of you. The colonel is coming, and you know your bedroom is the only well-furnished one in our house. Will you give it up to him for the little time he stays here?"

"My room," said Léda, "you ask me to give up my room?"

"Yes."

"Oh!" she said, rising suddenly, "take it and the others too, you may take them all."

Aly observed the countenances of both husband and wife and muttered inwardly,

"She has weak nerves—poor Bricord!"

"Are you angry about it? Does it vex you?" said Bricord, "well then, the colonel is not hard to please; people don't always sleep on feather beds in Africa; I will give him another room."

"I tell you, you can take mine," replied Léda.

"In that case," said Aly to Bricord, "will you shew me which is Madame's room that I may go and prepare for him."

"I have something to arrange there," said Léda, "in an hour it will be at your disposal."

She went out immediately; Aly Muley resumed his seat, and poured himself out a glass of wine. Bricord discontented and confused, went and seated himself near him.

"She has been ill for some time past," said he, "she is the best of wives, so well educated, so clever."

"It seems business goes well with you," said Aly in a bawling voice, the farm is a good one."

"However," said Bricord, "if it vexes her to give up her room, the colonel would not be amiss in mine."

Aly looked at Bricord again, and then resumed:

"And raising horses, has that succeeded?"

"There is something very extraordinary about Léda, certainly," said Bricord rising, "I must speak to her. Wait a moment."

He went out, and Aly Muley soon heard him knock at a door, which however remained unopened. Bricord called Léda, she did not answer. He entreated with no better success, then pretended to grow angry, then softened again, and ended by obtaining a reply to the effect, that Léda wished he would leave her a moment's peace.

Muley, who had listened attentively, began a series of oaths accompanied by terms of disdain, which in polished language signified:

"Simpleton! booby! if I had a wife like that, I would break her bones, I would lock her up in the coal-hole."

Bricord entered whilst he was giving utterance to this menacing monologue.

"What's the matter?" asked Bricord.

"Nothing, I was thinking of the beautiful jewesses and the Moorish girls, in the street of Bab Azoun."

"My wife will come back directly," said Bricord with a huge sigh.

The two friends resumed their places on each side of the table, and kept silence a moment, Bricord, with a full heart, ready to confide all his secret vexation to his old comrade, would he but address the least question to him on the subject; Aly Muley positively decided not to speak a word which could lead to such a confession. Both were much embarrassed, when they were relieved by the arrival of a new personage.

The colossus who entered at this moment burst into a tremendous fit of laughter, and advanced towards the table, saying:

"Ah! thunder! I was sure I should find you there, Bricord, glass in hand, since I could not meet you in the fields, where I have been searching for you on all sides, to tell you some good news. Popineau scented a wild boar yesterday in the thicket of the Louches forest; we must have it to-morrow, that is if your master will allow us to pass through his woods; for Lalouette my huntsman tells me, that Montéclain makes a difficulty about it, and pretends to preserve his game. What the devil can a Parisian like him do with it? he could not put a ball into the cathedral door of Autun, at thirty paces."

"I have not heard that," replied Bricord, "but at all events, I will speak to the marquis about it to-day. He has given notice that he will call at the farm as he goes by, to settle some accounts that we have together."

"Ah!" said the Viscount Hector de Montaleu, "he it must have been, then, whom I saw in the distance with another person in Brias' carriage; they turned round the slope of the hill, and were coming in this direction."

"That must be the colonel," said Aly Muley, "for I left him at M. de Brias' house, and he was to have accompanied him as far as this."

"My colonel! my colonel!" cried Bricord hearing the name, which made him forget both Léda's ill-humour and Montaleu's presence. "I will run and meet him," he added as he left the room, regardless of Aly Muley's company or of the viscount's.

"Who is this colonel?" said Hector, left alone with Muley.

"It is my colonel," he replied, arranging the bottles and glasses which remained on the table.

"And his name?" asked Hector, retaining a bottle which was not quite empty, and pouring the remains into his glass, which he went to fetch off a sideboard, like a man accustomed to act in Bricord's house as as if it were his own."

Aly Muley drew himself up, looked full at the immense viscount, and replied emphatically:

"He is called Colonel Thomas Rien."

"What a funny name," said Hector, setting down his glass, and turning on his heel, apparently in no way struck by the importance of the personage whose title had just been so solemnly announced to him.

Immediately afterwards he left the lower room and ascended straight to Léda's chamber, where she had shut herself in, and suffered Bricord to knock in vain for admittance.

The manner in which Hector announced his presence was probably more agreeable to the lady than that employed by her husband, for the door was instantly opened, and quickly closed after him. Aly Muley went up two of the steps leading to this room, as if he longed to go and hear what was said; but he descended almost directly, shaking his head, and muttering, as he usually did:

"The wife has weak nerves; there is one chamber for the lady and another for the gentleman; and that of the lady, which is closed to her husband, opens for another in his absence. There might be something learnt here, but I have no orders—"

He drew from his pocket a steel and some tinder, lit his pipe, which he had filled while Montaleu was speaking to Bricord, and went off to the stables to see that Megador and Penny wanted nothing. Had Aly Muley been less discreet, he might have heard the following words rapidly exchanged between the tall Hector and the fair Léda:

"I waited for you two hours at the colliery," said the latter.

"How could I help it," said Hector, carelessly, "Lalouette detained me—about a wild boar."

"And you forgot me for that?"

"You see very well I did no such thing," replied Hector in a brutal manner, "since here I am."

"And you may just go back again," replied Léda; for here is my husband coming."

Hector went down; he entered the room below at the same moment that Brias came in from without, accompanied by the colonel and a man, who was still young and very handsome, tall, and very distinguished looking: this was Montéclain.

"Ah!" cried Brias, "here is the forest king, Hector de Montaleu, allow me to present him to you, colonel. Viscount, I introduce one of my best friends to you, Colonel Thomas Rien."

The colonel, examining Hector with a disdainful glance, bowed coldly. Hector, on his side, hardly bowed at all; and these two men said each to himself:

"There is a rustic I would willingly give a lesson to."

"That fellow with his sword displeases me mightily."

Montéclain had remained at the door talking to Bricord. Montaleu went up to him, while Bricord said to Thomas:

"What do you think of our Nimrod?"

"That he's a blackguard."

"Is Bricord talking to you of our hunt to-morrow?" said Hector to Montéclain."

"He has spoken to me about it, and I refuse my permision."

"What!" exclaimed Hector, "you refuse?"

"Precisely and positively," said Montéclain, as he entered the apartment, speaking in the sweetest and most careless voice.

"Do you know, Montéclain, you are not amiable?"

"Why should I be so to you, my dear Hector? I wished to be a deputy and member of the general council; you could have given me your vote and the votes of your friends; you thought it better to follow your uncle's advice, who attacked me with more spirit and courage than I believed him to possess; you voted for my opponent, I did not make you the least reproach. To-day you ask a favour of me and I refuse it."

"Always the same story," said Hector sneeringly, "what a mania you have for being deputy."

"It is as good an amusement as anything else," replied Montéclain; "I was almost as anxious about it as you for a ten-horned stag; you would not give me the pleasure, and I will not grant what you ask of me; nothing can be more just and reasonable, I think."

"Very well, very well," returned Hector bluntly, "we will speak of it later. For the present I wish you good day, gentlemen, for it seems to me time to go and arrange my toilette a little, that I may visit the lady you promised to present me to, Brias."

"You will find us at her house," replied Brias. "Display all your coquettish resources, my dear Trojan; you will have to do with a woman well acquainted with elegance and beauty. It would be a conquest worthy of you."

"The devil!" said Montaleu shrugging his shoulders; "but for the reason you know of, I swear I would not go to the house of this She-Tiger, as you call her."

As Montaleu concluded this phrase Aly Muley entered the room.

Hearing the word Tiger he stopped short, and cried out, his Gascon accent even stronger than usual:

"What do I hear, a She-Tiger in this country."

"Certainly," answered Montéclain laughing.

"In that case lend me your gun, Bricord, and if I have not relieved the country of her in three days, I will lose my name of Aly Muley, which I gained by twice risking my Christian skin against Infidels. This is really an amusing hunt, while as to your stags and boars, they may be shot under one's leg."

"Have you ever killed a She-Tiger?" asked Montaleu.

"No," said Aly Muley; "but I have killed four He-Tigers as large and fat as you; and that is why I want to kill a She-Tiger."

"Is it true?" said Montaleu, looking both at the colonel and Montéclain.

"What! is it true?" said Aly Muley, "I have a tool which a prince made me a present of, with which I flatter myself I would lodge a ball in the right or left eye of any living animal, be it quadruped or man."

"That's enough," said the colonel; "go and arrange my things, that I may dress."

"We must know first if the room is ready," said Aly Muley.

"You can go up when you will," said Léda, entering at the moment.

"Ah!" said Bricord, "it is my wife, colonel, there is my wife. She did not come to meet you, because she wished to prepare every thing for your reception."

"Ah, but why do you bow to her like that? Embrace her, I beg you will embrace her."

In spite of Bricord's recommendation, Thomas, contented himself with saluting Léda with cold politeness, while Hector de Montaleu, who had stayed at the door, looked on with an angry eye, equally irritated against Bricord and the colonel.

The husband's recommendation had displeased him; but the refusal of the new comer, had doubtless displeased him much more, for he went off immediately muttering the words:

"Insolent fellow!"

The colonel had followed his servant into the room prepared for him, and Bricord had carried off his wife, to make her read some papers which had been given him by Montéclain, so that the latter was left alone with Brias.

"How is it," he then said to his companion, "that a clever fellow like you can live on familiar terms with that stupid brute, Montaleu?"

"How can I help it, my dear Montéclain, I am not in a position to make an enemy of him."

"Do you owe him any money then?" said Montéclain.

"Not much," replied Brias; "and I avow to you, that he is one of the last men I ever would owe any to, could I procure it elsewhere."

"How much do you want to arrange your affairs," said Montéclain.

Brias seemed to reflect, and presently replied in a light tone;

"Thanks, Montéclain, if what I am about to try succeeds, devil take me if I do not find myself clear of Montaleu, after I have returned him his money; and if he is not satisfied with the manner in which I return it, I shall try to recall the fact that the skull of a Montaleu is not more difficult to aim at than the left arm of an Englishman."

"You are plotting some perfidy towards him, is it not so?"

"No, indeed. I assure you, to speak in his style, that I will only run after the animal, when he has suffered it to escape him."

"Ah, but," said Montéclain, after a bantering look at Brias, "this Julia de Monrion, is a very powerful enchantress it seems?"

"Why do you speak to me of her?" asked Brias angrily.

"Because this is your plan in the matter," replied Montéclain; "you will borrow a hundred thousand francs of Montaleu; with that you will arrange your affairs, appease the minister, and as, setting aside your mania for getting into debt, you are one of the most distinguished men in diplomacy, you will obtain the post which is promised you. Your commission once in your pocket, you will lay all at the feet of the old Marquis de Montaleu, that he may accept and offer it in his turn to Madame de Monrion, whose plebian vanity will be charmed at the idea of being the wife of a minister, and soon of an ambassador. In this manner you will at once have paid the fair one and the estate with the money of the lover and heir. Very pretty diplomacy."

"Devil take you, with your suppositions!" said Brias, "I hope you will not breathe a word of all that before Montaleu.

"I do not tell people's secrets, except to themselves; you are not always equally cautious yourself."

"On whose account do you say that?"

"On Bricord's," said Montéclain, lowering his voice. "As we were coming here, the colonel questioned me about this brave fellow, and despite all his circumspection, I saw that you had been revealing certain secrets to him—"

"Ah, bah!" said Brias, "people of that sort—"

"People of that sort," said Montéclain drily, kill the man who dishonours them."

"I do not see that it would be any great misfortune, were our Hector overcome by this new Menelaus."

"If you consider it proper that every Menelaus in the country should knock down the Paris of his Helen, I have nothing more to say."

Brias bit his lips.

"Listen to me Brias," resumed Montéclain, "we tread at this moment a burning soil; something fatal and terrible is going to happen in this country."

"What is it then?" said Brias.

"I know nothing of it," replied Montéclain, "but I am sure of it."

"Why so?"

"Because the devil is here."

Brias began to laugh and answered gaily,

"And to whom do you give this dreadful name?"

Before Montéclain could reply, Colonel Thomas entered saying;

"I am ready sir, and whenever you like, we will set out to visit the beautiful Madame Amab."

This sudden apparition which seemed to have replaced the reply Montéclain had not had time to make, struck Brias so vividly, that he could not help noticing the colonel more attentively, and be it that Thomas Rien's countenance bore an expression, which the young diplomatist had never before remarked, or that his imagination lent an aspect to the face which it did not possess, he thought he discovered there something so deadly and satanic, that he shuddered as he looked.

"In that case," said Montéclain, "let us go, and though it is early, we shall probably not be the first to arrive."

## CHAPTER XLIX.

### THE INVITATION.

On reaching Amab's house, they were informed that Felina was still at her toilette, but they would find Victor in his studio.

"Come and admire him, colonel," said Montéclain; "he is a man of great merit, this Amab. Indeed it troubles me horribly to see one of his standing lavish for a few *ecus*, which he does not profit by, the most serious, earnest talent of our epoch. He is one of those men who are always hoping to do something, but never perfect anything, because they do not understand that glory is the true fortune of the artist, as it is also that of the soldier. Is it not so, colonel?"

Brias remarked that Thomas did not reply, but a slight emotion of anger agitated his features, generally immovable in their stern gravity.

"Oh! oh!" said Brias to himself, "is this one also running after some dowry or inheritance? Another rival, perchance. I will be on the watch."

When they entered Amab's studio, they found him with Champmortain, who, after the usual salutations had passed, and he had been presented to the colonel, informed them with a joyous air, that he had at length induced M. Amab to part with the four pictures then in his studio.

Felina's jest was consummated.

Amab did not look so happy about the bargain as M. de Champmortain. The artist had been much perplexed after what had passed between him and his wife, in seeking the best means of leading the conversation to the subject of his pictures, and was not a little surprised when M. de Champmortain, on arriving, ascended to his studio, went into ecstacy over the paintings, and again offered to buy them despite their having been refused him several times before. Had M. de Champmortain been informed of the scene which had taken place between Victor and Felina he could not have treated the subject which had been so long pending between them in a more direct manner.

Amab, for his part, received very coldly the congratulations offered to Champmortain, although they were so many eulogiums for the artist, as testifying how fortunate the possessior of his works was esteemed to be. A moment after they were informed that Madame Amab awaited her guests in the drawing-room, where M. Hector de Montaleu had just arrived and been obliged to introduce himself.

"On my honour," said Brias, "I am delighted to hear it; if I had been obliged to present both Montaleu and the colonel at once, I should have been puzzled to avoid being impertinent to one or the other. Had I introduced the colonel on the same footing as Montaleu, my friend Thomas would justly have been offended, and had I said of each what I think, it is probable that Hector would have been dissatisfied with the very small place he would have had in my eulogiums."

They went down stairs, and the colonel was introduced by Brias.

"The name of M. Thomas Rien suffices," said Felina, "to ensure him a good reception from all who are not strangers to the young and glorious of our time, and I thank M. de Brias for presenting the colonel at my house before introducing him elsewhere. I hope he will not forget that we shall have some claim to his visits, if only by right of seniority."

"Madame," replied Thomas gracefully, "the right of seniority should only be advanced by those who have no other, and it is my wish that you should attribute to a truer motive my demand for permission to present myself frequently at your house."

A singular interchange of looks between Felina and the colonel followed these words. Brias remarked it, and turned towards Montéclain, who interrupted him by saying in a low voice:

"Brias, look at this cloud gathering on the horizon, it seems to me that I see in it combats, blood, murder, incendiarism, every disaster at once."

"Where is it?" asked Brias.

"Oh! it is too late," said Montéclain, "the wind has dispersed it all; it requires a quick glance to discover the warnings heaven places before our eyes."

They set out for a walk before dinner. Felina affected great reserve towards the colonel, was charmingly familiar with Brias, refined in her coquetry with Hector de Montaleu, almost respectfully polite towards Champmortain. As to Montéclain, he only obtained from her attention, so abstracted, as to be almost impolite. Felina either felt the utmost contempt for Montéclain or was afraid of him. Brias, who knew that Montéclain permitted no one to treat him thus carelessly, said to him, while Felina was leaning on Hector's arm:

"Is not this woman charming?"

"Which?" said Montéclain.

"Eh! what! Madame Amab to be sure!"

"Faith! it matters little to me," replied Montéclain.

"What is your motive, then, in coming to the house?"

"All I can tell you about it," said Montéclain, with his accustomed indifference, "is that I do not come here to buy pictures."

"Shall I repeat that to Felina?" asked Brias, pointedly."

"I will relieve you of the trouble by telling her myself."

"A moment, a moment," said Brias.

"And I will add," resumed Montéclain," that you thought the saying a malicious one."

"Devil take your mania for breaking windows about the smallest trifle."

"I break nothing, only I prefer meeting the danger you threaten me with."

Do you believe me capable of repeating words like those you made use of?"

"You—no—you are incapable of saying them, but she is capable of forcing them from you."

"You are very much afraid of Felina, it seems?"

"Yes—on your account."

"My vows are offered elsewhere."

"But it is her hand that directs all your plans of action."

"You take me for a Champmortain, my dear fellow," said Brias foppishly.

"Not so, not so, my dear friend, Champmortain you know buys pictures, and that gives him a claim you do not possess."

"Ah!" exclaimed Brias," for whom the conversation was growing embarrassing, "only look at Hector holding Madame Amab's parasol in the air; he looks as the King of Siam's elephant might do, carrying one in the end of his trunk to shade his sovereign's favourite lady."

"Look rather at Champmortain conversing with the colonel, and trying to obtain a clue to the mysterious look exchanged between him and Felina."

"Do you believe the colonel and Felina were acquainted before they met to-day?"

"Do you know anything of the colonel's life? or shall you ever know anything of Felina's projects? Stay, here is M. Amab approaching, he pretends to admire his peonies, because he sees no one to speak to. I will go to his relief; he is the only one here present who interests me."

"That is well done, Montéclain; we know you always befriendthe victims."

"You may depend upon me," answered Montéclain mockingly.

"Ah! but," said Brias, retaining him, "do you know, you will frighten me before you have done?"

"I will ask you one question, and if you reply frankly to it, will perhaos tell you more."

"Let us hear."

"Does Madame Amab know your intentions with regard to Madame de Monrion?"

"No, certainly not. I have been very cautious not to name them to her."

"I do not ask if you have told her, I ask if she knows."

"Unless she has guessed—"

"Or unless she has learnt it from one of your contractors, whose suits at law you have suspended, by announcing yourself on the eve of making a splendid marriage."

"How the devil do you know that?"

"From one of them, who knowing me in this country, wrote to ask if he might safely lengthen the line at the end of which you hunt, like a new dog, obliged to wear the collar."

"And you think one of these fellows may have written to Felina as well."

"That is what I ask you."

"Faith," said Brias, "there will come of it what come may. What danger do I incur, supposing Madame Amab does know my projects?"

"This, that despite all your folly, you are not an avenger."

"What do you mean by that?"

"In what interest think you has Felina pushed you on to excite Montaleu's projects of marriage? Whence comes it that by her insinuation you dictated the letter sent this morning to the old marquis? You know nothing about it. Well! this is why. Montaleu will be accepted, or Montaleu will be refused."

"The position is inevitable."

"If he is accepted, do you think there can exist in the world a more deplorable destiny for a woman, than that of belonging to the savage brute, the She-Tiger is caressing at this moment?"

"You are right; but he will not succeed, I know it."

"I think as you do. But in that case have you calculated to what excess such an animal may go, pricked on by so clever a hand as that of Felina?"

"Upon my soul, you frighten me. But after all what can she do? Tell Hector my plans. It will cause a duel."

"My dear Brias, you are lost. How is it that you a clever diplomatist, can only see the weapons which are aimed at your breast, and not the side strokes."

"What do you say?"

"The vulnerable side."

"What vulnerable side?"

"The Champmortain side."

"I'll be hanged if I know what you mean."

"The Sylvia side."

"On my honour Montéclain it is an infamous supposition; Sylvia is irreproachable. But indeed you make me tremble. Explain yourself."

"Impossible, here comes Felina and all her party. Come Brias be cool, they will attack us."

"You are wrong to disquiet yourself as to what these gentlemen are saying," said Felina to Hector, "It cannot be anything very interesting I should think. Probably they are regulating the destiny of Europe."

"You forget that our illustrious diplomatist had me to converse with," said Montéclain, "and I am incapable of comprehending such vast interests. We were talking of our neighbours—"

"And you were saying—"

"I do not know what," said Monteclain, "ask Brias. Was it good or evil?—that depends—"

"May we be the judges?" asked Thomas Rien.

"It would be taking too much trouble," said Felina, rather impatiently, for she saw at the end of the walk a domestic, who appeared to be carrying something on a silver tray.

Champmortain gave Felina a look, which seemed to say:

"That is what you expected."

Felina thanked him by a most animated smile.

"Brias," said Montéclain, in a low voice, "be all eyes and ears."

"Why?"

"I do not know—but some theatrical effect is being prepared."

The servant approached. There was a letter on the tray. Felina extended her hand to take it; but immediately drew it back, saying:

"It is for M. Amab."

Amab received and opened the letter. Hardly had he glanced over its contents before he turned pale, and crumpled it up convulsively between his clenched hands.

Felina seeing this movement, was not sufficiently mistress of herself to wait longer.

"What is it?" she asked coldly, "some bad news?"

"No, madam," said Amab in a choked voice, as he approached Felina, "an insult."

"To you?" said Felina, in a low voice.

"Judge for yourself," said Amab.

And he gave her the letter. Felina read it.

It was printed in the set form usually employed for letters of invitation, and was as follows:

"The Count and Countess of Champmortain beg M. Amab to honour them, &c.—"

In spite of her self command, Felina turned pale, and remained silent for a moment.

"Well," said Amab.

"I ask your pardon, gentlemen," said Felina, with a gracious smile, "it is the dinner hour, I think it would be well to return to the house."

"What!" said Amab, going up to his wife, "you say nothing?"

"Not a word, I entreat you," said Felina, "and I swear the reparation shall far surpass the injury."

"And you will permit M. de Champmortain to seat himself at your table?"

"That is my concern, I suppose—the insult is for me—allow me to act as I please."

She turned away from Amab, and joined her guests, who were talking of the beautiful sky, and watching from the corners of their eyes the *aside* of Felina and her husband. Champmortain was on thorns; he cast an imploring look at Felina, but she did not condescend to notice him, and while addressing some remarks to Montaleu, the colonel, and Montéclain, she took Brias's arm, and gently drew him towards the house.

We relate their conversation word for word; it is of great importance.

"Brias, I want to talk with you," said Felina to him.

"If you please, I am listening."

"No, not now, to-morrow."

"So be it—here?"

"No, in the forest."

"In the forest! in what part?"

"By the side of the Louches wood."

"With great pleasure."

"Or rather," resumed Felina, "in the pheasant grotto."

"Still better."

"Yet I should decidedly prefer the thicket which borders M. de Rudesgens' park."

"If you want a private interview," said Brias earnestly, "it is much frequented there."

"Ah!"—said Felina, "elsewhere then if you like; in the Louches wood. What is your hour, Brias?"

"Yours."

Felina reflected.

"Ten o'clock in the morning."

"That suits me."

"No," she resumed, "I could not go out before breakfast, without a thousand explanations."

"Later if you wish it."

"At noon."

"Very well."

"Or at two o'clock."

"As you like."

"How forgetful I am," said Felina, "I have business all the morning with M. Amab's notary. If it is indifferent to you, say five o'clock," she added, observing him as she spoke.

"Capital."

"Or if you dine out between three and four."

"You proposed five o'clock, and I should prefer it," replied Brias.

"Excellent," said Felina earnestly, "I also prefer that hour."

"And may I know nothing as to the cause of this interview?"

"It is more important than you think."

Brias insisted, Felina laughingly refused, and the subject was dropped. The dinner was charming, the conversation gay, rapid, full of amusing paradoxes. Champmortain, who was deeply disquieted, did the most absurd things from absence of mind, and Montéclain would not suffer one to escape unnoticed. As to Brias he had never been so brilliant; the colonel had his share of success, and such was Felina's address, that she contrived to make even Montaleu's absurdities pass for witticisms.

Amab alone was wanting in the heart of concealing beneath the bubble of frivolous conversation the resentment of injury which was burning within. He was sad and disagreeable, and they soon excluded him from the innumerable jests, the noisy, light, and foolish pleasantries which sped round the table, as if each of those present had no anxiety at heart.

During the evening after they had left the dinner table, Champmortain tried to approach Felina; it was in vain, he could not win even a look from her.

But he was informed at the moment of departure that he would obtain no private interview. Felina said to Montéclain;

"How do you return home?"

"I have my carriage."

"In that case M. de Brias will take M. de Champmortain, and the colonel can accompany you."

"I have my own horses," said Champmortain.

"So have I," said the colonel.

"Very well, you will be able to ride together," said Felina.

There was no possibility of remaining after this decided dismissal. The colonel and Champmortain took on horseback, the road to Lavordan Farm. Montaleu turned off another way, and Montéclain preceded Brias along their road; but when at some distance from the house he stopped his carriage, and permitted his friend to come up with him.

"What has happened?" cried Brias.

"Nothing, I only want a place by your side."

"Very willingly."

"Brias, what did Felina say to you?"

"Such a question passes the limits permitted even to indiscretion."

"Brias, you will be made to commit some tremendous folly."

"Ah! but Montéclain, are you joking or speaking seriously? I do not wish to accept from any one the puppet part you pretend they mean me to display, or that you seek to make me play yourself."

"The earth trembles," said Montéclain in a singular tone, "the heavens are covered with clouds, the wind moans in the valley. Woe to those who walk abroad in the woods at such an hour."

"Pshaw! Montéclain, were you illuminated

during your last journey in Germany? or are you pretending to play Mac Allan's part, since your pilgrimage into Scotland? Explain yourself more clearly."

"I cannot if you do not answer me frankly, what did Felina say to you?"

"Well! since you must know everything, she has asked me to meet her to-morrow."

"Is that all?"

"That is all."

"In that case, I am at a loss to understand; you will go?"

"Certainly."

"Will you let me be present?"

"Ah! here again your indiscretion becomes—"

"Do you know what tne letter was, which made Amab turn pale, and caused Champmortain to be sent away with us?"

"No."

"You have no idea?"

"No. But you, who see so many things in the clouds, have you not guessed?"

"Perfectly."

"Ah! the devil! What was it?"

"It will remain my secret as long as you keep yours."

"But I have none, I assure you."

"Well then, Brias, this letter contained your death warrant."

Brias started.

"You are mad, or wish me to become so."

"Will you allow me to be present at this meeting?"

"I shall go well armed."

Montéclain laughed.

"Do you think they are going to assassinate you?"

"But, the devil! if it was my death-warrant, the execution will probably take place to-morrow."

"Not yet; but I entreat you to agree to my being present, hidden close by."

"Do you know," said Brias, who tried, but unsuccessfully, to appear gay, "that your presence might be very inconvenient?"

"Peste! what a conqueror!" said Montéclain.

"With Felina?" said Brias foppishly.

"My dear fellow," said Montéclain sententiously "Champmortain has been in the field this two years, and I would not bet on his being victorious."

"I did not think him so great a simpleton."

"Because you do not know Felina."

Here the two friends separated, each returning to his own house.

## CHAPTER L.

### LOVE.

In the course of the same day, M. de Rudesgens, with his wife and daughter, had been to pay a visit to M. de Montaleu; they had stopped to dinner. In the middle of the evening, Sylvia had complained of being very unwell. Her mother had proposed to her to return home immediately, but she had declared that the jolting of the carriage would aggravate her illness, so it had been settled that she was to sleep at the castle of Montaleu.

The Countess de Monrion had therefore conducted Madame de Champmortain into a room contiguous to her own; and after she had been assured that everything which she required had been done for her guest, she had returned to her own apartment, leaving M. de Rudesgens very busy playing dummy against his wife and M. de Montaleu.

As soon as Julia was alone the kindly grace, the eager attentiveness, the benevolent and happy expression which usually adorned her countenance when strangers were present, disappeared immediately, to give place to a look of sadness and dejection, closely wrapped up in a long white combing gown, she strayed for some time about the almost royal chamber she occupied, taking up and laying down each of the articles that came to hand, and looking for something to fix her attention, but in vain. Two or three times she laid her small white foot on the lower step of the estrade, on which the spacious canopy bed stood, but each time she returned in sadness. She knew full well that no sleep awaited her there.

Then she went and seated herself in one of those ample gothic arm chairs, in which painters love to enthrone a graceful fair young maiden in the dark back ground of some rich tapestry. Happy the artist who could have seen Julia similarly placed, her flaxen head thrown back, her hands clasped upon her lap, and her blue eyes melting silently into tears as they gazed upon the sky.

Poor girl! By what thoughts was she disturbed? What misfortune did she fancy she saw hovering above her to make her weep thus? Perhaps she would not have dared to acknowledge it, for she appeared to be ashamed of the feelings she had yielded to. Indeed, she suddenly started up, opened the window, and leaned upon the ledge to inhale at once the fragrance and tranquillity of night.

Before her stood the castle, whose name she bore, inhabited by the woman who had sought to ruin her, and who, at one poisonous breath had extinguished in her soul the first flame which had kindled therein. One solitary light was reflected from that house.

"It is he, perhaps, who is watching," said Julia to herself. "Oh! miserable man, how he must lament, if he has ever understood how much I loved him! Oh! cursed be the woman who has withered that noble genius, although I feel at present that the union she broke off, would have produced no happiness to me. Alas! is not the one she bequeathed me equally dreadful? Who am I now? What future lot is fated to be mine? Scarcely protected by an old man who is on the brink of death, living in a world which is not my own, though it enchants me, I move along like a blind man with a name given to me as a reparation, and which is mine only by chance. I have his name, and title; but where is the authority of a life of honour acquired under a husband's protection? Death and absence have deprived me of the only indulgent affections this life affords. I am alone with life, what shall I do with it?

At this point, in her reflections, Julia's tears began again to flow, but this time she abandoned herself to them as well as to the thoughts which impelled them.

"Alas," said she to herself, "must I live and die thus with unshared affections, an empty soul, without hope, without love? O my God, take pity on this tumult of my wandering soul, on this burning thirst of love which I shall never quench. Whom now shall I love? Whom shall I venture to love without fearing to become more than ever the victim of some selfish passion, of some loathsome interest? Oh! the treason, the despair, the tears, the tortures of a despised passion, are preferable to this loneliness of the heart. To hope for nothing, to believe in nothing, to expect nothing—it is dreadful. Thus to move on in life without seeing a refuge wherein the heart may seek for rest, without apprehending a rock against which it may be crushed—this is death. To swim in the infinite void where no world which we can resch is visible, even though that void were lighted with heaven's

most glittering rays, is as frightful as to fall into the eternal darkness of hell. O God, remove me from this vortex. Leave me not alone with myself —I want to love. My heart is dying in weary solitude. Who will love me? Whom shall I love?

Thus did Julia think, if, however, we can call thinking those warm and earnest aspirings which expired in the gloom,—or that cry of a lonely heart to which nothing responded.

A new impulse made her discard in dismay these unavailing desires, and she crossed her hands in prayer, beseeching the Almighty to deliver her from these fatal thoughts. Thus she was plunged in tears and prayer, when suddenly she heard, beside her, an outbreak of the most cruel sobs, the most sorrowful lamentations.

She listened—it was Madame de Champmortain, who lay murmuring so near her.

Julia thought she was getting worse; she, therefore, hastened from her own room, and went into that occupied by Sylvia. Madame de Monrion stopped at the threshold, at once surprised and dismayed by what she saw. Madame de Champmortain, half-naked, was kneeling on the carpet, her hair fell down in disorder over her feet, and the unhappy woman, her head and body thrown back, her hands extended towards the sky, exclaimed, with convulsive sobs:

"My God! my God! my God! have pity on me!"

Madame de Monrion ran to Madame de Champmortain. The unhappy Sylvia looked up, and once more her tears burst forth, as she exclaimed:

"Oh! if it be you that are sent to my relief, have pity on me! Pity! pity!"

"Compose yourself," said Julia to her, sitting down by the side of her and endeavouring to raise her up.

"No," said Sylvia to her, "I am as I ought to be, on my knees before you, so pure and happy, whilst I am so guilty and so wretched!"

"Guilty! you, madame!" said Julia. "No, no—you are indisposed. I will comfort you as much as I can."

Sylvia buried her forehead in Julia's lap, which she inundated with her tears, after which she raised her suddenly, saying:

"Oh! stay, I must tell you all, my heart must give vent to its agonies, though you should despise me; though you should betray me, I must have some one to reveal my sufferings to!"

Julia, moved as she was by this cruel sorrow, knew not in what manner to approach it; she was so astonished to hear Madame de Champmortain accuse herself of being guilty, that she trembled to put any question to her. However, she ventured to say to her:

"Is it then M. de Champmortain who has caused you this distress?"

"Oh!" said Sylvia to her, "it is my fault rather than his, although he is, indeed, the primary cause."

"His levity of conduct, perhaps?"

Sylvia shook her head gently,

"But what is it then?"

"What is it," said Sylvia, with a distracted look, "it is an insane, jealous, tempestuous passion. Yes, I love to very madness."

"Poor Sylvia!" said Julia, her whole frame quivering beneath the glowing and powerful expression in which these words had been uttered.

"Listen to me," resumed Sylvia, "I will tell you all, everything. For two years I have been dying, for two years I have smothered my heart to make it still. I must speak at last. And better it be to you, than to him—"

"Than to him, you said; he is ignorant then."

"No—he knows—or rather he knows not. You would not understand me—were I not to reveal to you the desperate passion by which I am tortured. Listen then. You know it is about five years since I married M. de Champmortain."

"Yes."

"I did not love him. At that time I did not love at all. Educated according to the severe customs of a convent, I submitted to marriage as the fulfilment of a duty to my family; I felt neither love nor aversion for M. de Champmortain. His elegance, his readiness of manner, his invariable good humour, that exquisite good breeding which he showed in society, and, above all, the marriage rights which surrender the whole woman, except her heart, to him whose hand she has accepted, finally the respect I feel for everything pertaining to duty, persuaded me, at first, that I loved him. I mistook for love that servility of the soul which led me to obey his orders, and yield to his desires. I did, indeed, sometimes, hear those about me comment on those fatal and delirious passions which oppress the heart, torture and intoxicate it; but I looked upon those who said they had experienced them as madmen or affected babblers. Besides, I must tell you, Julia, that the rigidity of my life drove away from me the very appearance of such passions. In this manner did I live on peacefully, divided between my religious and domestic duties, and offering perhaps to M. de Champmortain a reserve which thwarted the freedom of his morals. Whether it be his fault or my own, I do not know. I no longer accuse those who fall, I pity them; however it be, I say, he gradually forsook his home. I did not love him, Julia, for his absence left me no blank, no vacuum, it merely affected the regularity of my habits. But at length there came a day, on which I suffered acutely; it was that on which I was informed that I was deserted for a worthless rival, for a woman who pollutes all who approach her, and whose fatal power you know still better than myself—Madame Felina Amab."

"She!" gasped Julia, with a shudder of affright. "Oh! then I understand your terror, your despair. I understand how deeply your heart must be wounded."

"No—" said Madame de Champmortain, in a panting voice; "no, my heart was not afflicted. I thought so then; but now I know what the heart's sorrow really is, and I no longer deceive myself. My vanity was wounded, my pride revolted. God has punished me for having harboured that fatal sentiment, by which the king of angels fell. What now I suffer is the chastisement which God has inflicted upon me; the abyss in which I am struggling, the fire which consumes me, is the hell into which I have been cast. O Lord," said Sylvia, clasping her hands in holy fervour, "have I not suffered enough? Wilt thou not extinguish this crater which is devouring both my body and soul! Oh! kill this love in my heart, or kill me along with it."

"But," said Julia, "had you not a right to complain of M. de Champmortain's desertion?"

"Certainly; but I ought not to have listened to the presumptuous suggestions of that well-founded anger. It was by them I was misled. Oh! heaven preserve you for ever from a like temptation! thus was I persuaded to punish my husband for his desertion by exciting him to dread my own. Injudicious friends of my own sex, with whom coquetry is a game which easy to themselves they imagine to be as easy to every one, persuaded me to turn upon my husband, and rouse his jealousy."

"Imprudent women!" said Julia.

"Among the numerous friends of M. de Champmortain, there was a young man who was famed for his success, for the brilliancy of his conquests, and the notoriety of his violated vows; he seldom came to see us. I hated him for the very reasons which induced other women to vie for his notice. It was that man—it was—M. de Brias, why should I conceal his name? you would undoubtedly guess it yourself—"

"M. de Brias!" echoed Julia, with terror.

"It was he," continued Sylvia, who observed this shock, "it was he whom I fixed upon purposely and deliberately to raise into a rival to M. de Champmortain; now that I am lost, I may tell you so. Had I known any other man more notorious for his numerous adventures, I should have preferred him. I retained a residue of justice in my misconduct; nor would I have given false hopes to a heart on which they might have inflicted a mortal injury. Oh! presumptuous fool that I was, methought I ought to inspire a love fatal even unto death, and yet I did not foresee that it was I who should be smitten. Finally, I seized the opportunity of a visit; I played my part with sufficient art to make M. de Brias believe that I had noticed him! He accustomed himself to return. I saw him often, then every day; he spoke to me of love, and I, still presumptuous, still too reliant on my own rectitude, I listened to him. O Julia! what a new world opened before me at that enkindling language which he poured into my soul! It seemed to me that my heart, hitherto locked up into a mantle of ice, was expanding its wings to life, to the light, to the sun, as the butterfly emerging from its prison. I felt myself rocked in an intoxicating atmosphere of moist and burning perfume; I listened with avidity, I trembled, I was in a maze. I tore myself from this delirium, and returned to myself; I wanted to pray, and instead of praying I muttered words of love which he had dropped. I condemned myself to see him no more, and saw him continually at my feet, sad, supplicating, with his eyes rivetted to my heart. By night, he passed across my dreams, and drove me all trembling from my bed. By day, he possessed my thoughts; everywhere, in company, at the theatre, at church, his name, his voice, his breath floated about me. I thought I was turning mad, I was more afraid of myself than of him, and his image in my fancy seemed more powerful than himself. I beheld him again. I saw him. O Julia! unhappy me! At his sight, at his voice, my soul recovered that supreme, that ineffable joy, wherein all one's being is dissolved into the single sensation of love. Again I was afraid, again I dismissed him. But there came a day when, seeing him in anger, and ready to depart. I told him that I loved him. This was three months ago. Then it was, Julia, that the struggle which is destroying me began. I left Paris to avoid the danger; he followed me here. He no longer entreats me on his knees, he commands, he orders, he exacts, he tells me that unless I forget, for his sake, my duties as a wife, my honour, my religion, my chastity, the modesty of my sex,—he says I do not love him—he threatens to desert me—to give me a rival. Julia! Julia! he says I do not love him. Yet when he speaks to me, when he implores me, he sees me turn pale, tremble, and shudder. I am not yet guilty!" exclaimed Sylvia, rising on her knees; "the last effort of that virtue which I have lost, and of which I was so proud, stopped me on the brink of the precipice. But, heavens support me! I have no strength left against him—nor against myself—I love him—I love him, and if abandoned to myself, an hour may possibly come when the remorse of having erred may appear to me with less terrors than this conflict within me."

"And yet you called yourself guilty," exclaimed Julia, "you who have so desperately resisted the love which is torturing you!"

"O! yes, I am guilty, Julia; woe to the woman who suffers one illicit sentiment to penetrate into her heart—she is on her way to ruin: in vain do I struggle, I feel that an invincible force is hurrying me on to my destruction. I have contended with my love, Julia; I have resisted that wild enthusiasm by which my whole soul is suspended on one of his words—that enthusiasm which urges me towards him still more than he allures me himself; but I shall not resist my jealousy, I feel I shall not. Do you know Julia, that there is a woman here, they say, capable of disturbing the reason of the most frigid hearts? He knows that woman, he goes to see her,—at this very hour he may be with her. If he loved her, as M. de Monrion did, as M. de Champmortain does!"

"Her again?" cried Julia.

"Yes, she, now—always! she would not fear, not she, to return that love, and to give him those fatal proofs, without which he says there is no love. Well! Julia, if he would leave me for her, if I cannot bind him to me except at the cost of my honor, I shall be lost Julia, I am sure I shall be lost."

"Oh! say not so, Sylvia, say not so: Heaven has supported you, Heaven will support you still."

"No, I am deserted; every day I pray for strength to resist, every, where at every hour; I macerate my soul and body—Satan prevails; I love the man more than ever. I tell you Julia, I am undone."

"Recall your reason; only compare the misfortune which a fault would produce to that which you suffer at present; it would be a thousand times more horrible. If you knew what terror, what hopelessness accompany one fault! Oh!" added Julia with a deep sigh, "may you never learn it!"

"But if remorse be a torture," said Sylvia sullenly, "crime has its joys which make us forget it. Do you know what I have done to day?"

"No," replied Julia alarmed.

"Well! that woman, that Felina—M. de Champmortain required my mother to invite her to her party."

"Did she consent!"

"Yes."

"And you?"

"I!"

"Yes, you whose existence she has disparaged by seducing M. de Champmortain—you surely have not permitted him to introduce this shameless rival into your house?"

'Oh! the time is gone by for that," said Sylvia. The wife's dignity does not revolt so proudly in my heart. Had it been for M. de Champmortain alone, I should have suffered that woman to come and triumph among our crowd of guests; but he too knows her, he sees her, he thinks her beautiful: he was to call upon her this very day. Well! I wished to return this woman some of the evil I suffer; I wanted to insult and humiliate her in his presence; I waited for the hour when she would be surrounded by that court of admirers who kiss the hem of her gown. I sent to her house the invitation so imperatively required by M. de Champmortain; but that invitation was only for M. Amab; whilst admitting the husband, I repulsed the wife; I repudiated her. They say she is proud! She must have been mortally wounded—she too must suffer. And I stopped here, to avoid the anger of M. de Champmortain, whom doubtless she asked to explain this insult."

There was something so wild and obdurate in the tone of Sylvia's voice, as to terrify Julia. Still she attempted to soothe that bewildered spirit, that volcanic brain. She endeavoured to persuade her that Brias could not love Felina; then, when once she had appeased the fury of this jealousy, she showed her the glory of self conquest, and the serene joy which rewards us for the afflictions of the struggle. Julia spoke and argued so well that the chaste persuasion of her candid soul fell like a reviving dew on that irritant despair.

And after the night had been spent in this long and painful communion, Sylvia said to herself,

"Oh! she is happy, she does not know what it is to love."

Whilst Julia muttered with deep concern:

"She is afflicted—but she loves."

The following day Sylvia had resumed her dispair, and Julia had retained her melancholy.

As the day advanced, a feverish anxiety seized upon Madame de Champmortain, and at length, when the clock struck two, Sylvia trembling, wild, and regardless of everything, fled from her sympathising friend, saying as she went:

"He expects me at three o'clock in the park—I must see him."

She tore herself away, in spite of Julia's tears and entreaties.

At three o'clock—of all those hours which the subtle She-Tiger had proposed to Brias, this was the only one he had declined—and the wood near Sylvia's park was the only spot that he had considered unfit for their appointment.

---

## CHAPTER LI.

### THE FIRST ASSIGNATION

ALTHOUGH Brias affected to feel very little esteem for Montéclain, the mysterious and indirect advice which that nobleman had given him had deeply impressed him: he had understood the difficult task he should have in conducting at the same time his conjugal scheme and his love for Madame de Champmortain. Not that this love was one of those passions to which men blindly sacrifice their dearest interests; far otherwise, Brias had coldly calculated that it would be for him an oppressive chain which would entangle the remainder of his life. Sylvia's passion terrified him. Accustomed to offer up his versatile affections to divinities who do not murmur at the change of rites, he had been from the first interested and almost overruled by Sylvia's love; a sincere and absolute passion which was a thousand times more ardent in its resistance than that of others when indulged. The libertine's curiosity had been excited by this desperate struggle, and he had eagerly sought to possess the final secret of that timorous spirit. He conceived in his fancy as a delightful image the decisive fall of that staggering virtue, and as Sylvia said, he had dared to exact it with the authority of a heart which complains of ingratitude, and which nevertheless was its own master.

Amidst the conflicts in which he pitilessly tortured the desolate heart of Sylvia, Brias had understood at last that conquest does not always imply happiness; he had sounded the future he was preparing for himself. Perpetual requirements, inexorable thraldom, furious jealousy, such was the fate which he foresaw in Sylvia's submission, even without computing in that future the serious and scandalous perils to which the imprudence of so ardent a passion might expose him.

These reflections which had often presented themselves to him before, assumed a new power, thanks to the singular hints of Montéclain, and Brias resolved therefore to break with Madame de Champmortain, as well to escape the dangers of such a connexion, as to feel himself free and unrestrained in his designs on Madame de Monrion.

But a fortunate rake is very loath to accept the part of a coward and traitor, and Brias thought, before breaking off the yoke, he ought to employ a means which though common in its use, would lay all the fault to the charge of his mistress.

It was already past three o'clock when Brias arrived in a thicket which ran along one side of the park of M. de Rudesgens. It was a private walk, fenced with palings, so that it was secure from the observation of the keepers and of idle saunterers. A small door in the park opened into this cool retreat, whilst on the forest side there was a hole in the palissade carefully concealed, by which one might enter. When Brias arrived, he thought he perceived that some one had removed the faggots which covered the hole; but he was reassured on seeing Sylvia a few steps before him.

"Did you come in that way?" said he to her.

"Yes," she answered coldly; "I am just returned from Madame de Monrion."

"Champmortain, whom I have just met going to Madame Amab's, told me you had passed the night at the house of Madame de Monrion, and that you purposed stopping there the whole day."

"I see I have done wrong, to come."

"Am I not come as well?" said Brias, like a man who might have dispensed with doing so.

"M. de Brias," rejoined Sylvia, making every exertion to subdue the agitation she felt, "I have just passed a night which has been useful to me; for it has opened my eyes as to the guilty imprudence of the steps which you have urged me to take. These measures must be suspended to day, and for ever."

Sylvia averted her lovely head to hide her tears. However, Brias did not hear, without some dissatisfaction to his vanity, a declaration so auspicious to his own designs. He wanted to be free, but not to be dismissed. Still he over-ruled this slight impulse of self love, and replied with well affected sorrow:

"I ought to have expected it. This was to be the reward of a sincere—a genuine passion. I will obey you madame."

"I dare say you will do it gladly," resumed Madame de Champmortain, bitterly, "for you will have greater liberty to devote to your friends the hours you waste upon me."

"Really, madame, I do not understand you," said Brias, alarmed at the insinuation.

Madame de Champmortain squeezed and crumpled in her hands the handkerchief with which she had wiped the tears she could not restrain.

"You do not understand me, sir," she replied; "be it so, let no more be said; all that remains is for me to thank you for having granted me this last interview."

"Madame!"

"It is true," continued Sylvia, tartly, "you could not be elsewhere; a more fortunate rival occupies at present the whims of that haughty beauty who, doubtless, will soon make you amends for the weary vexations of a ridiculous amour."

Here Brias distinguished the object of Sylvia's suspicion, and being relieved as to the secret of his designs on Madame de Monrion, he resolved to play with an open and bold hand the scene he had planned and prepared.

"I know not whom you allude to, madame," he resumed, in a tone of restraint; "but it would perhaps be fortunate for me if you were right. Yes, I swear to you, Sylvia, I shall bless the day when, broken by your cruel denials, my heart would derive from its pride or its despair sufficient strength to offer to another the love you reject."

"Ah!" said Madame de Champmortain, in an altered voice, "you need not wait for that happy time, it is come."

"You are mistaken, Sylvia," returned Brias, "but I will exert all my energy."

"What!" said Sylvia, with a satirical smile, "is a man like you reduced still to hope with a woman like her? You greatly surprise me, sir. What! a fortnight's assiduity has not triumphed over that virtue?"

"One cannot succeed in a quarter where no attempt has been made."

"Then what do you do there every day?" exclaimed Madame de Champmortain, breaking out. "You were there again yesterday, perhaps this morning, perhaps you will be there presently. Oh! you deceive me, I know you do—you deceive me."

"No, madame," said Brias, with affected pride, "I do not deceive, no, I do not love Madame Amab."

"Ah!" exclaimed Madame de Champmortain, angrily, "you guessed easily who it was."

"And suppose I did love her," continued Brias, "have I not the right? Am I not at liberty to tear myself by every means from an insane passion, which you deny every hope to—to a passion which you never participated in, which you disdain."

"Is it you who speaks to me thus, sir! But why then am I here? Why did I leave Madame de Monrion; why did I not return home? to come to you, at the peril of my honour."

"And to tell me," resumed Brias, with vivacity, "that it is time to put an end to all connexion between us."

"Which you are eager to obey."

"Think you it is not sufficient humiliation, madame? Think you I did not judge myself unworthy of you, when I saw how coldly you repulsed me? I do not complain, madame, if I do not appear to you to deserve the requital I have so often sued for on my knees. But you will permit your victim to escape from his torture."

"And go to seek elsewhere a more indulgent heart."

"Well! be it so, madame," said Brias with a pretended burst of passion, "and if the person you accuse would but accept the vows which you so unfeelingly reject, I would invoke blessings upon her."

"And moreover, you would love—or rather you love her already—"

"Be it so, madame," said Brias, who at length gave credence to this much desired rupture."

"But what is there about her?" suddenly exclaimed Madame de Champmortain;—"what fascinating charm does she possess to please you all—this woman whom you prefer to me? Is it because she has neither modesty nor reserve? Is it because she surrenders herself without a struggle, without remorse to her shameful caprices?"

"Well, madam, if she does this, at least it must be acknowledged she does not play the part of an odious coquette, who demands and exacts your love, who inflames and bewilders it, and who, when her victim falls at her feet and supplicates her, repulses him with disdain. Perhaps she is guilty —but she loves, and in love, Sylvia, the only crime is to be callous."

"Ever," resumed Sylvia shuddering with anger and grief, "ever the same reproach, the same threat. I do not love you, you say; my God! what then must I do?"

Brias had before witnessed these paroxysms of grief, in which Sylvia's mind seemed on the point of wandering, yet he had always seen her issue triumphant from the struggle. He foresaw that it would be the same this time, and he wished to strike the last blow.

"You must," said he to her in an agitated voice, you must respond to my passion. Yes, Sylvia, you must—or I will no longer believe in your love, so strong to resist mine, so strong to resist itself—"

"No—" said she, "no; I had rather die—I had rather see you love another. No—no—I will not—no, never—"

"Farewell, then, madame," said Brias; "farewell for ever."

"Farewell," said she in a stifled voice.

Brias looked at her and saw her sinking on a grass seat, where she remained all in tears and annihilated.

Seen in that attitude her beauty was irresistible, all the passion she inwardly restrained with so much power, quivered in her disordered features, in the convulsive palpitation of her lips, in the fixed wildness of her eyes. Brias hesitated. The whimsical desire of contemplating once more the sorrows of this woman's love prevailed over the prudence necessary to his designs; he returned and said to her:

"So then, it is decided, Sylvia? your mind is made up?"

She turned away without answering.

"Farewell, then!" he returned.

"Where are you going?" she suddenly exclaimed, detaining him as she spoke.

"What do you care, madame?"

"Where art thou going, Frederick?" she repeated, in a wild voice.

"What did you say, Sylvia?" asked Brias, startled into feeling by that exclamation.

"What did I say—I know not; but tell me, Frederick, what would you have me do? What is it you require?"

"Unless your heart prompts you, it would not behove me to tell you."

"You love me, do you not?"

"Is it you who can distrust me?"

"And you will never return to see that woman?"

"Never."

"Well! Frederick—this evening—to-night—in this pavilion. No—no," she continued with another gush of desperation, "never—never—no, leave me—avoid me—I do not love you—"

Brias thought he had fulfilled all the requirements of a rupture, and burying his head in his hands, he drew off once again repeating:

"Farewell then madam, farewell!"

He passed into a narrow walk, and was issuing from the underwood, when all at once Madame de Champmortain, appeared before him, pale, bewildered, half frantic, and said to him in a hoarse and panting voice, such as Clytemnestra must have used when speaking to Egisthus:

"Well! since thou wilt go, Frederick—since thou requirest it, come this night into this pavillion —come, I will be here."

Brias stopped amazed, stunned by his good fortune, and Sylvia added:

"Now leave me."

"This night then," said Brias.

And he moved away with rapid strides, hoping at the bottom of his heart, that a return of conscience would prevent Madame de Champmortain from coming to the rendezvous.

Scarcely had Brias departed, before Sylvia, who stood rooted to the spot, let her head drop, and her arms hang loosely by her sides. Her eyes were dry and fixed. Her face did not exhibit that agitation which springs from suspense, anxiety, or remorse. All it contained was the hopeless expression of an inexorable resolution. She would doubtless have long continued in this posture, had not a slight rustling noise broken upon her deep consideration.

She raised her head at the sound, like a frightened hind, and beheld, standing before her a woman who was examining her with a look of gentle pity. The woman advanced towards Sylvia, who drew back in alarm."

"Who are you, and what do you want with me, madame?" said she to her.

"I am Madame Felina Amab, and I desire to speak to you."

"I know you not, madam," rejoined Madame de Champmortain with indignant pride.

"True, madam, but I desire to be known to you."

"I desire no such thing, for my part," said Madame de Champmortain trying to escape.

"And yet it is the only expedient to save you," said Felina, boldly placing herself before her.

"Is this violence madam?"

"No madame, it is a prayer."

"You forget that there can be no communion between us."

"You deceive yourself, madam," said Felina coldly, "you forget the suspicions which you have just exposed to M. de Brias and which concern me."

"What, madame," exclaimed Sylvia, looking at Felina with amazement, "you were—"

"Yes, madame," returned Felina, "I was there."

"Merciful heaven!" said Sylvia, in a tone of desolation, "I am undone."

"No, madame," said Felina, mildly; "if I had wished to ruin you, I should have brought M. de Champmortain to this place."

Sylvia appeared not to hear her.

"Undone!" she repeated, in a voice almost inaudible, "undone! and by whom!"

"No, madame, you are saved, and by a woman whom you have insulted in the most flagrant manner."

All the lofty spirit of Sylvia was restored to her.

"Well, madame," said she, with an imperative gesture, "go and tell M. de Champmortain everything; he will believe you—he is accustomed to it —this is enough between us."

"Not yet, madame," said Felina, "you have insulted me, and if M. de Champmortain's attentions had been the cause of it, I should not have forgiven you. I consider that the person who makes assignations like the one I have just witnessed, has no right to blame any one; but I forgive you that insult, because it was dictated by the true and genuine passion which has subdued you."

"Madam, I await your exposure; but I have already told you that I have had enough of your insults."

Felina could hardly refrain herself, she resumed however with composure:

"I have borne with yours, madame; and, if you consider my words as insults, you who are religious must understand better than ever the goodness of that maxim of our creed, which orders us not to do unto others what we do not wish them to do unto us. But, madame, believe me, and listen patiently to what I have to say. I come here neither to threaten, nor to be revenged; I come here to vindicate myself. You accused M. de Brias of soliciting my love; M. de Brias, madame, has something better in view than to carry on an intrigue with a married woman, he who has pursued so many of them, and who pursues them still; M. de Brias, madame, loaded with debts, and arrested in his career, can only be rescued by a rich marriage. This he expects, this he is in pursuit of, and if you have remarked any coldness in him towards yourself, it proceeds from his apprehension that the hand and fortune of Madame de Monrion may escape him."

The moment the word marriage had fallen from Felina, Sylvia had listened to her with eager curiosity and increasing anxiety.

"Madame de Monrion!" she repeated in a stifled voice, "does he want to marry Madame de Monrion?"

"Be sure that he does, and as my assurance may not be a sufficient pledge with you, I can give you the proofs of what I tell you."

"The proofs!—I must have the proofs!" cried the wretched Sylvia—"you have them? Oh! give them to me, madame, give them to me—and I swear to you—But no, it is impossible: you hate Madame de Monrion, and you are deceiving me."

"I hate Madame de Monrion; but I do not deceive you."

"Well! the proofs—shew me the proofs!"

"Follow me then, madame, to an appointment which I have solicited of M. de Brias to speak to him about his own affairs, and the proofs shall be afforded to you."

Madame de Champmortain was on the point of accompanying Felina, when all at once she stopped; a terrible conflict arose between her dignity and her wrath; she endured at once, in all their severity, the shame of her situation, the tortures of jealousy, and of anxiety. Felina watched her with a ferocious joy, whilst she was thus struggling with desperation between these dreadful feelings. At length, passion prevailed, and she cried out with fearful excitement:

"Undone, either way undone, I had rather know the truth!"

---

## CHAPTER LII.

### THE SECOND ASSIGNATION.

Madame de Champmortain followed Felina, who led the way to a shady by-path, where she had ordered her carriage to be secreted; they got into it together, and on a signal from Felina the vehicle was rapidly driven off.

Sylvia, who was a prey to the most terrific despair, preserved a sullen silence, whilst the She-Tiger insinuated the most shameful slanders against her rival, sliding them one by one into her heart. To speak truly, Sylvia hardly heard what she said; for she was measuring the gulf down which she had fallen. In a single day the secret of the passion she was resisting with all the strength of her soul, had been detected by the woman who might infatuate her lover, and who had already despoiled her of her husband.

But in that jealous and desolate soul, the shame of being in Felina's power felt very far short of the anger she felt at the idea of being the dupe of her fortunate rival. Too well Felina knew the heart of woman not to continue the recital of her calumnious reports, although Sylvia appeared not to listen to her. At that moment, it was all received as empty unmeaning words; but the artful woman foresaw the clamour they would raise when, by and by the memory of these tales should return to Madame de Champmortain.

In this manner they reached the place of the rendezvous selected by Madame Amab. She perceived De Brias walking about at a quick pace. The carriage blinds were immediately let down.

"Stop in the carriage—" said Felina; "I will keep within hearing, on your account."

She ordered the coachman to stop, alighted, and made a particular sign to the driver, who followed her step by step.

De Brias hastened to join her.

"You see I am punctual," said she to him.

"I am equally so; the hour is not yet come."

"And now," said Brias, "may I be informed to what I am indebted for this flattering solicitude?"

"To something of the highest importance to you and possibly to me."

"If that be the case" said Brias, lowering his voice, "we might choose another walk, or tell your coachman to stop."

"He has first, the inestimable advantage," replied Felina, "of being deaf and dumb; and, secondly, in the eyes of those who might happen to meet us, he is too respectable a witness, not to remove all suspicion as to the propriety of our interview."

"Your foresight is admirable, Felina; speak, therefore, and tell me for what reason you have granted me this interview, I who have been so forgetful as never to solicit one from you."

"It is a want of gallantry which I forgive you," rejoined Felina, gaily. "When a man's mind is stuffed and crammed with assignations, with actions at law, and stamp papers of every kind, he seldom thinks of serious matters. I want to speak to you about yours. Tell me; do you know what has brought down Montéclain to these parts?"

The question appeared to embarrass Brias, who gave a stealthy glance at the copse.

"Why," said he, "I suppose he is come to see and look after his estates."

"No, M. de Montéclain is come here to *look after* Madame de Monrion."

"He?" said Brias, starting; "impossible! he would have told me so."

"It is necessary," returned Felina, "for me to relate to you a little anecdote, which you may not have heard perhaps. There is somewhere or other a certain M. Villon, formerly a clerk in the house of M. Thoré, and now become the master of that old established business. This M. Villon, ex-adorer of fair Julia Thoré, has retained for Madame de Monrion a sort of passionate worship, which would lead him to commit the most extravagant actions to prevent his idol from becoming the wife of such a ruined bankrupt diplomatist as yourself, and one, if I am not mistaken, who is less in love with the person of the countess, than with her fortune."

"You are mistaken, Felina; if abundance of love can supply the place of abundance of wealth, there is no man can possess better claims than I to that lady's hand."

"What!" cried Felina, in a sarcastic tone, you love her so intensely, you say so to me—"

---

*Note.*—We are getting into the plot. The marvellous fecundity of invention, the power of intellect, the ever present vigilance, the comprehensive arrangement, the ebullient anger, malice, and revenge, the immeasurable dominion over others, of this satanic woman, begin to appear in a fierce shower of proofs and instances, and we challenge every critic in the kingdom to point out another female character drawn with so large and bold a hand, since the death of Scott

"I was forgetting that you mortally hate her on account of the name she bears. But what signifies my love, whether great or little? I must perhaps give up all my hopes and expectations."

"Have you received such pressing news from Paris, then?"

"No," answered Brias, abruptly.

"Can it be the arrival of Montéclain?"

"No—no, for I am sure, Montéclain is not even acquainted with the Countess de Montrion."

"That is true; but he is very desirous to know her."

"But for what purpose?"

"On account of that M. Villon, whom I mentioned to you just now."

"True, I had forgotten him. Well! what connexion is there between that worthy M. Villon and the Marquis de Montéclain?"

"I will tell you. Some months ago, I went to the ball at the Opera, and was sitting on a bench in the green room, when somebody took a seat close beside me: this was Montéclain, who, according to his custom, felt dull and *ennuyé* there, as he does at all times and in all places. We are too bitter enemies he and I for me to seek even to injure him at the risk of diverting him. I preferred to leave him to the tedium of his reflections, and was about to leave the place, when I perceived M. Villon. I called him to me, and the chinaman, who had been languishing for an hour, looking about him in vain among all those black satin faces not one of which answered to his look, sat down by my side. There are certain secrets between Madame de Monrion and M. Villon."

"What do you mean?" exclaimed Brias, reddening—do you intend to slander the countess?"

"True, true, I did not express myself clearly; —I should have said *there had been* secrets between Mademoiselle Thoré and M. Villon."

"Either one way or the other, it is a calumny levelled against the chastest virtue and the noblest soul I have ever met with."

"And undoubtedly the first who has taught you to understand the meaning of true love," resumed Felina.

"She has at least taught me to understand the love which respects the object of its worship."

"Felina was seized with a sudden and violent fit of coughing; she had just heard a feint lamentation issue from the carriage. Brias stopped short, for he too, had been struck by the sound. But Felina immediately continued:

"What's to be done, my dear Brias, we all have our diversions and mental abstractions: just now it was you who forgot that I hated Madame de Monrion, and you confessed to me your love and admiration for her; in my turn I forgot that love and admiration to give vent to my hatred; we are even—as for the rest, will you break off the interview? for you appear to me quite unprepared to take good advice."

"You might come to the point less indirectly."

"Yes, if you did not interrupt me."

"Speak, I am attentive."

"Well, I was saying that I had called M. Villon and that he was seated between M. de Montéclain and me. I availed myself of the freedom of my mask to say all I knew of Julia Thoré's marriage, and I hit so accurately that the unhappy chinaman fell into the most outrageous and absurd passion. He threatened me, I believe, and as I only laughed in his face, he appealed to Montéclain and asked him if it were not allowable for an honest man to correct a woman, who ventured to assail with scandalous comments, the chastest virtue, the noblest soul. Yes indeed, he employed the very same words as yourself, Brias. It is one of the privileges of the love that ady inspires to suggest the same silly things to her adorers. In spite of his *ennui*, Montéclain had listened to us all along, and when M. Villon appealed to him, he merely shrugged up his shoulders, and replied with that absolute insolence for which he has no equal:"

"You are a simpleton to notice such stuff. Don't you recollect Madame Felina Amab, formerly Madame de Cambure?"

"At this disclosure, I thought that the Chinaman would have sprung up at my throat; but he restrained himself, and I left him laughing heartily, though very angry with Montéclain, who had rescued a victim from me. However, I did not lose sight of them; they began to talk to each other. I went round the saloon several times, observing that they kept up a most animated conversation the whole time. I stopped for two hours in a box, and when I returned to the saloon, there they still sat together on the same bench. How many things Montéclain may have learned of Madame de Monrion during that colloquy. You know the man, you know with what art he attains his ends."

"He?" said Brias; "I think he is very careless about such intrigues, and quite innocent of the designs you ascribe to him."

"Say no more," answered Felina. "Ah! you think Montéclain a careless man, a very innocent. I knew he was a superior mind, but I did not believe him to be capable of persuading a diplomatist of your ability that he had nothing in him."

"All this is very well," said Brias; "but what connexion is there between that meeting at the opera ball and Montéclain's presence in this country?"

"This—that Montéclain, who never tells any thing to any one, who is not acquainted with Madame de Monrion, who is not even thinking of her, has written to—"

Felina could not proceed, for Montéclain suddenly stepped forward, and said to her with a smile:

"What! do you open my letters, madame?"

Felina recovered herself with wonderful rapidity from the surprise of this unexpected appearance, and replied:

"No, sir, no; but if you wish your correspondence to remain as secret as your thoughts, you ought not to entrust your letters to an awkward domestic who, instead of delivering to Madame Amab the note in which you thank her for her invitation, hands her another letter directed to M. Louis Villon."

"But what of that letter, madame?"

"I only read the superscription; but that was all that was necessary to inform me that the Marquis de Montéclain kept up a continuous correspondence with M. Villon."

"And what do you infer from that, madame?"

"I leave you to draw conclusions yourselves, gentlemen; the object I had in view is attained; and that was, to caution all those who hear me as to the real designs of each."

Thereupon she curtseyed, and opening the carriage door herself, she hastened into it, and shut the door more quickly still.

"I understand her object," said Brias; "she wants to ruin Madame de Monrion."

"Brias!" exclaimed Montéclain, in an altered voice, his eyes rivetted to the carriage as it rolled along.

"Or else," continued Brias, "to make us cut each other's throats."

"Brias!" cried Montéclain, again pointing to the carriage."

"Unless she wants—"

"Brias!" resumed Montéclain, in a thundering voice, "Felina was not alone in her carriage, there was somebody with her."

"Champmortain, perhaps," said Brias, terrified.

"No; it was a woman."

"A woman! what woman?"

"Madame de Champmortain."

"Impossible!" exclaimed Brias, changing colour.

"I only saw her foot and satin buskin, and the world does not contain two so pretty and small, not excepting those of Madame de Monrion, which I am not acquainted with."

"Sylvia, Sylvia," cried Brias; "and has she overheard, then, what I said. But no, it is impossible; why, it is scarcely an hour since I left her exclaiming vehemently against Felina."

"Did I not tell you yesterday that the woman was hatching some vile plot—and you only laughed at me."

"No—no—no—it could not have been Madame de Champmortain," resumed Brias. "How? By what art? By what surprise and stratagem?"

"I cannot say!—but I am sure of it. Brias, you did not tell me all."

"On my honour! I concealed nothing from you."

"So you think; but don't you know that with this serpent, compared with whom the one in Genesis was but an apprentice, every word, every modulation of the voice is a new peril. How did she propose this meeting to you?"

"Why, most naturally."

"Did she appoint the hour and the place at once."

"Stay till I recollect myself. No; she first proposed the morning, then noon, then two o'clock."

"I understand," said Montéclain angrily, "you accepted all these hours, save one."

"That is true."

"And she will have led you about through the whole forest, until she came to a spot which you objected to as unfit."

"Just so. You make me tremble, Montéclain!"

"Are you acquainted with mathematics, Brias?"

"What an out of the way question!"

"Answer me: do you know why the straight line is the shortest way from one place to another?"

"Because it is, that's all," said Brias shrugging his shoulders; "that is not to be proved."

"You are wrong, Brias; it is one of those principles the truth of which is proved by showing the absurdity of all surrounding ones. When a mathematician has proved that every line we can draw by the side of a straight line is longer than it, the truth is obtained that this is the shortest. So, when Felina found that every hour in the day and every place in the forest were indifferent to you, except one certain hour and one precise spot, it was mathematically demonstrated to her that you had an appointment at that hour and place. *Ergo:* she was present at your appointment with Madame de Champmortain."

"But, for what purpose?"

"I know not what you may have said at that rendezvous; but know you not that Felina has no other way of passing off her vices upon the world than to screen them with the protection of other women's faults? Now that she is in possesion of your secret and Madame de Champmortain's, don't you see what fatal power she has over you both?"

"Fortunately," cried Brias with a candour which forced a smile from Montéclain, "fortunately Sylvia is innocent; she has never forgotten her duty."

"Very well, Brias," said the marquis, "but she has been sufficiently imprudent to appear altogether culpable; she is timorous enough to believe it, and God knows to what account Felina may be able to turn such a circumstance and such a disposition of mind."

"I must see her," exclaimed Brias impetuously.

"Will she allow it? Can you effect it?"

"What's to be done then?"

"She has enthralled Madame de Champmortain through you. You must enthrall Felina through Champmortain."

"God help us! Sylvia knows the truth, and her husband's desertion has now become indifferent to her."

"Undoubtedly; but M. Amab does not know it and he is a man likely to kill his wife."

"You do not know him, Montéclain; he might kill Champmortain, but he would never hurt Felina."

"I believe you are right," replied Montéclain. "But, zounds, now I think of it—we have a most valuable ally."

"Who is it?"

"Colonel Thomas Rien."

"How so?"

"To horse, Brias; we must see him before he visits Champmortain to-night. Come, and I will explain the thing as we ride along."

---

## CHAPTER LIII.

### THE RESULT.

CHAMPMORTAIN, who had gone to pay his usual visit to Felina, in order to ask for an explanation of the coldness she had on the previous evening evinced towards him, had just come back, vexed and irritated at not having met her. He was informed that his wife had not returned, and he was preparing to go to M. de Montaleu's, when he perceived the carriage of Madame Amab. At first, he was delighted that his wife was absent. Champmortain firmly believed that Sylvia had sent to Felina the invitation he had required. But he had some doubt concerning her behaviour towards Madame Amab. There are many ways of blending great impertinence with most perfect politeness; and in this art women display a most wonderful talent.

He therefore considered it a favourable circumstance that this first visit would take place only between Felina, M. and Madame de Rudesgens, and himself. The conquering pretensions of M. de Rudesgens were a security for his amiability; and the terrible history with which he had threatened his mother-in-law, made him easy concerning the manner in which she would receive Felina. He was, therefore, most strangely surprised when he saw his wife alight from Felina's carriage. Sylvia was pale and agitated; Felina calm and pensive. These two ladies seemed to be on the best possible terms together.

At that moment a strange and yet natural feeling was experienced by Champmortain.

Spurred on by Felina, whose ambition, dominant above all, was to be admitted into a society which till now had kept their doors shut against her, he had required and obtained for her an invitation to the party which was to be given at the chateau of M. de Rudesgens.

Assuredly, after that victory, he would have been much dissatisfied, if the reception given to Felina had sufficiently shown that she ought not to avail herself of the invitation; and yet he was still more dissatisfied with the kind of sudden intimacy which had sprung up between Sylvia and Madame Amab.

The husband wished, it is true, that his wife should receive his mistress, but he did not wish at

all to see his mistress the intimate friend of his wife. Champmortain knew Felina too well not to be convinced that an intimacy of such a kind was improper for Sylvia. Madame Amab might indeed be seen in his drawing-room among a hundred other women; that was of little consequence; but an intimacy with his wife might be attended with more serious results. For an instant, therefore, he was grieved at his success.

Before Champmortain had come down to the sitting-room, in which M. and Madame de Rudesgens were, Sylvia had presented Felina to her father and mother; she had related to them that as she was returning on foot from the house of M. de Montaleu, she had met in the wood with Madame Amab, who was coming to pay her a visit, and that this lady having stopped, she had accepted a place in her carriage, Sylvia added, that she was delighted with that meeting, which had given her an opportunity of better knowing and more fully appreciating a charming neighbour.

Whilst Sylvia was speaking, M. de Rudesgens, surprised in his morning gown, exhausted all his eloquence in begging pardon for being in that negligé, and Madame Rudesgens stiffened herself into constrained courtesy, being quite astonished both at the eagerness of her daughter and the overflowing politeness of her husband.

Champmortain entered the saloon just as M. de Rudesgens disappeared to go and decorate himself. Until now, Madame de Rudesgens had confined herself to curtsying and biting her lips, but she gave way to a most graceful smile when Felina said:

"Indeed madame, had not Madame de Champmortain positively told me, that it was to her mother she presented me, I could not have believed it, and I should have thought that she had a sister."

"It is true, Madame; I was still very young, indeed, when I married M. de Rudesgens," replied the mother, assuming a playful countenance.

Champmortain was still dissatisfied, he advanced and bowed to Felina, in a frigid and ceremonious manner. She curtsied to him with a perfect modesty, and continuing to address Madame de Rudesgens, she said to her:

"Madame, permit me to leave aside ceremonious words with a lady of a superior mind, and allow me to tell you candidly how happy and flattered I am with the invitation you had the kindness to send me; for, though the invitation was in the name of Madame de Champmortain, yet I indulge the belief that it was submitted to the approbation of her mother."

"Undoubtedly, madame."

"You double the price of it, madame, and, at once, you show me the truth of what I have heard so many times, that it was impossible to unite more grace and kindness to more distinction and virtue."

Champmortain became quite alarmed. He thought that his mother-in-law would perceive that Felina was mocking her; but, as yet, he knew not how robust is human vanity. These outrageous flatteries, which ought to have upset Madame de Rudesgens, on the contrary tickled her most agreeably. She smiled, displayed her graces, and the conversation assumed that vulgar turn destined to fill up a visit of ten minutes. Felina withdrew after that short stay, notwithstanding the entreaties of Madame de Rudesgens.

The ladies had accompanied her to the door of the saloon; Champmortain wanted to go farther. Felina stopped him, saying, in a low voice:

"Until to-morrow! be prudent.

When she had departed, Champmortain looked at his wife; she was buried in deep reflections. He addressed his mother-in-law.

"Well! madame, you have seen that terrible person whom you refused to receive. What do you think of her?"

"She is, I believe, a very good woman, who has been much slandered, as generally are all those who have the misfortune to be beautiful," answered Madame de Rudesgens, applying to herself with a deep sigh, the last part of her sentence.

"She is considered a woman of intellect," said Champmortain, smiling.

"A woman of intellect, perhaps," said Madame de Rudesgens; but I believe that she is possessed of tact, judgment, and superior discernment."

"And above all," said Sylvia, in a tone full of conviction, "her ideas soar above those of common people: she is an extraordinary woman."

"What! you have been able in a few brief moments to form an opinion about her?" resumed Champmortain.

"We have been together more than an hour."

"And what did she tell you?"

Sylvia looked at her husband with a sarcastic air, and answered, while leaving the saloon:

"You, perhaps, would be the more embarrassed for it, if I repeated to you what she trusted to me."

Champmortain did not find a word to answer, and his mother-in-law was probably going to ask him the explanation of that sentence, when M. de Rudesgens came in quite radiant, rubbing his hands, and with the appearance of a debauchee.

"You are come too late," Madame de Rudesgens said to him; "the dove has taken her flight."

"Bah!" said he, laughing, "very well, very well."

"You take it joyously, sir."

"But I have no motive for being sad."

"You are an old madman," said Madame de Rudesgens to him, shrugging her shoulders. Besides, Madame Amab is not what you fancy—she is a woman of merit, of intellect."

"I believe so."

"And all your gallantry will only end in making you appear ridiculous."

"I request you to believe so," answered M. de Rudesgens, saluting ironically his wife, who retired at that moment.

Then, suddenly turning towards Champmortain, he exclaimed:

"Ah! Champmortain! the trick is excellent. Having been surprised in deshabille, and having only just retired to dress myself, I was returning into the saloon, when I heard the salutations of departure. As you opened the door, I nimbly threw myself aside; and the door was scarcely shut, when I offered myself to the eyes of Madame Amab. I must confess it, Champmortain, I have not played a friendly part towards you. I told her, I believe that I asked her the permission to repair the impoliteness of my son-in-law, offering her my hand to her carriage; and when she had placed her hand in mine, I could not help adding, upon my word, that a man must be the worst of blunderers to yield to another so fine a hand. I said two or three more charming things, and the deuce take me, but I believe that I pressed her hand, for she blushed.

"She is able to do so," said Champmortain, peevishly.

"Decidedly, she is delightful; but I leave you. I wish to be discreet."

At these words, M. de Rudesgens turned on his heels, and went to promenade his triumph through the park.

"What!" said Champmortain, to himself, "she has bewitched them all."

And after this observation, he withdrew, more dissatisfied than ever with Felina's success, although he had exerted himself beyond all due limits to obtain that she should be admitted.

Now, we are going to interrupt this narrative, whilst we communicate to our readers a few letters, written by several personages connected with this history.

A letter from Colonel Thomas Rien to Madame Muller, at Cologne:—

"20 May.

"My Mother,—I wrote to you yesterday, and I told you the circumstances of my arrival. I named all those whom I had met in this country, and what I had heard about them. I have not seen either M. de Montaleu or the celebrated Madame de Monrion. I expected to meet them at M. de Champmortain's, where I passed yesterday evening. But they did not come. I had, in the morning, received the visit of Montéclain and Brias, a visit which astonished me much, as you will see.

After a few insignificant words Montéclain exclaimed suddenly:

"Colonel, do you remember the amouscade of Cherchell?"

"Yes, indeed!" said I; "had it not been for you who, with the butt end of your horsewhip, broke the head of the Arab who held me, with his pistol on my breast, that would probably have been my last campaign."

"True colonel, and you remember at that moment, before rushing back among the enemy, you said to me:

'My turn will come, I hope.'"

"Since you bring those words to my recollection," said I to Montéclain, "it is because my turn has come."

"You have guessed right."

"What am I to do?"

"A very important thing, the secret of which is to die here."

"Speak, I listen to you."

"You are to request Madame Amab, to keep secret everything she saw and heard yesterday."

"I do not know Madame Amab, said I to him."

"I believe so."

"I saw her yesterday for the first time."

"I believe so. But I shall consider as an eminent service the eagerness with which you will address her that request in your own name; for you must not tell her that it has been suggested either by me or by Brias."

"But what authority can the request of a stranger exercise over Madame Amab?"

"Colonel," Montéclain answered, "I do not discuss the extent of your authority, but I rely upon it."

"M. de Montéclain," said I then to him, "this becomes a joke which I might consider improper. I repeat that I do not know Madame Amab, and that you require me to play a very unbecoming part with regard to her."

"Colonel," Montéclain answered with his sardonic countenance, "you do not know the extent of your power, as before the ambuscade of Cherchell, I did not imagine that with a blow of my horsewhip I could save the life of a man. I gave a rough blow—that is all. Well! tell roughly, if it be necessary, to Madame Amab, that you require of her not to mention what she saw and heard yesterday, and I swear that you will succeed as I succeeded."

"If the question was only to acquit a debt," said I to Montéclain, I would consider this in a different light. But you require me to be true to my word; be it so. Service for service, I will do what you wish."

"Thank you, colonel," answered Montéclain, "we shall be quits, and henceforth, we are at full liberty to pursue, each our purpose, without being hindered by any fear, any consideration whatever."

"He immediately retired with Brias, who stood the whole time examining me, as if I had been some rare animal he saw for the first time."

"What is the meaning of all this, mother? does this man know me then? He knows, perhaps, that I am—at least he knows my connexion with Felina. Why do I say my connexion? I spoke the truth when I said that I did not know Madame Amab, that it was the first time I saw her. He knows then something else, he knows the mysterious lie which unites and binds us together for the same vengeance. On the day of my introduction to Felina, we avoided exchanging a single word which was not connected with the general conversation, my intention was to delay my visit for a few days in order to rouse no suspicion.

"I could not resist the uneasiness which had been caused by the words of Montéclain, and I hastened to Felina. She had just come in, her husband was in the saloon, and left us alone for a few minutes, I availed myself of the opportunity to tell her what Montéclain had asked of me. She explained to me the cause of the recommendation, and then alluding to my request:"

"Does that come from you, Thomas?" she asked.

"No matter," said I to her, "it must be so, it is a debt which I pay."

"She had no trouble to guess the person who had induced me to make the request, and she answered me:"

"Well! I will be silent. But you may tell Montéclain from me that he is a simpleton; I had not the least desire to make use of the secret of Madame de Champmortain either against her or against Brias. I have already derived from it all the advantage I wanted."

"When am I to see you again?" said I.

"At the party to be given by Madame de Champmortain."

"Her husband came in again and I withdrew."

"Towards evening I went to Rudesgens' hotel, and there I understood what Felina had not had time to explain to me. She has transformed Madame de Champmortain into an implacable enemy to Madame de Monrion, whose name is here in every mouth. Madame de Champmortain has not spoken a single word against her; but as M. de Rudesgens was launching out into praises of Madame de Monrion, and as he appealed to the testimony of his daughter, the latter turned towards Brias, and said to him:

"It is you who can say whether these praises are deserved; for I believe that you know her more intimately than any one of us."

Although these few words were pronounced with an easy voice and a charming smile, they contained a fund of inexpressible rage. Brias stammered like a fool. With regard to Montéclain, to whom I said that I had done what he wished, he displayed a humour which bordered on sublimity. He courted Madame de Rudesgens with a constancy and an air of good faith which threw the old lady into ecstasy, and drew from her incredible looks and sighs. Then he took delight in teasing M. de Rudesgens, and making him relate his good fortunes, a circumstance which brought on between the old marquis and his wife a furious quarrel, at which he laughed with all his heart. Brias looked like a naughty boy who has been placed in a corner to punish him. Champmortain was a prey to *ennui*, and appeared uneasy; his wife in sullen and gloomy silence nursed her jealousy and anger. Montéclain alone appeared careless, and made a free use of his mind. Who is that man? What is his purpose? What is he aiming at? I thought I knew him, because I was acquainted with what the world says of him. I should like to speak to Felina about him; but I must wait until the day after to-morrow. This I will do. I shall not forget that you have recommended me to take her for my guide. I know your tenderness for her, and I shall say nothing which may hurt your feelings. But I wish the woman whose early years were entrusted to your care had profited better by the advice which was no doubt given her by your experience and virtue. However, I neither accuse nor judge her. She had to suffer from poverty and contempt; she pursues her revenge. Am I not also actuated by the same feeling. I will inform you of what she says of Montéclain. She must know him. They have both of them the appearance, nay the attitude, of two enemies who, fully appreciating one another, are afraid to begin the attack. We shall see.

I cannot repeat to you what I have heard of Madame de Rudesgens. That woman has forgotten her past life, and without the written proofs possessed by Felina she never would be brought to a confession. Besides, she appears to me to be of good faith in her hypocrisy. She is right; her faithfulness to M. de Rudesgens may be considered as a virtue whose merit is sufficient to blot out all the frailties of her youth. But I return to my visit.

"In order to tell you what took place last evening, I must add that after many subterfuges, and whilst Montéclain engaged universal attention, Brias approached Madame de Champmortain, and addressed a few words to her in a supplicating voice.

"I believe," answered she drily, "that I am becoming deaf; be so good as to speak louder; I do not hear you."

The imprudent Brias murmured with despair the name of Sylvia, which I caught.

"You are right," said she rising, "it is time to take tea."

Then Brias being greatly chagrined attempted to play the part of an indifferent man, and began to talk at randon, uttering absolute nonsense, at which Madame de Champmortain had the cruelty to laugh as well as we. This was too much for poor Brias, and he has fallen into a languid consumption. About half past eleven we withdrew, and I left those gentlemen at the door of the chateau. Montéclain had continually displayed a silly frivolous mirth, and I heard him laughing as I went away. Such is the state of affairs. After to-morrow I shall certainly see M. de Montaleu at the party which is preparing. I will observe him closely before I come to the terrible explanation which is to take place between us two. I only saw him for an hour during a conversation which I had with him fifteen years ago, and which decided my fate. He at that time appeared to me to be a model of ingratitude and sternness. He is considered in every respect as a man of honor and probity. That is only a mask no doubt, and I must believe so. But make yourself easy, mother, I will pull that mask off his face.

Your ever devoted son,

THOMAS.

---

## CHAPTER LIV.

ARTHUR DE MONTECLAIN TO M. LOUIS VILLON.

23rd May.

"I TOLD you so, my dear friend, the horizon was loaded with thick vapours, pale lightnings darted through it unexpectedly, low murmurs were heard in the air; we live in an electric atmosphere, everything forbodes a storm; and the storm has burst out.

"It was indeed a splendid *soirée;* the Chateau of Rudesgens was radiant with light; and flowers spread their perfume in every room. All the pomp and grandeur at the command of wealth were there exhibited.

"M. de Rudesgens wore a most exquisite dress, it was that of a young gentleman, who having left school, for the first time, is admitted to a fashionable ball.

"Madame de Rudesgens, over-excited by the extraordinary elegance of her husband had attempted to throw him into the shade, and she was glittering with diamonds.

Champmortain would have been very well, had he not betrayed the arrogance of making people believe that he still possessed the slender figure for which he was remarkable at the age of twenty-five. All his art had proved inadequate to hide the effects of good cheer upon his girth.

Madame de Champmortain was beautiful like a woman who has the happiness to be so, who wishes to be and knows that she is so.

She wore a white robe of india muslin, with a few natural flowers that adorned her head. But the whole formed such an admirable simplicity and such an exquisite elegance, that I should not wonder if Felina had presided at the toilet. The unfortunate Sylvia appeared to be happy and cheerful. Felina is indeed a terrible master, and I should not be surprised if Champmortain had to pay for the education of his wife.

Desirous of seeing the arrival of every one, I went in good time to the chateau of Rudesgens, but already about thirty persons had preceded me there, and among them I met some old friends of my father, who knew me when I was a child, and they related to me the uninteresting tricks of my first years. I likewise found there some little girls whom I used to dance on my knees some fifteen years ago, and who have since become grown up women hungry for matrimony.

"All this tells me that I am old, and in fact I am now thirty two; and I am nobody, thanks to that old Montaleu, who tries to redeem by moral discourses the immoralities of his youth; who exhibits enthusiasm for virtue, and severity for vice, though he has been a warm adherent to vice, and a scoffer at virtue. He is a vulgar Armenian, who tries to hide the bad practices of his past life, under the veil of hypocrisy.

"But I know you entertain for him the most profound esteem; he is the heavenly protector of the star towards which your looks are perpetually directed. I promised you to respect him, and above all, to watch over your star. I therefore lay aside my legitimate hatred, and continue my narrative."

Brias alighted from his carriage, with his head cast down and his forehead darkened by ill-humour. Brias is certainly no fool, but he does not possess the least tact. Any one in his place may be calm or tortured by despair, may be delighted or very much vexed; all this is natural. Madame de Champmortain is well worth the trouble of playing a little comedy on her account. Brias pretends that she would not believe in it. So much the better; women are always grateful for the trouble we take to deceive them. I examined Brias when he entered the drawing-room: he was received by Sylvia just like the rest of the company. That circumstance made him turn pale; and this must have made her very happy for a moment.

He was looking for some one; and his eyes met those of M. de Rudesgens, who brought him towards the place where I was; he wanted to speak to him of the beautiful Madame Amab. Just then she appeared in the drawing-room. Nothing could be better than the manner in which she entered. She was beautiful, calm, and modest. She showed herself both happy and embarrassed with the extraordinary welcome given to her. She accepted with her looks cast down the place which Madame de Champmortain had reserved for her by her own side. M. de Rudesgens was delighted with it; having discovered him, she saluted him with a kind of refined cunning which seemed to refer to the recollection of a first meeting. All my attention was fixed on Felina, and I watched her looks as they wandered timidly about her. This led me to detect at the corner of a door the corpulent Hector de Montaleu, bridled up in his white satin cravat, and pinned with diamonds. He was abominably ugly. When this vast individual is met with in the fields, his long leather gaiters, his velvet jacket, his fur cap, his whip, his shooting pocket, and his dogs, he has about him some rustic beauty, which leads you to believe, that with a decent deportment he might appear a handsome cavalier in a drawing-room. But full dress makes him look quite vulgar. It is not so with Colonel Thomas Rien, who was near him. His tall fine figure was admirably displayed through a black coat buttened up to his white cravat; he wore a commander's ribbon."

"Since you pretend to know it, my dear Villon, I will not contradict you. I am willing to believe that this Colonel Thomas is the son of some good German woman, half *illuminate,* that is, more than half-cracked, who has retired into a convent at Cologne; that your excellent Madame Muller, who is also Felina's god-mother, gave birth to the colonel, I do not gainsay; but, depend on it, there is in that man some blood of high breed. His aqueline nose, the extraordinary gracefulness of his lips, the fire of his blue eyes, shaded by fair and thick brows, bespeak a noble origin. The late M. Muller never existed, you may believe me, and one day I will tell you the name which might be assumed by him who has chosen the name of Rien, as a challenge thrown down to the world."

"But I proceed. The assembly was now pretty numerous, and the drawing-room began to be too much crowded. Madame de Champmortain, with incredible affectation, heaped women upon women, without any regard to their exquisite toilettes. The musicians had already executed several preludes, dancing was expected, but Madame de Champmortain did not give the signal, and she lavished the most ridiculous attention on Madame Amab. By the by, I was forgetting M. Amab: That individual had been received by Champmortain, who had got rid of him by handing him over to Montaleu, who then left him alone. Suddenly the door was opened, and I saw a fairy enter.

"Villon, my friend, you said to me one day, I shall love her all my life, and without any hope, for, now the distance which separates us is insuperable; but if at any time my fortune and my life could spare her a grief, I should believe that I had not entirely lost my time on this earth. You told me that, and knowing that she was to come to the country where I am, you added: 'Watch over her protect her, and if any danger threaten her, let me know, and I shall go and save her.' You told me all that, Villon, and though there is between me and *her* a secret, which you know, and which she does not know, a secret, which has prepossessed me much in her favour, I confess, that if I did not laugh in your face at the time, it was because I pity crazy people.

"Well! Villon, if there is a madman in one of us two, it is not you, it is I who am that madman. I have seen her, Villon, beautiful, candid, majestic, *naïve*,—a pure image of the angels through her beauty, and dressed like a duchess. When I saw the celestial fire of her eyes, the adorable smile of her bewitching lips, the whiteness of her shoulders, the perfect form of her arms, her childlike hand, and her fascinating figure. Villon! Villon! I remained dazzled, annihilated, confounded! I felt contempt for myself, and I thought you had an uncommon share of insolence.

"What! you love her, Villon? On my soul, I should not dare to do so.

"No! I shall not love her. But if I loved her, if I loved that woman, I would make myself her slave, her lackey, I would worship her on my knees I would place her on a throne, on an altar; or rather I would shut her up in a fortress, I would mount guard at her door, I would ill-treat her, I would kill her, if I believed she had a look for any other than myself. But, be reassured Villon, I shall not love her, I have not the least wish to become stupid and ridiculous.

"However, bear in mind that this does not apply to you. Your nature can bear such love, so much the better. As for myself, I am too passionate, too imperious to accept such a power. I am above all too selfish. If I loved your star, your holy virgin, your Julia, I should belong no longer to myself.

"Well! she was Julia, she was the Countess de Monrion, and she held the arm of M. de Montaleu. That execrable old man passed under my eyes without rousing in me the least desire to break his head. For he was under the protection of a fairy.

"You will ask me how I was able to see so many things, to discover so many perfections during the short space of time that a woman enters a drawing room. But I must tell you that this short space of time was prolonged in a most insulting manner. Madame de Monrion having come up close to a double row of women who devoured her with their eyes, began to look for the mistress of the house. The latter was with Felina, and bent towards her in a manner which clearly showed that she did not wish to see Madame de Monrion.

"At length Julia perceived Madame de Champmortain and advanced towards her. M. de Montaleu stopped her on recognising Felina. He hoped, no doubt, that Madame de Champmortain on perceiving them, would come to them, and spare them the displeasure of finding themselves face to face with Madame Amab.

Madame de Champmortain was implacable, she continued obstinately and attentively bent towards Felina, so as not to see either M. de Montaleu or Madame de Monrion. This situation was soon perceived. Madame de Monrion remained calm, but M. de Montaleu stepped back, as if to retire. A few discreet voices called out to Madame de Champmortain, to rouse her from the too deep attention she was paying to Felina, the person next to her even pushed her with her elbow; she remained impassable. This began to assume a scandalous appearance when M. de Rudesgens, whether he guessed the incredible intention of his daughter, or that he believed in a real absence of mind, crossed the room rapidly, took Julia's hand, and led her to Madame de Champmortain, saying, loud enough:

"My daughter, here is Madame de Monrion, who has been too long waiting for you."

The old Amadis, with his ridiculous affectation, has shown more sense and good breeding than that blockhead Champmortain, who saw everything, was vexed by what he saw, and only wiped, with a trembling hand, the cold perspiration as it ran from his forehead.

Madame de Champmortain, thus addressed, turned carelessly, rose as slowly as she could, made the least possible curtsey, and throwing a vacant look around her, said, languidly:

"How do you happen to come so late, Madame? There is no room left in the drawing-room; I must of necessity conceal you in yonder corner."

She took Julia by the arm, conducted her to the door, where she met her mother, and desired her to place the countess in an apartment in which there were none but men. As M. de Montaleu was engaged with M. de Rudesgens, he did not see this last piece of impertinence.

Several persons appeared more or less affected by this scene. First, Champmortain was a prey to such vexation, that he was covered with perspiration, and he burst his gloves: then Brias looked as besotted as a drunken man; and, lastly, there was Amab, whose pale face had turned green.

With regard to Colonel Thomas Rien, he opened his fiery eyes to their full stretch to contemplate the most beautiful of the beautiful.

Felina is always a great master in little things; she had looked at Madame de Monrion with a charming smile, then turning towards her neighbour, she said, with her melodious voice:

"This is a very beautiful person."

I left the place where I had been standing myself, at a moment when Felina appeared to be looking for some one. I went directly to her, and said:

"Here I am."

"Have you seen her," said she to me, without pretending that I was not the person she was looking for.

"Yes," answered I, without asking to whom she alluded.

"Have you forgiven M. de Montaleu."

"I have not."

"Where are you going?"

"I am going to look for her."

"Is that all? and do you begin your attacks with obstinate glances, just like yonder little man, who scarcely reaches up to Montaleu's waist, and who is ogling me?"

"He is a very pretty fellow," said I; "he is the son of my apothecary."

"I advise you to present him to the daughter of your china-man."

"I ought first to be introduced myself."

"You might request my husband to render you that service."

"If he dared you would not forgive him; I prefer to ask Brias to do me that favour."

"If he dared, Sylvia might forgive him."

"I will not expose him to such a terrible chance of pardon. I will not ask to be introduced to her; I shall be quite satisfied with looking at her."

"Why do you look at her?"

"To see her."

"Is it then a very extraordinary pleasure?"

"It is the first time I understand it."

"You had never seen anything so beautiful then?"

"Never."

"In order to be witty, you become impolite."

"And, in order that you should not follow my example, I leave you."

I was not sorry to have thrown that first grain of pepper on the triumph of Felina. If she abhors the virtue and good fame of Madame de Monrion, she does not the less detest her beauty. I was sure to cause a quicker outbreak of the bad intentions premeditated against that angel whose wings have been cut, and who cannot return to heaven; so I went to continue my part of observer.

When I arrived in the second saloon, Julia was there alone, between three or four tall and over-mature girls, who twisted their eyes to see her without looking at her. She was evidently wounded, and her eyes looked everywhere for a protector. There were in the first saloon, Champmortain, the master of the house, Brias, who knew her, Amab, whom she had loved, and who, I expected, would have come to her; no one stirred beyond the reach of Felina's look. Colonel Thomas had followed me into the little saloon, where the beautiful deserted woman was seated. He looked strangely at her, I promise you. Was it hatred, admiration, or love? I cannot say; but his eyes threw various rays, which alarmed her when she met them. And the consequence was that she turned towards my side. I probably, and without suspecting it, played the same part as the colonel, for she appeared equally displeased with my attention.

Fortunately for me, the signal for the dance was given. A certain number of male dancers were, therefore, compelled to come to the second saloon. Madame de Champmortain set the example. Since a week the first quadrille had been promised to Brias, who had had the good sense to ask for it before all of us. He remembered it, but Madame de Champmortain passed under his nose with a certain Baron de la Trottière, who is said to have conquered the favours of a roulade singer, who has her residence at Issoudun. That baron has the reputation of being a first-rate fencer.

This awoke Brias from his prostration; I saw the moment when he was going to seize the tall baron by the throat. I stopped him in time and said to him:

"Stop, no nonsense—a moment's courage, invite Madame de Monrion."

Brias obeyed me like a desperate man; and like all weak minds, he carried things to the last extremity, and went straight on to place himself opposite Madame de Champmortain. O, my dear Villon, undoubtedly at that moment a superior power covered with an adamantine shield both Julia and Brias, otherwise they would have fallen perforated, burned, and crushed by the look which the fair Sylvia darted at them. I do not know what step Madame de Champmortain was going to take under the influence of her exasperation, when Felina, led by that vulgar Hector, appeared. At this sight, and as if that woman carried about her an atmosphere of bad thoughts, Sylvia was struck with a sudden inspiration; she made a sign to Felina to come opposite to her, and insolently aimed these insulting words at Julia:

"Pardon, madame, this is the *vis-à-vis* that I expected."

Brias stood confounded; Hector perceived nothing; and Madame de Monrion fell almost fainting into an arm-chair which happened to be behind her.

"Champmortain, who had witnessed the unexpected stroke, made a motion to approach, but he was nailed to his place by a look from Felina. The colonel who had examined everything withdrew with a dissatisfied countenance.

"Brias quite distracted, did not know what to say to Madame de Monrion, except that he was very sorry, and would try to find another *vis-à-vis*. I was for a moment tempted to engage for the quadrille one of those over-mature girls who were forgotten on their seats, and to come to the assistance of Brias and Madame de Monrion; but all the grief, all the fright which were depicted on that beautiful face, could not prevail upon me to appear to do anything for a person in whom the venerable Montaleu took an interest.

"He had just entered, proud of his virtue, proud of his good fame, of his peerage, and of himself; his appearance venerably foppish, drove back all pity to the bottom of my heart; I abandoned Brias to his fury, and Julia to her humiliation. At length she perceived him, she glided towards him and took him into an ante-chamber. I found means not to lose sight of them.

"Old Montaleu was unwilling to believe what Julia told him. And yet she wept; the immaculate widow, the white fairy, the chaste Venus wept. And her holy and sincere tears made no more impression on the varnished leather that covered the heart of virtuous Montaleu, than dew drops on a tin armour. If those tears had addressed me either as a brother, a husband or a lover, I take heaven to witness that I would have re-entered that ball room like a drunken man, that I would have thrown myself in the midst of that insolent quadrille, in order to slap the faces of Champmortain, Brias, the colonel, the tall baron, and M. Amab, and all the men who should have raised their voices, and I would have done this not only to avenge that fair child who was weeping, but also to forget there were present two women, one of whom deserved to be publicly flogged, and the other to be sent to a penitentiary.

"But I know not Madame de Monrion, I do not wish to know her, and I left her under the unfeathered wing of her noble peer. Do you know Villon, what answer the venerable object of your worship gave to this sad distress?

"No one here," said he, "would have dared to insult me thus."

"The wretch! but had he not been under the protection of her whom he was bound to protect, I would have nailed the insult on his forehead, in order to teach him to display more pity and dignity. How is it, Villon, that among all those men there was but one who showed a good feeling towards Julia, and that man was old Rudesgens, the incarnate ridicule? It is because at the bottom of that ginger box covered with dried lemon peel, there is still the heart of a father—it is because Rudesgens has a daughter. A father, however stupid he may be, has one sense more than other men."

However, this was to have an end. M. de Montaleu pretended that he was going to have an explanation which would show Julia that she had completely mistaken the intentions of Madame de Champmortain. He sent a lackey to desire M. or Madame de Rudesgens, or M. de Champmortain, or even Madame de Champmortain, to come and speak to him. But M. de Rudesgens was nailed to a whist-table, Madame de Rudesgens was dancing, Champmortain could not be found, and Madame de Champmortain requested that they would wait for her. Brias entered at that moment. He was very much confused at the meeting, and inquired for me.

"I beg your pardon," said M. de Montaleu to him. "Madame de Monrion had your arm when she was obliged to withdraw from the quadrille. Tell her, I beg you, that Madame de Champmortain had no bad intention when she found herself compelled to fulfil an engagement which no doubt had been previously taken."

Brias cast down his eyes without answering.

"Do you then think, sir," said Montaleu, "that Madame de Champmortain had the intention of insulting my niece?"

"What are you saying, my friend?" said Sylvia

who entered at that moment. "I, far otherwise, I only wished to be agreeable to the queen of beauty, to your divine niece, by giving her an opportunity to talk more privately with M. de Brias."

Julia merely replied to Madame de Champmortain:

"Oh! madame!"

That word was said with an eloquent look, which proved that she knew more than anybody else.

"This at least is an allowable love, I know," answered Madame de Champmortain, "a love of which the imprudence will soon, I hope, be legitimated by marriage. As for me, I wished to do something to hasten it, and I am excessively sorry to have so badly succeeded."

M. de Montaleu, who, like a wise man, never knows anything, seemed to ask the angles of the walls to explain these words. Madame de Monrion looked at Sylvia with so touching a pity that I was quite moved by it.

"Oh! madame," answered she, "into what hands have you fallen?"

She thought she had guessed and understood everything, and she had pity on the mad jealousy of Sylvia. M. de Montaleu took the hand of his niece, and talking aloud to a servant whom he called:

"My carriage, and tell M. de Champmortain that I expect to see him to-morrow morning."

He retired after that bravado. Sylvia had a moment's hesitation, and perhaps she would have said something better calculated for an explanation, if that confounded Brias, the most awkward diplomatist I ever knew, had not taken into his head to say to Madame de Champmortain:

"Ah! madame, I know whose hand it is has pushed you to insult the purest virtue; but I swear that I will chastise her for it.

This rekindled the furious jealousy of Madame de Champmortain.

"It is your duty as a betrothed," answered Sylvia.

I fancied that the drama had drawn to an end, when suddenly the big Montaleu, walking like a carriage horse, came in and exclaimed, with a crushing levity:

"The betrothed to whom?"

"To your beautiful cousin, Madame de Monrion."

Hector, who pretended it required several mouthfuls to eat an ice, almost swallowed up Brias at once; but the presence of Madame de Champmortain stopped him directly. However, he could not wait till she had entirely disappeared, and he approached Brias and said, in a sinister voice:

"Brias! I must kill you."

Madame de Champmortain stopped and uttered a stifled cry; she was afraid.

"Ah! you will indeed oblige me very much," replied Brias.

Sylvia heard the answer too, and I do not know what she was going to do when her husband appeared. Sylvia went away under the protection of Felina who happened to pass. Hector boiling with rage, stopped Champmortain to ask him to be his second against Brias.

Champmortain asked for an explanation, but at that moment a servant entered and gave him a note written with a pencil.

"From whom?"

"From the Marquis de Montaleu."

"Is he gone?"

"I believe that he could not very well do otherwise," said Brias.

Champmortain read the note.

"Well!" he suddenly exclaimed, "here is another affair."

"What! my old rogue of an uncle wishes also to fight?" asked Hector.

"I do not think so; though the note is pretty dry. But," resumed Champmortain, "something new has then taken place?"

"Probably," said Hector, "for I have seen nothing."

"Gentlemen," said Champmortain, "be so good as to re-enter the ball. No scandal, I pray. We will all endeavour to have an explanation to-morrow."

They returned to the ball.

"What do you say of this, friend Villon? Is it not a pretty beginning of discord, a charming prelude to a general fight? for Felina stirring up the mess, it is probable that in a few days, Amab, the tall baron, the colonel, myself, and several others, shall all be mixed up in a quarrel."

In the meanwhile, expecting to be useful to Brias, were it only to prevent him, through despair, from getting himself killed by that huge ox Hector; I repaired to the saloon. But there I sought in vain for the Rudesgens, and the Champmortains; they had availed themselves of the *whirl* and obstructions of the dance to disappear. Felina had vanished along with them, as likewise Hector and Brias. Amab was playing with the colonel and two wealthy iron masters.

As usually happens, the two rich men won the money of the artist and the soldier. They were in Madame de Champmortain's bed-chamber and I was very much astonished to see the boudoir which is next to it was shut. A low murmur of voices was heard from the door. There was a secret consultation.

I took the place of Amab, who had already lost too much, and gave myself the pleasure of stopping the luxuriant, exhilarating, and devouring good luck of the merchants by winning from them a few hundred sovereigns.

I never beheld two money bags so much astonished as they were, when they met with a man, who by the boldness of his attacks, beat down the insolence of their good luck. However I played only with one eye; for the other was fixed on the door of the boudoir. It opened at length, M. and Madame de Rudesgens came out first, the Sexagenary zephyr had a countenance both confused and triumphant; Madame de Rudesgens was exasperated.

"It is the horror of horrors," murmured she.

"Well!" rejoined her husband, "it was so in the good old time; we belong to that period."

The word which shut the mouth of M. de Rudesgens was lost for me in the rustling of the rose satin of his wife, who, light as a child rushed into the hands of a young dancer. The marquis followed her. A moment after Champmortain came out with his wife—she had wept—an explanation, a scene had taken place—undoubtedly concerning the insult done to Madame de Monrion. I began to hope that Felina had thrust herself into an undertaking where she would leave some marks of her venomous claws. I relied upon the anger of Brias, when to my great surprise, I saw him appear with Felina, whom he listened to with conviction on his countenance, and, to crown all, Hector followed them. He appeared to be on good terms with Brias, though a gloomy cloud darkened the summit of that Atlas. An infamy had just been accomplished, and in order that my conviction should be full, a few minutes afterwards, I saw Brias waltz with Madame de Champmortain. The foolish woman was delighted with the pardon that she had no doubt granted, and did not conceal her love for Brias.

But that pardon? where and when had it been obtained? how had a reconciliation taken place between Brias and Hector? No kind of information could be obtained from them. I looked again al Champmortain; he alone was gloomy and dissatisfied. He is not Felina's dupe, though he is under her power. Until now he has sacrificed to her his fortune and consideration only; but he is not the man to allow Felina to sport with the honour and prospects of his wife. I sifted him with regard to Madame de Monrion, and foolishly asked him what had become of her.

He answered me without ceremony, that he did not care much about her. I could get no other information. I began to sing inwardly: *What is then this mystery?* Or, if you prefer it, *I understand nothing of it.*

After humming this tune, I went to whisper it in Felina's ear, who answered me:

"As I have made them all pledge their word of honour not to speak of it to any one else, it is probable that the whole ball will know it this evening."

In fact, an hour afterwards I knew it. But you, my dear Villon, you shall not know it. It is a new trick of Felina's, a marvellous arrangement of a little history which is not unknown to me. Besides, sleep in peace, friend Villon; I am here, I am on the watch—and why am I on the watch? for both our sakes; I am sitting up to write to you; for, almost immediately after I left that abominable crowd, a prey to the madness of all the bad and ridiculous passions which Felina chooses to excite in them. It was an hour after midnight when I left; now it is four o'clock in the morning, and I am just going to bed. Answer me with one word only. Were I to fall in love with Julia, would you forgive me? Yes or no. Good morning.

MONTECLAIN.

## CHAPTER LV.

### THE ORPHAN.

THE next morning M. de Montaleu entered early into the apartment of Julia. She had gone to bed; her eyes were red with tears, and also for want of sleep; but at this moment a firm and immoveable resolution had succeeded the despair which had kept her awake.

"I have come to talk with you concerning the affair of yesterday," said M. de Montaleu to her. "I wrote, as you are aware, a word to M. de Champmortain; I hope that he will do me the honour to give me an explanation, otherwise I shall go to him for it. But, in order that this explanation may be complete, you must answer me candidly. Something must have taken place between you and Madame de Champmortain which ha sled her to insult you publicly. Answer me, Julia. I am your protector, I consider you as my daughter, I wish to know the whole truth.

Madame de Monrion listened to M. de Montaleu with a calm and resigned countenance. When he had done, she answered, with a firm voice:

Sir, I am the daughter of honest persons, and I am proud of their name, but I understand that the obscurity of my birth may hurt the susceptibility of those who belong to another class. Madame de Champmortain's intention was to make me understand that I had no right to have a place in her house.

"Madame de Monrion has a right to be admitted into any house; the lady I call my niece has a right to be received everywhere with consideration," replied the Marquis.

"You have seen, sir, that it is not so."

"You do not tell me the truth, Julia," said M. de Montaleu. "You came to this country, six months ago, and the house of M. de Rudesgens was eagerly opened to you. Madame de Champmortain received you in Paris as a friend, and she treated you as one a few days ago. This change has taken place since the night she passed here. You know how she departed, notwithstanding your urgent request to detain her. Have you, by chance, been deficient in consideration towards her?"

"No, sir."

"I know that such was not your intention, but perhaps, little accustomed to certain susceptibilities of a world that you do not know completely, you may have hurt the feelings of Madame de Champmortain."

"You see, sir," said Julia with a sad smile, "that it is I who am probably wrong. The best thing that can be done is therefore for me to renounce a world for which I was not born."

"You are not calm, Julia, and you answer me with bitterness. Perhaps a trifle—tell me all. Remember whether anything has taken place, or has been said between you and Madame de Champmortain, which was not quite proper."

"If anything, not altogether becoming has been said between me and Madame de Champmortain," replied Julia with firmness, "I prefer to forget it, rather than to remember it."

"You cause me a true grief, Julia, you have not accustomed me to find you so cold, and I will add, so haughty. I ask of you some information which may be useful to me in the explanation I wish to have, that information you refuse to me."

"Since you have pronounced the word, I accept it—you are right—that information I refuse to you."

M. de Montaleu appeared very much irritated.

"Do not forget," exclaimed he, "that you bear a name which was that of my sister, and that if I am ready to have it protected in you against every injury, it is because I suppose that you will not expose it to any reproach."

"This name, sir," said Julia, "you know how I received it. It was given to me as a reparation, and whatever may have been the crime which compelled me to accept it, I am convinced that he who gave it to me on his death-bed, would have had it respected in me, if he had lived. It is because I have that conviction, it is because I respect this name that I will not leave it exposed to odious outrages, and that I wish to leave this country."

"Julia, Julia," said M. de Montaleu, surprised at the firmness of this resolution, "it is the same as to tell me, that I am unable to protect you."

"No, certainly, sir," answered Julia with an inexorable mildness, "but it is to refuse to engage you in a struggle which would be so much the harder for you, that I am determined to desert it."

"It is also to tell me that you wish to leave me," said M. de Montaleu, in a voice more agitated than perhaps he wished it to have been.

"Do not say so, sir," answered Julia, "you would render too sorrowful a wise resolution, which, I hope, will spare you more grief for the future than it can cause displeasure for the present."

"But what is the cause of this resolution?"

"It is useless I should tell it to you," replied Madame de Monrion.

"Indeed! this is strange," resumed M. de Montaleu, wounded to the quick. "I have called you about me as my daughter, and being unable to give you the name, I wished to secure to you the rights—"

"Oh! sir, sir," exclaimed Julia, quickly, "do not persist in this thought! do not, I entreat you, raise enemies for me, who never would forgive me your beneficence."

"What does this mean, Julia? Do you accuse my nephew, Hector?"

"No, certainly, sir."

"However, he alone can complain of my resolutions with regard to you; and his motives of complaint would have easily disappeared if you had allowed me to give a favourable answer to the demand he addressed to me."

"Be so kind as to forgive me, sir, if I recall to your memory that you do not entertain yourself an excessive consideration for M. Hector de Montaleu."

"I know his faults, they are those of a violent nature, of a course education, and of a life rather too rustic; but Hector is an honest man, he bears a great name, he is young, brave, and he is justified in his pretensions. Besides, I have not yet answered him formally. Listen to me, Julia, I have much reflected on this subject, I comprehend that your delicacy may be offended with the suit of Hector, but on the other side this marriage would reconcile many interests."

"This marriage is impossible, sir," said Julia, with a sorrowful effort.

"Impossible!"

"Pardon me, sir," said Julia, with a strong agitation; you have been my friend, my protector; your wish has been to replace the parents which I have lost by a fatal event. Believe me, believe me, sir, never was gratitude more sincere, more profound than mine; but when I am convinced that my presence in your house may become the cause of misfortunes, from which you perhaps would have as much to suffer as myself, believe me, my noble friend, that I shall have the courage of a separation which breaks my heart, but which is necessary. I must depart."

"And what will become of you alone in the world, without friends, without parents?"

"I have a brother, sir."

"A giddy fellow, without steadiness, without consistency, and a child besides."

"Misfortune soon makes people grow old, sir, and the dignity which my brother may now want, he will acquire under the necessity of protecting his sister."

"There is in all this something very extraordinary, and I thought I deserved your confidence," rejoined M. de Montaleu, bitterly.

Julia, who, up to that moment, had preserved a painful but immoveable firmness, could not any longer master the despair which she had long controlled. Her tears flowed apace, and in spite of her sobs, she exclaimed:

"Allow me to depart, sir. I entreat you, do not compel me to tell you the motive of Madame de Champmortain's insolence."

"She had a motive then?" exclaimed the Marquis, eagerly.

Precisely then the bell of the chateau announced the arrival of several strangers; and M. de Montaleu was informed that M. de Rudesgens, accompanied by Champmortain and Brias wished to see him.

"Wait for me, Julia," said he, "we cannot part thus. You cannot go away without having seen me again."

"It would perhaps be better," said Madame de Monrion, bitterly.

"Reflect, that if you were to depart at this moment, it would be to accept as just the outrage which you received yesterday."

M. de Montaleu left the room. Julia, with sorrowful vexation at heart, had her eyes on him as he disappeared. But suddenly she appeared to have become stronger in the resolution she had taken, and she exclaimed:

"Yes, I will go. But I will not do like them, I will not forget the weak and the orphan."

Immediately she wrapped herself up in her mantle, took a purse out of her desk, and instantly departed from the house, without being observed.

---

## CHAPTER LVI

### THE REVELATIONS

When M. de Montaleu entered the drawing-room, he coldly saluted those who were waiting for him. There was something ceremonious and solemn in Champmortain and Brias; and even M. de Rudesgens himself endeavoured to assume an austere gravity.

"I only expected you, M. de Champmortain," said Montaleu; "but I am glad that M. de Rudesgens and M. de Brias have accompanied you."

"We have all been of opinion," said Champmortain, "that it was better the explanation you have asked should come from the lips of the oldest and most sincere of your friends. What M. de Rudesgens is going to tell you, will account for the presence of Brias, who more than any other had a right to be astonished at the conduct of Madame de Champmortain, since it was he who gave his hand to Madame de Monrion. Your nephew, Hector de Montaleu was also to be present at this explanation; but he has refused, and we appreciate his scruples. His presence on this occasion might have been misinterpreted; he might have been supposed to be actuated by interested views. He has therefore abstained, and you will think, with us, that he has acted properly."

"Of this I shall be better able to judge when I have heard what Rudesgens has to tell me. Speak, my friend, I am listening to you," added M. de Montaleu, making a sign to his visitors to sit down.

They sat down; and M. de Rudesgens, after having taken an easy attitude in his arm-chair, coughed, and breathed, and then began in a cavalier tone, through which was visible a lively satisfaction on account of what he was going to say.

"Listen, Montaleu, though I speak before my son-in-law, whose conjugal principles I should be sorry to shake; though I speak also before M. de Brias, a young man who is to believe in the impeccability of grey hair, I must, however, recall to your memory that we have been—"

"Young that we have not always been—"

"Moral, as a proof I will give you a certain adventure of Cologne."

M. de Montaleu frowned, and rejoined in a severe voice:

"Some recollections of my youth may have given me regret, but not one has left remorse."

"You believe so, and I will not renew a discussion which nearly caused us to fall out."

"Besides," said M. de Montaleu, gravely, "I do not see that these recollections can have the least reference to the business which brought you here."

"Pardon me, my friend, it was necessary to bring back to your recollection that the strongest minds have had their passions and errors. Now," resumed he, with an adorable foppishness, "happy those who have the liberty to continue those passions as long as they are led by their heart."

"I beg your pardon," said M. de Montaleu, drily, "but I do not suppose that you came here only to make a parade of moral principles more or less accommodating. I beg you will come to the point, and in order to avoid every useless paraphrasis, I ask you to tell me plainly the motives of Madame de Champmortain's conduct towards Madame de Monrion. We are old friends, Rudesgens, I can hear everything when a man of honour speaks to me clearly; but I am not a man to bear everything, even from a friend, when he dares not confess to me the motives of his conduct or of the conduct of a member of his family."

"Ah! but this is the difficult part——," answered M. de Rudesgens, fidgeting in his arm-chair.

"Come, Montaleu, you must have some idea of it, guess a little. Everything is known; the deuce take it. This is the truth, everything is known."

"M. de Champmortain," said the Marquis, impatiently, "can you speak more clearly than M. de Rudesgens? I confess that all this has no meaning for me."

"And I confess," rejoined Champmortain, "that it would be painful for me to say certain things to a man whose long friendship with my family has taught me to respect—"

"I will then apply to you, M. de Brias," resumed M. de Montaleu, more and more astonished. "Our slight acquaintance must allow you to speak freely to me."

"Pardon me, sir," said Brias, in a penetrated tone, "I could not refuse either my presence or my testimony to the justification of Madame de Champmortain; but there are questions so delicate, that I hardly believe to have a right to know them, and that I think I have not the right to speak of them."

"Gentlemen, let us beware," said M. de Montaleu, with a high bearing; "so much consideration may become an injury. What has then taken place that you hesitate to tell me of it? Whatever it may be, this hesitation is not admissible, unless you think that I have authorised what has been done—or that I am an accomplice in it—if not the author?"

"Now we approach the truth," said M. de Rudesgens, playing with his ruffles.

Then he placed his elbows on his knees, and with a shrewd air, his eyes half closed, a smile on his lips, he resumed:

"Come! Montaleu, allow me to ask you certain questions, and to bring to your recollection certain dates. You arrived here, last year, towards the end of the season?"

"In the first days of October."

"Madame de Monrion was still in mourning, our relations with her were confined to a few mutual visits."

"I know all that well. Julia was unwell, and

the remembrance of the frightful death of her parents still haunted her."

"She was unwell," repeated M. de Rudesgens, "that is right. You know that towards the middle of October you left home to go to Nevers—that absence lasted a week, I believe?"

"Ten days; in fact, as long as the elections of the council-general lasted; for I wanted to prevent the nomination of Montéclain, who offered to stand, and I fully succeeded."

"Do you know that during that time, Madame de Monrion took a journey to Issoudun?"

"She went there to settle an affair with the person who had bought the house of her father. I was so well informed of that journey to Issoudun, that I went to fetch her back."

"And how did you find her there?"

M. de Montaleu stopped, as if struck with a circumstance which revived in his memory, but which he had not noticed at the time.

"I did not find her there," answered he, examining M. de Rudesgens; "for, on the eve of my arrival she had left precipitately."

"Well, my dear Montaleu," said M. de Rudesgens, "on the very day of your useless journey to Issoudun, a young woman arrived towards nightfall at the hamlet of Saint-faron, you know, that little place concealed among rocks and woods, and about three miles distant."

"Well?"

"Well! this young woman handed to a peasant woman of the hamlet a fine boy, two days old, with a birth certificate, in which he was named Jules, and was declared born of unknown parents."

M. de Montaleu was quite astonished while listening. However, he said:

"What can this have to do with Madame de Monrion?"

"This young woman," continued M. de Rudesgens, "gave, at the same time, twenty-five sovereigns for the nursing of the child. Eight days after she returned, and kissed him, complaining to be obliged to forsake him, for she was going to leave the country. It was towards the end of October."

M. de Montaleu started.

"The epoch at which we departed," exclaimed he.

M. de Rudesgens pursued:

"This unknown woman did not, however, forget the child; clothes, gifts, and money, were sent from Paris to the nurse; then the fine weather returned, and with it the presence of the unknown woman. Finally, since—a month—visits have been frequent at the hamlet of Saint-faron, and the young and beautiful woman appears delighted with the health of that dear child."

"And this young and beautiful woman?" said M. de Montaleu, in a voice which betrayed anger and surprise.

"It is Madame de Monrion," said M. de Rudesgens, casting down his head.

M. de Montaleu threw a rather wild look on Brias and Champmortain, who bowed without pronouncing a word.

"Impossible!" exclaimed M. de Montaleu, "impossible. You have been told a lie."

"Your grief and your astonishment justify you at least in my eyes," said M. de Rudesgens, "for I must confess it, my dear Montaleu, the concordance of your absence and that of Madame de Monrion, had led certain people to believe that you had pretended to go on one side, while Madame de Monrion went on the other, with the understanding that you both would join again at the same place and same time for the birth of this offspring, of a weakness the excuse of which is for you in the beauty of Madame de Monrion, and is for her in the hope of securing one of the largest fortunes in this country."

"I am dreaming! I am dreaming! I am dreaming!" repeated M. de Montaleu!

Then he rose and resumed abruptly:

"And here are three noblemen, honourable sensible persons, who dare to make themselves the propagators of such calumnies! And tell me, Rudesgens, tell me, gentlemen, who has taught you all these fine things?"

"The nurse herself," said M. de Rudesgens.

"The nurse!" repeated the Marquis; "how! have you seen that woman?"

"Though my daughter, who held all these details from a person well informed, had revealed them to us yesterday, when my son-in-law asked her the cause of her conduct towards Madame de Monrion, yet we would not have dared repeat such things had we not had proofs of what we were to bring forward."

"Proofs!" repeated again the Marquis de Montaleu.

"Yes! proofs!" continued M. de Rudesgens. "M. de Champmortain, M. de Brias, your nephew and I, who yesterday were present at the explanation of Sylvia, repaired after the ball to the house of the peasant woman. Her name is Jeanne Dromeray, she is the wife of a wood-cutter of the hamlet of Saint-faron, at some distance from the village; and in the middle of the forest. We have questioned her. We must confess it, Montaleu, she has confirmed all the details which I have just related. Since six months, no other woman than that who had brought the child has come to visit him. No one else has inquired after him. Then I asked her if she knew the name of that lady. This question appeared to confuse her. Urgently pressed, she at length has confessed that this lady had told her that she was called Madame Thoré."

"This is, in fact, the name of her family," said the Marquis, with terror; "but, nevertheless, it might also be the name of some other."

"M. de Brias communicated to us the same suggestion," resumed M. de Rudesgens. "We have pressed the nurse to tell us if she knew this lady under another name. She also has confessed, that desirous to know her, she had followed to the door of your park; that the lady went in after having been saluted by a game-keeper who happened to pass."

"And! then—" said the Marquis, in a trembling voice:

"Then," continued M. de Rudesgens, "the nurse approached the game keeper, and asked him who was the lady who had just entered the park?"

"The Countess de Monrion," answered the man.

The old marquis bent his head as if crushed by that terrible news. But after a moment of sorrowful and solemn silence, he arose abruptly.

"Gentlemen," said he, with anger, "I must see the woman. You must follow me. There is in all this some infamous plot. Do you not think so, M. de Champmortain? added he, in a tone full of sarcasm.

"I only know what M. de Rudesgens has told," rejoined Champmortain, rather embarrassed.

"And you, M. de Brias," demanded the marquis.

"Believe, sir, that I excessively regret to have been mixed in all this. The only part which fits me in it, is to keep an absolute silence on everything which is going on; and this silence I promise it to you."

## CHAPTER LVII.

### CIRCUMSTANCES GROW WORSE.

A FEW minutes afterwards, De Montaleu, old De Rudesgens, Brias, and Champmortain went in their carriages, to repair to the village of Saint-faron, or to speak more correctly, as far as carriages could proceed on such a road. M. de Rudesgens rode in the same carriage with M. de Montaleu; Brias and Champmortain followed them in a phaeton.

"One word, Rudesgens," said Montaleu, when they were alone, and let this word be the last on an affair which I hate to hear mentioned."

"I understand that the conduct of Madame de Monrion affects you painfully."

"I do not refer to Madame de Monrion, but to that affair of Cologne, which you have so awkwardly thrown in my face."

"Pardon me, my dear marquis," said M. de Rudesgens, "but, on my soul, if I have recalled the past; it was because I believed you were the real author of the present feat. You have been wise Montaleu; you have shunned matrimony, you are at liberty to roam about as formerly, as in the time of Sophia."

"Rudesgens, you know what has been my irrevocable determination with regard to that unworthy woman. Pray! let us speak no more of her."

"Let it be so, keep your opinion, I keep mine; and I am sure that Sophia was innocent. This makes you angry, let us speak no more of it. But, what do you think of Madame de Monrion."

"I say that it is impossible, that this affair cannot be true. Julia is free. She can marry whom she likes. No! it is not true. There is in all this some infamous plot, or a deplorable error."

"Try to see through it more clearly than we do, I wish it with all my heart."

"But who can the wretched man be?"

"The wretched!" repeated M. de Rudesgens. "The epithet is unjust. It is not the one I applied to you. When I thought that—"

"It would have been the height of infamy,"

"And the most charming of triumphs, resumed M. de Rudesgens. Ah! she is indeed the most adorable person."

The marquis shrugged his shoulders.

"And yet," continued M. de Rudesgens, "she is perhaps the only woman to whom I have never spoken of love. I believed her to be a saint. Ah! my dear marquis. the respect one has for women now and then, always turns out an illusion, I shall be caught no more."

While the venerable zephyr continued this foppish talk, Champmortain and Brias remained a long time in silence; they were equally sad and thoughtful. Champmortain saw with fear the disturbance which the mere apparition of Felina had brought into his house, and he was so much the more dissatisfied that he could only accuse himself of this misfortune. Brias reflected on the terrible situation in which he and Sylvia were placed. In fact, Felina was the confidant of their amours; she would be able to work their destruction on the very day when this crime would be necessary to her vengeance. Though no evidence supported him, Brias was convinced that Julia was innocent, though he did not and dared not defend her; for he was prevented by the fear that Madame de Champmortain would suffer from the least effort he might make to justify the countess.

Champmortain was the first to break silence.

"This is a very silly affair, Brias," said he to him.

"A very sad one," replied Brias.

"Do you know who told these particulars to my wife?"

"Did she not tell you?"

"She absolutely refused; but you know something, I am sure. You are not at all mixed up in all this, and yet you appear more afflicted than any of us."

"Believe me, when I tell you!" said Brias, impatiently, "I wish I were a thousand leagues away from this country."

Whilst conversing in this manner, they reached that part of the wood where carriages could go no further. They had therefore to proceed on foot along the narrow footpaths.

Struck by the terrible revelation which he had just heard, M. de Montaleu had at first bent his head under this cruel accumulation of circumstances; but by degrees he had recovered from this first alarm, and he was convinced that the information he was about to find at Saint-faron would explain and remove this calumny. The party had now a full sight of the dwelling of Jeanne Dromeray, when the marquis stopped suddenly. He had that moment recognised Madame de Monrion, who was crossing the threshold of the cottage, and going rapidly away. Brias and Champmortain were obliged to support him.

"Unfortunate woman!" murmured M. de Montaleu. And a tear which rose up to his eyelids showed how sincere and deep were the tenderness which he felt for Julia.

"In whom are we now to believe?" added he, in a stifled voice.

There was so much despair in the noble old man that Brias, whose remorse at what he witnessed, spoke louder than any feeling in the hearts of his companions, forgot the prudence he had imposed on himself, and said to M. de Montaleu:

"Enter, sir! enter! perhaps you will discover that all this is a calumny or some fatal error."

"No!" said M. Montaleu, in a tone of despair, "no! you have seen this woman, and she has told you that Madame de Monrion—"

"Must be the mother of this child, whom she alone came to see. But enter—"

"No!" resumed the marquis. "I have too long forgotten that I have no authority over Madame de Monrion. She is now nothing more than a stranger to me, and henceforth everything I might do to discover her secret would be but a mean and vulgar curiosity. I have nothing to do here—now—"

As he pronounced these words, a bitter and sardonic laugh was heard issuing from a cluster of trees close to them. They all turned, and were very much surprised to see Montéclain in the costume of a cavalier, and who, as he continued to approach them, laughed repeatedly. He saluted Brias, Champmortain, Rudesgens, in a friendly manner, and bowed his head to M. de Montaleu, in a way which was rather like an impertinence than a salute.

"What were you doing there?" asked Brias.

"I was admiring," answered he, laughing, "the logic of M. de Montaleu, who cannot go and question this woman, although it might exonerate his niece, whilst he has received as good evidence the revelations which condemn her."

"M. de Montéclain," said M. de Montaleu, in a high tone, you forget to whom you are speaking."

"To my most deadly enemy, I do not forget it: to him, who, in a public assembly of electors, made it his task to describe me as a wretched debauchee; to him who has made it a point of honour to bar every career my ambition might lead me to pursue."

"No, M. de Montaleu, I do not forget to whom I am speaking, I remember it too well, on the contrary, not to profit by every circumstance which shall give me the power to return you a part of the evil you have done me."

"And as you are not able to attack me," replied M. de Montaleu in a rage, "you wish to strike a poor woman."

"Nothing could depict the ineffable contempt with which Montéclain looked at M. de Montaleu. He shrugged his shoulders, and turned his back on him, advancing towards the cottage Madame de Monrion had just left."

"Where are you going?" exclaimed M. de Montaleu.

"To this woman; I have something to do here," answered Montéclain disdainfully.

Immediately he hastened into the hut, M. de Rudesgens, Brias, Champmortain looked at each other with a stupified countenance, and M. de Montaleu murmured in a low voice;

"No! I will not go there, but I must see Julia."

And accordingly he went away likewise, followed by his friends.

## CHAPTER LVIII.

### A GREAT PROJECT.

The ferocious Hector de Montaleu had returned home after the ball, and contrary to his custom had not enjoyed that heavy sleep which is the happy lot alike of brutes and of persons of sanguine constitution who drink hard; he had spent the rest of the night in walking. A mighty project was being revolved in his thoughts. Hector was not habituated to the troublesome exercise of reflecting, combining the various chances of a project, foreseeing its obstacles, and finding the best means to evade them or break them down. When his brutal passions were fired, he went directly forward and without heeding the consequences, proceeded towards their gratification.

He was of noble birth, rich, and endowed with great bodily strength; he said to himself, that after all he could get off by paying for the silence of those who would have a right to complain if they belonged to the mob, and by killing in a duel those of a superior class who might find fault with him.

But on the present occasion, his usual expedient was not of any avail; for in this case, skill was necessary to accomplish a thing which would afford him a great triumph, and transform him into a hero. We shall not attempt to explain how the idea of such a project had occurred to him, and how it had been brought to maturity in his thick bains, we might as well undertake to relate the works of Hercules.

Suppose a man, who by chance, and in the midst of a tempest, has discovered the beginning of a silver vein in a sand mountain. He digs with activity, works hard, and all at once perceives the direction of the vein; but quite as suddenly the sand tumbles down, and annihilates the work so laboriously accomplished. The man sets to work again, and ten times in succession his work is destroyed by the same accident.

The maturing of Hector's project had encountered nearly the same chances as we have here described.

As Montéclain had written to Villon, Hector was present at the little meeting which took place n the boudoir of Madame de Champmortain. It was there that Sylvia, to whom on the eve Felina had communicated the strange information which the next day M. de Rudesgens related to M. de Montaleu, it was there, we say, that Sylvia, related the extraordinary history of the child confided by Madame de Monrion to the woman of Saint-Faron.

Hector had at first listened to those details and their dates with looks of amazement, and more than once a kind of indistinct and stifled groan, had shown the interest he took in that history. Several times he would certainly have interrupted it, if while he was looking for a sentence in his thick intellect, and attempting to open his heavy jaws, other more active minds and tongues more ready, had not deprived him of the chance of speaking. He therefore allowed the narrative to proceed to the end. He likewise left the boudoir, without having uttered a single word, but entirely confounded by the revelation. It was in the middle of this intellectual storm that the first glimpse of an idea became visible to Hector. He said to himself that he might derive a great advantage from that revelation. Another man in the same position, would in less than ten seconds have discovered how he was to proceed; but even ten hours were not sufficient to enable Hector to clear that idea from the thick confusion which reigned in that mind of compact matter. But he became aware that the twelve thousand pounds a year of his uncle might one day belong to him. Such a vein well deserved that the vigourous viscount should move even mountains in order to seize hold of it. He set to work with so much ardour and perseverance, that at length his project assumed a visible form, and he was able to trace the line of conduct he would have to follow in order to accomplish his object.

As it will be seen, if the plan was laboriously combined, it bore the marks both of audacity and skill. One obstacle alone threatened to oppose his first proceedings. And perhaps that obstacle did not really exist. This was the thing to be ascertained. Accordingly Hector went up to the top floor of his chateau, settled the blinds of some of the windows in a certain manner, opened one ot them, hung out a long red curtain, and came down again when he had seen a signal from the Lavordan Farm, informing him that he had been understood.

A few minutes after, Brias, Champmortain, and M. de Rudesgens came to fetch him, that he might hear the questions which would be put to Jeanne Dromeray. He accompanied them, listened very attentively to what was said, but did not open his mouth.

But we are wrong—he opened it once and uttered a few words of immense signification, but they passed off unnoticed. Hector said in a low voice:

"Has no other woman ever come here to see this child?"

"Never," answered the nurse.

Hector heaved a deep sigh; and his flushed face expanded with satisfaction.

The party went away and we have already expressed through their mouths under what delicate pretence Hector had refused to accompany them to his uncle's mansion.

It is written somewhere that however bad an actor may be, there is generally a character or a moment in his life when he is sublime: in the same manner, there is in the life of the greatest boor, and of the biggest fool, a day when he displays all the resources and all the presence of mind of a man of genius. Such a day had shone for Hector.

Therefore, whilst Brias, Champmortain, and M. de Rudesgens were gone to relate to M. de Montaleu the result of their visit to the nurse of Saint Faron, Hector took his way by a narrow path through the forest to the farm, where his signal had been so well understood.

The reader, we presume, has not forgotten that it was in that farm-house, belonging to Bricord, that Colonel Thomas Rien lodged. After the ball was over he, like the rest of the company, had returned home in a state of great agitation. He had dressed himself very early the next morning; and when going out had taken with him to a short distance from the house his faithful spahi, Aly Muley.

The latter was a native of Pezenas, a town in the south of France, whose real name was so very ridiculous that we cannot write it. That name, which signified a *coward*, had been a source of annoyance and quarrels to him who bore it. The Gascon had, therefore, sworn to take the name of the first Arab he should kill. So one day as an Arab stood under his sword, he asked him for his name; the unfortuuate Arab obeyed; but before he had had time to articulate all his different names, he was a dead man, and the Gascon remembered only the name of *Aly*.

The comrades of Aly continued their jokes, and persuaded him that the name he had assumed was merely a christian name. He swore again to add to it the family name of the first prisoner he should surprise. An opportunity soon occurred: in the course of a razzia, Aly pursued an Arab who was driving cattle before him; but he was attacked in his turn, his horse was killed, and he was very fortunate in laying hold of a mule on which he made good his retreat. His comrades did not fail this time to compliment him on his prisoner, whose name they gave him. As *mule* in French becomes *mulet*, so by a slight change in the spelling *mulet* became *muley*, and henceforth the Gascon was called *Aly Muley*. It was that person with whom we are as yet but slightly acquainted that Colonel Thomas Rien ordered to attend him.

"You know what I have recommended to you," said the Colonel. "I wish to be made acquainted with every step of M. Hector de Montaleu. The hour at which he usually goes out approaches; you might already be on the watch."

"Make yourself easy, colonel," answered Aly Muley, "I have an eye on the barometer of the marches and counter marches of M. Hector de Montaleu."

"What do you mean by barometer?"

"I ought, perhaps, to have said thermometer; but be perfectly easy."

"Is he here, then?"

"No!"

"You know, then, that he is at home?"

I don't."

"Is that the way that you execute what I recommended you."

"Do not trouble yourself in the least, colonel, I know my business. Since three days that I have been here, I have had sufficient time to become acquainted with the habits of the animal. As long as the mistress stays at home quietly, I am sure that the deeds of Montaleu the nephew are quite harmless, that is to say, he confines himself to beating about the brambles, or drinking Macon wine with some gamekeeper, twice I have happened to lose sight of him, but I always have found it again by following the track of Madame Léda."

The colonel made a motion of illhumour and impatience.

"I cannot help it. You told me to look and I have seen. Two or three times I have felt a desire to send a ball into the left eye of the viscount; but I am not her husband; and the article of the code which allows Bricord to kill the man who —you understand, would not protect me. I have, therefore, put back my desire in the scabbard."

"And you will do well to do the same with your tongue."

"You must know, colonel, that I am as discreet as a midwife. But it appears that all the husbands of this place are lodged at the sign of the Big Stag; for in my solitary walks by the side of the avenues of the forest, I have met Madame Amab, whom you visited on the day of your arrival, walking with a gentleman who is no relation of hers, legitimately speaking; and another time I have seen the wife of that gentleman stealing into a copse where another gentleman was waiting for her; and that gentleman was not her husband, was not the man I had seen with Madame Amab."

"Enough," said the colonel drily; "I want to know what M. Hector de Montaleu is doing. and I do not intend that your observations should go beyond my instructions."

"You told me to observe what road was followed by that brave Nambrude, as M. de Brias calls him: well! I can't help seeing this or that lady who is passing, can I?"

"Very well! but do you know what are M. Hector de Montaleu's intentions to-day—to-day above all?"

"Be perfectly easy on the subject, colonel; Madame Léda is now engaged in adorning and making herself attractive, and every moment she is looking at the clock in the kitchen—she will put me on the track, and when I have got her at the end of my eye, I will follow her step by step without being perceived. Eh! don't you hear that she is shutting the door? it is herself."

"Go, then!"

"I need not hurry myself, colonel—provided I see in what direction she proceeds; I can safely allow her an advance of ten minutes, and though her foot is nimble and her leg fine, two minutes after I shall be on her heels. I will finish my pipe and then be off."

The colonel left the farm to go and pay a visit to Madame Amab, whilst Aly Muley ran after Léda, who had arrived at a crossing where several avenues met. Aly Muley walking through the wood with a step as silent and nimble as that of the fox in search of its prey, came in sight of Léda at the very moment Hector de Montaleu appeared at the end of one of the avenues.

Léda, nimble and joyful, ran to meet her homeric lover, for he had hoisted on the highest window of his chateau the signal which informed the too credulous Parisian that a pressing *rendezvous* was desired.

Léda wno, for some time past, had observed on Hector's countenance that tint of lassitude which is the sure presage of expiring love, had suddenly hoped for a revival of his passion. Poor woman! she had spoiled her eyes with reading all the fantastic theories of love, and as it is ever the case with ill-directed minds, dangerous and guilty notions had taken possession of her heart, in the same manner as weeds stifle the good seed in an ill-cultivated soil. From all her pernicious books Léda had not derived even that vulgar wisdom which teaches us that love, like the strongest tree and the weakest plant never recovers its luxuriant life after it has once begun to decay.

Léda was, therefore, cruelly disappointed when her own joyful smile was repulsed by a gloomy look and a frigid reception. Another sorrow fell on the suffering heart of the poor woman, and she siad with a timid voice:

"Why have you desired to see me?"

"We have to speak of serious matters," answered Hector in a brutal tone. "Have you brought the key of the hut?"

"Here it is," said Léda taking the key out of her pocket.

## CHAPTER LIX.

WHEN they had shut the door, Aly Muley approached, and applied his ear to the wall of that singular retreat; but to his great annoyance, he found that the walls had purposely been made so thick that only a low murmur could be heard.

The Gascon perceiving that it was useless to attempt to listen to the conversation, took up his station at a spot which allowed him to have a glance at the door, and then began to smoke his pipe.

Hector, as if he feared to hear something to disturb the combination of his project, hesitated to speak.

"Why have you invited me here?" Léda said, at length, to him.

I want to know," replied Hector, looking at his victim with a threatening countenance, "whether you have kept the promise you made me?"

"I have made so many promises to you," answered Léda, "that I do not know to which you allude; but whichsoever it may be, I am sure that I have kept it."

"Thus you never have once visited the child?"

"Oh! no, never, never," said Léda, with tears. I never have seen the poor innocent creature; you would not allow me."

"It would have been imprudent, Léda, people naturally would have been led to endeavour to explain why you took an interest in that unknown child, and in the end they would have discovered the truth, and you would have been undone."

"Am I not undone as it is, and to the crime which has dishonoured me, have I not added the crime of a mother discarding her child?"

"The devil confound your high sounding sentences, Léda! I tell you that we are here to talk of serious matters, and not to be bothered about crime and dishonour. A terrible danger has to be averted."

"A danger to you, Hector!" exclaimed the poor woman. "Oh! if my life is necessary to save you, take it."

"I dread no danger," said Hector, brutally. "I fear no man, not even your husband. You alone are concerned."

"Myself."

"Yes, yourself, Léda! the child is discovered, and they seek to find out to whom he belongs!"

Hector took good care not to tell Léda to whom the child was attributed. He was afraid of rousing an impulse of courage and generosity in the heart of that unfortunate woman."

"Discovered!" exclaimed Léda. "In that case I am at the mercy of Madame de Monrion."

"Perhaps! she may be compelled to remain silent."

"And how could you compel her to be silent?" she asked.

"I may perhaps tell you; but I cannot succeed unless I know everything which took place at that time."

"How many times have I attempted to tell you all that I then suffered; but you always most harshly refused to hear me."

"And where would have been the use," said Hector, in a passion, "to have listened to your complaints at that time? Of what use to have talked about a matter which appeared so fortunately settled. But to-day it is the object of my serious attention, for your own sake."

"The affectation with which Hector pronounced the last word; ought to have taught the unfortunate Léda that he himself was especially concerned. But the deluded woman, blinded by passion, took it for a revival of tenderness, and answered him in a grateful tone

"Well! I will give you all the particulars which so many times you have refused to hear."

"Above all," said Hector, "do not omit the least circumstance."

"You know that I took down the history of that event in writing."

"And that you destroyed it, I hope, as I had ordered you?" replied Hector, in a tone which betrayed both anger and alarm.

"Yes, I destroyed it; but I can recollect the least expressions, so deep they were printed in my heart by despair. But it is useless for me to repeat the complaints contained in my narrative."

"Omit the complaints," said Hector, abruptly, "and come to the fact."

Léda uttered a low groan.

"After all," added Hector, "do as you please; I can listen to everything."

He was right. As long as a faint feeling of compassion for that unfortunate woman had existed in the heart of Hector, he had repulsed her tears and complaints; for they disturbed the brutal tranquillity of his coarse selfishness; but at this moment he was too much engrossed by his selfish and covetous views to be in the least disturbed by the recital of her sufferings.

Léda repeated, from memory, the following narrative, which, as the reader knows, she had written:

"My husband had been absent during four months, in consequence of important business he had to transact in Brittany. His departure delighted me, as his absence would allow me to indulge more freely the guilty passion which united me to a nobleman of the neighbourhood. He was possessed of every kind of attraction, beauty, fortune, and rank."

"The intoxicating pleasure I enjoyed with him without foreseeing its frightful consequences was suddenly disturbed by a terrible event. I was warned by the laws of nature that I was a mother; and these same laws revealed to my conscience, awakened too late that the being who was to call me his mother, had no right to the tenderness and the name of the man who was my husband. In the first moment of that terrible discovery, I thought I should go mad—I wished to die; but I had not the courage to execute my project of suicide, and I went to communicate my despair to the author of my shame. Alas! he who was bound to console me, received me with harshness—I had hoped for his protection, and he gave me none but appalling counsels—"

"Which you ought to have followed," said Hector, interrupting the poor woman.

She cast down her eyes, remained silent for a moment, and omitting the cruel conduct of her seducer, she continued thus;

"My husband came back, but did not, any more than the other persons in the house, discover my real state. I was very earnest, but my suffering alarmed him without awakening any suspicion. He remained two months at the farm; and when the harvest was over he returned to Brittany. I again found myself alone and face to face with the man upon whom I had a right to rely. But the nearer the fatal period approached, the more he showed himself gloomy and dissatisfied. He reproached me for not having followed his criminal advice. Finally, one day after a terrible explanation, he dared to tell me, that he would do nothing for me, and he deserted me a few days before the birth of the child who was to be proscribed and devoted to shame, and whom he ought to have protected. Oh! what grief tortured my soul, what terrible thoughts crowded in my mind, in presence of that cowardly desertion! I ought to have cursed him, I ought to have proclaimed my shame and his own; but I still loved him: so much does crime debase and pervert the human mind. My wish was to sacrifice myself alone."

She made a pause.

"Continue," said Hector, in a mild voice; for she had reached the point which Hector considered the most important, and upon the perfect knowledge of which in some measure depended the success of his scheme.

Léda deceived by his accent less brutal than usual, resumed her narrative with eagerness.

"I felt that the fatal moment of my delivery and shame was near at hand. I wrote to my husband a letter in which I confessed my fault, and announced my determination to die. But I did not name him who had led me to violate the most sacred duty of honour."

"Are you very sure of that?" inquired Hector with anxiety.

"No! I did not name him, for the man I am unworthy to call my husband, is a generous and high spirited man. Had I named the accomplice of my crime, he would have killed him—"

"A peasant!" said Hector, with deep contempt.

"The distance which birth had placed between them, would not have stopped him; and if my seducer had refused to give him satisfaction, he would have killed him without pity, he would have gratified his vengeance even through a crime, if necessary—"

Hector bit his lips, wrinkled his eye brows, and made a wry face, which showed that he believed in the assertion of Léda.

"Well," added he, "you did not name me in your letter, you were right."

Léda resumed her narrative.

"I had determined to leave my husband's house a few days after the writing of the letter; but I was suddenly informed that my husband, recalled by the Marquis of Montéclain, our landowner, was to arrive on the next day."

"There was no room for hesitation: I placed on a table the letter I had written, and set off a few hours before the arrival of my husband. I took a carriage for Issoudun, expecting to proceed from that town to Paris. But I had more courage than strength. Arrived at Issoudun I was a prey to such dreadful sufferings, that I felt I was absolutely unable to proceed any farther. I looked for an obscure inn, and concealed myself in it. It was then that my situation appeared to me in all its horror."

"Come to the point," said Hector abruptly.

"Don't interrupt me, Hector," replied Léda; "and since you have desired to hear this narrative, you must for once at least know what I have suffered."

And she resumed with an authority which for a moment subdued the brutal indifference of Hector.

"Yes, it was then that my situation appeared to me in all its horror. I was alone, forsaken by the man who ought to have protected me; alone with the sorrow of my soul and the sufferings of my body; alone in a low, damp and cold room; alone half dead on a wretched bed, stifling my cries, without help, trembling every moment to see my husband appear. The least noise rendered me a prey to the most frightful fears. Every moment I fancied I saw him enter, terrible and implacable. I felt my blood freeze in my veins. I expected to die. But God gives to those who are about to become mothers a supernatural strength. I conquered my suffering and even my fears, and in the silence of the night I gave birth to a child who was destined to have neither a name, nor acknowledged parents; a child cursed and repulsed by the man who ought to have received him in his arms."

Hector shrugged his shoulders. Léda did not see it; her sight was obscured by her tears; and in spite of her sobs she exclaimed:

"Oh, to what dreadful suffering I was a prey! I do not know the joy with which heaven fills the heart of a mother at the sight of her newly-born child. Ah! Hector! Hector! you had killed in me all the feelings which elevate the soul. That poor child! like you, I cursed him, I devoted him to death."

A low exclamation, the meaning of which escaped Léda, interrupted her.

"It was a crime; was it not? but I did not condemn him alone, I condemned myself also with him. Yes, I had resolved to die. I trembled lest any one should arrive."

"The morning had not yet come; I hoped to be able to go out unperceived. I had carefully covered up my child. O! wretched condition! I was going to kill him; and yet I was afraid to hurt him. I was ready, I was on the point of leaving that house to go and commit a double crime, when suddenly I heard the voice of my landlady answering another voice and saying:"

"At the end of the passage, the door in front."

"The room thus indicated was my own."

"I threw myself half dead behind the door before I was able to extinguish the light which I had kept near my bed. I did not see the door open, nor did I hear the voice which called me. I fell on my knees, pressing my poor child against my heart, and I exclaimed: Pity! pity on him at least."

A heavy sigh escaped from the breast of Hector. Something human and compassionate had at length penetrated into that hard and cowardly heart; but he resisted this impulse of pity, and murmured the word:

"Proceed!"

"Instead of the threatening and terrible voice which I trembled to hear, it was the voice of an angel that answered me. I opened my eyes, I raised my head, and I found myself face to face with a woman of extraordinary beauty. I was so much astonished, so much stupified, that I did not recognise her immediately. I took her for one of those celestial creatures whom God sends to mortals to console them in their dreams. But it was no dream, it was reality; it was a noble lady in the neighbourhood of our farm, who also had suffered, according to report, and—"

"It was Madame de Monrion," interrupted Hector.

"Yes!" resumed she, "it was herself."

"What did she tell you?"

"She had pity on me, sir, she consoled me, and informed me how she had come."

"This," said Hector, "I do not recollect well."

"I will repeat it again," said Léda.

"On the day my husband arrived she was at the farm; she had come there with a servant to purchase a horse for herself. She found M. Bricord very much astonished at my absence, and questioning all the servants to know if I had not said where I had gone, and how long I should be absent. She was astonished to see him repeat his questions, even after a maid servant had told him that I had left a letter for him. Madame de Monrion called his attention to the fact."

"Then my husband, imposing silence on his vanity, requested Madame de Monrion to follow him to my room. She consented. It was there that he confessed with confusion, what he never had dared to tell me—that he did not know how to read. Alas! the unfortunate man had concealed his ignorance, lest I should not consider him worthy of me. He was ashamed of not being possessed of those vain advantages of education which do not protect the heart against the most guilty weakness."

"In short," said Hector, "he confessed to her that he did not know how to read."

"He did," continued Léda, "and he requested the countess to be so kind as to make him acquainted with the contents of the letter I had left for him. Madame de Monrion had broken the seal, and was going to read it, when a providential chance engaged for a moment the attention of my husband. A servant had come to inform him that one of his neighbours wanted to see him. My husband exchanged a few words with that man, addressing him from the top of the staircase, and requesting him to wait for him. The neighbour likewise added:

"By the bye, I have been told that you were uneasy on account of your wife. I may inform you that I met her a few hours ago on the road to Issoudun."

The countess started on hearing this information for the interruption caused by the arrival of the neighbour, had allowed her to peruse the letter, and she had seen in it the confession of my fault, and the fatal resolution I had taken of dying."

"You had told me, I believe," said Hector, "that you intended to go to Paris."

"True! such was my design when I set out, but while writing to my husband, I had felt that I must die—I told him so, and Madame de Monrion believed it."

Léda continued thus:

"During that short interval, Madame de Monrion conceived a most noble and dangerous design; she resolved to save me, by extemporising with admirable presence of mind, a letter quite different from the one I had written, she said to my husband that I informed him I was going to Paris where I was called by my mother who was ill."

"Very well!" said Hector, "but I presume that she did not leave that letter in your husband's hands, for he might have shown it to some one else."

Léda appeared embarrassed and answered,

"That letter, he desired to keep, and Madame de Monrion could not prevail upon him to relinquish it."

"The devil!" murmured Hector, "you assured me that he had it no longer."

"I have many times asked it of him and he always answered me that he had burned it. I have myself carefully searched for it in every part of the house, and I must have found it, had it still existed. Besides, the behaviour of my husband since that time, proves to me that the letter has completely disappeared."

"And my name was not written in it," said Hector.

"I have already told you so," replied Léda with a deep sigh. "Gracious heaven! are you so ashamed then of the love which you once had for me?"

"What more reproaches—you must know," replied Hector abruptly, "that I could not save you, if by chance you had named me, especially to Madame de Monrion."

"Madame de Monrion did not ask any questions about it."

"But how did she discover you at Issoudun?"

"Whilst my husband hastened to Nevers to vote for M. de Montéclain, Madame de Monrion started for Issoudun where she had heard I was gone. Once in that town, she succeeded in discovering my retreat. She arrived just at the moment when I was going to accomplish my terrible sacrifice. My resolution was to die, Hector in spite of her prayers and representations; and it was only after she had sworn before God never to reveal my secret, that I consented to do what she wished."

"And she swore so?" said Hector in the tone of a man who wishes to be quite sure of the fact.

"Yes, she did; and it would be a horrible perjury if she did not keep her word."

"She will not fail to keep it, I hope," answered Hector with a satisfied smile.

"It was then," added Léda, "that she induced me to write to my husband a letter dated from Issoudun. After that, I set out for Paris, and from that city I wrote again, so that he believed and still believes the fable invented by Madame de Monrion."

"And he will believe so to the end," said Hector rising up.

"Some time after—"

"I know the rest," said Hector carelessly; your husband went to fetch you and you came back with him."

"After an illness which cruelly altered me no doubt, for I did not find you the same."

"I forgot one thing," said Hector, "when she took the child, was there any one in her confidence?"

"She had come to the place with a servant whom she dismissed, and then she set out alone in a hired carriage which she left at a little distance from Saint Faron; after that she walked on and committed our child to the charge of Jeanne Dromeray."

"All is right," said Hector, "without noticing the supplicant looks of Leda.

Now," said she to him, "that I have related to you all the circumstances of that deplorable event, will you inform me of the danger which is threatening me."

But Hector already listened to her no longer; the explanation he had heard gave him full confidence that no obstacle could oppose his mighty project. He could think of nothing else but that. He was joyful, and showed his satisfaction through his vulgar smiles, and exclamations of delight. Léda, the poor woman whom he had ruined was nothing more to him; he would have crushed her under his feet, had she been an obstacle in his way. Léda was obliged to repeat her question several times before she could obtain an answer.

"Well!" said he brutally, "what do you want of me? what do you ask?"

"But," resumed Léda, "did you not tell me that our child had been discovered, and that the inquisitive were endeavouring to find out who were his parents?"

"True!" said Hector; "and now more than ever you must keep your secret. Bear in mind that the least indiscretion would cause your destruction; and were Madame de Monrion herself to accuse you, you must deny it—"

"Before her! to her face!" rejoined Léda; "I never should dare to do so."

"It is, however, absolutely necessary," resumed Hector, in a gloomy and imperative tone. "This is not all: as slanderers may accuse another woman to be the mother of the child, beware not to take up her defence, or to confess the truth."

"But this is a scandalous course that you propose to me."

"Ah!" said Hector, whose threatening anger was excited by any kind of resistance, "you shall hold your tongue—such is my will."

He threw a gloomy look around him, and added, in a hollow voice:

"You shall hold your tongue, or I shall know how to compel you to do so."

"We dare not express the cruel thought which at that moment crossed the mind of Hector.

He seemed to consider the solitude of the place where he was, fixed his looks on that woman, whom with one single blow he could annihilate, with the secret of which she was possessed, and which disturbed him. A purple redness covered his face; his eyes floated in their orbits like those of a drunken man, and he exclaimed:

"Ah! wretch! If I thought you would dare to speak!"

Léda, frightened, fell on her knees, and answered in a trembling voice:

"I will be silent."

"It is well," said Hector, opening the door abruptly, as if to run away from the temptation to which he was a prey. But he suddenly stopped on hearing, at a short distance, the voices of two persons who were talking with some degree of vivacity. Hector thought he had recognised the voice of Felina, and then that of Colonel Rien. They were disputing with some vehemence, and appeared to be near and opposite the hut."

"Take care, Thomas, you wish for vengeance, and you recoil before the means which would secure it."

"Yes, when those means are disreputable."

"And there is no other," rejoined Felina, fiercely, when the purpose itself is not honourable. Honour, reprobates vengeance; call it to your assistance against your resentment, and then you will have a right to blame the way I follow to gratify mine. Reflect upon it, Thomas, I hope soon to see you again."

"Yes," said the Colonel, "I will see you again, it is necessary."

They parted, and Hector saw them rapidly disappear. An instant after he left the hut with Léda. She returned to the farm a prey to greater sadness and desolation, whilst the Viscount de Montaleu, with a smile on his lips, a triumphant air, and carrying his head high, proceeded at a quick pace to his uncle's house.

Hector and Léda firmly believed that they had not been perceived. But Aly Muley had been watching them, and Felina herself, who had retreated into a clumpse of trees, had at length divined the use to which that wretched hut was converted.

---

## CHAPTER LX.

### SECRET THOUGHTS.

After having left the house of Jeanne Dromeray, Madame de Monrion hastened to return to her uncle's chateau. She did not perceive the carriages of MM. de Montaleu and De Rudesgens, which had been removed from the spot; but she was very much surprised to meet M. de Montéclain, who having perceived these carriages, had dismounted from his horse in order to approach the hut more privately. Up to this moment, Madame de Monrion had not the least suspicion of the frightful calumny to which she was exposed. However, this man, whom M. de Montaleu had represented in such unfavourable colours excited in her a real terror. On seeing Julia, Montéclain suddenly stopped; he seemed to wish to approach her; but almost immediately he passed on, bowing to her respectfully. She continued her way, but turned her head round to mark the direction taken by Montéclain. He was still standing in the same place, motionless, and with his head uncovered.

When Julia left the chateau, she was a prey to a profound grief. She was well aware that the insult she had received from Madame de Champmortain had been directed by another and more experienced hand. She recognised Felina's hatred, and understood that Sylvia's jealousy had been excited against her. Madame de Monrion, who had been able to judge of Madame de Champmortain's violent passion, foresaw that under Felina's incitement, it might be carried to a terrible excess. Her pride had at first resolved to face the struggle, but after many fits of anger and many tears, she had at length adopted the resolution of making her escape.

The outrage she had received was not, after all, Julia's most cruel grief. In the night, and after the horrible scene had taken place, the Countess de Monrion had examined her situation, and had found that really she was alone. M. de Montaleu had, it is true, assumed the air of a protector, but she was far from being satisfied with his quiet indignation. She thought of her father's generous anger, and of her mother's tears and consolations on such an occasion, had they lived. Charles himself, her brother, who was looked upon by M. de Montaleu as a giddy and thoughtless young man, would have given vent to one of those bursts of wrath which intimidate the most insolent, and make the outrage recoil on the head of the guilty party.

Among all those who would formerly have protected her, and whose protection was beyond her reach, Julia did not forget the man whose name she bore, and who on his death-bed had appeared to her so just and so great.

"Oh! as for him," said she to herself, "I do not know what he would have said and done, but I am confident that he would have made me stand like a queen, in that drawing-room which I left stealthily and pursued by shame. Had he lived, indeed, he would not have had to avenge such an outrage, for they would never have dared to offer it to me."

Then she asked herself how it was that in a drawing-room where so many gallant and proud men witnessed the outrage, not one of them had stood up in her defence; not a single generous thought, not a single chivalrous cry had been raised in her favour?

Julia was burning with indignation.

Without pondering on her future destiny, without attempting to foresee the misfortunes by which she might be threatened, Julia resolved to depart. There was in everything around her a hateful and menacing aspect.

However, before she executed her desperate design, she thought of fulfilling a sacred duty. It was exactly at the moment when she had secured the existence of the deserted child, and her chaste pity had been transformed into a shameful crime that she met Montéclain.

"This man," said she to herself, walking on, "this man is doubtless one of the accomplices of the insult that I received yesterday. He is the enemy of M. de Montaleu. He has probably begun with me the retaliation which another has provoked; and the ironical respect which he has just shown me is but one insult the more. But why have I just met him on my passage? Why, yesterday at that festival, did he notice me with so persevering an attention? He knew indeed of the outrage that was prepared for me, and he wished to witness to his satisfaction my grief and confusion."

Such were the thoughts in which Madame de Monrion indulged, in order to persuade herself that Montéclain was her enemy.

This requires an explanation.

Married to a man considered as one of those debauchees who are the despair of their families, she had seen him make such noble amends for his conduct towards herself, that she had preserved a friendly respect for the unfortunate Monrion. In her solitary thoughts she had often grieved for his loss; she fancied she might perhaps have discovered, in the heart of that misguided young man some flowers of love which had not yet blown, and noble feelings which had been stifled by the narrow minded severity of M. de Montaleu.

These were the thoughts which wandered in the vacant and unoccupied heart of Julia, when for the first time she heard of M. de Montéclain. He was represented to be just as Monrion had shown himself to be. Both were equally known for the seductions they had carried on, for their extravagant expenses, the scandal of their intrigues, their notorious duels, and their disdain for amiable and modest virtue. M. de Montaleu, who freely expatiated on the follies and vices of Montéclain, never alluded to his generosity, courage, and intellect. But by his silence he acknowledged its existence. Besides she knew that, independently of his severe principles, M. de Montaleu hated Montéclain, as the fatal model which had led Monrion to his destruction. Julia, grieved for the loss of her husband, she had not known, and she therefore felt a strong curiosity to become acquainted with Montéclain, so similar to him.

That thought, that desire of forming a correct opinion of the man who was no more, through the man who still lived, had often occupied Madame de Monrion's mind. Thus, on the previous day, the moment she was insulted, she fancied she heard a secret voice of her heart, pointing to Montéclain, that told her, "This man will protect you." She therefore felt a sorrowful astonishment on witnessing his indifference; and of all those who saw the insult he was the one she despised the most for not having repulsed it.

This disappointment added considerably to the violence of the grief she felt. She discovered that Montéclain's conduct grieved her, and she was vexed on account of this kind of grief. Her pride was humbled, she was ashamed of having given access to a hope without foundation.

Such were the reasons which induced Julia to persuade herself that Montéclain was an accomplice of the insult she had received. But did she entirely succeed in working herself up into that belief? It is doubtful; and she resolved to depart, because probably she feared her own heart as much as the malice of her enemies.

She was in this state of mind when she arrived at the chateau. She dreaded the explanation that was to take place between herself and M. de Montaleu, and was thinking of the means to elude it, when she heard that the Marquis had left the house in company with MM. de Rudesgens, Brias, and Champmortain.

Julia seldom saw the world as it was. Who does? The delicate and exalted instinct through which she discovered so many things, often led her into fanciful notions. She imagined that M. de Montaleu, not satisfied with the explanations given to him, had required a terrible satisfaction. She felt regret at the precipitate orders she had given for her departure. A prey to uneasiness, she inquired after the cause of the marquis's absence, she could not obtain any information. She therefore resolved to wait till M. de Montaleu's return. We must not forget to say that the first thing she did on her return was to send a servant to inform Léda that Madame de Monrion wished to see her immediately, for we shall soon see with what consequences the message was attended.

In the meantime Julia's uneasiness increased every moment; her lively imagination represented to her the old marquis wounded and dying for her; her anxiety for him had become so keen that she had resolved to return to the forest, when she perceived the marquis's carriage. Her heart was a prey to cruel fear; but she was relieved when she saw him alight in good health, but gloomy and dissatisfied.

The carriage of Madame de Monrion was in the court-yard. M. de Montaleu stopped and looked at it. The servants were engaged in settling conveniently Madame de Monrion's luggage. He could not, therefore, entertain the least doubt concerning her departure.

Consequently, Julia was excessively astonished to see M. de Montaleu pass on to his own apartment.

The interview she had before dreaded was now the object of her desire; and she found fault with M. de Montaleu for avoiding to see her. What crime then had she committed? What had she done that he should disdain to come to her. At first despair, then indignation filled her soul. Pride advised her to depart without seeing again the man who had offered her his protection, and who now abandoned her when she was most in need of it. But her various emotions soon subsided, and gave way to a sentiment which was more in harmony with her noble and dignified nature.

Julia wished not to depart either as a fugitive or as an ungrateful person. She thought that she ought to take the first step out of deference to the age of M. de Montaleu, for the affection he had shown to her, and for which she ought to be grateful, even though that tenderness had been powerless in protecting her. Therefore, after having waited for more than an hour, she sent her lady's maid to ask for an interview. The servant brought her the following note:

"It would perhaps be better for us to see each other no more. However, if you wish to speak to me, come, I am waiting for you. Only, in order to avoid explanations which would be painful to us both, I inform you that I know all. Now, decide if you ought to come."

Julia, the gentle, the mild, the timid, when soothed with any mark of benevolence; Julia, the reserved and blushing girl, when the object of praise; Julia, the woman who was so easily disconcerted by the admiration she excited, had scarcely perused this note before she rose up, exhibiting in her deportment a mixture of pride, resolution, and dignity; a sudden fire shone in her eyes, and her nostrils distended, like those of a generous steed on the approach of battle, she entered M. de Montaleu's apartment, with the stately agitation of an offended queen.

---

## CHAPTER LXI.

### THE ACCUSATION.

JULIA found the marquis sitting in a large arm-chair, with his head resting on the palm of his hand; he was absorbed in deep and sullen thought. He heard Julia come in but did not look at her. It would have been too painful to him to see her tremble and ashamed of her fault, to witness the confusion of the woman whom he had loved, as being so pure, so candid, so charming, so rare and inestimable.

The expression of that grief was so powerful that it stopped the impulse which had brought Julia there. She remained silent; M. de Montaleu, for whom this interview was more cruel than his letter had expressed, was the first who broke silence.

"What do you want with me, *madame?*" said he to her with affected coldness.

"I come sir, to ask you to explain this note," answered Julia with the same coldness.

This reply prompted the marquis to raise his head and his eyes, and his indignant look met the calm and proud countenance of Julia. She was almost justified in his mind. Her pure and holy countenance resplendent with beauty, grace and conscious innocence, was to him like a meteor of light, which suddenly showed him the truth. But the marquis was an old man; he had learned too well in his long career, how skilful duplicity is, in putting on the mask of virtue; and there was perhaps in the bottom of his soul, some personal, sorrowful, and fatal recollection, which prejudiced him against this instinctive testimony of his heart. He cast down his eyes in order to avoid a light which might be deceitful, and withdrew to the deceitful obscurity of experience, trusting only to appearances, which loaded Madame de Monrion with suspicion.

"Listen to me, madame," answered he, after a short silence, "I do not wish to accuse you. I am happy I confess, not to have the right of doing so. If nature had given it to me, I should have too much to suffer, not only for what you have done, but also for the assurance with which you present yourself before me to ask for an explanation of a note, which you understood better than you are willing to acknowledge."

"M. de Montaleu," said Julia bitterly, "a judge usually informs a prisoner of the crime for which he is condemned."

"I am not your judge, and I do not condemn you."

"Why then do you expel me from your house?"

"You forget, madame, that you desired to go away; I allow you to do so."

"But sir," said Julia with dignity, "to allow me to depart as you do is indeed to expel me."

"Are you not free, and have you not full liberty to do as you please?"

"M. de Montaleu," said Julia with some irony, "let us not play upon words. You believe that I deserve the insult which I received yesterday; you believe so since the visit of M. de Rudesgens, his son-in-law, and M. de Brias. I come to ask you candidly what accusation has been laid to my charge?"

"If you are able to hear it, madame, I am not possessed of sufficient courage to repeat it in your face."

"But it is something very infamous then?" exclaimed Julia in a burst of indignation. "And yet you tell me in your letter that it is true? So then you consider that infamy, whatever it may be, as a truth? I must, I will know it, sir!"

"Take care, Julia," replied M. de Montaleu quickly and in a sad and threatening voice.

"I must know it," resumed Madame de Monrion with a cruel bitterness, "for judging from the manner in which the calumny which attacks me is received and trusted, I begin to believe that I must remain to defend myself. For, I warn you I will never allow falsehood to strut at its ease behind me as no doubt it would were I away."

M. de Montaleu knew nothing of Julia's nature

but her amiable gracefulness, her laughing kindness, her melancholy thoughtfulness; he never had suspected her deep passion and resolution. He was astonished at this sudden revelation. The marquis was undoubtedly a just man, but he had a right to think that Julia had just exhibited herself in a new light, and had until now displayed much art in concealing her real character. More over Madame de Monrion had cruelly wounded the old man's vanity, by giving him to understand that she would protect herself, which he had been unable to do.

"Madame!" said he rising, "the words calumny, falsehood are often heard in the mouth of the guilty—"

"And very often in those of the innocent, who are condemned."

"You forget whom you are addressing, madame—"

"And you sir," added Julia with a violent energy, "you forget that I came to ask what is the accusation laid to my charge. Why sir, you would not turn out of your house a lackey, without telling the reason. Have I less claim to your esteem?"

"Madame, madame," said M. de Montaleu, "you are carried too far by your anger."

"Not by my anger, sir, but by my despair, for you know, sir," resumed Julia, "that I am alone in the world, that I have neither mother nor father to protect and console me. My brother is far away from me. And you, sir, of whom I beg the charity of one single word, not to defend me, but to enlighten me; you, I admit, who opened for me the door of that world where I did not desire to enter, but in which you said I should find happiness and respect; you have seen me insulted, you know the reason of that insult, you hold the accusation in your hand, you refuse to open it, to let me know its nature, you refuse to speak. Who am I then? and what is it? Sir, sir, you who were formerly so severe to the man whose name I bear, you ought to know that no person has a right to sport with the life and character of a woman. Well! you have allowed others to attack that character; my life! Oh! my life! you would almost tempt me to throw it at the fect of my enemies, to be trampled upon by them!"

This time the cry of that high-minded indignation reached the heart of M. de Montaleu; he doubted the fault, and doubted no longer, Julia had a right to the explanation she was craving, but along with this new feeling a fear entered into the mind of the marquis. How, if Julia were innocent, should he dare to make known the infamous accusation laid against her? She was, it is true, called *Countess* de Monrion, but if her heart were not depraved, her mind perverted and full of deceit, her soul must have remained ignorant and candid.

M. de Montaleu hesitated, attempted to speak, then stopped short; but again conjured by the ardent and supplicating look of Julia, he said to her:

"Tell me, where did you go whilst I received the visit of M. de Rudesgens and his friends?"

This question was so very different from anything Julia expected, that she remained astounded; she blushed and appeared to be a prey to a cruel embarrassment, the hopes of M. de Montaleu, vanished at the sight of this sudden confusion. However Julia recovered and replied with a slight irony:

"Am I reproached for my visits to the village of Saint Faron?"

She was still a thousand miles away from the accusation laid against her. In his turn, M. de Montaleu was very much surprised at this calm assurance. If it were not the sign of innocence it betrayed the most shameless audacity

"Doubtless, you know," said he, looking earnestly at her, "who is the child whom you go and visit?"

"I know it," said Julia, composedly.

"Do you know his parents?"

Julia hesitated; determined to protect the secret of Léda, she was anxious to avoid saying anything which might lead to a suspicion, and she replied:

"Allow me not to answer this question; I have assumed the duty of a protectress to this child, I will be a mother to him; I cannot say more."

"But then you do not know, Julia, to what you are exposed by this silence?"

"To despicable calumnies, no doubt, I know, sir," resumed Julia, with a profound disdain; "to see me expelled from your fashionable world, like a woman who has lent her assistance to some guilty intrigue, and who, by protecting it, shows she is an accomplice in it."

M. de Montaleu went up to Julia, with his eyes fixed on her own, as if to read those thoughts of hers which her words did not express.

She continued:

"If it is on that account, and I do not believe it, that Madame de Champmortain has been led by her austere morals to insult me in her own house, I will not conceal from you, that I will expose her to repeat her insolence; for, I shall not desert this innocent creature."

The marquis stretched his hands towards Julia, and exclaimed, with deep emotion:

"Julia! Julia! I thank you; for now it will be in my power to justify you."

"To justify me, what for? for an action which I am ready to proclaim aloud before all."

"But you do not know, unfortunate child, that this fault—"

M. de Montaleu stopped this time, he unaffectedly recoiled before the word that he was going to utter; he was frightened at the terrible blow which he was going to inflict on that young and innocent soul—and began to murmur in a terrible and hollow voice:

"Oh! the monsters! the monsters!"

"Do not curse them so violently, sir; the religious and sincere rectitude of Madame de Champmortain must, I conceive, have been alarmed, at a conduct which displays more freedom than ought to be possessed by a person of my age and position. Probably in my place she would not have acted as I have done; probably she would have been right, according to her own notions; I believe, according to my own, that I have acted well."

M. de Montaleu walked to and fro with agitation. For him the innocence of Julia was certain, complete; but it was necessary to inform her of the misconstruction assigned to her generous pity. He was uncertain, troubled; at length he believed he had found out the means of preserving this noble child from the horror of hearing the calumny with which she had been stricken.

"Julia," said he to her, "listen to me, and answer me, I entreat you, I ask it as an act of mercy; I ask it on my knees. Tell me who is the mother of this child."

"I cannot."

"Julia, I ask it for me, I who want to know it for me, do you understand?"

"I have sworn before God not to tell it; the honour and the life of another are concerned."

"But, poor child, your honour is also concerned."

"My honour!"

"Well! Julia, my child, my daughter, my innocent daughter, I am sure of it," said M. de Montaleu, surrounding her with his arms, "you must not, by devoting yourself to conceal the fault of another, allow people to impute it to you."

"Sir!" exclaimed Julia, starting back from M. de Montaleu.

"I wish to have the power of justifying you."

"Sir!" resumed Julia, retreating still farther, as from a threatening spectre.

"For, you are innocent, I am sure of it."

At these last words, Julia, with a bewildered look, raised her eyes to heaven; confused sobs, inarticulate sounds issued from her throat. Wild with despair, she walked in the apartment, raising her arms towards heaven, and letting them fall at every step, as if she was stifled.

"Julia! Julia!" said M. de Montaleu, attempting to stop her.

But Julia did not hear him, and her grief breaking at last through that strangulation which impeded her breath and voice, she cried out:

"My mother! my father! My father! my mother! Where are they? My father! my mother, my mother!—"

She continued thus in a panting voice, and a frightful delirium, whilst M. de Montaleu held her.

"Julia!" said he to her, "I will be your father, I will protect you as he would have done; I will console you as your mother would have done, your holy mother."

Julia, at length, melting into tears, and recovering the consciousness of the truth, exclaimed:

"Ah! they are no more, they have left me, they have left me alone in this world. Oh my God! My God!" added she, falling on her knees, and stretching towards heaven her supplicating hands, "why did you not let me die along with them?"

Then she hid her head in her hands and gave vent to her sobs and tears, and heart-rending exclamations. What grief! what sadness! what horrid anguish were revealed through her desolation!

This young heart was broken, this immaculate soul was bleeding, this delicate and pure mind was polluted.

When exhaustion had diminished the violence of her sobs, and the abundance of her tears, M. de Montaleu took her on his knees, and said to her gently:

"Come! Julia, my daughter, console yourself, no one in the world will believe in this calumny."

As if these words had opened both the heart and the eyes of Julia, she looked at him fixedly, and said to him, in a short dry tone:

"You believed in it yourself?"

"Grief misled me, I acknowledge, as just now it misled you; but a single word has been sufficient to make me believe in your innocence."

The recollection of all that had taken place between herself and M. de Montaleu gradually returned to the memory of Julia, and a new feeling—indignation was mingled with her grief. She removed gently from M. de Montaleu, and said, in a voice which betrayed the restraint she exercised over herself:

"I thank you, sir; but this justification which you have accepted, I cannot give to every one. I cannot go and exhibit to every eye the horror and despair to which I was a prey."

"No, Julia, no," said M. de Montaleu, "I shall justify you, this duty is my concern, and if the tenderness of a man who wishes to be your father is not indifferent to you, you will tell me the truth."

"The truth!" replied Julia, quite astonished.

"You will give me the proofs with which I shall confound calumniators."

"The proofs!" said Julia, looking again at him with a suspicious air, "Proofs!" repeated she, "do you want proofs!"

"Not for myself—"

"For whom then?" said Julia, proudly, "for her who insulted me? To her, sir, I leave her conscience for judge. For the woman who has incited her? Oh! it would be too much ignominy to justify oneself before her."

"Julia! be more calm, I must avenge you now."

"I do not know what you intend to do now, sir," resumed Julia, restraining herself; "but, if any one had come and told me that he had *seen* you commit anything dishonourable, whoever might have been the accuser, I would have answered him in his face that he lied."

"Julia!" said M. de Montaleu.

"But, I grant," resumed she, in a sardonic tone, "that I should find it a more difficult task, if at first I had admitted the accusation, which afterwards I wished to destroy."

"Julia, I conceive your anger, but the world has its requirements, its tyrannies; it will be respected even when it acts unjustly. You do not know it, child!"

"I know it sufficiently to despise it," answered Julia.

"Julia!" resumed M. de Montaleu, with a slight impatience, "be more calm. These expressions—"

"Hold! sir," said Madame de Monrion, who began to feel that her grief was reviving, "forgive me. The education I have received has not sufficiently taught me perhaps to lend a polite word to the feelings which I experience; I do not know this world which accuses me, you are right; but the world in which I have lived, in that world of obscure citizens which yours may be justified in disdaining, if an insult like the one of which I was yesterday the object, had been done to me—yes, sir, instead of my father, who is no more, instead of my mother who died with him, instead of my brother who is absent, some man would have been found, some friend, some stranger, a father, a young man, who would have come and taken me under his protection. But in this noble drawing-room, filled with illustrious names, with men renowned for their courage—not a single one was moved at the sight of my grief, not a single one came to offer me his hand, not a single one was found to say to me aloud: 'Madame, resume your place.'"

As Julia pronounced these words, the door of the apartment opened, and a voice, both grave and rude, answered her:

"There shall be one, at least, Madame, to defend you against calumny."

This was Hector de Montaleu, who, in spite of the protestations of the servants telling him that his uncle was not at leisure, had reached the door and heard Julia's last words.

Julia turned her head, uttering a cry of surprise and shame, and M. de Montaleu rose to prevent his nephew coming in. But Hector was already in the room, and had shut the door after him.

"I know all, my uncle," said Hector. "I know all that has been related to you, and if I did not come this morning, it was in order not to sanction such calumnies by my presence."

"You know, then, that she is innocent," exclaimed the marquis, with joy.

Hector hesitated, and raised his eyes on Julia, who examined him with curiosity; then making an effort of courage, he answered:

"I do not know it, my uncle, but I am sure of it. I do not ask my cousin for any explanation of her conduct, any proof of her innocence. I have faith in her virtue. I have faith in her; and the best proof I can give you is, that after all that has been said against her, I come to you, my uncle, who stand in the place of a father to her, I come a second time to ask you for her hand."

Julia drew back before this greatness of soul, and

the marquis was overwhelmed. His nephew, his coarse nephew, this frightful eater, this prodigious drinker, this dreaded and violent boor, whose natural brutality delighted only in the barking of dogs, in the clamour and tumult of hunting, in boisterous revelries, this low and coarse fellow, as the marquis in fits of anger, used to call him, had just assumed the part of a hero full of generosity and delicacy. The aristocratic vanity of the venerable marquis prevailed over his long prejudice, and he exclaimed, offering his hand to Hector:

"Ah! I knew well that one day the blood of the Montaleus would work in you."

Julia was astounded at this magnificent performance, so artistically prepared; but, in the midst of the surprise she experienced, in the midst of the disturbance not yet entirely appeased, which had been caused by the scene that had taken place between herself and her uncle, in the midst of all this, the false and unsteady light which gushed from Hector's restless eye, the constrained accent in which he spoke, warned her that beneath this action, apparently so heroic, some odious calculation might lurk. She had no time to ponder on this feeling of aversion, for the marquis, immediately turning towards her, said:

"Excuse, Julia, the roughness of his demand; so true and so noble an impulse is to be met neither by delay nor precaution."

"Neither by reflection, nor by anything," added Hector, in a delighted and triumphant tone.

"It is the reason for which," said Julia, bowing modestly, "that I entreat the Viscount de Montaleu to allow me not to answer immediately. If, after some time, and in spite of all that has been said against me, he perseveres in his resolution, then I will answer, as I am bound to do, to a proposal, the generosity of which I fully appreciate."

"I will persevere till death," replied Hector, assuming a still more heroic attitude.

"And when you have the right to do so," added M. de Montalou, "you shall punish the infamous wretches who have invented this calumny."

"Certainly," answered Hector, with an embarrassment, which did not proceed from a want of courage, but from the fear that the truth might be discovered while they were in search of the calumniators.

"I know" resumed M. de Montaleu, "that it is Madame de Champmortain who has repeated this atrocious invention, but some one has suggested it to her; and this is the guilty wretch who deserves to be chastised. It is not either M. de Rudesgens, or Champmortain, or Brias, they were all three too much afflicted when they came to repeat this atrocity to me. It is, perhaps, Montéclain."

Julia turned pale.

"Since you cannot positively name the guilty person, accuse no one," said she, mildly. "And, now, allow me to withdraw."

At the very moment she was about to leave the apartment, a maid came to announce that the mistress of Lavordan farm, Madame Bricord, would not be able to obey her orders to visit her until the next day.

At the name of Madame Bricord, the generous colossus, the terrible and gallant Hector staggered. This confusion escaped the marquis, who was speaking to Julia; but Julia saw it, and the transient suspicion which had crossed her mind, appeared there again, clearer and more tangible.

"But you promise not to depart," said the marquis.

"I promise nothing, sir," answered Julia. "I want to collect myself, and I make bold to ask you for a few hours of retirement and freedom."

## CHAPTER LXII.

### THERE IS SUCH A REPORT.

Now let us repair to the ground floor of the Lavordan farm. The colonel and Bricord were sitting each on one side of the chimney,—in the middle of the room there was a table, around which Léda and her female servants were engaged with needle work. The colonel was thoughtful and somewhat anxious; but Bricord, proud of enjoying his society, was radiant with pride and joy. He had at first intended to invite all his neighbours to the banquet which the colonel had kindly accepted in his house, but his gallant guest had expressed a desire to sit down to a family meal, and it was not without astonishment that he had supped at the same table with more than twenty servants, with the beautiful Léda presiding over them.

In fact, if any vestiges of the ancient patriarchal life still exist in France, they are only to be found in the dwellings of our farmers.

The colonel had at first beheld with real satisfaction the picture of a laborious, calm, and sedentary existence, very different from the strolling and adventurous life of the soldier. But whether the comparison brought sad reflections on himself, or he thought of the misfortune and crime concealed beneath this show of happiness, he had gradually become thoughtful; and a deep silence had for some time prevailed in that large hall when Aly Muley came in suddenly humming an opera tune.

"Ah! here you are," said Bricord to him; "where have you supped?"

"I never sup until I have first dined," replied the Gascon pretty merrily. "Now, as No. 1 has not yet taken place, I could not pass on to No. 2."

Thereupon he began to hum his tune again whilst one of the maids was laying at the other end of the table a plate, a fork, and a knife for him.

"What the deuce are you singing there?" said the colonel.

"It is, at least I imagine so, a tune which I heard a Parisian lady sing at Algiers. It is true that I introduce embellishmsnts here and there, for we people of the south are all great musicians. However, colonel, I can tell it to you with the words in all its simplicity."

He began again singing the ritornella.

"Why," said Léda, "it is, I believe, the tune of Meyerber: *He is coming*."

"Precisely," said Aly Muley, "I feel flattered, and this shows that you have a musical ear, Madame Bricord."

"Well! but what the deuce have you been doing all day long?" inquired the farmer.

"I went to select a house and farm in this neighbourhood," said Aly Muley, "for I, also, intend to withdraw from service in order to live peacefully."

"Ah! ah!" rejoined Bricord, "that is right. You will do well to settle in this country, you will marry and have a good wife like mine."

"Fill my glass," said Aly, "there is a piece of ham in my throat which I cannot swallow."

As he pronounced these words the door opened, and the Viscount Hector de Montaleu entered. Aly began again to hum the tune: *He is coming*.

Hector was received as an old acquaintance whose presence was an habitual occurrence; but he appeared annoyed to meet the colonel. However, they saluted one another in a rather friendly manner.

They both felt that their private designs required that they should not be hostile to one another. Bricord, delighted to see so important a personage as the Viscount de Montaleu conversing with his colonol, went and sat down by Aly Muley, and began to talk with him in a low voice.

Hector and Thomas had already exchanged a few insignificant sentences, and had hardly anything more to say when their attention was attracted by an exclamation of Bricord, who said in a voice betraying both astonishment and doubt:

"Where did you hear of that?"

"Who knows!" answered Aly Muley; "no where and everywhere; by listening in an antechamber, by walking in the neighbourhood of a park, by looking at the sun and the moon."

"But it is not possible," said Bricord.

"I do not say that it is possible, I merely say that it is so reported."

"And you ought not to repeat it," resumed Bricord. "To pretend that—it is, I am sure, a horrid lie. Madame de Monrion is such an excellent lady, she is quite incapable—It is, indeed, so very stupid that I cannot understand any one could say so."

"I do not pretend to say that it is not stupid; but it is what people say."

"But what is it, then?" asked Hector, who could not restrain his impatience.

On hearing the name of Madame de Monrion, the colonel had listened more attentively, and Léda had started.

"A mere absurdity," said Bricord. "Aly Muley tells me he has heard that the Countess de Monrion is concealing a little child in the hamlet of Saint Faron."

Thomas detected the sudden terror that Hector betrayed; whilst Léda, bending her head over her work, endeavoured in vain to conceal the convulsive tremor that shook and agitated her hand.

"It is a lie!" exclaimed Hector with passion.

"I do not deny it"—rejoined Aly Muley very coolly, "but so they say; and to speak the truth," added the spahi, "it is not said, as Bricord has just repeated, that she is concealing a child, but her own child."

"Her own child!" exclaimed Léda in a hoarse voice, and raising her head.

She was pale, lividly pale, and her wild glance swept rapidly from Hector to her husband.

"You see," resumed Bricord, addressing Aly, "that I am not the only one who is astonished at this infamous invention. Don't you think, Léda, that it is impossible. You know her, she always has been very kind to you. And even to-day, she sent for my wife in order to make her some present as usual."

Léda had again bent her head down over her work, but her hands searched in vain for it, her eyes had become dim, and she could hardly breathe.

"Simpleton," cried Bricord abruptly, "look how your tale has unsettled my poor wife; she is so good, so kind-hearted. Come, Léda, compose yourself."

He embraced her, and took hold of her hands. The unhappy woman began to weep.

"And you did not call upon Madame de Monrion?" asked Hector, addressing Léda.

"No—no," replied Léda in a broken voice.

"Who, then," said Bricord, "would have presided over the entertainment accepted by the colonel?"

"In that case," said Hector, "if what this man relates be true, you had better not go."

Léda stood up, and with an expression which made Hector shudder, she replied:

"Oh! sir, I shall go, I shall go; and I ought to be there already."

"It would be useless," said Hector abruptly, "I have just come from my uncle's, and Julia was not there."

Aly Muley looked at the colonel, whose ardent glance surveyed at the same time Hector, Léda, and the farmer.

"Excuse me, viscount," said Aly; "what are you saying to Léda, that she had better not go to the chateau, if this be true? So then you believe that it may be true?"

Hector rocked himself in his chair like an infuriated bear, and the handle of the bellows which he chanced to have in his hand was crushed.

"I say, I say—" answered he in a rough and gloomy voice, "that when such misfortunes occur in a family, it is better not to meddle with them."

"The viscount is right," said Aly Muley; "that concerns the uncle and the nephew, when there is neither father, mother, nor brother."

"No doubt," said Hector; "and no one knows the danger that there may be in meddling with such matters."

"But!" said Léda in a voice which made Hector tremble, "if she is calumniated—if it is another who is guilty—is she to be forsaken—abandoned? is it—"

"It is always necessary to be prudent," interposed the colonel in a grave voice. "Besides," added he, "the best thing we can do is not to speak of matters of such importance."

"In that case," said Aly Muley, with his cool and impudent assurance, "I am sorry I brought in the news, though it is already spread about everywhere; and they say, too, that it was on this account that the countess was expelled from the ball of Madame de Champmortain."

"Expelled!" exclaimed Léda, rising with a frightful resolution; "expelled!—Madame de Monrion—expelled—and for—"

"For a ridiculous report," said the colonel, advancing towards Léda, and making her sit down again.

"Yes," said Aly Muley with a cruel persistency, "a ridiculous report in which nobody believes, be sure of it, Madame Léda. And what I say is so true that this very day, a rich man, nay! a nobleman, has been to solicit the hand of the countess, in spite of everything that is said against her."

Hector rose; the blood rushed so violently to his head that he staggered, and one might have believed that his eyes were springing from their orbits. The colonel himself could not restrain a start of surprise on hearing this news. With regard to Léda, she had fallen into a moral prostration; with her head bent and her eyes fixed on the ground, she was as still and motionless as a statue, whilst a hissing and choking respiration issued from her half-open mouth. Fortunately for her, Bricord was seized with a transport of enthusiasm at this intelligence, and exclaimed, in a loud voice:

"The man who did this is a brave fellow. It is thus that such reports ought to be answered—for—though I am of opinion we cannot be too severe with those who swerve from the right path, yet I think we are bound to extend a helping hand to the poor honest woman who is the object of infamous reports. I am nothing, unfortunately, but I wish I were something—a viscount or a marquis—that I might have a right to say to this young lady: 'I honour and esteem you.' Therefore, Léda, you shall go; since the countess has asked for you."

"There is, then," said Léda, recovering a little strength, "some one who has asked for the hand—"

"It is another foolish tale of this simpleton, Aly," said the colonel abruptly.

"Why not?" said Bricord, "there are still some honest people left—and if our master, M. de Montéclain, were not on bad terms with the old marquis, I should not be surprised if he were the man."

"Or some one else, perhaps," said Aly Muley, "who has his own private reasons for believing that the countess is innocent."

At this last word, the unhappy Léda fixed a wild look on Hector. A livid pallor overspread the villain's face, succeeding the purple hue which covered it before: his eyes were still bloodshot, and shone like burning coals. Léda raised her quivering hand towards him, and said in a convulsive and inarticulate voice:

"What, you!—you!"

Here strength failed her, and she fell back in her chair. There was no expression in her blank countenance, no thought in her look. Bricord astonished at this extraordinary disorder, was silent for a moment, then sweeping the whole circle with an anxious and terrible look, he exclaimed:

"But why does she take so painful an interest in all this?"—

"Did you not tell me," interrupted the Colonel quickly, "that your wife was sickly, nervous? She has been much fatigued to-day. The best thing she can do is to go and rest herself."

"Undoubtedly," said Hector, in a troubled voice, and at the same time approaching her. "To-morrow she will see that these are false reports, which deserve no kind of attention."

For a moment, an awful, a frigid silence pervaded the hall. The farmer walked about like a man whose brain has been disordered by a violent blow.

"Go and rest yourself, madame," said the colonel, gently, to the unfortunate woman who sat on her chair, immoveable and prostrate.

"Yes," said Bricord, in a hollow tremulous voice, "go to bed—Léda, go."

Léda obeyed, but Bricord did not embrace her, as was his usual custom. She rose like an automaton, and retired accompanied by the two housemaids, who were obliged to support her. Bricord followed her with a terrible look. When she had disappeared, he put his hand to his forehead several times, like a man seeking for the clue of some thought which at once inflames and perplexes him.

Then he exclaimed abruptly, looking at Hector:

"And now I want to know—"

Scarcely had he uttered these few words, when the door suddenly opened, and a new personage came upon the stage.

This was Montéclain, who entered with his usual air of levity and carelessness.

"Ah! upon my word," exclaimed he in a lively tone, "I am fortunate indeed. I knew that I should find you here, my brave Bricord; but I thought, colonel, that you had gone to pay a visit to Madame Amab, and I was going to request our friend to transmit to you an invitation. I have just sent to your house, Montaleu; and though you did not vote for me, and I have not allowed you to hunt in my estates, I hope you will not refuse me?"

"What is the object of your request?" inquired the colonel."

"To hunt to-morrow a wild boar that has been seen and reported to me by my valet," said Montéclain with a roguish look.

Montaleu, in spite of the strong emotion which he had just felt, could not help bursting into a kind of laughter.

"And it is he, doubtless, who is to direct the chase?"

"You laugh," said Montéclain, with a most serious countenance. "Well! I bet that I who in your opinion cannot send a ball into the portal of a cathedral, shall bring the animal down, whilst you are unable to touch it."

"I accept the wager; what do you lay?"

"What you like."

"The right of hunting in your estates against two hundred guineas."

"Accepted," said Montéclain. "Colonel," resumed he, turning towards Thomas, "we have settled this matter this very evening with Brias and Champmortain, whose house I have just left. I have written to M. Amab; Madame de Champmortain, and no doubt Felina, the intrepid Amazon, will mount and follow the chase; and a dinner at my house shall celebrate our triumph."

Bricord remained sitting on his chair, with his head covered with his hands; his thoughts wandered through a terrible suspicion. Several times he had alternately rejected and admitted the frightful supposition which had offered itself to his mind. Montéclain availed himself of this agitation to say to Hector:

"To-morrow!"

"To-morrow!" replied Hector, hastily withdrawing.

"Shall I make one of the party?" said Aly Muley.

"Certainly, my good fellow," answered Montéclain. "Now Bricord," added he, "you must come with me to the chateau, and give some directions to my servants."

"Excuse me, marquis," said the farmer, rising like a man who has just awoke from a frightful dream; excuse me, but my wife is unwell!"

"A nervous complaint. Come and sleep at the chateau,—I hope you will not abandon me—my honour is at stake."

"Your honour?" said Bricord starting.

"My honour as a huntsman—"

"After all," resumed Bricord in a hollow voice, "I had rather not remain here."

But almost immediately he added, looking Montéclain full in the face,

"Besides, I have something to say to you, marquis."

## CHAPTER LXIII.

### THE SPY.

MONTECLAIN had retired with Bricord, and the colonel had returned to his chamber.

"Well!" said Aly Muley, when they were alone, "are you now sure of what I told you? Are you sure that Madame de Monrion is as innocent of the birth of the child of Saint Faron, as I am of the assassination of the late king, Henry IV."

"Yes," replied the colonel thoughtfully.

"How I made them both tremble and almost faint!" resumed Aly laughing.

"You have gone too far, for I saw the unfortunate woman was about to betray herself."

"Does she not suffer from nervous illness?" said Aly, laughing contemptuously. Such a complaint is a fine discovery indeed—to have diseased nerves, that means I have a right to laugh, to cry, to abuse my husband, to vex my servants, to grow pale, to tremble, to faint, to strut about, not to answer, not to understand, not to remember—with the word nervous, Bricord will be cozened."

Thomas was not listening to the soldier's talk, who was arranging his master's bed whilst speaking.

"But now that I think of it," said the colonel suddenly, "how did you learn that Hector had applied for the hand of Madame de Monrion?"

"Did I not follow the big Lovelace to the mansion of the marquis? Do you suppose that when he left the hovel where he had remained more than two hours with his beautiful Léda, that all my curiosity was gratified?"

"Still you were unable to penetrate into the chateau."

"Undoubtedly; but he came out along with his uncle, the two walking side by side, the best friends in the world, swinging their arms, and uttering deep sighs."

"'Well,' said the old marquis, 'your intention to marry Julia, shows the elevation of your sentiments.'"

"What a noodle," said Aly Muley, interrupting his narrative.

"'But,' continued the marquis, 'you must have other motives besides a blind confidence to believe in her innocence.'"

"To be sure he has, and excellent ones, the big scamp!" remarked Aly.

"And what did he answer?" inquired the colonel.

"Ah!" said Aly, "the ass is not so dull as he is big.

"'Never,' said Hector, 'will I commit the injustice to ask an explanation of Madame de Monrion.'"

"'I understand," said the uncle; 'but you might give it to others.'"

"Ah! the old peer of France," said Aly Muley laughing, "what a prodigious dolt he is! But, my good man, what would become of his generosity, if he told you the truth, by book and rule."

"Well!" resumed the colonel, "did the marquis appear disposed to favour the intentions of his nephew."

Aly cast at his master that kind of glance with which he no doubt examined a lion when he resolved to attack him; then, after a moment of silence, and as if he had made himself sure that the shot would safely produce the intended result.

"I believe," answered he, "that you ought to inform the old marquis of the snare into which he is led by his nephew, if you do not wish to see him become possessor of the beautiful lady, and of the inheritance which ought to be yours."

At this answer, the colonel, who was walking thoughtfully to and fro, stopped like a wounded lion, to see whence the ball had come by which he has been so suddenly struck. The colonel darted at Aly a look as threatening and as terrible as that of the king of the desert. Aly examined him with the anxiety of the huntsman about to leap aside and let pass the first spring of his terrible enemy's rage.

"What did you say, villain?" exclaimed the colonel in a choking voice.

"I said," replied Aly, "that it would be a crime

to allow a red and brutal animal like the viscount to marry a young and beautiful woman like Madame de Monrion, and I say that it would be still more stupid to allow him to pocket his uncle's inheritance, which after all is yours."

A hollow and terrible exclamation interrupted the soldier's speech.

"Ah! you have spied me, wretch!" he exclaimed.

And, in the first impulse of his wrath, he flew at Aly, who foreseeing the attack, leaped nimbly on the other side of the table, near which he stood, and put it between himself and his master.

"You have spied me, wretch!" resumed he. "Ah! you shall pay dearly for this!"

"Stop a moment, if you please, colonel," resumed Aly; "you are subject to most unreasonable fits of rage. You let me go like an unchained dog on the track of the viscount, and yet you pretend that I ought not to smell the game that passes under my nose. This is requiring of me more than I can do; I am not yet sufficiently trained for this."

"But, rascal," said the colonel, who, after a moment's reflection, had seen the injustice and impolicy of his conduct, "if you had not followed me, you would not have listened, you would not know—"

"You mean, colonel," replied Aly, "that if you had not come so close to the bushes where I lay in ambush to watch the hut in which the viscount had shut himself up; you mean that if you had not quarrelled with Madame Amab, within reach of my eyes and ears, I should not have heard you, and I should not know that—"

"Stupid oaf!" said Thomas, "could you not warn me of your presence?"

"Colonel," said the sly Gascon, who was gaining ground, "there are things which one does but of which no one boasts. I don't know that it would have been indifferent to you, had I exclaimed, from the thicket in which I lay, 'Halloo! I say, colonel, take care, I am here spying on your account.' But this I know, I was not disposed to tell the beautiful lady who accompanied you the business in which I was engaged, out of friendship for you."

The colonel, still angry and impatient, continued to pace the room.

"Since you heard me so well from the thicket, could they not hear me from the interior of the hovel," said he.

"Not at all! I had already tried the thing. Since I, who was without, could not hear what was said within, though they talked there pretty loud, there was no danger they could hear anything said outside. For, after all, colonel, a wall is not like a man, who may be deaf with his right, and hear well with his left ear."

The colonel had ceased to listen; he seemed to think that all the designs which had brought him to that country had been deranged by the discovery of Aly Muley. He was devising new combinations; for every moment he stopped as if to speak to the Gascon, and almost immediately resumed his walk, as if dissatisfied with his resolution. At length he approached Aly, and said to him:

"Why, when I met you in the wood, after I had left Madame Amab; when you informed me of the rendezvous of Léda and Hector; why, when you communicated to me your suspicions concerning the child, and we agreed about the scene of this evening in order to ascertain the truth, why did you not warn me that you had listened to me?"

"Listened! colonel, no; I did not listen, I only heard, which is very different."

"No matter; why did you wait till this evening?"

"Because I know you, better than you know yourself, colonel; because we were alone, in a lonely and deserted walk, remote from any habitation, and you would have flown at me as you did just now."

"But you could have avoided as you did just now, the first impulse of my anger?"

"No doubt, colonel, and even I might have run off and left you behind; but as you would have considered me a traitor you might, before any explanation, have sent a ball into my back—"

"Commit a murder, wretch—" exclaimed the colonel, turning pale through indignation.

"No, colonel—but a fatal shot. You are the bravest of the brave, colonel, and a man who is so does not assassinate. But there is in you something yellow and green, which, when you are very angry, rushes from your heart to your head, and maddens you for a minute. Here I was sure to let the minute pass off without injury. That was my reason for delay."

The colonel offered him his hand.

"You are still my faithful Aly, are you not?"

"Thunder and lightning!" exclaimed Aly, "I was devoted to you before I knew your history. But now that I am acquainted with the injustice committed against you on account of your mother—all my life belongs to you; and, if necessary, I would plant a ball in the right eye of your cousin—"

"Silence! Aly," said the colonel. "So I may rely on you?"

Aly Muley turned his head a little, and appeared embarrassed.

"What!" resumed Thomas, "do you hesitate?"

"No—but there are things which it is better to say immediately. You can, if you choose, send me back to my regiment, and may the Cathedral of Marseilles fall on my head, if I ever whisper a word of what I have heard. But, if you desire me to remain and to serve you, I mean to make my conditions."

"Ah!" said the colonel, grinning with disdain, "I see you are provident, you wish to secure a part of the prize."

"If the colonel succeeds," said Aly Muley, "and if he thinks that a good servant deserves to have a little money advanced to him to buy a little bit of a farm, I shall most obediently conform to his opinion; but this is all dependent on your free will. If you do so—good! if not—I shall return to Africa. But there is something else which I require, colonel."

"What is it?"

"It is, perhaps, very silly; but I cannot help it. I was in the ante-chamber of M. de Champmortain when Madame de Monrion went through it, scared like a hind on hearing the barking of dogs. What an angel of a woman! colonel; what eyes! and then—I am unable to express it. But she is a child, this countess, a poor sweet child, without any other protector than this old conceited peer of France, and they are all against her, and they wish to reduce her to dust, to dishonour her, colonel—no—it never shall be done, and I will never assist you—"

"If you had heard well," said the colonel, admiring Aly's enthusiasm, "you would know that I refused to lend myself to this scandal of Madame Amab, though I was not yet sure that it was a calumny."

"Yes—yes—yes—" said Aly; "but she has proved to you as clear as daylight, that you will succeed in nothing so long as Madame de Monrion is with the old marquis. She told you that it was for your good that she had acted in that manner. That lady is called Felina; she might be called a serpent, a viper—and you will not follow in her steps. Am I right, colonel?"

"Never," replied Thomas, "never will I raise my fortune on the dishonour of an innocent woman; I would prefer to renounce at once both my rights and my revenge."

"Good! well spoken!" said Aly.

"But I am embarrassed and grieved at one thing," resumed Thomas; "I fear that the justification of the countess will lead to the ruin of another poor woman, whom I saw suffer so much this evening, that the contempt I felt for her has almost been changed into pity."

"Pity for Léda!" said Aly, showing his white sharp teeth with a cruel expression; "for the wretch who has deceived an ex-spahi, a brave soldier, who picked her up in some conservatory where it is not sure that she preserved her duty. Pity for that! Then what do you feel for Bricord, who twice preserved your life? No—colonel—no. That you should care nothing for the canvass dauber, whose wife has so good a kitchen; I understand—so much the worse for him; he is rightly served: he who buys a brokenkneed horse must expect that it will stumble. You may even feel for Madame de Champmortain; he plants her here, and she plants on his forehead. Besides, colonel, the rich and the noble are not very particular abcut it; they have so many means to console themselves elsewhere. But a comrade, like Bricord, who lives and breathes only for this spouter of high-sounding words, for this insolent warbler who looks with disdain upon her husband and his comrades. No, no pity!"

"What! exclaimed Aly, "she heard what I said and she did not cry out, 'it is not true, the countess is innocent!' she did not expose herself. She is less than nothing—and I will crush her without mercy, as I will the other viper."

"You do not reflect, Aly," resumed the colonel, that it is not upon her you would inflict the greatest evil, but upon Bricord. He never would console himself if he were informed—"

"He would kill her, colonel, and he would serve her right."

"Yes, but he would die of despair himself."

"Psha!" said Aly Muley, quite surprised, "do you think so?"

"No doubt, Aly: however it may be possible to justify Madame de Monrion, without destroying this unfortunate woman. We shall see, besides it is very lucky that Montéclain took Bricord with him; otherwise I do not know what might have happened."

"Umph!" said Aly, "this other is a queer customer too. He cannot stop a minute in his chateau. While walking I have met him more than a dozen times, and he always comes upon you like a man who has a notion of what you have just said."

Just then, the colonel imposed silence on the Gascon by a sign. They listened, a slight noise was heard beneath their window, then they heard a slight coughing.

"What is that?" said the colonel.

"That blockhead of a viscount, I am sure, who comes to turn about the nest, now that the kite is gone."

"They listened again, and heard the name of Léda distinctly uttered.

"It is he, by all the devils!" said the Gascon. Stop! stop! I will send him something."

He took up a gun, threw open the window, and cried out:

"Who is there? answer or I fire."

Immediately a jeering and impatient voice replied:

"Do not take that trouble, Aly Muley, you have just committed a blunder, which will be more certain to kill than any of your balls."

It was the voice of Montéclain who hurried away immediately.

## HAPTER LXIV.

### CONVERSATION.

Ah, come now," said Brias to Montéclain, as he finished a cup of tea, "what mad idea induced you to organise this hunt so suddenly yesterday evening, and to invite every one to it, even that ogre Montaleu, whom you blamed me for being acquainted with?"

"A quarter of an inch since last year," said Montéclain buttoning his hunting coat. "I am growing stout, Brias, it is time for me to get married."

"What, you Montéclain, do you wear your last year's coats?"

"I am only too glad it was of no use to my valet, but for that I should have been impelled to hunt in a black one. I could easily improvise the hunt, but not the coat."

"Yet you had arranged the scheme long ago."

"No, the idea struck me on leaving the forest, a moment before we reached Champmortain's."

"At least you are certain there is a wild boar in the forest?"

"There always is a wild boar; only we do not always know where to find it."

"It seems to me there is some kind of mystification in the arrangement you have made."

"I never mystify any one, Brias—"

"However, you have not done this for nothing."*

"Perhaps it is for nothing that I have done it."

"You say—Oh!—you make puns too?"

"Why not? Nearly all great historical sayings are closely allied to puns."

"Come now, Montéclain, leave off acting the mysterious a moment, I am not to be deceived by concealments. You have some scheme, some object?"

"Seeing that you are a clever diplomatist, do me the honour of divining them."

"Well then," said Brias, "was Felina right? are you an interested party in all that is passing here?"

"If you did not think so, you would not question me with so much obstinacy."

"Is it," resumed Brias, "because your meeting with this M. Villon has induced you to turn your glances towards Madame de Monrion?"

"Why not?"

"It is very fortunate," said Brias, "that the discovery of the charming peccadillos, committed by this angel of purity, forbids the pursuit of my intended conquest, but for that, I should probably have sustained a defeat, which would have humiliated me greatly, even when coming from you."

"You renounce it then?"

"Can you ask?" exclaimed Brias, "do you think I am desirous of adopting some little Villon? for I begin to believe the ex-countess—"

Brias stopped short in the middle of his speech, so much was he surprised by the terrified manner in which Montéclain was looking at him.

"Well," said he, "what is the matter with you?"

"Ah! my poor Brias," said Montéclain, "my dear unhappy friend, with a head so well organized as yours, a man who has addressed such a remarkable memorial to the minister, on the Syrian question, who, in every particular, had foreseen England's conduct in the affair of the Marquis Islands, who has frightened the ministerial council by so clearly proving that Canada might be reco-

* The word nothing in French, is *rien*, the name assumed by the colonel, in consequence of his illegitimate birth."

vered by us in four and twenty hours—you believe—you think—that Madame de Monrion has committed the peccadillos, of which she is accused! Ah! there must be a horrible poison in the mind of a debtor to confuse his mental faculties."

"Then you do not believe it?" said Brias.

"To believe it, is not the part I have to play."

"What do you mean?"

"That you no more believe it than I do, Brias. Are we children then? Have you looked in this woman's face? Is there in that satin skin a wrinkle in which remorse could hide itself? Have you ever seen a doubtful ray in the clear look which pours forth her soul, like the waves that flow from a crystal fountain? Is not her smile open and fresh as a spotless flower? Come, come Brias, you who accuse me of employing artifice with you, do not try to deceive me by giving yourself the air of a simpleton."

"So you would marry her?"

"I desire to do so, furiously desire it, I tell you Brias. But—"

"But what?"

"There is that old Montaleu, who is one of my enemies."

"He believes her guilty, and will consequently leave a clear field open to you—"

"You are wrong, Brias, the good man is ashamed of his folly—"

"Then he knows now that she is innocent?"

"Wrong again. He believes, but does not know it."

"And you, you know it, perhaps?"

"Yes, I know it."

"Tell me all about it."

"Before thinking of others, think of yourself."

"What do you mean?"

"I will tell you."

Montéclain seated himself opposite Brias, and began thus:

"Now, listen to me, friend Brias, you are in Felina's clutches."

"By no means."

"Let us say no more about it," said Montéclain rising, "every one for himself."

"You pretend that I am in Felina's clutches?"

"Yes, mad diplomatist, you who think it very clever, the day after a defeat, to say to a power which would ally itself to you, 'we have still plenty of cannons, men, and horses,' when it is clear you have no longer anything. Yes, you are in Felina's clutches; she can cut you to pieces, devour you—annihilate you. Do you not know it."

"I know that she has surprised Madame de Champmortain's secret and mine—but Sylvia is innocent, I swear it—"

"Will she be so long? Had you not, this very day an assignation with her? Were you not to meet her in Madame Amab's house?"

"And if that were true?"

"What you, Brias," exclaimed Montéclain, "you—a gentleman, you expose the woman you love, or rather, that you do not love, to accept the protection of a Felina! Why Brias, were she guilty, and she is not, poor woman! were she guilty, she is still called Madame de Champmortain. It is a name as noble as your own, Brias. When a woman like that is loved, she may be seduced, stolen from her husband, carried off, ruined—but it should be done boldly, and without polluting her with the foul mire of this impudent courtezan."

"You are preparing yourself for the tribune, Montéclain," said Brias, trying to laugh; "the devil! I cannot be more careful of Madame de Champmortain's connexions than her husband, and he permits her to see Madame Amab."

"It is a husband like stupidity, to permit his wife to receive improper company, but all he sees in this visit, is a call which, though objectionable, will have no further consequences. But, on your side, it is an indignity, for you know that it is a rendezvous, in which you will place yourself, as well as Sylvia, at the mercy of this woman."

"Good heaven," said Brias, impatiently, "are we not so already, thanks to the meeting she surprised in the forest?"

"Is it my fault? Did I not warn you beforehand—?"

"Who could suspect—?"

"That arsenic was poisonous? Every one, Brias, except diplomatists, who, by dint of pretending to divine the most subtle of subtleties, cannot see the wiles which force their eyes out. I am not so skilful as you Brias, but everytime I know positively I am in the presence of a first-rate thief, I consider it prudent to take my departure. You, who are clever, put your hands in your pockets, and while you are saving your purse, he steals your watch."

"But what would you have me do?"

"Nothing for the present; for this hunt has broken your appointment."

"Did you then contrive it for that purpose?"

"And for many other reasons besides."

"May one inquire about them?"

"We shall see," said Montéclain; "only promise me that, during the hunt, you will not obey any look, or yield to any provocation which might entice you to turn out of the way to follow either Sylvia or Felina."

"Pardon me, dear and illustrious Montéclain; but neither a little boy, twelve years old, nor a grenadier of the Emperor Nicholas's guard, is ordered to march with more authority than you seek to possess over me."

"Brias, we are both children of this country; we have known Sylvia from her infancy; I love her as you do yourself, with sincere affection; for you do not love her otherwise. Were you not misled by your part of a seducer, you would be grieved and afflicted at any misfortune which might befall her. In pity for her, in honour to yourself, do not assist Felina in effecting her ruin; or, if your love is so sincere, so imperative, that you cannot subdue it, let her ruin be your work alone. It is not customary among us to take bullies to avenge our injuries; leave then to impotent age the employment of corrupt harredans. Brias, you alone can withdraw Sylvia from Felina."

"Eh! my dear friend, she is passionately attached to this woman."

"Still, I venture to hope she prefers you to her. Even to-day, Brias, you must have the courage to tell Madame de Champmortain, that you will not visit her so long as she consents to receive Madame Amab."

"But it would ruin Sylvia. Felina is capable of informing Champmortain of the rendezvous she surprised—"

"Well! both you and Sylvia will deny it, that is all. Have you not foreseen that a lie is the last resource of those who fail in their duty?"

"Doubtless; but wherefore should we seek danger when it may be avoided?"

"Brias, you are a booby; let us say no more about it. I will take other means," exclaimed Montéclain.

He rang the bell with a violence which proved to Brias how much his opposition had annoyed him."

"Where is Bricord?" said he to the servant who came in.

"He is getting ready to go out with the dogs; he has already settled the several stations."

"Tell him to wait for me. You know what I ordered?"

"Yes, my lord, all is ready."

"Come then, to horse, Brias."

"Well," said the other, as with some confusion in his manner he approached Montéclain, "I will take your advice. I promise you not to see Sylvia to-day."

"Wise at last!" exclaimed Montéclain, "and if you will render me a great service, I can make the task lighter to you. Apply all your energies, all your horsemanship to keep up with Bricord; do not leave him for a minute."

"This is rough work. Bricord would tire the wild boar himself."

"Fear nothing, it is not in the animal's track that he will proceed."

"Another mystery?"

"Which you would have known an hour ago, if you had not cavilled. Know then—"

"I beg your lordship's pardon," said Bricord coming in, "everything is ready for the hunt. The huntsmen are well instructed, and for that matter Lalouette is just come; M. Hector de Montaleu places him at your lordship's disposal, and I shall have occasion to go by the farm."

"What! an enemy," exclaimed Montéclain, laughing, "Montaleu's huntsman; no, Bricord, you are my general, and I will owe my triumph to none but yourself."

"My lord," replied Bricord, in a serious and positive tone, "I must return to the farm."

"How!" said Montéclain reproachfully, "on the only day I demand a service of you, you refuse me? I shall not forget it, Bricord."

"Ah! my lord," said the farmer in a trembling, tearful voice, "do not tell me that. I would stay, but you see I must go back to the farm; I must indeed."

"Very well," said Montéclain coldly, "you shall go, but presently. I shall have to speak to you in my turn. Wait for me there. Brias, a word, I pray you."

He drew him into the adjoining cabinet.

"Brias, get to horse," he said with that earnestness which imposes obedience; "ride quickly to the farm, see Léda; tell her to go out, to hide herself; let her come here. Bricord will run home without stopping; let her plunge into the Navarette wood, and gain the park by the subterranean passage. Here is the key of the vault which passes under the Autun road. She must remain hidden there all day. Make haste, Brias, or the poor woman is lost."

"What! Bricord—"

"Knows nothing, but suspects everything. I will detain him till you return."

"Is this another of Felina's tricks?"

"No, a blunder of the colonel's, and an imprudence of his soldier's. But for them the unfortunate creature would have been in safety since yesterday evening."

Brias set off, and Montéclain returned to the room where he had left Bricord. He was waiting for him with downcast eyes, in the attitude of a man resolved to commit an act which he knows will displease, but ready to brave all the rebukes it is likely to bring down upon him. In the new position of affairs, Montéclain's only object was to gain time. He, therefore, left Brias in his embarrassment, and pretended to be absorbed by his displeasure.

"You have something to say to me, my lord," said Bricord, after a few moments passed in silence.

"Yes, indeed," said Montéclain, answering drily, "I have something to say to you; or rather, Bricord, you have something to say to me. Yestesday, on leaving your house, did you not tell me you had something to ask me?"

"It is true," said Bricord embarrassed.

"Why did you not do so?"

"On arriving here, your lordship went up to your room directly, I wished to see you, but was told you had shut yourself in."

"Undoubtedly; but I came down again, and you said nothing to me. During this morning you have had opportunities of speaking to me a dozen times."

"That's true, my lord," replied Bricord hesitatingly. It is because I have thought the matter over—there are some things one ought not to say—you understand," he added, stifling the tears which rose up his eyes, "if it is as I believe—or rather, if it is not so—what will you have—but—I have nothing to say."

Montéclain beheld with profound pity the unhappy man's efforts to conceal the tortures which were racking his heart.

"Yet," said he in a gentler voice, "when you left the farm, I heard you say in a singular tone: 'I had rather not stay here.' And you added, looking at me with an almost menacing air: 'Besides, I have something to ask you.' What made you speak thus?"

"I was wrong, my lord—I ask your pardon," said Bricord.

"But what is the matter, after all, Bricord? What does this way of treating me mean? You know we are not the best friends in the world, the Viscount de Montaleu and I."

Bricord turned pale.

"And that has not prevented you lending him your help, in his hunting parties, as often as he has asked for it—now to-day I want you to help me against him."

"My lord," returned Bricord, between his closed teeth, "I must go to the farm, I must see Léda. A suspicion is come into my head, and you see I cannot go hunting like that, by the side of—. Some misfortune would happen, its certain."

"Ah, but, my good fellow, have you gone mad since yesterday? No doubt it was something in connexion with the suspicion you wished to ask me—my advice probably?"

"No, my lord—no, I have thought about it, you would refuse me, or you would deceive me again."

"Bricord—"

"Ah! hold"—cried Bricord, in a burst of passion, I cannot read writing—but I will read in her eyes, in her voice, in her alarm—"

"Ah but," said Montéclain, who saw the storm increasing in Bricord's heart, and thought it would be less terrible if it burst before him, "who has offended you? who are you talking about?"

"No one—that is my business only,—" said the farmer. "I must go, my lord, it is necessary.—After all," he added, exciting himself to a rebellion which did not come from his heart, "I am not your valet, I am your farmer—my lease does not say—"

"Very well," said Montéclain, "but from the moment we come to this, all our interests must be regulated. Here," he added, opening a secretary, "is an account for reparation, which appears to me exorbitant."

"I will pay it," said Bricord.

"No," replied Montéclain coldly, "you have already accused me of having deceived you."

"I said that—I—my lord?" cried Bricord; "I said that you had deceived me, you who have placed me at ease, have made my fortune?—I did not say that—"

"You said it just now, Bricord, in speaking about the matter you now shun."

"Ah!" said Bricord, "yes, it is true."

"In what then have I ever deceived you?"

"Well!" said the farmer, "since I must say all—since you wish it; my lord, do you remember the letter my wife wrote me when she pretended to be gone to Paris to see her mother?"

"Well! what of that letter?"

"I got Madame de Monrion to read it to me."

"You told me so then, and moreover that you mistrusted the lady, and you begged me to read the letter again."

"Yes, my lord, and you told me that it contained just what Madame de Monrion had said, that is to say, that my wife had been to see her mother who was ill in Paris; but this letter was a lie—this letter did not contain what you told me."

"How!"

"Yes—yes. First, as to Madame de Monrion—I noticed well—she trembled—she stammered—a man can read, or he cannot—and she can—she did not go straight forward. That is why I came to you."

"I found exactly the same thing as the countess."

"Yes—yes—after having questioned me—after having made me tell you all, then, you repeated to me, what you had drawn from me. And then, it is because last night I recalled everything—I dug into my head—and I am sure they were not the same words. Besides, that letter you would never return it to me."

"I told you the reason why; there was an account at the end of it which I required."

"In that case," said Bricord, "if there was an account, you must have taken care of it. Will you give it back to me?"

"I think it would be very difficult to find it," said Montéclain, embarrassed. "I may have burnt it."

"You see how it is—" cried Bricord, "I was sure of it. Adieu, my lord."

Brias returned at this moment.

"Bricord," exclaimed Montéclain, "it is possible I may have it yet."

"I thank you," cried Bricord, as he departed. "I require none to help me to make out the truth."

"Well! Brias," exclaimed Montéclain.

"Léda was gone out," replied Brias; "Madame de Monrion sent to ask for her this morning, and she left the farm a few moments after."

"In that case," said Montéclain, "I do not fear that she will return then."

Just then, the sound of the horns, ringing suddenly through the castle court, announced the departure.

## CHAPTER LXV

### THE COAL MINE.

Brias had been told that Madame de Monrion had sent to fetch Léda. In fact, the day had scarcely dawned when Julia had sent a second time to the farm to beg Madame Bricord to come to her house.

Léda had replied that she was coming to her, but instead of taking the road leading to the Marquis de Montaleu's chateau, she turned hastily aside, and plunged into the forest. She soon came to the lonely hut, where we have already seen her in company with Hector de Montaleu. This time also a particular signal from the fierce viscount had informed Léda she would find him there; for, scarcely had she slipped into the lock an imperceptible key before the door opened, as of itself, and she found herself face to face with her brutal accomplice.

We have related how Hector's dull understanding had contrived with great difficulty to mark out for itself the route which should lead to the conquest of Julia, and the inheritance of the old French nobleman. Proud of the skill he had discovered in himself, Hector had rushed forward with the blind speed of a wild boar towards the magnificent result he had proposed; but all at once this victorious plan was thrown into confusion by the indiscretion of an awkward man. Léda had been informed of her lover's skilful projects. She could annihilate them with one word, but that word would ruin her, and Hector hoped she would not utter it. However, he was not easy; Léda's jealousy or grief might prefer death to the triumph of a rival, and her own abandonment. So Hector, whose obtuse mind had attacked this difficulty on all sides, without finding the means of overcoming or turning it aside, had exclaimed, "I will compel her to hold her tongue."

When Léda entered the coal-house she had reached that degree of despair, at which the soul, in its dread of some other peril, loses all fear of certain dangers. Léda, who trembled at the idea of appearing to her husband as a criminal, would fearlessly have braved death or suicide. The soul which retains a fear, and feels a courage like this, is not quite lost. Hector experienced a feeling of satisfaction in seeing Léda enter.

"You are come at last," he said, "I have been waiting for you this hour."

"I have often waited longer than that for you," said Léda, "when the intelligence of a wild boar, or the drinking of a bottle of wine has detained you anywhere."

"Are we going to quarrel," replied the viscount, "when we are threatened with a terrible danger?"

"What danger?" said Léda.

"Did you not hear that fool of a soldier yesterday? and did you not notice Bricord's face?"

"No, indeed," said Léda, "I only looked at yours. I never saw a man so frightened."

Hector turned with the astonished look of an enormous bull dog, who feels himself bitten by an insignificant cur. The blood mounted to his face.

"Listen, Léda," he replied, harshly, "spare me your epigrams, and reproaches; I am not in the humour to hear them. Besides, we must take some resolution. Let us see, what do you purpose doing?"

"I? what does it matter to you, viscount? Have you not severed your life from mine? Why should the future husband of the Countess de Monrion, trouble himself with what the miserable wife of farmer Bricord may do?"

"I understand you, Léda, that is what wounds and irritates you. But let us talk reasonably, Léda; I cannot be your husband; I cannot kill Bricord. I must think of my future fortune."

"And of Madame de Monrion."

"Of her," said Hector, "devil take me if I care about her! All I wish for, is, that the fortune of the Montaleu's may not pass into the hands of this silly prude."

"And to that end you will marry her? It is very clever. So much the more, because no one knows better than you that she is innocent of the crime imputed to her."

"You are laughing at me, Léda!" cried Hector, violently. "I told you, you must form some resolution."

"That resolution is already formed. You have acted according to your fancy, I shall act according to mine."

"And how will you act?"

"Did you consult me about demanding Madame de Monrion's hand?"

"Ah!" said Hector, "this is the tone you take, when I come here to save you, to shelter you from Bricord's anger?"

"I do not ask you for your protection."

"Then what are you come here for?

"Did you not give the signal which informed me you wished to speak to me? I am come, what have you to say?"

Hector did not reply. His anger was kindling by degrees, and Léda provoked him with that tenacity and imprudence which make women so formidable."

"Léda," said Hector, with a determined air, "listen to me attentively. I have formed a project, and this project must be accomplished. I wish to secure to myself my uncle's fortune, and my marriage with Madame de Monrion, is the only means by which I can succeed. If you love me, you should help me to accomplish it."

These last words began to disturb Léda's affected tranquillity. She started, whilst a disdainful and menacing smile agitated her lips.

"You say, that if I love you—I must help you to marry—my rival. Very well. And how shall I help you?"

"By saving yourself, and denying with firmness and constancy that you have anything to do with the existence of that child."

"And what will be the consequence?"

"That Julia, accused on every side, will be obliged to accept the proposals of the only man who will and can save her."

On hearing this reply, which displayed to their fullest extent Hector's heartless and selfish calculations, Léda allowed a sharp insolent titter to escape her.

"Ah!" she exclaimed, "happy woman! what a noble husband I shall have procured her, to reward her for having tried to save me."

"Léda," said Hector in a threatening tone, "you shall be silent."

"Doubtless, in order that Madame de Monrion may not know that you have basely turned against her the protection she granted to an unhappy woman, and may not order you to be driven from her house."

"Léda, you shall be silent."

"Yes," returned the farmer's wife, with clenched teeth and sparkling eyes, "in order that my husband may not discover that you have abused the friendship he has shown you, and may not strike you after he has killed me."

"Léda!—"

"And may not kill you, though you are a viscount—"

"Léda," repeated Hector in a terrible voice, "you shall be silent."

"And if I were not silent?" cried Léda, measuring Hector with a flashing glance, "if I were not infamous enough to suffer another to perish beneath the burden of my fault? if I were tired of living as I am, in falsehood and fear? if my heart revolted at last at the thought of deceiving the man who has sought my happiness, for one who despises and forsakes me? if I were to confess my crime and yours?"

A dull, terrible, furious cry replied to this attack. Hector approached Léda, and seizing her two wrists in his large powerful hands, he threw her on her knees before him, and lifted his clenched fist against her. Léda bent her head. Montaleu checked himself immediately, and breathless with the fury which had carried him away, he said, tittering:

"But you dare not say it, Léda, you dare not say it; Bricord would kill you, you know he would."

"Well! let him kill me!" cried Léda in the last transport of despair, "he has a right to do it."

"You are mad."

"No, sir, no; but it shall never be said of me, that you dishonoured, and then flung me aside, to gratify the avarice which prefers your fortune to my love. I will not; do you hear, I will not, loaded as I am by you with shame and affliction, add to it the shame of having ruined her who took pity on me, and the grief of seeing you laugh at my sufferings."

"You are mad, Léda," repeated Montaleu, whose face, injected with blood, became almost blue."

"No, I am not mad, you shall give up Madame de Monrion, or I will tell everything."

"Léda!"—cried Hector in a choked voice.

"Ah!" resumed Léda, who had reached that paroxysm of blind anger which sees nothing, not even death hovering above its head. "Ah! you have advanced towards your object without troubling yourself about the poor woman whom you are going to crush in your path. Well, then, this woman whom you have so insolently disdained—this woman will stop you, she will expose the base cunning of your conduct."

"Léda," repeated Hector again, pressing his head between his clenched hands, as if he felt it ready to burst, "Léda, hold your tongue!"

"No"—replied Léda, "you have made me tremble enough and suffer enough. No, I tell you—I will speak—I—"

At that moment Hector seized her with his two iron hands; any one passing by might have heard a cry of despairing anguish, but all of a sudden the forest echoed with the joyous sound of the hunting horns.

A moment after, Hector went out of the hovel. A livid paleness had succeeded the dark red tint which his face displayed a moment before. His lips trembled convulsively; his haggard eyes rolled in their sockets. When he tried to put the key into the lock, to fasten the door, his hands trembled so violently that it was some time before he could manage it. Nevertheless, he closed it with a double lock, went with a wavering step to seek his horse, which he had tied up a few yards from the coal-house, and after having mounted it, not without trouble, darted at full speed across the thicket, whose briars tore the breast of the noble animal, while the branches struck Hector's face. He soon gained a long alley, where he would perhaps have continued to ride in the same frenzied manner, had he not perceived, at a considerable distance, a group of horsemen, advancing at a gentle pace.

---

## CHAPTER LXVI.

### THE HUNT.

Bricord, on leaving Montéclain's chateau, repaired immediately to the farm.

Until this day, no suspicion had entered the farmer's mind. Plunged in the obscurity of unlimited confidence, his wife's happiness had been the sole object of his life. Good, because he was strong, confiding, because he was incapable of deception; modest, because his heart was truly great; never had he arraigned against Léda, her caprices, her denials, or her despondency, he had never reproved her either for her repeated absences, or the reception, sometimes too gracious, sometimes too cold, to be natural, which she gave to Hector. Bricord had an ever ready excuse at hand for Léda's faults; this was, that he was unworthy of her, that he had not obtained for her all the happiness he had promised.

It was in the midst of this profound security in Léda's honour, that suddenly there crept in a suspicion that he was deceived. Bricord had not understood the crafty calumny which had cast on

Madame de Monrion the shame of Léda s crime, but he had seen her terror: this alarm had been succeeded by the desperate anger she had shewn at the announcement, that some one had demanded Madame de Monrion's hand, and this anger, Bricord had seen reflected in the disconcerted countenance of Hector de Montaleu. Then a something glittering, painful at the same time, like a red hot iron, had traversed the darkness in which he had hitherto lived so tranquilly, and he seemed to have a glimpse of scoffing phantoms lurking around him, and pointing with mocking looks at Léda and Hector.

Then it was that Montéclain arrived.

During the night which Bricord passed at the chateau, this suspicion, which, like a distant light, had shed at first only a doubtful ray upon the past, stimulated by the patient raging breath of jealousy, had continued to glitter, illuminating, with its sinister gleam, the part which he had traversed in obscurity. All that had been excused by the perfect faith of the confiding husband, became an accusation in the mind of the jealous husband.

The singular coincidence which had summonsed Léda to Madame de Monrion, the same day on which the latter was smitten with a dishonourable imputation, had at first turned Bricord's suspicions into another direction. For a moment he said to himself that Léda was perhaps Julia's confident, but then, when recalling Léda's words again, more distinctly, he remembered she had said that Julia was the victim of her generosity. Bricord was unable to pierce to the bottom of this abyss of perfidy, but his look was fixed upon it, and he strove to see into it distinctly.

As firm in his resolve to discover the truth, as he had been in his confidence, he left Montéclain's chateau to go and interrogate Léda.

On arriving at the farm, he met the colonel and Aly Muley, who were quitting it for the rendezvous of the hunt. Thomas stopped him to ask if he was not included in the party.

"Presently, colonel," replied Bricord, "it is probable I shall rejoin you, and perhaps you may have a finer hunt than you expect." He entered the farm.

"Where is Leda?" said the colonel to Aly.

"Madame de Monrion has sent for, and she set out long ago."

"Probably the countess has prepared everything for the unhappy woman's flight," said the colonel to Aly

"Let us go quietly, that we may see what Bricord is going to do."

The farmer went straight up to the little room occupied by Léda. Not finding her there, he came down again, and hurried through the premises, without addressing a word to the servants, or to the men at work in the yards. Again his search was a useless one.

Then he looked about him with the aspect of a man who feels his senses are leaving him. He called to one of his servants, but in a voice so hoarse, so changed, that she turned round laughing and said:

"Who called me in that unearthly voice?"

"I!" said Bricord.

The poor servant stood dnmbfounded on seeing Bricord's pallor and the sinister look he fixed on her.

"Where is my wife?" said the farmer.

"Why sir, the Countess de Monrion sent for her about an hour ago, and she went out directly after."

"Good!" said Bricord leaving the yard."

At the same moment, a servant on horseback entered at full gallop:

"Hey!" he cried, "M. Bricord, the servant, where is Madame Bricord?"

"Well!" replied the girl, she is at your house."

"Not so," returned the servant, "I came here once before this morning, and Madame Bricord told me she was coming directly, yet no one has seen her. I do not know what the countess wants with her, but I never saw her so impatient before."

"It is strange," said the servant girl, "and M. Brias has been here to inquire for her too."

Bricord had stopped to listen, and was devouring the servant with his flashing eyes.

"Ah!" he said, "so my wife is not at your house?"

"No, since I am come to fetch her. Try then to tell me where she is, I have orders to ride after her."

Bricord leant against the post which was near him.

"Don't you know where she is?" said the man to the rest.

"I know," said Bricord.

"In that case," said the servant, "send her to us directly; its an urgent matter it seems.""

Bricord let him pass, without seeing him, and stood for a moment annihilated. His trembling lips muttered disconnected words.

"She is—she is with him," said he, "where then—where?—oh!—at his house—yes—good—"

He returned into the house, and having taken his gun, was going to leave the farm, when suddenly the horns resounded for him, as they had resounded for Montaleu."

"Oh!" cried Bricord, "if he is with her, he will not have time to be at the hunting appointment."

Immediately he runs to a stable, saddles and bridles one of the intrepid coarsers he was training, and armed with his gun and hunting knife, he darts off at full speed in the direction taken by the colonel and Aly Muley.

He had soon overtaken them.

"Where are you riding to like that?" cried the colonel spurring his horse up to that of the farmer.

"To the hunting appointment," answered Bricord, "if he is not there, I will go on even to his house."

"Who are you speaking of?" said the colonel.

"Leave me, colonel," said Bricord, making his horse go at a frightful pace.

But the colonel was sufficiently well mounted to keep up easily with Bricord.

"Bricord!" he cried, "Bricord! answer me; what is it about? what do you want?"

"You shall see—"

At that moment they reached a cross way, where the different roads met which intersected the forest, when suddenly they perceived Hector de Montaleu riding tranquilly by Felina's side, while Madame de Champmortain preceded them by a hundred paces, with her husband and M. Amab.

Hector's quiet look checked Bricord's fury for a moment. Nevertheless he said to him in a disordered voice:

"What, viscount, you are not yet at the meeting."

"It is my fault," said Felina; "M. de Montaleu, has been losing his time with me. I have detained him more than an hour."

Bricord hung down his head; his mind had attached itself to the idea that Hector was in his own house with Léda, and he found him in company with another woman, with whom he had been upwards of an hour. This last circumstance confused his suspicions. But what had become of Léda, since she was not at Madame de Monrion's? The unhappy Bricord, struggling with his doubts, like a madman in his chains, which only leave him at liberty to move a few steps in a narrow circle, pricked straight before him, then stopped suddenly, retraced his steps, went to the right, then to the left, and at last not knowing which course to take, was going to return to his own house, when all at once Montéclain and Brias appeared.

The sight of the latter recalled to Bricord what the maid-servant had said. In fact, Brias had been to ask for Léda at the farm. This significant proceeding, nevertheless, excited no personal suspicion against Brias in the farmer's mind. Only the feeling which had hindered his confiding in Montéclain, the idea that the nobles and the rich sustained each other, and connived together for the dishonour of a man who was nobody, made him think for a moment that Brias might be Montaleu's confident.

Bricord then was going to ask him why he had been to the farm, when Montéclain advanced rapidly towards him.

"That is capital, Bricord," he said, gaily, "you have not forsaken me. In that case, I will no longer bear you a grudge, for I must tell you I was so wounded by the manner in which you left me, that I sent to fetch Léda, to arrange with her some way of regulating our affairs, that we might break off all connexion together. Happily Brias did not find her, and since you are come, we will say no more about this misunderstanding. And now, Bricord, let us all ride off to the hunt, and cut the grass beneath Montaleu's feet; I confide my honour to you.

Bricord, bewildered, not knowing what to do, replied at hazard, and promised to do his best.

The company finding themselves assembled, took the road to the thicket, where they expected to attack the animal.

"Shall we draw out the beast to the entrance of the inclosure?" said Hector.

"Oh! nonsense," said Montéclain, "I mean to have a set on with the dogs, there is no good hunt without that."

"We ought," said Hector, "to be sure of turning the beast, for it is very possible she has made off on hearing the sound of the horns. Boars, you know, are not fond of that kind of noise."

"Yours are not," said Montéclain, with immovable assurance; "but mine are capable of holding their ground for more than an hour."

"In which case," said Hector, "it will be prudent to shoot."

"No, in the name of all the devils," said Montéclain, "should he overthrow dogs and horses, I mean to kill him with my own hand."

"With the needle you have at your side?" said Hector, laughing.

"Do not alarm yourself," Montaleu, returned Montéclain, with a disdainful smile, "the needles I handle make holes which no other needle would be able to mend."

The conversation soon became general, and nothing was heard save discussions on the quartans, or four-year-old boars, the pigaches, and the signs by which a boar, its age, sex, and trace might be known, all which was intermingled with the terms peculiar to hunting.

Nevertheless, the hunt soon began; the pack of hounds were let loose. Montéclain, exposing himself, like the lowest huntsman, urged them on by crying, in an animated ringing voice:

"Hola! there, my man; hola! hola! there."

Contrary to his expectation, or rather to the opinion he had expressed, the boar took his course, forcing a point which must draw off the hunt very far from its starting place. Montéclain darted on his track with so much ardour and spirit, with so many cries, and bravadoes, that Hector, beguiled by this false demonstration, precepitated himself with rapidity in the same track; the jealous hate he bore Montéclain, his vanity as a huntsman, his desire to vanquish, in some struggle, the man whose disdainful superiority wounded him on all occasions; silenced in Montaleu's mind the remembrance of the scene which had lately passed in the coal-house. Bricord, on his side, lost in his suspicions, unable any further to penetrate the truth, instinctively attached himself to the steps of Hector. Brias, the colonel, Champmortain, and Amab, accompanied Felina and Madame de Champmortain, and the whole party were soon hurrying away in the same direction, as if animated by the most ardent enthusiasm, though assuredly there was not one among these individuals who was really interested in the matter.

Brias wanted to speak to Sylvia, who wanted to speak to him. Champmortain wished to remain alone with Felina, who wished to remain alone with the colonel. Among them all, there was only Amab, who, satisfied with having found an opportunity of flying from himself, nevertheless felt no desire to approach any one. He did not even take that common interest in the chase, which is excited by the sight of other people's passions. Amab was a poor lost man, desolate, consumed in the depth of his soul, with a secret despair, whose agonies he sometimes forgot in the inspiration of his pencil, and sought at this moment to deaden by the excitement and turmoil into which he had plunged.

In the mean time, the cavalcade, influenced by the secret desires of each, performed its evolutions rapidly and skilfully, though with imperceptible dullness.

Felina had gradually disengaged herself from the horizontal line they had followed at first, and advanced in front, side by side with the colonel. Champmortain, who aspired to the favour of a conversation, followed them close; Amab drew near to Champmortain, while Sylvia and Brias, who were obliged to be tender of their less powerful horses, suffered themselves to be left alone behind.

"Well, Thomas," said Felina, to the colonel, "you know the news?"

"What news?" said the colonel, "that Madame de Monrion is innocent of the crime imputed to her."

"Bah!" said Felina, "do you believe that? I avow that for my part, I should require very convincing proofs, after the story of the village of Saint-Faron."

"You know better than I do that she is innocent," said the colonel, sternly.

"Where could I have learnt such intelligence? All I know is, that Montaleu, who would marry a rag-picker, if her basket was filled with bank notes, will marry the countess, and take the bantling into the bargain."

"I believe he can do so better than any on—"

"Yes, he is of a make to bear all possible ridicule; it is true the dowry is a magnificent one."

"I did not mean that. You pretend not to understand me, Felina. Hector marries her because he knows to whom this child belongs."

"Ah! he is in Madame de Monrion's confidence?"

"Felina," returned the colonel, "are we talking seriously? or do you think you can treat me as you do M. Amab, or Champmortain?"

"Reassure yourself, colonel," replied Felina, with a smile of unspeakable disdain, "I have no wish to do you this honour."

The colonel repressed the anger excited by this impertinence; and resumed after a moment's silence:

"Understand me well, madam, I do not intend—I will not be mixed up in an affair of which the object is to injure an innocent woman."

"Colonel Thomas Rien, who wishes to mix you up with it but yourself, when you come preaching to me of Madame de Monrion's innocence? For heaven's sake, sir, prove it, bring it to light; I *will* not, I do not *intend* to prevent you from doing so. Do better still, marry the marquis's beautiful protégée. Do it, if it please you, sir."

The colonel, whose obstinate and impetuous nature was at once surprised and irritated by this contemptuous language, rejoined, with violent anger:

"A word, Felina: you swore to my mother, that you would assist me in my projects."

"And I am still ready to do so."

"You know what is the object of my life?"

"Yes, the re-establishing of your mother's honour."

"You hold it in your hands, you!"

"That is true."

"What price do you put upon it?"

"The ruin and dishonour of Madame de Monrion," said Felina, flinging the words at him in a voice of derision.

"Never," replied the colonel, indignantly.

Felina stopped her horse suddenly, and permitting Champmortain and Amab to come up to her, said to them joyously:

"Come, gentlemen, come! must I set you the example? A race at full speed, Victor, and you too, M. de Champmortain, let us show the colonel that the African horses, which parade so proudly under a magnificent uniform, cannot keep up with us in this country bristling with difficulties."

All three set off at a gallop, leaving the colonel sullen and discontented. He looked about for some one to join; but just as he was preparing to approach Brias and Sylvia, he saw them turn rapidly in another direction, as if they wished to cut off the hunt. Thomas, thus deserted by every one, would perhaps have decided on returning to the farm, had he not perceived Montéclain, who was approaching at full speed. Thomas suffered him to approach, and was going to ask him, why he appeared thus to forsake the hunt, when Montéclain, suddenly stopping him, said:

"Colonel, will you save a woman's life?"

"Do you doubt it?"

"Well, then, do not leave this alley, it is the only one which leads from this part of the forest to Lavordan. Bricord is going to return there, he has just said so to Aly. Detain him for a quarter of an hour or ten minutes."

"What has happened, then?"

"You shall know, colonel; but, for mercy's sake, keep Bricord from going. I shall ride over to Lavordan—and hide Léda, who may possibly have returned there—but here he comes—adieu."

Montéclain disappeared at full speed, and the colonel went to meet Bricord.

## CHAPTER LXVII.

### AN ENCOUNTER.

THE previous night had been a cruel one for Julia. At first, confident of her innocence, she was almost astonished at the unskilfulness of her wicked accusers; but on recalling by whom this accusation had been brought to M. de Montaleu, she was obliged to acknowledge that men of some consideration had been found to give faith to this calumny; and to remember that M. de Montaleu had believed it.

Once engaged in this train of reflections, and arguments, she had recalled the circumstances of her journey to Issoudun, and her return to Saint-Faron. The thousand precautions, a feeling of pity had induced her to take, to conceal from all eyes another person's secret, could not have been better combined had it been necessary to hide her own fault. All she had done to protect Léda might be turned against herself.

Arriving at this result, an unspeakable terror took possession of Julia, and she saw clearly that she was, in a manner, at the mercy of the guilty woman's generosity, or remorse. Then she no longer sought, as she had done before, for a means of saving Léda, but applied every energy of her mind to discover in what was past, some means of saving herself.

Nothing offered itself to her agitated spirit. She had set out alone; she had returned alone. She alone had appeared in Jeanne Dromeray's house. Her head wandered. She was on the point of running to M. de Montaleu, telling him all, and imploring his support and advice; but the remembrance of her promise to Léda stopped her. Then amidst this tide of fears, doubts, and griefs, the consciousness of her innocence, rose up like the ark of salvation above the waters of the deluge.

Julia took refuge in it, and kneeling down regained a little tranquillity. But soon her fears returned; solitude and the darkness of night lent their fearful aid to her ardent imagination, and more than once, at the moment she clung with clasped hands to this plank of safety, she seemed to see Felina's fatal and menacing shadow, set her proud foot upon it, and plunge her again into the abyss wherein she was doomed to perish.

It was after such a weary night as this, that Julia, wishing at last to know what she had to hope or dread from Léda, sent for her to come. Léda, surprised by the early arrival of Madame de Monrion's messenger, had replied that she was going to obey her summons immediately

A whole hour had passed in vain expectation, and Madame de Monrion, whose impatience and anxiety increased every minute, sent a second time to the farm. The servant whom we have seen arrive there at the same time as Bricord, and on this occasion without meeting with Léda, had scarcely left the chateau de Montaleu, when the old marquis entered Julia's room, and began to settle himself there with all those precautions and tedious solemnities which commence an interview of long duration. Almost always, at the theatre, these entrances are received by the public with a feeling of ill-will and alarm; at this moment, and for reasons easily understood, Julia experienced a sentiment rather analogous to that of the spectators, and it required all the deference she owed to M. de Montaleu to prevent her eagerly entreating him to postpone this interview to some future time.

The marquis, having taken his place, thus began:

"Julia, particular reasons, which were derived from the memory of a deceived affection, induced me to renounce matrimony for ever. Nevertheless, the want of some object to love, the desire to bequeath my fortune to a man not undeserving of the favour, made me look around me for some worthy inheritor of both these benefits. My hope and my choice turned first towards Hector de Montaleu. He is my brother's son, and the inheritor of my name. My tenderness and my fortune were destined to be his. I must confess to you, that my heart was soon repulsed by so coarse and narrow minded a character, under which I did not at that time expect to meet either courage or generosity. Younger, and at the same time handsome, witty, spirited, full of grace and energy, the young Count Gustavus de Monrion grew up in my house. He was my sister's son, but did not bear my name, and for a long time I resisted the allurement he exercised over me, before I determined to turn my hopes in that direction. The affection I bore Gustavus was very powerful, since neither his faults nor his follies could subdue it."

"Because there was a noble heart beneath those faults, a proud sincerity beneath those follies," observed Madame de Monrion.

"Be it so," said M. de Montaleu; "but have the goodness to listen to me. After Gustavus's death, I saw myself alone, and should perhaps have turned my thoughts towards Hector, had not the misfortune which made you an orphan, imposed on me the duty of protecting you, and afforded me the consolation and hope that I should have a family in my old age. I love you as a father, Julia; but you know not perhaps, that a man with a name like mine, must not listen exclusively to the dictates of affection. Very often in my solitary hours of reflection, I have grieved that Hector de Montaleu was not different from what he seemed to me. He bears my name, he will inherit my title, and were he worthy to become your husband, I should by uniting you, and securing to him my fortune, accomplish at once my duties to you, to him, and to myself."

"You can assign him your fortune, without his becoming my husband," said Julia softly.

"Julia," said M. de Montaleu eagerly, there is a strange thing in your destiny. Placed by an unheard of chance, between the two heirs given to me by nature, and both of whom had shewn themselves too long unworthy of my tenderness, you have alternately awakened in their souls, the noble instincts they had received from their ancestors. The first generously repaired the insult he had offered you; the second offers triumphantly to contradict the calumny by which you are pursued. Julia, you demanded of me an interval of some hours, to collect yourself, before replying to Viscount Hector de Montaleu's offer; this reply I am now come to seek, and I hope it will be in accordance with my wishes, and such as the viscount's noble confidence deserves."

This conclusion might have been easily foreseen, yet Julia started with indignation. In fact, she no longer doubted that Hector and Léda were accomplices. Nevertheless, she restrained herself."

"I thank you, sir," she replied in a circumspect voice. "Long since, I comprehended that the affection you showed me, would be a serious blow to the sacred rights of your family. I again entreat you, as I have always done, to restore to M. Hector de Montaleu, the legitimate hopes, given him by his relationship; but permit me to decline the proposal he has deigned to make me."

"What! you refuse?" exclaimed the old marquis.

"Yes, sir I refuse—"

"Despite the generosity of this proposal?"

"My lord," returned Julia with noble decision, "though accused myself in the most infamous manner, I shall accuse no one in return. I expect the justification of my honour from those who hold it in their hands. If it does not come, then I will tell you what signifies the generosity of M. Hector de Montaleu."

"I do not understand you."

At the same moment the gallop of a horse was heard entering the court yard. Julia saw that it was the servant whom she had sent to the farm.

"Perhaps," she eagerly replied to M. de Montaleu, "perhaps you will understand me better immediately."

The servant so impatiently expected, entered the apartment.

"Well," said Julia, "where is Madame Bricord?"

"She was not at the farm, madame."

"How! where is she then?"

"No one can tell. It seems M. de Brias also came to look for her, without finding her, and I left M. Bricord very uneasy at his wife's absence. They say she has disappeared—"

"Disappeared!"—repeated Julia with terrible fear; "it is impossible. Why she has abandoned me then, she—"

Here she suddenly broke off, and glanced round with a look of dismay.

"What does it mean?" asked M. de Montaleu, "what can there be in common between you and this woman?"

"There is this, sir, that—No," she resumed, "it is impossible." And addressing herself to the servant, who still stood there with that malicious curiosity common to those who are servile and wicked:

"She must have left a letter for me."

"Nobody said so. But if your ladyship wishes it I will return."

"No," said Julia quickly, "I will go myself,—order my carriage, I am going out."

The servant left the saloon.

"What does all this signify, Julia?" said M. de Montaleu. "How comes it that Madame Bricord is initiated into matters which concern you?"

"Sir, you have a right to know the whole truth; but I have not the right to tell it you, until this woman by abandoning me shall have delivered me from my vow; then, sir, you shall learn whether or not I had good reason to reject the unworthy proposal of M. Hector de Montaleu."

Julia then left the marquis, and some minutes later, reached the Lavordan farm. She had scarcely entered therein, and had not yet had time to ask for Léda, when Montéclain rode into the court, in breathless haste.

"Is Madame Bricord here?" he cried, leaping from his horse, without seeing Julia.

"No, my lord," replied the servant, to whom he had addressed himself, "this is the second time she has been asked for, and here again is the Countess de Monrion."

Montéclain turned about eagerly, and saluted Julia with so profound a respect, that for the first time for many days, she felt herself raised again to the position, from which slander had attempted to degrade her. Nevertheless, she continued confounded by the presence of this man, whom she had so often heard accused of levity and misconduct. Montéclain himself was embarrassed, despite his assurance; he guessed the motive which had brought Madame de Monrion to the farm, but it was very difficult to commence such a subject with a woman who must consider him as her enemy. Nevertheless, Julia's pale looks and agitation deeply affected him.

"Pardon me, madam," he said, "you wish to see Madame Bricord, and I desire it as eagerly as you do; perhaps, forgive me for the supposition, perhaps there is some connection between the motive which has conducted you hither and that which brings me."

Julia, with her eyes cast down, and trembling in every limb, replied in disconnected words, uttered in a broken voice:

"I think not, sir. I came—I—but what does it matter?—she is not here. It is enough—"

A deep sigh escaped from her breast, she raised towards heaven the tearful azure of her beautiful eyes, and murmured in a feeble tone:

"Mon Dieu! mon Dieu! what remains to be done now?"

"Madame," said Montéclain, slowly approaching her, "I have no other right than that of feeling the deepest respect, to demand a moment's conversation; but if the prayer of a man of honour, whose whole heart has revolted at the idea that some have dared to outrage you, if this prayer appears sincere, deign to hear me for a moment."

"But, sir," said Julia, looking at him fearfully, "I have not the honour of knowing you; you do not know me—"

"Madame de Monrion," said Montéclain, in a firm voice, "I do know you, I know that you are holy, I know that you are pure, I know that you are good and generous, and I know that you have been outraged and calumniated. Will you hear me, madame? it is necessary, I swear it is, yes, I swear it to you, by the memory of him whose name you bear."

Julia raised her eyes to Montéclain, who stood there before her, with his head uncovered, like a subject before his queen, like a faithful worshipper before his saint, and pointed with his hand to the inner room of the farm-house. She passed on before him, all confused and trembling; yet, amidst all the confusion, tremour, and grief to which she was a prey, a singular, a vivid hope began to gleam in her soul. It was not merely the hope of being saved; it was not only a light which discovered her approaching justification, it was likewise a soft and lukewarm heat which soothed her suffering soul. The star which she saw ascending her horizon gave forth both light and heat.

She entered; Montéclain followed her. She sank upon a seat; he approached, and looked at her. Never had a more charming embarrassment, a more touching grief, a more ingenuous confidence, animated a lovelier face. Montéclain forgot himself as he gazed; he felt his knees bend beneath him; it seemed to him that he could not speak to her, except it was to say:

"Madame, I adore you, my fate is in your hands."

But Julia, embarrassed by this long silence, ventured again to look at Montéclain. The look of burning admiration that she met obliged her blushingly, to veil her eyes with their long lashes.

"What have you to say to me, sir?" she asked, tremblingly.

"Pardon me," replied Montéclain, "you ought to have been informed of it already. To leave your heart in grief for a minute, is a crime. Madame de Monrion, I am acquainted with the truth of all that passed at Issoudun."

"You, sir!" said Julia, with a quick start of surprise.

"Yes, madam, I know by what admirable subterfuge you concealed Bricord's misfortune, I know with what holy devotedness you have striven to repair a poor woman's fault. You understand now why I admired you just now in silence, why I would have knelt before you to ask your forgiveness."

"My forgiveness, sir, for what then?"

"For myself, who left you exposed to two days of suffering, when I was able to exonerate you."

"I had no claim to your benevolence."

"Calumniated virtue has a claim to the testimony of every honourable man, madame, and I value too highly, your esteem, not to seek to justify myself in your eyes."

Julia bowed gently, but already did she listen with secret joy to that serious penetrating voice, which addressed her in language she loved to hear, with an accent she had only heard in her dreams.

"Informed like you of Léda's flight," continued Montéclain, "I was secretly associated with your good action. At the moment you fell a victim to it, madam, something of happiness, allow me to say so, was mingled with the indignation I felt."

"M. de Montaleu has shown himself your enemy, sir," replied Julia, hesitatingly, "and I can understand that you hoped for vengeance, in the humiliation he would feel on my account."

"Oh! madame," returned Montéclain, in a tone of such deep reproach, that Julia was moved by it, calumny has not alighted on you only, he who has given you so infamous an idea of me, that you can lend such an interpretation to my words is an enemy I cannot pardon. And yet, it is true, your misfortune has given me the only vengeance I wish to obtain from the man who could believe in your dishonour, and who for two continuous days, could find no other protection to offer you than the base insulting alliance of M. Hector de Montaleu."

"Oh! I have refused him, sir."

"Well! madame, this joy, so ill-interpreted by you, arose from the right chance had given me, of saying to you, 'madame, there is a man known to you only by the evil you have heard of him; to confound your calumniators, to crush your enemies, this man offers you his support, this man belongs to you.'"

"Sir," returned Julia, agitated to the depth of her soul, "a few words will suffice for my justification, I expect them from your justice."

"You are right, madame," said Montéclain, "what I can do for you, demands neither courage nor devotion, you are right, there is nothing in this to persuade you that I would give my life to spare you a single tear."

"Sir!" said Julia, whose heart throbbed with indiscribable feelings.

"I must tell you all, madame," resumed Montéclain eagerly. "If I have delayed to proclaim the truth, it is because I have hoped to save the poor woman also, whom we have both come here to seek."

"And if it be possible to save her, sir, I beg you will do it."

"I confess to you that her absence leaves me in a most cruel suspense. Yet by retarding your justification until to-morrow, it might be possible—"

"Ah! sir," cried Julia eagerly, "now that I know I have some one to defend me, I can wait."

She stopped, filled with confusion, at this lively emotion of confidence.

"Ah! thank you, thank you, madame, thank you," said Montéclain, with overflowing pride, "you confide your honor to me, you commit to my faith, this treasure of purity and innocence, thank you, I shall bear it in my heart, as a chaste and sacred deposit, as I would bear the honor of my sister if I had one, of my mother if she were still living. I will restore it to you madame, pure, and bright, and worthy of you. But add yet more to this confidence, and permit me to save you entirely."

"Is it not enough that you destroy the calumny by which I am pursued?"

"No, madame, this calumny has been too cleverly combined not to render it necessary to trace it back to the calumniator, and brand her with her infamy. Permit me to speak to you with open heart, as a man of honour, to the woman he respects, whose fortune and life he would extricate from these reptiles, who may not always be crushed perhaps with the same facility. There is a woman, madame, who detests your beauty, your mind, your virtue; a woman, who has, perhaps, some right to seek to punish in you an injury of which you are ignorant."

"Me?"

"Yes, you, madame; permit me to conceal the nature of this injury, you would not understand it. Know this much only, that of the two offenders, one was M. Amab, the other your brother; she has punished the first, by rendering an honourable name contemptible; in you, she would punish the second of her insulters. The report she has spread is her first attempt; but it is not enough to destroy her plans, she must suffer and atone for the shame of them. Were I to produce to-morrow the proofs which exonerate you, it would suffice her to say in excuse, that she had believed in appearances which had deceived everybody; and for those who do not know her, this excuse would be sufficient. This attempt having failed would give birth to another. She will never rest until she has either produced your ruin, or met with her own.

"But, sir," returned the trembling Julia, "what can she invent more infamous?"

"Madam," said Montéclain, "with a skill you do not suspect, she has enchained to her cause, Champmortain and Brias, two honourable men, whose lives and happiness she holds in her hands; she has joined to these the unfortunate Sylvia, whom she seeks to ruin, that in her she may acquire an accomplice; she can excite against you, the brutal jealousy of Hector de Montaleu; in fact, the plot in which she hopes to take you is so well constructed, that she may perhaps convert into your enemy, a man whom you do not know, who has only seen you once, and who more than all those who surround you, has need of your disgrace, to obtain his object."

"But who, sir, who is he then?"—said Julia terrified.

"Colonel Thomas Rien, madam."

"He? the stranger who arrived here yesterday?"

"He, madam, to whom she can offer the choice between your ruin, and that of the hopes of his whole life, and who in spite of honour, will perhaps decide against you."

"But what will become of me then, sir? Who will protect me?" said Julia, in tears.

"I was Monrion's friend, madam; give me your hand, as to a brother, and in the name of all that is most holy, I swear to you that if this woman had stirred up against you all the interests, and all the hatreds of the universe, I would baffle and defeat her designs, and replace you radiant and honoured in the place from which she seeks to make you fall."

"Ah! sir, so much interest testified by a man who does not know me, affects, astonishes, and almost renders me proud; but I know not if, in my position, I can accept a protection like yours."

"You can, madam, for I deserve it. A life marked by too many follies, perhaps, would authorize a soul like yours to distrust a devotion which should declare itself inspired by the love which springs to life beneath your glances, like flowers beneath the sun; but if the Marquis de Montéclain has lost the right to inspire belief in a too tender passion, he has at least preserved that of being considered an honest man, he deserves to be every one's friend, and it is with this title that he says to you; 'Confide yourself to him.'"

"Well! be it so, sir," said Julia, rising up with

confidence. "I trust myself to you. I accept the succour you offer me, and I tell you fearlessly, that I shall be happy in the gratitude I shall owe you. Already, sir, you have restored strength and confidence to my soul. It is so pleasant to believe in the existence of generous and disinterested hearts, that you have almost consoled me for the misfortune which has befallen me. I am but a poor child, an orphan—but the prayers of innocence are precious in God's sight, and I, who can do nothing to thank you, will at least pray for you."

Montéclain seemed about to speak; but he stopped himself immediately, and looked at Julia; then, after a moment's silent contemplation, he exclaimed:

"Oh! madam, you would inspire the most infamous with honour, the most cowardly with courage; go in peace, madam, and depend on me."

As he bowed to salute her, Julia held out her hand to him; he still retained it, when the door opened, and the colonel appeared with Bricord.

They seemed much surprised at this meeting.

"Pardon me," said the colonel, "I accompanied Bricord, who was coming here to know if his wife had not returned."

"You have not found her then," said Montéclain.

"No, my lord," returned Bricord, "no more than you who sent to inquire for her this morning, or the countess, who wanted to speak to her, it seems, since she has come so far as our house."

"Well! said Montéclain, "since all our researches are useless, let us return to the chase."

"Let us wait for it rather—," said the colonel, whose eager look examined alternately the agitation of Julia, and the affected indifference of Montéclain. "It seems to me that it cannot be far off."

"You are right. In truth," said the marquis, "for a boar hunt, it appears to me, it has been carried on very silently."

"It is possible, my lord," said Bricord, "perhaps there is some one who wished to surprise people here, who are not here."

"Adieu, M. Bricord," said Julia; "I wished to speak to your wife, but I think now there is no occasion to do so."

She bowed to the colonel and Montéclain; the latter offered her his hand, and said as he conducted her towards her carriage:

"I must warn you of all, madame, our meeting may perhaps be misrepresented like your good action."

"How so, sir?"

"They may see in it a meeting concerted between us—"

"And if it were so, sir, where would be the harm?"

Montéclain dared not reply. He feared to affect the candour of her soul, by telling her what they might suppose.

Madame de Monrion had reached the farm-door, where her carriage was stationed, and her servant was opening the door of it, when suddenly there appeared on the road, Brias, Amab, Champmortain, Hector, Felina, and Madame de Champmortain. At the sight of Julia and Montéclain, they all stopped: astonished, wondering, and stealthy looks were exchanged, and by some incredible cowardice, only one of these men dared to bow to Madame de Monrion; this was Hector. But the cold look and haughty salute which Julia returned him, was but a poor requital for this interested deference."

"Ah! I understand you now," she said to Montéclain, "as she was getting into her carriage."

"And you do not fear this new slander?"

"Now, more than ever, my life and honor are in your hands," said Julia, "I have no fear, sir."

She got into her carriage, and was obliged to pass the cavalcade, which had drawn up along side of the road. Felina burst into a loud laugh, Sylvia tried to imitate her, whilst all the men kept their eyes cast down, so deeply were they conscious that they were countenancing an infamous transaction by their silence.

Hardly had Julia disappeared, when Montéclain, as if he had not seen the sneers exchanged between Felina and Madame de Champmortain, shouted joyously:

"To the hunt, gentlemen, now all to the hunt!"

---

## CHAPTER LXVIII.

### A RARE SUPPER.

THE dining-room of the castle de Montéclain was sparkling with lights which were reflected on the gilding of a magnificent canopy, and darted emerald and ruby-coloured rays across the Bohemian glasses, with which the table was loaded. The wines were numerous and choice, the viands as exquisite as they were abundant; ten assiduous domestics constantly directed by their master's eye, every moment strove to provoke with wine and meat the appetites of the guests; gaiety encircled the table.

The hunt had been crowned by the animal standing at bay, in first-rate style, when Montéclain had redeemed the promise made to Hector de Montaleu in the morning, by killing the boar with his own hand. To the hunting party were joined at dinner, M. and Madame de Rudesgens. Thus all the inhabitants of the Lavordun valley were assembled, except the Marquis de Montaleu, and Madame de Monrion.

They had reached the second course, that period of the repast when the appetite, over-excited by violent exercise, is partially appeased, and the choicest morsels are superseded in the mouths of the guests, by a *bon mot*.

They were conversing, they were beginning to joke, and the genial gaiety of the master of the house, the excellence of the wines, and that freedom of the country, which is never felt in town parties, gave a noisy feverish tone to the general gaiety, which might have raised a suspicion that, but for the presence of Madame de Rudesgens and Madame de Champmortain, it had been easy to turn a joyous feast into a frantic revel.

Hector de Montaleu was already growing clamorous.

M. de Rudesgens, spruce, playful, half recumbent in his chair, flung into the general conversation a thousand delicious souvenirs, uttered in the shrillest tone of feeble treble; anon in the lowest and most familiar voice, the aged cupid would insinuate the most satanic declarations into Felina's ear. In her turn, she excited the ancient Annibal by appearing charmingly embarrassed, whilst she lulled the watchful jealousy of Champtmortain by soft semi-fervent glances, which seemed to dedicate to him the happiness she felt in being thought so beautiful.

Sylvia was radiant with a strange transcendant happiness hitherto unfelt, of which Brias doubtless alone divined the cause; for, in their language there were a thousand words indifferent to all around, which they referred to each other by keen intelligent smiles. Even Amab, relaxing from his wonted mood, suffered himself to be borne along by the general gaiety, like a man who is resolved to avail himself of whatever amusement life could yet bestow; he sat near Madame de Rudesgens, in whom his eager politeness aroused such sweet emotions, that she forgot to watch over her fickle and erratic lord. Besides, had not Felina told her, that if she intended to seduce Amab, she should be obliged to revenge herself on the charming Annibal. The old Artémise was therefore placed upon a par with one of the most renowned Parisian beauties.

The colonel alone seemed unwilling to give himself up to mirth, though he was always ready with a repartée.

As to Montéclain, he stirred up the fire of conversation with unwearied activity, addressing his guests collectively and individually. It was one of those delightful banquets, of which we all carry away with us a pleasant remembrance without being able to say precisely whence it sprung.

Yet, by a strange acquiescence there was one name, known to all the guests, an adventure interesting to all, which, as if by common consent, had been discarded from the thousand subjects which had engaged the conversation; it seemed as if every one hesitated to take the first step on that burning and rugged ground, with its sudden shelves and precipices. It was, and it could have been no other—the dull and burly Hector, who first ran his head roughly against the barrier, which apparently protected this dangerous soil.

The conversation had returned to Montéclain's triumph, and the guests did not spare Hector on his misfortune.

"Bah!" he exclaimed, "it is frequently with hunting as with cards: the best hands fall to the dullest. According to all rules of sport, the beast should have taken his course in the direction of Saint-Faron; but, no such thing; while I strained my horse to follow the track, the boar changes his direction, brings us back to the point whence we set out after three leagues of useless running, and is suddenly checked on the Lavordun farm, where Montéclain's horse was resting at his ease, whilst his master was conversing with Madame de Monion.

That circumstance, and that name stopped the conversation in every mouth; each look was turned towards Montéclain. There was a moment of singular silence.

Every one was desirous of questioning the master of the house, on this mysterious meeting, but no one dared. Montéclain seemed regardless of the incidents.

"I must acknowledge it," he said, in the most careless tone, "chance rendered my game a fine one."

"Yes, indeed," returned Felina, "it favoured you in every way, for it occasioned you to meet with the charming countess. How is the child? I heard that you went yesterday to inquire about it."

"It is quite well," said Montéclain, as if speaking on a very indifferent subject.

"And the mother," said Madame de Rudesgens bitterly, "is wonderfully well, also it appears—"

"I cannot give you any intelligence respecting her," said Montéclain, "for I do not know where she is—"

Hector turned pale, and Sylvia took up the thread of the conversation:

"Nevertheless, she looked quite glowing as she was leaving the Lavordun farm."

At this remark, Montéclain burst into a laugh so joyous, so prolonged, and breathless, that every one was hushed into silence.

"What! madame," he said to Silvia, "what, a woman like you, with a mind so just, is it possible that you can have been led to believe this fable for a moment, which is not even malevolent, so stupid, so clumsy it is! Who the deuce then has invented this absurdity?" he resumed, continuing to laugh; "it is quite pitiful. I can forgive its wickedness, but not its stupidity. For indeed, pardon the word —but it is stupid—it is stupid."

Felina grew pale in her turn.

"And how," she asked, "do you explain this strange concurrence of circumstances? The flight to Issoudun, the return, the child brought back by Madame de Monrion? Perhaps you could give us some excellent information on the subject; for you are acquainted with the nurse—"

"And you have private interviews with Madame de Monrion," cried M. de Rudesgens, "happy mortal that you are."

"Ah! this is marvellous," said Montéclain, laughing with still more hilarity and mirth; "is it perchance after accusing the venerable uncle of our heroic Hector, that you now desire to make me likewise one of the party?—Ah! poor Madame de Monrion!—"

"It is a serious affair, notwithstanding," said Thomas.

"A ridiculous one, my dear colonel, a ridiculous one, that is all."

"You are very sure then that the countess is innocent?" said Felina.

"But we all are so," said Montéclain, "and you above all—Hector as much as you, and the proof is, that he went yesterday to solicit her hand—and you also, colonel, you know she is innocent."

"But once more then," said Brias, "how do you explain the departure, the return, and this child?"

"Hold," said Montéclain, "that reminds me of a rather singular story which was related to me in Germany, I think;—it very much resembles this."

"Let us hear it," said M. de Rudesgens, "a scandalous story—bravo!"

"Nevertheless," said Madame de Rudesgens, "I hope that M. de Montéclain—"

"Oh! madam," replied the latter, in a peculiar manner, "re-assure yourself, I will be discreet and prudent."

"We are waiting," said M. de Rudesgens.

"Well then," resumed Montéclain, "it was in the year 1811 or 12, at Cologne—"

At that name and date, Felina and the colonel were confounded, M. de Rudesgens raised his head, and Madame de Rudesgens opened her eyes with unspeakable terror.

"Two young girls at that city, were courted by two French noblemen—"

"Ta, ta, ta," said M. de Rudesgens; "that was in our time, Artémise—we ought to have some notion about it—"

"One of them was very rich, and the other very poor," continued Montéclain, "and by a just compensation, the rich young lady was admired by the poor noblemen, and the poor girl by the rich one—"

"Ah! but—but—but—that is singular," said M. de Rudesgens, while his wife with disordered looks, her whole body trembling, seemed ready to lose all consciousness, "What do you say about it, Artémise?"

"I say," replied Madame de Rudesgens, in an almost inarticulate voice, "that M. de Montéclain has no doubt excellent reasons for believing Madame de Monrion's innocence, and that for my part, I am quite of his opinion. There has been a mistake—or a calumny."

Felina fixed a serpent look on Madame de Rudesgens, saying to her in a bitter voice:

"Do you think so, madam?"

The colonel, on his side, looked menacingly at the poor woman, and added in an agitated tone:

"You think Madame de Monrion is suffering for the fault of another; you think that like the unhappy Sophia Muller—"

On hearing this name, Madame de Rudesgens looked with terror at the colonel; it seemed to her

that his face was suddenly lit up; she uttered a sharp cry, and then fainted away.

Sylvia, much alarmed, ran to her mother, while Felina looked at her with glad and threatening curiosity.

The colonel remained lost in reflection; Brias and Champmortain appeared to be dreaming, while M. de Rudesgens, went up to one and all, crying out:—

"But what does it all mean? what is the matter with Artémise?—Tell us Montéclain, what the devil was it happened at Cologne?"

"It is dreadfully warm in this dining room," said Montéclain, open the windows."

"But I will know," said M. de Rudesgens.

"What?"

"The story of Cologne."

"It would not be strong enough," said Montéclain, with imperturable coolness; "some salts, bring some salts."

"But," resumed M. de Rudesgens, "I do not speak to you of Eau de Cologne, I want to hear the story."

"Good," replied the other, it was an invention—I should not have been able to proceed any further with it."

In the meantime Madame de Rudesgens came to her senses, and Montéclain approaching her, said softly:

"I ask you a thousand pardons, I always forbid my people to put flowers in this apartment. That has made you ill. But you are better, are you not?"

Then as Madame de Rudesgens fixed on him a frightened look:

"Fear nothing," he said in a low tone.

This incident had disturbed the banquet. Madame de Rudesgens asked permission to retire.

"Colonel," said Felina approaching Thomas, "shall we take you back to your house?"

"No," replied Thomas who appeared as thoughtful as the rest, "I shall stay where I am."

"I must see you however."

"To-morrow."

"No, this night."

"Where, then?"

"At the colliery, in two hours."

"I will be there."

Amab had listened to and observed all.

During this dialogue Montéclain, assisted by Sylvia, was escorting M. and Madame de Rudesgens to their carriage.

"Accompany your mother," said he to Sylvia, "and tell her not to be alarmed."

A moment after he returned with Amab, Brias, Champmortain, the colonel, and Hector de Montaleu.

"M. de Montéclain," said the colonel, "I must ask for a private interview."

"With me?" said Montéclain, "I shall be at your command whenever you please."

"Immediately!"

"That is impossible," said Montéclain, "I have a very pressing matter to settle first."

He rang the bell violently.

"Well!" he said to the servant who entered immediately, "what news from the farm?"

"Nothing, except that Bricord has searched everywhere about it, without finding his wife."

The servant went out.

"Do you know what can have become of her, Champmortain?" said Montéclain rocking himself to and fro.

"I; I did not even know that she had disappeared."

"And you, Brias?"

"I cannot understand it at all."

"And you, Hector de Montaleu, have you no idea what has become of Madame Bricord?"

"I! I!" said Hector, "I have not quitted the chase all day."

"M. de Montéclain," said the colonel impatiently, "the subject on which I have to speak to you is, perhaps, more important than the search for this unfortunate woman!"

"I do not think so," said Montéclain, fixing at the same time a piercing look on Montaleu's disordered countenance. "Gentlemen," he added, "we must find the unhappy Léda; it must be done, and I entreat you to lend me your help."

"Why do you take so deep an interest in it?" said Champmortain.

"I will tell you," returned Montéclain, "listen to me well. The tale that I began at table, and which was interrupted by Madame de Rudesgens' fainting away, would have made you understand under borrowed names, the misfortune which has befallen Madame de Monrion. The poor child is suffering from the fault of another."

"And what woman is base enough," cried the colonel, "to let another be calumniated in her place?"

"A woman sufficiently timid and abandoned was found to do so formerly," replied Montéclain, "but the unfortunate creature who is the cause of it to-day must not be thus accused; she sought to save by her silence, not herself, but her accomplice."

"Do you not know him; can you not name him?" said Brias, looking scornfully at Hector.

"No," said Montéclain contemptuously. "When the accusation is one of cowardice, I must have certain, incontestible proofs."

"How is it," said Champmortain, "that knowing the name of the mother, and the child, you are ignorant of the father's?"

"This is how," replied Montéclain. "This is what happened six months ago in this country."

Thereupon he related to them the history of the letter of which Madame de Monrion had so generously concealed from Bricord. He added how this letter had been presented to him by the farmer, and how he had himself assisted in this noble subterfuge.

"And do you still possess that letter?" cried Brias.

"Yes."

"What! holding in your hands Madame de Monrion's justification, you have not produced it?" said Amab.

"No, gentlemen, no, and I demand from you all your words of honour that you will not make known this justification until the moment I shall tell you to do so."

"So be it!" they replied.

"Have the kindness to listen to this letter, and you will understand my motives."

Montéclain drew a letter from his pocket, and read as follows:

"When you shall read this letter, Peter, you will have a wife no longer. Do not let this afflict you, for I deliver you from one who was unworthy of you. In your absence, I yielded to the seductions of a man who has punished me for it, by his base desertion. The day is come when my crime can no longer be concealed; perhaps you would forgive me, for you are good and great; but you would not forgive him, who has dishonoured me, and had I lived, you would at last have wrested from me the secret of his name. All infamous as he is (and Montéclain laid great emphasis on these words), all infamous as he is, I still love him yet too fondly to deliver him up to your vengeance, and prefer carrying with me to my grave his name, and the proof, soon a living one, of my adultery. Adieu."

Montéclain stopped, and looked at his auditors, who were listening to him with profound surprise.

"This letter," he added, in an agitated voice, "bears the date of the 21st of October, of last year. It is the day on which it was found by the husband, the day it was shewn to Madame de Monrion, the day it was brought to me. On that very night, the woman you suffered to be driven from your house, Champmortain, set out alone in pursuit of the unfortunate creature bent on self-destruction, consoled her, brought away this child, provided it with a nurse, and imposing silence on the mother restored her to her husband."

"But she must know the accusation, which weighs upon her benefactress?" said Brias.

"Yes," said Montéclain, "and doubtless it is on that account she has taken flight; on that account she has hid herself; for she knows well it is death to her. Unless," he added, looking at Montaleu, she has forestalled her husband's vengeance, by accomplishing to-day the fatal design she announced in this letter, six months ago."

"Do you fear it then?" said the colonel.

"I know not what to think of the unfortunate creature. But what do you think, gentlemen, of him whom she does not name, who, knowing that an innocent woman is the victim of a crime in which he has shared, has not justified her?"

Montéclain's looks here wandered round the listening group, but were fixed for a moment on Montaleu, whose face had assumed an impassive look.

"I think he is a coward," said Brias.

"So do I," said the colonel.

"Excuse me," said Champmortain; "there is perhaps an excuse for his conduct; do not forget that he could not justify Madame de Monrion, without ruining the woman who gave herself up to him."

"Ah!" rejoined Montéclain, bitterly, "you see then, gentlemen, that it is a dangerous thing, and one which may lead to the most cowardly actions, to seduce the wife of another; that the hour may come, when to guard the secret of the imprudent woman who has yielded herself to you, you may be compelled to behave with infamy"

"And what would you do were you in the place of the man you speak of, with such contempt?" said Hector de Montaleu, between his clenched teeth."

"I would not do what you have done, viscount," said Montéclain, "looking him full in the face; I would not have gone to ask for the victim's hand."

"So then," said Champmortain, "Montaleu, you are the man—?"

Hector was on the point of answering; but he stopped himself suddenly, a livid paleness covered his face, and he replied, after a moment's silence:

"But Montéclain is mad. I am hardly acquainted with this Leda, and do not know what has become of her."

"Indeed?" said Montéclain, fixing on Hector an anxious and dismayed look.

Then he seemed to drive away the idea which had crossed his mind, and resumed, in a firm but more cordial tone:

"Viscount, no one here doubts your courage. I do not think, then, it is fear which makes you silent, but you must take some resolution. You wish to save Léda, I wish it likewise, it is for that reason I brought Bricord away yesterday evening, it is for that I have sent so often to inquire for his wife at the farm, it is for that I went there myself. More interested than I can be to save her, you have anticipated me, you have concealed Léda somewhere. It is well—but you should not stop there, you must conclude Madame de Monrion's justification by declaring and signing the truth before us all. You must then leave this country, and take with you the unfortunate Léda to Paris, to some foreign country, or where you will, and though it may happen through you, that an honest man may die of grief, this victim will at least have been spared."

"M. de Montéclain," said Hector, whose face wore a frightful expression of ferocity, "I thank you for your advice, but do not accept it. I have nothing to say, nothing to declare. I have solicited Madame de Monrion's hand, because in my eyes she is superior to calumny. But I will not dishonour another woman by boasting of favours I have never obtained. Which of you dare affirm that I am the lover of Madame Bricord?"

The colonel and Brias, both started simultaneously as if to speak—"

But Montéclain prevented them by exclaiming:

"I, sir, I say it—"

"And I answer that you lie," said Hector, passionately.

Montéclain sat and looked so confounded, that he did not immediately reply to this gross insult. He remained immoveable at first, then, after quietly folding the letter which he held in his hand, he walked about the drawing-room, pulled a bell, and finally approached Thomas:

"Colonel," he said, "you are Bricord's friend, I entrust this letter to you, it belongs to him. I leave it to your prudence to choose the moment for returning it to the unhappy man, though I have reason to suspect that the unfortunate Léda has nothing more to fear from the danger of this revelation."

As Montéclain finished these words, the domestic he had rung for appeared.

"Shew M. de Montaleu to the door," said Montéclain without even turning towards Hector.

"M. de Montéclain, I shall be at your orders when you will."

"John," said Montéclain, speaking again to the domestic, "go and fetch some help, and take M. de Montaleu away."

"Montéclain," cried Hector, with blood in his eyes, his mouth full of foam, as he advanced towards him with upraised fist, "you are a base villain, and I will chastise you."

"Come, come," said Montéclain in a low voice, "you think you have to do with poor Léda."

Montaleu drew back terrified; he cast on all those who surrounded him a look full of rage and menace, while Montéclain, with his finger, pointed to the door. A deep and stifled roar gushed from the chest of the colossus; he strove to speak, but could utter nothing but inarticulate sounds, and he rushed out of the apartment.

The spectators of this scene were amazed, confounded by its result. Brias was the first to testify his astonishment.

"What;" said he, "you, Montéclain, you receive the lie from this clown? You rest contented with driving him from your house, as old Montaleu might have done."

"Brias," returned Montéclain sadly, "I will not interfere with the rights of the executioner."

A general cry of horror responded to this observation.

"What do you say?" cried Champmortain.

"I say that in order to be so convinced of Léda's silence, Montaleu must have murdered her."

There was a general exclamation.

"Not a word of all this, gentlemen, night is a good adviser, we will see each other again to-morrow; but I suppose there is not one among you who is not convinced of Madame de Monrion's innocence; I ask nothing of you, but you owe her some reparation."

"And she shall have it," said Champmortain.

"I swear she shall," said Brias."

"To-morrow," resumed Champmortain, "I and those of my family who have offended her will go and testify our respect. And as to this wretch, Hector—"

"You will be silent," said Montéclain. "As yet we have no proofs. Colonel, you will not restore this letter to Bricord until you have shown it to M. de Montaleu; if I had been able to bear it myself and accompany these gentlemen, I would not have yielded to any one the right of avenging this base slander against Madame de Monrion; but you know that my relations with M. de Montaleu—"

"Exactly so," said Brias. "At what hour would the colonel like us to wait upon him?"

"You will find me at M. de Montaleu's, doubtless," said the colonel. "I have to pay him a visit."

"To-morrow, then."

"Now, colonel," said Montéclain, "I am at your service."

Here Amab, Champmortain, and Brias, took their departure; the colonel and Montéclain were left alone together.

## CHAPTER LXIX.

### CRIME FOLLOWS CRIME.

THE night was dull and gloomy; the wind shook the forest trees somewhat roughly, and awoke them to a plaintive murmur, which, had it been beneath a clear blue firmament, might, perhaps, have been listened to as a soft song; but beneath the dark and dismal sky which enveloped nature, sounded on the ears like a desolate groan. Felina had just reached the outside of the hut designated by the name of the *colliery*. She approached it cautiously, and listened a long while, her ear riveted to the door. Several times she thought she heard painful sighs; but the continual rustling of the trees prevented her distinguishing whether these lamentations came from the inside or the outside of the cabin. In order to convince herself that she was not mistaken, she knocked loudly at the door, and at the same instant a more distinct cry informed her there was some one within. Then she fixed her lips to the crevices of the door, and called softly:

"Léda! Léda!"

No one answered.

"Léda," resumed Felina, "it is a friend; it is some one who wishes to save you."

Still the same silence.

"Let me in," continued Felina, "I am a woman, do not be afraid."

All remained silent.

Felina thought she had deceived herself; but, at the same moment, the fall of a piece of furniture within the hut convinced her that some one was shut up in the cottage. She listened more attentively. A deep groan reached her ear.

Felina shuddered. That morning on meeting Hector in the neighbourhood of the colliery, she surmised that he had just left Léda. The agitation of Montaleu made her likewise suspect that some scene of violence had passed between them. Moreover, she heard during the hunt that Léda had disappeared, and she had no doubt that the poor woman was concealed in the colliery. But the idea of a crime had not yet presented itself to her mind.

She sought on every side for some place where she might make herself better heard. But as we have said, this cabin had no other accessible entrance than the door, and the holes opened in the roof to let in the light were much too high for Felina to reach. For a moment she seemed to hesitate, but her resolution was soon taken; she went as far as her carriage, which had remained hidden at some distance from the colliery, and a moment after returned with the deaf and dumb coachman, who usually drove her. A sign to him from Felina was sufficient to explain her wish to enter the cottage. The deaf and dumb man went quickly round it, shook the door violently, and having convinced himself that it was strong enough to resist the most violent attempts, he availed himself of the rough branches which overgrew the cabin, and in an instant stood upon the roof.

He had soon discovered and broken one of the small windows made in the roof, and disappeared by that opening. Almost immediately a hoarse savage cry gave Felina warning that the deaf and dumb man had discovered something extraordinary. He reappeared a moment after, and sprang to the ground, making signs of the keenest terror. Felina did not give him time to explain the cause of his alarm; she knew it. She made him understand that he must force the door, or find some means of withdrawing from the cabin the unfortunate creature he had found there. The man returned to the carriage and brought out a key, a turnscrew, with all the implements generally employed to repair an accident on the road; he then re-entered the colliery by the broken pane. Felina soon heard him busily employed, and a quarter of an hour had not elapsed before the door was opened. Felina went eagerly inside, and immediately stumbled against a body lying on the ground; she lifted it up, life had not forsaken it; she caused the poor wounded creature to inhale some salts, for it was Léda whom she had thus discovered; almost immediately the unhappy woman heaved a deep sigh, and some confused words escaped her, among which Felina only heard:

"Mercy! mercy!"

To whom were these words addressed? To the terrible lover, come as she believed to consummate his crime? Or to the husband whose vengeance had discovered her? It mattered little to Felina. At a fresh signal from her, the dumb man lifted up poor Léda, and conveyed her to the carriage. Felina seated herself by her side, and the equipage proceeded rapidly towards Madame Amab's dwelling. But, instead of entering directly into the chateau, they stopped at a little door opening on the forest. The deaf and dumb man again took Léda in his arms and carried her to a private staircase which went up to Felina's room. There they placed the wounded female, who was received by Dorothy, Madame Amab's faithful attendant, and they were at length able to judge of the state she was in: the face and arms were covered with bruises, the head was swollen, the eyes almost starting from their sockets. Poor woman! she had long dreamt of love under its most romantic forms; often had foreseen that death might come to her in vengeance, or in chastisement, and in this case imagination had shewn her the poignard, or the poison draught, as the agent of this deserved punishment. Alas! even this illusion was not realized, and the rude churl on whom she had lavished all the tenderness of her soul, had crushed her brutally beneath his iron grip.

"Dorothy," said Felina, "put this unfortunate creature into my boudoir. That is sufficient to tell you that no one must know of her presence here. There must be everything she requires in the chateau. I suppose leeches will be sufficient. When she has regained her senses, soothe her, tell her she has nothing to fear from any one, but do not inform her where she is. I will question her when I return."

"Madame is going out again, then?"

"Yes, I must see the colonel this very night. Oh! how strange it is," she added, "everything sooner or later seems to be discovered—"

The maid looked at her mistress with an astonishment that sufficiently proclaimed she had never seen her so agitated.

"Ah!" resumed Felina, lifting to heaven her flashing eyes, "now, indeed, I shall be revenged."

She went into her room, took from a casket a dagger and a pair of small pistols, which she carefully examined.

"When M. Amab comes home, what shall I tell him?" said the maid.

"That I am asleep, as usual."

"But nobody has seen you come in—"

"True."

She rang the bell: a servant entered; she desired him to call the cook. He came; she gave him some trifling orders, and having sufficiently made known that she had returned, she said to her maid:

"As to the carriage, you will say that I sent it back to M. de Montéclain's, to fetch my husband. Lutz will have lost himself in the forest. I will give him his lesson."

While speaking thus, she dressed herself in man's clothes, with that marvellous rapidity which characterized alike her slightest actions, and her most important resolutions.

Some minutes after, she again got into her carriage, and resumed her way to the colliery.

The carriage stopped at some distance as before: she alighted by herself, with her weapons, and directed her steps towards the hut she had recently quitted. Few, even of the bravest men would have exposed themselves to Felina's situation, for she had foreseen that Montaleu would take advantage of the night to return to the colliery, and he was the person she sought for at this moment. In fact, the hour of the colonel's probable arrival was still distant. Within a few paces of the cabin she drew forth her dagger, armed herself with one of her pistols, and leaning her back against a tree, called out in a clear voice:

"Monsieur Hector de Montaleu!"

She had hardly uttered these words when Hector, coming out of the cabin, approached the spot where his name had been pronounced.

"This way!" resumed Felina. "Fear nothing; It is I, Madame Amab."

"You!" said Montaleu, "you! And how came you here? Oh! if I knew—" he added, advancing towards her.

"M. Hector de Montaleu, replied Felina, "take care; I am prepared to blow your brains out, however difficult it may be."

"What are you come here for?" said Hector, who was not alarmed by this threat.

"I am come to offer you a treaty of alliance. Therefore, let us have a friendly explanation."

Hector appeared to hesitate.

"Well!" he said, "will you come into this cabin?—"

"Why not?" replied Felina; "it does not seem to detain the prisoners confined in it."

"You know what has become of Léda then?" said Hector, alarmed.

"She is in my house; quite ready to denounce you, if I have not returned in two hours; quite ready to keep silence if I tell her you consent to what she expects from you."

"How did you discover her?"

"We have not time to enter into all these explanations. Léda is in my power; that is all. I can ruin, or save you. It is for you to decide whether you will serve me, or be my enemy."

"Serve you in what?" said Montaleu; "what can I do now? I am about to be accused—"

"By whom? by Léda? "she will not do it."

"No, but by Montéclain, who suspects me, who will say—"

"What will he say against the testimony of Léda herself?"

"But will she pardon me then?"

"She will pardon you if I wish it," said Felina.

"And what must I do then to insure your keeping her quiet?"

"Madame de Monrion must be ruined."

"She, whose hand I have demanded?"

"Yes, the woman who knows this child belongs to you, whose look this morning should have warned you that she has prepared an insulting refusal."

"But then, if she knows it, she will tell it."

"She must be able to prove it, and when Léda is no longer there to make any confession, when you firmly deny this charge, it will fall back upon her, and add to the shame of her weakness, that of having accused the innocent."

"You deceive yourself," returned Hector, "there is a letter which exculpates Madame de Monrion."

"What letter?" said Felina, in an agitated voice.

"The letter that this fool Léda wrote to her husband the day she left the farm to kill herself, when she was so charitably succoured by Madame de Monrion. For," said Hector, in an almost feeling voice, "the poor woman's generous action has cost her very dear."

"But the letter, the letter," replied Felina, impatiently.

"Well! it is in that letter, which Bricord asked Madame de Monrion to read to him, that Léda declares she shall soon be a mother."

"I do not understand you. Then Julia did not read this letter to the farmer?"

"No. Pitying Léda, she told Bricord that his wife informed him she was gone to visit her sick mother. Then it was she ran after her, and—"

"Ah! now I understand. Julia then has this letter in her possession?"

"No; for Bricord, mistrusting Madame de Monrion, carried it to Montéclain, who deceived him by the same ruse as Julia."

"And he has it!" cried Felina, in an accent of angry despair. "Ah! that man—that man—must I always find him in my path!"

"Oh! as to him," returned Victor, "that is my business. Give me some assurance that I shall not be sought after for having ill-used Léda in a moment of angry feeling."

"Come, now," said Felina, "do not hide the truth by subterfuge; you mean to say: 'for having wished to kill her.' Well! I will save you from this danger, I; and in your turn, what will you do to Montéclain?"

"Oh! as to him I will kill him outright," said Hector, passionately.

"It is possible, but in the mean time he will save Madame de Monrion, thanks to this letter."

"He has it no longer."

"He no longer has it!" cried Felina, joyfully; "but who then?"

"He has given it to Colonel Thomas Rien, that he may return it to Bricord."

"To Thomas?" said Felina, in a low voice; "to him?"

"Yes. But, that letter, I care very little about it, for, after all, if it exonerates Madame de Monrion by saying to whom the child belongs, it does not accuse me."

"But it saves them," returned Felina, "and this letter, I want to have it, I will have it!"

"And by what means?"

"The colonel is coming here presently. I will ask him for it."

"And if he refuses you."

"He will not refuse me."

"But in case it should so happen?"

"He will not refuse me I tell you. Ah! if he dared, if he should prefer the honour of this Julia, to that of — Oh! no, no, let him not refuse me that; for then he would be my deadliest enemy."

"And then your vengeance would escape you."

"Yes," said Felina, "it would escape me, and I warn you it is not merely to save you that I will force Léda to be silent."

"What!" said Hector, "you would suffer her to accuse me?"

"Why should I prevent her? What does all this matter to me, the moment my revenge is thwarted by that letter?"

Hector advanced a few steps in the wood; he returned, went away again, and ended by saying:

"You shall have the letter, you shall have it."

Felina did not reply. Montaleu's brutal ferocity raised a feeling of terror in that soul, which crime itself could not have awakened.

"He will give it me!" she resumed, after a moment's silence. Yes, yes, he is too eager for his own vengeance to refuse it me."

"We shall see," said Montaleu.

"Silence!" exclaimed Felina. "Do you not hear the sound of a horse?"

"Yes," said Hector, "it is he."

"Go back into the cabin, and do not come out till I call you."

"How will you call me?"

"I will exclaim, *Adieu colonel.*"

"Very well."

Montaleu returned into the colliery. Felina went back to the green lane, but behind her she heard the sharp click of a gun, which was being tried.

She was frightened, and ready to retrace her footsteps; but it was too late; the colonel had stopped, and dismounted from his horse.

The next moment Felina was beside him.

---

## CHAPTER LXX.

### AN OLD STORY.

NEARLY two hours before this meeting, Colonel Thomas Rien was left alone with Montéclain; the colonel dull, thoughtful, absent; Montéclain, careless, free, and entirely at his ease.

"M. Montéclain," said the colonel, "you understand the explanation that I expect from you."

Montéclain replied only by nodding assent. He rang the bell.

"Tea and pipes," said he, "and let no one interrupt us on any account."

"M. the colonel's spahi is down stairs," said the servant, "and wishes to know if he is to wait here, or go and walk?"

"Go and walk?" said Montéclain, looking at the colonel, who was embarrassed, for this Aly Muley's method of asking whether he should go in pursuit of of Hector de Montaleu.

"Tell him to wait for me," replied the colonel, hastily, too eager for the explanation which he expected from Montéclain to think about Hector.

Montéclain signed to his servant, and the tea and pipes which he had ordered were immediately brought. Montéclain took one of the pipes, and throwing himself carelessly on a divan, said to Thomas:

"Then, colonel, you wish to know what means this story of Cologne, the first lines of the first chapter of which I so learnedly quoted during the false gaiety of our supper, and the principal personage of which you have so impetuously named."

"Yes, I wish to know who told you of that fatal adventure which happened thirty years ago."

"And of which you have just made the discovery? It can be of little consequence to you to know from whom I learned it, provided that you are certain I am not ignorant of any of the particulars."

"Indeed?" said the colonel, blushing.

"Judge for yourself."

"It was in 1812. M. de Montaleu, then devoted to the service of Napoleon, as he has since been to that of Louis XVIII. and of Charles X., and as he is now to that of Louis-Philippe, exercised the office of Prefect at Cologne. He there met with two persons who interested him in different ways; for one he felt friendship, for the other, love. These two persons were Lord Annibal de Rudesgens and Miss Sophia Muller."

At the mention of the latter name, the colonel sighed deeply.

"At that time, Lord Annibal de Rudesgens was in a slight difficulty; he was smitten with the fortune of Mademoiselle Artémise Van Marken, the daughter of a contractor, strongly suspected of having sold immense quantities of merchandize which he had never delivered. I may mention, by the way, that the Emperor Napoleon adopted a policy on this subject which purists in sound morality, must deem hateful, and which, for my part, I admire from the bottom of my heart. Permit me to dwell upon this subject, because this opinion of the great man is that which has dictated my line of conduct even up to this day, and will dictate it in the affair which is now about to be disclosed."

"Explain yourself clearly."

"It was impossible that the Van Markens, whatever they might be, could steal by hundreds of thousands of francs, and by millions, without having accomplices among the generals of the armies, whose substance they pillaged on so large a scale. Napoleon knew this; but like that tutor of Louis XV., who pitilessly flogged a poor unfortunate child for the faults of his royal pupil, the emperor severely punished the civil pillagers, for the extortions committed by the military thieves. In the same manner as it appeared to the worshippers of monarchy, improper to submit the royal child to the punishment of the cane, so did Napoleon think it unsuitable to dishonour the glittering planets which he had drawn into the solar system, of which he was the centre."

"That is true," said the colonel, "and this is one of the dark spots in the bright career of that man, in whose genius so much justice resided."

"And still more good sense, believe me. Evil, it must be owned, is a guest so frequently found in the best reputed houses, that I think it is a greater misfortune to society to unveil it everywhere and always, than often, and in certain places, to hide it. The publicity of great offences is a principle of social dissolution, which we must of necessity renounce, unless we wish to see society fall into decay before half a century. If Napoleon had publicly branded all the men of his army and his administration who deserved this punishment, the gigantic power he had established, would not have lasted six months. Besides, colonel, whatever may be said, the great qualities of a man are considered to compensate for his faults or his vices. There is with me, and with all of us, an immense difference between the general who had gained a battle, the administrator who had organized a province, the learned man who had endowed the world with a useful discovery, and who abuse, the first his victory, the second his power, the last his science, to enrich themselves, there is, I maintain, an immense difference between these people and a sharper like this Van Marken, who, having performed nothing either illustrious or useful, has no excuse for his robbery."*

"This, no doubt, appears to you a very loose morality; but I believe it to be more useful than that strict consciencioùsness which in its miserable generality abstracts from the valor and position of the individual to condemn the single action."

"To make an end of these metaphysics, I enter on the business which engages our attention, and I say to you, there are several women seriously implicated. Madame de Rudesgens, already very guilty; Sylvia, about to become so; Léda, whose fault is glaring; and lastly, Felina. Madame de Rudesgens has for her excuse, the prescription, and that is a voucher in my eyes as it is in the eyes of the law. Sylvia has the misconduct of her husband for her palliation. Léda has her misfortune; but Felina, the fierce Felina has nothing to excuse her. I will save the rest if I can, and I will ruin her if necessary. I shall respect the position of the one, the temptation of the other; the misfortunes of the third; but I shall be pitiless towards the last named, who cannot throw into the scale a single hour of kindness, or even of affection, one charitable action, nothing, not even a great talent. In her, wickedness and adultery are as naked and hideous as theft was in the case of M. Van Marken. This granted, colonel, I continue my recital."

* This is bad logic. Whoever cheats other people, is a cheat; whoever robs other people is a thief, however great his former actions may have been. His other actions, indeed. His other actions have nothing to do with the case itself, for which we condemn him. When Dr. Dodd was hanged for forgery by George III., that great and good king did not look at his cloth, but his misdeed; and when Marshal Ney was shot for high treason, a long life of heroic actions did not prevent his execution. In both these cases the law stood paramount above the weakness of the human heart and the still greater weakness of the human understanding.

Thomas had listened with a dissatisfied attention to Montéclain's strange declaration of his principles, and his countenance was still more clouded when he so plainly expressed his hatred for Felina and his projects against her.

"I am listening to you," said he to Montéclain, coldly.

"This then is what happened. The emperor appointed a committee to examine into M. Van Marken's accounts, and it was whispered in the ear of the president of this committee that, although it might be quite necessary to examine the affairs of the contractor, he must not spy too closely into those of the officers, his accomplices. The result of this divided justice was, that nothing was thoroughly examined into, and that the president of the said committee, the virtuous Montaleu, could walk at his ease amidst all the money and dirt it was his business to rake up."

"Do you think he profited by it?"

"Not personally; but he enriched by this means the old friend with whom he had met at Cologne. Lord Annibal de Rudesgens, in love with Antémise Van Marken, saw with despair, in the ruin of the contractor, the ruin of his hopes. The ruined marquis wished to become rich; the rich girl wished to become a marchioness. Montalieu, who was the president of that committee, appointed to deprive Van Marken of his treasure, managed matters so well, that he found contracts of marriage hitherto unknown, imaginary documents left by the deceased wife of Van Marken, and constituting her daughter heiress to a fortune quite independent of the riches stolen by her father, so that the contractor, stripped of everything, disappeared in the dungeon of one of the Cologne prisons, whilst the beautiful Artémise remained on the surface of the soil, radiant with her millions, now become a legalized spoliation. The emperor had certainly some knowledge of this transaction, but the Marquis de Rudesgens married, recognised the emperor's authority, and took the oath of allegiance. The emperor was persuaded that this Annibal was worthy of his consideration: the eagle let fall his eyelids over the lightning of his glance, and this matter was concluded. Did you know all this, colonel?"

"You may imagine that this is not what interests me in the affair. The origin of M. de Rudesgens' fortune has nothing to do with my concerns."

"An enormous mistake, colonel, a mistake which you will acknowledge immediately, and which would drive you from the right road, if I did not enlighten you upon the very complicated turnings of this very simple story."

"I will hear you," replied the colonel.

"Pray observe," said Montéclain, putting his lips to a cup of tea, "that I am now relating external matters; I show you the front of the building, afterwards we shall examine the inside. Now, whilst the honorable M. de Montaleu contrived so rich a marriage for his friend Rudesgens, he cultivated on his own account, a tender passion of the first order. He had met on the other side of the Rhine, a beautiful young girl, a great enthusiast, very pensive—"

"Take care," interrupted Thomas in a firm and serious tone, "take care, you are speaking of my mother."

"I expected this observation," said Montéclain, with an ironical smile, "and I accept it, only colonel, do not forget it at the end of our conversation. In every explanation, I keep within the limits proposed to me, as in every duel I accept the weapons which it pleases my adversary to select. In warning me to be circumspect towards you, you oblige yourself to be so towards me. Do not forget it."

"To what does this recommendation tend?"

"You will see," said Montéclain, "I have told you that you will leave my house, either as a brother or an enemy."

Thomas appeared surprised, and repeated once more:

"I will hear you."

"M. de Montaleu met Miss Sophia Muller, beautiful, poor, and but ill protected by a father sunk into the most degrading debauchery. M. de Montaleu seduced Miss Sophia Muller, and—"

"By promising to marry her," interrupted the colonel in a voice trembling with anger, "for without this promise, which the scoundrel never kept, my mother, my poor and noble mother would never have yielded to this wretch. But proceed, sir, proceed."

"No, no," said Montéclain, "finish the story, you know a version differing from mine—it is for you to enlighten me."

"Will you dare deny that M. de Montaleu, promised my mother that he would marry her?"

"I do not say that—you know it. I dispute nothing."

"Why, then, do you not continue your recital?"

"Because you are not calm, colonel; because if we dispute five minutes in this tone, we shall fight in a few hours—because I do not wish to divulge," added he, accentuating his words, "what may implicate me in this secret to a man whom I do not see disposed to make a fair compensation for all the wrongs of each."

"Do you constitute yourself the defender of M. de Montaleu?"

"God forbid! But who knows if I may not presently have to speak to you of some one who has, perhaps, also suffered wrongly in this affair, and to whom I will not allow the epithets of scoundrel and wretch to be applied?"

"Speak, then, sir," said the colonel, "I will be calm."

"It is probable, as you say, that M. de Montaleu gave that common promise of marriage which too many accept as an excuse for their own weakness rather than as a serious hope. Do not chafe with impatience, colonel; it is necessary, in order that justice may be done, that everything should be shown in its true light."

"Proceed, then," said Thomas, "and do not stop again. If I must drink the cup even to the dregs, do not distil it drop by drop in my heart."

"Be it so, and let us finish with facts. Sophia Muller bore the penalty of her frailty; and was on the point of telling her seducer that she was about to become a mother, when he forsook her abruptly, without deigning to say more than this: that he confessed the baseness of his conduct, but that he rejected favours lavished upon others, and which were still shared with several gallants."

"Yes, it is true," said the colonel angrily, "he wrote this to her, the wretch! and he left my mother."

"He did more, he quitted the country; the emperor had just summoned him to the Council of State, and he set out."

"Leaving behind him a poor woman in misery and dishonour."

"All that is quite true, colonel; but you know what was the cause of this abandonment."

"Yes, I know it. One day, before she was acquainted with M. de Montaleu, at a time when the misconduct of my poor mother's father had reduced her to the last extremity, when he took from her the money she had so hardly earned, to waste it in debauchery, a strange man presented himself at her dwelling, and offered her what she thought a large fortune, namely, ten thousand francs, if she would lend assistance to another woman who had been cruelly deceived. My mother consented; she was conducted to a mean house where there was a woman who had just given birth to a girl. The offered reward would be given to my mother, only on condition that she should take this child, and, to prevent any suspicion, should present it to the magistrate as belonging to herself and a servant named Joseph Miras."

"You are rightly informed, colonel, and the register of the birth of this child, then named Gertrude, proclaims that she was born of Sophia Muller and Joseph Miras. Every precaution was taken to assure the authenticity of this register."

"It was poverty, sir; the most dreadful poverty, that drove my mother to this desperate action, in which she sold her honour for a morsel of bread."

"I neither accuse nor blame, colonel," said Montéclain with some emotion, "I recall the facts to your recollection, considering that they ought to be perfectly established between us, before we discuss what we should be for one another."

"I think we have now nothing more to learn."

"Pardon me, colonel, more than you imagine. M. de Montaleu was, as you say, very guilty towards your mother, but it is only just to acknowledge that it was difficult not to believe such proofs, such testimonies of culpability."

"My mother was innocent, sir," said the colonel.

"Yes, colonel, she was more than innocent, for she faithfully executed the compact for which she had been bought. She brought up the little Gertrude, and the supposed mother often met at the house of the nurse with whom she had placed the child, the supposed father of it. Now, can you not understand that M. de Montaleu, having known of this register, having heard of the visits your mother paid to the nurse, and her frequent meetings with the man, the titles to her intimacy with whom she had attested and signed, had good reasons for believing that he had been deceived by a clever intriguer, and thought himself justified in disclaiming the new paternity which was attributed to him?"

"But my mother informed him of all this, sir; he knows it."

"Would you have believed it had you been in his place? And if, at the present time, you did not know the error of Léda, the complicity of Hector de Montaleu; if, above all, you did not know what implacable, perfidious, enraged hand, has directed the accusation brought against Madame de Monrion; if you had been captivated by her; if she was not protected by her past virtue, by her position, by her liberty even; if, in short, in yielding to you, she had given you the right to believe she was not above such weakness, tell me, would you not have thought her guilty, and might you not have turned from her with contempt?"

"But my mother has justified herself, sir."

"Without proofs; in saying that which was true, but which was not credible. But there is yet another thing, which is now the most important of all. When you were born, the real father of the child who had been entrusted to your mother, fearing that she would neglect it to think of her son, wished to settle a fortune on this child; a document was prepared to this effect; a sum of fifty thousand francs was destined for her dowry at the time when she would be marriageable. It was the interest of this sum which was employed to educate you, as well as the girl who was then called Gertrude, until the day when a new career was opened for you both."

Montéclain stopped, and looking at the colonel, said to him:

"Well, colonel, am I rightly informed? Is there any circumstance of which I am ignorant?"

Thomas, who, whilst listening, had had time to repress his feelings, to subdue his impatience, to prepare his answers, turned away from Montéclain's searching glance, and replied:

"All that you have just said is correct; it remains to me to know what interest has impelled you to find out such secrets, and why you appear disposed to make use of them against some of those whom they concern."

"Colonel," said Montéclain, "we do not play in an equal manner; I show you all, or nearly all, that I hold in my hand; you have not yet said a word to me respecting what you know or intend to do."

"M. de Montéclain," replied the colonel with haughtiness, "since you know so much, you ought to understand that I come here to avenge my mother's honour, and that I have the right to do this."

"Doubtless; but I ask you in what way you propose to do it?"

"That is my secret."

An expression of anger shone in Monteclain's eyes.

"Look round this room, colonel," said he, "and learn one thing: it is in this same place, between these four walls, which bear witness to the confidence I have placed in you, that I can declare to you that I am perfectly ignorant who you are, that I can destroy with one word the proofs of your mother's innocence, proofs which you are come into this country to seek."

"Is it really M. de Montéclain who speaks to me thus?"

"Himself, who thus speaks to a man who has allowed him to tell all his secrets, and who so carefully keeps his own."

The colonel blushed; but replied immediately:

"Is our position equal, sir?"

"When your confidence shall have been equal to mine, I will answer that question."

"Since you know so much, you doubtless know also upon what ground I found my hope?"

"Yes, colonel, I know it. The document which settled a fortune on this Gertrude enclosed a sealed paper which was to be given to her on the day of her marriage or of her majority. This paper, although it was not destined for that purpose, contains the complete vindication of your mother. You see that I know all."

"It is true, sir, and you know consequently, I suppose, that this Gertrude—"

"Is no other than Felina—who, although she has possessed this declaration for more than ten years, has not informed you of its existence until a few months since."

"In truth, sir, said Thomas, this amazes me; how is it that you are so well informed?"

"That is my secret. But this paper, sir, do you know it? have you seen it?"

"Never."

"Do you know what it contains?"

"No."

"Do you know how, and by whom it can be explained?"

"That information I expect from Felina, and no doubt, she alone can give it me."

"Perhaps so, colonel. But you know something that she is ignorant of, and that you do not tell me."

The colonel began to walk about the room impatiently, then, after a moment reflection, he returned to Montéclain.

"Are we friends or enemies, sir?" said he, holding out his hand.

"I have told you, colonel, that that is a question which can be decided only when we shall have told each other everything. I have commenced; I expect you to imitate my example."

"What then is it that you desire to know?"

"To ask you for it, colonel, would be to detract from your frankness."

THE BOAR HUNT.

"Well! then," said Thomas, "I know not what will result from it, but I warn you that if you are capable of denying what you have told me, I will not allow the man to remain alive who would have gained my secret only to abuse it."

"In asking of you, some days since, a service which acquited you of any obligation towards me for that which I had rendered you at Constantinople, I have anticipated your wishes. I desired to render you as free towards me, as I am towards you."

"Speak then."

The colonel had taken breath, as though he were about to assert an enormity, and looking at Montéclain in an uneasy manner he said:

"I suspect Madame de Rudesgens of being acquainted with the birth of Felina."

"I also have this thought," returned Montéclain smiling. "But, tell me, what induced you to suppose it?"

"Merely a word used in conversation, respecting one of those stories which are repeated in the world, and which for ten years awake no attention until the day when some one guesses the terrible secret, heretofore hidden under frivolous speeches."

"Proceed," said Montéclain.

"I will repeat the story to you, exactly as it happened, and you will easily understand how this anecdote roused my suspicion, which the confusion of Madame de Rudesgens has now changed into certainty. It took place a short time ago in Africa; I was dining with some officers and Brias—"

"I believe," interrupted Montéclain, "that no envious and wicked men have ever done so much mischief by their most skilful calculations, as this boy has caused by his indiscretion."

"They were conversing as usual upon a thousand of those nameless adventures, the greater part of which, acquire celebrity by being arranged and embellished by the wit of the narrator, when Brias related to us one which was entirely new, quite recent, and of a simple truthfulness:

"'I was dining,' said he, 'at Champmortain's house with the pope's nuncio, the ambassador of Prussia, the ambassador of Spain and several others. We had among the guests the Cardinal de Lampierri, one of the most eminent men of Rome, whom the emperor had particularly distinguished, and to whom, although he was then very young, he had in 1811, presented a curacy at Cologne.

"'Notwithstanding the presence of the two Eminences, many scandalous secrets were related, when Champmortain spoke to this effect: 'I am sure, that in spite of our pretended knowledge of the heart of things, of men, and of society, these gentlemen (he alluded to the nuncio and the cardinal) must smile with pity. How many secrets, how many errors how many crimes even, have they alone had confided to them in the confessional!

"The cardinal smiled.

"But," cried I, (I put myself in the place of Brias,) "how can you endure life with this fatal and desolating knowledge of the world and of man? Surely it must afflict the stoutest heart."

"We forget very much," replied the cardinal, "and of all the confessions I have received during a long ministry, it would be with difficulty that I could relate any of them, were I permitted to do so. One alone," added he, "is ineffaceably impressed on my memory, because it took place the first time that I sat in the confessional box, and greatly surprised my youth, and the little knowledge I possessed of the crimes and errors, hidden by the world under so brilliant an exterior."

"What was it then?" enquired all the company.

"Ah!" replied the cardinal carelessly, "it was an avowal which has since been so often repeated to me that I now find it a very common thing. It was this: A young girl about to be married, confessed to me that she had no right to wear at the altar the virginal wreath so dear to her future husband, and that she had hidden, with a skill that shocked me, the fruit of her guilt."

"This very insignificant revelation," said Brias, "was quickly forgotten, and it is certainly not here that the point of the story lies."

"This revelation related by Brias," continued the colonel, interrupting himself in his narrative, "had already struck me. The Cardinal Lampierri had been curate at Cologne under the sovereignty, and you can readily understand what interest I took in an anecdote, which I already imagined bore some resemblance to that which had placed me in so miserable a position. I begged Brias to proceed, and he continued thus."

"The dinner was finished, the cardinal's words were completely forgotten, and Champmortain's drawing rooms were already beginning to fill, when an august lady, very devout, and horribly nun-like in virtue, made her appearance, and on learning that the Cardinal Lampierri was present, neglected no means of bringing herself into notice until she was presented to him."

"He was seated near her, whilst I, Champmortain, and another, were conversing together behind his chair. Suddenly, amidst a thousand enticing questions from the lady to the cardinal, respecting his merit, his success, his great fortune, his introductions, we heard the two following speeches:

"You know me, then, madame, for you recal my past life, which I thought was unknown."

"Yes," replied the old lady, primly; "you do not suspect that you are speaking to your first penitent?"

"This," continued Brias, "was indeed an unexpected event. The cardinal narrowly escaped falling backwards. I ran away to have my laugh out with—"

"With me," said Montéclain; "I was the third auditor of this singular revelation."

"What! you knew—"

"Yes, colonel, and the story is so diverting that I should have known it for one of Brias' relating; but it appears to me unpardonable that he should have employed the true names."

He wished to add a last feature to the story by saying that the said lady's son-in-law had heard the conversation, and from that time made use of it to conquer the opposition of his virtuous mother-in-law, who was foiled in the malevolent investigation with which she annoyed his household.

"Then he did not name Madame de Rudesgens?"

"No, but two hours afterwards, whilst questioning Brias about the Count de Champmortain, I learned that he was the son-in-law of M. de Rudesgens, who was married at Cologne to a young lady named Van Marken. Some days afterwards, I wrote to my mother to ask her to make enquiries respecting this lady, and from her I heard that Mademoiselle Van Marken lived at Cologne in 1812, that her marriage with M. de Rudesgens had been celebrated about two months after the birth of Felina, and from all these facts, from the dates corresponding so well, I had concluded that Madame de Rudesgens was perhaps the woman who held the secret of my mother's honour, and after what has passed this evening, I own to you that I have no longer any doubt of it."

"And you are right, colonel. But how is it that you have not warned Felina of a suspicion which ought to interest her much more warmly than yourself, since it might lead her to find out her mother?"

"Because the present is a fatal time, in which it appears that interests and circumstances are driven by an invisible and all-powerful hand towards the same end. At the moment in which the frivolous indiscretion of Brias, in Africa, gave me this first ray of light, a letter from Felina informed me that for nearly ten years she had possessed a document which proved my mother's innocence. In return for a silence so long kept, I have thought myself authorised to keep this part of a secret which is common to us, in order to be able to discuss the conditions which she intends to make before giving up this document."

"And you do not suspect what it may enclose?"

"No; I only know that it is addressed to M. de Montaleu."

Montéclain reflected for some time. In his turn, he appeared to hesitate to intrust the colonel with the last part of his secret. He was about, however, to tell him all, when, in spite of the formal order which he had given, they were interrupted by the entrance of a servant, who announced that Bricord wished particularly to speak to his master. Montéclain was angry, but the servant added that Bricord appeared to be out of his mind, and threatened to do some mischief.

"Will you not deliver to him the letter, of which you have made me the depositary?" said the colonel.

"No, not until I am sure that Léda is in safety. Besides, you must show it to-morrow to M. de Montaleu."

"What will you say to him, then?"

"That I have given you this letter, that you may read it to him—"

"But he must know that I am here."

"Well!" said Montéclain, "set out, while I go to receive him. I cannot be supposed to know what he has come to ask of me."

"But directly I return to the farm he will question me; what shall I tell him?"

"The truth, of course; but, I will have prepared him to expect it. However, if you prefer it, remain here."

"The fact is," said the colonel, "that I must see Felina to-night. She is to give me her positive conditions—"

"That serves our purpose admirably. Go, colonel, and take my word as a gentleman, that if Felina refuses you the writing which contains your mother's justification, I engage myself upon honour to furnish you with sure means of obtaining this vindication."

"I take your word, and I go, although I am ignorant as to the means you have of keeping it; but you are so well acquainted with the particulars of this mournful story, that I need no other proof to convince me that you are able to do what you have promised. I leave the rest to your honour. When shall I see you again?"

"I will retain Bricord long enough to allow of your seeing Felina; for, once informed that you possess this letter, he would be just the man to follow you into the forest and surprise you, even at Madame Amab's house."

"That reminds me," said the colonel, "to ask another favour of you. I will leave you Aly Muley—"

"Yes, I know he is very inquisitive. We will all three be at Bricord's house in two hours from this time. Will that suffice you?"

"Perfectly."

"See Felina, then; judge her, and I hope that the conversation you will have with her will lead you to repudiate such an ally, and bring you over to our side. For the rest, colonel, this is my formal condition. I do not wish that Madame de Rudesgens, I do not wish that Sylvia should suffer for anything which may happen here. I will save Léda if I can; I do not speak of Madame de Monrion; she has no need to be protected by any one; and now, adieu for the present!"

"Adieu!" returned the colonel.

He went out, and Bricord was almost immediately admitted to Montéclain.

---

## CHAPTER LXXI.

### THE LETTER.

When Felina and Thomas Rien met, they remained for a moment silent.

"It is you, Felina?" said the colonel.

"It is I," replied she. "Well! have you reflected?"

"Yes," said Thomas, "and my reflections have caused me to persevere in the resolution which I communicated to you in the conversation we held at this same place."

"Indeed?" replied Felina, in an ironical tone. "So, the gentle light of the chaste Julia's beautiful eyes has, in a few days melted those strong resentments which were to break and destroy everything around him who has ruined your mother?"

"No, Felina, no; but it is not in helping you to ruin a woman by calumny, that I wish to avenge my mother, whom calumny has ruined."

"This is a sort of antithesis proper for a course of rhetoric, but quite useless to the object you have in view."

"I would rather renounce it altogether, than obtain it by unworthy means."

"Have you a memory, colonel?"

"Why that question?"

"Because, when I wrote to you in Africa to inform you that I possessed a document which proved your mother's innocence, you replied to me, in a letter, which appeared to embody all the fire, all the anger of the lions of the desert. 'Ah!' you said to me, 'I can at length prove to the man who seduced my mother, and abandoned her to her misery, and despair, to the man with whom I have expostulated, and who has repulsed me with disdain, that he has been ungrateful, infamous, and cowardly. Oh! this proof, may I but possess it one day, one hour; and when I have acquired the right of casting all these epithets in his face, I will insult him everywhere. I will cast into the mire the insulting hypocrisy of his false virtue. I will give to the few days of his remaining life, all the sufferings endured by my mother for thirty years.' These were your very words, Thomas; for, if your memory fails, mine, you see, serves for us both. This is what you wrote to me! I then asked you to come; I expected you as a companion in vengeance, you who have been my companion in misery and destitution; you arrive, and instead of this terrible avenger, of this son armed for chastisement, I see a man who considers how far his right can go, who shrinks from the task he had promised himself. What then has taken place Thomas, having the power to change you thus, if indeed you ever have been that which you boasted of being?"

The colonel made no reply. Felina continued:

"Who then has destroyed these threatening hopes and broken these furious resolutions?"

"You, Felina," replied the colonel, severely, "you alone, by making my assistance in the ruin of Madame de Monrion, the condition upon which you offer to help me."

"Do you not demand mine to ruin M. de Montaleu?"

"He is guilty."

"According to your opinion."

"Has he not devoted me to destitution?"

"Madame de Monrion, or one belonging to her has done me more injury than you have ever suffered."

"I do not constitute myself the judge of your griefs."

"In that case I claim to be ignorant of yours."

"Assure yourself of one thing, Felina, and that is, that I will not lend you any assistance against Madame de Monrion."

"Be assured, in return, that I will not furnish you with any against M. de Montaleu."

"Felina," said the colonel, angrily, do not forget that my mother brought you up and protected you."

"Do not forget, colonel, that she was paid for it, and that it is to the fortune settled on me, you owe the education which has made you what you are."

"You insult me, Felina—"

"You provoke me to answer you as I do."

"It is enough," said the colonel, "I shall perhaps find other assistance which will not cost me so dear."

"From Montéclain, doubtless?"

"Perhaps so."

"Ah!" said Felina, with a disdainful pity, "return to Africa, colonel, renew your career as a soldier; battle fields teeming with horsemen, marches distinguished by treasons and dangers, furious frays, bloody combats, fierce victories. These are your lot—you are young, you are brave, you have in your brain and in your breast the burning thought and the unwearied courage which produce great commanders; go, and you will become a hero; but do not risk your fortune in our world, do not turn your hopes towards these unknown labyrinths in which we walk: you would be more awkward there than the most obscure and disdained among those you despise; a simpleton such as Brias would stun you with his empty and boasting talk; a fair and languishing little girl would bring you in adoration to her knees, and, to put your misery to its height, a Montéclain, the clothed nullity of insolence, the spacious illusion of frankness, the ever wakeful cunning disguised with carelessness, would make you betray the friend of your infancy, the companion of your sorrows; he would make you abjure the vengeance promised to your mother. Go, go, colonel, you are not strong enough for the struggle in which you have engaged this time. Abandon it before being conquered, spare a shame to your pride, and to my friendship the regret of having led you to it."

"What does this mean, Felina, and what interest has Montéclain to deceive me?"

"You have conversed with him for an hour, and you ask me this! What! he has promised to serve you better than I can do, and he has not told you how he will keep his promise?"

"No," replied Thomas, whose faith began to be shaken by Felina's sarcasms."

"If that is the case," returned Felina, "what has he given you for all your secrets, which you have no doubt confided to him?"

The colonel did not reply. A cruel doubt arose in his mind. In fact he had learned nothing respecting Montéclain's projects, while this man had torn from him his every one."

"Once more," cried he, at length, "what interest could he have in deceiving me?"

Felina tittered with audible disdain; then after a moment's silence, she resumed:

"Montéclain has told you much evil of me, I know; but I am convinced he did not tell you that I was foolish enough to confide my secrets to one who admits himself to be my enemy."

"Your enemy, because I will not assist in a calumny, which is moreover useless; for, I tell you plainly, this pretended fault of Madame de Monrion is no longer believed by any one."

"And you are among the number of those who are convinced of her innocence?"

"Yesterday, I was convinced of it, you know, and the discussion we had together proved it to you; to-day, I am certain of it."

"I can easily believe it, for I know that you have the proof of it."

"You know it—"

"A proof which has been given you in the presence of Champmortain, my husband, Hector, and Brias."

"And which of these gentlemen has so correctly informed you?'

"My husband, perhaps, in wishing to humble me by the triumph of one whom he had loved, and for whom he cherishes, in the depths of his heart, a devotion anything but flattering to me.'

"Ah! it is M. Amab?"

"Or perhaps Hector de Montaleu, whom I sanction in his pretensions to the hand of the beautiful Julia."

"It is a cowardice of which he is quite capable."

"Or it may be Brias, who fears that I should inform Champmortain of the secret assignations which he obtains from his wife."

"He is indiscreet enough for that. But it is of little consequence to me who is your informer," said the colonel, coldly. I merely wish you to understand that if I yesterday refused to lend my aid to a plot, the heinousness of which I guessed even then, notwithstanding all your attempts to persuade me of the truth of your calumnies, I am to-day still less disposed to afford you the assistance you require."

"What then is your object in coming here?"

"To demand of you the writing which you have promised me."

"On certain conditions."

"Well! name them to me."

"They can be easily accomplished: give me the letter which Montéclain has delivered into your hands, and I will give you what you require."

"Give you that letter!" cried the colonel, "that letter upon which Madame de Monrion's honour depends!"

"In exchange for that upon which your mother's honour depends—this ought to be the desire of a good son."

"It would be an act of cowardice," said Thomas, scarcely able to restrain his indignation.

"The cowardice would perhaps be to sacrifice the honour of your mother to that of a woman whom you do not know."

"Madame—madame—" cried the colonel, in a voice so altered, that Felina moved softly away from him, "you have in your possession a document which belongs to me. I will have it—do you hear. I will have it."

"A document which belongs only to me," said Felina, jeeringly, "and you will have it. You are mad, Thomas."

"Give it me—I will have it," replied he, exasperated.

"Colonel," continued Felina, with insolence, have you ever had any other mistresses than the miserable moorish women of Algiers, poor creatures, subdued by flogging and slavery? If you have, you ought to know that a woman grows firmer and stronger under threats, and will die rather than yield. It is in this, sir, that the weakest are powerful—and I am not," added she, haughtily, "one of those who have strength for resistance only."

"Ah!" resumed Thomas, his voice trembling

with anger, "there are some women who lament their weakness! Ah! they make it a shield which protects them better than the most resolute courage."

"And it is just, colonel; there ought to be in this world beings so protected by human respect, that clever and insolent aggressors cannot be allowed to submit them by fear to obedience and contempt. If I were a man instead of a woman, you would have struck me, and I should go out from this interview to be either killed or dishonoured. Do you think that is right?"

"I admire the right which permits a man of honour to have satisfaction for infamy which the law cannot punish."

"But this right is as much the privilege of the veriest scoundrel, as it is that of the man of honour. You wish to obtain from me the remittance of a document for an honourable object, as you profess, and you threaten me because I refuse it; a wretch might wish to obtain it for a crime, and he would not act differently. Calm, therefore, these useless and ridiculous furies. You are come here to avenge your mother; I have called you here myself, to help my vengeance. You have already deserted my cause. I desire nothing from you; but I pity you. It may perhaps suit you to desert the cause of your mother for that of Madame de Monrion, do it; but do not ask me what sentiment will banish from my heart the pity with which you inspire me."

"You refuse me this document then," said the colonel.

"It is yours in exchange for the letter which Montéclain has confided to you."

"Never, never," said the colonel, "let what may result from it. Adieu."

"The result will be," said Felina angrily, "that Montéclain will marry Madame de Monrion, and reap for her the fortune which belongs to you, and which you are come hither to seek."

"What!" said the colonel, "can that be Montéclain's object?"

"Will you give me the letter?" continued Felina without replying to him.

"Could he have mocked me thus?"

"The letter! the letter!" said Felina.

"Would he who knows all my secrets, dare to make use of them?"

"To cause you to be hooted by the Marquis de Montaleu as an intriguing subaltern—to induce your father to expel you as a bastard whom he denies."

"Ah! if I thought that—"

"The letter, Thomas, the letter!"

"Never—never. Ah! I wish to know how far the baseness and perfidy of this world can extend; but I do not wish to share it. Adieu, Felina, adieu."

"Colonel!" cried she, as he was leaving her: "colonel!" repeated she, whilst he deigned not to make her any reply.

"Ah!" muttered she, as Thomas Rien mounted his horse, and rode rapidly away, "ah! may God save him, for he has condemned himself."

She then called with a loud voice:

"*Adieu, colonel, adieu!*"

She had scarcely pronounced these words when Hector de Montaleu stood by her side.

"What!" said he, in a sharp and hissing tone, this man is the son of my uncle?"

"Yes, and he has a right to that inheritance, which you thought belonged to yourself—"

"Which he comes here to seek?"

"And which he will take away from the lawful heir, on the day when it shall become known that the latter has allowed to rest on Madame de Monrion a charge which he might have destroyed with one word; for he possesses Léda's letter."

Hector uttered a harsh and terrible cry.

"In one hour, he will have given it to Bricord."

Hector's breathing became quick and oppressed.

"And Léda, once convicted of the crime which ruins her, will no longer hesitate to betray her accomplice."

"Ah!" said Hector in a voice no longer human, "I will have the letter."

He immediately darted forth in pursuit of the colonel. Felina, immoveable, her ear extended, listened to the footsteps of Hector who had taken a different path from the road Thomas had followed. For a minute, she heard at the same time the heavy tread of the colonel's horse, and the dull sound of Hector's steps: then, by degrees the sounds grew fainter, and returned only at intervals to her ear, until, at length, both were lost in the sad and solemn silence of night.

Felina listened still.

---

## CHAPTER LXXII.

### CORRESPONDENCE.

"*De Montéclain to Louis Villon.*

"FRIEND VILLON, in one of my previous letters, I told you we were all immediately about to engage in a dreadful struggle, which would probably cause blood to be spilt. Nevertheless, at that time, I only foresaw sundry sword-thrusts honestly, if not honourably exchanged in a duel: my expectations have been surpassed; blood has flown; but it is a case for the king's attorney.

"I will relate the fact. Yesterday Bricord came to my house, to demand the restoration of his wife's famous letter, I had given it to Colonel Thomas, who had a rendezvous with Felina.

"Wishing to prepare Bricord for his misfortune, I had calculated on being present when this fatal missive was read; for I own I feared everything from Bricord's anger and despair. If I had been justified in quoting the name of the man who had dishonoured him, I should not have hesitated to tell him all—for then this anger and despair would have been wasted on an object, Bricord would have killed Montaleu, and in doing so would have conferred a service on this wretch; for Léda has disappeared. What has he done with her? Has he concealed or murdered her? I know not what to think. But no matter, Bricord would have attacked Montaleu, like a brave soldier as he is, and on my soul! unless the viscount had accepted the peasant's challenge, there are some among us here, who would have loaded him with insult to his dying day. But a game like this may not be played without clear proofs, and I foresaw that Bricord, seeing himself alone with his dishonour and despair, would visit on himself the rage by which he was consumed. I wished then that this frightful intelligence, since it was necessary he should hear it, might be revealed to him in the presence of Thomas, to whom he is attached, and of one of his comrades, whose authority and advice would prevent the suicide, his bewildered state led me to anticipate.

"I detained him a full hour, falsely arguing against the jealous clear-sighted instinct which had enabled him to discover all. Still, however, I suffered him to accustom himself to the idea that his wife had committed some serious imprudence; while, at the same time, I suggested to his heart the possibility of forgiving her. I repeated so frequently that perhaps Léda had been led away in a moment of folly, or overcome by violence, that

Bricord's anger had almost all turned against the seducer. Having obtained this point, I thought it was time to go to the farm, where we should rejoin the colonel.

"I will tell you everything in his presence. I said to Bricord, 'and he will tell you what is to be done.'

"Yes—," was his reply, "I shall believe him, for he is neither noble nor rich, and will not take part in the treason every one here is plotting against me."

"We set out with Aly Muley, and reached the farm. Thomas had not yet returned. As I was aware of his engagement with Felina, this delay occasioned no surprise to me; for she knows perfectly well how to choose her time so as to baffle and mislead the reason of the wisest, by her crafty reasonings.

"We waited for an hour; the absence of Thomas began to make us uneasy. A doubt crossed me as to his honour.

"Had Felina induced him to join her party? I knew not what to think. Bricord, on his side, suspected the colonel; he accused him of wishing, like me, to screen the guilty by his silence. Aly Muley alone guessed the truth; he maintained that Thomas must be in some danger, and vowed and swore that he would go and seek him. I contended with his fears, but was obliged to yield to them at last, when nearly another hour had passed without Thomas re-appearing. I began myself to feel astonished, but dared not imagine a crime to be the cause: at length we set out, and entered the forest. Aly Muley escorted and guided us through the darkness with incredible skill, until we reached the ruined house called the colliery. This cabin, which no one yet had ever seen unclosed, had apparently been the scene of some event: the door was broken open. We entered it. Aly had brought with him a match and candle, and, having lit the latter, we examined the place carefully; Bricord discovered some drops of blood on the floor.

"The colonel has been murdered here," he cried.

"Aly Muley shook his head, and with an expression that made me shudder he murmured:

"No—no—it is a woman's blood."

"A woman's!" cried Bricord, "what do you mean?"

"Ah!" resumed Aly Muley, "I understood it but too well, my colonel! my colonel! what have they done with him? Oh! I swear on my life and soul, that I will kill any one who has touched him, man or woman, noble or peasant; I will burn him in his chateau, if I cannot get at him in any other way."

"We continued our researches, and examined the ground. Footsteps of different lengths were mingled around the cabin—the feet of a man and woman had passed that way, and left these marks in different directions. At last we reached a spot where the earth had been recently disturbed and turned up by the pawing of a horse.

"The colonel has been here," said Aly Muley. This is where he tied up Mogador. There is no other horse in the world that has so fine a hoof!"

"Aly sought for the track, and discovered that it led towards Bricord's house.

"You see," said I, "he must have left this place whilst we were coming to seek him."

"That is possible," he answered, "let us return to the farm."

"Ah! but," observed Bricord, who, divided between the fears for Thomas, which Aly Muley had suggested, and all those passions murmuring within him, felt all his own suspicions revive, "what did you mean by saying just now: '*It is a woman's blood?*'"

"Listen, Bricord," answered the soldier, "I am here to obey the colonel's orders, we are going to see him, he will tell you about your business. But if a misfortune has happened, if his enemies have dared—. But it is not possible—he is at the farm. And if he were not there, I would tell you my mind—and then, Bricord, you understand me—we two should have to settle the account."

"Do you not likewise calculate on my aid?" I said to Aly.

"Pardon, my lord," replied Aly, "but you are not one of us—it is possible that the colonel, like you, is the son of a good family—but that has not served him; he is what he is, because he has shed his best blood in the service of France, because he has been our comrade, has fought in advance of us, has slept in the rain while his cloak covered the sick—because, whilst he was like a lion in the fight, he was as good as a mother to the soldier—it is—ah! thunder of—!" he went on in broken accents,—"my colonel, my colonel! Where is he now, my poor colonel?"

"Aly Muley wept while speaking thus, and I felt the tears rising in my own eyes, when suddenly we thought we heard some distant sound in reply to Aly's sorrowful exclamation. He uttered a cry which made me start.

"It is Mogador—," he exclaimed.

"Mogador?"

"Yes, it is he—"

"We listened again, and this time clearly distinguished the neighing of a horse.

"Ah!" said Muley, "the poor beast utters a cry of complaint, the colonel is dead—"

"You are crazy," said Bricord.

"Ah! I have heard it once before—one day when he was stretched on the ground and the Arabs surrounded him to cut off his head—Mogador cried out like that. But you know it well, Bricord, you heard it, for it was you who saved him—colonel! colonel!" he began calling out in broken accents.

The horse again replied to this lamenting voice. We directed our steps in that direction, guided by the sounds which conducted us towards the noble animal.

At length we arrived, by the light of the dawning day, we saw Mogador at a distance, his head hanging down, and bending over a ditch by the wayside; he pawed the ground with his foot, and kept neighing as he swung his head; the noble animal seemed to be communing with some one. We ran forward, and there, at the bottom of the ditch, we beheld the poor colonel, bleeding from the breast, and extended on the ground.

"Never, Villon, never, by my soul, have I seen anything to equal Aly Muley's despair; he fell on his knees beside the motionless body, weeping and sobbing like a child, or like a mother. How holy, surpassing all I had ever imagined, was the grief of this soldier, down whose manly face, embrowned by the sun of Africa, tears were fast streaming, whilst he prayed with clasped hands and eyes upraised to heaven!

"As to Bricord, he tore his hair, and accused himself of the colonel's death, saying that if Thomas had not come into this accursed country, to see his old soldier, he would not have been assassinated in this cowardly manner

"Happily I had preserved my composure. A simple remark which I made had revealed to me, if not the murderer's name, at least the motive which had induced the committal of this crime. The colonel, like many military men, was in the habit of keeping his coat carefully buttoned. Now the colonel's coat was unfastened: doubtless it had been opened in order to search the side pocket, in which papers are usually carried. I examined this pocket, it was empty. Léda's letter, which I had given him, had disappeared. Two wretches alone were interested in the suppression of this letter: Felina and Hector. It was dreadful to think of. But I had no time to bestow on these reflections. Whilst I was still searching, to convince myself it had disappeared, I thought I felt a slight palpitation: I applied my ear over the heart, and bent down over the colonel's mouth.

"He is not dead," I exclaimed.

"Ah! Villon, my dear Villon, how good, how honourable must that man be, when he is loved like this! To the lamentations uttered by these two rude soldiers, to the tears which flooded their sun-burnt faces, succeeded a moment of mute surprise, and then a mad, an incredible joy. Bricord fell on his knees, crying:

"'My God, my God, grant that this may be true, and I will forgive everybody.'"

"Aly Muley embraced me. The poor fellows, in their delight that the colonel was not dead, would have left him to die, had I not reminded them that something must be done. We lifted him up into a sitting posture. The ball had struck him in the chest, but a deep sigh showed the respiratory organs were still in action.

"A moment of debate followed. Bricord wanted to carry him to the farm, and Aly Muley was also of the same opinion; but as we were nearer to my house than the farm, this consideration decided the question in my favour. Poor Aly Muley was so overcome with grief and hope that he could not lift the colonel; I and Bricord took charge of him, whilst the soldier, mounting Mogador, rode off to the chateau in search of a litter. In the meantime Bricord and I began to move forward. Ah! my friend, how dreadful is the aspect of death! I have seen it on battle-fields, I have been present at fatal duels, I have beheld the torn and bleeding victims of horrible assassinations, and the calm white bodies of people dead in their beds, but, to speak the truth, I had never yet touched the dead. I had now taken hold of the colonel's arms, and sustained him, by passing mine under his shoulders. I cannot tell you what a shudder passed through me as I felt that strong, intelligent, ambitious head, so full of ardour and future hope, roll inert and helpless about my breast. I thought that I likewise had a share in the death of this noble soldier, in whose misfortune my father was so largely concerned, for—. But, Villon, the hour for confidence is not yet come—let me conclude this frightful recital.

"Slowly and gently we pursued our way, when, at the turning of an alley, we were unexpectedly stopped by a carriage, which was going by; it would have passed, but suddenly drew up at a cry which came from the inside; the door opened, and I recognized Madame de Monrion.

"Yes, it was herself!

"Villon, this woman is descended from heaven, she possesses charms which are not of earth; when she moves quickly, it is as angels fly; when she walks, her motion is all grace, her look is like a ray of light, her voice a tone of music, her word an authoritative command. She approached, pale, alarmed, inspired by that holy christian love which every hour forgets itself to minister to others.

"I will not tell you how she inquired, or how I answered; but whilst Bricord and I hesitated, she covered the colonel's wound with a handkerchief which had wiped away her tears, for she had wept much, poor injured spirit; and whilst I was again explaining to her that we were expecting some servants with a litter to assist us, she had already caused the colonel to be placed in her carriage; and all that, Villon, had been done, and commanded with the chaste simplicity of one, to whom right actions, pity, and devotion are as natural as the light they look upon, as the air they breathe; whilst the coachman drove the carriage (in which Bricord had seated himself beside the colonel) at a foot pace, she came and walked with me, as I followed behind, and then for the first time asked the cause of this wound. Was it a duel, or an accident?

"No, madame," I answered, sadly, "it is an assassination."

"An assassination!" she repeated, with alarm. "In this country—and for some paltry sum of money—"

"No, madam, from revenge—or some timorous apprehension."

She fixed on me an indescribable look of astonishment, curiosity and grief. I know not what instinct, derived from divine foreknowledge made her appear to understand that she was not quite a stranger to this unfortunate event.

"Assassinated!" she said in a voice that touched me like that of a mother who is anxious about her child.

"Yes," I replied, "and doubtless for having refused to aid in the committal of a crime."

The calm and holy courage which, a moment before, animated this sweet fair child of heaven, melted away on hearing this word, crime; she became pale and trembling.

"What crime?" she said, "and committed against whom?"

"You will know one day madame, but permit me to ask, where you were going at this early hour?"

She coloured but did not seem offended; nevertheless she answered in a trembling voice;

"I was going to the village of Saint Faron. Oh!" she continued with feverish indignation, "I will not abandon the orphan—I will struggle—I will go every day—"

"It is useless," I replied, "Jeanne Dromeray is no longer at Saint Faron; the child you took under your protection is gone with her—"

"They have been driven away," she cried.

"No, madam, they have been placed where this woman will not be exposed to perfidious influences, nor the child to the dangers which threaten it from the anger of a deceived husband and the ferocity of a guilty father."

"I thank you, sir," she replied softly,

"Oh! Villon, Villon, there have been moments of burning passion in my life, when I believed myself happy; I have experienced and satisfied immoderate wishes; I have seen after months of torture and suspence, some women bow their heads beneath my look, while the trembling avowal of love fell from their lips; well! never, on my soul, never has anything in the world, conveyed to my heart a joy, at once so sweet, so powerful, so strange as those simple words 'I thank you.' She had then understood at once, that I had done this, she believed me capable of a little good. Villon, I felt the tears rising in my eyes; I—but the former man still whispers within to prompt me, for I resisted I know not what impulse, which incited me to go down on my knees before her. And yet, tell me who is more worthy of adoration than the being who bears in herself the gift of doing so much good with a single word. Ah! Villon my friend, I who think myself a clever man, I, who have sometimes driven back crime, and unmasked hypocrisy, who have accepted a challenge from all the wicked and often vanquished them, who could at need punish remorselessly and revenge myself with éclat, how humiliated, how poor, how little did I feel myself before this woman. Should I employ my life, my fortune, my abilities in striving to do good, never could I impart to anyone the thousandth part of that heavenly joy with which she has filled my soul. Oh! the only true power is that of doing good, for you must understand me, Villon, she has made me, not a happier, but a better man."

"But I must conclude."

"Some steps farther on, we met Aly Muley with my people; he looked into the carriage, assured himself that the colonel was as well as he could be, spoke to Bricord, recommended the coachman to avoid the ruts, and having taken all these precautions, went up to Madame de Monrion to thank her, for Bricord had told him what had occurred. Then Aly Muley placed himself before her; uncovered his head, seemed to hesitate what he should do or say, then fixing on Julia a tearful look, and stammering like a man who cannot express himself and speaks at hazard, he said abruptly:

"Madame—yes madame, it is true—if you had lived in other times you would have been the Virgin Mary."

"Is it because these words were addressed to her or because they were spoken by the rough soldier whose despair I had witnessed, that I conceived them to be both sublime and pathetic?" I took Aly Muley's two hands into mine and pressed them silently, unable to utter a word."

"Well! yes," he said sobbing, "it is true—it is—"

Then to conceal his tears he hastily turned away from me.

"Julia had stopped. I turned towards her. Aly Muley's words had been more powerful than all I could have said; she appeared to me happy and consoled. The secret of celestial souls is known to the simplest hearts.

"I am already very far from home," she said, "allow me to return."

"Alone?" I asked.

"I am not afraid."

"Allow some of my people to attend you as far as your residence."

"If one of them would drive my carriage, my coachman could accompany me."

"She bowed and was going to leave me."

"Madame," I said, "you were to have received a visit this morning from those gentlemen, whose object in coming to your house, was to salute you respectfully, and ask you in the name of all that is honourable, to pardon them the suffering they have occasioned you for some days past. There will now be only two, the third is in this carriage. Another would fain have accompinied them; but the hatred of M. de Montaleu forbids him all access to your presence. Permit him to profit by this chance meeting to say to you—"

"Why did my voice fail me? Because I could not pronounce the word that rose to my lips; because I wished to speak of respect, and my heart was overflowing with admiration. Julia was before me, her eyes cast down, happy, not I think because of my agitation, which she did not understand, but from the joy she experienced in regaining the world's esteem. She awaited the conclusion of my phrase; I could not express it and said to her, so little did I possess of the worldly science in which I believed myself an adept."

"Adieu, madam. Allow me to think of you, as I sometimes think of my mother, who was beautiful, holy, and is now in heaven."

"She departed, and we soon reached the chateau. The village doctor had already arrived, and one of my servants had ridden off towards Nevers, to bring another. The colonel has been bled, but the ball is not extracted from the wound. Nevertheless, he has spoken a few words, and these words were: "My mother—my mother!—" A moment after he opened his eyes, and muttered again, "My mother! my mother!"

"Villon, when you receive this letter, hasten to my house. With the key which I have enclosed, you will open a secretary, in rosewood, placed in my bed-room, to the left of the chimney-piece. You must press the bottom shelf; where you will find a hollow place beneath it, in which, among other papers, you will see a packet, with this inscription: 'To my son.' Take it, and immediately without losing a minute, get into a carriage, and come here. Spoil the horses, destroy the carriage, but come—come.

"They tell me the colonel has again called on his mother. Make haste, Villon—and forgive me. Yes, forgive me, for it is true! I promised you I would protect—and I love her!

"MONTECLAIN."

## CHAPTER LXXIII.

### STRANGE INTERPRETATIONS.

ON the morning of this same day, Madame de Rudesgens had summoned her daughter to her side. The peevish proud Artémise had quite recovered from the shock and terror of the foregoing day. Sylvia, who had left her so overcome and indisposed, that she had not dared to speak to her of the occurrence at supper, now found her stiffer and dryer than usual. Madame de Rudesgens had communed with herself, during the night, in her solitary alcove; she had looked a great danger in the face, and was resolved to turn it away from her own head by making it burst on that of another. Madame de Rudesgens understood the great art of diversion, as will be seen.

"My daughter," she said to Sylvia, "we must converse seriously, but it must be in the presence of your father. I will send for him."

It suited Madame de Rudesgens' projects only to see her husband in Sylvia's presence; therefore, as soon as she was protected by her daughter, she sent in search of the victorious Annibal.

He, too, had reflected much during the night. His wife's fainting fit had greatly disturbed him. Doubts which, dated from the period of his marriage, and which had been buried beneath a union of thirty years, were re-awakened from the depths of his memory. Perhaps at that time the millions of Mademoiselle Van Marken had lulled to rest in M. de Rudesgens' soul certain feelings awakened by the conduct of Artémise. Be that as it may, he had been silent at the important moment. The newly received millions, covered with a golden shield any stain on the character of Artémise. He held his tongue. To recriminate afterwards, when the peevish rigour of Madame de Rudesgens disturbed the seductive projects of her Annibal, would have been to confess either his folly or his good nature; so he always preserved a dignified and prudent silence. One of the reasons which had come in aid of M. de Rudesgens' philosophy, was the profound conviction that the suspicions he had conceived had never entered the mind of any one else. Only one of his friends had warned him; but this friend had left France at the time of his marriage with Artémise, and had died in a foreign country. No one then had the shadow of a suspicion. Thirty years of repose about the matter had rooted this faith in M. de Rudesgens' soul. He had even succeeded in persuading himself that connoisseur as he was in that kind of thing, he had been mistaken, and in fact he did better than reason, and reason falsely; he thought no more about it.

But all at once this secret, so profoundly buried, on which forests had had time to grow up,—this secret, we say, is evoked, and threatened to be dug up again, some one appears who strikes the earth with his foot, and says:

"Here is the trace of a crime."

M. de Rudesgens had trembled to the very mar-

row of his vanity. To have a finger pointed at him after glorying for thirty years in his wife's virtue, after having suffered all the bitterness of this virtuous happiness, after having been furiously reprimanded for the least fault, and all that to turn out at last a husband deceived before, and perhaps after marriage; for the colossal vanity of the little marquis this was a prodigious vexation, which he would have avoided at any price. It was therefore with eager haste that he approached the august offender who had made him pay so dearly for her repentance. With his present idea that an explanation was about to take place on the subject of the fainting fit, the previous evening, he was surprised to find Madame de Champmortain present. He looked at his noble spouse: never had she appeared to him so steeped in vinegar; he understood directly that the quarrel would be a terrible one, and that Madame de Rudesgens had prudently sheltered herself behind Sylvia, fully convinced that he would not dare, in her presence, to utter certain charges and accusations that a daughter ought never to hear.

Nevertheless, he preserved his little grave and pinched up manner, fully resolved to seize this time, a part of the dominion he had coveted all along.

" You desired me to be called?" he said, taking a chair. It seems to me that Sylvia—"

" I have called her also; for what I have to say to you, concerns the whole family."

" But I," said the husband drily, " I have things to say to you that Sylvia—"

" Sylvia ought to hear every thing," rejoined the wife, still more drily.

" Allow me," said M. de Rudesgens, " I intend, before anything else, to have an explanation which—"

" You intend," said Artémise, again interrupting him, " do you intend to tolerate much longer the scandals which are passing in your house?"

" Scandals!" cried M. de Rudesgens, " what scandals? Madam, if there has been any matter for scandal, or if there still exists any, you know by whom it is caused."

The heroic Annibal hurled this sentence at his wife's head, with a tartness he believed irresistible; but, instead of seeing her guilty forehead bow down beneath the terrible insinuation, the ancient Céladon saw her face about, like a paroquet bristling its feathers.

" M. de Rudesgens," she said, in a choking voice, you will explain to me what you mean, you will explain it instantly, I desire it—speak—speak then,

Annibal; when we are guiltless of wrong we should dare to say everything."

The old marquis was seized with a furious longing to humble the insolent bawling of his wife; but the thought that Sylvia was there stopped him. He stretched himself carelessly in an arm-chair, and replied in his most disdainful manner:

"We will speak of that by and by, let us begin by what may be said in our daughter's presence."

"Ah!" said Artémise, "you are silent now, as you always are, because you know what you have made me suffer by your misconduct."

"Mamma, you wished to speak to me," said Sylvia, who had too often witnessed similar scenes to be much disturbed by them.

"Ah!" replied Madame de Rudesgens, wiping her eyes, "you do not know how much I have suffered—and it is in order that you may never have to submit to the same griefs and the same humiliations, that I wish to put an end to what is going on in our house."

"And what is going on there?"

"You know well what it is, Annibal, and you close your eyes that you may not see it; who knows even if you do not lend a helping hand? Birds of a feather flock together. Besides, who knows if there are not two of you instead of one?"

"To do what?" said M. de Rudesgens, taking his shell comb and arranging his hair in an indolent manner.

"You understand me very well, sir; you know all—and yet you allow it."

"But what is it?"

"Have the goodness to tell me, I beg, whether you approve of M. de Champmortain's conduct towards our cherished and adored daughter, towards this poor forsaken child?"

At these words, Madame de Champmortain bent down her head, and coloured. In fact, she felt she had no longer the right to complain of M. de Champmortain's infidelity, and felt horribly embarrassed by the necessity she was placed in of taking cognizance of this ill conduct, and reproaching him with it. M. de Rudesgens turned round on hearing the attack made by his wife on his son-in-law. He rose, with flashing eyes, stood ten feet higher than before, and approaching Madame de Rudesgens, said, with an accent she had never heard from him before:

"Madame, you are a bad mother."

Whether this accusation was applicable, in Madame de Rudesgens' thought to some distant souvenir, or whether she considered it a reproach addressed only to her present action, all her audacity seemed to forsake her at these words.

"I," she murmured with an effort, "I a bad mother!"

"My daughter," said M. de Rudesgens, "leave the room—"

"But I will not allow it. She shall learn at last—" cried his wife.

"Leave the room!—Sylvia," said M. de Rudesgens, with an anger which was not intended for his daughter. "Go, my child, go—"

But Madame de Rudesgens, whose plan of warfare would have been entirely deranged by Sylvia's absence, darted furiously before her.

"Stay, Sylvia, stay," she cried, or if you obey your father, prepare never to see me again."

Sylvia hesitated a moment.

"Remain, Sylvia," said M. de Rudesgens, sadly, "I will never place you under the frightful obligation of choosing between us. Stay with your mother: but believe me my child, do not be misled by the suspicions they strive to call up in your mind. If the evil you are about to hear of does exist, which I do not believe, a prudent mother would have taken every precaution to conceal it from you. A mother who had considered your happiness, would have removed this evil by wise representations, and left you in ignorance. But, whatever may be said to you rely on me for consolation and protection—"

"After having protected M. de Champmortain's profligacy—"

"Go on, madam, go on!" said M. de Rudesgens. "But I warn you if you have calculated that the disturbance you are about to raise in your daughter's home will make me forget certain matters—you are deceived."

M. de Rudesgens had at last discovered the secret aim of his wife's enterprise. Touched in so sensitive a place, she began to exclaim, with angry violence:

"What does this mean? what do I wish forgotten, sir? What do these accusations, these words of double meaning signify? Sir, I will have an explanation, I will have it: otherwise, sir, I shall not forget that if we cannot dissolve our union, we can at least separate our lives and fortunes."

M. de Rudesgens drew himself up, and would perhaps, in his reply, have gone beyond the bounds which Sylvia's presence prescribed, had not the latter eagerly stopped him, by saying:

"My mother, my father, listen to me I entreat you; in mercy be calm, both of you. It is on my account that this discussion has arisen, it is for my happiness that my mother takes one view of the subject, while you, my father, take another. Well, then, I must tell you, you are both in error."

"How?" exclaimed the proud Artémise sharply.

"What do you mean, Sylvia?" said M. de Rudesgens.

"My father," returned Sylvia, with extreme confusion and agitation, I know all my mother thought she was revealing to me."

"What! you know," said Madame de Rudesgens, "that your husband is the lover of—"

"Yes, my mother, I know it, and I will not and cannot make him a single reproach."

"What!" resumed M. de Rudesgens, "you believe in your husband's infidelity, and speak so calmly of it?"

Sylvia cast down her eyes, whilst tears trickled down her face.

"Poor child!" said Madame de Rudesgens, "she has learnt to know what grief and patience are by seeing her unfortunate mother suffer. Come, my daughter—come to your mother's arms, we will weep together."

Sylvia continued to weep bitterly, while M. de Rudesgens looked at her attentively. He tried to explain to himself this calm resolution, so little in accordance with all he had been compelled to suffer, and which it seemed to him could not be the result of a saintlike resignation. He was too skilful in such matters not to suspect some other cause; nevertheless, he deemed it prudent to accept this view of the case, and said to his daughter, soothingly:

"Sylvia, you are right, it is not by vain recriminations, by furious outbreaks and acrimonious reproaches that a wandering husband can be brought back."

At this enumeration of his trials, Madame de Rudesgens lifted up her head angrily, and threw flashing glances at her spouse; the latter took no notice of them, but continued:

"But if I approve of this indulgence, Sylvia," and he folded her in his arms as he spoke, it is because I believe it to be the noblest virtue of a pure heart."

Sylvia drooped her head, and her tears flowed more abundantly.

"Yes," replied Madame de Rudesgens, "she pardons him, because, poor child, she has neither malice nor resentment."

"Sylvia, you are an angel—"

Sylvia's tears fell faster.

"Alas!" she said, hesitatingly. "I have no longer the right to—"

"Sylvia," cried M. de Rudesgens, hastily interrupting her, "you forgive him because you are good, that is all—"

"Oh! no, no," said Sylvia, in despair, turning towards her father, it is because it is no longer my right—"

"Oh! hush," said her father, in a low voice; "not before your mother," he added, drawing her to his heart.

He was right. Hardly had Sylvia suffered a word to escape her, which could awaken the belief that she had lost the right of complaining of her husband, ere her mother fixed on her an inquisitive and almost cruel look. In fact, Sylvia's fault would have served still better than that of Champmortain, to divert from herself the storm with which she was threatened by her husband's suspicions.

"What are you saying to her?" cried Madame de Rudesgens, angrily interrogating her husband, "let her speak, let her confide in her mother, who will understand her and all the sorrow she has to bear."

"Her sorrow," said M. de Rudesgens, "she has no other than what you cause her by your foolish suppositions."

This word would have been the signal of a terrible explosion, had not M. de Champmortain suddenly entered without being announced; he was accompanied by Brias.

The alarm depicted on Sylvia's countenance, and the looks of the last named gentleman, at once enlightened M. and Madame de Rudesgens.

"I beg your pardon," said Champmortain, "if I had known you were already prepared for company, I should have come in sooner to announce some news that I am sure you will be delighted to hear."

"What is it then?" asked M. de Rudesgens.

"Yesterday, after your departure, Montéclain shewed us a letter, which proved Madame de Monrion's innocence in a glorious manner."

"Indeed?" said Sylvia.

"Yes, madame," replied Brias, to whom she had put the question, by her look.

Sylvia smiled bitterly.

"And what does this letter say?" asked Madame de Rudesgens, sharply.

"You will know hereafter," replied Champmortain; "for it contains a secret we are not yet at liberty to reveal."

"So this adorable creature is innocent," exclaimed old Rudesgens joyfully; I was sure of it."

"What a singular pleasure," said the sour Artémise.

"It is a pleasure which every man of honour ought to feel," rejoined Champmortain, with severity; "and M. Amab, the colonel, Brias, and I were delighted to hear Madame de Monrion justified. Is it not so, Brias?"

"Certainly," said the latter, whom Sylvia was watchfully observing.

"Ah!" she said, sneeringly.

"But the pleasure afforded us by this justification is of little consequence," said Champmortain; it now concerns us to think of what we owe to Madame de Monrion, to M. de Montaleu, and above all to ourselves. I am come, then, to beg you ladies, and you M. de Rudesgens, to join Brias and myself, and accompany us to M. de Montaleu's house, where we shall meet the colonel, in order to present ourselves before Madame de Monrion, to whom we owe an atonement for the insult she received at our house."

"An atonement," said Sylvia, whose jealousy was suddenly awakened by the sight of Brias' confused mien; that is to say a humiliation for our house."

"Sylvia," said her husband, in a gentle but firm voice, I can understand that false reports may have deceived you sufficiently to excuse a cruel insult towards Madame de Monrion. You know that I blamed this insult at the very time I knew its motive. You have taken a great responsibility on yourself by condemning Madame de Monrion, and a young woman commits a serious fault by thus taking upon herself to execute so severe a judgment, passed on appearances entirely false."

Madame de Champmortain turned pale with anger, and replied, bitterly:

"It was allowable in me to believe in these appearances, when my informant was a person in whom I know you have absolute confidence."

"Of whom are you speaking?" said Champmortain, angrily.

"Of Madame Amab, sir, who is, I believe, more your friend than mine."

"Therefore," returned Champmortain, after a moment's hesitation, "therefore it is I told you I excused your conduct, imprudent as it has been; but I am astonished that you are not as happy to learn you have been deceived, as I doubt not Madame Amab is."

"You are right," said Sylvia; "I am perfectly happy, as much so as yourself, as much so as M. de Brias, who will be at liberty, now Madame de Monrion is justified, to resume his projects of marriage."

Sylvia's jealousy had carried her beyond all prudence. Brias turned pale, Madame de Rudesgens looked threatening·.s to Champmortain, he cast on his wife a look of such astonishment that she began to feel terrified. He was going to speak, when M. de Rudesgens exclaimed, quickly:

"We have nothing to do at present with M. de Brias' marriage projects. The most important point is this, that we have injured a woman who did not deserve it, and some reparation must be offered her."

"Yes," said Champmortain, who had regained his self-command, "and it is for that purpose I am come to beg that Madame de Rudesgens will kindly accompany us."

"I!" cried the old lady, sharply, "I to go and make excuses to a little affected prude."

"We will do without you," said Champmortain, somewhat rudely; "but I hope Sylvia will accompany me—"

At these words Sylvia drew back; she saw herself humble and repentant before this woman to whom she had first confessed her love, and whom she had then so outrageously driven from her house.

"I, sir," said she, in a voice tremulous with anger, "I to go and make excuses to Madame de Monrion—never!"

"Sylvia," returned Champmortain, sternly, "what means this refusal to fulfil a duty sacred to every honourable woman? You will come, Sylvia?"

"Never, sir."

"And she will do right," said her mother.

"And she will do wrong," said M. de Rudesgens, "she must come."

"Never," replied Sylvia, wilfully persisting in her resolution.

"And to what motive must I attribute this refusal?" said Champmortain, angrily. Madame de Monrion's innocence is very hateful to you then? No doubt she interferes with your projects—your affections—"

"M. de Champmortain," said M. de Rudesgens, "you forget that you are speaking before a person who does not belong to your family."

"M. de Brias, in fact," said Champmortain, ironically; "but there are friends who are as good as relations, is it not so, Brias?"

The latter, thus unluckily brought upon the stage, strove to retire into that neutrality so difficult for a lover who is placed between the husband and the wife. In fact, he cannot on one side blame the husband without incurring the risk of being banished by him from the abode to which he is attracted by love, and on the other he knows what punishment awaits him, if by chance he should deem it advisable to take the husband's part against the wife.

Brias was a clever diplomatist, and the case was one to demonstrate his talent; but the position was too pressing, and he could only stammer out the following words:

"I confess, for my own part, I do not understand the reasons which prevent Madame de Champmortain from taking a step of mere propriety, the consequence of which she can herself control."

Brias, in seeking to calm Sylvia's suspicions, only increased those of Champmortain, who replied, in a sardonic tone, addressing himself to his wife:

"Well! madam, what do you think of it? Have M. de Brias' counsels shown you the folly of your refusal?"

Happily, Sylvia had perceived the imprudence she had been led to commit, and she replied:

"The advice and opinion of M. de Brias can in no way influence my conduct; but you can understand, sir," she added, looking earnestly at her husband, "that I feel it extremely disagreeable to go and make apologies to a woman who is innocent, according to you, because I have perhaps listened too readily to the information of another woman, whom you, sir, compelled me to receive."

Champmortain changed countenance. Sylvia, seeing her advantage, continued:

"Had you not imperatively required my mother and myself to receive Madame Amab at your house, I should have known nothing of these pretended calumnies, I should not have used them against any one, nothing of all this would have happened. The atonement for so much evil, if evil there is, should come then from him who has caused it. As to me, sir, I formally declare to you, for the last time, I will not go."

The discussion had already been pushed too far, Champmortain devoured in silence the cruel lesson he had just received. He turned towards Brias, and said:

"Then, sir, we will go together, and when this honourable duty has been fulfilled," he added, addressing Sylvia, "I shall return, and I hope to learn the serious motives of a refusal which greatly surprises me, I warn you."

"I am of your party," exclaimed M. de Rudesgens; "for, as I bore to M. de Montaleu the unfortunate explanation of Sylvia's conduct, it is only just that I should testify the grief I feel at having caused her so much annoyance. I do not ask you to accompany me," he added, turning towards Madame de Rudesgens; "I leave you with your daughter."

Then he added again, in a lower voice:

"I also must have an explanation."

"You must," replied Madame de Rudesgens, bitterly, "go and flutter about this interesting victim."

"I must," replied her husband, hastily drawing her into a corner, "I must go and prevent an explanation between Champmortain and Brias, which might have deadly results; I must save the honour and the future life of our child, madame; think of it. And for that, understand me well, I will consent to remain in ignorance of all that concerns you. I will forget the right I have to a personal explanation."

"Sir," said his wife, in an arrogant voice, "I do not know what you mean."

"Ah!" said M. de Rudesgens, with an accent which at last made his wife fear him, "contrive to save Sylvia, or I give you my word as a nobleman, you shall suffer for the misery from which you had not been able to save her. Come, gentlemen," he added, addressing Champmortain and Brias, who were anxiously observing him, "it is time to visit Madame de Monrion."

The three men went out, and the daughter and mother remained together.

## CHAPTER LXXIV.

### THE LESSON.

Felina retired to her boudoir and seated herself at the foot of Léda's bed. Dorothea's assiduous cares had partly removed from the unhappy victim of Hector's brutality the traces of his horrible violence: Léda seemed tranquil. Felina, on the contrary, was pale and exhausted; her eyes sometimes fixed, sometimes wandering, denoted excessive agitation; the dark circles round them told of want of sleep, the wrinkles on her forehead revealed terrible thoughts, while in a low tone she murmured incoherent words.

Many times rising impatiently, she opened the red window curtains, then resumed her place, saying:

"Will he never come?"

Placing herself opposite to Léda, she examined her curiously. The latter, a smile on her lips, her eyes sparkling and joyous, began repeating a melancholy song, in an almost imperceptible voice. Felina was looking at her, and was perhaps going to interrupt her, when the slight sound of an opening door stopped her. Dorothea entered, and made a sign.

"Is it he?" said Felina. "Dorothea, watch over this woman."

Felina went into her room, where she found Hector de Montaleu.

Like Felina, he seemed to have passed a night of anguish and terror. His eyes were dim, his face pale and haggard; never had the roughest hunting days, never had nights of the maddest debauch reduced so low the herculean strength of this colossus. Felina smiled on seeing him thus. Such prostration promised her a docile slave.

Hector trembled, and cast down his eyes, on perceiving Felina.

"You have got the letter?" asked Madame Amab.

A sign of the head in the affirmative, was Hector's only reply.

"What have you done since this morning?"

Hector looked at Felina with stupid astonishment, as if to ask her how she could suppose he had done anything.

"I ask you," resumed Felina, impatiently, "what you have been doing all the morning?"

"Why," returned Hector, with an almost besotted look, "nothing. What could I do?"

"What you would have done, if the event of this night had not occurred at all."

"And what should I have done?" said Montaleu, with a grovelling smile.

Felina, who had noted Montaleu's dejection with

pleasure, trembled at the thought that perhaps all the energy of this ferocious character was crushed. She looked at him attentively, while with drooping head and eyes fixed on the ground, he seemed lost in profound stupor.

Then, with a voice at once soft and shrill, with the suppleness of a serpent, and the look of a basilisk, she resumed:

"What! the Viscount Hector de Montaleu has been turned out of the Marquis de Montéclain's house, and has not yet demanded satisfaction?"

"He will refuse it to me," returned Hector in a dejected voice.

"Why?"

"Why!" said Hector, with a shudder, "why!" he repeated, "do you not know they have found the body of—?"

"Yes, I know it, and I know also that they expect him to recover."

Hector drew back with affright.

"To save him?" he repeated, "then he will speak, then—"

"What will he say?" asked Felina, anxiously.

Hector seemed to seek for a reply, but could not find one.

"I do not know," he said.

"He will say," replied Felina, "that he had a rendezvous with me in the forest; that after leaving me a gunshot from a thicket struck him in the breast, and that he fell from his horse, and then—that he remembers nothing more; for he was so completely senseless you thought him dead."

Hector raised his head like one lost in darkness, who sees the glimmering of a far off light.

"Ah! yes," he said, with a deep sigh, "it is true; he cannot say anything else."

"Who knew that you were in the forest at that hour? No one, except myself."

"And you, will you keep silence?"

"Yes, but on one condition. It is that you will do all I am going to propose to you."

The guilty man, in the hands of this Delilah, had lost his strength, and hanging down his head, without even knowing what was required of him, he replied:

"I shall not be able."

Felina stamped her foot angrily; but recovered herself almost immediately.

She wished to arouse this emasculated energy, and for that purpose she felt it was necessary to make Hector understand his only remaining means of safety, with the patience of an attentive mother, seeking to impart some complicated idea to the indolent mind of a child.

"Let us see," she said to him, "if you had not met me in the forest, if nothing of all this had happened, should you not this morning have sent a challenge to M. de Montéclain, who has driven you out like a lackey—?"

"True," said Hector; "but I forgot that; I have not done it."

"Well then! since you now acknowledge that you ought to have acted in this manner, you must do it at once."

"But," returned Hector, who was so overwhelmed that he could hardly understand the sense of Felina's words, "suppose he refuses me?"

"Then you will treat him before every one like a coward and a calumniator."

"A coward!" said Hector, "Oh! no—no—that would not be believed! Treat him as a calumniator. Why?",

"For trying to make people believe you to be the father of this child."

"Ah!" said Hector, despairingly, "call him a calumniator—when it is the truth—I shall not be believed."

"But," resumed Felina, interrupting him, "have you not already told Montéclain to his face that he lied?"

"Oh! yes, that is true."

"Then it was he drove you from his table, and you swore to demand satisfaction for this outrage?"

"Yes, that is true again."

"Well! then ought you not to adhere to what you said?"

"Yes," replied Hector, who seemed incapable of being roused by anything from his depression, I ought to do it."

"Have you not everything to fear if you do not? Will it not be said that you admit the truth of Montéclain's accusation?"

"Yes."

"While, if you persist in denying it, Montéclain will have told a lie."

"Ah! yes," returned Hector, always born down by the same thought; "it would have been possible, had I not met with you; and if to obtain that letter—"

"That letter exists no longer, or else it is in your hands."

"Yes," he replied, and he spoke in the desolate tone of a wretch who being hedged in by his crimes, can discover no issue for escape; but they would want to know why that letter had disappeared."

"Who can say you have taken it? and why should you be accused? That letter does not implicate you, and you have no interest in getting hold of it."

"That is possible," said Hector, whose remorse constantly intervened between his intelligence and Felina's reasonings; but you had an interest in it, and then—"

"I!" said Felina, disdainfully; "you need not trouble yourself about me. I shall know how to defend myself if I am accused. But you, if you wish to be saved, must not rest satisfied with defending yourself, you must turn upon him and become the accuser!"

"Accuse—who?" asked Hector, looking at Felina in a stupified manner.

"Listen," she replied, "and if you can, understand me well."

She went up to Hector, took his hand, and said, as if she required all the powers of persuasion to reach a mind so buried in darkness:

"Look at me, and listen to me. Yesterday, on leaving Montéclain's chateau, you returned home indignant at the odious accusation he had dared to bring against you, and resolved to avenge it?"

"Yes, yes," said Hector, hesitating, "and—and after that—"

"This morning you must go in search of witnesses, to demand satisfaction of Montéclain for his insult."

"And who would you have me apply to?—to Brias, to Champmortain, who were both of them present when I was insulted?"

"Brias and Champmortain, exactly," said Felina, in an assenting voice.

"Those who saw Léda's letter?"

"But," said Felina, with patient pertinacity, "this letter does not name you."

"What does that matter?" said Hector; "they have seen the letter; they know that Léda is the mother of the wretched child, saved by Madame de Monrion; and they will ask who is the father of this child."

"Very well. But," rejoined Felina, marking each word with a stress, "let us suppose that Léda were not guilty—that she is not the mother of the child."

"But the letter," said Hector, despairingly, "the letter?"

"If the letter were false?"

Hector fixed on Felina a look of terror.

"If this letter," continued Felina, making both her look and word penetrate into Hector's troubled mind, "suppose this letter, at first entrusted to Madame de Monrion, and preserved so long by Montéclain, to be an invention, to visit on the innocent the consequences of the fault they are themselves guilty of."

"Montéclain and Julia?" said Hector, looking fixedly at Felina.

He thought he understood her, but almost immediately resumed in a desolate voice:

"Why should they have concealed themselves? Are they not both free?"

"That is no reason why a woman should avow her fault."

"But why should they not have married?"

"Because M. de Montaleu, who has made Julia his heiress, would never have consented to her marriage with Montéclain, whom he detests and despises."

"Ah!" said Hector, raising his head, yes—yes—good. Ah! yes."

He rose and drew his hand across his forehead, as he pronounced these words. Thanks to Felina's perfidious speech, an infernal light had at last penetrated the frightful darkness in which he was struggling.

"Proceed—proceed?" he said, in an agitated, inquiring voice.

"What signification," said Felina, with a triumphant smile, "has this pretended letter, read first by the Countess de Monrion, and immediately afterwards by Montéclain, which, six months ago, according to these two confidents, stated that Léda was gone to visit her sick mother, in Paris, and six months after is found to contain the avowal of a fault?"

"In fact—it is true—yes—it is possible," rejoined Hector, that does appear extraordinary. But," he added, stopping before Felina, "it is certain that at this period Julia and Montéclain did not know each other."

"Who told you so?" continued Madame Amab; "did they not both live in Paris, that town where all are lost in the noise and crowd? Did they not both come into the country in October last? Supposing they did not know each other, how could they have come to an understanding so quickly, for the purpose of concealing Léda's fault from her husband, by both reading what the letter did not contain? This coincidence is inexplicable. And since then, who has been to the village of Saint-Faron."

"Julia—Julia only."

"Julia and Montéclain!"

"Indeed?"

"Did not Messieurs de Montaleu, Brias, Champmortain, and De Rudesgens see Montéclain enter the nurse's cottage a moment after Julia had left it? They had perhaps come together."

"The nurse can say the contrary."

"The nurse has disappeared, and do you know where she is concealed? In Montéclain's chateau."

"Impossible."

"I am sure of it," said Felina. "Let this woman say what she will—it is Montéclain who will have dictated it to her. And yet again, how is it that these people, who do not know each other, have been surprised conversing tête-à-tête at Bricord's farm, while Montéclain occupied us all in the pursuit of a wild boar? How is it these people who never see each other, just met so opportunely this morning in the forest?"

"You are right," said Hector. "In fact, yes," he resumed, as if endeavouring to sum up all that Felina had said. "Yes, the letter is false. To-day they pretend it contains an avowal of Léda's, and they have arranged together the invention of this fable. In fact, it is impossible to believe that each should have had the same idea of deceiving Bricord. They did not tell a lie then, but they tell one now."

"That is it," said Felina, with satisfaction; "and after that—" she resumed, as a master makes a child repeat the lesson he has just taught him.

"And then," continued Hector, "never have I or Léda been to see this child while Montéclain has been there, and Julia likewise."

"Very well," said Felina, "go on?"

"And then, they met the day after the ball, and since, at the farm, while Montéclain amused us with the hunt; so this morning again; and the nurse is hidden in Montéclain's house. Ah! I understand," exclaimed Hector, slyly, "you are right. And he who drove me out so insolently, who insulted me. Oh, he shall pay dearly! he—"

Hector stopped suddenly short, as if his ferocious enthusiasm had that moment encountered some formidable obstacle.

"But who will explain the colonel's wound, the substraction of the letter?"

Felina resumed the snakelike fascination, the sharp and penetrating voice, with which she had poured, drop by drop, into Hector's thick brain the subtle poison of her infernal combinations.

"The assassination of the colonel, and the disappearance of the letter, may be explained by the interest of the guilty parties; and if Montéclain has concealed his intrigue with Julia, lest she should lose your uncle's inheritance, has he not a real interest in getting rid of the heir, who is come to lay claim to this immense fortune?"

"But the letter?"

"If it were a false one, would he have risked a a denial of it by Léda?"

"That denial would have availed nothing."

"But understand me then, this letter is false, and consequently not in Léda's writing."

"Well?" said Hector who did not understand.

"Since you say it is a forgery," said Felina with the gesture and intimation of one who is unfolding a subtle train of reasoning to a mind of limited comprehension, "it certainly cannot have been written by Léda. You understand—the letter is false, and it is Montéclain who has written it; now if he could shew it to Champmortain and the rest who do not know Léda's writing—he would have been afraid to have it examined by people who do know her writing, you understand—consequently he would do all that was possible to conceal it from those who would have exposed the cheat by declaring it was not in Léda's hand. If the letter is a forged one, it is his interest to destroy it after it has once served his purpose—do you understand me?"

"Yes, yes," said Hector who was listening attentively.

"Very well then!" resumed Felina, with a cruel smile, "you understand also why Montéclain should have given it to the colonel, whom he meant to make away with, and from whom he was very sure of getting it back.

Montaleu looked with strange fear at Felina; the profound duplicity of this woman, this prodigious art for giving to the circumstances which might have ruined them, a probability, a meaning, a result, which might be the ruin of others, terrified him.

"Oh!" he said in a tremulous voice, "you would cause the innocence of a saint to be questioned."

"And still better, the guilt of an assassin," replied Felina disdainfully.

Hector looked at her angrily.

"Oh!" she said, "now we are in this track, we

must march directly on to the end, or else perish in a few hours."

"It is frightful," said Hector.

"It must be done, or else you may expect to be denounced by Montéclain, and accused of causing Léda's disappearance."

"Léda!" said Montaleu, placing himself before Felina, "have you thought of her? How do you account for her disappearance? Has Montéclain effected that too?"

"Léda!" repeated Madame Amab with a triumphant smile, "Léda!"—Know then that I found her last night, wounded and lost in the forest, and that an hour hence, I shall send her back to the farm."

"But she will speak!" cried Montaleu.

"No."

"She will accuse me of being the father of this child!"

"No."

"But she will say that I struck her?"

"No, I tell you."

"What have you promised her then?"

"Nothing."

"With what have you threatened her?"

"With nothing."

"Has she consented to join in this plot?"

"Léda can no longer either help or injure us."

"Is she dead then?"

"*No, she is mad!*"

---

## CHAPTER LXXV.

### MOTHER AND DAUGHTER.

A moment after Champmortain, M. de Rudesgens and Brias had set out together for Madame de Monrion's house, Felina called at M. de Rudesgens' and demanded an interview with the old marchioness. The latter, with that skill so common to women, but which sometimes denotes or passes for genius in great captains, had determined as we have seen to carry the war and disorder into another family, to avoid the disturbances which might break out in her own.

After all she had just said against Felina, Madame de Rudesgens' was in no way disposed to receive her, and was going to reply that she was not at home when Sylvia stopped the servant who had announced Madame Amab, saying:

"Show her up to me this moment.

"What!" said Madame de Rudesgens in a low voice, "in spite of what you know?"

"Yes," replied Sylvia, "it must be so mother; for if I know—she knows also—"

"What?" asked Madame de Rudesgens frightened.

"Be cautious," returned Sylvia, "we are not alone."

She turned to the servant who was waiting and said:

"Shew Madame Amab in."

"But what is it?" said Madame de Rudesgens immediately, what does she know then?"

"Oh! mother, mother," said Sylvia, hiding herself in her arms, have you not guessed the truth?"

Felina appeared at that moment. Any one who had seen her during her interview with Hector, and had been present when she entered to Madame de Rudesgens' would have trembled at her look. This woman whose face a few minutes before, had been disordered by watching, by the sinister thoughts to which she was a prey; had now as if by enchantment, recovered all that quiet assurance which characterized her beauty, the clearness of her glance, the grace and confidence of her smile. With so much power over herself, so much self-command, there was every reason to fear such a woman. The manner in which she looked at Sylvia and Madame de Rudesgens, had something in it at once disdainful and cruel. The bird of prey making a stoop over the nest which contains the victims he is going to devour, must thus look upon them; the powerful assassin who strikes a defenceless prisoner in his cell, must exhibit the same disdain in the presence of an enemy too easily exterminated.

Felina came forward, and in her sweetest, most delusive voice, said to Madame de Rudesgens:

"Well, madame, have you recovered from the effects of your illness of yesterday?"

"Perfectly," returned Madame de Rudesgens, "the heat, the noise, an unfortunate indisposition—"

"And perhaps," said Felina graciously, "some unfortunate recollection revived by M. de Montéclain—"

"Madame," said Madame de Rudesgens with sudden anger, "I do not understand you."

"Will you permit Sylvia to retire, madame," rejoined Felina, "then perhaps I should be better able to make myself understood."

Madame de Rudesgens was alarmed, and detaining Sylvia, replied:

"My daughter should never have an interview with any one at which her mother may not be present, and I presume you can have nothing to say to me which my daughter may not hear."

"As you please, madame," answered Felina, "I am the most accommodating person in the world; I can keep a secret ten years, whilst in the neighbourhood of the people interested in it, or divulge it before an assembly of a thousand persons. Let Madame de Champmortain remain then, since you think it proper."

"You are too kind madame," said Sylvia in a tone of intreaty, "to have anything to say to my mother to give her pain, whether it relates to herself, or to other people."

"You are mistaken, Sylvia," returned Felina seriously, "what I have to say to Madame de Rudesgens is terrible and may become a source of great misery to her."

"To me!" said Madame de Rudesgens whose acrid temper, was growling sullenly in spite of the alarm she experienced.

"To you, madam," said Felina.

Madame de Rudesgens drew herself up proudly, and rejoined:

"Do you hope to threaten me as you have doubtless threatened this unhappy child?"

"Madame Amab never threatened me, mother," said Sylvia. "All she did was by chance to surprise an innocent interview. I swear to you—she knows the feelings I cannot control—but—I may say—that never—"

"Sylvia," rejoined Felina, sadly, "you are weak, and passion may render you cruel; but you will suffer as much by the evil you commit, as by that you feel. Leave us, I entreat you; you must not learn as I have done, that all in this world is falsehood and hypocrisy; leave us—leave us."

"Really, madam," cried Madame de Rudesgens, while Sylvia listened to Felina in fearful surprise, "really, this passes the bound of propriety; do you forget that you are in my house, and that it is in the presence of her own mother you are desiring a daughter to withdraw? Do you not understand madam, that if any one ought to leave this room, it is you?"

"Remain, then, Sylvia," said Felina, "and you madam," she added, "turning towards Madame de Rudesgens, "are you sure you have a right to drive from your house the pretended daughter of Sophia Muller and Joseph Miras?"

At these words, as if a hideous and dreadful phantom had suddenly risen before Madame de Rudesgens, she fixed on Felina a look of despair, and stretching out her trembling hand towards her, repeated, in a broken hollow voice:

"The daughter of Sophia Muller and of—you!—"

"Yes, I," returned Felina.

"Sylvia! Sylvia!" said Madame de Rudesgens, with a hasty gesture, but without taking her eyes off Felina, "Sylvia! go away, go away."

"No," replied Felina, sternly, "let her stay now to learn—"

"Oh!" said Madame de Rudesgens, with a despairing cry, clasping her hands, "not before her, not before her."

These were the very words M. de Rudesgens had spoken to Sylvia. Unhappy mother, unhappy child, obliged thus to conceal themselves from each other!

"Go, Sylvia, go," added Felina, after a moment's hesitation: "but remember, one day, that I, the forsaken banished child; I, the degraded woman, whom all may insult with impunity, remember that I pitied you—that I did not revenge myself as I might have done."

"Go, go, Sylvia," said her mother, wildly, "go."

Sylvia went up to her mother, took her hand, and would have kissed it; but Madame de Rudesgens folded her in her arms, and held her there a ong time, whilst her tears fell fast upon her. Felina contemplated them; a death-like pallor spread itself over her face, and when Sylvia had left the room, she exclaimed:

"Ah! yes, that is the darling child, the beloved daughter, who is not threatened with being driven away—"

"What do you want with me? what do you demand?" interrupted Madame de Rudesgens, who had hardly strength enough to speak.

"I want to be revenged," returned Felina, coldly.

"On me!" cried Madame de Rudesgens, 'what have I done to you, then?"

"Oh! nothing at all, really," said Felina, with ironical malice, "nothing at all; a mother, who, to conceal her own fault, refuses to own her child; who, whilst possessing herself an enormous fortune, condemns her almost to misery; who, to ensure the possession of a great name, endows her, by means of a forged deed, with that of a lackey and a miserable woman. The mother who does that has a right to ask her child, 'What have I done to you, then?'"

"Do you wish for money?"

"No."

"Do you want a fortune?"

"No."

"Then, in heaven's name, what do you want?"

"I have told you; I want to be revenged."

"But, on whom?"

"On Madame de Monrion."

Though that name ought to have alleviated the terror experienced by Madame de Rudesgens, she stood as if frozen, so unpitying, so threatening was Felina's accent.

"On Madame de Monrion?" she repeated.

"Yes, on the woman to whom your husband, your son-in-law, and your daughter's lover are just gone to apologize for the insult offered her in your house."

"But," returned Madame de Rudesgens, "it appears that these gentlemen read a letter yesterday, which proved Madame de Monrion's innocence."

"That letter is a forgery," said Felina. "Madame de Monrion is guilty, she must be so, for I will have it—"

"You require it!" said Madame de Rudesgens, consulting the expression of Felina's face.

"And you will require it too," rejoined Felina. "And Sylvia as well."

"But what can I do against this poor woman?"

"What! you who know so well what measures ought to be taken in defence of your own honour—don't you know how to injure that of others? Oh! you are too modest, madam; I came to solicit your advice—"

Madame de Rudesgens hung down her head, equally vexed and afflicted to be obliged to submit to the implacable authority Felina imposed on her. No feeling of tenderness or repentance, no natural emotion had affected these two women. It was not the meeting of mother and daughter, but the compact of two guilty wicked beings."

"But," exclaimed Madame de Rudesgens, angrily, "what infernal hand has torn aside the veil? Who informed you of this secret?"

"You, madam, you. For a long time I knew I was not the daughter of Joseph Miras and Sophia Muller. With the act which endowed me with a certain fortune, was found a writing which was to be given me on my wedding day."

"This writing, whose was it?"

"My father's."

"Your father's—the writing of—"

Madame de Rudesgens stopped short."

"It is impossible. He swore that he had never named me, that my name had never been written."

"Neither is it mentioned."

"He wrote so to me on his deathbed."

"His deathbed!" repeated Felina; "he is dead then?"

"You did not know it?" said Madame de Rudesgens, regretting that she had suffered herself to be overcome by the fear which the terrible apparition of this abandoned daughter had called up. "You do not know who he is then?"

"Well! no," returned Felina; "it is useless to surprise secrets which we ought to tell each other without subterfuge. The writing which was given me on the day of my marriage, is addressed to M. de Montaleu."

"M. de Montaleu!" said Madame de Rudesgens, "and he knows?"

"Not yet, nor shall he ever know it, if you like."

"But what does this writing say?"

"Here is a copy of it," replied Felina.

Madame de Rudesgens took it anxiously, and read as follows:

"My friend, at the moment of setting out on a long journey, I confide this letter to a notary, that on her wedding day it may be delivered to the person who will bring it to you herself. It may be that one day, in spite of the care I have taken to secure her fortune, she may fall into poverty and abandonment; I depend on you to come to her assistance, and compel, if necessary, the woman who has induced me to forsake her, who has forced me to commit an action unworthy of an honest man, to receive her under her protection. Gertrude Sophia is not, as recorded in the certificate of her birth, the daughter of Joseph Miras and Sophia Muller; she is my child, and her mother is a woman known to you, whose fortune you have protected. At the time the child was born, this woman was on the point of marrying one of our friends. To conceal her faults from every eye, and to prevent the deserted child from making inquiries after those she belonged to, her mother got two poor creatures for a sum of money to acknowledge her as their own daughter. Joseph, a servant of her

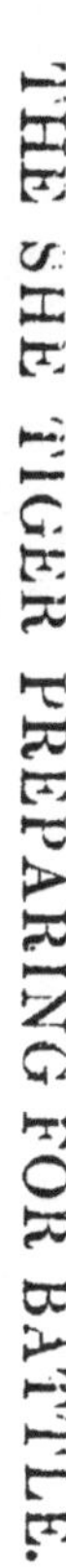

THE SHE TIGER PREPARING FOR BATTLE.

mother's, undertook to find an accomplice, and availed himself of the misery of a poor woman, named Sophia Muller, to persuade her to accept the bargain. But, as I have already said, the day may come, when my child will be forsaken by her supposed mother, as she has been by her real one. If this should happen, I commend her to you. Take care of her, and, if necessary, apply to her, whose immense fortune may readily make up for the wrongs of her first desertion. I do not name her to you, you will easily recognize her in the woman we used, between ourselves, to nickname the Fairy of diamonds.

"On the other hand, my friend, as it is possible that the child I am compelled to forsake may be unworthy of your interest; as she must not abuse the secret I only dare confide to you, as it might possibly make use of my name and her mother's, did I reveal them here, to create disorder in two families, I leave it to your prudence to judge whether you ought to give her this information, to decide what you can do for her, to protect, or leave her in her abandonment, according to her merit. I sign this writing with a name, and attach to it a seal, both known to you, as well as my writing, and now I can go, for I depend on you."

The writing was signed, MATHEUS LUDWIG, and the seal shewed a pistol, with the motto: *Lethum quam lutum.*

Madame de Rudesgens stood for a moment with her eyes fixed on the writing; she looked at Felina, and then again at the paper.

"Oh!" she said to herself, "she has no other proof than this useless writing, which M. de Montaleu would have refused to understand, for he hates and despises her, and I, like a fool, have entirely surrendered my secret."

Madame de Rudesgens tore the paper, angrily.

"It is but a copy," said Felina, coldly, "the original is in my possession."

Madame de Rudesgens did not reply, she was seeking for some means to deny all she had owned to Felina.

The latter seemed to guess as much, for she instantly resumed:

"Do not repent, madam; for if this revelation had not come from me, it would have come from another."

"From whom then?"

"From Sophia Muller's son."

"But fifteen years ago, when he presented himself to M. de Montaleu, to obtain an acknowledgment from him."

"M. de Montaleu drove him away, and you, who, by a single word, might have corrected the old marquis's mistake, you suffered him to do so."

"He was a wretch whose nature bespoke every possible vice."

"Indeed?" said Felina.

"So Montaleu told me; that young man, who was hardly fifteen, threatened him with his vengeance: he spoke of punishment, and I know not what."

"And what do you think has become of him?"

"He most probably died of want, or in the depths of some prison: he can never have been anything but a miserable wretch."

"What ever he be," said Felina, "this man is here."

"And he knows—the truth?"

"He ought to know it—for he was present yesterday at Montéclain's supper."

"At Montéclain's supper! Then doubtless this man is the unfortunate man who waits upon the colonel?"

"Ah!" said Felina, casting an angry glance on Madame de Rudesgens, "you are all alike; you, whose life has been moulded by birth and fortune, cannot conceive that any man, whoever he be, may be worth anything in himself; because you flung him back into misery and ignominy you think he must live in them. All that is great, strong, and powerful of itself, you are a stranger to. Madame de Rudesgens, the child you condemned to shame and abandonment, bears to-day a name more celebrated throughout the world than that of your noble husband. The child discarded by M. de Montalieu, and whom you would look for amidst the sweepings of anti-rooms, was seated at your table, equal by his fame to those around him; the son of M. de Montaleu is Colonel Thomas Rien."

"And he knows the truth?" said Madame de Rudesgens, for she had paid no attention to Felina's oratorial display.

"It is probable he knows it, like myself; and now, madam, you must give me one last piece of information—what is the name of the man who assisted you to hide your shame?"

"His name?" said Madame de Rudesgens, turning pale.

"The name of him who directed to M. de Montaleu this letter, which shall crush you, if I choose?"

"What, do you not suspect it?"

"Perhaps I do."

"But," resumed Madame de Rudesgens, in a low tone, "who then could have told Montéclain this horrible tale, except—"

"Except his father, is it not so?" cried Felina, with transport.

Madame de Rudesgens only replied by a mute sign.

"Oh! Montéclain! Montéclain!" resumed Felina, whose whole face was lit up with a fierce and threatening joy, "woe to thee, now!"

"What do you mean to do then?"

"Mother," said Felina, terrifying her with her fiery glance, "Madame de Monrion must be dishonoured, and Montéclain must die."

"But why?—but how?"

"The work is in progress; you must help me to accomplish it, or else you, my mother, and Sylvia, my sister, shall perish with me."

Thus did Felina hold in her hands the will and liberty of action of all those around her; of Champmortain, of Brias, of Madame de Rudesgens, of Sylvia, and the ferocious Hector, whose faults, whose crimes, had made them all her slaves; Léda, whose resistance and remorse were lost in madness; the colonel, whose honour and resolution were shackled on a bed of death.

## CHAPTER LXXVI.

### THE HEART OF A GENTLE BEING.

MADAME DE MONRION had just returned home, after her last meeting with Montéclain.

For two days past, Julia's heart had been a prey to emotions so terrible, so divided, that at this moment she could hardly tell what she felt. The gross outrage offered to her by Madame de Champmortain striking her in the midst of the innocent tranquillity in which she lived, had wounded at once her pride and the only affection she was at liberty to avow, that is the one she felt for M. de Montaleu, whose protection she had found so cold and impotent.

As we have said, she suffered also from the fact that no one rose to avenge her wrongs; this abandonment made her feel most bitterly that she was alone in the world, and the indifference of a man on whom she had depended, rendered this solitude still more desolate and frightful.

Then the dreadful blow inflicted by M. de Montaleu had fallen upon her, abating in Julia's heart the high confidence she felt in herself. In fact, he had taught her two grievous truths: that the most irreproachable virtue is no safeguard against the hatred of the wicked, and that it has no claim to those devoted and exalted affections which exist in one's family alone.

M. de Montaleu's tardy repentance, occasioned by the burst of despair, had not consoled Julia. Shortly afterwards, Hector de Montaleu's proposal so well received by his uncle, had proved to her still better that her existence and happiness were at the mercy of a credulous old man, and on the wicked audacity of one who wanted to speculate on the scandal of a calumny.

Then for the first time she had met that Montéclain, of whom she had so often dreamed in the silence of night; whose apathy in Madame de Champmortain's drawing-room had so deeply wounded her; she had seen him as she had imagined him; respectful, serious, and generous. All he had said at the farm during their first interview had been to Julia a singular revelation of the power this man exercised over her. He had promised to assist her; and she had calmly relied on his honour. He had bowed before her in rendering homage to her innocence, and she had risen again to the position in her self-esteem, whence M. de Montaleu had suffered her to descend. She had parted from him proud and happy.

But, during the night which followed this first meeting, Julia's joy and confidence were disturbed by painful reflections.

This man who exercised such power over her, who, as a stranger, had occupied her thoughts, and who now, when scarcely known, already governed her, was he not renowned for the infernal address by which he had succeeded in deceiving so many women? Was it not said that he made a sport of their dishonour and despair? Had not M. de Montaleu depicted his heart as one too implacable to recoil from any means of vengeance? Was he not one of those who strike a father through his daughter, a husband through his wife, a brother through his sister?"

Julia's heart gave the lie to her fears, but her reason continually renewed them in a thousand new shapes. Where then was the truth?

These were the thoughts which tormented Julia's mind, and this is why Montéclain met her in the forest shedding tears, forced from her by the painful conflict between her feelings and her fears. In all that concerned her personally, Julia had confined herself to a simple protestation against the calumny: this was publicly to take a last succour to the forsaken child, she had so daringly protected, and thus to shew her contempt for the accusation brought against her. At the sight of Montéclain, all the terrors of her agitated soul were effaced; the mute homage which he offered her, the eager respect she received from him, and those by whom he was accompanied, had once more recalled to Julia's heart hope, confidence, and faith; but hardly had she left him, before her fears returned. Alas! had she not been once already deceived by another, or rather by herself? Had she not loved Amab with a love he did not return? Then it was she sat down to write the following letter:

"My brother, I write to you at Florence, where you were residing some days ago; will this letter find you there? I hope so: but, in whatever part of Italy you receive it, set out immediately; come back to Paris, I shall be there. Charles, your presence is necessary to me.

"I told you a long time since, how I had saved a poor woman from the suicide to which she was driven by despair, and from the punishment which threatened her. This action which you praised, and boasted of as one of sublime charity, has been employed against me, as the pretext for an infamous slander. But this is not my real cause of unhappiness, the calumny has been quickly acknowledged to be one: what alarms me, and makes me, implore you to return, is myself. Charles, I remember that when I once before fondly yielded to the hope of being loved, when my imagination invested with the noblest qualities one who had never looked on me save with admiration, I remember your cold reason passed a judgment on him which was just, but which my prepossessed heart refused to believe. I attributed it to your carelessness and frivolity, while I was in fact deceiving myself. Well! Charles, my brother, now again I am afraid of being duped by the same illusions.

"There is a man here who has undertaken my defence. To see him, to listen to him, it would seem that no other respect ever equalled his, that no homage was ever more sincere, and yet this man passes for one of those who deceive with the greatest facility. He has never told me that he loves me, but he will tell me so, I am sure of it, and I do not wish to hear it; he would find it too easy to deceive me; I should like so much to believe him!

"Forgive me, Charles, I have but one safeguard against him, that of flight; I will leave this country where he is, before another interview shall have disclosed to him the empire he possesses over my weak heart. If I were to meet him again, renowned as he is by his courage, his terrible adventures, his fascinating qualities, his inflexible language, his proud contempt, his supreme confidence in himself, if I were to meet him again as I have already seen him twice, generous, simple, good, and bashful, before me, like a young man subdued by his first love, he would too easily perceive the joy I experience in beholding him thus.

"And if the agitation which flatters me, the modesty which enchants me, were only a part admirably played. If I revealed all my heart to this man, while he perfidiously concealed his own from me, what would become of me Charles?

"Not that I fear, not that I fly from the apprehension of a fault! Whatever power the presence and language of this man exercise over me, they could never prevail against the love of virtue bequeathed to me by our sainted mother. I am not like one whom I have beheld here in anxiety and alarm, I do not fear that he will allure me into the forgetfulness of all my duties. He will not destroy me in the world's judgment, but he might kill me in myself.

"You do not understand me, Charles, for I am mad, I feel I am. He has not said he loves me; well then, I wish him never to say so. I will not incur the danger of listening to him, of believing him, and being deceived. When I shall be far away from him, if he forgets, if he despises me, I shall not have the right to complain, and deprived of all love, I shall be able to say in the depths of my soul, 'Had I remained, he would have loved me.'

"See to what extent I love him, my brother, since I would prefer hereafter a faith in this supposition, to the fear I now feel of being deceived. I am going to set out then, I shall arrive alone in Paris, and remain there in concealment. Then you will come to me, and I shall be better able to reveal to you the feelings of my soul.

"I am alone here; there is no one near me of whom I can ask support and advice, except him, whom I have trusted as I should have done an old friend of my infancy, for I have confided my sorrows to him unreservedly, in the hope of being justified by him. When he offered to devote himself to my cause, I accepted the offer as I should have done yours. I held out my hand to him, as I would have done to poor Villon; when he promised to revenge me on my enemies, I felt as secure as if a king had come to my assistance; when he said to me, 'Madam, I honour and respect you,' I felt myself re-instated in my former position, as if my father had blessed me. He has possessed himself of every feeling of my soul—my friendship, my confidence, my admiration.

"Oh, my brother, do you not see that it is this terrible power which alarms me? Oh! if this man deceives me! if he has practised through me the vengeance which he has vowed to M. de Montaleu! I dare not, I will not believe it. I should suffer too much in accusing him, and yet I am afraid to believe he is sincere. This evening I will leave this country. I will not see him again—he would penetrate my feelings, and if he asked me if I loved him, I could not tell him a lie. Come, then, come, you, whose reasons is calmer, will tell me if I may love him, if I may—. Oh! my brother, if this were only a vain terror, if it were but the result of all I have already suffered, if my fears were an outrage to him—if he could love me sincerely. Oh! my brother, how happy I should be! how proud! And how could I ever love him enough to repay him for my happiness? But no—I must go, I must—"

Julia had written thus much of her letter, when the door of her apartment opened suddenly.

---

## CHAPTER LXXVII.

### A NEW MISFORTUNE.

JULIA'S sudden interruption was occasioned by the entrance of M. de Rudesgens, Champmortain and Brias.

"Pardon us, Madame," said M. de Rudesgens, in his most gallant tone, "we asked, when we entered the house to see M. de Montaleu; but we were informed that he was closeted with some one, who has doubtless already informed him of the motive which dictates this solemn proceeding, and as he has forestalled us with M. de Montaleu, we wish to forestall him with you. We are more fortunate than he is, madam."

"What is the matter in hand, then, gentlemen?" said Julia, who could not doubt their motive in coming.

"As the object of our visit here," resumed Monsieur de Rudesgens, "interests you as much as it does our old friend, as joy and peace cannot be too quickly restored to a suffering heart, we are come, madam, to offer you the assurance of our esteem and consideration."

"Madam," added Champmortain, "you who have a right to be severe, will only be indulgent, I am sure of it, and will pardon Madame de Champmortain."

"Oh! tell her," cried Julia, eagerly, "that I only ask her permission to love her as a sister."

"Thank you, madam," said old Rudesgens, "that is truly kind—thank you. But you must know all: there is some one who is not here, who has done better than us all; it is a man of whom you have heard a great deal of harm, who has been guilty of loving and being loved by many, and that has given him a bad reputation. But this man has a heart as noble as his name; he might have been your enemy, he has constituted himself your defender; he might, by merely keeping silence have caused you suffering, but Montéclain does not war against the weak, nor against women; he possessed the proof of your innocence, the letter of the farmer's wife, he showed it to these gentlemen, and you have to thank him through us."

Julia listened to M. de Rudesgens, trembling at once with joy and fear. Montéclain had kept his promise, and at this she was rejoiced; but, at the same time he had acquired in her heart a too powerful claim upon her gratitude, and this it was which alarmed her. Another thought was mingled with these feelings. She remembered the meeting of that morning, and Montéclain's mysterious words, she answered, in a deeply agitated voice:

"I thank you, gentlemen, for the step you have taken, and the eagerness you have manifested in taking it, but let me ask you to whom did M. de Montéclain confide the proof of my innocence?"

"To Colonel Thomas Rien," replied Champmortain.

"To him!" cried Julia, with a shudder; "it is for that reason, then, he has been assassinated?"

"Assassinated!" repeated the three men, looking at each other in terror.

"Then he is not with M. de Montaleu?" said M. de Rudesgens.

"Assassinated," resumed M. de Champmortain, "but by whom?"

"By whom?" cried Brias, angrily; "why, by the man who, by suppressing the proof of Madame de Monrion's innocence, would extinguish that of his infamy at the same time."

Just as Brias had uttered these words, the door of Julia's apartment was again opened violently, and M. de Montaleu came in, hastily followed by Hector.

M. de Montalieu was pale, his features were disordered, he appeared to be trembling at once with anger and horror. As to Hector, his countenance was animated by a savage inflexible resolution. It was that of a man in a deadly track, who, with eyes looking fixedly onwards, marches on to the end he aims at, without daring to look at the road he is pursuing or the miry precipices he must cross over. The aspect of the uncle and nephew was so strange that Brias, M. de Rudesgens, and Champmortain remained speechless. Julia shuddered; she felt that Hector's presence foreboded some new misfortune. Excited once more by the feeling which governed her, she cast a despairing glance around, as if to seek for some defender. Instinctively she drew near to those who had come to offer their testimony to her innocence, and waited for M. de Montaleu to explain himself; for the latter had stopped, as if suffocated by the emotion he felt.

"Well!" said M. de Rudesgens, more astonished than any one by this impetuous entrance, "what is the matter? What has happened?"

"What is the matter?" said Hector, with the furious courage of a criminal driven to extremity. "The matter is—"

"Silence!" interrupted M. de Montaleu, authoritatively. "Silence, Hector! A justification of your conduct was due to me alone; if others demand it of you, I am to judge whether you ought to give it them."

Champmortain, Brias, and M. de Rudesgens looked at each other again, as if to ask what signified M. de Montaleu's passion, aud Hector's justification. Julia continued motionless, ignorant how misfortune could reach her, unable to divine one of Felina's perfidious machinations. She only felt that some terrible blow was aimed at her; she fixed an eager look on Hector; but this time he was not disturbed by it, he did not look down; his brow, like his heart, was bronzed by Felina's lessons.

"Tell me, gentlemen," said M. de Montaleu, suddenly, with a bitter smile, tell me why you are come to this house? Speak, I entreat you."

"We came," replied M. de Rudesgens, drily, "to testify to Madame de Monrion our regret, our esteem, and our respect."

"And what induced you, gentlemen, to make this solemn ovation to Madame de Monrion?"

"A letter, which I have seen with my own eyes," said Brias firmly, "which Champmortain has also seen, and which in our presence was given to Colonel Thomas Rien."

"Indeed!" said M. de Montaleu, in a very sarcastic voice, "and by whom was this letter written?"

"By the person to whom the child at Saint-Faron belongs, the unhappy wife of farmer Bricord."

"Really!" replied M. de Montaleu again, "and do you know the writing of this unfortunate creature?"

Brias and Champmortain looked at each other, and Brias was obliged to reply:

"It is true we do not know the writing, but Montéclain affirmed—"

"Ah!" said M. de Montalieu, contemptuously, "Montéclain affirmed—, and on the affirmation of M. de Montéclain, of the man who all his life has sported with the honour of women, of the man who never curbed his passions, of the man whose conduct I denounced before all his fellow-citizens, who in your presence threatened to revenge on me the justice I had visited on him; on the affirmation of such a man you believed in the authenticity of that letter!"

"What!" exclaimed Brias, "do you suppose it is a forgery?"

"I affirm, and swear, that it is," said Hector de Montaleu, in a firm distinct voice.

This man was no longer confused, he no longer hesitated; he had, in a manner, passed through, and been tempered by the fire of hell!

"So, then," said M. de Rudesgens, "this letter was fictitious."

"But what interest could Montéclain have in ruining that wretched woman?" said Champmortain.

"It was not her ruin he sought," replied M. de Montaleu, "it was the Viscount de Montaleu, it was my nephew, the inheritor of my name, whom, in default of me he strove to dishonour, it was he Montéclain strove to strike in his inability to reach me."

"To whom then does this child belong?" asked M. de Rudesgens.

"Ask that," returned M. de Montaleu, casting a look full of indignation and contempt towards Julia, ask that of her who concealed it in the hamlet of Saint-Faron, of her who alone has been to see it, of her whom we met there, and who returned there again this morning."

All eyes were turned upon Julia. She was motionless, dumb; she looked and listened as if all that was being said before her was not the condemnation of herself. There was no despair in that silence, but only a strange astonishment. Julia asked herself at that moment whether she were not a prey to some abominable dream, or whether she had not at once been deprived of her memory and reason.

"But," resumed M. de Rudesgens, in the tone of a man who shrinks back from a conviction which subdues, yet grieves him, who then is the father of the child?"

"Go," rejoined M. de Montaleu, in a clamorous voice, "go and ask him who went secretly to visit it, him whom we met there, who, at the moment I speak to you, has concealed the child in his chateau. Go and ask the generous defender of Madame de Monrion, go and ask Montéclain."

Thus was the system developed, which Felina had imparted to Hector, and which the latter, inspired by the perfidious lessons of that woman, had in his turn persuaded M. de Montaleu to believe. Already had new doubts forced a passage into the minds of Champmortain, M. de Rudesgens and Brias. Julia stood silent and still, her gaze intently fixed on Hector. Brias turned towards her:

"Madame!" he said, "you have heard?" Julia made no reply.

"Madam," said Champmortain, "all this is untrue: is it not so?"

"Permit—permit M. de Montaleu to conclude," she replied, in a short hissing voice.

"I think I have said enough," he replied, "to enable you to understand—"

"No," said Julia, with a frightful smile, "you have not yet explained Léda's disappearance."

"Those who have so often inquired for her at the farm could explain the matter to us better than those who have not concerned themselves about her," rejoined M. de Montaleu.

"Ah!" said Julia, "it is well; but how do you account for the assassination of Colonel Thomas Rien."

"He who had given him a fictitious letter would seek to wrest it from him at any cost."

"And would he have done so by an assassination?" cried Brias.

"Either he or I did it," said Hector, "make your choice between us—"

For the first time, Julia turned her eyes from Hector, and looked one after the other at M. de Rudesgens, Brias, and Champmortain; but all three stood uncertain and faltering before this incredible audacity. Perhaps their conviction was still wavering; but how few men would have dared to take the responsibility of the terrible choice offered to them, especially when they had no direct interest in the matter! Julia left them time to reply; then seeing they remained silent, she rose, went straight up to M. de Montaleu, and said to him in a solemn voice:

"Adieu, sir, the malediction of heaven is on your house. And you, gentlemen," she added, turning towards the rest, accuse yourselves alone for the inevitable misfortunes which will strike you and yours. Adieu!"

"What!"

"Threats?" cried M. de Montaleu, angrily.

Julia stopped; the supernatural strength which had supported her till now seemed giving way; for a moment she believed herself capable of entering upon the discussion of the thousand fatal circumstances accumulated against her; but she felt that she should lose the desperate energy which alone preserved her from a burst of cries, tears and sobs; she would not suffer M. de Montaleu to behold a second time a spectacle which had justified her once already, and was preparing to leave the room when a servant announced the Marquis de Montéclain.

"Montéclain!" was the universal exclamation.

"It is he!" cried Julia, on perceiving him. "Thank heaven, thank heaven!" she added, "retreating to the further end of the room, whilst he, pale with sparkling eyes, but calm and master of himself, advanced up the room.

Julia sank upon a chair, motionless as before. One would have thought she was a careless spectator of these terrible scenes, who had quietly resumed her place, to watch their farther development. At this moment one fatal thought occupied her mind. Something cruel had glided into this pure and simple soul, an unknown feeling had thrilled through that heart; this being created by heaven a thing of goodness and openness, had been led by the wickedness of mankind to say:

"I too will be implacable; I too will be revenged."

Thus calumny, which ruins the feeble by crushing them beneath the weight of shame, sometimes ruins the strong and just also, by inspiring them with anger and revenge.

M. de Montaleu, on seeing Montéclain exclaimed:

"You here, sir, in my house! what do you want here?"

"There is at my house," replied Montéclain, in a voice perfectly composed and serene, "a man who is almost at his last hour, and who wishes to speak to you M. de Montaleu. This man has desired me to come and demand an interview with you. That is why I am here."

"Who is that man?" said M. de Montaleu.

"The son of Sophia Muller," replied Montéclain.

"The son of Sophia Muller," repeated the old man, "I will not see him."

"Very well," replied Montéclain, "I have discharged the commission I undertook. You have all of you heard, gentlemen, that M. de Montaleu has refused the interview demanded of him by the dying man who sent me here."

"It is enough, sir," returned the marquis, with a gesture which commanded Montéclain to retire.

"Pardon me, sir," said Montéclain, coldly, "but in this chamber, I am Madame de Monrion's visitor rather than yours, and I shall await her orders before quitting it."

"You are mistaken, sir," said Julia, "I am not mistress here."

"Ah!" said Montéclain, smiling contemptuously, "the crime is accomplished then?"

"Sir," said M. de Montaleu who was trembling with anger, "you forget that you are in my house!"

"No, my lord," replied Montéclain, bowing, "it is for that reason I ask your permission to address a single question to M. de Brias and M. de Champmortain."

"Make haste, then," said M. de Montaleu, "and do not give me time to recollect that you had the insolence to drive my nephew out of your house?"

"Montéclain bowed again, and turning immediately towards Brias and Champmortain, he said:

"Have you kept the promise you made me yesterday, gentlemen?"

"We came here for that purpose," rejoined Brias, in a sad embarrassed tone; but the Marquis de Montaleu has communicated to us circumstances so singular—"

"Indeed!" said Montéclain, looking at Brias, with an air at once satirical and terrible; and these circumstances have caused you to hesitate, they have left a doubt in your mind?"

"But,"—began Brias.

"Repeat them to M. de Montéclain," exclaimed Julia, eagerly throwing off the determined resignation, in which she had taken refuge.

"It is useless, madame," replied Montéclain, "I know them all. I am come from Madame de Rudesgen's house where Madame Felina Amab has been relating them, as M. Hector de Montaleu has related them here."

"And you have dared to enter my house," said M. de Montaleu.

"Yes," replied Montéclain, "because I knew you were all here, and I had a promise to make to each of you."

"To you, first, Brias," he said, with an accent which made those who listened to him shudder, "to you whom I sought to save, I promise ruin; to you M. de Rudesgens, ridicule and despair both; to you, Champmortain, dishonour, and perhaps death; to you, M. de Montaleu, the shame of the past, the remorse of selfishness; and to you, Viscount Hector de Montaleu, I promise either the galleys or the scaffold."

At this terrible harangue, every mouth opened to utter threats, every hand seemed to rise, as if to crush the imprudent offender who had come to brave all these men. But Montéclain remained calm, proud, haughty, and whether it was that his look intimidated the most resolute, or that the false position in which each of them found himself warned them that Montéclain was able to keep his threatening promises, all stood still whilst he went up to Madame de Monrion, and said:

"And, to you, madame, I promise, the pity, the respect, and the admiration of the world."

"I need more than that," said Julia, rising, and holding out her hand to him.

"Ah!" said Montéclain, softly, "you do not ask for vengeance?"

"No, sir," she replied, blushing, but I ask for a refuge—a home.

"Come, then, madam," rejoined Montéclain, and that I shall open to you, however modest it may be, will be more sacred than the mansion in which you have twice been insulted."

He immediately took Julia's hand and led her through the midst of the men he had just provoked. Each, as he passed him by, uttered the word of provocation exacted by the outrage he had received; but Montéclain disdained to reply until he had nearly reached the doorway, then turning round he said to them:

"Gentlemen, this day still belongs to you. Reflect. Until this evening I shall wait for your excuses—but to-morrow—"

"To-morrow," said Hector, furiously, "you will have to answer to me for your insults."

"To-morrow," returned Montéclain, "I shall suffer justice to take its course; to-morrow it will be too late for you all. Adieu."

---

## CHAPTER LXXVIII.

### THE CHATEAU DE MONTECLAIN.

Colonel Thomas was lying in a large room in the chateau de Montéclain.

Bricord was seated at the head of his bed, whilst Aly Muley remained at the foot. The farmer and soldier looked at each other, as if communicating in this manner the thoughts they could not express aloud. Montéclain, anxious and uneasy, walked up and down the room. A window, covered with thick green curtains, scarcely sufficed to light the immense apartment, with its sombre hangings; a profound silence was observed by the four men.

All at once, Bricord and Aly Muley rose, by a simultaneous impulse, as if in the mute language of their looks they had deliberated and resolved upon some project in common.

They advanced a few steps as if going out; Montéclain stopped them.

"Where are you going?" he said.

"Where I ought to have gone long since," replied Bricord, "to Viscount de Montaleu's house."

"And what would you do there."

"Do you not know what I shall do, now you have confessed the truth? I shall demand satisfaction."

"For what?" said Montéclain, coldly.

"For what?" cried Bricord, "are you making game of me, my lord, that you ask such a question? Has not this wretch seduced my wife? my wife, do you hear?"

"You forget that, according to the plan Felina has settled, this seduction is a lie, invented by me and Madame de Monrion; you forget that, in this manner he has obtained a right to refuse you."

"Ah! he had better not refuse me," replied Bricord, "or, on my soul, I will kill him like a dog."

"What! threaten him," returned Montéclain, "and let it be said I have incited you to do so! Offer him violence, that in the position he has taken up he has a right to repel by every means of defence!—for when you accuse him of being your wife's lover, he will reply that it is not true."

"But I will tell him—"

"That I and the colonel have assured you of the existence of the letter, in which your wife confesses her fault: but this letter they declare to be forged—this letter, besides, does not name him."

Bricord struck his forehead in despair, and sank down upon a seat.

"M. de Montéclain is right," remarked the colonel, it is not yet time."

"Ah! but, cried Aly Muley, "is it to be borne then, that upstarts, thieves, and rascals of every kind, have a right to walk with heads erect, and commit the most infamous deeds in the world, whilst honest people must stand looking on with heads down, without whispering a word! No, sapredieu! no! I can understand what you say to Bricord, that it is not yet time, but, in the name of all the devils! no one in the world shall prevent my going to the house of this great marquis, this white cravated old fellow, who knows that his son is lying here with a ball in his chest, and leaves him here, saying, 'Go, die, be in pain, what do I care about it.' Oh! no, no! I will go and tell him the truth! A mummy, to whom the good God has presented a son who would make the king of the French proud, and who disowns him, and who—. Ah! I will go to him, and tell him my mind!"

"Stop," said the colonel, "stop. I no longer wish to avenge myself in that manner. Montéclain, you will keep your word; you will repair the evil done by your father."

"Yes," said Montéclain." "and I thank you that you have not cursed him."

"At such an hour as this is for me," returned Thomas, "a man no longer curses; there is too much need of God's pardon not to think of pardoning others."

"Do you suffer greater pain?" cried Aly Muley, hastening towards the bed.

"I have acted contrary to the doctor's orders," said Montéclain, "in relating to you what took place in M. de Montaleu's house; but, in my opinion, it was better to inflict this blow than leave you in a frightful state of suspense."

"But what do you propose to do, then?" asked Aly Muley.

"The king's attorney will be here this evening at nine o'clock; if those to whom I am going to write do not reply to me as I desire, his commission will be a fearful one; if they still obey the voice of honour, it will be limited to the punishment of those for whom human justice has no pardon; and now, keep watch beside the colonel. It is time to take some resolution."

Montéclain left the apartment after having pressed the colonel's hand, who smiled trustingly on him. He returned to his own room, and a few minutes later, two servants started off on horseback to convey sundry letters which he had placed in their hands. He himself took his way to Bricord's farm.

During the scene which passed in M. de Montaleu's house, Julia had been sustained by that energetic feeling with which the innocent are inspired by misfortune, which enables them to contemplate with desperate courage all that is most frightful in the wickedness of mankind. In moments like these, the soul attains a degree of exaltation which causes it to feel a kind of insensate joy in seeing lies and accusations accumulated against itself. It is like an insatiable thirst for pain which continually calls for sharper pangs; the heart full of despair seems to cry out: "Again! again!" and the time comes at last when the innocent being, struck on every side, willingly assists the aggressors, pointing out to them the place they have spared.

But, when the violent paroxysm is passed, when the ardent desire to measure in all their horror the baseness and infamy of others is appeased, then this fleeting energy gives way to profound dejection and absolute despair. Such was Julia's situation when Montéclain conducted her to the farm, after leaving M. de Montaleu's chateau.

"Have the kindness to wait for me here," he said to her, "and I hope soon to offer you a shelter more deserving of you."

Julia did not reply; all the strength which had supported her in the presence of her enemies, abandoned her when she found herself alone with her protector. A lingering sense of dignity had preserved her from giving way to tears and cries in his presence. She would not reveal to Montéclain all the weakness of her soul. Women are warned by a secret feeling of modesty that there is danger in revealing to those they love, sufferings which are unknown to them. The lover of a woman is hardly ever her confident.

But when Montéclain had retired, and Julia was left alone with her grief, she could yield to it freely. It was one of those terrible moments of life, when the noblest hearts of the most upright spirits, suffer a dreadful shock. Doubt is awakened within them, and sometimes like the vanquished of Pharsalia, they exclaim, "Virtue is a mere word."

At other times, and this danger is the greatest of all, weariness and disgust penetrate into these desolate souls, along with doubt, and after saying: "What good is there in virtue?" they say, "What good is there in life?"

Soon after, Julia, exhausted by tears and hopes, sought to tear herself away from the thought of death, which had taken possession of her. The unfortunate girl gathered up all her remaining strength to give the necessary orders for her departure. She sent to M. de Montaleu's to ask for her carriage and horses that she might instantly depart: she wished, at the same time, to fly from her enemies and her protector, and the latter alarmed her more than the others did.

But this was no reasonable project formed for a particular purpose. She fled instinctively, like the child who, having gone into a cavern, is surprised by the murmurs which frighten it, and rushes out, and does not stop until it is at a sufficient distance from the dreadful cave to dare regard its entrance and reflect on the cause of its fear. In the same way, Julia wished to place herself at a distance from all those who had injured her, free to stop afterwards, to reflect and devise some plan.

The thought of flight haunted her, and was predominant over all the rest; she felt she could not think of herself whilst she should continue in the place where she had suffered so much. She was waiting with mad impatience, when she saw the nurse of Saint-Faron enter her room with the child, which had caused her so much sorrow. Julia, on beholding this woman and this infant, was seized with terrible alarm.

"What are you come here for, unhappy woman?" she said to the nurse.

"I am come," replied the poor woman, "to present to you the child you took compassion on, in order that you may bless it."

"That I may bless it," murmured Julia, "I! I!—"

She looked at the child a moment.

Suddenly snatched from her disordered fears by its innocent looks, and brought back to the thought of the duty she had imposed on herself, and was about to forget, strengthened all at once in the cause she was ready to desert, she took the child in her arms, and exclaimed:

"Ah no! I will not abandon thee."

At that moment she was noble, she was proud, she was sublime.

"Who sent you here, then?" she said to the nurse.

"I did, madam," said Montéclain, coming in.

Julia uttered a cry, and pressed the child to her heart, as if it were a shield against the agitation caused by Montéclain's presence; she sheltered herself behind her noble action, the better to resist the empire of him who had been her accomplice therein.

"You, sir," she exclaimed, "you sent this child to me, and why?"

"I will tell you, madam," replied Montéclain, bowing to her.

Was it a prepossession, or a peculiar charm attached to, Montéclain? or, rather was it that exquisite sense of the heart which warns us when our feelings are sincere? Whatever the cause, from the moment Montéclain appeared, Julia felt herself surrounded, as it were, by respect, kindness and justice. She seated herself, holding the child on her knees, resembling at that instant in beauty and candour the holy virgin, to whom Aly Muley had compared her. It was with some difficulty that Montéclain refrained from telling her he loved her, and kneeling in adoration before her; but it was not yet time for him to speak; he subdued the vivid emotion by which he was agitated, and went on with downcast eyes, so much did he fear to look upon her thus charming and beautiful:

"I sent this child to you, because the sight of it alone could recall all you had done, all which remained for you to do. In fact, the cry of this innocent creature has been more eloquent to your heart than my reasonings, protestations, or prayers, could have been. Do I deceive myself, madam, in saying that I left you lost in despair, doubting everything in this world, and that I find you again strong, resigned, and resolute to combat for your cause?"

Julia coloured; this man, who penetrated so well her secret feelings, astonished and alarmed her.

"Yes, sir, it is true," she said, "I am stronger since I have seen this child again, for I had forgotten it, and you have reminded me that I have yet a duty to fulfil."

"And I knew you would adhere to it," added Montéclain, with courage and pride.

"I thank you," said Julia, confused and trembling.

"But, believe me, madam," resumed Montéclain, "there is no other woman in the world to whom I would have dared send for consolation and hope, the being who had occasioned her so much sorrow. Thousands of others in your place, as innocent and calumniated as yourself, would have cursed and driven it away. But you, madam, have taken it to your arms, you hold it on your knees, you press it to your heart still bleeding from the wounds it has cost you; you are not only innocent and good, madam; you are great and you are holy!"

Julia shuddered at Montéclain's words; this language, flattering as it was, she believed to be sincere. Did not Montéclain's voice tremble? Was not the sparkling adoration in his eyes bright with the moisture of tears which he could with great difficulty restrain? Oh! how much less powerful had he been, if he had spoken to her of his love! She strove to stammer out some words, but her voice was lost in tears, which flowed gently; and as in lowering her head to conceal them from Montéclain's sight, they fell on the forehead of the child who was smiling at her, she wiped them away with her kisses, as if they had been the traces of a confession she sought to efface.

Montéclain turned away, for he felt the resolution he had made of not crying to Julia from the depths of his soul: "Madame, I love you," growing weaker. There was a brief moment of silence, at last Montéclain resumed:

"Madam, thanks to God and to you, my hope has not been deceived, a moment of calm has returned to your soul, and enables me to say to you what otherwise you would not have been able to hear. You wish to fly, madam, you ought not."

"I ought not, say you, and what can I do here?"

"Wait for your justification."

"In order to wait, sir," said Julia, with bitter despair, "I must have an asylum in which I could remain."

"This may suffice for one day, madam, and this evening you shall have one worthy of you, or I will have placed you under protection no one can gainsay. This evening, madam, you will either return triumphant and venerated into M. de Montaleu's house, or you will be placed under the shield of the law."

"I will not return to M. de Montaleu's house," replied Julia, bitterly.

"Notwithstanding it would be better thus."

"Is it you who tell me so? You, sir, after the threats you made him?"

"Yes, madam, it is I who say so; for of these threats there are some I will keep, I swear it; but there are others from which I hope to be absolved by the repentance of the guilty."

"Ah!" said Julia, looking sweetly at Montéclain, "you will pardon those who have only been feeble and deceived."

"You cannot be approached with impunity, madam; for we learn from you feelings unknown before. The man who believed himself strong, because he had been implacable, who made it his glory that he had left no attack unanswered, no injury unavenged, no fault unpunished, has learnt within the last few days, in what consists true strength, true glory, and true greatness. Yes, I will pardon, madam; by following your example, and that of heaven, I will pardon all those who between this time and this evening, shall come and testify their repentance."

"Only till this evening?"

"The period cannot be lengthened; a crime has been committed, the blood of a man has been shed, that of a woman also, perhaps; the magistrates have been informed—this was my duty; this evening, a king's attorney will come into the country bearing the torch of justice into this shadowy labyrinth of crime and intrigue. Woe to those who suffer him to arrive before they have sheltered themselves from his strict inquiries behind your pardon!—for then everything must be told. Once in presence of the judge, I will not for anything or any person tell a lie; I will clearly expose the faults of some, the crimes of others, and if the law only strikes some among them, shame at least will alight on all!"

"Oh! they will repent, I hope so," said Julia, as if she were praying.

"Angel of heaven!" murmured Montéclain, in a low voice, "who would not love thee?"

"You were saying;" inquired Julia, who had not heard the words, scarcely articulate, of Montéclain

Recovering from the new emotion he experienced, he replied, in a voice he strove to subdue:

"I say, madam, that it is necessary you should come this evening to the chateau de Montéclain."

"I!" exclaimed Julia, startled.

"You, madam."

"To your house, sir?"

"Madam, you will find there to receive you, either some friends in whom you may confide, or a magistrate who will be ready to listen to you."

"In your house?" repeated Julia.

"In my house, madam, and never has this dwelling, to whose old walls the pictures of my ancestors are appended, where more than one queen of France has accepted the hospitality of my forefathers, been more honoured than it will be by your presence."

Julia did not reply; her whole soul was moved, and incited her blindly to obey this man, whose language charmed her. She dreaded to think how her most chaste and innocent actions had been perverted by calumny; but the next moment she was angry with herself that she no longer dared to repose in him the generous confidence which a few days before would not have permitted her to hesitate; she trembled likewise at the thought of wronging one who, without knowing her, had devoted himself to her cause, and that to which she was henceforth attached.

She remained before Montéclain, with her head depressed, a blushing face, and heaving bosom. He understood her hesitation.

"Is it necessary to say more?" cried Montéclain eagerly, "must I swear to you on my honour as a gentleman?"

"No," she said, rising suddenly, "I will go."

"Oh! may heaven reward you madame!" returned Montéclain.

"I will not wrong you," said Julia interrupting him, "by saying I am a poor woman alone in the world, with a heart so dismayed, that it no longer knows good from evil; I will not tell you that it is easy to draw me into a snare, where the loss of my honour may be consummated, no sir, I will not say all this—I believe you to be an honest man."

Montéclain bent one knee to the ground before her.

"Thank you madame, thank you," he said in a deep exultant voice.

Julia looked at him thus, without appearing either surprised or alarmed, and continued:

"But I will say to you; my strength is exhausted

I can bear no more, without losing my reason or my life, poignant emotions like those I have suffered from for some days past. I would not begin again the contest I endure, even at this hour: spare me, sir, and whatever reception awaits me in your house—whether it be friends or a magistrate who receive me, enable me to leave it delivered from the horror of all these accusations."

"I swear to do so, madam."

"And now sir, I will go—in my turn, I swear it, I will go.

"Thank you, madam, thank you again," said Montéclain, fixing on her a disordered glance; "I go to await you. "Oh!" he resumed rising with proud and joyous emotion, "it is not you who will be re-instated to-day, it is I, I in whom you will have had confidence, whose dwelling you will have sanctified, I whom you have accepted as a defender whom you have raised up to yourself,—thank you, madame, thank you—I shall expect you."

He departed.

---

## CHAPTER LXXIX.

### A SEPARATION.

In another part of the valley, two of the characters of this history left their respective dwellings at the same time, after having each read a letter delivered by one of Montéclain's servants; these two individuals were Sylvia and Brias, and they went to meet each other.

No rendezvous had been arranged between them. Brias, incited by the anxiety he felt, went out with the chance of meeting Sylvia, and she, without knowing where she was likely to meet Brias, went towards the spot in which they were accustomed to repair. Brias was already there. They hastened one towards the other, they trembled, were agitated, and disturbed, as if alarmed at this encounter.

"Ah! I was looking for you," exclaimed Brias, on perceiving Sylvia.

"I too was looking for you," rejoined Madame de Champmortain in an agitated voice. "Hold Frederic, read this; it is a letter I have just received from Montéclain," she added as she gave it to him

"And here is one that has just been given me," replied Brias, in his turn placing a letter in Madame de Champmortain's hand.

Brias read as follows:

"Madam, it is a strange arrogance on the part of a man whose life has often merited the censure of honest people, to wish to advise you who have never committed any action to be ashamed of. Nevertheless I will do it, for if my advice has not the respectable authority of virtue, it will perhaps have that of experience, which is more powerful still.

"You are young and beautiful, madam, full of passion and sensibility; you have been neglected, your pride has been mortified, by finding yourself forsaken.

"If there is an excuse for desiring to seek consolation elsewhere than in mute resignation, this excuse is greater for you than any one. But permit me to say, madam, grief has no sincere and noble consolation, save in duty. I could tell you how many lives I have seen compromised and lost, because the heart, indignant at its sufferings, has one day revolted, exclaiming, 'I too, will revenge myself!' But I will take no other example than your own. For by yielding to the cry of a pardonable anger, you have been enmeshed in the intrigues of a lost woman, who has made use of the shadow of a fault to render you the accomplice of her cruelties, her assistant in propagating calumnies. Governed by the fear inspired by this woman, whom you despised for so many reasons, you have struck another, who, in the bottom of your soul you know to be innocent.

"And now what has happened? I have been mixed up with those odious lies, and forced on pain of being considered the meanest of men, to shew in all its purity the innocence of her who has been so detestably outraged, to expose in all its baseness the infamy of the woman who has attacked her, and necessarily to explain the motives of those who have lent a hand to these calumnies.

"What can I do, madam? I know not. My conduct can only be dictated by that of my enemies. To every one who still maintains that Madame de Monrion is guilty, I must reply by exposing the secret interest which makes him speak aloud against a truth he cannot really be ignorant of.

"Oh! madam, how painful it is to be compelled whilst saving the honour of one woman to touch that of another! You will not reduce me to this grievous necessity. You will join with me in rendering homage to suffering virtue; it is the noblest courage of that virtue which is wavering; and this you will display. This return would absolve one one who was guilty, it would be the crown of triumph to that contest in which you have not been overcome. Oh! come, madam, unite with me; prefer the sad tranquillity of undeserved misfortune, to the gloomy joy of vengeance. I see, I feel that you suffer, and I know what is necessary for your consolation: it is to remain worthy of yourself.

"As yet, you only know the torments of a guilty hope, never learn those of an irreparable fault. Shame bends the head low, and you are too much accustomed to raise yours not to die rather than bow beneath the weight of a fault. Dare to look around you, see to what a depth of infamy the woman who seeks your ruin has fallen, to what misery she is reduced, whose absence continues inexplicable. Drive from your soul the thirst for vengeance which alone has bewildered you. Come, I expect you! In pity for yourself, who merit the respect of all, come and extend your hand to a woman whose innocence will shine the clearer for your testimony, and will reflect on your's the purest lustre. You and I, madam, are the last descendants of names once powerful, and still respected. If God has not permitted us to add to their celebrity, He will not suffer us to tarnish their honour by deserting the oppressed. You will not force me, madam, to forget the profound sentiments of affection and respect I bear you, by leaving me alone to defend Madame de Monrion. Ask, either your father, your husband, or Madame de Rudesgens to accompany you this evening to my house; one of them will consent to do so, I hope, perhaps all. Oh! come, madam, come! it is your duty, and your happiness to do so!

"Monteclain."

Whilst Brias was reading the letter, Montéclain had written to Sylvia, the latter was reading that he had addressed to Brias. It was thus expressed:

"Brias, not many days ago, I said to you: 'Employ all the power a man of honour can have over the woman he loves, to tear Madame de Champmortain from the grasp of the wretch who seeks her ruin.' I added, 'Do not suffer her to run blindly towards the abyss in which they seek to precipitate her; and, if you love her sincerely, prefer her safety to her love. Save her, though she should hate you for doing so.

"You promised to do this, Brias, and you have

not kept your word. Surprised at a rendezvous by Felina's incredible audacity, you delivered yourself up to her, bound hand and foot; you did more, you delivered to her the honour, the fortune, the life of a woman, who has committed no other fault than that of wanting strength to endure her husband's total neglect.

"And now, what is your position, Brias? Has not Felina profited cruelly by your weakness? She has bound you, a man of talent, spirit, and judgement, like a slave, to accomplish her odious design. This yoke, which you were incapable of flinging off with disgust, does not fall most heavily on you; but on the unfortunate Sylvia. A successful, or unsuccessful duel would relieve you from the terrible position in which you are both placed; but, who will save her if ever Champmortain should be acquainted with your secret rendezvous? and he will hear of them. From whom, do you ask? Well! Brias, from me.

"You had promised an atonement to Madame de Monrion, and you, as well as Champmortain, have listened silently to the stupid atrocities invented by Felina, repeated by Hector, and commented on by M. de Montaleu. Was this conviction on your part? No, it was terror. You recognized in these lies, so basely put together, so audaciously uttered, Felina's work, and each of you, trembling for his own faults, allowed her to say and do what she chose, without a protestation, without a complaint. It is not your belief of what was said against me that angers me, it is your suffering a woman to be maligned without one touch of pity, without one transport of noble indignation.

"Brias! Brias! what were our fathers, and what are we? I grant your liberal philosophy that they had all the brutal vices of irresponsible power; they did justice with the sword or the poignard, they resorted to violence with the weak. They had in fact all the vices of the strong; but they knew nothing of the fear which accepts a lie for truth; they preferred to wear their crimes openly, rather than to bow before base cowardly perfidy.

"Oh! Brias, what must this young and beautiful woman, so outrageously insulted, so coldly abandoned, think of our nobility? She a child of the middle class, you laugh at so much, she does not laugh, she weeps, and each of her tears falling on your escutcheon, will leave there an indelible stain. Well! I, Brias, will not play the part you accepted so gaily. Justice shall be done to all; so much the worse for those who suffer by it. I will relate, I will tell everything. And, in order that it may not be couched in empty phrases, denied with contempt, I will make out a deed of judicial accusation, in which, names, deeds, and intentions shall all be revealed.

"I have made Madame de Monrion's cause my own. She shall triumph, I promise you. Do not knit your brows in reading what I say, Brias, nor glance at your sword. I will not fight. Attacked with a lie, I will reply with truth. I will speak, at least, if I am not assassinated like Colonel Thomas Rien.

"And now, Brias, in the name of that honour, which ought to be the imperishable gem of our coronets, I ask you, will you avoid all scandals, will you save yourself, or rather, will you save Sylvia? Come, then, this evening, at eight o'clock, to my house; everything shall be decided there, I swear to you, all shall be arranged. Forgive me, Brias, if in this letter some offensive expressions have escaped me; they are ill-suited to a man determined not to give satisfaction for them, but I have not time to be calm; danger threatens you more than me. At nine o'clock a police magistrate will come to unravel the thread of this roof of falsehoods, already stained with blood. Brias, throw aside your vanity, I forget mine with you; I do not wish to act the just man, and to set myself up for an irreproachable Don Quixote; I love Madame de Monrion, I have loved her as I have never yet loved; this woman has revived my life, my hope, and my faith; she has restored me all the feelings of youth; I am as strong in her virtue as if it were my own, but I have also a heart full of her indulgence; I wish to save you all, come to my assistance. I entreat you, I hold out my hand to you; for once in your life taste and enjoy the happiness which springs from the thought of a sacred duty nobly accomplished. This evening, Brias, I shall fully expect you. There are words you have never been able to resist: honour and friendship. Come; and until then, avoid Champmortain. This evening I expect you.

"MONTECLAIN."

When Sylvia and Brias had each perused the letter received by the other, they looked at one another.

"Well!" said Sylvia, who was pale and trembling, "will you go?"

"I will do as you wish, Sylvia; in a moment like this I have only the right to obey you. Command me to impose silence on Montéclain, and unless he has covered himself with a cuirass of stoicism impervious to every insult, I will force him to be silent."

"A scandal, a duel, more blood, you mean?" said Sylvia, wiping away a few tears. "No—no," she added, in a broken voice, "it is enough."

"Do you wish," replied Brias, that I should silence all pride, and yield to his threats? I will do it."

"Frederic," replied Sylvia, sadly, "you might yield to his prayers; for he supplicates as much as he threatens you. But that is not the principal thing: you will go to Montéclain's house, I entreat you to do so; I will go too."

"As you please," said Brias, whilst Sylvia was stifling her sobs.

For a moment Sylvia continued silent; her tears were suffocating her. It was evident she had not said all, and her courage faltered before what remained to be said. She resumed, in a stifled voice:

"This will suffice to save us, at least I hope so; but it is not enough for my honour, for my future—"

"What do you require, madam?" what do you wish?" returned Brias.

"M. de Brias," she said, sobbing, "you must depart, you must leave this place."

One of the most detestable delusions played by vanity, is that of pretending to accept as a sacrifice, the part which is necessary, and sometimes wished for.

"I must go!" cried Brias, "I must leave you! oh! Sylvia! Sylvia! what do you ask?"

"Frederic," she answered with an effort, "must I alone then have courage? Will you not take pity on me?"

"But what will become of me when far from you?" said Brias.

"You will soon have forgotten me sir," said Sylvia with a fresh burst of tears, "the world, your own affairs, your embarrassments will assist you to eradicate from your heart the remembrance of a woman you have loved like many more—"

"What do you say Sylvia!"

"And I," she resumed, despairingly, "I am going to remain alone in the presence of my husband, whose suspicions are awakened; of my mother, ready to arm herself with my fault, that she may extend to me, the tyranny she exercises over my father; I shall be alone Frederic, with your memory, with my love, my regrets, my remorse—and yet I do not hesitate. Unable to fly from you

I ask you to leave me. You will do so, will you not? taking his hands in a supplicating manner. You will take courage, you will not render this separation too difficult for me."

Oh! vanity, thou vile and inane sentiment! Brias could not determine to obey the unhappy Sylvia without setting himself up for a victim.

"You wish it?" he replied in a tone, which he did his best to make reproachful, "well then! I will go—without having obtained a single token of the love you profess for me, without having moved you for a moment by that which is burning me."

"Ah! Frederic! Frederic," said Sylvia shrinking back fearfully, "be silent. Alas! when I pardoned you for seeking your fortune and rejecting my love, you told me you would never ask anything of me which I should have to blush for. Ah! it would be dreadful to abuse my grief—you will not do it."

The man of conquering pretentions is a savage, blind beast; Brias seized Madame de Champmortain's hands.

"Oh! Sylvia," he said, "into that future in which we are both to live isolated, will you not bear the remembrance of one hour's happiness? Shall not our thoughts there meet and mingle? What shall so much love have been given in vain, and nothing rest between us? Sylvia, this evening, to-night?"

"Ah!" cried Madame de Champmortain, with equal despair and indignation, there is nothing then in men's hearts save one thought, one desire, one wish? A woman's dishonour is the only triumph which satisfies them? No, sir, no—never. Do not go to M. de Montéclain's, let him disgrace me, if you will; but leave me, sir, leave me."

"Oh!" said Brias, "forgive the rashness of desperate love."

"No," she rejoined with sorrowful anger, "you have neither pity nor generosity; you leave me all the weight of grief. You do not excite me to the performance of my duty. You do not wish me to continue innocent; you wish to lose me. No, you do not love me."

"Well, then!" returned Brias, "I will go, I will leave this place, I will never see you again."

"Ah! heaven!" said Sylvia, at that terrible word, never!

"To-morrow," continued Brias, "I shall be far from you."

"It must be so. I wish it," said Sylvia,'sobbing. Go; but—think sometimes, Frederic—that you have left here a woman who suffers, who loves you, whose affections, whose wishes follow you. And now, farewell."

Brias took Sylvia's hand; it was hot and feverish; he kissed it ardently, and departed, saying, in a stifled voice:

"Adieu, then, madam."

He had taken but a few steps, when Sylvia pressed her lips to the place where Brias' had touched her hand: then, leaning against a tree, she gave way to her tears. Women alone possess fortitude. Sylvia had crushed her heart unhesitatingly, though she loved Brias, and believed in his love, whilst he, who did not love her, had left to her all the effort of this separation.

When her grief had exhausted itself in tears, Sylvia returned home; the part she must play all her life was about to commence, she had resigned herself to it courageously. She expected inquisitive questions from her mother, remonstrances from M. de Rudesgens, jealous suspicions from M. de Champmortain, and she was resolved to shut herself up in the right which her innocence and grief afforded her, of waiting in silence.

But when she entered, she was informed that her mother had that instant set out to visit M. de Montaleu. Champmortain, too, was absent. On his return from Madame de Monrion's house, a letter from M. de Montéclain had been given him, and he had immediately gone out again. As to M. de Rudesgens, he, too, had received a letter from Montéclain, and had shut himself up in his room.

"Oh!" said Sylvia to herself, "can he who does not love me have protected me thus, and spared me all the torments I have so well deserved?"

"Oh, God! if it be true," she added, in an attitude of prayer, grant that he may be happy, for he has a noble heart. Oh! he would not have left me without a word of encouragement, without a tear of pity."

Was Sylvia's thought a just one? Let the reader judge.

---

## CHAPTER LXXX.

### THE RUPTURE.

After visiting Madame de Rudesgens, Felina had returned home: her faithful Dorothy was waiting for her whilst watching over Léda.

"Well?" said the maid-servant.

"Well," returned Madame Amab, "I triumph. Julia driven from M. de Montaleu's house, has found no better refuge than Bricord's miserable farm."

"And Madame de Rudesgens?"

"Madame de Rudesgens is quite ready to say that she has long suspected the intrigues of Montéclain and Madame de Monrion, and her daughter will swear to what she does."

"What!" said the maid, "Madame de Champmortain too—"

"Her honorable mother promises as much; for I confess I had not the heart to threaten the poor little thing; I pity her Dorothy, and were it not that Champmortain so well deserves punishment, for his supreme folly in trusting her, I do not know whether I should not myself have withdrawn her from Brias' seductions, or rather from her own passion; for Brias does not love her."

"So then," said Dorothy, "all goes well on both sides, and our pupil, M. Hector has done wonders, it seems."

"As yet I only know the result, but I am curious to learn the particulars."

"I am surprised at his success; for between ourselves, madame, he is so dull, so stupid—"

Felina shook her head.

"Dull—yes," she replied, "stupid—oh!.. no For if this man had but an hour to reflect before each speech he makes, he would surpass us all, in cunning, audacity and lying; in the same manner, if he had time given him to employ his bull-like strength, no one would be able to resist him. For that reason he must have been admirable on this occasion, when I had foreseen and argued everything for him. Such an accomplice would be very dangerous, if ever he meditated a change. But I hope he will not have time for that."

"What will you do with him then?"

"I do not know."

"And with this unhappy creature?"

"With Léda."

"Yes madame."

"The day is declining, you will take her across the park, and go out by the little door; you will guide her some distance through the forest and then leave her."

"Alone, when night is coming on?"

"Yes."

"But what will become of her?"

"There is a God for the mad, as well as for the drunkard," said Felina turning away.

"There is one for everybody," said Léda, with the fixed smile of madness, so much more dreadful to behold than the darkest expression of anger or grief.

These words, pronounced in a calm, sweet voice, made Felina tremble. She fixed her eyes on Léda.

"The Orientals," she muttered, "respect idiots, and seek for Divine inspiration in their wandering thoughts. Perhaps they are right."

Felina reflected a moment."

"Come," she said to Dorothy, "let us make haste. I will accompany you as far as the pavilion in the park; it is strange that I have not yet seen Champmortain. He can tell me what has passed in M. de Montaleu's house."

Some moments later, the three women left the chateau by a private staircase leading to a covered walk. Felina and her maid conducted Léda as far as the door of the park.

At the moment Felina opened it Champmortain appeared on the threshold.

"Ah!" he said on perceiving Léda, "so the wretched woman was here?"

"You see," said Felina.

"Where are you sending her to?"

"To her husband's house."

"For some new infamy?" returned Champmortain drily.

Felina turned like a wounded lioness, and for the first time remarked the anger and excitement which agitated the count.

"Take away this woman," she said to Dorothy, "and return quickly—I shall want you."

Léda and Dorothy left the park, and Felina remained with Champmortain.

"Will it please you," said the latter, "to come into the pavillion?"

"What for?" asked Felina in a tranquil voice.

"I have serious things to speak to you about—"

"If you are going to reproach me as you did just now, it is useless. I am more careful of pleasant memories than you think; this pavilion recalls to me the time when you declared yourself happy with a look from me, proud of the least favour; it shall not witness your violence. We are well here—"

"We may be heard."

"You intend then to bawl out?" returned Madame Amab quietly.

"Felina!" said Champmortain.

"In that pavilion, I was called Felina," she replied carelessly, "but in the open air I am called Madame Amab."

'Well then! madame," returned Champmortain who trembled with indignation, "I come to warn you that your base actions have borne their fruits; this evening a magistrate is to arrive here: this evening all those who have the misfortune to be your friends will be punished, for having been feeble enough to—"

"To do what?" said Felina ironically.

"Madam," continued Champmortain, "scarcely had you entered my house before you sowed scandal and disorder in it!"

"Indeed!"

"You invented that abominable tale about Madame de Monrion."

"If you did not believe it, you should not have allowed Madame de Champmortain to drive an innocent woman out of her house. Besides, have you not offered her a splendid atonement?"

"It was my duty to do so, madame, but we found M. Hector de Montaleu there, who, inspired by you, strove to cast upon another the responsibility of those crimes which you hourly give birth to."

"Ah!" said Felina with a degree of uneasiness, "he attempted to defend himself, and succeeded badly no doubt?"

"He lied with such insolent audacity."

"That you dared not tell him he did so to his face," returned Felina with contemptuous irony, "and come to say so to me a woman; methinks the distance is as short from your house to M. Hector de Montaleu's, as it is from your house to mine."

"Felina, or madame, this has nothing to do with M. Hector de Montaleu, but with you."

"I do not understand you."

"You do not understand me?" said Champmortain, lowering his voice. "Do you know what Montéclain has just written to me?"

"Come, come!" said Felina, jestingly, "own it, speak the truth, it is not you who are talking at this moment, but Montéclain. And what does he say to you?"

"That this evening a magistrate will be in his house, that he will commence the inquiry relative to the colonel's assassination."

"And in what does that concern you?"

"What concerns me, madam, is, that this affair is henceforth inseparably united to that of Madame de Monrion, that the colonel was assassinated with a view to deprive him of the letter he had with him, which absolved Madame de Monrion from an aspersion which you artfully contrived should come first from Madame de Champmortain's mouth. It is because I, madam, and my wife, are going to be mixed up with your base intrigues—because you have been to my house to threaten my mother-in-law and Sylvia—lastly, it is because Montéclain, in order that this magistrate may understand the motive of my silence will not hesitate to say that I sought to conciliate the woman with whom—. Ah! madam, it will be a dreadful scandal."

"Better than that, M. de Champmortain," replied Felina, disdainfully, "for the scandal exists, but the punishment is to come. Montéclain will tell all, and I warn you, there is a man in this house, who will not forgive you for having seduced his wife."

"Indeed," returned Champmortain, "the contrary might be said, for generally it is not the seducer who is enslaved."

"The crime will be the same in my husband's eyes, count, and I believe you are frightened."

"Frightened!" said Champmortain, with disdain. "I think I have proved myself courageous enough for a duel."

"You mean to say for two," rejoined Felina, bitterly.

"For two?"

"Doubtless, for, after having satisfied the honour of a husband, whose wife you have seduced, is it not so that you understand it? You will have to ask satisfaction of the lover who has seduced your wife?"

"Indeed!" said Champmortain, bitterly.

"If the threatening Montéclain amuses himself by revealing the motives of your silence, he will doubtless take care to expose those of Madame de Champmortain and Brias."

"And what are these motives?"

"The fear of seeing their honest intrigues and innocent rendezvous divulged by a base intriguing woman."

"Mere folly!" returned Champmortain, shrugging his shoulders.

"A marital maxim, spoken with the conviction of those similarly situated."

"A new calumny, uttered with the assurance of women like you."

"Calumny," replied Felina, insolently, "is an arm which every one does not deserve to be employed; truth is sufficient in the case of Madame de Champmortain."

"Your rage bewilders you."

"And your fear makes you blind; but I am not so yet, and as I have seen—"

" You ?"

" Seen with my own eyes, seen, the rendezvous between Madame de Champmortain and Brias."

" A lie!" cried Champmortain.

" I have seen it, sir," said Felina, pale at last with the anger she had so long restrained."

" Infamous lies ! madam ; I was warned of all you might say to me on this subject. I expected it. Sylvia is to be sacrificed as Madame de Monrion has been. But I respect the lady who bears my name, madam, and will not suffer you to touch her."

" What !" returned Felina, with flashing eyes and trembling lips, you dare to say—?"

" I say," rejoined Champmortain, "that you lie as you have always lied."

" Oh !" said Felina, "the truth, where then is the truth ?"

" It cannot be in your mouth."

" But I have seen—"

" You lie."

" But why then did she receive me, this woman so pure ?"

" Because I wished it."

" But why did she recall the insolent invitation in which she had omitted my name ?"

" I did not see this invitation."

" I received it in your presence."

" You did not shew it me."

" I will shew it to you."

" I should believe it to be forged. Ah ! madam, it is time for every one to return to his position," said Champmortain. " You may have abused my fortune and my personal consideration ; you shall not abuse the honour of my name."

" But what are you come here for, then ?"

" To ask you to acknowledge that you accused Madame de Monrion falsely ; and as you may have been deceived by appearances, your excuse will be easy."

" What more ?" said Felina, in a cutting voice.

" In that case," returned Champmortain, " Montéclain will do all he can to save you."

" He ?" replied Felina, shuddering.

" One moment of repentance, and he will pardon you."

" He will pardon me !" repeated Felina.

" Yes, he will do all that is possible to spare the name of M. Amab from shame," continued Champmortain, " if a moment of repentance—"

" Of repentance," answered Felina, whose stifled voice revealed all the fury by which she was agitated. " Oh ! yes," she added, with the proud energetic spirit of rebellious demons, " I repent of having lowered myself to you sir, you, the most infamous of my enemies, for they are faithful to their hatred, whilst you question your love. Yes, I repent of having believed in your courage, your probity—deceiving and deceived husband, who come here to insult the woman who had dishonoured herself for you, and who glorify her who dishonours you. Yes, I repent of being the mistress of a coward. And now, sir, go. The magistrates are coming; they are as well acquainted with adultery and forgery as with assassination and calumny. Ah ! M. de Montéclain threatens you with scandal, and you obey the man who treats you as you deserve. I promise you to make your share larger than you think. I congratulate you, M. de Champmortain, you have an honourable family, and your virtuous wife has a sufficiently virtuous example in her virtuous mother to make you quite tranquil on her account. Go, sir."

" Felina," said Champmortain, " I have warned you, as I ought to have done ; I will now carry your answer to Montéclain."

" Tell him," replied Felina, proudly, " that I will myself bring him that which it becomes a woman like me to make to a man like him. Go."

" Speak lower, madam," said Champmortain, " I am not accustomed to obey such orders."

" Take care ! I have a husband less patient than you are, and I am capable of telling him the truth, were it only to see your terror in his presence."

" If ever he learns it," rejoined Champmortain, " he will find me ready to answer him."

" It will be sooner than you think, perhaps."

" Adieu," said Champmortain.

" We shall meet again," replied Felina. " Before the magistrates, the ascused defend themselves, and the accusers are sometimes silent. We shall meet again."

Champmortain retired. Felina, who had been hitherto sustained by her anger, stood overcome, crushed, after he was gone.

For the first time in her life, she had just seen one of those whom she believed in her power, turn against her ; and what was he ? a worthless man in Felina's eyes, ordinary in mind, in heart, in everything. That Montéclain braved her, she could understand ; his was a character steeped in fire and ice ; that Brias strove to resist her, he had the art of cavilling and retreating diplomatically ; but Champmortain, a man of common narrow ideas ; she could not understand it.

In this, Felina was wanting in the profound science of the human mind. In fact, when by dint of address, coolness, caresses or sarcasms, she had succeeded in drawing the adversary she was about to attack, to the ground she had selected, he must possess very uncommon skill to avoid being vanquished by her ; but, whether from an instinct of weakness, or a privilege of his mediocrity, Champmortain had remained immovably fixed to the idea with which he had come there.

For him, Felina was an embodied lie, a living wickedness : strong in this idea, he had not stirred from it a step ; he had not discussed the probability of Sylvia's fault for a moment, he had simply answered Felina : " You lie ;" he would have made the same reply to the most brilliant proofs ; he was so convinced that all Felina said was false, that he would have denied the sun if she had appealed to it.

Hence it happened that Felina, so formidable to the most skilful, when she accused falsely, found herself powerless against a fool, when the truth was on her side.

Is it because the hand that can handle the poignard cannot hold a sword ?

Suddenly she seemed to awaken from the torpor into which she had fallen, and addressing Dorothy, who had just come in, she said :

" My carriage."

" Madame is going out ?"

" Yes."

" Madame must take care then. I do not know if I deceived myself, but it seemed to me that some one was watching us in the wood whilst I was leading away the poor idiot."

" Montéclain, doubtless ?"

" No, madam ; the master."

" My husband ?"

" Yes, madam."

" If that be all," said Felina, " do not be uneasy."

" But, if madame has made any appointment with M. de Champmortain ?"

" Oh ! no, no."

" Are you going to meet M. Hector de Montaleu ?"

" I am not going to the colliery," said Feina.

And as Dorothy looked at her with astonishment, Felina continued :

" I am going to the house of my oldest enemy. I am going to the Marquis de Montaleu's."

" You ?"

" Yes, I. Oh !" she added, " my vengeance will be so much the sweeter, when it comes to me through him."

## CHAPTER LXXXI.

### CONFESSION.

After the scene that had passed at his house in the morning, M. de Montaleu had remained alone, a prey to the deepest melancholy. He was, at the same time discontented with himself and with all the world.

He felt as angry with those who were right as with those who were wrong. This is easily accounted for. M. de Montaleu, just though he was stern, though he wished to be, had attained an age when rest for the heart and mind, is desired above everything beside. The egotism of old men is complained of, but this egotism is too often only weariness and disgust. The longer we engage in the struggles of the world, the less interest we feel in it. Has it not, in fact, been acknowledged ten, a hundred, nay a thousand times, that if defeat is mortification, victory is often deception? Success would be too mighty a power were it always productive of happiness. This is why old men dread new events, and carefully withdraw themselves from them. With some, this apprehension becomes an implacable mistrust, which predicts evil in everything. This calculation is perhaps a wise one. If they are deceiving themselves, so they reflect, they have also the chance of a pleasant surprise.

With others, this disgust of the same struggles, this fear of the same results becomes a kind of obstinate credulity. They turn away from anything which might wound the sensibility which still remains to them; they make themselves blind and deaf for the woe which passes under their eyes, or cries in their ears.

This class, and M. de Montaleu was one of its number, do all in their power to avoid being disturbed in the luxurious, half obscure retreat to which they retire. Thus it happens that when they are dragged from it by rumours and violence which it is impossible to help hearing, they at first curse with fury those whose faults have caused these rumours to break out, and soon afterwards those who are made the heralds of them. Thus, in the minor troubles of life, I have seen turned away with the same degree of anger, by an indulgent old man, the servant who robbed him, and the servant who gave him information of the robbery. Both had disturbed the idle ease in which he delighted to live. Let us turn from this anger to a sincere grief; let us see M. de Montaleu suddenly surprised in the gentle and noble confidence in which he lived, his white head reposing on the lap of a virtuous child, and we shall well understand the anger that he felt, both towards the woman who had deceived him, and towards those who had revealed to him her error.

Julia had for some days found herself forsaken by this old man who loved her. It was now M. de Montaleu's turn to feel very lonely, separated from the child to whose affectionate attention he was accustomed. Disgust of life, or rather those impatient feelings which make life a sorrow, are seldom experienced except by youth, at the moment in which it is submitted to one of those terrible undeceptions which follow any great hope. Old age is exempt from this, and yet M. de Montaleu felt so forsaken, so miserable after Julia's departure, that in deep discouragement he said:

"Ah! it would have been better to die before seeing my last hope in this world, fall to the ground."

M. de Montaleu was in this frame of mind when Madame de Rudesgens' visit was announced to him. He was alarmed by it.

He would no doubt hear fresh information, more certain particulars respecting Julia's error, Montéclain's being an accomplice, respecting events of which M de Montaleu, to say the truth, did not render a very exact account to himself, but in which he heartily disliked being concerned. This reluctance of M. de Montaleu to hear the sharp voice of Madame de Rudesgens adding the venom of her own commentaries to all these unfortunate circumstances, this reluctance, we say, had perhaps determined the marquis to refuse to the aged Artémise the interview she requested of him; but she had gained admittance to his apartment before he had time to make his reply, and the manner in which she entered told M. de Montaleu that a great misfortune had just happened, and that a dreadful catastrophe was impending. Madame de Rudesgens did not wait for M. de Montaleu to dismiss the servant who had announced her, she herself bade him depart, with a troubled voice and a quick gesture; she then ran to the door, secured the fastenings, and returned to the marquis saying, in a frightened voice:

"My friend! my good and poor friend! I am lost."

"You, madame," said the marquis, quite astonished by this extraordinary trouble, "why and how?"

Madame de Rudesgens threw herself on a couch, untied her bonnet, used her smelling bottle, fanned herself with her handkerchief, in short, gave to herself all those attentions which a woman exacts who is ill and has no time to spare, and continued, with angry despair:

"I am between the hands of two scoundrels, marquis; between two wretches, who have sworn my ruin. If I do not help Felina to dishonour Madame de Monrion, she will tell all—if I do not assist Montéclain to save her, he will tell all."

"But what will they tell?" inquired M. de Montaleu, with some impatience.

"Montaleu," said Madame de Rudesgens, fixing a supplicating look upon the marquis, "you must pardon me, you first of all."

"I?" returned M. de Montaleu, "but for what?"

"My friend, my old and good friend, you must know all. You understand, a woman never owns these things. I have suffered injury, I feel it; I should have been able to confide it to you, to you alone, and you would have been charitable to me, I am certain of it; but what can I do—the fear of shame—and then I have so cruelly expiated my fault. M. de Rudesgens' misconduct has so punished me, that I thought myself privileged to keep silence; but if you do not come to my assistance, Montaleu, I am ruined."

And Artémise began to shed real tears, which astonished M. de Montaleu so much that he now felt the importance of the event which Madame de Rudesgens was about to communicate to him.

"Let us see, my dear," said he, gently, "calm yourself, and then explain what is the matter."

Madame de Rudesgens heaved deep sighs, wiped her eyes several times, and at length resumed, with downcast look and hesitating voice:

"You, doubtless, remember the time when I received the homage of M. de Rudesgens at Cologne?"

"Ah!" said M. de Montaleu, whose brow darkened as he heard that town and that distant time mentioned; "it is of your marriage with M. de Rudesgens that you wish to speak to me."

"No, my friend," replied Artémise, trembling more and more; "not of that, but of a dreadful terrible, frightful event, which preceded this marriage, by two months only."

The marquis looked at Madame de Rudesgens attentively; and, as all the dates of the events which had taken place at this time recurred to his memory, he repeated, in an anxious voice:

"Two months before your marriage? do you say."

"Yes," replied the guilty Artémise, whose strength appeared almost to fail her.

"But what happened?" said M. de Montaleu, quickly.

Madame de Rudesgens wept afresh, and suddenly cried out:

"I was a young girl, without experience, without guidance, without protection, for my father was already in prison; I had often met at the house of an old friend of my father, a young French officer. (She weeps.) He was charming, Montaleu. (She sobs.) He was handsome, he was brave, he was clever, and he loved me."

Madame de Rudesgens burst into tears.

Well?" said M. de Montaleu.

"He told me," continued Madame de Rudesgens, "that he could interest you in my favour, you, upon whom my fortune depended. And," added she, sobbing more and more, I believed in his love."

The marquis started, and leaning towards Madame de Rudesgens, he inquired, with a slight trembling in his voice:

And when did this happen?"

"Nearly a year before the decision which restored to me my fortune, and determined my marriage with M. de Rudesgens."

"But why," said M. de Montaleu in a tone full of anxiety, "why did you marry M. de Rudesgens, when it was the duty of your betrayer to repair the fault he had caused you to commit?"

"He was married," replied Madame de Rudesgens in a voice scarcely audible.

"Married!" repeated the marquis, "and you were ignorant of it, of course?"

Madame de Rudesgens did not reply.

There was a moment's silence between the two speakers, and M. de Montaleu at length continued:

"But how does it happen that a connexion which has doubtless been broken more than thirty years can be a subject of terror for you to-day?"

"Because," said the mournful Artémise stammering, "because—in spite of all the precautions which were taken at that time, the child born of this unfortunate union has finished by discovering—"

Madame de Rudesgens stopped, and M. de Montaleu who took more interest in the events which had taken place thirty years before, than in the fears which she now experienced, resumed quickly:

"And what precautions did you take to hide the birth of this child?"

"Oh!" cried Madame de Rudesgens, "it was he who wished it—"

But she stopped as if something had suddenly warned her that any falsehood would be unveiled. She then continued in some confusion:

"No, it was not he, it was I who wished it. You can understand the terrors of a poor young girl, Montaleu; he could not marry me, since he was already married, and the slightest circumstance would have awakened suspicion in the mind of M. de Rudesgens; I should have been lost, for he would have forsaken me after having publicly sought my hand. It was therefore necessary that an impenetrable mystery should hide the true birth of this child."

M. de Montaleu listened in wondering anxiety, whilst Madame de Rudesgens, trembling more in proportion as she approached the last avowal, resumed, letting fall these words, scarcely articulated:

"It was then that a devoted servant named Joseph Miras, went to propose to a poor girl named—"

"Sophia Muller, was it not?" cried M. de Montaleu, suddenly raising himself by a quick movement.

"Yes," replied Artémise faintly.

"He went to propose to her," continued the marquis trembling with emotion, "to recognise as being his, the child which belonged to you."

"It is true."

"And the poor girl accepted, and afterwards—Oh!—"

M. de Montaleu stopped, and raising his hands to heaven, he cried with deep despair:

"Oh! Sophia! Sophia! thirty years of misery and desertion, because it has pleased a miserable woman to brand thee with her error!"

"She accepted voluntarily," cried Madame de Rudesgens, "and we were at any rate able to relieve her misery, for you did not know her at that time."

"It is true," said M. de Montaleu, in a tone of the deepest sadness, "poverty placed her in your power, and sold her honour to you. Oh! poverty! poverty!" added he, "what a weapon it places in the hand of the rich to ruin and calumniate the poor! But I understand you; I understand how necessary it was for you to hide the fault you had committed; but what coward has been able to assist you in this shameful bargain?"

Madame de Rudesgens trembled from head to foot.

"Do not call him thus," replied she, "do not insult him, above all before his son; for, he has written to me, he would tell all."

"But what more then?" cried M. de Montaleu, in the greatest agitation.

"It was I," said Madame de Rudesgens, stammering, "it was I alone, who, unknown to him, made this fatal bargain—he heard of it only at the moment when he was setting out for the new world, and he was then ignorant of your connections with Sophia Muller."

"It was Montéclain, then?" cried M. de Montaleu.

"Yes, yes."

"He, whose son threatened us all so insolently this morning?"

"Yes."

"He who came to ask me to visit on his deathbed the unfortunate child whom I have repulsed denied, driven away?"

"It is true," repeated Madame de Rudesgens, who could scarcely support herself.

"And you," resumed M. de Montaleu, with indignation, "you who, since the departure of Montéclain, of your lover, have learned all the misfortune which your infamous fraud had brought upon the unhappy Sophia; you who know all that I have suffered from believing her guilty, you have not had a moment's pity either for her or me, you have not been to make me this avowal."

"Oh! pardon me, pardon me," cried Madame de Rudesgens, with despair.

"And my son is dying," cried M. de Montaleu, whose tears at length forced their way, "and he is in the house of my enemy, who has received him, whilst I have driven him away; who has also received a poor child, innocent perhaps, whom I have in the same manner repulsed! And why? because I have around me people without heart, without honesty, without honour."

"Montaleu! Montaleu!" cried Madame de Rudesgens, interrupting the marquis's anger, "you must come with me this evening to Montéclain's house, and you will thus frustrate the perfidious intentions of Madame Amab."

"Madame Amab!" repeated M. de Montaleu, "Felina? But in what way is this woman mixed up with the affair?"

"Have I not told you, then?" said Madame de

DEATH OF THE SHE TIGER.

Rudesgens; "Felina is this child whose birth has been attributed to Sophia Muller. Felina is—"

"Your daughter!" said Montaleu.

"Yes, my daughter," repeated Madame de Rudesgens, hiding her head between her hands.

M. de Montaleu looked at her for a moment in silence, and said to her, in a tone less severe:

"Oh! you are punished cruelly enough. Felina is your daughter!"

"My daughter!" continued Madame de Rudesgens, in a low voice, and, as though the report of her own words had frightened her; "my daughter, who has threatened to reveal everything to my husband, if I do not assist her to ruin Madame de Montion."

"Who is innocent, is she not?" cried M. de Montaleu, with delight, and who weeps now, who suffers like my poor murdered son. Murdered—but by whom?"

"My friend," replied Madame de Rudesgens, "Montéclain expects me at his house this evening. 'Come, he writes to me, and any proof which can compromise you shall be destroyed; come, and bring M. de Montaleu; he must pardon you first; without that, all my efforts will be useless; tell him that his son demands it; tell him that, since I have been at his house, he can come to mine; only I will try to shew him how a gentleman opens his house to the enemy who does not fear to enter it.'"

M. de Montaleu was silent. His pride still struggled against the feelings of his heart; at length, he cried out suddenly:

"Well! be it so, I will go, and if I have done Montéclain wrong, I will not shrink from repairing it by owning it before all the world. At what hour shall you repair to his house?"

"He expects us at eight o'clock," said Madame de Rudesgens. You will certainly come, will you not? M. de Montaleu was about to reply, when a knock was heard at the door; he unfastened it, and the servant announced the arrival of Madame Felina Amab.

"This woman at my house!" cried M. de Montaleu.

"She says," replied the servant, "that she has an important writing to put into your hands."

Madame de Rudesgens, trembling and bewildered, but restrained by the presence of the servant, fixed her wild eyes upon M. de Montaleu.

The marquis pitied her, and said to her in a low voice:

"Is it necessary to admit her?'

"I do not know," replied Madame de Rudesgens, almost inaudibly.

"Must we send her away?" returned M. de Montaleu.

"Oh! no, no! that would perhaps cause my ruin."

"Admit Madame Amab," said M. de Montaleu, aloud.

"Oh! my friend," cried Artémise, as soon as the servant had withdrawn, "you alone can save me, you alone."

Felina's voice was heard almost immediately, and Madame de Rudesgens, frightened, concealed herself in an adjoining closet.

Felina appeared.

She stopped on the threshold of the door.

M. de Montaleu made her a sign to approach, and pointed to a chair.

"It is useless, sir," said Felina, in a calm voice; "these vain forms of politeness are unnecessary between us; we hate and despise each other—"

M. de Montaleu bowed, without making any reply.

Felina continued.

"I come to speak to you on a subject, on which perhaps the safety of my life depends. It is a question of honour, sir, and I place it with confidence in your hands; have the goodness to read this," added she, offering him the original of the letter, the copy of which she had shown to Madame de Rudesgens, "and tell me who is the author of it, and who he is whose name I suppose I have a right to learn."

M. de Montaleu, still preserving the same silence, took the document which Felina handed to him.

She looked at him attentively, for this letter contained Sophia Muller's justification, and Madame Amab expected an explosion of rage from the marquis. M. de Montaleu already knew the contents of this letter. He could not, however, hide the emotion which this appeal to its truth caused him to feel. He held in his hands the written proof of Sophia's innocence, and he appeared to hesitate for a moment. The paper trembled in his hand. Felina, who devoured him with her looks, at length said to him:

"Well! marquis, what is the name of the man who wrote you this letter? What is the name of the woman who, by abandoning her child, has forced you to abandon yours?"

M. de Montaleu folded the paper, and returning it to Felina, said, in a firm voice:

"I do not know this writing, madam."

Felina remained astounded.

"Nor this signature?" said she.

"No, madam."

"Nor this inscription?"

"No."

"You know nothing, I suppose?" cried she, with frightful transport.

"Nothing," repeated M. de Montaleu, coldly.

Felina neither uttered a cry, nor spoke a word, she indulged in no gesture of prayer or threat; she bowed stiffly to M. de Montaleu, and went out.

At the same moment, Madame de Rudesgens came out of the closet in which she had concealed herself.

"Oh! thanks! thanks! my friend," cried she, you have saved me!"

"But Montéclain will restore to me my son?" said M. de Montaleu.

"Oh! come! come!" returned Madame de Rudesgens: "he expects you."

---

## CHAPTER LXXXII.

### THE INSANE WOMAN.

It was evening. Julia, still at the farm, saw with anxiety the hour approach in which she must keep the promise she had made to Montéclain.

Julia, as we have said, having decided to leave the country, had sent for her carriage from M. de Montaleu's house. She received with it some things necessary for her journey, and what was of still more consequence, all the papers which belonged to her. Amongst these, Julia found the letter she was writing to her brother that same morning, when she was interrupted by the arrival of De Rudesgens, Champmortain, and Brias; Julia read it again, and concealed it in her bosom near her heart.

This disclosure of her secret feelings, by bringing her back to herself, renewed her fears with respect to Montéclain. More than ever governed by the imperious charm which that man exercised over her, she was still more frightened by this empire.

Julia's whole heart, all that was generous and confiding in her nature, cried to her: "Go, do not hesitate, go;" but almost immediately the remembrance of what Montéclain had been, the recollection of the illusion by which she had formerly been deceived; the recent but terrible experience, she had just had of the perfidies of the world, cried to her, on the other hand: "Take care, it is perhaps another trap; beware!"

Any other woman, in Julia's place, would probably have encouraged these dictates of prudence; but she was so afraid of being ungrateful towards Montéclain, that she let the evening pass away in the midst of her painful perplexity, when suddenly the arrival of Bricord and of Aly Muley was announced to her.

The nurse de Saint-Faron and Léda's child were with Julia in the room, to which she had withdrawn. She feared lest the farmer should know that this child was in his house, and hastened down stairs into the lower hall, where Bricord had remained with the spahi.

All the farm servants were assembled, and were looking inquisitively at their master, whose pale face expressed nothing but calm and firm resignation. Aly Muley and Bricord took off their hats when Madame de Monrion appeared; all the servants did the same.

The presence of Aly Muley and Bricord restored Julia's confidence; she had a just perception of the intrinsic worth of a man, without reference to the costly or mean garment which might cover him. It was neither a marquis, like M. de Rudesgens, nor a peer of France, like M. de Montaleu, who tendered her assistance. Here were two peasants, two noble hearts, two honest men; and Julia felt both confident and strong.

"Madam," said Aly Muley, in a grave and almost bold voice, "we are come to conduct you to M. de Montéclain's castle."

"You will accompany me, will you not?" said Julia; "and you also M. Bricord?"

"We will accompany you there, madam," replied the farmer. "But, you might enter it fearlessly, even were you quite alone. There is something in yourself which protects you better than the presence of such poor men as we could do; it is because you are good, madam, because you have pity on the guilty and the unfortunate; I know all, madame," added Bricord, his voice broken with emotion; "I know that you have not wished to say a word in your own defence—that you have had fear only for another. I wish to be able to tell you all the feelings of my heart. But," added he, wiping away the tears which rolled down his cheeks, "I cannot—I do not know how."

"Come, enough of this," said Muley, speaking in a loud voice to hide his emotion; "we must not say so much to madame; she will hear what she ought to hear, she will see what she ought to see; that will suffice."

"Oh! my friends, my friends!" cried Madame de Monrion, holding out a hand to each.

She stopped whilst the two men pressed in their hard hands hers, so delicate and white. She then resumed:

"Yes, you are my friends, are you not?"

"Oh!" said Bricord, in a low voice, and stammering, "God will reward you, you will be happy; yes, yes," added he, in a still lower tone, "consent to be Marchioness of Montéclain, and you will see, and you will see; you will be happy."

Julia cast down her eyes to hide at the same time her joy and confusion. Bricord had just given a name to the hope which had for some hours agitated her breast. During this time Aly Muley did his best to recover from the emotion which had gained the better of him, and muttered between his teeth:

"Devil take me! I thought I was going to become a saint. Come, madam, added he, "it is time to set off, they are waiting for you."

Madame de Monrion stepped into her carriage, accompanied by the blessings and good wishes of those who had witnessed this scene. She took the road to the castle of Montéclain. Bricord and Aly Muley followed the carriage on horseback.

They were scarcely a quarter of a league from the farm, when Bricord suddenly stopped, uttered a stifled cry, and galloped quickly towards a path which crossed the road they were travelling. His movement was so rapid, that Aly Muley, plunged in his own reflections, did not notice the farmer's disappearance until he was quite out of sight. He supposed that Bricord had returned to the farm to give some orders there, and he continued his journey, feeling persuaded that his companion would soon rejoin him.

Aly Muley was mistaken. It was not a forgotten order that had induced Bricord to give up the mission he had accepted to accompany Madame de Monrion.

At the end of the path he had just followed, he thought he saw a white and flitting shadow. Notwithstanding the distance, and the twilight which already enveloped the whole forest with partial darkness, it seemed to him that it was Léda.

Arrived within a few steps of his wife, the farmer jumped quickly from his horse, and ran towards her to prevent her flight, for he supposed that at the sight of him she would try to escape. But Léda quietly looked at him as he approached, examined him attentively, and while Bricord was considering in what way he should accost the woman who had so cruelly offended him, whom he always loved, and who had suffered so greatly, Léda said to him, in a gentle and melancholy voice:

"Friend, can you direct me to farmer Bricord's house?"

"Farmer Bricord's house," repeated he, cold with terror at the question. "Do you ask me for the house of farmer Bricord?"

He examined Léda more attentively. She was calm, her lips were smiling, her eyes glittered with joy. Bricord trembled, and was frightened.

"Yes," replied Léda, in a confidential and mysterious tone. "I wish to find out where he lives; I must go and see him to-night, I must comfort him. I am dead, you must understand, and he loved me so much, that he must be very sorry for it."

"Léda," cried Bricord, "Léda, Léda, do you not remember me? Do you not hear me? You are not dead, since you are here, since you speak to me."

Léda smiled, and replied softly:

"I know very well that I am dead—he has killed me, the coward, he has killed me; but, do you see, God has permitted me to rise from my tomb to expiate my fault, and to come and console him whom I have treated so ill; lead me to his house, I pray you: he is good, he is generous, he will thank you. I will tell him that you have had pity upon a poor wandering spirit; come, I beg you."

Bricord, distracted, weeping, sobbing, instinctively, took the road to his farm.

"Léda," said he, in the midst of his sobs, "Léda, return to your better self, I will pardon you, I will love you, I will forget all."

"Do you know," said Léda, supporting herself on his arm, and speaking in a low voice, "do you know what I shall do? When I arrive there, I shall seat myself at the head of his bed, and, during the night, I shall stoop down to his ear, and sing him the songs he used to love; I will comfort him, I will tell him that those who are good and brave like him, must live and pardon, for God has told me that I shall not rest in my grave until he whom I have deceived shall come there and pray for me."

"Oh! I will pray to Him, I will pray to Him," replied Bricord, "but it will be that He may restore you your reason. Oh! poor woman! you have suffered greatly then? he has ill-treated you, the wretch!"

"Do not say that, sir," replied Léda, "my husband would kill him, I should meet him among the dead, and he would do me still greater harm."

Whilst speaking thus, they had approached the farm. Léda looked at the house, and suddenly stopped.

"Thank you, sir," said she to Bricord, "I recollect now, that is really our house, where I lived so miserably, where I might have lived so happily. It was my fault, sir, I did not wish to be happy. Poor Bricord," added she, "how he must suffer from being alone! Do you know him? Have you seen him since I died? Has he cursed me such? Has he wept for me a little?"

"He has pardoned you, Léda," said Bricord, whose voice could scarcely be heard through the sobs which suffocated him. "He pardons you—he calls for you—he waits for you."

They were now at the entrance of the farm-yard; the servants still much excited by Madame de Monrion's departure, were all assembled and conversing among themselves about recent events, when Léda and Bricord suddenly appeared. At the sight of them, a quick surprise, sudden terror, closed every mouth, and the group of servants silently made way for Léda, who walked up to the house with a firm step.

"Oh! my children! my children!" said Bricord, speaking to his servants, who looked at him in utter astonishment, "she is mad!"

They all approached to look at her more closely.

"Let me pass," said she, with that uniform and gentle voice in which she had always spoken, "let me go to him, I have many things to say to him."

The servants drew back, and Léda entered the lower room. She stopped there, and looked around her.

"Yes," continued she, "it was certainly here, it was for me that he had this place arranged, this table, these curtains, these flowers, this couch, were for me. Poor Peter!" added she, mournfully, how he loved me! But, be tranquil, my children, the happiness that I have not given him during my life, shall now be his. Believe me, death teaches many things; it teaches us where duty, virtue, and goodness are; thus I love him now, and I come to him to tell him that I do so."

"Oh! my children, my children!" cried Bricord, "let us pray God to restore her to reason. Oh! my God!" cried he, falling on his knees, have pity on her and on me!"

All the servants imitated their master's example, and Léda remained alone standing in the midst of those who were praying for her.

Suddenly, a weak cry was heard above the murmur of all these suppliant voices. Léda started; the pleasing and calm expression of her countenance gave place to one of despair and terror; her eyes glittered, her head was bent forward; she appeared to listen and expect. A fresh cry resounded, weak and gentle, which was answered by a passionate cry from Léda. She immediately ran out of the room, rushed panting up the staircase which led up to her own room, pushed open the door, and found herself in the presence of the nurse de Saint-Faron, who held the poor, abandoned child on her knees, and was trying to send it to sleep.

At this sight, Léda uttered another cry, at once despairing and joyful, the cry of the intelligent and awakened soul, a cry proceeding from the inmost depths of a mother's heart. The nurse arose, frightened by this apparition.

"It is my child," said Léda, in a distracted voice.

The nurse drew back, whilst Bricord and the servants were hastening into the room, and she replied, trembling:

"No! no! It is the child which Madame de Monrion placed under my care."

"It is he!" cried Léda, advancing towards the nurse.

And, as the latter still drew back, Léda fell on her knees at the nurse's feet, and said to her in an imploring tone:

"Oh! let me see him, let me see him."

The stupified servants looked at one another, and the nurse was hiding the child in her arms, when Bricord said with an accent of deep pity:

"Give it to her, it is hers."

At these words, Léda, about to seize her child, turned and looked at Bricord. A frightful scream escaped her. She pointed towards her husband with her hand, convulsively agitated.

"Ah!" murmured she, in a broken voice, "you—you—and I—I—"

She arose slowly; she glanced with distraction upon all those who surrounded her.

"They—they—" continued she, in the same short and broken voice, "and I, here—here—"

A light seemed to burst in upon the unfortunate woman; she pressed her forehead with her hands, as though a burning grief had entered there with recollection, and immediately disappeared from the room before any one could detain her.

They sought her on all sides, they called her; but they discovered nothing, they heard nothing. Bricord alone understood that she was no longer insane.

They went out of the farm with torches, they ran in different directions. It was a moment of tumult and agony. Bricord seemed in his turn to have lost his reason. He could not have felt more terrible despair if Léda had been innocent; for, to the noble heart of this man, misfortune was a title almost as sacred as virtue. He took Léda's infant in his arms, and ran out, crying:

"Léda! here is your child; he calls for you, do you not hear him?"

The servants went backwards and forwards, the men searched the thickets and in the ditches. Each eager in the pursuit, gradually went to a greater distance from the farm.

Bricord suddenly found himself opposite the little river which flowed at the bottom of the valley of Savordan.

It was at a spot where the course of the water, kept back by a narrow bank, formed a cascade, the noise of which, joined to that of the mill which was built on this bank, prevented the cries of the peasants from being heard.

Bricord drew back on perceiving, through the darkness, a man on horseback, standing at the edge of the river, below the mill.

"Whoever you may be," cried he, tell me—"

"Ah! is it you, Bricord?" said Aly Muley, "I came to know why you left me?"

"But why have you stopped there?" enquired Bricord, struck with an ominous presentiment.

"Because," replied Aly Muley, "I fancied I saw a white shadow pass, which ran towards the river, and then I thought I heard a loud shriek, and the sound of a body falling into the water."

On hearing these words, Bricord uttered a terrific cry of despair, which esounded through the valley.

## CHAPTER LXXXIII.

### VIRTUE TRIUMPHS.

When Julia arrived in the court of Montéclain's castle, she was greatly surprised to see that Aly Muley and Bricord were no longer with her. Their absence alarmed her; the thought of having been drawn into a snare, crossed her mind for a moment, but she drove it away with indignation. She might not have had faith in Montéclain, but that she felt ashamed of suspecting that Aly and Bricord had lent their assistance to a crime.

Two servants, bearing torches, opened the carriage door. They lighted the vast flight of steps before the castle. Julia entered the hall, where two more servants, with torches, walked before her, and silently introduced her into an ante-room, illuminated as for a feast, but vacant.

This singular reception astonished Julia, and made her tremble; at length she reached the door of a second room, which was opened for her in the same manner, whilst one of the servants announced, in a loud voice:

"The Countess de Monrion."

Julia entered, and found herself in the presence of M. de Montaleu, the Colonel, Brias, Champmortain, Sylvia, M. de Rudesgens, and of his wife. M. de Montaleu was seated near the colonel, whose hands he held in his own; Brias was conversing with them; Sylvia and Champmortain were speaking together with tenderness; Madame de Rudesgens was smiling at her husband.

On Julia's entrance, they all rose with one accord. Brias was obliged to support the colonel. Julia stopped. There was a moment of solemn silence; every one hesitated. But at length M. de Montaleu, advancing towards Julia, called out:

"My child! my daughter—my daughter!"

Julia threw herself into his arms, happy, overwhelmed, intoxicated with joy. All that she had suffered was forgotten.

Dearly as she had paid for this moment of joy and triumph, she did not regret her sufferings, for it was not herself only who triumphed, it was Montéclain also, who had kept his word to her, Montéclain who did not deceive her, Montéclain, to whose house M. de Montaleu had come.

Julia wept and sobbed aloud. In disengaging herself from M. de Montaleu's embrace, she perceived Sylvia, who had approached her, and was looking at her in a supplicating manner.

She took her in her arms. Her heart was full of pardon for every one. She embraced Madame de Rudesgens, and old Annibal also. She gave her hand to Brias, and to Champmortain, saying to them all: "Thanks—thanks—" as if she owed them gratitude.

Then, after having been from one to the other, her eyes still wandered round the room in search of some one, but he was not there.

"Oh!" thought she from the inmost depths of her heart, "if this generosity should not be his act!"

But this thought did not last a moment. Besides M. de Montaleu immediately turned her attention to something else.

"My child," said he, "permit me to present to you my son, Colonel Thomas Rien de Montaleu."

"Your son?" said Julia astonished.

"That shall be explained to you, most beautiful lady," said M. de Rudesgens kissing Julia's hands. "Regard him always as a brave gentleman, a man of honor, an honest man, a—"

"Ah!" said Julia, pressing the colonel's hands, "I know how much I owe to this gentleman,—I know it is on my account that his life is in danger —that it is for me he suffers."

"I suffer no longer," said Thomas, "happiness is a good physician. Do you not feel it so yourself, madam?"

"Oh! yes!" replied she with emotion.

She then turned towards the other persons present, and exchanged with them some words of pardon and thanks; but she remained uneasy and surprised: Montéclain did not appear.

Each one seemed to guess the reason of Julia's surprise; but no one appeared willing to explain the cause of this absence.

She was going to speak; she was about to question M. de Montaleu, when a servant came in and told Brias that M. de Montéclain wished to speak to him. He went out. A moment afterwards M. de Rudesgens was summoned; then Madame de Rudesgens; at length Champmortain and his wife were called out in their turn. Julia was left with M. de Montaleu and his son.

"Oh!" said she trembling to M. de Montaleu, "why are they all sent for?"

"I hope you will see them again presently, unless—"

M. de Montaleu and the colonel were now summoned.

"What! will you leave me alone?" cried Julia.

"You will see me again at any rate," said M. de Montaleu smiling. "Adieu, for the present, my child."

The colonel and M. de Montaleu went out, and Julia was left alone. She stood for a moment motionless in the middle of the large drawing room glittering with wax lights. For the first time she looked at the place to which she had come, and saw hanging around her a great number of portraits, all of which seemed to be looking at her inquisitively. Julia was in a state of inexpressible anxiety; she foresaw for herself a great event; but she scarcely dared to hope that it would be a happy one."

He would come no doubt; but what would he say to her? Oh! was she not too much flattered? Might he not merely have prepared a justification for her innocence, a homage to her misfortune.

Julia felt almost suffocated. Her heart beat violently and stopped suddenly. Her anxiety was so great that she pressed her hand upon her heart, in doing which she felt the unfinished letter, the confidant of her hopes and fears, which she had that same morning written to her brother.

She looked around her with terror, as if to implore protection against herself: her eyes interrogated all the dumb countenances which surrounded her, and seemed to ask their support and advice. Her glance wandering from picture to picture could not make out one friendly countenance, until it fixed at length on the portrait of a sorrowful, but young and beautiful woman, who, with a look of love was bending over a cradle.

This countenance Julia recognized. It certainly was the high and thoughtful forehead of Montéclain, it was his proud lip, his Roman nose, his intelligent eye, his affluent black hair; it was his mother.

Julia stopped at this picture, and joining her hands, she murmured, in a low voice:

"Protect me, madam, protect me!"

A slight noise startled her; she turned round and perceived Montéclain.

He approached, bowed respectfully, and made her a sign to be seated. Julia returned his salute, and seated herself upon the chair placed below the portrait, for she was unable to support herself.

"You must pardon me, madam," said Montéclain, gravely, "for having taken away one after another, all the friends about you; I must explain to you why I have done this.

Julia bowed. She trembled violently, for she felt that this interview would decide her fate.

"To put an end to the thousand schemes and artifices which were at work to injure you," continued Montéclain, gently, "I had sent for some papers from Paris, which have just arrived; and I have placed them in the hands of each of those whom they concern."

"You have done what was right, I am sure," said Julia, in a weak and faltering voice.

"Stay," returned Montéclain, "let me tell you all. Brias, liberated from his debts, leaves this country to-morrow, and France itself soon after."

"That is well," said Julia, "but poor Sylvia?"

"Madame de Champmortain will soon restore to her husband the affection which he had lost by his own fault, and which he will now be happy to recover."

"Oh! that is indeed good news! sir," said Julia.

"I hope," continued Montéclain, smiling, "that I have obtained for M. de Rudesgens more comfort in his home, by proving to his wife that those who themselves have need of indulgence ought to show it to others. I have also warned M. de Rudesgens that his conduct was unjust in now seeking to throw light upon suspicions which he formerly repelled when coveting the fortune of Mademoiselle Van Marken."

"You are right, sir," replied Julia.

"To conclude," continued Monteclain, "I have transmitted to M. de Montaleu the written proofs of the innocence of a poor mother who has long suffered, and I have afforded him the right to recognize as his son one of the bravest men of our time, one of those hearts which bestow renown on the name they adopt, or add a glory to the name they receive."

"Oh! thanks for them all, sir. Some you have saved from danger, others you have restored to happiness. God will reward you for what you have done."

"I have done but little for them," replied Montéclain; "yet, I boast before you, madam, of all that I have elicited from your looks of goodness and indulgence; proud of what little good I have done, and which you inspired me to do, I ask you now whether you are satisfied?"

"Ah! sir," said Julia, whose anxiety made her voice tremble, "can you think me so unjust, so ungrateful?"

"No, madam," replied Montéclain, "no; I think you just, I think you grateful, and that is why I ask your permission to tell you all. Yet, before I proceed, remember this: your friends are still within this castle; at the slightest appeal from you, they will come forward. This is my house, madam, but whilst you are here, it is yours. If what

I am about to say, appear strange to you, madam, if even one of my words alarm you, at least fear not that I wish to take advantage of your presence here to address you in language unfit for your ears. You are queen and mistress in this house, madam; you are seated in the place where my mother used to sit, below the likeness of her, who sees and hears me, and who protects you."

"Indeed, sir," said Julia, her eyes cast down and her heart overflowing, I have no fear, no apprehension."

"More even than this is necessary, madam," added Montéclain, "you must take courage."

"Courage!" repeated Julia.

"Yes, madam—but understand my meaning. You think yourself under an obligation to me; you consider that you owe me gratitude, and you are too generous, too kind to wish to occasion sorrow to the man who came to your help. Well! madam, that must be forgotten; I must be frank, I must confess all."

"You! sir?"

"Yes, madam; all that I have done for some days past, all which I have just now boasted of I have not done for others, but for you alone."

"For me—sir?" said Julia, violently agitated by the much-desired word.

"For you alone," said Montéclain, "and I have done it because I love you, madam."

Julia blushed, and could scarcely refrain from bursting into tears.

"Why," continued Montéclain, gravely, whilst avowing this love, "should I use language which would tell you but half what I feel. I love you, madam, not only because you are beautiful, virtuous and high-minded; but because you have made me understand the power of goodness, the charm of innocence, and the superiority of virtue; I love you not only for what you are, but also for what you have made me."

Julia's heart was throbbing violently; her face, burning with blushes, was hung down; she longed to hide herself in a mother's arms; she breathed with difficulty, and could not speak.

Montéclain continued:

"Yes, madam, I love you, and that in itself is not surprising; but no doubt it will much surprise you that I dare to ask you for your love?"

"My love?" murmured Julia, sinking back in her chair with agitation.

"Yes, madam," resumed Montéclain, in a sad and gentle tone; "and it is to you alone that I wished to trust; it is from you alone that I desire an answer. Do not misunderstand me, madam, I might, according to custom, have employed your friends to tell you the desire of my heart, and mine to request your reply. The former, perhaps, judging you amiss, might have spoken to you of my name, of my rank, of my fortune, and led you to believe that I relied upon them to gain your favour. The latter, too much prepossessed in their good opinion of me, might have spoken to you of my courage, my generosity, and the harvest of glory I might expect to reap in my old age. Others again, more severe or just, might have told you the story of my past life, its follies, and errors, and led you to spurn my affection. None of them would have deceived you, yet none of them would have told you the truth. I alone ought to open my heart to you: you alone should hear my confession. Madam, until the day when I saw you for the first time, I had not lived. This is the truth; I declare it to you in the presence of my mother, who is looking at me. No, I had not lived with my heart, with my soul, with my true spirit; for, since I have known you, I have been conscious of another mind, another soul, another heart. It is, therefore, not the man of whom you might be told much evil and little good, who speaks to you, it is he whom you have created, who belongs to you, who now addresses you, and asks you faithfully if you will accept his affection and his name."

"But, sir," said Julia, trembling; "I do not know—"

"You can tell me all, madam; you can reply that you do not believe in my love, or that you disdain it; you can tell me that you pity me, and that you do not love me; and, I promise you that whatever your answer may be, I will accept it with respect. I shall only grieve that I am not worthy of you, whilst I shall be grateful to you, for this; that you have had faith in my honour, and came alone to this house, without fear, without hesitation: that, madam, is an honour of which you will not forbid me to be proud."

Julia, confused, overwhelmed, her heart full, happy, intoxicated by what she heard, frightened by what she felt, her love and her modesty each striving for the mastery, Julia, whose heart beat with joy, but whose pure thought shrank from an avowal, whose lips could not pronounce the expression of her happiness, turned round and murmured softly:

"Do not ask me to reply to you; do not exact—"

"Oh! madam," said Montéclain, "I told you that you must have courage. You pity me, do you not? You are as grateful for my love as for your safety, for you feel that I love you, and you dare not tell me that you do not love me."

"Oh! no, no," said Julia, gasping for breath, I dare not—I suffer."

And as whilst speaking thus, she laid her hand upon her heart, she felt the letter she had written to her brother; she started.

"You suffer?" said Montéclain, tenderly; "I ought to have foreseen that you would hesitate to tell me the truth. I might even have known it; for yesterday, and to-day again, you wished to leave me."

"Yes—" said Julia, looking at him, at length, "I wished to leave you, and this is the reason—"

She handed him the letter, and hiding her face in her hands, burst into tears. For the first time in her life, her maidenly heart was unveiled, and she was oppressed by her happiness.

Montéclain read the letter rapidly; his hands trembled, his eyes sparkled with joy, his countenance appeared illumined with heavenly light, and he already knew to what an extent he was loved, whilst Julia still wept and hid her face.

Montéclain took her hand, and raised her up. She felt nothing, she had no longer either thought or will; he turned her gently towards his mother's portrait, and said to her in a voice of deep tenderness:

"Julia, when you become Marchioness of Montéclain, come and sit here, and this holy picture shall say to you from Heaven: 'My daughter, I thank you.'"

"And my mother, who is with her," replied Julia, "shall tell yours that you may trust in me as I trust in you."

At that moment, a loud noise was heard in the ante-room. The door was opened almost immediately, and they announced:

"*The king's attorney!*"

---

## CHAPTER LXXXIV.

### THE CATASTROPHE.

All those who were scattered about the neighbourhood, on hearing Bricord's cry, had run to the spot whence it proceeded. Those in the mill and the out-houses near were awoke; in an instant both sides of the little river were thronged with people, whilst shrieks and exclamations rang in the air.

"Where is she? where is she? It is Léda—it is Bricord—was heard on every side; for the former likewise had thrown himself into the water.

Three times he had risen to the surface, three times he had dived again; but a minute (a century to those who looked on) had now elapsed without his reappearing. The water, deep and disturbed by those rapid eddies which revolve at the foot of cascades, only returned the broken reflections of the torches held over the bank.

A frightful silence succeeded the tumult and noise which a moment before had animated the whole valley.

Suddenly the water divides, a hand appears and falls back again. Another cry is heard—a dull sound resounds amidst the silent expectation of the motionless group. Aly Muley, in his turn, had thrown himself into the river. This heroic action is hailed by a thousand cries. The bystanders exchange sinister prognostics, and gloomy doubts: "They will all perish, say some; the river is full of those dreadful holes, and powerful whirlpools, which entangle the bravest and strongest swimmer in the long grass floating on the water:

It is no longer either for Léda or Bricord they fear; it is for Aly Muley.

At length he appears, and more self-possessed, more skilful, more prudent, he seeks to gain the shore. They throw him a cord, which he lays hold of, and they pull him to the bank, dragging the half-exhausted farmer after him. Both, covered with long slimy grass, had torn themselves by desperate efforts from the grasp of those innumerable fibres which had enveloped them in their heavy network.

Bricord soon came to himself, and his first cry was:

"Léda! where is Léda?"

One of Bricord's servants would then have leapt into the water, but Aly Muley held him back, saying in a low vice:

"It is useless to expose a man's life to bring up a corpse. She has been under water at least five minutes."

"Five minutes!" cried Bricord, starting up; "she might be there ten, twenty minutes, an hour even, and yet recover; let me go."

Aly Muley was obliged to hold him in his arms, while those who surrounded him assisted, and yet they would not have been able to restrain him, had not the miller appeared with nets.

"We shall find her now," said Aly.

"Living or dead, I will have her, I will have her," cried Bricord, in a voice, which made all those who approached him shudder.

Aly exerted himself to explore these unknown depths. He took a wooden bowl, placed a candle in it, and pushed the bowl down the current.

Every eye watched with anxiety this vacillating light, floating like a red star on the shadows above the river. The bowl and the light which it carried swung to and fro for a moment, then, impelled by the current, they floated rapidly down the river. Soon after the bowl suddenly stopped, remained still, and then began to turn, swinging backwards and forwards. It had encountered the body, which formed an obstacle to the current of the water.

At each motion it made there were low whispers and words hurriedly exchanged by a hundred persons walking slowly in the train of this mournful star of death. At length, it stopped. The large net, dragged by the miller and a few others on one side of the river, and by Aly Muley and Bricord on the other, had accompanied the march of the funeral torch.

The rope held by the miller was thrown over to Aly Muley's side, and the net, thus bent, was drawn to the bank, which at this point was high and steep, and rose above one of those deep gulfs which made this river so dangerous. The net was heavy, either because it was shackled by the glutinous weeds it tore up, or because it sustained a heavy body. Their expectation was deep, their anxiety awful.

The net was soon brought to the shore; nothing more remained but to raise it out of the water; every hand lends it help; they have nearly done; the water which streams from the meshes envelops the net with a transparent veil through which a white object is perceived.

"It is she! there she is!" they all exclaim together.

Their efforts are redoubled; the net drawn up with force gives a sudden jolt to the lifeless body. The sight is deceived by this motion, and the same voices cry out:

"She lives! she moves!"

All hands are stretched out. Bricord advances to seize the body of the unfortunate Léda; but suddenly the net breaks, and she falls back into the stream with that dull and hollow sound produced by deep waters.

It was an awful, a cruel moment. It was next to certain that they had found nothing but a corpse, yet everybody was struck with horror, as though the unhappy Léda had that moment expired. The valley resounded with Bricord's cries; he fell down on a stone, mourning and weeping like a child, calling on Léda, promising her his pardon, his love, the forgetfulness of the past—happiness for the future. Poor noble heart, prostrated by the death of the woman who had outraged his love, and, who was so cruelly punished!

"She was alive," cried he, "she was alive; you have killed her. Let me seek for her; I will find her, I will rake the bottom of the water with my nails to find her."

They retained him easily, however, for all his strength was now exhausted. Meanwhile, Aly Muley let down the net at the spot where Léda had just fallen. But the net came up empty; the current having dragged the body still farther down. Bricord, overwhelmed with sorrow, remained lying on the stone where he had fallen, sobbing, weeping, biting the ground, hollowing the earth beneath his contracted fingers, whilst Aly Muley continued his search. The bowl was again launched on the water—they followed it again, it stopped as at first, and the net drawn up as before, at length exposed to view the body of poor Léda.

They placed her on the bank, disengaged her from the weeds with which she was covered; a few women offered themselves as bearers, and, followed by the frightened people, bent their steps towards the farm. This corpse thus borne by women in the middle of the night, thus lighted by flickering torches, amidst a gloomy silence, was at once solemn and mysterious. Bricord had, before this, been conveyed to his house. When the procession arrived Aly Muley saw him on his knees in the middle of the hall. As the corpse was brought in, Bricord rose slowly, approached, and stood contemplating it for some time.

Aly Muley began to fear that Bricord himself had lost his reason: he wished to remove the ghastly spectacle from the eyes of the unfortunate farmer.

"Place it upon the bed," said he.

"No," said Bricord abruptly, "no—"

"But what do you wish to do?" enquired his friend.

"Aly," replied the farmer, without taking his eyes off the corpse, "Aly, over the mantel piece, you will find my old sword, take it down—"

"I have," said Aly, who dreaded the explosion of this terrible calm.

"Take yours also, Aly," continued the farmer,

in the same firm and quick tone, and without looking away from Léda's body.

"Here it is—"

"Good," said Bricord, still persisting in his stedfast gaze.

"What are you going to do then?" said Aly to him.

Bricord pushed aside those who supported the corpse, and hastily snatching it from them took it in his arms, threw it across his shoulders, and cried to Aly Muley:

"Now, follow me."

## CHAPTER LXXXV.

### THE DISCOVERY.

The magistrate whose presence had been announced at Montéclain's house, had summoned before him all the personages of this story who were assembled there. He took his seat and commenced questioning them.

"Sir," said he to Montéclain, "a letter has been received from you warning the magistrates that Colonel Thomas Rien, a few hours after leaving your house, was struck by a gun-shot; you added further that a woman dwelling in this part of the country, had been missing for some days. You have requested the investigations of justice respecting these facts, which, from some expressions in your letter, I am inclined to think, are connected together. Have the goodness to tell me everything that is calculated to afford me information on the subject."

Montéclain was about to reply, when the colonel spoke.

"Pardon me sir," said he, "I have already thanked M. de Montéclain, as I ought, for the eagerness with which he has exerted himself to discover the perpetrator of the wound I received. His friendship for me, and the grief produced by this accident have for the moment persuaded him that it was the result of a crime. For my own part I am convinced that an unfortunate accident has been the sole cause of my wound."

The company looked at each other with astonishment; the colonel continued:

"I am quite unknown in this country; therefore I cannot, I ought not to have enemies here. Had this been a crime, it must have been that of a wretch who wished to rob me; now no such attempt was made."

"But," said the attorney, "how can you account for this shot?"

"I believe, and every one here must think the same," replied the colonel, "that it must have been some poor poacher, who thought he was firing at a stag or a wild boar, that he fired accordingly, and that chance alone directed the ball towards me. But as to myself," added he, looking round in a significant manner, "I neither will, nor can believe that it resulted from crime."

"Is your opinion the same as that of the colonel?" said the magistrate to Montéclain.

"I own myself to have been deceived, and must be excused for having been too quickly alarmed."

"Are you of the same opinion, M. de Montaleu?" said the kings attorney.

"Yes," replied M. de Montaleu in a hesitating tone, "I think—I believe that the colonel is right in speaking as he has done."

Then, while the magistrate was taking notes of these different answers, the Marquis de Montaleu whispered to Thomas:

"Thanks, my son, thanks for your generosity towards this wretch."

"He bears our name father," replied the colonel in the same tone.

"I do not see," said the magistrate, "that it is needful to take further notice of this affair: it only remains to discover the unfortunate creature who has disappeared. Who is this woman?"

"She is the wife of one of my farmers," replied Montéclain.

"I know him, she left his farm two days ago, and has not been heard of since."

What would have been very easy to explain, had they all been willing to speak the truth, became very embarrassing by their desiring to spare Hector, or rather the name of Montaleu, the scandal of an ignominious charge.

"Let us hear," resumed the king's attorney, upon whom do your suspicions rest? Is it an abduction, a flight, a sequestration, an assassination?"

"It is nothing of the kind—" said Champmortain. "It is not three hours since I met Madame Bricord in the forest, very composed and looking very well, she was walking towards the farm."

On hearing this, Montéclain rose with anxiety.

"Léda at the farm!" cried he.

He rang the bell.

"Where is Bricord?" enquired he.

"He has not returned to the castle," was the reply.

"What!" said Montéclain to Julia, "did he not accompany you?"

"He was no longer with me when I arrived here."

"And Aly Muley?"

"He had left me also."

"Oh! the fools! the madmen!" cried Montéclain with grief, "they must have committed some mischief—"

Montéclain had scarcely uttered these words, before a loud noise was heard; many voices resounded in the court; the doors were opened violently; hasty footsteps crossed the ante-rooms, and Aly Muley came in, pale, agitated, his hair in disorder, his looks wild; he fell breathless, on a chair; blood was upon his face and hands.

"You are wounded?" said the colonel anxiously.

"Yes—no," replied he bluntly, "it is my blood—no—it, is the blood of others."

"The blood of whom?" inquired Montéclain and the magistrate at the same time.

"I am going to tell you," said Aly Muley whose teeth chattered, whilst his whole body shook convulsively.

Every body leant forward to listen. Aly continued in a hollow tone:

"We had just dragged up the poor woman—'

"What woman?" interrupted Montéclain.

"Bricord's wife," replied Aly. "But you do not know what had taken place. Scarcely had we left the farm to follow the countess's carriage, when Bricord left me. I imagined he had forgotten something, and went on without him. But when I had arrived near the castle, and found that he did not return, I felt uneasy about him, and knowing that the good lady was no longer exposed to danger, I returned to the farm. I was riding along side of the river, below the mill, in the alley of willow-trees. All at once I descried a white shape close before me, and then—I heard something fall into the river.

"I ran forward, but nothing was to be seen—the water was as smooth as glass—I had not been there half a minute when Bricord came up—calling after his wife—after Léda—

"She is there," I said to him, pointing to the river.

"Poor Bricord threw himself in, rose, dived again, and then disappeared altogether; at length I pulled him out, and afterwards—her also—"

"Léda!" cried they all.

"Yes, but dead—lost. She had been insane it seems; but having seen her child—that had restored her to reason—she found herself with Bricord—then—oh! she did not know him, poor woman, she imagined that because he was a soldier, a peasant who could neither read nor write, he could not possess a heart of gold. Yes—yes," said Muley, "as brave as a lion—as good as it was possible to be—poor Bricord!"

"Go on, continue your story!" cried the colonel.

"She was taken out of the water, we had her brought to the farm. Then Bricord looked at her so calmly, so steadfastly that it made me shudder. We were all assembled, without knowing what he wanted, when he told me to take down his sword, and bring my own. I did as he bade me. I may have been wrong. But at that moment I felt so afraid to thwart him, that I should have granted him anything he asked me. Hear what followed. No sooner had I taken the two swords than he lifted up the body of his wife, like that of a sleeping child, and said to me as when we used to march together: 'Follow me!' Well! I followed him."

A feeling of terror shot through the hearts of those who listened to Aly Muley.

"Well? go on," said Montéclain.

"We went," resumed Aly Muley, "or rather, Bricord went, and I followed him. It was a terrible sight. He bore the poor woman in his arms, her head hanging over his shoulder; her arms falling over his back, and swinging to and fro as he walked; I could not look another way, and with my two swords under my arm, I was afraid of this corpse; it drew me on, it fascinated me—I would have followed it to the end of the world without complaining. Suddenly—"

Aly Muley stopped.

They approached him with fresh anxiety.

"Well?"

"It is nothing," said he, "but it froze the blood in my veins—Bricord stopped suddenly—I was walking close upon his heels; I was not aware that he was going to stop, and I knocked my head against that of the corpse, her cold lips met mine. Oh God! I was afraid."

"Finish your story," said the colonel.

"Yes—yes—I will," replied Aly Muley, "Bricord stopped, because he heard the sound of voices. This restored me, they were the voices of Hector de Montaleu and of Madame Amab."

Everybody started, foreseeing some frightful result.

"It was Hector!" said M. de Montaleu in a trembling voice; "and what happened?"

"You shall see," replied Aly Muley. "Bricord stood still for a moment, then he advanced, but it was with a wolf's step. In this manner we reached the corner of a crossway; the two accomplices were disputing. He was on foot, she in her carriage."

"Where are you going?" Hector was saying to Madame Amab.

"What is that to you?"

"Ah!" said the viscount, "you urged me to commit a crime, and now you abandon me."

"What!" said M. de Montaleu, interrupting the soldier.

"Proceed," said the king's attorney, in a commanding voice.

Aly resumed.

"You are a coward," she replied; "you ought to ask Montéclain to give you satisfaction for his conduct towards you."

"But you do not know then," said the other, "that I have asked Brias and Champmortain to be bearers of this challenge, and that they have both refused?"

"Because you wanted courage," was the reply.

The coachman whipped his horses, but Hector pulled the reins. The carriage backed, the horses pranced, they were nearly upset.

"What do you want?" cried Madame Amab.

"I want you to remain, for I am going to be arrested, because I have listened to your perfidious advice, because you have urged me to murder the colonel."

"Was it I," replied Madame Amab, "who made you assassinate the unhappy Léda? Let me go."

"Léda," said Hector, "Léda is mad, and I do not fear her."

"Léda is dead," cried Bricord, "and here she is."

"Saying this," resumed Aly, "Bricord came from among the trees and burst into the middle of the cross-way. On hearing his voice, the viscount turned round, with his hand raised to strike him; but he found himself confronted with Léda's corpse which Bricord held towards him."

"Look—look," cried Bricord, whilst the other drew back, "she is dead—it is your turn now."

"It was terrible," said Aly, in a hollow tone, "it made me shudder. Bricord continued to advance, the viscount to draw back. At length Bricord—Ah! my God! poor woman!—Bricord, unhappy man, threw the corpse at Hector de Montaleu, saying to him: 'Are you afraid to embrace her now?' She fell upon the ground between the two. It was awful to behold."

Aly Muley stopped, and Montéclain said to him, with an anxious voice:

"And Felina—what of Felina?"

"Oh!" replied Aly, in a blunt and bitter tone, "Madame Amab knew what she was about,—she wanted to escape; the coachman whipped the horses again. I declare to you that I should have let the carriage pass, for in fact I scarcely knew what I did, but I saw that the wheel was going to pass over the poor woman's body—*mille tonnerres!* then I darted forward, and struck the horses heads with the back of my sword—they groaned—they pranced—they drew back and overturned the carriage into a ditch, where it was broken to pieces, whilst Bricord, who held the other sword, said to the viscount: "Defend yourself!" The wretch wavered, he said he was not willing."

"Look," repeated Bricord to him, "see there upon the ground, the woman whom you have ruined—and killed. She is punished, it is now your turn."

"I must tell you," resumed Aly, "that the people had followed us one after another, so that by this time, there were more than twenty of us on the ground, some with torches."

"Will you fight?" Bricord continued to cry.

"No," said the people, "he must be arrested. One of the king's attornies has arrived."

This decided him.

"Give him your sword," cried Bricord to me.

"I gave it to him. Then—ah! mercy! I have seen men fighting, and you too, colonel; but nothing like this—they spoke not a word—nothing was heard but their breathing—it was like a rattle in the throat—and then such dreadful blows,—and at each blow a louder sigh—and the rattle returned more furiously—for, they were not fighting, they were murdering each other; they had their heads cleaved open, their arms cut, their chests laid bare; they struck every time. At length Bricord was suddenly arrested by Léda's body; he stumbled, and as he was recovering his footing, the giant—curses on him! dealt him a blow—it was the last; my poor Peter tottered and fell down over his wife's body."

"Dead!" cried Aly Muley's listeners, with horror.

"Dead," repeated Aly Muley. "For the moment I neither saw nor heard any more. I had thrown myself upon Bricord, when suddenly I heard a cry. It was Hector, who, covered with wounds, had dragged himself to the carriage. That man was made of iron and stone—and wounded as he was, he pulled out his accomplice, who was struggling at the bottom, as if she had been a child; he dragged her up to the two corpses."

"There, do you see your work?" said he to the wretched woman.

And with these words he raised his sword over her: but, at the same instant, there was the report of a pistol. The giant recoiled, roaring like a wounded lion; but he was not killed: then suddenly he fell.

"Unhappy man!" said M. de Montaleu.

No one replied to this exclamation.

"But Felina!" cried Montéclain.

"Ah!" returned Aly Muley, "she—you will scarcely believe it—it is dreadful—it seems impossible, but so it was—no sooner had the viscount fallen than she presented the mouth of her other pistol to the people saying:

"Make way—make way—or I will smash the head of the first who stirs."

I thought the viscount was dead, but he moved and cried out:

"It was she who made me murder the colonel."

On hearing this, I threw myself upon her, I caught hold of her, and told her that I arrested her, she would not yield, and sent a ball into my ribs—it took off the skin and glanced aside—I still retained my grasp—but as she was a woman, I could not strike her like a man—I held one of her hands tightly—but she had a small knife in the other—I tried to wrest it from her, she thrust it into my breast, but with more anger than strength—it was nothing—a mere scratch; I then said to her—I could swear before God that I did say so—besides there were witnesses to prove it—I said to her:

"Will you surrender? I will not hurt you."

She broke from me, I ran after her, she tried to strike me—I held both her hands.

"That is enough," I said to her, "you shall do no more harm to honest people."

She made no reply, but I thought I heard her teeth snap, and then a cry—scarcely a cry—a hissing, as if her throat were torn. I said to her:

"Follow me."

She fell on her knees, I tried to raise her—she fell back immediately, I shook her, I called her, I lifted her up. She was powerless! I took a torch, and examined her: her eyes were open, she was white as marble, and her lips were covered with blood. I shook her again, but it was useless! She was dead!"

Every body present was thunderstruck.

"Then," said Aly Muley in a faint voice, "I made my escape, and came here."

"The justice of God has overtaken them, said Montéclain. "It is far better than our own."

The marquis was right. Felina had not a wound upon her body, nor even the mark of a bruise. She had died at the thought of her own impotence.

## POSTSCRIPT.

Two months afterwards, the following letter was sent round by Montéclain to his friends:—

"M. the Marquis de Montéclain has the honour to inform you of his marriage with Madame the Countess de Monrion."

THE END.

www.ingramcontent.com/pod-product-compliance
Lightning Source LLC
Chambersburg PA
CBHW080839250626
47161CB00009B/3119
* 9 7 8 1 5 3 5 8 1 4 6 1 4 *